O9-ABE-533

LA FRONTERA

El viaje con papá ~ My Journey with Papa

Deborah Mills & Alfredo Alva

ilustrado por ~ illustrated by

Claudia Navarro

TO ISABELA, THIAGO & ANA SOFIA FROM UNCLE DENNY & AUNT MARY ANN

Barefoot Books

step inside a story

Cuando era niño, mi familia vivía en el pequeño pueblo de La Ceja, en el centro de México, en el estado de Guanajuato. Mi familia había vivido allí por más de 100 años.

Mi abuelo, mi tío Tomás y mi papá trabajaban en los pinos piñoneros. Todos los días caminaban cinco millas hasta el bosque para recolectar los piñones de los árboles. Se subían a los árboles y recolectaban los piñones en costales. Me encantaba ver a mi abuelo remendar los costales, y deseaba que mis manos fueran así de rápidas.

En el verano, yo trabajaba con papá en el valle amontonando el maíz para que se secara. El valle también estaba lejos de nuestro pueblo.

When I was young, my family lived in the small village of La Ceja in central Mexico in the state of Guanajuato. For over 100 years, my family had lived there.

My grandfather, my uncle Tomás and my father all worked in the pinyon pine trees. Every day they walked five miles to the forest to gather the pine nuts from the trees. They climbed the trees and gathered the pine nuts in their sacks. I loved to watch Abuelo, my grandfather, mend the sacks, and wished my hands could move as swiftly.

In the summer, I worked with Papa in the valley stacking corn to dry. The valley was also far from our village.

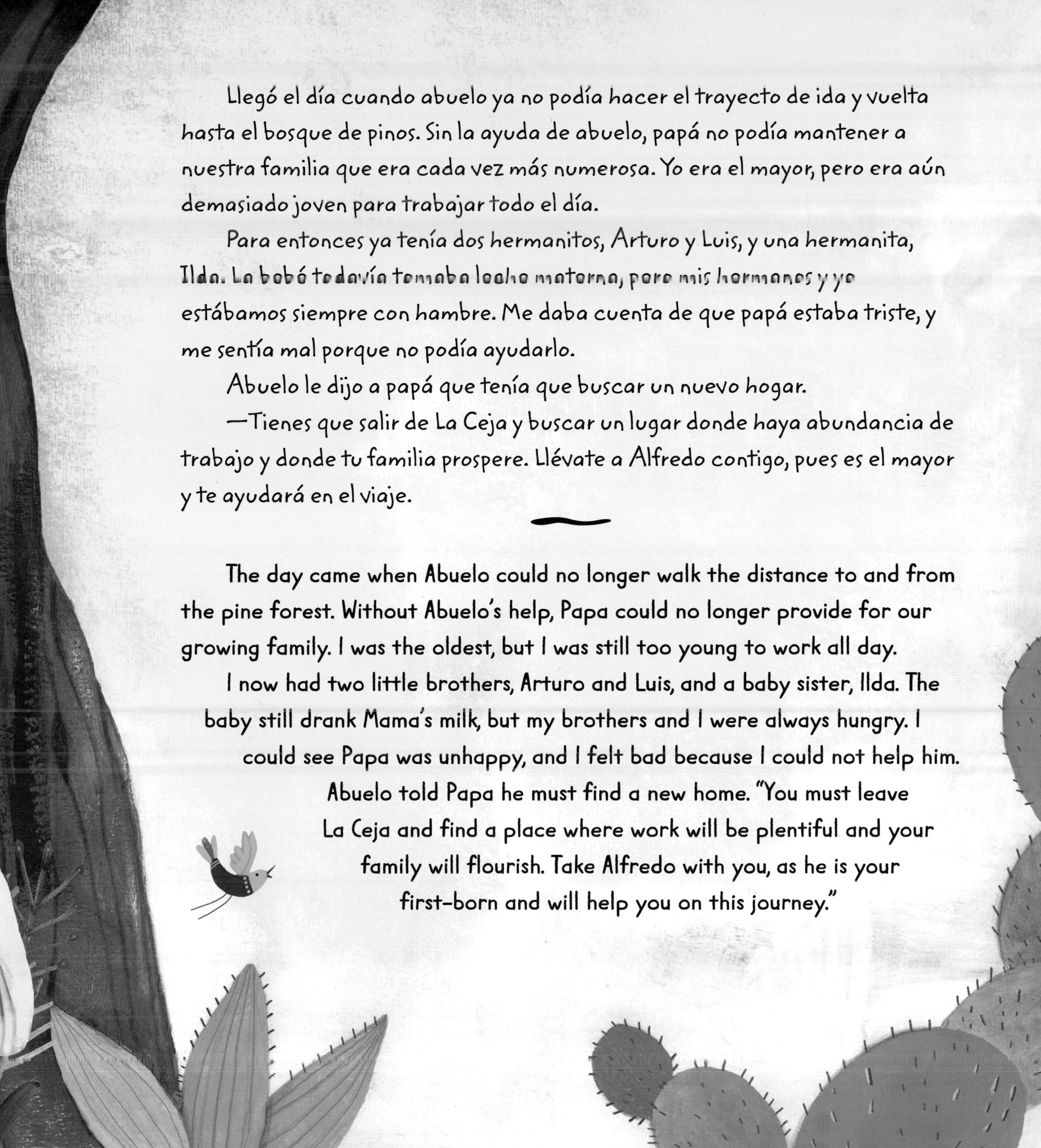

Llegó el día cuando abuelo ya no podía hacer el trayecto de ida y vuelta hasta el bosque de pinos. Sin la ayuda de abuelo, papá no podía mantener a nuestra familia que era cada vez más numerosa. Yo era el mayor, pero era aún demasiado joven para trabajar todo el día.

Para entonces ya tenía dos hermanitos, Arturo y Luis, y una hermanita, Ilda. La bebé todavía tomaba leche materna, pero mis hermanos y yo estábamos siempre con hambre. Me daba cuenta de que papá estaba triste, y me sentía mal porque no podía ayudarlo.

Abuelo le dijo a papá que tenía que buscar un nuevo hogar.

—Tienes que salir de La Ceja y buscar un lugar donde haya abundancia de trabajo y donde tu familia prospere. Llévate a Alfredo contigo, pues es el mayor y te ayudará en el viaje.

The day came when Abuelo could no longer walk the distance to and from the pine forest. Without Abuelo's help, Papa could no longer provide for our growing family. I was the oldest, but I was still too young to work all day.

I now had two little brothers, Arturo and Luis, and a baby sister, Ilda. The baby still drank Mama's milk, but my brothers and I were always hungry. I could see Papa was unhappy, and I felt bad because I could not help him.

Abuelo told Papa he must find a new home. "You must leave La Ceja and find a place where work will be plentiful and your family will flourish. Take Alfredo with you, as he is your first-born and will help you on this journey."

Me entristecía la idea de dejar mi hogar. Iba a extrañar a mi burro, Fernando. Habíamos nacido en el mismo año, y lo quería mucho.

Iba a extrañar a mi abuelo y al tío Tomás. Iba a extrañar los juegos con mis hermanitos y mis amigos. Y no quería ni imaginarme cómo sería dejar a mamá. Tenía hambre, sí, pero no quería que cambiara mi vida.

I was sad to think of leaving my home. I would miss my donkey, Fernando. We were born in the same year, and I loved him.

I would miss Abuelo and Uncle Tomás. I would miss playing with my little brothers and my friends. I did not even want to think about leaving Mama. I was hungry, yes, but I did not want life to change.

Al día siguiente llegaron unos hombres desconocidos al pueblo. Vi a papá hablar en voz baja con el hombre al que todos llamaban "Coyote". Papá le dio dinero. Él no aceptaba pesos, solo dólares americanos. Luego los hombres se fueron.

Le pregunté a papá por qué llamaban Coyote al hombre. Papá me dijo:

—Se llama así por el animal. El coyote es famoso por su comportamiento sigiloso y astuto. Es solitario y tímido con los desconocidos, al igual que este hombre. Pero necesitamos su ayuda en nuestro viaje.

The next day, strange men came to our village. I saw Papa talking quietly with the man everyone called "Coyote." Papa handed him money. He would not take pesos, only American dollars. Then the men left.

I asked Papa why the man was called Coyote. Papa said, "He takes his name from the animal. A coyote is known for its stealthy, wily ways. It is a loner and shy of strangers, just like this man. But we need his help to make the journey."

Tío Tomás anunció que íbamos a tener una fiesta de despedida, y que iba a asar el puerco de la familia. Toda la gente del pueblo vino a la fiesta, desde el más viejo hasta el más joven. La fiesta duró todo el día y toda la noche. Nos llenamos de tortillas, arroz, pan de maíz y mucho más.

Mi primo Francisco tocó el acordeón y hubo baile, abrazos y besos. Cantamos mi canción favorita, "Amor eterno".

Uncle Tomás announced that we would have a going-away celebration, and he would roast the family pig for the feast. All the villagers came to the party — the very old and the very young. It lasted all day and all night. We filled our stomachs with tortillas, rice, corn bread and much more.

My cousin Francisco played the accordion, and there was dancing, hugging and kissing. We sang my favorite song, "Amor Eterno," which means *Eternal Love*.

Mi mamá me llevó al pozo que había detrás de la casa y me pidió que me sentara. Me miró a los ojos y me dijo:

—Tienes mucha suerte de ir en este viaje especial con papá. Debes ser fuerte. Imagínate que eres un pajarito que no necesita mucha comida o bebida para seguir volando hacia el norte. Así como las golondrinas que vemos todas las primaveras.

—Y Alfredito, no te olvides, te amo mucho, mucho.

No me dijo que no la vería ni a ella ni a mis hermanos y hermana por muchos años.

My mother took me to the well behind the house and sat me down. She looked me in the eye and said, "You are so lucky to be going on this special trip with Papa. You must be strong. You must think of yourself as a little bird who does not need much to eat or drink to keep flying north. Just like the swallows we see every spring.

"And Alfredito — don't forget, I love you so, so much." She did not tell me that I would not see her or my brothers and sister for many years.

Papá y yo salimos temprano a la mañana siguiente. Caminamos hasta la estación de autobuses y esperamos el autobús para Acuña. Era temprano y no había nadie en la calle. Algunas personas estaban sentadas en las bancas esperando el autobús, pero nosotros nos quedamos apartados y en silencio.

Papa and I left early the next morning. We walked to the bus station and waited for the bus to Acuña. It was early, and nobody was in the street. A few people were waiting on benches for the bus, but we stayed separate from the others and kept quiet.

En Acuña nos encontramos con el coyote, el desconocido que había venido a casa.

—El coyote no nos puede decir nunca su nombre —dijo papá—. Sabe que tiene muchos enemigos, como el astuto coyote de quien tomó el apodo.

In Acuña, we met "Coyote," the strange man who had come to our house. "Coyote can never tell us his real name," said Papa. "He knows he has many enemies, like the sly coyote he is named after."

El coyote nos llevó a la orilla del río Bravo. Nos escondimos en la hierba alta hasta que anocheció. El coyote nos dio una llanta vieja para usar de flotador, y nos dijo que se encontraría con nosotros al otro lado, en Estados Unidos.

Papá y yo tomamos la llanta e intentamos cruzar, pero la corriente era muy fuerte. Nos deslizamos a lo largo de la orilla hasta que llegamos a un lugar menos profundo. La luna brillaba con fuerza sobre el agua. Se veía hermosa.

Nos pusimos los costales en la cabeza y nos metimos en el río en silencio y rápidamente. Cuando el río se hizo más profundo, papá agarró mi costal y me amarró a él con una soga. Yo me abracé a su cuello. La corriente era fuerte, pero el agua no llegó a cubrir la cabeza de papá. Yo no tenía miedo, pero me alegraba de que tuviéramos la luz de la luna para guiarnos a cruzar.

Coyote took us to the edge of the Rio Grande river. We hid in the tall grass until it was truly dark. Coyote gave us an old inner tube to float across, and said he would meet us on the other side — in the United States.

Papa and I took the inner tube and tried to cross, but the current was too strong. We crept along the shore until we came to a shallower place. The moon was so bright, shining on the water. It was beautiful.

We put our sacks on our heads and quietly and quickly waded in. As it got deeper, Papa took my sack and tied me to him with a piece of rope. I wrapped my arms around his neck. The current was strong, but the water did not go over Papa's head. I was not afraid, but I was glad to have the moonlight to guide us across.

Tan pronto como llegamos al otro lado, buscamos al coyote, pero no lo vimos. Yo estaba contento, pero me di cuenta de que papá estaba preocupado. El coyote había desaparecido, llevándose el dinero de papá.

—Ahora tendremos que encontrar solos el camino, Alfredo —suspiró papá.

Comenzamos a alejarnos de la frontera y del río Bravo. Yo corrí hasta que mis piernas no podían avanzar más. Entonces papá me cargó hasta que él también se desplomó.

As soon as we reached the other side, we looked for Coyote, but we did not see him. I was glad, but I could tell Papa was worried. Coyote had disappeared — and taken Papa's money with him. Papa sighed, "We must find our own way now, Alfredo."

We started running away from the border and the Rio Grande. I ran until my legs would no longer keep moving. Then Papa carried me until he, too, collapsed.

En la mañana me di cuenta de que había dormido encima de unas piedras.
Estaba tan cansado que no había sentido las piedras en toda la noche.

In the morning, I saw that I had slept on top of rocks.
I was so tired, I had not felt those rocks all night.

Comenzábamos a caminar todos los días al amanecer, y caminamos durante cinco días. No había senderos y las zarzas me rasgaron la ropa. Tenía muchos rasguños. Cuando me sentaba o dormía en el suelo, me picaban las hormigas rojas, y siempre estaba atento por si veía escorpiones o víboras.

Cruzamos una montaña grande. Era empinada y rodaban piedras que me pegaban en las piernas. No me quejé y me esforcé por mantener el paso con papá. Cuando me vine a dar cuenta, habíamos dejado atrás la montaña.

We started walking at dawn every day, and we walked for five days. There was no path, and the brambles ripped my clothes. I had many cuts. When I sat or slept on the ground, I got bitten by fire ants, and I was always watching for scorpions and snakes.

We crossed over a big mountain. It was steep, and rocks kept tumbling down, hitting me in the shins. I did not complain and worked hard to keep up with Papa. Before I knew it, the mountain was behind us.

Al otro lado había un valle gigante. Caminamos hasta llegar a las vías del tren. Las seguimos porque papá decía que la tripulación del tren llevaba jarras de agua, y que las iban dejando a lo largo de las vías. Vi una y corrí a recogerla.

On the other side stretched a giant valley. We walked until we came to train tracks. We followed them because Papa said the train crews carried jugs of water for us, and would drop them along the tracks. I saw one and ran to pick it up.

A veces dormíamos encima de algún tren de carga que estuviera parado en las vías. Era un buen lugar para esconderse, pero teníamos que saltar rápidamente al suelo cuando el tren comenzaba a moverse porque no sabíamos a dónde iba.

Sometimes we slept on top of a freight train that had stopped on the tracks. It was a good place to hide, but we had to hop off quickly when the train started moving, because we didn't know where it was headed.

Saltamos muchas vallas. Yo iba en silencio, hablar tomaba demasiada energía. Pero me sentía seguro con papá.

Él me miraba con una sonrisa y decía:

—Recuerda, pequeño, mi nombre es Raymundo y significa *Rey del Mundo*.

Eso siempre me hacía reír.

We climbed many fences. I did not talk much — it took too much energy. But I felt safe with Papa.

He would look at me with a grin and say, "Remember, little one, my name is Raymundo, and it means *King of the World!*"

It always made me laugh.

Le pregunté a papá a dónde íbamos, y me contestó: "A la Embajada". Yo no conocía esa palabra. En esos largos días de caminata, intentaba imaginarme qué sería eso de la Embajada. Parecía algo de categoría, como un reino o un palacio.

Yo le preguntaba:

—¿Cuánto falta para llegar a la Embajada? —pero él nunca me respondía.

I asked Papa where we were going, and he answered, "To the Embassy." I did not know this word. On those long days of walking, I tried to imagine what the Embassy could be. It sounded grand, like a kingdom or a palace.

I would ask him, "How much farther to the Embassy?" but he would never answer.

Al final del sexto día, llegamos a una choza destartalada. Tenía un letrero en español: *Está abierto. Tomen lo que necesiten y no destruyan nada. Gracias.*

Dormimos en la choza. Yo respiré aliviado. Estaba tan contento de no tener que dormir en el suelo y preocuparme por las hormigas rojas, las víboras o los escorpiones. Papá dijo que estábamos esperando a un hombre llamado Isidro, un amigo de abuelo.

Isidro llegó en su camioneta al día siguiente. Pude leer la placa: decía *Texas*. Me quedé profundamente dormido en esa camioneta segura y amiga.

At the end of the sixth day, we came to a broken-down shack. There was a sign on it in Spanish: "Está abierto. Tomen lo que necesiten y no destruyan nada. Gracias." *It's open. Take what you need and don't destroy anything. Thank you.*

We slept in the shack. I sighed with relief. I was so happy not to have to sleep on the ground and worry about fire ants, snakes or scorpions. Papa said we were waiting here for a man named Isidro, a friend of Abuelo's.

Isidro came in his pickup truck the next day. I could read the license plate: it said *Texas*. I fell fast asleep in his safe, friendly truck.

APR TEXAS
317 ELS

Isidro nos llevó a papá y a mí a la Embajada, que no era más que una colección de casas móviles destartaladas y muebles que la gente había tirado en el bosque detrás de una fábrica. Había un pozo viejo que aún funcionaba, pero el agua era de color café oscuro. Yo era el único niño en la Embajada.

Isidro took Papa and me to the Embassy, which was nothing more than a collection of broken-down trailers and furniture that people had dumped in the woods behind a factory. There was an old well there, and it still worked, but the water was very brown. I was the only child at the Embassy.

Dormíamos en un autobús viejo y comíamos en una choza de metal y triplay. Mi única amiga era una cría de pecarí, un puerco salvaje, que apareció por allí un día. Creo que había perdido a su mamá. Yo me sentía igual. Los dos estábamos solos, y con ella compartía todos mis pensamientos. Ella me recordaba a mi burro Fernando, en mi antigua casa. ¿Se estaría él preguntando a dónde me había ido?

We slept in an old bus and ate in a shack made of metal and plywood. My only friend was a baby javelina, a wild pig, who wandered in one day. I think she had lost her mother. I felt like I had, too. We were both lonely, and I told her all my thoughts. She reminded me of my donkey Fernando, back home. Was he wondering where I had gone?

Después de pasar unas semanas en la Embajada, comencé a ir a la escuela. Papá me enseñó el lugar donde me iba a recoger el autobús y me dio un billete de $100.

—Lleva esto siempre contigo —me dijo papá—, y no le digas a nadie que lo tienes.

Guardé el billete cuidadosamente en el bolsillo pequeño de mis jeans.

—Si alguien uniformado te para y te regresa a la frontera, usa este dinero para comprar un boleto de autobús de vuelta con nuestra familia a La Ceja.

After a few weeks at the Embassy, I started school. Papa showed me where the bus would pick me up and gave me a $100 bill.

"Carry this with you at all times," Papa said, "and don't tell anyone you have it." I put the bill carefully in the little pocket in my jeans. "If someone in a uniform picks you up and takes you back to the border, use this money to buy a bus ticket back to our family in La Ceja."

En México, todo el mundo iba caminando a la escuela, por eso me ponía nervioso tener que tomar el autobús escolar. Parecía algo peligroso. Mi padre me había dicho que estuviera atento a los hombres uniformados y yo creía que iban a estar en el autobús. Yo guardaba silencio y siempre me sentaba atrás.

Al pasar unas semanas me sentía más seguro en el autobús, pero en el salón de clase, me sentía solo. No hablaba inglés ni entendía nada. Sentía las miradas de los otros estudiantes y sabía que hablaban de mí.

In Mexico, everyone walked to school, so I was nervous getting on the school bus. It felt dangerous. My father had warned me to watch out for men in uniforms, and I thought they might be on the bus. I was very quiet and always sat at the back.

After a few weeks I felt safer on the bus, but in the classroom, I felt alone. I couldn't speak English or understand anything. I could feel the other students' eyes on me, and I knew they were talking about me.

EMERGENCY DOOR

Un día un niño llamado Antonio entró a nuestro salón y preguntó por mí. Era dos años mayor y hablaba español. Me di cuenta de que él les caía bien a los otros niños y que ellos estaban celosos de que viniera a verme.

A partir de ese día, todo comenzó a mejorar. Mis compañeros me ayudaban con la pronunciación de palabras en inglés. Usaban sus manos y caras para enseñarme los números, las figuras, los sentimientos, los nombres y las partes del cuerpo. ¡Cuántas palabras! Y como a mí se me daban bien las matemáticas, también los ayudaba.

Creo que mi maestra me había enviado a Antonio. Yo quería agradecérselo pero todavía no sabía las palabras adecuadas.

One day a boy named Antonio came into our classroom and asked for me. He was two years older and spoke Spanish. I could see the other boys liked him and were jealous that he was there to see me.

After that day, everything started to change for the better. My classmates helped me pronounce English words. Using their hands and their faces, they taught me numbers, shapes, feelings, names and body parts. So many new words! And since I was good at math, I helped them, too.

I think my teacher had sent Antonio to me. I wanted to thank her but did not know the right words yet.

STOP

Al terminar el verano, empecé a sentir que yo era parte del país. Ya podía hablar algo de inglés y podía conversar con mis nuevos amigos.

Siempre en el fondo de mi corazón estaba mi familia. Extrañaba a mamá, a mis hermanos y a mi hermanita, pero me gustaba mi nueva vida. Me estaba volviendo tejano. En noviembre de ese año, el presidente Reagan concedió la amnistía a millones de inmigrantes, lo que significaba que podíamos comenzar con el largo proceso de solicitar la ciudadanía.

By the end of the summer, I was beginning to feel like I belonged. I could speak some English now and could talk to my new friends.

Always at the center of my heart was my family. I missed Mama, my brothers and little sister, but I liked my new life. I was becoming a Texan. In November of that year, President Reagan granted amnesty to millions of immigrants, which meant we could begin the long process of applying for citizenship.

Cuatro años después

Un día papá me recogió de la escuela en su camioneta. Me dijo:

—Hoy vamos a hacer un viaje muy especial a una ciudad llamada El Paso, en la frontera.

Yo no quería ir, pero papá me prometió que esta vez no tendría que dormir encima de piedras ni preocuparme de coyotes. El viaje duró muchas horas. Era primavera, y recuerdo que las plantas silvestres a lo largo de la carretera estaban llenas de flores.

Four years later

One day Papa picked me up from school in his truck. He said, "We are going on a very special trip today to a town called El Paso, on the border." I did not want to go, but Papa promised me that this time I would not have to sleep on rocks or worry about Coyotes. We drove for many hours. It was spring, and I remember all the wildflowers were in bloom along the highway.

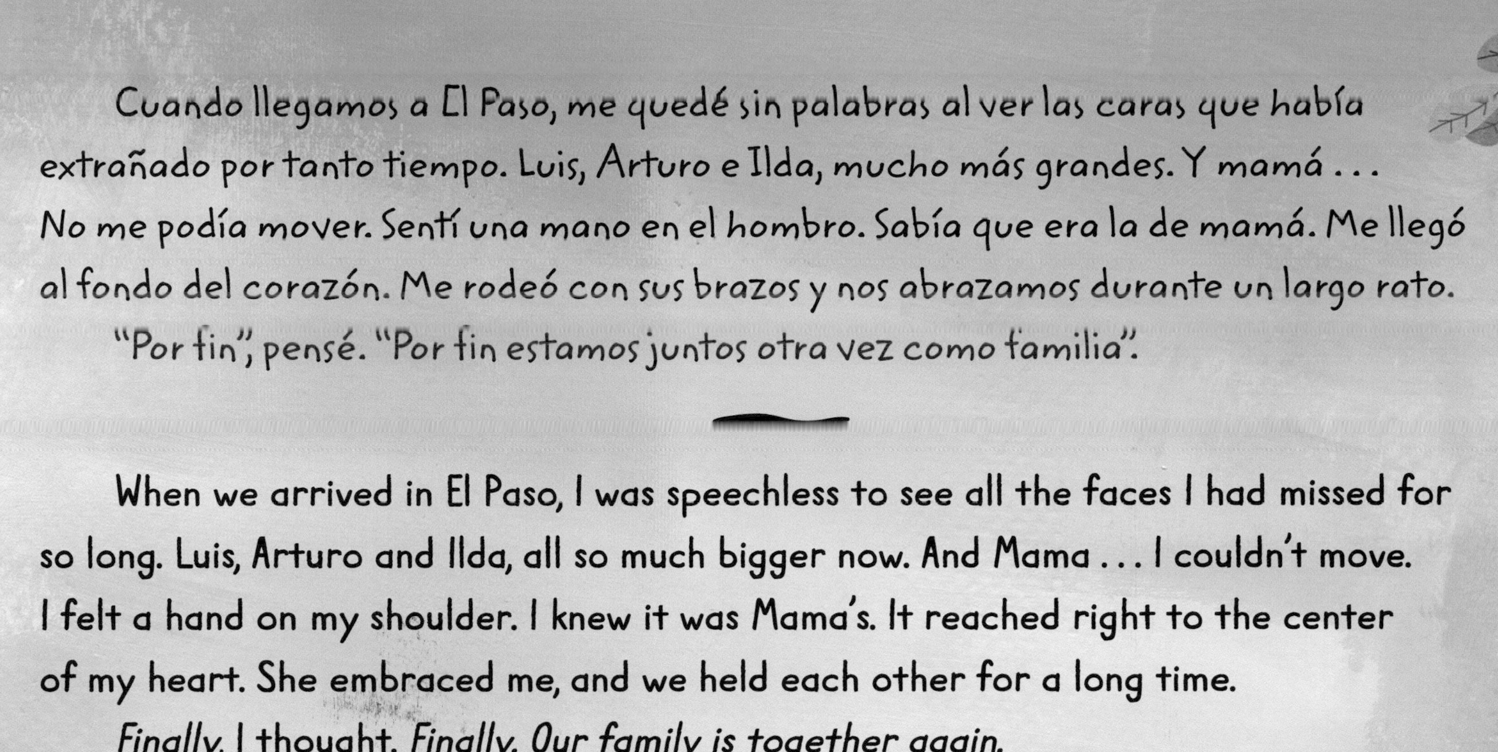

Cuando llegamos a El Paso, me quedé sin palabras al ver las caras que había extrañado por tanto tiempo. Luis, Arturo e Ilda, mucho más grandes. Y mamá . . . No me podía mover. Sentí una mano en el hombro. Sabía que era la de mamá. Me llegó al fondo del corazón. Me rodeó con sus brazos y nos abrazamos durante un largo rato.

"Por fin", pensé. "Por fin estamos juntos otra vez como familia".

When we arrived in El Paso, I was speechless to see all the faces I had missed for so long. Luis, Arturo and Ilda, all so much bigger now. And Mama . . . I couldn't move. I felt a hand on my shoulder. I knew it was Mama's. It reached right to the center of my heart. She embraced me, and we held each other for a long time.

Finally, I thought. *Finally. Our family is together again.*

Alfredo Alva con su familia en Texas, 2016 / Alfredo with his extended family in Texas, 2016

La historia de Alfredo / Alfredo's Story

Este libro narra la verdadera historia del viaje de Alfredo Alva a Texas en los años 1980. El padre de Alfredo trabajó de albañil especializado en cantería al llegar a Estados Unidos, y Alfredo también se hizo cantero. Todavía vive en Texas y tiene dos hijos. Todo el que migra de México a Estados Unidos tiene su propia historia. La familia de Alfredo pudo al fin reunirse y se hicieron ciudadanos americanos, pero las historias de muchas familias de inmigrantes tienen otros desenlaces.

Alfredo trabajó con su vecina, Deborah Mills, para escribir esta historia. Alfredo y Deborah querían compartir esta historia porque muchos niños experimentan viajes parecidos hoy en día: no solo en México y Estados Unidos, sino en todo el mundo. Escuchar estas historias contribuye a que las personas entiendan lo que es pasar por un viaje tan difícil como el de Alfredo.

This book tells the true story of Alfredo Alva's journey to Texas in the 1980s. Alfredo's father started working as a stonemason after they moved to the United States, and when Alfredo grew up, he became a stonemason, too. He still lives in Texas and has two young children of his own now. Everyone who immigrates from Mexico to the United States has a unique story. Alfredo's family was eventually reunited, and they became U.S. citizens, but many immigrant families' stories end differently.

Alfredo worked with his neighbor, Deborah Mills, to write this story. Alfredo and Deborah wanted to share this story because many children experience similar journeys today — not just in Mexico and the United States, but all over the world. Hearing these stories can help other people understand what it would be like to experience a difficult journey like Alfredo's.

Fronteras y cultura / Borders & Culture

Alfredo y su papá cruzaron el río Bravo, el río que comprende gran parte de la frontera entre México y Estados Unidos. Tiene casi 2,000 millas (3,000 km) de largo. En algunos lugares, el río es profundo y ancho, en otros, es más estrecho y poco profundo.

A veces las fronteras entre los países cambian debido a guerras o a que se crean nuevos países. En otros casos, las fronteras cambian porque la Tierra cambia. Cuando se usa de frontera algo como un río o una cordillera, la frontera se desplaza con el tiempo a medida que el terreno cambia.

Alfredo and Papa crossed the Rio Grande, the river that forms much of the border between Mexico and the United States. It is almost 2,000 miles (3,000km) long. In some places, the river is deep and wide; in others, it is more narrow and shallow.

Borders between countries can change sometimes because of wars or because new countries are formed. Other times, borders change because the earth itself changes. When a landmark, like a river or a mountain range, is used as a border, the border will move over time as the land changes.

Estados Unidos tomó cerca de la mitad del territorio de México en 1848, al final de la intervención norteamericana en México. Ese territorio se convirtió en Texas, Nuevo México, Arizona, California y otros estados. ¡No es de extrañar que esos estados tengan muchas tradiciones de la cultura mexicana!

The United States took about half of Mexico's land in 1848 at the end of the Mexican-American War. That land became Texas, New Mexico, Arizona, California and other states. It's not surprising that those states still carry on many traditions from Mexican culture!

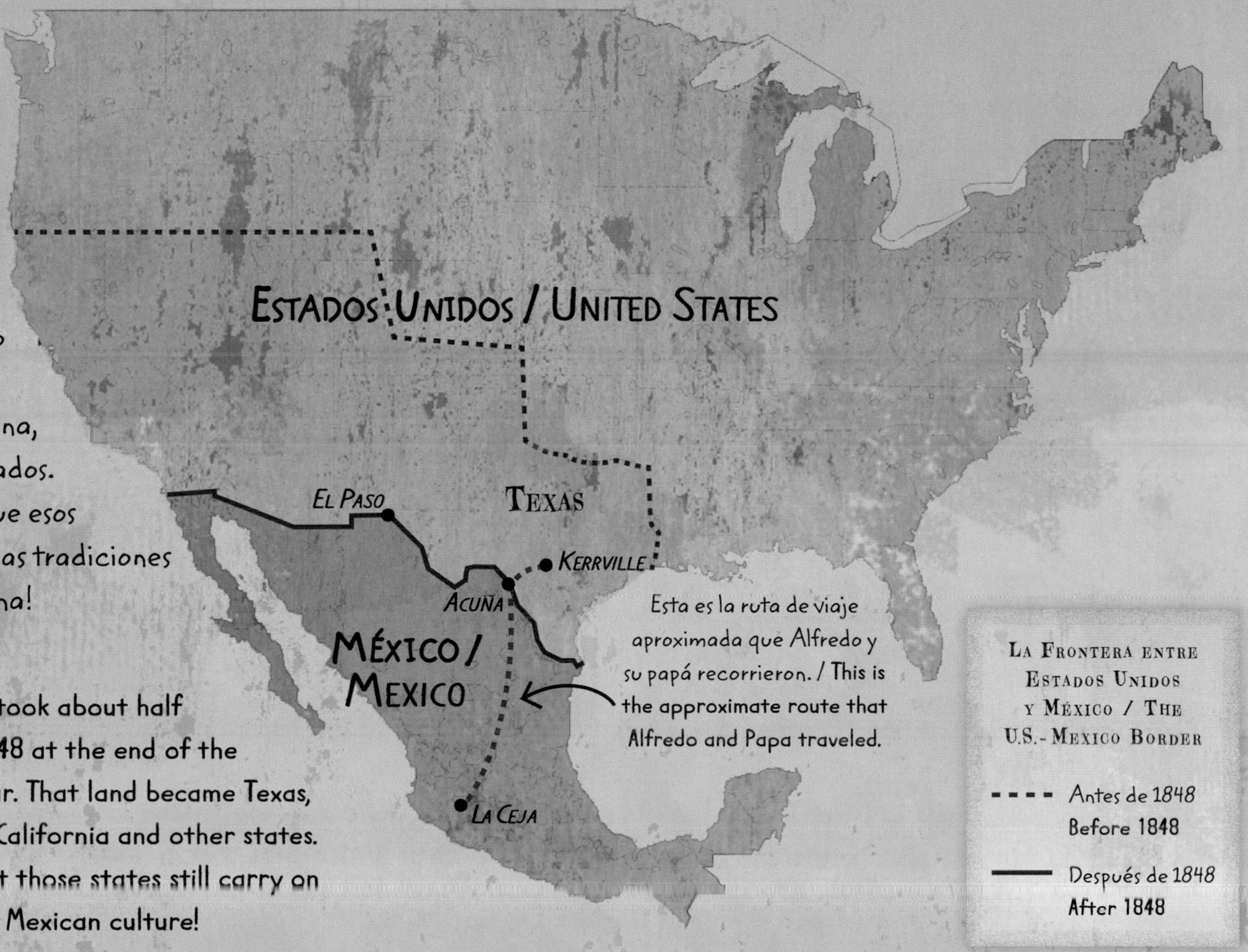

Estados Unidos / United States
Texas
El Paso
Kerrville
Acuña
México / Mexico
La Ceja

Esta es la ruta de viaje aproximada que Alfredo y su papá recorrieron. / This is the approximate route that Alfredo and Papa traveled.

La Frontera entre Estados Unidos y México / The U.S.-Mexico Border

- - - - Antes de 1848 / Before 1848

—— Después de 1848 / After 1848

Inmigración / Immigration

En todo el mundo hay gente que emigra (se traslada de su país de origen a otro). Se puede viajar en avión, carro, barco o, incluso, a pie, como Alfredo y su papá. Algunos inmigrantes le pagan a un "coyote" para que los guíe cuando cruzan de México a Estados Unidos, como hizo el papá de Alfredo. Estos guías toman el apodo de un animal muy listo, parecido a un lobo, que caza cerca de la frontera y que se llama coyote. Los inmigrantes deben pagarles mucho dinero a estos guías para llegar a salvo. Los coyotes no son siempre fiables y a veces le roban el dinero a la gente en lugar de ayudarla. En otros países, los guías que cruzan a las personas reciben otros nombres.

People immigrate (move from their home to a new country) all over the world. A person might travel on a plane, in a car, on a boat or even on foot, like Alfredo and Papa. Some immigrants pay a "coyote" to guide them across the U.S. border from Mexico, as Alfredo's papa did. These guides are named after clever, wolflike animals called coyotes that hunt near the border. Immigrants must pay these guides a lot of money in order to arrive safely. The "coyote" guides are not always reliable, and sometimes they steal money from people instead of helping them. In other countries, guides who bring people across other borders are called by different names.

Tomás Alva, tío de Alfredo
Alfredo's uncle, Tomás Alva

Tomás Alva recolectando piñones
Tomás Alva gathering pine nuts

La calle principal en La Ceja, México
The main street in La Ceja, Mexico

Photographs by Deborah Mills / Fotografías por Deborah Mills

La gente tiene diferentes razones para emigrar. A veces los inmigrantes sienten la "llamada" de otro país por las oportunidades de mejores trabajos o calidad de vida, o para reunirse con la familia; en otros casos, se ven forzados a dejar su hogar por problemas como las guerras.

People have many different reasons for immigrating. Sometimes immigrants feel "pulled" to a new place for better jobs or quality of life, or to reunite with family; other times they are "pushed" to leave home because of problems like wars.

Pic
SOC
MIL
186112

Dedicamos este libro a todos los inmigrantes del mundo.

We dedicate this book to all immigrants everywhere. — **D. M. & A. A.**

Para Pau y Santi, con amor

For Pau and Santi, with love — **C. N.**

Barefoot Books les agradece a las siguientes personas sus inestimables puntos de vista y reflexiones en la creación de este libro:

Barefoot Books would like to thank the following people for their invaluable perspectives and thoughtful input in the creation of this book:

- Sarahy Sigie, Barefoot Books, for communications translation and sensitivity reading
- Ouranitsa Abbas, Immigration Legal Representative
- Becky Kidd, Clinical Social Worker (LCSW-C), Esperanza Center
- María-Verónica A. Barnes, Director of Diversity Education, Lexington Montessori School (Lexington, MA)

Barefoot Books
2067 Massachusetts Ave
Cambridge, MA 02140

Barefoot Books
29/30 Fitzroy Square
London, W1T 6LQ

Text copyright © 2018 by Deborah Mills and Alfredo Alva
Endmatter text by Barefoot Books
Illustrations copyright © 2018 by Claudia Navarro
Photographs copyright © 2018 by Deborah Mills
The moral rights of Deborah Mills, Alfredo Alva
and Claudia Navarro have been asserted

First published in Great Britain by Barefoot Books, Ltd and in
the United States of America by Barefoot Books, Inc in 2018
All rights reserved

Graphic design by Sarah Soldano, Barefoot Books
Edited and art directed by Lisa Rosinsky, Barefoot Books
Translated by María A. Pérez

Reproduction by
Bright Arts, Hong Kong
Printed in China on
100% acid-free paper
This book was typeset in Hombre BT,
Might Could Pen and Zemke Hand
The illustrations were prepared in
graphite, acrylic and digital collage

Hardcover ISBN: 978-1-78285-388-6
Paperback ISBN: 978-1-78285-392-3

British Cataloguing-in-Publication Data: a catalogue
record for this book is available from the British Library
Library of Congress Cataloging-in-Publication Data is available upon request

1 3 5 7 9 8 6 4 2

Los gobiernos de cada país tienen leyes sobre inmigración. Estas leyes a menudo requieren documentos oficiales para que las personas puedan ingresar y permanecer en un nuevo país. Obtener estos documentos puede ser muy difícil. Alfredo y su papá ingresaron a los Estados Unidos sin esta documentación. Después de su llegada, cambios en la ley de inmigración les dieron la oportunidad de convertirse en ciudadanos estadounidenses.

Sin embargo, muchos inmigrantes no son elegibles para solicitar la ciudadanía. En este caso, el gobierno podría enviarlos de regreso al país que dejaron. Es por eso que el papá de Alfredo le dio dinero para que regresara a La Ceja, en caso de que lo enviaran al lado mexicano de la frontera.

Torribio Alva, papá de Alfredo, con su amigo Tito García / Alfredo's father, Torribio Alva, with a friend, Tito Garcia

National governments have laws about immigration. These laws often require official documents for people to enter and stay in a new country. It can be very difficult to obtain these documents. Alfredo and Papa entered the United States without this documentation. Changes in the laws after they arrived gave them the opportunity to become American citizens.

However, many immigrants aren't eligible to apply for citizenship. In this case, the government could send them back to the country they left. This is why Papa gave Alfredo money to return to La Ceja — in case he was sent back to the Mexican side of the border.

Alfredo y su papá en la casa de la familia en La Ceja / Alfredo and his father at their family's house in La Ceja

Xiclaly Alva, sobrina de Alfredo
Xiclaly Alva, Alfredo's niece

Cuando se mudan, los inmigrantes traen consigo parte de su cultura. Por ejemplo, alimentos tradicionales mexicanos como las tortillas, la salsa y el guacamole se han vuelto populares en Estados Unidos entre personas de diferentes culturas. Si vives en Estados Unidos, es muy probable que tus antepasados hayan venido de otro país, aunque fuera hace mucho tiempo. ¿Hay tradiciones o historias que tu familia trajo consigo?

Immigrants bring parts of their culture with them when they move. For example, traditional Mexican foods such as tortillas, salsa and guacamole have become popular in the United States among people of many different cultures. If you live in the U.S., most likely your family or your ancestors came there from another country, even if it was a long time ago. Are there traditions or stories your family brought with them?

future policy was not properly respected. For Vietnam, he wrote, one would start the examination with "Truman's turn away from Ho Chi Minh's OSS-supported nationalism."[95]

So Colby, who presided as DCI when those last estimates were written and who believed at the time that the war could still be won, joined with John Foster Dulles, and John McCone, and Richard Helms in seeing the origins of the war in clear hindsight. "I went to Vietnam with no reservations," wrote a diplomat about his youthful confidence in the Kennedy Administration's understanding of the need to win hearts and minds in an unconventional war. "Conveying the mind-set of the era was a Peanuts cartoon someone later stuck on the wall in our Saigon embassy showing Charlie Brown marching resolutely onto the baseball field with his bat over his shoulder and his glove slung over his bat. The caption read, 'How can we lose when we're so sincere?' "[96]

The intelligence community had reasons, and readers can find them here.

---

95 Colby, *Honorable Men*, p. 287.

96 Robert Hopkins Miller, *Vietnam and Beyond: A Diplomat's Cold War Education* (Lubbock: Texas Tech Univ. Press, 2002), p. 56.

Vietnamese attack, which had come too soon according to previous assessments, were blunted, Thieu's government would find itself in control of little more than the delta and Saigon. The continuing debate in America on further aid to South Vietnam was an unsettling factor fueling defeatism. It foresaw final defeat by early 1976, an assessment still too generous as it turned out. Outright defeat could be avoided only if there were changes in Saigon that opened the way "to a new settlement on near-surrender terms." [94]

Final Words

The papers in this collection generally reflect sound and realistic analysis and in some cases prescient commentary on likely outcomes, yet they also illustrate the bedeviling problems of reaching intelligence judgments. The first commandment for the analyst, as gleaned from the documents themselves, is (and has to be), "Thou Shalt Not Lose Thy Audience." National Intelligence Estimates, of course, constitute much less even than the tip of the iceberg of advice arriving in the Oval Office. To make an impact, the Estimate must conform at least in some way to the other information reaching the policymakers at the highest level. Presidential commitments usually do not wait upon the considered judgment of intelligence specialists, however much one might wish that were more the case. Dissents from policy assumptions appear, therefore, as in these documents, in later pages or within careful wording that sometimes seems to require a decoder ring.

The bane of clear thinking, the "a-little-of-this-and-a-little-of-that," is present in many of the papers, enabling the policymaker to take only what fits today's need to fill a gap. We know from Harold Ford's excellent study, *CIA and the Vietnam Policymakers,* that at least one crucial NIE was essentially turned upside down by DCI McCone and that in the 1967 Order of Battle controversy the CIA leadership knuckled under to the military and MACV. Yet, on occasion and at key turning points, the dissent and skepticism were plain to see, as in the 1964 Memorandum discussing the domino thesis, the August 1966 study of 300 pages on North Vietnam's will to persist, and the remarkable September 1967 "Memorandum" DCI Richard Helms sent in a sealed envelope to President Johnson, hoping he would find it "interesting."

The process of persuading a policymaker to reconsider assumptions is a long one. John McCone, perhaps recalling his own role in the 1963 Estimate, would say in retirement that Johnson (and Kennedy before him) had acted on flawed assumptions, but in the face of such determination intelligence analysts can only hope to set in motion a process of reconsideration. As the situation in Vietnam deteriorated, the analysis concentrated too much on the supposed weakening will in the US to stand up to the Communists. That was unfortunate but hardly surprising. Perhaps down deep at its core, the feeling was simply the reverse side of American hyper-optimism. That energy fueled insistence there were no limits to what American good will (and technology) could accomplish even in a place where the "best and brightest" had very little real knowledge about the history and dynamics of Vietnamese politics and life. The war became an endurance contest, but, it can be argued, the Estimates observed that energy alone could not sustain the effort against such odds. DCI William Colby, who succeeded Helms, wrote in his memoirs about "individual decisions" that might have changed history and where intelligence's ability to see past errors to help formulate

---

[94] Special National Intelligence Estimate 53/14.3-75, *Assessment of the Situation in South Vietnam*, March 27, 1975, p. 3.

As had always been the pattern, the darkest prospects were placed deep inside. Given the balance of forces within the south, the October 1973 Estimate said, "Preemptive offensive operations of any magnitude seem well beyond GVN capabilities." The Communists would undoubtedly be aware of the preparations, as they had been in the past, and, in any case, such operations could not be sustained without "a significant expansion of US military aid." And that was not likely to happen, the paper could have continued.[91]

With Watergate tides sloshing up against his desk in the Oval Office, Nixon's ability to rejoin the battle in Vietnam—even if he had wanted to, a doubtful proposition at best —was close to zero or below. In May 1974 an NIE gave as its best judgment that, while the picture was not entirely clear, Hanoi would probably not undertake a major offensive that year or in the first part of 1975. The paper argued that eventually the North Vietnamese would have to do so or risk that South Vietnam would become strong enough to withstand such a blow. But once again the bad news was tucked away in the back pages. The South Vietnamese economy, it said, was in a serious slump and the outlook was for a worsening situation with unemployment and rapid inflation. The problems were caused by increasing prices of critical imports and declining amounts of US assistance. What the paper did not say, however, was that this problem had been identified as early as the late 1950s, when the new Diem government in South Vietnam essentially lived off American support rather than adopting policies designed to plant a solid foundation for the economy out of fear of alienating his supporters.[92]

In December an Estimate revised the judgment about a likely attack, observing that Saigon's combat abilities had peaked in the first year or so following the ceasefire and were now in a gradual decline. "Without an immediate increase in US military assistance, the GVN's military situation would be parlous, and Saigon might explore the possibility of new negotiations with the Communists." In other words, the previous conclusion that North Vietnam could not come to power except by military means was now put in the questionable column, but the issue depended on Washington. The intelligence community still believed that an all-out offensive was not likely until 1976, when Hanoi could regard a US presidential year "as a particularly favorable time to launch an offensive."[93]

The perennial concern inside and outside the intelligence community about the political climate in the US is reflected here, alongside the speculation that military victory was (or had been) within reach if the will had been there to continue the fight. Although ONE papers had raised questions about the war from the beginning, expressed skepticism about the domino thesis, and deflated assumptions that escalation and bombing would deter the North Vietnamese, as the death agonies of the American-installed government in Saigon began, these later National Intelligence Estimates touched more and more on supposed deficiencies in American domestic politics. In the postwar debate over the "Vietnam syndrome" such arguments became entangled in current events and later wars.

The final Special National Intelligence Estimate in this collection, *Assessment of the Situation in South Vietnam*, published on March 27, 1975, assessed that even if the ongoing North

---

[91] *Ibid.*

[92] National Intelligence Estimate 53/14.3-1-74, *The Likelihood of a Major North Vietnamese Offensive Before June 30, 1975*, May 23, 1974, pp. 1,5.

[93] National Intelligence Estimate 53/14.3-2-74, *Short Term Prospects for Vietnam*, December 23, 1974, pp. 2, 6.

Then there was this gloomy summary:

> Thus, it is impossible at this time to offer a clear-cut estimate about South Vietnam's prospects through the mid-1970s. There are many formidable problems and no solid assurances over this period of time. In our view, the problems facing the GVN, the uncertainties in South Vietnam about the magnitude, nature and duration of future US support, doubts concerning the South Vietnamese will to persist, the resiliency of the communist apparatus in South Vietnam, and North Vietnam's demonstrated ability and willingness to pay the price of perseverance are such that the longer term survival of the GVN is by no means yet assured. [88]

No Vietnam Estimates were produced in 1972. This was a year of intense diplomacy with summits in both China and the Soviet Union. The spring offensive came, as predicted, and failed to bring down the Saigon government. Nixon could thus boast that his diplomacy had in fact isolated North Vietnam, at least in the sense that there were no threats from Beijing or Moscow when the US mined Haiphong harbor. In Paris the negotiations continued. Nixon and Kissinger had introduced the POW question into the negotiations in early 1969, perhaps seeking to gain both moral leverage and time for their Vietnamization policies to work. Now, however, the tables had turned, as the North Vietnamese used the POW issue as leverage in support of their demands that Washington agree to dismantle the political structure it had so carefully built in Saigon and allow it to be replaced with a coalition government. Eventually Hanoi dropped the demand that the Thieu government be replaced with a coalition, realizing that the United States would not insist upon a withdrawal of North Vietnamese forces from the South.

After a peace agreement had been negotiated in October, however, Nixon pulled back, partly because of South Vietnamese objections but also because he had little reason to fear losing the election. Infuriated, the North Vietnamese broke off negotiations. This gave Nixon the opportunity to say that the Christmas bombing forced them back to the table. The substance of the October draft agreement, however, was not changed by the bombing, as the final agreement in January 1973 still provided for the complete withdrawal of American troops and the continuing presence of North Vietnamese forces in the South. As one American diplomat, John Negroponte, quipped bitterly, "We bombed them into accepting our concessions."[89]

An October 1973 Estimate concluded that North Vietnam did not believe it could gain power through the political provisions of the Paris agreement and would launch a military offensive to try to reunite Vietnam. The Estimate did not predict success for Hanoi: ARVN's resolve had grown stronger, it insisted, and the US had not so far dissolved its commitment to Saigon. The ominous build-up of military supplies suggested it would not be longer than a year away. The unknown factor was the political situation in the United States and whether the President would have greater or lesser freedom of action. Obviously, Hanoi would take note of any changes in that regard. [90]

---

[88] National Intelligence Estimate 53-71, *South Vietnam: Problems and Prospects*, April 29, 1971p. 4.
[89] Berman, *No Peace, No Honor*, p. 240.
[90] National Intelligence Estimate 53/14.3-73, *Short-Term Prospects for Vietnam*, October 12, 1973, pp.1, 15.

immediate pressure from Hanoi. A joint American/GVN move against the supposed headquarters of the NLF/North Vietnamese would serve two purposes, then: protect Lon Nol and demonstrate that Vietnamization really was working. Nixon expected trouble with the antiwar movement and "up on the Hill," but the risks seemed worth it. On television, he told the nation that the operation would strike at the "heart of the trouble." It "puts the leaders of North Vietnam on notice that . . . we will not be humiliated. We will not be defeated."[85]

The explosion Nixon set off with the Cambodian "incursion" reverberated across the political landscape from Congress to Kent State University and back to the Lincoln Memorial, where Nixon tried to start a pre-dawn dialogue with college students from all parts of the country. Whatever time the incursion may have bought for Saigon, it did not do anything to improve Lon Nol's chances for surviving. A special National Intelligence Estimate in early August 1970 reported that in the four months since Sihanouk's ouster, half of Cambodia had been overrun by the Communists. Without outside support in the form of heavy military assistance, the outlook was grim. Lon Nol might survive until the end of the year, until the rainy season ended, but after that the Cambodians were in for it, with the prospect for heavy fighting against long odds.[86]

Hanoi would have to judge above all, concluded the paper, how the Cambodian situation would affect the will of the US to prosecute the struggle in Vietnam. The tone of this conclusion was very different from the pre-incursion Estimate as it reverted to the "test of wills" theme. Hanoi had never doubted the superior physical and material capabilities of the US, it asserted—without saying how those capabilities could have been used differently from Rolling Thunder to Cambodia—while North Vietnam's hopes had lain in its ability to out-stay the US "in a prolonged politico-military contest carried on according to the principles of revolutionary struggle." The public outcry against "the Cambodian adventure" might lead Hanoi to believe it had the upper hand now. Dean Rusk never said it better. "But it [Hanoi] must recognize that the contest in Indochina will continue for some time."[87]

Calling the incursion, "the Cambodian adventure," was something of a give-away, even if not precisely intended in that way by the August 1970 Special NIE. At the least it suggested Nixon's rash effort to test Vietnamization had made things worse, politically at home and militarily in Cambodia. In April 1971 a new NIE foresaw little change in the "reasonably good" outlook for Vietnam for that year but thought an enemy offensive was likely the following year when the US election season opened and the troop drawdowns continued. South Vietnam would continue to require substantial US support. It took note of serious problems in ARVN morale, while Hanoi's advantage was still the "apparent durability of the communist party apparatus." Besides the communist threat, moreover, the GVN faced other internal problems that might well produce tensions, growing anti-Americanism, and a government relying solely on coercive powers. Should that happen, the outlook would change to one of increasing instability "risking political disintegration."

---

85 Kimball, *Nixon's War*, p. 211.

86 Special National Intelligence Estimate 57-70, *The Outlook for Cambodia*, August 6, 1970, pp. 1, 41.

87 *Ibid.*, p. 33.

the United States would honor all its commitments, but the "Guam Doctrine" sent a shock wave through the SEATO area, particularly so in Thailand, where National Security Adviser Henry Kissinger attempted to draw a distinction between internal subversion, including guerrilla war, and an international conflict. "The general policy is that internal subversion has to be the primary responsibility of the threatened country."[81]

Along with the emerging *détente* policies Nixon hoped to pursue, balancing the Soviet Union and China, the Guam Doctrine could certainly be interpreted as removing Vietnam from the Cold War battlefront. A lessening of Soviet and Chinese anxieties about American intentions, on the other hand, might also produce a situation where Hanoi felt stranded from its sources of supply. The intelligence community estimated in early 1970 that Hanoi was indeed worried about the success of Vietnamization, i.e., shifting the ground war to the South Vietnamese. The Estimate was probably the most upbeat assessment since those in 1965 after the decision to send large numbers of American troops into the war. Enemy casualties "still" exceeded infiltration and recruitment rates, it said, and their military tactics were conservationist, aimed at avoiding heavy losses. Looked at in terms of the effort to build up South Vietnam's military forces, the paper seemed to be saying, indeed, that the "cross-over" point was in sight, ironically, not with American troop numbers going up but going down! [82]

But—and there was always a "but"—the North Vietnamese had other advantages. "The Communists attach considerable importance to controlling the adjacent Laotian and Cambodian border areas, which they probably believe can continue to serve as base areas and sanctuaries." There is considerable evidence that Nixon had renewed hope early in 1970 that the measured pace of American withdrawal and a National Intelligence Estimate's report of successes in regaining and pacifying areas previously under enemy control led him to think in bold terms about operations to clear out those sanctuaries and give Saigon a real chance beyond a decent interval.[83]

The Special Estimate put a positive spin on the Guam Doctrine, positing that Hanoi had been forced to revise its timetable after realizing that Nixon never intended to approach the Paris negotiations as a "face-saver" but only intended to leave gradually in pace with the GVN's growing strength and ability to handle the situation with minimum outside support. Vietnamization had added to Hanoi's fears that Nixon had outflanked antiwar sentiments, giving the President a great deal more flexibility with his timetable. The Nixon advantages kept mounting up. There was the Sino-Soviet split to factor into the equation. Indeed, the mood was close to self-congratulatory, if not giddy, about future prospects. "In these circumstances," the paper summed up, "the North Vietnamese leaders might deem it prudent further to scale down the level of military operations in the South, or even to move toward a cease-fire."[84]

For all the optimism, however, the mood in the Oval Office just before the Cambodian "incursion" at the end of April 1970 bordered on the desperate. Cambodian Prince Sihanouk's government had been overturned by a rightist general, Lon Nol, whose regime came under

---

[81] See, US Department of State, *Foreign Relations of the United States, 1969-1976*, (vol. I. Washington: G.P.O., 2003), pp. 91-3.
[82] Special National Intelligence Estimate 14.3-70, *The Outlook from Hanoi: Factors Affecting North Vietnam's Policy on the War in Vietnam*, February 5, 1970, pp. 1-6; and see Kimball, *Nixon's Vietnam War*, pp. 182-83.
[83] *Ibid.*
[84] Special National Intelligence Estimate 14.3-70, p. 17.

Beyond the bluff and bluster of the "madman" theory—a variation of the old story that Eisenhower planned to use nuclear weapons in the Korean War—the Nixon plan turned out to be a long and torturous road to a settlement that probably was worse than what Johnson could have obtained in 1968—but that also is speculative. In the summer of 1969 Nixon announced the first withdrawal of 25,000 troops, at the same time he was extending bombing into Cambodia. On July 17th, a Special National Intelligence Estimate asserted that despite the Communists' ability to maintain the numerical strength of their forces, "the Communists are suffering an erosion of their position in South Vietnam." The paper argued against itself at points, as had many other Estimates, asserting that enemy weaknesses had been revealed by the "alacrity with which the Communists responded to the March 1968 cutback in the bombing and the US offer to begin talks." A few paragraphs later, however, the paper said that while an operation against the administrative structure of the NLF was underway, "despite some attrition and disruption, the infrastructure remains basically intact and capable of engaging in roughly the same magnitude of operations as it has during the past four years."[78]

To prove the strength of the enemy was "eroding," the paper gave huge estimates of casualties. If these were not exaggerated, at 170,000 men in 1967, nearly 300,000 in 1968, and continuing at the same level in 1969, what the Estimate was really saying was that the will to persist had not slackened since August 1966. It had grown stronger. But the Estimate insisted, as had Westmoreland two years earlier before Tet, that the quality of the enemy troops was in decline. Yet even at this point the Estimate twisted back again to acknowledge there were adequate human resources within North Vietnam to make up for looming deficiencies in the south and the logistical support system "along the infiltration pipeline" remained sufficient. The Air Force, as it had always done when earlier questions arose about interdiction, dissented from this judgment. Its view was that the bombing had cut tonnage by 25% from 80 tons to 60 tons per day, "a logistics shortfall that should result in a reduced level of enemy activities during the last half of 1969."[79]

In the end, the Estimate mirrored positions in the debate over whether Nixon's "plan" sought only a "decent interval" or whether "Vietnamization" envisioned long-term survival of an independent South Vietnam. Former policymakers and historians continue to argue the evidence.[80] The Air Force dissent could be seen as a rebuttal, therefore, to those who argued that at best the war was stalemated. Finessing Vietnam to deal directly with Russia and China was not going to be easy, as the Air Force view suggested to some that victory was still possible. Above all, Nixon feared he could not control the political situation if he admitted the war had been a mistake or a tragedy of missed signals. Little wonder he played his cards very close to his vest.

At the same time the July 1969 Estimate was being written, Nixon was speaking at an air base on the Island of Guam, announcing a new "doctrine" that muffled the sound of clacking dominos. "As far as our role is concerned," he said of the future, "we must avoid the kind of policy that will make countries in Asia so dependent upon us that we are dragged into conflicts such as the one we have in Vietnam." One can interpret this sentence in many ways and add in his promise that

---

[78] Special National Intelligence Estimate 14.3-69, *Capabilities of the Vietnamese Communists for Fighting in South Vietnam,* July 17, 1969, pp. 1,3-4.
[79] *Ibid*., p. 20.
[80] See Larry Berman, *No Peace ,No Honor: Nixon, Kissinger, and Betrayal in Vietnam* (New York: The Free Press, 2001), and Jeffrey Kimball, *Nixon's Vietnam War* (Lawrence: Univ. of Kansas Press, 1998), for an introduction to the opposing positions.

When Johnson heard of the defection brewing, he demanded Carver give him the same briefing. On March 26, after sitting through the whole thing for an hour and fifteen minutes, he got up and left the room without saying a word. Then he came back, shook Carver's hand, and again left the room without saying a word. Five days later he addressed the nation and said that he was stopping the bombing of the north except in the region of the demilitarized zone. He also announced that he would not seek a new term for the presidency. Escalation was over.

The Elusive Quest

When the North Vietnamese agreed to come to Paris to open negotiations, it was no secret that their first purpose was to secure an unconditional end to all the bombing. After that was achieved they would move on to negotiations, but not with an eye to compromise. "The Communists see themselves more as revolutionaries opening a second front," read an ONE Memorandum on what to expect at Paris, "than as negotiators exploring the possibilities for compromise." They saw themselves as leading from strength, though realizing their position was not as strong as they had hoped it would be. The Americans should be prepared for the demand that the South Vietnamese National Liberation Front (NLF) be represented in a new coalition government.[77]

The question of NLF representation as an equal party to the negotiations was, of course, the hardest thing for the American delegation to accept. Secretary of State Dean Rusk had long ago vowed that the NLF or VC would not be allowed to shoot its way to the peace table. The intelligence Memorandum reminded policymakers that Hanoi's memory of the 1954 Geneva Conference and what happened when elections were not held two years later made Ho's heirs "chary" of negotiations that might fall short of its maximum goals. There was absolutely no chance they would back down from the demand to be an equal party at the negotiations.

The Memorandum also stated that the North Vietnamese would seek to manipulate the agenda in ways designed to exacerbate relations between Saigon and Washington. Over the long summer months of 1968, Johnson and his advisers wrestled with these conditions as the President attempted to find a safe exit out of the morass that had overtaken his administration and endangered his beloved Great Society programs. Finally, near the end of October in the election year, he thought he saw some light. In exchange for Hanoi's promise to initiate serious discussions and to stop the shelling of cities, the President declared a bombing halt over all North Vietnam.

Johnson had done so with the concurrence of General Creighton Abrams, who had replaced Westmoreland as commander of MACV. But that was only the first hurdle. South Vietnam's President Nguyen Van Thieu balked, holding out against the terms of any agreement that would place the NLF on an equal footing with his regime. His resistance no doubt helped to elect Richard Nixon, but the Democratic defeat cannot be said to have resulted from a Vietnam policy that seemed either too hawkish or too dovish. Nixon had neatly avoided talking specifics about what he would do to extricate the nation from the unpopular war that dragged on seemingly without end. Taking advantage of Lyndon Johnson's March 31 declaration that he would devote himself to finding a peaceful solution, Nixon promised not to criticize the President and said only that if LBJ failed he had a "plan."

---

[77] Intelligence Memorandum, *Hanoi's Negotiating Position and Concept of Negotiations,* May 6, 1968, p. 1-2.

levels.[72] George Carver had reached a similar conclusion, but when the offensive turned out to be a broad attack on cities across South Vietnam, he asserted Saigon had earlier sent "nothing which appeared to be very hard" that anticipated the upcoming attacks. But then this admission:

> While we may be undergoing a major multiple harassment without lasting military significance, the ultimate import will depend on their degree of success on the ground and the impact on American and South Vietnamese willingness to rebound. The boost to VC/NVA morale is in any case certain to be substantial.[73]

Tet has been debated ever since. In an unsigned memorandum on February 9, 1968, probably also by Carver, the "revisionist" argument was already developed in embryonic form. The Communist effort to rally people to the VC cause had failed, it began. Tet could not be considered a "final allied 'victory' but certainly represents an initial Communist defeat." No one had claimed the O/B conclusions were absolutely accurate, it went in a more uncertain tone. "The 250,000 figure is not our estimate of <u>total</u> enemy strength." Whether the figure of 60,000 enemy casualties was also not absolutely accurate, it concluded, "<u>Total</u> enemy strength (as opposed to main force strength) has indeed declined."[74]

"'Victory'" is a slippery, normative word," the memo said, "not a noun with solid content." So it is with the argument over Tet. The North Vietnamese/VC did not win a military victory, and they suffered very high casualties, but the victory the United States had sought since 1954 was now much farther off than beyond the next rice paddy or the one after that. The financial and social costs of the struggle, former Secretary of State Dean Acheson of the famous council of "Wisemen" told Johnson on March 26, 1968, would be as hard for the United States to sustain as the force levels for the enemy. The Wisemen's conclusion that the United States had to find a new way out of Vietnam rocked Johnson as nothing else had.[75]

The CIA briefer for the Wisemen was none other than George Carver. The landscape had changed rapidly since Tet. Martin Luther King had been assassinated, setting off riots in Washington, D.C., and other cities. Senator Eugene McCarthy had entered a Democratic primary in New Hampshire on a peace ticket and done amazingly well. Robert Kennedy was ready to join the race. However that might be, Carver later related that he had told the genro of American diplomacy, "You can't tell the people in Keokuk, Iowa, you want to get out and tell the North Vietnamese you're going to stick it out for two decades and make them believe you." But Carver made two substantive points that went beyond wit and clever expressions: the pacification program was in shambles, and the enemy had been underestimated and undercounted by half.[76]

---

[72] Rostow to Johnson, January 22, 1968, encl. Westmoreland cable of same date, National Security Files, Country File, Vietnam, Box 127, *Johnson Papers*. For the Saigon station warning, see Adams, *War of Numbers*, pp. 133-4.
[73] Carver to Rostow, January 31, 1968, National Security File, NSC Histories, Box 48, *Johnson Papers*. On the failure of Saigon to provide a better estimate of the attacks on cities, see Allen, *None So Blind*, pp. 256-8.
[74] Helms to George Christian, enclosing unsigned memorandum, February 9, 1968, Files of George Christian, Box 12, *Johnson Papers*.
[75] The Wiseman included, among others, Arthur Goldberg, George Ball, Robert Murphy, Arthur Dean, Douglas Dillon, Henry Cabot Lodge, Matthew Ridgway, Mac Bundy, and Clark Clifford.
[76] Thomas Powers, *The Man Who Kept the Secrets: Richard Helms and the CIA* (New York: Alfred A. Knopf, 1979), pp. 192-3.

problems, the more so in a social environment where basic data is incomplete and often untrustworthy." [67]

From there on it was practically pure MACV orthodoxy, portraying a growing problem for the enemy of maintaining force levels and increasing recruitment. "Considering all the relevant factors, however, we believe there is a fairly good chance that the overall strength and effectiveness of the military forces and the political infrastructure will continue to decline." According to a chart of the sort Rostow treasured, infiltration had fallen off dramatically in the first eight months of 1967, from a monthly average the previous year of between 7,000 and 8,000, to between 4,000 and 5,000.[68]

From such statistics it was possible to glimpse the cross-over point just beyond the next rice paddy. But Johnson never got there. The President even brought MACV commander General Westmoreland back to Washington to assure Congress and the public. The General made speeches, gave television interviews, and was guided along by Johnson at a Congressional briefing. "We feel that we are somewhat like the boxer in the ring," Westmoreland told Congressional leaders, "where we have got our opponent almost on the ropes. And we hear murmurs to our rear as we look over the shoulder that the second wants to throw in the towel."[69]

Johnson then urged the General to talk about what bad shape the enemy was in. "Tell them the story about the company that came down the other day and over 38 years of age and 20 of them didn't make it." Westmoreland was eager to oblige. "I talked to the President today about this, and made the point that North Vietnam is having manpower problems." The General then related how *his* intelligence—not those 12,000 miles away from the scene—had learned from a captured prisoner about a company of 120 men who left North Vietnam to head south to battle. Twenty men fell out sick or deserted. Of the rest forty were over 38 years old. "And 38 for a Vietnamese is an old man, I can assure you . . . So, they are having to go now to the young group and to the old group."[70]

Johnson and Rostow pinned their hopes on such microcosms even as the enemy assembled its uncounted forces outside the cities to prepare for a massive attack. On January 31, 1968, the Tet offensive began and with it a re-evaluation of the American role from the beginning. Helms continued to support Johnson loyally, but his memoirs echoed those of others who believed that the mistake was originally made by not exploring Ho Chi Minh's overtures to President Truman. "Some of the Americans who dealt closely with Ho in those early days saw him as a nationalist and idealist, a person whom the United States might profitably have supported."[71]

A week before the Tet attacks began, General Westmoreland sent the Pentagon his assessment of the enemy's anticipated winter-spring offensive. He agreed with the CIA station in Saigon that the incipient offensive had already demonstrated increased urgency and tempo, but he thought that it was really a somewhat desperate attempt to force diplomatic negotiations for a coalition government. It would be short-lived because the enemy had problems maintaining force

---

67 Special National Intelligence Estimate, 14.3-67,*Capabilities of the Vietnamese Communists for Fighting in South Vietnam*, November 13, 1967, p. 1; Adams, *War of Numbers*, p. 129.
68 *Ibid*, pp, 2, 7.
69 Congressional Briefing by General Westmoreland, President Johnson, and Mr. Rostow, November 16, 1967, *Johnson Papers,* Congressional Briefings, Box 1.
70 *Ibid.* (I have reversed the order of the last two sentences quoted from the minutes of the briefing.)
71 *A Look Over My Shoulder*, p. 309.

confidence. On and on he continued this litany of disasters, countering any and all arguments advanced in the Helms Memo.[62]

The hopeful conclusions of the Military Assistance Command Vietnam (MACV) about enemy numbers in the 1967 Order of Battle (O/B) controversy with the CIA were even more speculative than the Helms memo or Rostow's dire predictions. Here, indeed, was a high stakes dispute. MACV had been under intense pressure to show real progress in the war. On September 12, 1967, as CIA estimators were meeting with MACV counterparts, the President turned to General Harold Johnson and made it plain what he wanted: "On balance we have not been losing, the President said, and we will change it a lot more. The President said we should say that the enemy cannot hold up under this pressure." [63] Given the attrition strategy associated with graduated escalation—there were eventually half a million American soldiers in Vietnam—the only way to demonstrate progress was through body-counts. If the enemy suffered as many casualties as MACV claimed, it was possible to imagine that the situation in Vietnam was approaching the long-promised "cross-over" point where American reinforcements outnumbered the ability of the North Vietnamese/Viet Cong to put new men into the field.[64]

Many CIA analysts doubted MACV's estimates about the enemy's O/B, even those like George Carver, who normally landed on the optimist's side of the Vietnamese fence. The dispute raged through September to November, 1967, and ever afterwards in books and lawsuits. CIA analysts even had some deeply worried allies in the military concerned that MACV had underestimated the size of enemy forces. There is no question but that the Oval Office was also involved in the pressures that forced a "compromise" during a meeting in Saigon, as Rostow cabled the President, "The danger is press will latch on to previous underestimate and revive credibility gap talk."[65]

It was becoming harder and harder to close the credibility gap, and everyone was expected to put a shoulder to the castle doors. Helms's role continued to be an ambiguous one. He had sent the "secret" Memorandum to Johnson telling the president it represented not the work of one man but a consensus, yet he also now agreed the CIA must "compromise" on a lower figure, 250,000, for the O/B estimate. The DCI's complicity in accepting MACV's stonewalling undercut the logic of the September Memorandum and left Helms exposed to harsh criticism by some of his best analysts. [66]

George Carver had led the intelligence community delegation to Saigon that accepted the compromise and now rejoined the group, walking down the sunny side of the street. In the works for 144 days, the "compromise" Estimate had gone through twenty-two drafts, "the hardest-fought in agency history." "Our information has improved substantially in the past year or two," it admitted in an opening paragraph, "but the unconventional nature of the war poses difficult intelligence

---

[62] "Notes of the President's Meeting with Australian Broadcast Group," September 20, 1967, Meeting Notes File, Box 3, Johnson Library.
[63] "Weekly Luncheon with Secretaries Rusk and McNamara . . . ," September 12, 1967, *ibid.,* Box 2.
[64] See Harold Ford, *CIA and the Vietnam Policymakers*, pp. 86-7.
[65] *Ibid.*, p. 96.
[66] *Ibid.*, pp. 96-7; and see, Sam Adams, *War of Numbers: An Intelligence Memoir* (South Royalton, VT: Steerforth Press, 1994). In his memoirs, moreover, Helms places the memo in September 1968, months after the Tet offensive. This may be a simple mistake. *A Look Over My Shoulder*, p. 314.

leadership. "I believe that you will find it interesting," the DCI wrote in his cover letter.[55] In his memoirs, Helms noted that he sent the memo, *Implications of an Unfavorable Outcome in Vietnam*, in a sealed envelope with a blunt warning, "The attached paper is sensitive, particularly if its *existence* [emphasis added by Helms] were to leak." He wanted LBJ to be responsible for any further dissemination of the document. "The mere rumor that such a document existed," he added in his memoirs, "would in itself have been political dynamite."[56]

Even so, Helms closed his covering letter with an ambivalent nod to Oval Office convictions about the war. "It has no bearing on whether the present political-military outlook within Vietnam makes acceptance of such an outcome advisable or inadvisable."[57] Helms maintained as well that the Memo was not an argument for or against getting out; "We are not defeatist out here" [at Langley]. But the author argued gradual withdrawal could be managed to minimize damage to the nation's position abroad and lessen the domestic political fall-out. And it ended, "If the analysis here advances the discussion at all, it is in the direction of suggesting that the risks [of an unfavorable outcome] are probably more limited and controllable than most previous argument has indicated."[58]

For Lyndon Johnson, however, it offered very little political help as the proposed timetable would work out "to Communist advantage within a relatively brief period, say, a year or so." The Memo conceded the impossibility of disentangling such a process from the "whole continuum of interacting forces." "The view forward is always both hazy and kaleidoscopic; those who have to act on such a view can have no certainties but must make choices on what <u>appears</u> [*sic*] at the moment to be the margin of advantage."[59] Helms's "secret" Memo to Johnson apparently remained a deep secret. Robert S. McNamara writes that he did not see it until after he left office and returned to the Johnson Presidential Library to do research for his memoirs. That is not surprising. It is hard to imagine Lyndon Johnson immersing himself for very long in the cloudy speculations the author had imposed on his conclusions.[60]

He had come to see the CIA, Johnson told a visitor, just like a problem the farmer had milking his cow. As the pail filled up, the cow kept swishing its muddy tail in the clean, warm milk.[61] Comments Johnson made to Australian journalists about the domino thesis, with the assistance of National Security Adviser Walt Rostow, might be seen as his response to the memo. Turning to the National Security Adviser, the President asked him to summarize the consequences of pulling out of Vietnam. Rostow gave the domino thesis a new spin by suggesting the first reaction would be "an immediate and profound political crisis," not in Vietnam, but in the United States. Out of this turmoil, he argued, the forces behind a "powerful isolationism" would emerge triumphant. Johnson then led him on to a further conclusion: "They would say our character had worn out?" Rostow replied, "Yes." And while we were divided and preoccupied by the debilitating debate, the USSR and China would seize dangerous initiatives. NATO "could never hold up" as America pursued its lost self-

---

55 Helms to Johnson, September 12, 1967, NSF, Country File, Vietnam, Box 259, *Johnson Papers.*

56 Richard Helms, *A Look Over My Shoulder: A Life in the Central Intelligence Agency* (New York: Random House, 2003), pp. 314-5.

57 Helms to Johnson, September 12, 1967.

58 Memorandum, *Implications of an Unfavorable Outcome in Vietnam*, September 11, 1967, p. 33; Robert S. McNamara, with Brian VanDeMark, *In Retrospect: The Tragedy and Lessons of Vietnam* (New York: Vintage, 1966), pp. 292-3.

59 *Implications*, p. 5.

60 McNamara, *In Retrospect*, p. 293.

61 Johnson's story was related to me by George Allen.

troops were taking place in exactly the same locations where the Vietminh had emerged out of hiding to attack the French.[53]

Eighteen months of bombing, it said, had not reduced North Vietnam's ability to send supplies to the south through alternative routes in Laos, and the number of enemy forces had very likely been underestimated. Destruction of North Vietnam's small industrial base would not mean much because Russia and China supplied the necessary war materials. It might, in fact, make it easier to divert manpower resources to other tasks in support of the war.

The Lao Dong (Communist) Party controlled the war in both parts of Vietnam, it went on, and while that might confirm Washington's insistence that the war had begun as an "invasion," it also suggested that the "will to persist" could not be localized and reduced to the leadership cadre in Hanoi. As it happened, North Vietnamese leaders were in Moscow at the same time McNamara was reading the report he had requested, and, while admitting their problems, refused to listen to Russian arguments that they should show more interest in negotiations. The Communists were no doubt disappointed by the failure to win the war when Saigon was in disarray but not so much as to force any revision in strategy. They were waiting also for pressures to build up in American domestic politics just as they had in France before the end of that war. Whether that was an invalid comparison—policymakers hated that analogy—there were ominous similarities. Just as in the first Vietnam war, the enemy had suffered horrendous casualties over the past year, and now as then there was no indication of a loss of will to continue.

However devastating to arguments that the war could be won with a little more or even a lot more bombing, the Memorandum also gave some comfort to those who believed that the other side was hurting and that morale had become a problem for the enemy. Like some other papers, *The Vietnamese Communists' Will to Persist* held out some hope that if American military successes continued the enemy might feel the need to reconsider its strategy in about a year's time, but it was presented in the final paragraph of the summary and not as a major theme. McNamara certainly found little in the paper to confirm the stream of optimistic reports from military headquarters in Saigon. In a conversation about the study with analyst George Allen, McNamara said he found it very interesting and asked "what we might be doing wrong in the war." The Memorandum had raised fundamental questions about whether any change of strategy or tactics would produce different results, however, and Allen's comments did not encourage new expectations. The Secretary of Defense had begun to reassess the entire situation, including his past confidence that quantitative measurements showed the war being won. It was a process that would take another year and culminate in a famous memorandum to President Johnson on November 1, 1967, advocating changes in the bombing policy and heavier emphasis upon seeking negotiations.[54]

Admiral Raborn's successor, Richard Helms, something of an old Vietnam "hand," ordered another Memorandum meanwhile that revisited the domino thesis one last time in the Johnson Administration. The burden of the paper suggested that, yes, an American withdrawal would be de-stabilizing in the Southeast Asia area, but the impact could be managed. The greatest concern would be how to avoid a US loss of self confidence, and that was a matter for skillful political

---

[53] *Ibid.*, Appendix IX, p. 4.

[54] George W. Allen, *None So Blind: A Personal Account of the Intelligence Failure in Vietnam* (Chicago: Ivan R. Dee, 2001), pp. 212-7.

the recommendations of Walt Rostow and General Maxwell Taylor to violate the 1954 agreement which restricted the military assistance group provided for the South Vietnamese. . . ."[48]

McCone's dissent had been couched in super-hawk terms—no troops without massive air strikes—but he never expected the President would accept that recommendation, and it appears the DCI, "desperately unhappy," had used a dramatic ploy, his resignation, to force consideration of the pitfalls of the policy LBJ had accepted from his other advisers. By early 1966 the brief moment of optimism within ONE had passed. On January 19, 1966, it assessed that the North Vietnamese had judged they could absorb "a great deal more bombing" and that they still had "political and military advantages" that promised ultimate success or at least a far more favorable settlement than the United States was willing to accept. A major finding was that the Soviet Union really did not have much influence over Hanoi's decisions. Although Moscow would prefer that the war be de-escalated because of its own concerns with European issues, it could do little but persevere in supporting the North Vietnamese and wait for some opportunity for diplomacy. Another Estimate a few days later, one vigorously contested by the Air Force, concluded that even with bombing the ports and other attempts to interdict the movement of supplies into South Vietnam for the VC, Hanoi could still move "substantially greater amounts than in 1965." [49]

The Air Force dissent complained that the Estimate had excluded consideration of what bombing would do to the "psychological fabric" of the enemy and thus to "North Vietnamese will to continue the war."[50] In August the CIA corporately addressed the question of "will" directly in a 300-page "Memorandum." The comprehensive study had been requested by Secretary of Defense Robert McNamara, who would explain after the war that he had sought this intelligence study out of unhappiness about the analysis he received daily from his own Defense Intelligence Agency and other places. Chock full of tables and statistics—perhaps intended to impress the Pentagon "boss" in the language he knew best—the Memorandum covered every "measurable" aspect of the war conceivable.

The Memorandum detailed the ways the North Vietnamese coped with interdiction as no other paper had done before it, talking about the speed with which roads and bridges were repaired. In one section, for example, it discussed the imaginative ways the North Vietnamese dealt with bombed out railroad bridges by using large barges with tracks installed on the decks![51] In contrast to the mobilization of civilian resources in the North, it pointed out, American military forces in the South required a supply and support system that required up to 80 percent of their manpower. And in another remarkable section, almost in passing, the Memorandum talked about VC taxation of GVN petroleum trucks in enemy-controlled territory.[52]

The Memorandum thus covered almost every aspect of the war, going back to the 1954 Geneva Conference. Indeed, the story of the French defeat had rarely been told so well as in these pages. With a sense of irony about current policy, this section noted that ambushes of American

---

[48] Institute of International Studies, UC Berkeley, Conversations with History, *John McCone Interview*, April 21, 1988, http://globetrotter.berkeley.edu/conversations/McCone, downloaded February 28, 2005.
[49] Memorandum, *Reactions to Continuation or Termination of the Pause in Air Attacks on the DRV*, January 19, 1966, pp. 3-4; Special National Intelligence Estimate 10-1-66, *Possible Effects of a Proposed US Course of Action on DRV Capability to Support the Insurgency in South Vietnam*, February 4, 1966, p. 3.
[50] Memorandum, *Reactions to Continuation or Termination of the Pause in Air Attacks on the DRV*, pp. 3-4.
[51] Memorandum, *The Vietnamese Communists' Will to Persist*, August 26, 1966, Appendix I, pp. 20-31.
[52] *Ibid.*, Appendix IV, p. 2; Appendix V, p. 17.

Thus the argument over the way the war should be fought and with what forces had already commenced even before the decision to send 100,000 troops at the end of July 1965. It was a bad omen. An ONE Estimate admitted the intelligence agencies had no real answer to questions about the impact of sending troops but feared the US might "acquire both the responsibility for the war and the stigma of an army with colonialist ambitions." The outcome would depend not on military measures but on the total "effectiveness" of the US effort. As for the American belief that the new troops would smash the VC in a set battle, it was more likely the VC would adapt to American strategy and continue to seek victory through protracted conflict without ever "letting US/GVN forces engage them in decisive battle."[46]

Here again the analysis was on target. In September 1965, however, the estimators sounded a bit more hopeful—and "hawkish." In the past, a new National Intelligence Estimate said, Hanoi had reason to doubt that the United States was willing to undertake a protracted war, feelings strengthened by repeated "US soundings and overtures for negotiations." Now with military successes and other tangible evidence that Washington was willing to increase its commitment, the Vietnamese *mise en scène* had changed. And it might result in the North Vietnamese moving toward political and diplomatic initiatives.[47]

The Estimate seemed to confirm the views of hardliners in Johnson's war council. Curiously, moreover, it followed the resignation of John McCone as DCI, to be replaced first by Admiral William F. Raborn and then by Richard Helms a year later. McCone's departure has long been a subject of some controversy. Clearly it was connected with differences with the President over Vietnam, but it had been assumed these extended only to the way LBJ was waging the war. McCone was a conservative Cold Warrior brought in by John Kennedy in the wake of the Bay of Pigs debacle to demonstrate that the Administration was not soft on Communism in the Caribbean or anywhere. But in retirement McCone revealed in a series of interviews that he had had doubts about Vietnam from the beginning and was unhappy when JFK took the first step up the escalation ladder.

Johnson's decision to send 100,000 troops in July 1965 made McCone "desperately unhappy," he said, and "That is when I parted company with them." In those debates, McCone had argued sending troops in such numbers without unleashing America's full power in air strikes was wrong. "I took the position that if you're gonna be in a war, you'd better win it!" But it was the military and Secretary of Defense Robert McNamara McCone blamed most for ignoring CIA Estimates that Vietnam promised only more escalation and huge numbers of casualties.

What do you do in such a situation, asked the interviewer? "You have to do your best to persuade those who are not willing to accept your analysis that they are wrong and ought to take a second look." What, then, should Johnson have done differently in his conduct of the war? "In the first place, he should not have conducted it. You see Kennedy made a mistake when he accepted

---

[46] Memorandum, *Reactions to a Further US Buildup in South Vietnam*, June 10, 1965, pp. 2-3; see also, Special National Intelligence Estimate 10-9-65, *Communist and Free World Reactions to a Possible US Course of Action*, July 23, 1965.

[47] Special National Intelligence Estimate 10-11-65, *Probable Communist Reactions to a US Course of Action*, September 22, 1965, pp. 2, 9.

The signal could be seen in America, and that satisfied Johnson's immediate need, but it was too weak, apparently, to impress either North Vietnam or South Vietnam. In the post-Tonkin dawn, Johnson had to risk his footing on the slippery slope he could see before him or pull back to reconsider his next step. He could not stand still. In October ONE produced an Estimate on the continuing disarray of the Saigon government. One of the gloomiest in the entire series of NIE's during the war, it acknowledged that things were as bad as they had ever been, even before the November coup. "Indeed, we cannot presently see any likely source of real leadership."[43] By early 1965 the political situation had reached the point where only drastic measures would convince the South Vietnamese to remain loyal to Saigon. Out of that dark foreboding was launched the bombing campaign, Rolling Thunder, the albatross that strangled diplomatic options instead of bringing Hanoi to its knees.

The first air attacks in early February 1965 were said to be in retaliation for a VC strike against an American base, Pleiku, in the central highlands, killing eight Americans and wounding many more, but planning for a sustained offensive against North Vietnam had been in the works for some time. What put an exclamation point on the American attack was the presence of Soviet Premier Aleksei Kosygin in Hanoi. Kosygin had come to repair relations with the North Vietnamese leaders, who had criticized Moscow's supposedly inadequate aid program and cautionary political advice. An intelligence Memorandum drew another darker conclusion from the visit, however. The assessment, made on February 5, 1965, was that Kosygin was there, in effect, to be in on the kill when Vietnam fell and steal glory from the Chinese. "We accordingly believe that the Soviet leaders seek to share—and guide—what they believe to be a Communist bandwagon." As the Russians saw the situation, it argued, the United States was not going to intervene and a Communist victory was drawing near. They expected Washington was close to being ready to negotiate a face-saving exit.[44]

This Memorandum, which, in fact, could have served as a basic rationale for the bombing campaign that ensued, is something of an anomaly among Estimates not only for its portrayal of Russian policy towards Vietnam but for its suggestion that Kosygin's visit presaged a new Soviet forward attitude in Southeast Asia, and it may have reenergized a theoretical US concern with Soviet profit-taking from "wars of national liberation." But there was concern developing with the question of whether the bombing was suitable punishment for the "crime" of attacking Pleiku. An ONE Estimate went to the core of the problem. Hanoi had anticipated a "prolonged and grinding struggle." It was bolstered not simply by material support from Russia and China but by doctrinal belief in the inevitable success of a "people's war" and recent memories of victory over the French. "Our present Estimate is that the odds are against the postulated US attacks leading the DRV [Democratic Republic of Vietnam] to make conciliatory gestures to secure a respite from the bombing; rather, we believe that the DRV would persevere in supporting the insurgency in the South." Air Force Intelligence dissented from this Estimate, arguing not for the last time in the Vietnam war that the selective bombing since Rolling Thunder began "may well have led Hanoi seriously to underestimate the extent of US determination to exert the necessary power to force discontinuance of DRV support for the insurgency in the south."[45]

---

[43] Special National Intelligence Estimate 53-2-64, *The Situation in South Vietnam*, October 1, 1964, p. 8.
[44] Special Memorandum No. 7-65, *The Dimensions of Kosygin's Trip*, February 5, 1965, p. 1.
[45] Special National Intelligence Estimate 10-6-65, *Probable Communist Reactions to Certain US Actions*, June 2, 1965, pp. 3-4.

Within weeks the political situation was literally set afire with the Buddhist protests and self-immolations on street corners in the middle of the day. The Kennedy Administration and American television audiences watched these scenes with horror, and ONE could now use straightforward language in assessing that unless Diem addressed the Buddhist issue, "disorders will probably flare again and the chances of a coup or assassination attempts against him will become better than even." At the same time, the new paper added, Washington's "firm line" had increased Diem's uneasiness about US involvement in his country. "This attitude will almost certainly persist, and further pressure to reduce the US presence in the country is likely."[39]

The story of the October coup and the divisions over its wisdom within the Kennedy Administration is a never ending controversy. An ONE memorandum on "South Vietnam's Leaders" written in late August or early September, 1963, unfortunately has not been located. A pointed rebuttal to that memo dated September 4, 1963 argued that the Buddhist protest had been overblown, however, and that the war could still be won with Diem. The what-ifs in the aftermath of the coup and Kennedy's assassination continue to swirl through Vietnam literature like October leaves in the wind, never settling for long on solid historical evidence.[40]

Years of Escalation

In May 1964 a Special National Intelligence Estimate said it was impossible to set any meaningful odds about whether Hanoi's leaders would prefer to lower their expectations rather than face "the destruction of their country." Already bruited about in Washington were a variety of escalatory steps, including bombing attacks on North Vietnam. In response to an American escalation, ONE did not see a strong military reaction by China, and especially not by the Soviet Union, unless American troops actually crossed the so-called demilitarized zone. Two weeks later, in early June, Sherman Kent, chair of the Board of National Estimates, sent a memorandum to DCI McCone challenging the very premise of the "Domino Effect." If one looked at these as a pair, the first describing the likely reactions of Beijing and Moscow and the second arguing the loss of Vietnam and Laos would not mean Communism's inexorable spread across Southeast Asia, Vietnam's fate shrank back to its territorial limits.[41]

But the domestic political implications of "losing" a country, any country, to "international communism" alarmed presidents and their West Wing advisers. Lyndon Johnson was especially nervous about Vietnam in an election year. "Using troops is the very last thing we want to do," LBJ told David Lilienthal, "or getting stuck with a "sink-hole kind of 'war' . . . just before an election here."[42] Moreover, his "crisis managers," National Security Adviser McGeorge Bundy and Defense Secretary Robert McNamara, assured him that the best way to show his determination not to lose Vietnam was to send a signal. So LBJ sent planes to bomb North Vietnamese PT-boat bases on August 4 and submitted the Gulf of Tonkin Resolution to a compliant Congress.

---

[39] Special National Intelligence Estimate 53-2-63, *The Situation in South Vietnam*, July 10, 1963, p. 1.

[40] Memorandum to DCI, September 4, 1963.

[41] Special National Intelligence Estimate 50-2-64, *Probable Consequences of Certain US Actions with Respect to Vietnam and Laos*, May 25, 1964, and ONE Memorandum, *Would the Loss of South Vietnam and Laos Precipitate a "Domino Effect" in the Far East?*, June 9, 1964.

[42] Lilienthal, journal entry, June 16, 1964, *The Papers of David Lilienthal*, Mudd Library, Princeton, Box 208.

signaled Washington's determination to avoid defeat. When it came down to it, the reaction to American escalation would be counter-escalation. The paper thus skipped around an underlying issue: what use were signals in the kind of war being waged in Vietnam?[35]

Kennedy increased American forces in Vietnam and turned for advice to British counter-insurgency expert Sir Robert Thompson, whose methods had been credited with success in Malaya. These centered on programs at the village level and things like the Special Forces, or "Green Berets." Kennedy met Thompson the first time in early April 1963 and was pleased by his reports that the war was going well in Vietnam, the strategic hamlet program, in particular. Indeed, if things continued to go well, the President should announce he was reducing the number of American advisers by one thousand by the end of the year. This would demonstrate confidence in the Saigon government and weaken Communist propaganda.[36]

The upbeat attitude that spring engulfed as well the office of DCI John McCone out at CIA headquarters in Langley, Virginia. The Office of National Estimates had been at work on a new Estimate since the previous fall, and as it went forward to interested parties, including those in the military who claimed to "know Vietnam best," it received heavy criticism for being too negative. At McCone's orders ONE revised its original paper so that the first sentence now read: "We believe that Communist progress has been blunted and that the situation is improving."

The story of McCone's dramatic intervention is told in detail by former senior CIA analyst Harold P. Ford, whose book, *CIA and the Vietnam Policymakers: Three Episodes 1962-1968*, explores the fundamental issue present in all Estimate writing and analysis.[37] The analyst is the modern messenger whose penalty for bringing bad news might not be so severe as in ancient times, but who does risk "banishment" of sorts if his conclusions fail to serve a policymaker's need to appear in control of events. Once around that corner the analyst can qualify optimistic assessments with reference points that nudge the reader to reconsider assumptions. The danger is that no one reads beyond page one. And even after these analytic judgments become sharper, as they did in later years, policymakers could always extract paragraphs where the light at the end of the tunnel shined brightest.

In the specific case of NIE 53-63, published on April 17, 1963, the Estimate followed the first sentence affirming that Communist progress had been blunted with a judgment that while the North Vietnamese would not introduce regular military units in an effort to obtain a quick victory, the Communists hoped military pressure and political deterioration would in time create circumstances for a *coup de grâce* or a political settlement that favored their cause. The document proceeded down that path, observing along the way "some promise" in political and security matters and raising doubts here and there about the government's ability to translate military success into political stability. It was all there in the fine print.[38]

---

[35] Special National Intelligence Estimate, 10-4-61, *Probable Communist Reactions to Certain US Actions in South Vietnam*, November 7, 1961.

[36] Peter Busch, *All the Way with JFK? Britain, the US, and the Vietnam War* (Oxford: Oxford Univ. Press, 2003), p. 94.

[37] Harold P. Ford, *CIA and the Vietnam Policymakers: Three Episodes 1962-1968* (Washington: CIA Center for the Study of Intelligence, 1998), pp. 14-19.

[38] National Intelligence Estimate 53-63, *Prospects in South Vietnam*, April 17, 1963, p. 1ff.

This was an especially bad time to hear such news. The Eisenhower Administration was looking very old and tired. First term successes in the Cold War were yesterday's news, and the headlines since the 1956 Suez Crisis were about disturbing trends. Above all there was Fidel Castro in Havana. Democratic candidate John F. Kennedy kept repeating at every whistle stop that the Republicans had allowed the Communists to take power only 90 miles from Florida.

Such rhetoric was sure to bring a challenge to JFK to prove he could do better. Eisenhower himself challenged JFK on the day before the inaugural. Laos was critical to American security, Ike lectured the former junior naval officer. He had to be prepared to intervene to stop the Communist threat. Kennedy sidestepped Laos, however, and chose a diplomatic path. The real trouble, he knew, was brewing in Saigon. Was Diem a friend any more, or was he just getting in the way? Inside CIA's Saigon station, as in Washington, opinions differed on that crucial question. When a disaffected South Vietnamese Air Force colonel launched a coup attempt, one CIA officer, George Carver, Jr., got caught in the middle while attempting to report events on the scene.

The episode had multiple consequences. Carver had to be recalled from Saigon and became a powerful voice against Diem, but then, after the 1963 coup, a powerful voice for staying the course. The Embassy's "neutrality" during the short-lived 1960 coup, wrote DCI William Colby in his memoirs, convinced Diem and his brother Nhu that they could not absolutely rely on the Americans and that they would have to deal with the United States as "yet another outside force" with a potential for help but also for opposition.[33]

The first months of the Kennedy Administration brought the Bay of Pigs debacle and the blustery atmosphere at the Vienna Summit. In Vienna, Kennedy and Soviet leader Nikita Khrushchev agreed to try to neutralize Laos, and a conference followed in 1962. Laos was not the prelude to US involvement in Vietnam; instead, it was the Bay of Pigs far away in the Caribbean that had the greatest impact on Vietnam policy. In the aftermath of the failed landing and the subsequent humiliating capture of a Cuban exile brigade trained by the CIA with Kennedy's approval, Walt W. Rostow, then an assistant to National Security Adviser McGeorge Bundy, wrote to several officials warning against involvement in Laos, urging immediate attention to Vietnam. The first thing to consider, he argued, was the need to dispel "any perception that we are up against a game we can't handle." Holding the line in Vietnam would demonstrate to the world that we could "deal with indirect aggression."[34]

This variation on the credibility theme placed great emphasis on a general issue—"a game we can't handle"—rather than support of any particular friend. The distinction is an important one, and it bespoke commitment to whoever occupied the Saigon presidential palace. In November 1961 the intelligence community responded to "hypothetical" questions about likely North Vietnamese reactions to a much stepped-up military presence and accompanying warnings that Hanoi must cease support for the Viet Cong (VC) or face air attacks. The Communist bloc would launch an intense international campaign to brand the US as an aggressor, it averred, but probably not much more would happen. Inside South Vietnam, however, one could expect attacks on American installations. The three Communist governments—Russia, China, and North Vietnam—would continue to feel confident the VC held the upper hand, but they would have to recognize such steps

---

[33] William Colby, *Honorable Men: My Life in the CIA* (New York: Simon and Schuster, 1978), pp. 164-5.

[34] Rostow quoted in, Lloyd C. Gardner, *Pay Any Price: Lyndon Johnson and the Wars for Vietnam* (Chicago: Ivan R. Dee, 1995), p. 44.

slowly improving, but Hanoi had to rely on Soviet help in obtaining supplies from Burma. Politically there were signs that the Marxist bond with China had not eliminated traditional distrust and that Hanoi hoped to balance Beijing's influence with closer ties to Moscow. Here was yet another suggestion that North Vietnam was something of an independent actor, but with China making threatening gestures in the Taiwan Straits and Sputnik later orbiting the globe, such maneuvers by Hanoi made little impact on US policymakers.[29]

The North Vietnamese, said the July 1956 Estimate, were infiltrating the Saigon government and trying to promote sympathy for Hanoi's claim to be the only legitimate nationalist force in the belief that such combinations of soft power and subversion would undermine the Diem government. But absent a major guerrilla effort to disrupt South Vietnam, the immediate security picture was encouraging. Moreover, one objective of America's Vietnam policy seemed to be working well: Japanese trade was increasing at the expense of French imports. It remained to be seen whether the government would prove effective over the longer run in dealing with economic and social problems, and here the Estimates expressed serious reservations. [30]

By mid-1959 these reservations had hardened into outright alarm at South Vietnam's unwillingness or inability to lay a foundation for future economic progress, unlike the North Vietnamese, who, whatever their methods, now had "generally realistic" policies in place. So far, American foreign aid, in the form of dollar grants to pay for imports, an Estimate warned, had provided the South Vietnamese with a relatively high standard of living. But how long could that last? Diem refused to take any measures that might reduce that standard, code words for saying he would not tax his wealthy supporters or inquire too closely into what was being raked off by speculators. He hoped American investments and Japanese war reparations would make such tough decisions unnecessary. But he would listen to no advice about how to run his government or the South Vietnamese economy. "Diem has indicated that South Vietnam expects the maintenance of large US aid and special consideration from the US as a reward for its steadfast support. Failure to receive such special consideration could lead Diem to assume a stance of greater independence *vis-à-vis* the US." The analysis and judgment were both on the money. For the moment, however, the lull continued as the North Vietnamese appeared unlikely to go beyond propaganda, subversion, and paramilitary action, convinced it would "mean war with the US." Diem would not change, however, and therein lay the future predicament that would divide policymakers.[31]

American military assumptions at this time posited the real danger to South Vietnam as a Korean-like invasion from the North, which fit in well with Diem's desire to keep American attention diverted from internal domestic practices. In August 1960 a brief Special National Intelligence Estimate questioned those assumptions with a dire warning about the internal situation. Even within urban groups and government circles, it said, Diem's leadership was under mounting criticism, while out in the countryside the Viet Cong, supported and guided by Hanoi, had stepped up their guerrilla warfare. "These adverse trends are not irreversible, but if they remain unchecked, they will almost certainly in time cause the collapse of Diem's regime."[32]

---

[29] National Intelligence Estimate, 63-56, *Probable Developments in North and South Vietnam Through Mid-1957*, July 17, 1956, pp. 4-5.
[30] *Ibid*., p. 14.
[31] National Intelligence Estimate 63-59, *Prospects for North and South Vietnam*, May 26, 1959, pp. 5-6, 8.
[32] Special National Intelligence Estimate 63.1-60, *Short-Term Trends in South Vietnam*, August 23, 1960, p. 1.

After a few months in Saigon the General became convinced that Diem would fail—sooner rather than later. By April 1955 when he returned home to report to President Eisenhower, Collins and the CIA were at odds over the capabilities of the Diem government. "Diem stinks," summed up his view. "If chaos is to be averted, Diem must go." For their part, intelligence agencies were hardly in love with Diem's one-man (or one family) rule, but they thought the General overlooked some significant questions, and, even more importantly, exaggerated the likelihood that whoever or whatever replaced him would have a better chance of success in the volatile climate of Saigon politics, where criminal sects (in some cases guided by French interests) controlled the police.[24]

Estimates also pointed out that dismissing Diem might not be so easy, as he might well manage to set up an alternative power center leading to civil war inside South Vietnam. "We believe that the resolution of the present impasse and the implementation of the Diem solution [building a nationalist government] would to a critical degree depend upon firm and substantial US and French support." The Estimate also suggested that if Diem thought he was about to be removed from office, he might precipitate a fight with the Binh Xuyen sect that controlled the police. If he won, thereby increasing his prestige, "He would be in a better position to proceed with proposed programs for strengthening South Vietnam."[25]

In the event, that is exactly what happened. Diem initiated a "war" against the sects and effectively ended the debate in Washington.[26] Henceforth he would be "Our Man in Saigon"—for almost a decade until the Buddhist crisis. The episode was notable also for bringing out relatively strong and unambiguous views about alternatives, something that would not usually be the case in future papers. When the time for elections came and passed, a National Intelligence Estimate in July 1956 noted that the co-chairs of the Geneva Conference, the United Kingdom and the Soviet Union, had implicitly approved an indefinite postponement of the reunification issue. [27]

If there was a betrayal of Geneva, then, it might be argued, both London and Moscow were accessories after the fact. The outlook in Vietnam now was for a lull in the struggle as both sides strengthened their bases. In North Vietnam, the first priority was to develop more effective controls over the people and the economy. Violence and intimidation had been employed "selectively" but not on a scale comparable to what had occurred in China after the Communist triumph. Between 30,000 and 100,000 landlords had been put to death in North Vietnam, said another Estimate, and the backlash at these methods had caused the regime to lose popularity and forced reconsiderations that slowed down socialization of agriculture.[28] Rice production, a key measure of success, was

---

[24] The "crisis" of April-May 1955 can be followed in a series of Memoranda to the Director of Central Intelligence and in National Intelligence Estimates, beginning with, *The Crisis in Saigon*, April 4, 1955; *Memorandum for the Director of Central Intelligence*, April 23, 1955; National Intelligence Estimate, 63.1-2-55, *Possible Developments in South Vietnam*, April 26, 1955; and Special National Intelligence Estimate, 63.1-2/1-55, *The Current Saigon Crisis*, May 2, 1955.

[25] National Intelligence Estimate 63.1-2-55, *Possible Developments in South Vietnam*, April 26, 1955.

[26] For the fullest account of Diem's "strategy" and the likely involvement of CIA agent Edward G. Lansdale in prompting the beleaguered Vietnamese leader to act or lose power, see, Anderson, *Trapped By Success*, pp. 103-115. The documents printed here do not resolve the questions about Lansdale's role. They are not action papers but they do suggest what the thinking was in opposition to General Collins' efforts to change policy. The debate was the last significant turning point until the summer of 1963.

[27] National Intelligence Estimate, 63-56, *Probable Developments in North and South Vietnam Through Mid-1957*, July 17, 1956, p. 2.

[28] National Intelligence Estimate 63.2-57, *The Prospects for North Vietnam*, May 14, 1957, pp. 2-3.

As the Geneva Conference delegates returned home, intelligence Estimates suggested that Ho's path to power still might come through elections, or, equally likely, when whatever regime the French and/or the Americans put in place began to falter. "Although it is possible that the French and Vietnamese, even with firm support from the US and other powers, may be able to establish a strong regime in South Vietnam," concluded the Estimate of August 3, 1954, "we believe that the chances for this development are poor and, moreover, that the situation is more likely to continue to deteriorate progressively over the next year."[19]

There was a loophole in the Geneva Declaration, however, that might at least gain some time. "There is no provision for forcing the parties to implement or adhere to the agreements." Even with pressure from the supervisory team from India, Canada and Poland, the elections could be put on hold indefinitely. With guidance and material aid the three states that once made up French Indochina—Laos, Cambodia, and Vietnam—"might" thus attain viability and permanence. The energy and resourcefulness required for "building national states" would not "arise spontaneously among the non-Communist Indochinese," it cautioned, "but will have to be sponsored and nurtured from without."[20]

Our Man in Saigon, 1954-1963

Vietnam had been divided, of course, and that put it in a separate category. Still, there was something to work with here, especially since the new leader in Saigon, Ngo Dinh Diem, did not recognize the Geneva Declaration as binding upon his government. The intelligence analysts thus foresaw a small window for creating a viable South Vietnam in the two-year period before all-Vietnamese elections were supposed to reunite the country. It was a small window in physical terms as well, one that permitted only a few weapons and military replacements to squeeze through, not nearly enough to fight a big war. Until the deadline for elections passed, the analysts believed, there would not be a widespread resumption of guerrilla activities, much less an attempt at an all-out military assault. Communist bloc fears of bringing on a full-scale American intervention still ruled out such adventurism, but, equally important, the North Vietnamese Communist leadership needed time to consolidate their rule.[21]

During the Geneva Conference, Bao Dai, the puppet "emperor" of Indochina, had named Ngo Dinh Diem his Prime Minister. Although Diem was considered pro-American, the initial American reaction was one of wait and see. Besides being staunchly anti-Communist, he had a virtue Dulles could appreciate: he disliked and distrusted the French. Diem had only one program, writes historian David Anderson: obtaining "greater and more direct U.S. assistance."[22] Dulles felt he had little choice but to gamble on Diem. "Frankly, Collins," the Secretary of State confided to General J. Lawton Collins, who was being sent to Saigon as Chief of Mission, "I think our chances of saving the situation there are not more than one in ten."[23]

---

[19] NIE 63-5-54, *Post-Geneva Outlook in Indochina*, August 3, 1954, p.1.
[20] *Ibid.*, pp. 3-4.
[21] National Intelligence Estimate 63.1-55, *Probable Developments in North Vietnam to July 1956*, July 19, 1955, p.2.
[22] David L. Anderson, *Trapped by Success: The Eisenhower Administration and Vietnam, 1953-61* (New York: Columbia Univ. Press, 1991), pp. 51-61.
[23] Oral History of J. Lawton Collins, Mudd Library, Princeton.

An Estimate held, however, that the defeat need not signal a total collapse, if only because non-Communist Indochinese themselves hoped "that the US might intervene in Indochina." In new Estimates a shift was underway from talking about French prospects to possible American intervention. High-level gossip around Washington had increased even as French outposts around Dienbienphu surrendered to the Vietminh.[15]

Vice President Richard M. Nixon, for example, during a speech early in 1954 had launched a trial balloon of sorts (though perhaps not meaning to) about putting ground troops into Vietnam. It whooshed out over an audience of newspaper editors, spun around crazily for a few seconds, and dropped to the floor. But when President Eisenhower described the situation in Southeast Asia as a row of dominoes during a press conference on April 7, 1954, the image captivated the media. Ike's successors were stuck with it for all time. One after another they were called upon to confirm its validity. Eisenhower had talked about losing raw materials and people as country after country toppled over behind the "Bamboo Curtain." Like the intelligence Estimates noted above, Eisenhower stressed Japan's still shaky economic place in the "free world." Japan was the last domino; when the others fell, that vital Asian nation would also pitch over "toward the Communist areas in order to live."[16]

The Geneva Conference concluded on July 21, 1954. Its final declaration established a "military demarcation line" at the 17th parallel. The line "is provisional," it said, "and should not in any way be interpreted as constituting a political or territorial boundary." Negotiations should begin for all-Vietnamese elections in 1956, read the declaration, in order to reunite the country. Under Secretary of State Walter Bedell Smith told the conference that the United States was not prepared to sign off on the declaration; yet, in somewhat ambiguous terms, he added that the United States would not condone threats or the use of force to disturb the demarcation line. As for the proposed all-Vietnamese elections, Smith said the United States had an established policy for nations divided against their will: "We shall continue to seek to achieve unity through free elections supervised by the United Nations to insure that they are conducted fairly."[17]

Reporting on the Geneva Conference, Secretary of State John Foster Dulles mused on the "fundamental blunder" that had allowed the situation to come to this pass where a Communist political victory seemed imminent. "Originally," Dulles wrote in a private memo, "President Roosevelt was against this [a French return to Indochina] on the ground that France did not have a good record as a colonial power and its return would not be accepted by the people." But his successors failed to carry out his intentions to pressure the French to grant eventual independence, with the result that the Communists took charge of the resistance. Dulles determined to rectify the blunder by all-out support for a Vietnamese alternative to Ho, Ngo Dinh Diem.[18]

---

[15] National Intelligence Estimate, *Consequences Within Indochina of the Fall of Dien Bien Phu*, April 30, 1954, p. 2.

[16] National Archives, *Public Papers of the Presidents of the United States: Dwight D. Eisenhower, 1954* (Washington: G.P.O, 1960), pp. 381-90.

[17] Smith's statement can be found in United States Senate, Committee on Foreign Relations, *Background Information Relating to Southeast Asia and Vietnam*, 90th Cong., 1st Sess. (Washington: G.P.O., 1967), p. 83.

[18] Memorandum, July 9, 1954, *The Papers of John Foster Dulles*, Seely Mudd Library, Princeton University, Princeton, New Jersey.

Once the term "international communism" became accepted usage, assertions of Ho Chi Minh's independence from Moscow and Beijing seemed contradictory and intelligence Estimates that called attention to North Vietnamese resistance to Russian or Chinese domination at odds with Cold War orthodoxy. Occasional hints at treating Ho as an Asian Tito never matured into anything substantial. Why that was so is easy to understand: while it might be useful to have a Tito around to demonstrate how the Soviets treated the unorthodox as an enemy, two Titos would be one too many. The exception that proved the rule would then become a challenge to the reality of the frozen monolith of international communism.

However that may be, Estimates continued to assess a French defeat as likely. Paris could not really afford to continue the war in Indochina and yet meet its defense obligations in Europe, asserted a January 10, 1952 Memo prepared in the Office of National Estimates. "In the absence of either some form of internationalization of the Indochina problem or of substantial additional US aid, public sentiment for [French] withdrawal will gain steadily and perhaps accelerate."[12] Hope that the French would agree to "internationalization" had spurred Dulles's drive to create SEATO. Then the enemy could be called "international communism," by far the best way to counter charges of neo-colonialism and put the conflict over emerging nationalism in Asia into a global context

Unfortunately for Dulles's plan, the French saw a better avenue, one that might leave them with influence in Indochinese cultural and economic affairs. They placed their hopes for extricating themselves from the war on the 1954 Geneva Conference. No matter what arguments the Secretary of State posed, neither the French nor the British would agree to join in creating SEATO until after the Geneva Conference had met and explored ways to end the fighting. A Memorandum to the Director of Central Intelligence (DCI) assessed that the Russians and the Communist Chinese—the latter making their debut as a world power—would seek to exploit such weaknesses in the "Western façade." On the other hand, said the Memo, neither Communist power would back a play by Ho Chi Minh's delegation to swallow Vietnam whole. The likely strategy of the Russian and Chinese Communists would be to negotiate a narrow truce, expecting to cash in later when a coalition government emerged to hold all-Vietnamese elections. The other side might even settle for a simple cease-fire with no other conditions but agreement on a future conference to settle political questions. A principal object of Communist policy was to avoid American military intervention.[13]

The Memorandum also drew attention to significant differences in Soviet and Chinese reasoning about a ceasefire. The Soviets wished to advance their post-Stalin peace campaigns, while the Chinese feared an American military presence in a neighboring country. Both were anxious for a truce. That left Ho Chi Minh either to continue waging war without blessings from his backers or to shift from "armed liberation" to political warfare. His prestige at a high point, the Memo concluded, Ho could feel confident about achieving a political victory.[14]

The Dienbienphu fortress fell as the Geneva Conference discussion of Vietnam began on May 7, 1954, ruining French plans for V-E Day celebrations. In one city where the parade had not been canceled, an honor guard marched under black crepe banners instead of its regimental colors.

---

[12] Memorandum for the Director of Central Intelligence, *Critical Developments in French Policy toward Indochina,* January 10, 1952, p. 2.

[13] Memorandum for the Director of Central Intelligence, *Probable Communist Strategy and Tactics at Geneva*, April 19, 1954, pp. 2-3.

[14] *Ibid.*, p. 4.

By the time of the October 13, 1950 Estimate, *Consequences to the US of Communist Domination of Mainland Southeast Asia*, however, any lingering attraction for a "neutral stance" about the French war in Indochina had completely disappeared. Instead, Washington worried the French would fail and add to America's woes. The post-war rush of events—the Russian atomic bomb, the triumph of the Communists in China's civil war, and, above all, the Korean "conflict"—had swept the agenda clean of smudged "what ifs" and "on the other hands." As America's own Indochinese involvement deepened, nevertheless, the old debate surfaced here and there in rueful comments about "missed opportunities" to support Indochinese nationalism.

Given this tense atmosphere, it was surprising that the October 13, 1950 Estimate asserted that Communist domination of mainland Southeast Asia "would not be critical to US security interests but would have serious and immediate and direct consequences." That statement did not go unchallenged. Both the Army and State Department entered caveats declaring that not enough attention had been paid to the long-term consequences of such a loss, whether considered in terms of America's global position or repercussions in countries surrounding the areas of conflict. The Estimate focused on the narrower question of what such a loss would do to the ability to win a global war. It was all a matter of degree to the intelligence agencies preparing the Estimate, but the dissents presaged the emergence later of the "US credibility" issue and the "domino thesis."[9]

The October 1950 Estimate contended that while the Soviet Union would gain "bargaining power" through control of rice supplies in Southeast Asia, the loss might be compensated for if, relieved of the Indochina burden, France paid more attention to Europe's defense. There could be no trade-off, however, if prospects for Japan's reintegration in the world economy were damaged by the "loss" of Southeast Asia. Japan's economic well-being had already become a worrisome matter for policymakers. At the 1945 Potsdam Conference President Truman and his advisors had made it clear they would not divide Japan into occupation zones, as had been done with Germany. Taking sole responsibility for Japan's rehabilitation required finding trade outlets as well as implementing democratic reforms. "Exclusion of Japan from trade with Southeast Asia," warned the October 13, 1950 paper, "would seriously frustrate Japanese prospects for economic recovery." After a peace treaty was signed, it went on, and American soldiers came home, the need for alternate outlets would "impel an unoccupied Japan toward a course of accommodation with International Communism."[10]

Secretary of State John Foster Dulles soon made "international communism" the cornerstone of his ideological foundation for American foreign policy. The term did not appear in the original Southeast Asia Treaty Organization protocol in 1954, but a year later at a Bangkok meeting it was included in the communiqué. "I called attention to the fact that it seemed rather extraordinary," he told a press conference, "when we were making all this effort to combat something, that we couldn't even give it a name. And so the words 'international communism.' I think that from now on it will be respectable in this circle to talk about international communism."[11]

---

[9] ORE 29-50, *Consequences to the US of Communist Domination of Mainland Southeast Asia,* October 13, 1950, p. 1.

[10] *Ibid.*, p. 4.

[11] Quoted in, Lloyd C. Gardner, *Approaching Vietnam: From World War II Through Dienbienphu, 1941-1954* (New York: W.W. Norton & Co., 1988), p. 347.

attitude toward the national aspirations of these areas," it warned, "and at least partially meets their demands for economic assistance, it will risk their becoming actively antagonistic toward the US."[7]

Such criticisms reflected an ongoing debate within the US government over the "colonial issue," one that continued to confront policymakers with unattractive alternatives. Before World War II Americans got little closer to the actual struggles in Asia than reading Pearl Buck's best-selling novels about the poor peasants of China. All that changed with Pearl Harbor and its aftermath. Where tradition and sentiment had been the principal factors in the national outlook, now there were many things to consider about the crumbling colonial system and what would emerge out of its ruins. The Japanese had been driven out, but it was far from clear that the nationalists who rose up in their wake would be friendly to US interests, especially if Washington aligned itself with the colonial powers.

The colonial "question" thus burst forth with a new immediacy, but it still took second place to concerns about the crises of recovery and reconstruction in devastated Europe. How would France recover, for example, if not by restoring the pre-war trade patterns? The onset of the Cold War sharpened the dilemma, pitting the potential short-run costs of weakening the European colonial powers against the long-term matter of good relations with the new nations.

Indochina was a special problem from the outset. In that restive French colony American OSS (Office of Strategic Services, a precursor to the Central Intelligence Agency) officers attempting to rescue downed American fliers behind Japanese lines encountered Ho Chi Minh, a venerated leader of the nationalist rebellion. One of the OSS group, Archimedes Patti, had no illusions that Ho was anything but a dedicated Communist, but he also took very seriously the Vietnamese leader's assertion he would not allow any other power to replace French rule. He desired American support, Ho told Patti, and conveyed a desire for American support in letters to President Truman. President Franklin D. Roosevelt, as the OSS group knew, had sometimes indicated—in pretty strong terms, actually—that France should not be allowed to return, at least not without a commitment to eventual independence.

But how FDR proposed to implement his avowed policy was far from clear. When Roosevelt's successor did not challenge the French effort to re-occupy Indochina, Patti was left with a deep sense of foreboding:

> It was for me a time of sober observation because I remained totally convinced that no amount of opposition would deflect the Vietnamese from pursuing their independence, whatever the cost or however long it might take. To me it was regrettable that our own nation was not coming to terms with that reality and charting a course which would serve our own best interests—perhaps just staying completely out of it and maintaining a truly neutral stance, both materially and in our planning concepts.[8]

---

[7] ORE 25-48, *The Break-Up of the Colonial Empires and Its Implications for US Security*, September 3, 1948, p. 3.
[8] Archimedes L.A. Patti, *Why Viet Nam? Prelude to America's Albatross* (Berkeley: Univ. of California Press, 1980), p. 381.

Introduction

By Lloyd C. Gardner

Lloyd Gardner is the author or editor of more than a dozen books on American foreign policy. In the last two decades he has specialized on the Vietnam War. His books on Vietnam include *Approaching Vietnam: From World War II through Dienbienphu* (1988), and *Pay Any Price: Lyndon Johnson and the Wars for Vietnam* (1995). In addition, he has organized three conferences at the Lyndon Baines Johnson Library and co-edited with Ted Gittinger the volumes that resulted: *Vietnam: The Early Decisions* (1997); *International Perspectives on Vietnam* (2000); *Vietnam: The Search for Peace, 1964* (2005). Professor Gardner received his Ph.D. from the University of Wisconsin in 1960 and is Research Professor of History at Rutgers University, where he has taught since 1963.

The Vietnam Watch[6]

The papers in this volume bring together intelligence Estimates and Memoranda covering the entire Vietnam war. Some have been declassified here for the first time. Although they are but a tiny fraction of CIA input into the Vietnam War deliberations and debate, they represent a fascinating, indeed indispensable, inside look into the efforts of the intelligence specialists to provide decisionmakers with a reasoned analysis of prospects for the success of American policy. One can read in them the convictions and doubts of the intelligence community as they change over time. They are often ahead of the curve and occasionally lag behind the pace of events. While there is always a desire for a "scoreboard" conclusion, intelligence assessments have to be evaluated in context. This introduction will attempt to provide the context within which the Vietnam analysts worked and how they viewed developments in South Vietnam until the fall of Saigon in 1975.

The First Indochina War, 1945-1954

Beginning in 1948 Central Intelligence Agency analysts produced a series of papers for policymakers on dimming French prospects for winning the war in Indochina. The first of these, *The Break-Up of the Colonial Empires and its Implications for US Security*, was published on September 3, 1948. While the Cold War had not yet spread to Asia, the Estimate offered a sobering look at the incipient rivalry developing with the Soviet Union—and the already evident appearance of a "colonial bloc" in the United Nations. Unlike most later papers in the series, moreover, it directly criticized US policies. At risk, the paper said, were needed raw materials and access to military bases previously controlled by the colonial powers. "Unless the US itself adopts a more positive and sympathetic

---

[6] I should like to express thanks to several people who prepared the documents for this volume and offered great help with my understanding of the process and personalities involved: John Allen, George Allen, Tom Elmore, Robert Layton, and John Carver.

Editors

John K. Allen, Jr.
Mr. Allen is a 30-year CIA veteran who served in operations, analysis, and the management of analysis. He was posted to Laos in the 1960s, and as an analyst followed Laos and Cambodia during the latter stages of the Vietnam War. He served on the NIC as an NIO in 1994 and 1995. He is a graduate of Virginia Tech, Harvard University, and the Air War College.

John Carver
Mr. Carver is a 40-year CIA veteran with an additional 10 years on contract. He is an Asian expert with analytic experience in politics, leadership, economics, and science and technology. He lectured on China at the CIA in the 1970s. He is a graduate of the University of Pennsylvania.

Tom Elmore
Mr. Elmore is a 40-year veteran of the CIA, having served primarily in analysis and the management of analysis. As an analyst he focused on China, and as a manager he served as Director of the Office of East Asian Analysis. He taught at The George Washington University, studied China at Harvard University, and has degrees from Rutgers University and Johns Hopkins University. Mr. Elmore is a recipient of the Distinguished Intelligence Medal.

Advisers

George Allen
Mr. Allen is a veteran of 55 years with the Intelligence Community. As an analyst he focused on the Indochina wars from 1949-1968, serving two years in Vietnam. He attended the Imperial Defence College in London. Since retiring from CIA in 1979, he has taught courses on intelligence analysis for the CIA, served as an adjunct professor at the Defense Intelligence College, and has lectured at the Army, Navy, Air Force, and National war colleges. He is a graduate of the University of Utah. His book, *None So Blind: An Insider's Account of the Intelligence Failure in Vietnam,* was published in 2001.

Bob Layton
Mr. Layton is a 32-year CIA veteran, having served primarily in analysis and the management of analysis. He was ONE Staff Officer for Indochina from 1965 to mid-1967 and then again from mid-1969 to 1973. He headed an analytic unit in CIA's Saigon Station from mid-1967 to mid-1969. From 1973 to 1976, he was the Assistant NIO for Southeast Asia. He is a graduate of Wake Forest University and has had additional graduate training at Duke, Princeton, and Harvard.

On the Estimative Process and Product Process

NIEs and the other national intelligence products are the most authoritative intelligence assessments in the US Government. The Estimates and Memoranda in this collection do not, however, represent the totality of the intelligence on Vietnam. Indeed, from the early 1960s on, INR, DIA, and various subcomponents of the CIA churned out streams of assessments and reports on Vietnam that dwarfed ONE's production, which to a degree was a distillation of these broader streams.

The process that generated most of the documents in this collection changed little over the 30 year span involved. In ONE, staffers, usually seconded from CIA subcomponents, produced an initial draft usually based on terms of reference and scope notes. This draft was subjected to several internal reviews, the last one by ONE's Board. The Board was a group of 8-15 senior CIA officers, retired ambassadors and senior military officers, and scholars from outside government, charged with overseeing the national intelligence estimative process. In the case of the ONE Memoranda in this collection, these papers then went directly to the Director of Central Intelligence (DCI), who forwarded them to senior policymakers, often with a covering note.

Once approved by the Board, NIEs, SNIEs and other formal estimative products were sent to the Community's constituent agencies, whose senior substantive experts then met at coordination meetings to record their agreements or disagreements. As a final act, the heads of the individual agencies met as a group—known variously over time as the Intelligence Advisory Council (IAC), the United States Intelligence Board (USIB), and, most recently, as the National Foreign Intelligence Board (NFIB)—to approve the Estimate or, where disagreements had not been reconciled, to register formal dissents from the majority view. The DCI then signed the assessment and forwarded it to relevant policymakers, as many as 300 in the case of Vietnam.[4]

The documents that emerged from this process were unique in several respects. Rather than the product of a single individual or agency, they reflected the collective judgments of the Intelligence Community as a whole. They tended to be more future-oriented than the analytic products from individual intelligence agencies.[5] Finally, because of the high level of the intended audience as well as of those involved in the final approval deliberations, the products of the estimative process constituted a formal historical record of the views the Intelligence Community provided policymakers at a given time.

---

[4] For a detailed description of this process see Sherman Kent, *The Making of an NIE*, available at http://www.cia.gov/sci/books/shrmankent/making.html. This is a particularly valuable essay by the individual who headed ONE from 1952 to 1967. The process used by ONE changed little during the early years of the NIO system.

[5] The one document in this collection that does not fit this model and was not a product of the process described here is the 315-page assessment published on 26 August 1966 entitled, *The Vietnamese Communists' Will to Persist.* This document was prepared jointly by ONE and several other CIA components in response to a request from then Secretary of Defense Robert McNamara, whose change of view on US involvement in Vietnam at about this time is well documented. It is included in the collection because ONE had a significant role in its preparation, because it reflects the depth of the evidentiary base and the rigor of the basic research and analysis that ONE drew on in its own assessments on Vietnam, and because it is so historically significant.

Foreword

This collection of declassified estimative products is the first such release by the Central Intelligence Agency (CIA) of documents exclusively on the Vietnam war and is one of the largest such releases to date. Of the 174 documents that comprise the collection, 38 appear at least in part in this volume, and all are on the accompanying CD in their entirety. The intent is to add to the scholarship of the period and to make the documents more readily accessible to the general public.

All but 18 of the documents were produced by the Office of National Estimates (ONE), which was established in November 1950 for the sole purpose of producing such "national intelligence" assessments. ONE was replaced in 1973 by the National Intelligence Officer (NIO) system, which remains an integral part of today's National Intelligence Council (NIC).[1] Fourteen documents in the collection published between 1973 and 1975 were produced by the NIO system, and four documents published before December 1950 were produced by ONE's predecessor organization, the Office of Reports and Estimates (ORE).

The documents fall into two broad categories: 1) formal products of the national intelligence estimative process, and 2) memoranda put out unilaterally by ONE. The most important difference in the two categories is that the products of the formal process—mostly National Intelligence Estimates (NIEs) or Special National Intelligence Estimates (SNIEs)—were coordinated with the constituent agencies of what is now known as the Intelligence Community[2] while the ONE memoranda for the most part were not. Importantly, however, both the formal products and substantive ONE memoranda in the collection were written for and disseminated to the highest levels of policymaking, including in many cases the President. Few of the ONE memoranda have been declassified before, and many of the NIEs and SNIEs published between the late 1960s and 1975 have not been previously released.[3]

---

[1] The fact that there were no formal estimates or ONE memoranda published on the Vietnam war during 1972 is at least in part attributable to ONE's looming dissolution. For more information on the NIC, visit its website at http://www.cia.gov/nic/NIC_home.html.

[2] As constituted for most of the Vietnam war, the Intelligence Community consisted of the CIA; the Department of State's Bureau of Intelligence and Research (INR); the Defense Intelligence Agency (DIA); The Joint Chiefs of Staff; the National Security Agency; the intelligence organizations of the Air Force, Army, Coast Guard, Marine Corps and Navy; the Federal Bureau of Investigation; the Department of Energy; and the Department of the Treasury.

[3] Some of the documents in this collection have been declassified and released previously through Freedom of Information or Executive Order channels or have appeared, at least in part, in the Department of State's *Foreign Relations of the United States* (FRUS) series.

Note: Documents are complete unless otherwise noted.

Contents

ORE: Office of Reports and Estimates	ONE: Office of National Estimates
NIE: National Intelligence Estimate	USIB: United States Intelligence Board
SNIE: Special National Intelligence Estimate	SM: Special Memorandum
IIM: Interagency Intelligence Memorandum	SE: Special Estimate
IM: Intelligence Memorandum	M/H: Memorandum for Holders

Preface

The National Intelligence Council (NIC) is delighted to publish this historic collection of intelligence documents related to the Vietnam War. The documents—38 in this book and 174 in the companion CD—show how the US intelligence Community viewed critical developments over a 27-year period, ranging from analysis of the implications of the post-World War II breakup of colonial empires to the Communist takeover of Saigon in 1975. A number of these documents were declassified and published in other circumstances, but many are being made public here for the first time. As such, they undoubtedly will be of immense interest and value to historians and scholars, academics and diplomats, and comprise in sum a unique historical record of a challenging and controversial chapter in US foreign relations.

The documents are estimative intelligence products, that is, reports that projected the impact of current trends into the future to give policymakers and military commanders a heads-up about where events were likely to lead and their probable impact on US security interests. Because they reflected the careful scrutiny and final agreement on conclusions by various Intelligence Community analysts and agencies, they were considered the most authoritative assessments of the Intelligence Community.

Any collection of this magnitude can only be the product of extensive collaboration. Work started in September 2004 under the auspices of NIC Chairman Robert Hutchings and Martha Lutz and her team in the Information Review Office of the Director of Central Intelligence. We are particularly grateful to the editors—John Allen, John Carver, and Tom Elmore—and their advisors for their selection of the documents. The same professional trio performed similar functions for the publication of *Tracking the Dragon: National Intelligence Estimates on China During the Era of Mao, 1948-1976*. We thank Professor Lloyd Gardner of Rutgers University, a renowned academic authority on the Vietnam War, for his masterful introduction to this volume. Within the NIC, Mathew Burrows and his analytic and production staff helped turn the documents into a professionally finished book, and the CIA's Imaging and Publishing Support Service provided the usual high-quality printing.

Finally, we wish to recognize with this publication the signal contributions of a generation of senior officers and analysts from the various agencies of the US Intelligence Community.

David F. Gordon

Vice Chairman, National Intelligence Council

NIC 2005-03 April 2005

ESTIMATIVE PRODUCTS

on

Vietnam

1948-1975

This paper was prepared under the auspices of
David F. Gordon, Vice Chairman,
National Intelligence Council.
Inquiries may be directed to (703) 482-3578.

This publication is also available on the NIC Public Web site at: www.cia.gov/nic
under Declassified NIC Publications.

To obtain a copy of this publication, please contact:

Government Printing Office (GPO), Superintendent of Documents, PO Box 391954
Pittsburgh, PA 15250-7954, Phone: (202) 512-1800, Fax: (202) 512-2250
http:\\bookstore.gpo.gov GPO Stock 041-015-00242-2 ISBN 0-16-074937-9

Vietnam: Major Developments, 1945-1975

US Presidents	Date		Events
Franklin D. Roosevelt Harry S. Truman	1945	March	Japanese oust French colonial rule; Emperor Bao Dai asserts Vietnamese independence.
		September	Ho Chi Minh establishes government of Democratic Republic of Vietnam; Bao Dai abdicates.
	1946		French troops return to Indochina. Ho Chi Minh negotiates with French for Vietnamese independence.
		December	Hostilities break out.
	1947		French move to restore colonial rule, Ho seeks to negotiate Vietnamese independence.
		December	Hostilities break out between French and Ho's "Viet Minh" forces.
	1949		France installs Bao Dai as head of Vietnamese government. Military stalemate continues.
	1950		Paris grants Vietnam partial independence "within French Union." US begins military and economic support for French war; US MAAG established in Saigon. Peking begins military aid to Viet Minh.
		October	French driven from posts on China border. Fighting intensifies as Viet Minh gain strength.
Dwight D. Eisenhower	1953	December	French seize Dien Bien Phu.
	1954	April	Multi-power conference opens in Geneva.
		May	Viet Minh overrun Dien Bien Phu.
		June	Bao Dai names Ngo Dinh Diem Prime Minister of SVN government.
		July	Geneva agreements divide Vietnam at 17th parallel, Viet Minh controlling North and Diem in South. US and Diem government agree to observe terms. Lansdale team arrives in Saigon to help Diem. Gen. Collins named US Minister to Vietnam.
	1955		Diem proclaims independence from France. US begins direct assistance to SVN military. Diem rejects talks with Hanoi to reunify country. Eisenhower pledges US support for SVN independence.
	1956		Diem government adopts constitution. US adds 350 advisors to MAAG Saigon. French withdraw military forces from Indochina. Diem cracks down on Viet Minh supporters in SVN.
	1959		Hanoi approves support for "patriotic movement" in the south, establishes infrastructure to move cadres and supplies to SVN via Laos.
	1960		Hanoi calls for reunification of Vietnam by force. Soviets begin support of Pathet Lao and North Vietnamese forces in Laos. Diem survives coup attempt by SVN paratroopers.
John F. Kennedy	1961		JFK administration moves to bolster Lao government. VP Johnson pledges increased assistance to SVN government.
		October	Taylor-Rostow mission recommends massive increase in US military assistance.
	1962		US establishes MACV, begins deploying combat support to aid SVN military.
		March	US forces reach 5,400; US pilots fly "combat training" missions with SVN air forces, provide helicopters for SVN operations.
		July	Geneva accord sanctions "neutral" Lao government with Communist forces controlling Laos along Vietnam border.
		December	US forces in SVN reach 11,300.
	1963	June	Diem government suppresses riotous Buddhist opposition.
		August	Diem proclaims martial law, students demonstrate. SVN generals extend feelers for US support of possible coup. USG indicates sympathy.
		September	USG threatens to cut aid unless Diem reforms.
Lyndon B. Johnson		November	With tacit US support, military seizes power, executes Diem. Viet Cong increase activity in countryside. Kennedy assassinated.
	1964		Successive coups throughout year as SVN generals vie for power.
		March/April	Deteriorating military situation leads LBJ administration to plan escalation. Hanoi increases flow of troops and supplies to south.
		August	Tonkin Gulf incident leads to overwhelming Senate endorsement of US policy in Vietnam.
	1965	February	After attack on US forces at Pleiku LBJ authorizes bombing of NVN.
		March	US Marines landed to protect US air base in Da Nang. Hanoi begins infiltrating regular combat forces to SVN.
		July	LBJ orders major increase in combat forces. Escalating stalemate ensues through 1967.
	1968	January	"Tet Offensive" hits all major towns and cities, is ultimately driven back with heavy losses but stuns public opinion.
		March	LBJ curtails bombing in North, calls for talks with Hanoi and announces he will not run for re-electon.
		April	Peace talks begin in Paris.
Richard M. Nixon	1969		Nixon continues Paris talks, announces "Vietnamization" plan, begins withdrawal of military forces.
	1970	May	US and SVN forces invade Cambodia to disrupt enemy base areas.
	1971	February	SVN military strikes into Laos to disrupt "Ho Chi Minh Trail" supply network in Central Laos but is driven back after heavy fighting.
	1972	March	Hanoi's "Easter Offensive" surges across DMZ, temporarily occupying most of two northern provinces in SVN.
	1973	January	Ceasefire agreement signed in Paris, but Hanoi and SVN forces continue jockeying for position in SVN.
Gerald R. Ford	1975	March	Hanoi mounts all-out offensive, occupies Saigon in late April, ending the war.

ORE 25-48

The Breakup of the Colonial Empires and Its Implications for US Security

3 September 1948

APPROVED FOR RELEASE
DATE: JAN 2005

THE BREAK-UP OF THE COLONIAL EMPIRES AND ITS IMPLICATIONS FOR US SECURITY

ORE 25-48

Published 3 September 1948

CENTRAL INTELLIGENCE AGENCY

CONFIDENTIAL

THE BREAK-UP OF THE COLONIAL EMPIRES AND ITS IMPLICATIONS FOR US SECURITY

SUMMARY

The growth of nationalism in colonial areas, which has already succeeded in breaking up a large part of the European colonial systems and in creating a series of new, nationalistic states in the Near and Far East, has major implications for US security, particularly in terms of possible world conflict with the USSR.[1] This shift of the dependent areas from the orbit of the colonial powers not only weakens the probable European allies of the US but deprives the US itself of assured access to vital bases and raw materials in these areas in event of war. Should the recently liberated and currently emergent states become oriented toward the USSR, US military and economic security would be seriously threatened.

World War II gave a tremendous impetus to the colonial independence movement. The UK withdrew from India-Pakistan and Burma, while the Dutch and French, exhausted by war, appear unable to suppress the Indonesian and Indochinese nationalists by force, or, despite any temporary compromise solutions, to be able to arrest their eventual achievement of genuine independence. Growing nationalism in French North Africa threatens French hegemony. While the colonial issue in most remaining dependencies is not yet acute, native nationalism in many of these areas too will exert increasing pressure for autonomy or independence.

This marked postwar development of the colonial independence movement has resulted from: (1) the release of bottled-up nationalist activities in the Far East as a result of Japan's defeat of the colonial powers in World War II and its encouragement of local nationalism in occupied areas; (2) the postwar military and economic weakness of the colonial powers, which has made them less able to resist nationalist demands and led them to grant concessions or even independence to their dependencies; (3) the increasing tendency of liberal-socialist elements in the colonial powers to favor voluntary liquidation of restive colonial possessions; (4) widespread support of colonial independence movements by a large group of recently liberated and other sympathetic states, particularly the USSR; and (5) creation of the United Nations, which has provided a forum for agitating the colonial issue and a mechanism for its liquidation.

Because of these factors, further disintegration of the remaining colonial empires appears inevitable. Belated concessions by the colonial powers, at least on the limited

---

Note: The information in this report is as of 9 August 1948.

The intelligence organizations of the Departments of State, Army, and the Navy have concurred in this report; the Air Intelligence Division, Air Intelligence Directorate, Department of the Air Force, had no comment.

[1] In this paper the term "colonial" is used in a broad sense to denote the relationships between the metropolitan powers and their dependent and semi-dependent areas, whether these be colonies, mandates, protectorates, or treaty relationships. Similarly the phrase "colonial issue" is meant to encompass all differences between the colonial powers and their dependent areas arising from the development of local nationalism.

scale presently contemplated, do not meet the basic nationalist demand for independence and are unlikely to be more than temporarily effective, except in more backward areas. The colonial powers appear unwilling for the most part to recognize fully the force of nationalism in their remaining dependencies and to take the leadership in guiding these toward genuine independence or self-government.

As a result of the rapid breaking up of the colonial systems, a new power situation is developing in the former colonial world. No longer can the Western Powers rely on large areas of Asia and Africa as assured sources of raw materials, markets, and military bases. In contrast to the ever closer integration of the Satellites into the Soviet system, there is an increasing fragmentation of the non-Soviet world. This process is already largely completed, with many of the most important colonial and semi-colonial areas, like India, Burma, the Arab states, and the Philippines already independent, and Indonesia and Indochina well on the road. These new states will be free to choose their future alignments, which will be largely conditioned by the attitudes of the Soviet and Western Power blocs toward the colonial issue and their economic demands.

The colonial independence movement, therefore, is no longer purely a domestic issue between the European colonial powers and their dependencies. It has been injected into the larger arena of world politics and has become an element in the broader problems of relations between Orient and Occident, between industrialized and "underdeveloped" nations, and between the Western Powers and the USSR. The newly independent and older nations of the Near and Far East strongly sympathize with the aspirations of still dependent areas, to which they are bound by racial and religious ties. These nations are further bound together in varying degree by two other issues which tend to set them off against the colonial powers and the US: namely, the growing economic nationalism of the "underdeveloped" areas and the underlying racial antagonism between white and native peoples. All intensely nationalistic, the Near and Far Eastern nations tend to unite in opposition to the Western European powers on the colonial issue and to US economic dominance. As a result there has been a tendency toward the formation in the UN and affiliated bodies of a so-called "colonial bloc," whose members have already brought colonial disputes into the UN and will likely take the lead in attempting in this manner to hasten the liberation of further colonial areas. The colonial issue and economic nationalism, therefore, will continue to be a source of friction between the colonial powers and the US on the one hand, and the states of the Near and Far East on the other. The gravest danger to the US is that friction engendered by these issues may drive the so-called colonial bloc into alignment with the USSR.

The USSR is effectively exploiting the colonial issue and the economic nationalism of the underdeveloped areas as a means of dividing the non-Soviet world, weakening the Western Powers, and gaining the good will of colonial and former colonial areas. Ever since World War I the USSR has sought to infiltrate the nationalist parties in dependent areas and, more recently, to play up the colonial issue and the so-called economic imperialism of the Western Powers in the UN. The poverty and underprivileged

position of the population in these areas, their latent hostility toward the occupying powers—past or present—and the existence of leftist elements within them, make them peculiarly susceptible to Soviet penetration.

Consequently, the good will of the recently liberated and emergent independent nations becomes a vital factor in the future strategic position of the US in the Near and Far East. In addition, the restoration of the economic contribution of their colonies is important to the economic stability of the Western European powers, which the US is endeavoring to create. Short-sighted colonial policies, however, will in the long run cause the colonial powers to lose the very economic and strategic advantages in their dependencies which they are anxious to retain. Unless, therefore, the European colonial powers can be induced to recognize the necessity for satisfying the aspirations of their dependent areas and can devise formulae that will retain their good will as emergent or independent states, both these powers and the US will be placed at a serious disadvantage in the new power situation in the Near and the Far East. Moreover, unless the US itself adopts a more positive and sympathetic attitude toward the national aspirations of these areas and at least partially meets their demands for economic assistance, it will risk their becoming actively antagonistic toward the US.

(Continued...)

CONFIDENTIAL

THE BREAK-UP OF THE COLONIAL EMPIRES AND ITS IMPLICATIONS FOR US SECURITY

1. Development of the Colonial Independence Movement.

A major trend in the twentieth century world power situation is the development of a strong colonial independence movement which is in process of breaking up the colonial systems and creating a series of new, nationalistic states. The primary cause of the break-up of the European colonial empires is the growth of native nationalism in these areas, simultaneously with the decline in power and prestige of the colonial powers. This striking growth of local nationalism is primarily the result of: (a) the rising level of political, economic, and social development in dependent areas, with resultant growing sensitivity to inequality of treatment; (b) the short-sighted policies of the colonial powers, whose discriminatory treatment of subject populations and exploitation of colonial resources without attendant benefits to these populations have aroused strong resentment; (c) a deep-seated racial hostility of native populations toward their white overlords, due largely to these policies, which has taken the form of a reaction against "white superiority"; (d) the exposure of colonial areas to Western ideas of nationalism and the right to self-determination, which has made them increasingly conscious of their dependent status; and (e) the meteoric rise of Japan, whose defeats of the European powers in the Russo-Japanese War and especially World War II punctured the myth of white superiority. The colonial powers, while exposing their dependencies to the technological advances and democratic ideals of the West, failed to reckon with their aspirations to achieve the same type of national self-expression which the West exemplified.

While nationalism in dependent and quasi-dependent areas first reached significant proportions in the early twentieth century, it was given its greatest impetus by World Wars I and II. These conflicts, particularly the last, greatly weakened the colonial powers, thereby reducing their ability to control their colonial holding by force. At the same time, reliance of these powers on colonial resources and manpower forced them to grant concessions which greatly advanced the nationalist cause. In World War I Great Britain also fanned Arab national aspirations in order to hasten the downfall of the Turks. President Wilson's insistence upon the self-determination of peoples and the creation of the League of Nations gave a powerful stimulus to colonial aspirations for independence.

The period between wars saw further development of nationalism in dependent areas, particularly in the Near East and India. The repercussions of the world depression of the 1930's, which forced the colonial powers to retrench in colonial development, and shattered the world raw material price structure, increased colonial resentment and led to pressure for self-government and a larger share of the proceeds of economic exploitation. Indigenous nationalists, resentful of political, economic, and social discrimination against them, tended to attribute the depressed state of colonial

CONFIDENTIAL

(Page 4 Blank)

(Continued...)

economies to the ineptitude of the great powers. States like Iraq and Egypt, which had been under British tutelage, tended to assume a more independent course in their affairs. The US groomed the Philippines for independence, while Britain was forced to make some concessions to the growing pressure of Indian nationalism. The aggressive policies of Japan, whose propaganda stressed the racist doctrine of "Asia for the Asiatics," greatly stimulated the racial hostility of East toward West.

World War II delivered another blow to the declining colonial empires. When the colonial powers proved unable to defend their Southeast Asian possessions against the Japanese onslaught, Japan, capitalizing on local feelings, set itself up as liberator of the Asiatic peoples from white oppression. Although the Japanese actually kept a tight rein on Southeast Asia, they granted a shadowy "independence" to Burma, the Philippines, Indochina, and Indonesia which further stimulated their national ambitions. At the end of the war most Allied Far Eastern dependencies were wholly unwilling to revert to their former status, and the exhausted Allies have been unable to re-establish the *status quo* ante. The UK labor government, no longer willing or able to hold off the violent demands of the Indian nationalists, granted independence to India, Pakistan, and Burma and dominion status to Ceylon. A weakened France was forced to recognize the independence of its Levant mandates, Syria and Lebanon. The US fulfilled its promise of freedom to the Philippines. Korea was freed from Japanese bondage. France and the Netherlands, unwilling to relinquish their rich Southeast Asian possessions to the native nationalists, became embroiled in an uneasy struggle with indigenous regimes established in these areas.

2. Current Status of the Colonial Independence Movement.

As a result of the stimulation of native nationalism in the chaotic war and postwar periods, the remaining colonial world is in a ferment of nationalist activity. This movement is in varying stages of growth in different areas, depending largely upon the level of local political, economic, and social development, but in most of them the eventual goal is independence. In the more backward areas of Asia and Africa, which are at a relatively early stage of political and economic growth, nationalism is still inchoate. On the other hand, in relatively highly developed areas like Indonesia, Indochina, and French North Africa, it has reached an advanced stage.

The two most critical colonial issues are in Indonesia and Indochina, where the Dutch and French, exhausted by war, have been unable to suppress the local nationalists by force and, despite temporary compromises which may be worked out, are unlikely to be able to arrest the eventual achievement of native independence. The Dutch and the Indonesian Republic are attempting to negotiate a settlement designed to bring the Republic within a Netherlands-dominated United States of Indonesia while allowing it a large degree of autonomy in all but foreign affairs and defense. In Indochina the French have been unable either to suppress the nationalist Viet-Minh Party or to reach mutually acceptable agreement with it. In view of the protracted strain of pacification expenditures on the unstable French economy, it is likely that France eventually will have to make sweeping concessions to the Nationalists. These will constitute but another step along the road to independence.

While nationalism in French North Africa has not yet reached the fighting stage, the development of militant native independence movements in Algeria, Morocco, and Tunisia is a growing threat to French hegemony. In Tunisia and Morocco, both protectorates, the nationalists have concentrated on restoration of national sovereignty under the existing dynasties. A bureau has been established at Cairo where exiled North African leaders like Abd-el-Krim coordinate the nationalist program. French North African nationalism is stimulated by common Moslem ties with the chauvinistic Arab League, which, while as yet giving little overt support to North African nationalism, may be expected to step up its activity as soon as the more pressing Palestine problem is settled. Mounting nationalism in Libya, particularly among the Cyrenaican Senussi tribes, is complicating the disposal of this former Italian colony.

Although nationalism in other dependent areas has not yet attained critical proportions, there exist well defined movements in several regions which foreshadow similar problems. In most of these areas the demand at present is not so much for immediate independence as for a greater measure of self-government. In Malaya the heterogeneity of the population and the relatively enlightened British colonial administration so far have retarded rapid growth of nationalism, but the success of neighboring areas in achieving self-determination cannot help but stimulate it to some extent. France's suppression of the 1947 rebellion in Madagascar has set back the Malagasy nationalist movement several years, but tension will recur. In the relatively backward Central African colonies the low stage of development has limited the growth of nationalism, and will do so for a long period. The Zik movement in Nigeria and the United Gold Coast Convention, though neither very strong, are examples of rising nationalist movements in this area.

3. The Colonial Issue in World Politics.

The colonial independence movement is no longer purely a domestic issue between the individual European colonial powers and their dependencies. It has been injected into the larger arena of world politics and has become an element in the broader problems of the relations between the Orient and Occident, between industrialized and "underdeveloped" nations, and between the Western Powers and the USSR.

a. External Support of Colonial Independence Movements.

The newly liberated and older nations of the Near and Far East strongly sympathize with the aspirations of still dependent areas, to which they are bound by racial and religious ties. All intensely nationalistic, these countries resent the political and economic domination of adjacent areas by European powers. States like India and Egypt have already brought colonial issues into the UN and may be expected increasingly to take the leadership in attempting to hasten in this and other ways the liberation of remaining colonial areas. Moreover, many of these states are exploiting the colonial issue in their own self-interest, with a view to supplanting the Western Powers in certain areas. India and China both have ambitions to dominate Southeast Asia, and the latter also aspires to replace Japan as the major power in the Far

East. Some of the Eastern states covet portions of the moribund colonial empires: Egypt the Sudan and Cyrenaica; Ethiopia—the adjacent former Italian colonies; and China—Hong Kong.

The colonial issue, therefore, will be a major source of friction between the Western European powers and the rising nations of the Near and Far East. To the extent that the US supports the European powers on this issue, it too will incur the ill-will of these new, nationalistic states.

b. *Economic Nationalism and the Colonial Issue.*

The nations supporting the colonial independence movement are bound together by another major issue, closely related to the struggle for political independence, which also tends to build up antagonism toward the Western European powers and the US. This is the development, more pronounced since World War II, of economic nationalism in the "underdeveloped" countries. These countries, most of them with a colonial background, find that though they have achieved political independence, their undeveloped economies, producing mostly raw materials and agricultural products, are still tied to those of the industrialized Western nations which provide markets for their goods. They are in essence still semi-colonial areas, for their economic dependence upon the metropolitan economies tends to vitiate their political independence. Therefore native nationalists have not been wholly satisfied by the achievement of political independence; they demand economic independence as well.

The aim of this economic nationalism is to attain greater economic self-sufficiency through development of a diversified economy, usually by industrialization. It has led the underdeveloped countries to favor tariffs, import restrictions, and other trade barriers to protect their infant industries. This attitude has characterized not only the recently liberated countries but many long since independent, like the Latin American nations, which still have semi-colonial economies. It was most clearly displayed at the recent Havana Trade Conference, where the underdeveloped countries strongly opposed multilateral free trade and charged that the US and other industrialized nations were stunting their economic development in order to keep them permanently dependent.

With the largest segments of the colonial systems either already liberated or in the last stages of liberation, this aspect of the colonial problem becomes increasingly important. The economic nationalism of the underdeveloped nations conflicts sharply with US trade objectives and these countries tend to resent US economic dominance. On the other hand, they urgently need external assistance in their economic development, and the US is at present the only nation able to supply it. The desire for US loans and private investment will have some effect in tempering the antagonism of these states toward US policies. However, the underdeveloped countries display an increasing tendency to demand US aid as a natural right, irrespective of any concessions on their part, and to feel that the US will be forced to invest abroad because of insufficient internal demand for its existing capital resources.

c. *The Colonial Issue in the UN.*

Colonial problems have been brought increasingly into the UN, which native nationalists and their supporters have found an ideal forum for agitating the colonial

issue. There is a pronounced tendency toward the formation in the UN of a colonial "bloc" consisting of formerly dependent states like India and the Arab nations, others like China and Iran with strong racial and religious sympathies toward colonial peoples (also characteristic of the first group), and yet a third group like many Latin American republics and Australia, which sympathize on liberal, humanitarian, and economic grounds. The colonial bloc has consistently sought to broaden the UN trusteeship system. China, India, the USSR, the Philippines, and the Arab states contend that Article 73 of the UN charter, which binds members to promote the progressive development of self-government in their dependencies, implies that the UN should have broad supervisory powers over these dependencies. Critical colonial situations like the Indonesian question and Egypt's demand that Great Britain withdraw her troops have been brought before the Security Council as potential threats to world peace. The underdeveloped countries have insisted on emphasizing their own economic problems in UN economic bodies. Thus, through the UN, the colonial issue has been placed squarely on the world stage and local colonial problems have become matters of global concern. The colonial "bloc" and the USSR may be expected to bring more and more of such problems before the UN and to attempt to use it as a mechanism for liquidating the colonial empires.

d. *Soviet Exploitation of the Colonial Issue.*

The USSR is effectively exploiting the colonial issue and the allied issues of economic nationalism and racial antagonism in an effort to divide the non-Soviet world, weaken the European allies of the US, and gain the good will of the colonial "bloc." In pursuit of these objectives, the USSR is: (1) giving active support through agitators, propaganda, and local Communist parties to the nationalist movements throughout the colonial world; and (2) consistently injecting colonial and Allied problems into UN and affiliated activities.

The Soviet regime has always looked upon the so-called "depressed areas" as a fertile field for penetration, and since 1918 the Comintern has stressed the importance of stirring up discontent in these areas. As a non-colonial power, the USSR is in the fortunate position of being able to champion the colonial cause unreservedly and thereby bid for the good will of colonial and former colonial areas. Its condemnation of racial discrimination pleases native nationalists and tends to exclude the USSR from the racial animosity of East toward West. The Communists have sought to infiltrate the nationalist parties in dependent and formerly dependent areas and have been, as in Burma, Indonesia, and Indochina, among the most vocal agitators for independence. The Soviet Union has found the World Federation of Trade Unions an effective weapon for penetrating the growing labor movements in Asia and Africa and for turning them against the colonial powers.

At the San Francisco Conference in which the UN Charter was framed the USSR fought for a provision categorically demanding eventual independence for all colonies. Since that time, it has frequently injected the colonial issue into UN discussions and has strenuously supported the colonial "bloc" on all colonial and allied questions brought into the UN. Persistent Soviet support of the colonial "bloc" on

purely colonial issues may win adherents from the colonial "bloc" for the USSR on other major issues between the USSR and the Western Powers in the UN. Thus the Soviet Union clearly recognizes the potential of the colonial issue for weakening its opponents and has made of it an important element in the power struggle between the Western Powers and the USSR.

4. Inevitability of Further Colonial Disintegration.

Under these circumstances, some further disintegration of the remaining colonial empires appears inevitable. Native nationalism in these dependencies will increase as the inhabitants, spurred on by the example of the already liberated nations, seek to emulate them. Indonesia and Indochina are apparently already in the final stage before full independence, and crises will arise in other colonial areas as local nationalists clamor increasingly for self-government. The USSR and the colonial "bloc" will lend external support to these groups and utilize the UN as a means of assisting them. The weakened colonial powers, stricken by war and economic crisis, will find it difficult to cope with these insistent nationalist pressures.

The colonial powers, belatedly aware of the threat to their empires, have shown some willingness to liquidate the most troublesome of their possessions and to make concessions in others. The Western European socialist parties, now a major influence in many governments, appear more willing than their conservative predecessors to adopt colonial reforms although their colonial policies to date have shown little change. Some of the colonial powers have adopted more progressive colonial policies, offering concessions to their dependencies in an effort to stave off the demand for independence. The UK in particular, after recognizing that independence for India and Burma was inevitable, is cautiously promoting greater self-government in its remaining colonies and has earmarked large sums for their economic development (although Britain's present economic weakness has prevented full development of these schemes). The Netherlands has granted substantial concessions in Indonesia, although clearly determined to make every effort to keep this rich area under her control. France, too, while making minimal reforms in critical areas, seeks to draw her dependencies closer to the mother country in a French Union.

These concessions, however, at least on the limited scale presently contemplated, appear unlikely to do more than temporarily placate local nationalism and at most delay the demand for liberation. Differences in race, language, and religion, intensified by a strong East-West antagonism, make Dutch and French plans for integration of their colonies into French and Netherlands Unions unlikely to succeed in areas like Indochina, Indonesia, and French North Africa where native nationalism is already well advanced. Moreover, stimulation of colonial economic and social development and granting of greater political autonomy may well promote local nationalism rather than weaken it. As the colonies become more highly developed, they will become more conscious of their dependent status and more insistent upon independence. They also will be better able to create viable economies and to function as independent states. Under these circumstances limited concessions are likely to be effective, in

the long run, only in relatively small or backward areas which would in any case be likely to remain under a protecting power.

5. Emergence of a New Power Situation in the Former Colonial World.

As the result of the gradual disintegration of the colonial systems and the emergence of young, nationalistic states, a new power situation is in the making in the former colonial world. No longer will the western colonial powers control large areas of Asia and North Africa which are sources of manpower and raw materials and provide assured military bases. The economic and political policies formerly imposed by the colonial powers on their colonies will give way to a welter of conflicting national policies. This process is already largely completed, with many of the most important dependent and semi-dependent areas, such as India, Burma, the Arab states, and the Philippines already independent, and Indonesia and Indochina well on the road. These new and emergent states will be free to determine their own economic policies and future alignments.

For a long period, however, these new states will find it difficult to stand alone. Though actively promoting their own political and economic development, they will remain for some time semi-dependent areas, forced to rely on the great powers for protection and assistance. Their relatively backward stage of political, economic, and social evolution, their lack of developed resources, and the absence of technical skills and education among the mass of their peoples make them dependent upon outside help in their development. Militarily, they will be unable to withstand any major power. Economically, they will still be undeveloped countries, tied to the larger metropolitan economies. The effect, therefore, of the disintegration of the colonial systems and the withdrawal of the colonial powers is the creation of a power vacuum in the Near and Far East.

There is danger that unless the Western European nations, and with them the US, can secure the good will of these newly liberated and as yet dependent areas, they may become aligned with the USSR. Several factors: friction over the colonial issue, economic nationalism, and the racial antagonism between East and West, may tend to orient these areas away from the US and the Western Powers. The newly liberated states will entertain some hostility toward the former colonial powers, and as these powers belong to the Western bloc supported by the US, this hostility will extend in some degree toward the US also. US support of the colonial powers in the UN also has tended to make the dependent peoples and their supporters suspicious of US motives. In the economic sphere, the new and undeveloped countries tend to resent US economic dominance and to fear that the US and other industrialized nations intend to keep them economically dependent. The USSR, pursuing an assimilative racial policy and able to represent itself to colonial peoples as largely Asiatic, escapes much of the resentment of colored toward white peoples; while US treatment of its Negroes, powerfully played up by Soviet propaganda, embarrasses the US on this issue. Racial restrictions in areas like South Africa and Australia also arouse colonial resentment. Moreover, the poverty and backwardness of the colonial and former colonial world, combined with the restrictive policies of the colonial powers, has en-

hanced the appeal of radical political philosophies and tended to place leadership of indigenous nationalist groups in the hands of extremists. This tendency is evident in the existence of active pro-Communist parties in such areas as China, Indochina, Burma, and Indonesia. Thus the basic backwardness of these areas, their resentment toward the past or present dominating powers, and the existence of strong leftist elements within them, make them peculiarly susceptible to Soviet penetration. Should the USSR in turn, however, become in the eyes of these areas a threat to their independence, they would actively oppose Soviet domination too.

6. Implications for US Security.

The break-up of the colonial systems and the creation of a series of new nationalistic states may adversely affect the present power balance of the US and Western Europe versus the USSR, particularly if these new states become friendly toward the USSR and hostile toward the US and its allies.

a. The loss of their dependencies weakens the colonial powers, which are the chief prospective US allies. These nations rely upon their colonies as sources of raw materials, military manpower, and revenue, and as strategic military bases. France, for example, draws heavily upon its North and West African empire in most of the above respects; and the breaking away of these areas, especially North Africa, would seriously weaken its strategic position. UK withdrawal from India and Burma already has substantially affected its strategic capabilities in the Middle and Far East. The Netherlands would be weakened economically by the defection of its rich Indonesian possessions.

b. The drift of the dependent areas away from the orbit of the colonial powers deprives the US itself of an assured access to bases and raw materials in many of these areas, an increasingly serious loss in view of global US strategic needs and growing dependence on foreign mineral resources. Bases in French North Africa and the Middle East, for example, would be strategically vital in event of conflict. The growing US list of strategic and critical materials—many of which like tin and rubber are available largely in colonial and former colonial areas—illustrates the dependence of the US upon these areas. The US has heretofore been able to count upon the availability of such bases and materials in the colonial dependencies of friendly powers; but the new nations arising in these areas, jealous of their sovereignty, may well be reluctant to lend such assistance to the US.

c. Possible Soviet domination of certain former dependent areas or their orientation toward the USSR would create a major threat to US security. Such a possibility is strongest in Asiatic peripheral areas around the USSR, where the danger of Soviet penetration is acute. Soviet control of areas like Iran, Burma, Indochina, Indonesia, or Korea, whether through occupation, alliance or friendly neutrality, would help complete Soviet control of the Asiatic continent, make the USSR more invulnerable to external attack, assure its access to vital materials like oil, tin, and rubber, and place it astride strategic sea lanes.

d. Colonial antagonism toward the US would hamper the US in its relations with colonial areas should their metropolitan powers fall within the Soviet orbit in event of

war. While governments-in-exile probably would be formed, they might prove unable to control their dependencies, which might seize this opportunity to further their own nationalist aims by revolt. Were the US forced to occupy these territories for strategic reasons, its task would be much more difficult if they were hostile.

e. The colonial issue also tends to create recurring crises which promote world unrest. Increasing resort to the UN to deal with the swelling chorus of colonial grievances and the pressure in behalf of dependent peoples by a large bloc of sympathetic states tends to magnify these grievances out of all proportion to their local significance. The USSR, seeking to promote any unrest in colonial areas, will quickly exploit its disruptive possibilities.

Consequently, the good will of the recently liberated and emergent independent states becomes a vital factor in the future position of the US in the Near and Far East. The breaking up of the colonial systems and the gradual withdrawing of the colonial powers from these areas has faced the US itself with the problem of filling the gap left by their withdrawal. The US stand on the colonial issue and economic nationalism will have a major effect on the attitudes of these colonial and former colonial areas. Yet the US is currently in an unfortunate position vis-à-vis the USSR with respect to such issues. On the one hand, the US has historically sympathized with the aspirations of dependent peoples for self-government and has pledged itself to this end in the Atlantic Charter and in the United Nations. As a result, the dependent and semi-dependent areas have come to expect and demand US backing in their struggle for independence. To the extent that the US acquiesces in or supports restrictive colonial policies on the part of the Western European nations, it will jeopardize its position in these areas. Such a policy will lay the US open to charges of inconsistency and imperialism and may lead to loss of the voting support of the colonial bloc in the UN. It will allow the USSR, in particular, to pose as champion of the colonial cause and thus gain the good will of the dependent and former dependent areas.

On the other hand, the European colonial powers are the chief prospective US allies in its power struggle with the USSR and it is difficult for the US to oppose these powers on colonial issues. These nations are anxious to retain as much of a hold as possible on their dependencies, partly for economic and strategic reasons, but also for prestige. Should these countries lose the benefits of their colonial empires, it would hamper their economic recovery and possibly threaten the stability of governments friendly to the US.

If, however, the colonial powers do not basically modify their present colonial policies, they will in the long run lose the very strategic and economic advantages in their dependencies and former dependencies that they are seeking to retain. Such restrictive policies will not arrest the development of local nationalism but may in fact so aggravate it as to alienate the local populations and minimize the possibility of retaining any benefits whatsoever. Moreover, attempts at forcible retention of critical colonial areas in the face of growing nationalist pressure may actually weaken rather than strengthen the colonial powers. French and Dutch efforts to suppress local nationalism by force in Indonesia and Indochina, for example, are a drain on funds

urgently needed for reconstruction and may create such antagonism that no profitable economic development will be feasible for an extended period.

The colonial powers must fully recognize the irresistible force of nationalism in their dependencies and take leadership in guiding these dependencies gradually toward eventual self-government or independence, if they are to retain their favored position in these areas. A policy of far-reaching colonial reforms, designed to foster colonial political, economic, and social development, would do much to neutralize the more violent aspects of native nationalism and to substitute orderly evolution toward the inevitable goal of independence for the violent upheavals characteristic of the present situation. Only through such a new cooperative relationship can the colonial powers in the long run hope to retain their close ties with these areas and the maximum of political and economic advantage. Unless the colonial powers can be induced to recognize this necessity for satisfying the aspirations of their dependencies and can devise formulae which will retain their good will as emergent independent states, both these powers and the US will be placed at a serious disadvantage in the new power situation in the Near and Far East.

In the economic sphere, since the US plays a dominant role in world trade and is the nation currently most capable of supplying the capital needs of the "underdeveloped" countries, the attitude of the US itself toward the efforts of these areas to achieve greater economic self-sufficiency will have a great effect on their goodwill. US failure to adopt a more sympathetic attitude toward the economic nationalism of the underdeveloped countries or at least partially to meet their demands for capital assistance will stimulate the charges, already heard, of US economic imperialism and seriously affect US relations with these areas.

The US, therefore, is faced with a serious dilemma. On the one hand US encouragement of colonial self-determination and economic development may itself incur the charge of US imperialism and run the risk of alienating the colonial powers. On the other hand, the US may be unable to afford to let its policy on colonial issues be swayed by the colonial powers if such support of its allies tends to alienate the dependent peoples and other non-European countries, lay the groundwork for future disruption, and in the long run weaken the power balance of both the US and the Western European nations vis-à-vis the USSR.

ORE 29-50

Consequences to the US of Communist Domination of Mainland Southeast Asia

13 October 1950

SECRET

COPY NO. 217
FOR THE ASSISTANT DIRECTOR
FOR REPORTS AND ESTIMATES

CONSEQUENCES TO THE US OF COMMUNIST DOMINATION OF MAINLAND SOUTHEAST ASIA

APPROVED FOR RELEASE
DATE: JAN 2005

(b)(3)

ORE 29-50

Published 13 October 1950

CENTRAL INTELLIGENCE AGENCY

SECRET

235016

CONSEQUENCES TO THE US OF COMMUNIST DOMINATION OF MAINLAND SOUTHEAST ASIA[1]

SUMMARY AND CONCLUSIONS

Communist domination of mainland Southeast Asia would not be critical[2] to US security interests but would have serious immediate and direct consequences. The gravest of such consequences would be a spreading of doubt and fear among other threatened non-Communist countries as to the ability of the US to back up its proclaimed intention to halt Communist expansion everywhere. Unless offset by positive additions to the security of non-Communist countries in other sensitive areas of the world, the psychological effect of the loss of mainland Southeast Asia would not only strengthen Communist propaganda that the advance of Communism is inexorable but would encourage countries vulnerable to Soviet pressure to adopt "neutral" attitudes in the cold war, or possibly even lead them to an accommodation with Communism.

Domination of the Southeast Asian mainland would increase the threat to such Western outposts in the Pacific as the island chain extending from Japan to Australia and New Zealand. The extension of Communist control, via Burma, to the borders of India and Pakistan would augment the slowly developing Communist threat to the Indian subcontinent. The fall of the Southeast Asian mainland would increase the feeling of insecurity already present in Japan as a result of Communist successes in China and would further underline the apparent economic advantages to the Japanese of association with a Communist-dominated Asian sphere.

The countries of mainland Southeast Asia produce such materials on the US strategic list as rubber, tin, shellac, kapok, and teak in substantial volume. Although access to these countries is not considered to be "absolutely essential in an emergency" by the National Security Resources Board, US access to this area is considered "desirable." Unlimited Soviet access to the strategic materials of mainland Southeast Asia would probably be "desirable" for the USSR but would not be "absolutely essential in an emergency" and therefore denial of the resources of the area to the Soviet Union would not be essential to the US strategic position. Communist control over the rice surpluses of the Southeast Asian mainland would, however, provide the USSR with considerable bargaining power in its relations with other countries of the Far East.

Loss of the area would indirectly affect US security interests through its important economic consequences for countries aligned with the US. Loss of Malaya would deprive the UK of its greatest net dollar earner. An immediate consequence of the loss of Indochina might be a strengthening of the defense of Western Europe since French expenditures for men and materiel in Indochina would be available to fulfill other commitments. Exclusion of Japan from trade with Southeast Asia would seriously frustrate Japanese prospects for economic recovery.

Communist domination of mainland Southeast Asia would place unfriendly forces astride the most direct and best-developed sea and air

[1] Assumption: (a) that major US policies in the Far East will be implemented substantially as now conceived; and (b) that Communist control of Southeast Asia will result in denial of the area to US and pro-Western nations.

[2] By "would not be critical to US security interests" is meant that the loss of the area to Communist domination would not have a decisively adverse effect on the capabilities of the US to win a global war.

Note: The Office of Naval Intelligence has concurred in this estimate; for dissents of the intelligence organizations of the Departments of State, Army, and the Air Force, see Enclosures A, B, and C, respectively. The estimate contains information available to CIA as of 15 September 1950.

(Continued...)

routes between the Western Pacific and India and the Near East. The denial to the US of intermediate routes in mainland Southeast Asia would be significant because communications between the US and India and the Near East would be essential in a global war. In the event of such a war, the development of Soviet submarine and air bases in mainland Southeast Asia probably would compel the detour of US and allied shipping and air transportation in the Southeast Asia region via considerably longer alternate routes to the south. This extension of friendly lines of communication would hamper US strategic movements in this region and tend to isolate the major non-Communist bases in the Far East — the offshore island chain and Australia — from existing bases in East Africa and the Near and Middle East, as well as from potential bases on the Indian sub-continent.

Besides disrupting established lines of communication in the area, the denial of actual military facilities in mainland Southeast Asia — in particular, the loss of the major naval operating bases at Singapore — would compel the utilization of less desirable peripheral bases. Soviet exploitation of the naval and air bases in mainland Southeast Asia probably would be limited by the difficulties of logistic support but would, nevertheless, increase the threat to existing lines of communication.

The loss of any portion of mainland Southeast Asia would increase possibilities for the extension of Communist control over the remainder. The fall of Indochina would provide the Communists with a staging area in addition to China for military operations against the rest of mainland Southeast Asia, and this threat might well inspire accommodation in both Thailand and Burma. Assuming Thailand's loss, the already considerable difficulty faced by the British in maintaining security in Malaya would be greatly aggravated. Assuming Burma's internal collapse, unfavorable trends in India would be accelerated. If Burma were overcome by external aggression, however, a stiffening of the attitude of the Government of India toward International Communism could be anticipated.

SECRET

CONSEQUENCES TO THE US OF COMMUNIST DOMINATION OF MAINLAND SOUTHEAST ASIA

1. Consequences of the Loss of the Entire Mainland.

Psychological Effects.

The most serious immediate and direct consequence resulting from the loss of the Southeast Asia mainland to Soviet-dominated Communism would be psychological and would derive from the proclaimed US intention to halt Communist expansion everywhere. Indochina, of all the countries in mainland Southeast Asia, has become a publicly declared symbol of this US determination. In consequence, the loss of Southeast Asia would spread doubt and fear among other threatened non-Communist countries throughout the world. This unfavorable reaction would be lessened to some extent, however, if events in other "sensitive" areas of the world—Korea, for example—clearly demonstrated that the advance of Communism was not inevitable. To the extent that the loss of the area was not counterbalanced by significant reversals for the forces of Soviet Communism elsewhere, "neutral" attitudes would be encouraged, and some countries on the perimeter of Soviet power might well accommodate themselves to Communism.

The loss of mainland Southeast Asia would add to Communist prestige internationally, the more so because the area is remote from the USSR and has long been exposed to strong Western influence. The loss would lend credence throughout the world to Communist propaganda regarding the inevitability of victory and the International Communist movement would be encouraged to strike bolder and harder blows at other areas of the non-Communist world.

Strategic and Political Effects.

If the fall of the Southeast Asia mainland should precede or accompany an outbreak of general East-West hostilities, Soviet forces deployed in the area would be in a position to threaten US lines of communication in the Far East. Unfriendly control either under conditions of "cold war" or following the outbreak of hostilities would directly threaten Indonesia and India and increase the pressures, primarily psychological, already being exerted from China on the Philippines. Both Indonesia and the Philippines are important elements in the island chain which represents the outer perimeter of US defenses in the Pacific and controls access from mainland Asia to the Australia-New Zealand area.

The fall of mainland Southeast Asia would increase the susceptibility of both the Republics of Indonesia and the Philippines to Communist pressures. Both subversive action directed from the mainland and economic pressures would have increased effect following the loss of faith in the West and the anxiety inspired by the proximity of aggressive Communist military power. Although the two Republics might not succumb to Communist pressures immediately, the stage would be set for their eventual voluntary or involuntary inclusion in the Communist orbit. The outcome of this eventuality, in turn, would be to place both Australia and New Zealand within closer range of Communist military and psychological pressures. This increased threat would not, however, alter the domestic or international orientation of either of these two Commonwealth countries.

The extension of Communist control westward to the borders of India and Pakistan would augment the slowly developing Communist threat to the Indian sub-continent. Covert Communist activities would be facilitated, indigenous Communists would be encouraged, and the two major nations of the sub-continent would be exposed to direct Communist military and economic pressures. The attitude of the Government of India toward International Communism would probably be stiffened, however, if any of the Southeast Asia countries, particularly neighboring Burma, were overtly attacked by Com-

munist China. On the other hand, the trend toward Communism on the Indian sub-continent could be accelerated if it should appear that the fall of Southeast Asia was brought about by indigenous forces in fulfillment of their nationalist aspirations.

To the north, Japan's feeling of insecurity — a result of that occupied nation's weak and dependent position — has already been aggravated by the Communist victory in China. Although this feeling has not prevented apparently willing Japanese support of the US-UN position in Korea, Communist acquisition of mainland Southeast Asia would undoubtedly strengthen grave concern in Japan over its future at a time when efforts are being made by early peace negotiations to assure that country's future on the side of the West. The apparent economic advantage of association with a Communist-dominated Asian sphere would impel an unoccupied Japan toward a course of accommodation with International Communism.

Economic Effects.

Rubber, tin, shellac, kapok, and teak, which are produced in substantial volume in the countries of mainland Southeast Asia, are on the US strategic list. In the case of each of these commodities, however, one or a combination of the following factors apply: substitute or synthetic materials are available, alternative sources of supply exist, or present US stockpiles are at levels which are reasonably adequate to permit the US to wage war in the near future. As a result, the National Security Resources Board and other US agencies concerned with the acquisition of strategic materials do not consider access to mainland Southeast Asia as "absolutely essential in an emergency." Thailand, Malaya, and Burma are designated by these agencies as areas to which US access is "desirable" but not "essential." Because of the paucity of strategic materials available for export from Indochina, that country is not regarded as one to which access is necessarily "desirable."[1]

[1] *Areas to which Access by the US in War is Essential or Desirable as a Result of US Deficiencies in Resources of Vital Materials.* NSRB, Materials Office, April 24, 1950. Confidential.

Unlimited access to the strategic materials of mainland Southeast Asia would probably (using the terminology of the NSRB study cited above) be "desirable" for the USSR but not "absolutely essential in an emergency." Consequently, solely from the viewpoint of strategic materials, denial of Soviet access to the area would not be essential to the over-all strategic position of the US and its allies.

In addition to rubber and tin,[1] the most important commodity that the Communists would obtain by control of mainland Southeast Asia would be rice. Thailand and Burma are the largest rice exporters in the world; Indochina produced a large rice surplus in the prewar period and could do so again under conditions of relative stability. These countries consequently play a most important role in the economies of the food-deficit areas of Malaya, India, Ceylon, Japan and a lesser role in the economies of China, Indonesia, and the Philippines. Communist control over the rice surpluses of mainland Southeast Asia would give the USSR a powerful political and economic weapon in its relations with other countries of the Far East.

An indirect but nevertheless extremely important consequence of the loss of mainland Southeast Asia would be its effect on British plans for achieving the full economic recovery of the sterling area. As a result of huge US purchases of tin and rubber, Malaya is the UK's greatest net dollar earner. The loss of Singapore's profitable entrepôt trade would

[1] It is believed that the present flow of natural rubber to the USSR and its Satellites, together with the output of synthetic rubber, is sufficient to meet current requirements and provide additions to stockpiles. Hence, unlimited access to and control over the rubber producing areas of Malaya and Thailand would not appear to be of great urgency to the USSR at this time.

The Soviet orbit requires imports of approximately 10,000 metric tons of tin annually to meet its peacetime requirements on a restricted basis and to permit some stockpiling. The USSR may be getting as much as 6,000 tons of tin annually from China at present and probably can acquire all of its minimum import needs from this source within the next few years. Unrestricted access to the output of tin from Malaya (55,000 tons in 1949) or even from Thailand (7,800 tons in 1949) would provide the USSR with a large surplus of this strategic metal for possible re-export to Satellites and the West.

also have serious implications for the UK's still tenuous economic position.

An immediate consequence of the loss of Indochina might be a strengthening of the defense of Western Europe since French expenditures for men and materiel in Indochina would be available to fulfill other commitments.

Japan, too, would be adversely affected. Exclusion of Japan from trade with mainland Southeast Asia would seriously if not completely frustrate Japanese prospects of economic recovery which would permit Japan to achieve economic independence and an acceptable standard of living. Furthermore, unless Japan were able to trade with the Communist bloc, the additional dollar expenditures for requisite imports would increase Japan's dependence on US aid.

Military Effects.

Communist domination of mainland Southeast Asia would place unfriendly forces astride the most direct and best-developed sea and air routes between the western Pacific Ocean area and the Near and Middle East (see accompanying maps). The denial to the US of intermediate routes in mainland Southeast Asia would be significant because communications between the US and India and the Near East would be essential in global war. In the event of such a war, the development of Soviet submarine and air bases in a position to interdict war and air transportation through the East Indies, together with the extension of Soviet naval and air capabilities into the Indian Ocean, probably would compel the detour of US and allied shipping and air transportation in the Southeast Asia region via considerably longer alternate routes to the south.

The loss of Singapore would close the Straits of Malacca, while the proximity of potential Communist bases would necessitate the protection of friendly shipping in the narrow alternate passages of the East Indies. These factors would probably force the use of the long route south of Australia.

Loss of mainland Southeast Asia would produce a gap in the chain of available airfields which rim the Asian continent and provide mobility to Western air power. Mingaladon near Rangoon and Don Muang near Bangkok, both of which have facilities for handling C-54 transport aircraft, lie on the most direct route between Karachi and Manila. The denial of this route and the loss of Singapore would mean that air traffic between allied bases in the Near East, the Asian offshore island chain, and the US west coast would have to be routed via Australia.

This considerable extension of friendly lines of communication in the Southwest Pacific would tend to isolate the major non-Communist bases in the Far East—the offshore island chain and Australia—from East Africa and the Near East as well as from the Indian subcontinent.

The loss of mainland Southeast Asia would not eliminate communications between the US and the Indian sub-continent since air and sea routes from the US over the Atlantic represent substantially shorter lines of communication. If, as a result of global hostilities, the Mediterranean were also denied to US and Western shipping, the Cape of Good Hope route would probably remain a more desirable alternative to routes south of Australia. An active submarine menace in the Atlantic as in World War II, however, would probably necessitate increased routing of shipping over less vulnerable Pacific Ocean routes. Air transit via North or Central Africa will, in any case, continue to be the shortest and quickest route from the US to the Near East and India.

Communist domination of Southeast Asia would deny actual and potential military facilities to the West. Singapore is the only major naval operating base between Capetown and Sydney or Yokosuka and its loss would compel withdrawal of naval forces in the region of Southeast Asia to less desirable peripheral bases at Subic, Surabaya, and/or Trincomalee. Although there are no airfields in mainland Southeast Asia currently capable of handling medium bombers, there are a number of installations currently able to handle large transport aircraft. A few of these installations are capable of development into medium bomber bases. Their utilization, however, would be against secondary rather than decisive objectives.

Soviet exploitation of naval and air bases in the area would increase the threat to existing lines of communication. Soviet activities in this area would probably be confined largely to submarine and air activity in contiguous waters. Larger-scale military operations staged from Southeast Asia bases would be unlikely, however, since such operations would have to be supported from industrial bases west of Lake Baikal over long, circuitous and poorly developed lines of communication.

2. Consequences of Partial Loss.

Events in Indochina and Burma will strongly influence the means and timing of the extension of Communist control over the remainder of mainland Southeast Asia.

Indochina.

If it is assumed that Indochina would be the first portion of mainland Southeast Asia to be lost, it would provide International Communism with several important advantages. Indochina has become the symbol of US intent to resist the expansion of Communism in Southeast Asia and the defeat of the French despite widely publicized US aid would furnish the Communists with such valuable propaganda themes as the defeat of "imperialism" by the forces of nationalism and the inability of the West to halt the steady advance of Communism. The forces of International Communism would acquire a staging area from which military operations could be launched against other countries in Southeast Asia, whether on the mainland or across the South China Sea. From a Communist-dominated Indochina, political pressures could be exerted in Thailand, which, unless substantial outside aid were forthcoming, would probably result in the complete accommodation of that country to International Communism in a matter of months. Finally, control over Indochina would make available to Communist China the substantial rice surpluses which Indochina is capable of exporting under conditions of internal stability.

Burma.

Whether it is assumed that Burma would fall before or after Indochina, control over that country would give the Communists access to its large rice surpluses. It would also provide them with a base from which political pressures could be exerted against India, Malaya, and Thailand. Although the terrain makes large-scale military operations difficult, infiltration of neighboring countries by armed troublemakers would be a relatively simple operation.

If the loss of Indochina accompanies or precedes the loss of Burma, political pressures against Thailand and military infiltration of Malaya would probably result in the whole of mainland Southeast Asia falling under Communist domination within two years, unless large-scale outside support were forthcoming.

Communist control of Burma might accelerate unfavorable trends in neighboring India. If Burma were a victim of overt aggression from China, however, a stiffening of the attitude of the Government of India toward International Communism would probably result, although popular reaction might tend toward accommodation.

Thailand.

As indicated above, Thailand, in the absence of substantial outside support, would probably submit to Communism within a year after Communist victories in either Burma or Indochina. If Thailand were under Communist control, the already serious security problem presented by the Thailand-Malayan border would be aggravated and would add to the difficulties of the British Security Forces in Malaya, already heavily occupied.

Although unrestricted access to Thailand's tin and rubber is not essential to the war requirements of the Soviet bloc, it would cushion the USSR's economy against the effects of an extended and costly war. Thailand's large export surpluses of rice (1,200,000 tons in 1949) would meet the import requirements of the food-deficit South China areas (200,000 tons annually) and place the Soviet bloc in a powerful political and economic bargaining position among the rice-importing countries of Asia.

Because of the close political ties that have developed between the US and Thailand, US prestige would suffer severely in the event that Thailand is lost to Communism.

Malaya.

Although unrestricted Soviet access to the rubber and tin of Malaya is not essential, it would be a desirable contribution to the Soviet economy. If it is assumed that the rubber and tin resources of Thailand would be available to the Soviet bloc prior to the establishment of Communist control over Malaya, it is probable that the Soviet bloc would find only a fraction of the Malayan resources worth exploitation.

Possession of Singapore, the most important naval base in the Far East, would increase the operational capabilities of the Soviet Navy, particularly its submarine fleet.

Because of its proximity and close relations with Indonesia, increased infiltration of Communists from Malaya to Indonesia would occur.

ENCLOSURE A

DISSENT OF THE INTELLIGENCE ORGANIZATION, DEPARTMENT OF STATE

We do not necessarily disagree with the major conclusion of this estimate as stated in the opening sentence of the Summary and Conclusions, but we feel that the narrow interpretation given the terms of reference makes it impossible to reach this conclusion with the certainty suggested by the present paper. Determination of the seriousness of the fall of Southeast Asia Mainland to Communism would appear to require much more detailed consideration of the snow-balling effects of such an event, primarily in terms of its impact on other areas and on the world position of the US. It is realized that the results of a chain reaction are difficult to predict. The estimate does, however, contain sufficient indication of such a reaction to warrant much closer attention to the factors that are involved.

In addition, we would also consider as relevant and indispensable to the estimate:

1. A more thorough evaluation of the significance of the area to the US world position and;

2. A consideration of various alternative circumstances under which the loss of Southeast Asia Mainland might occur, and of how these circumstances might affect the US world position.

ENCLOSURE B

DISSENT OF THE OFFICE OF THE ASSISTANT CHIEF OF STAFF, G-2, INTELLIGENCE, DEPARTMENT OF THE ARMY

The Office of the Assistant Chief of Staff, G–2, Intelligence, Department of the Army, dissents from ORE 29–50 (Revised) for the following reasons:

a. The principal conclusion in this study, that Communist domination of the area would not have a decisive effect on the capabilities of the U.S. to win a global war, does not appear to place sufficient emphasis on the seriousness of the long-range consequences to the U.S. of the loss of mainland Southeast Asia.

b. It is felt that while Communist domination of mainland Southeast Asia, considered *in vacuo*, would not have a decisively adverse effect on U.S. military capabilities to win a global war, nevertheless such a Communist gain would immediately, directly, and most seriously affect over-all U.S. strategic interests and might ultimately become "critical" to the U.S. security position when considered in conjunction with possible losses in other areas.

ENCLOSURE C

DISSENT OF THE DIRECTOR OF INTELLIGENCE, UNITED STATES AIR FORCE

1. The Director of Intelligence, U.S.A.F., has reviewed ORE 29–50 (Revised), "Consequences to the US of Communist Domination of Mainland Southeast Asia," and dissents from subject estimate for the following reason:

a. The estimate is seriously misleading, primarily because it fails to give a balanced presentation of the consequences to the United States—medium and long-range as well as short-range—of Communist domination of mainland Southeast Asia. While certain medium and long-range factors are discussed individually in the text, these are not adequately reflected in the Summary and Conclusions. It is believed that, from the medium and long-range points of view, the strategic, political, military, and sociological effects of the loss of mainland Southeast Asia may well be more serious than the immediate and direct psychological effects and could have a critical effect on the capabilities of the United States to win a global war. The loss of a specifically designated area of the world cannot be assessed adequately without considering its effect on the entire global situation. It is the view of the Director of Intelligence, U.S.A.F., that the loss of mainland Southeast Asia, when taken in conjunction with the resultant weakening effect on adjacent areas and adverse developments in other parts of the world, could be critical to United States security interests.

2. It is recommended that footnote 2 of page 1 be deleted, and that the first sentence of the Summary and Conclusions be rewritten as follows: "Communist domination of mainland Southeast Asia could be critical to United States security interests; it would have serious immediate and direct, as well as long-range, consequences."

(Continued...)

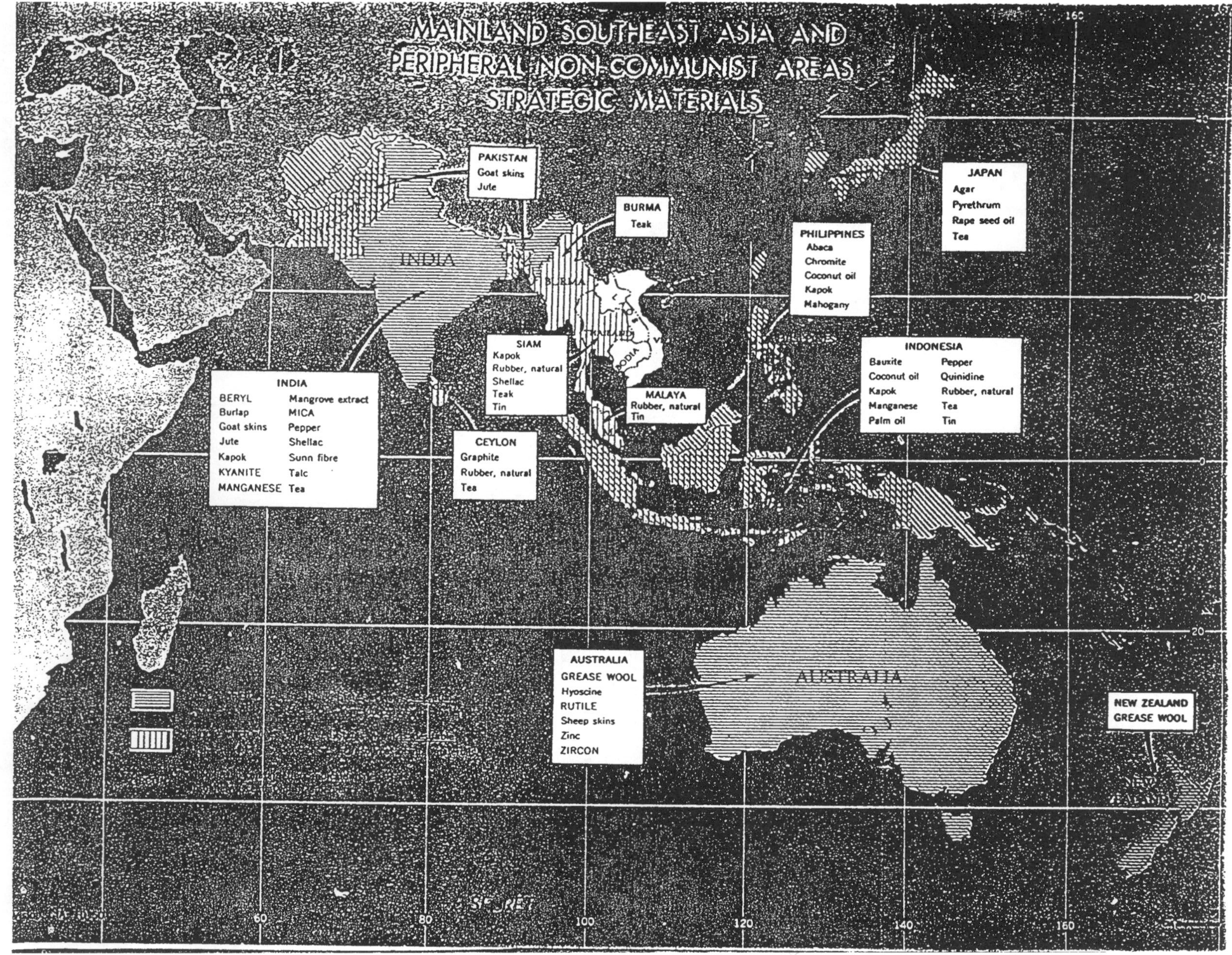
MAINLAND SOUTHEAST ASIA AND
PERIPHERAL NON-COMMUNIST AREAS
STRATEGIC MATERIALS
PAKISTAN
Goat skins
Jute
BURMA
Teak
JAPAN
Agar
Pyrethrum
Rape seed oil
Tea
PHILIPPINES
Abaca
Chromite
Coconut oil
Kapok
Mahogany
INDIA
SIAM
Kapok
Rubber, natural
Shellac
Teak
Tin
INDONESIA
Bauxite
Coconut oil
Kapok
Manganese
Palm oil
Pepper
Quinidine
Rubber, natural
Tea
Tin
INDIA
BERYL
Burlap
Goat skins
Jute
Kapok
KYANITE
MANGANESE
Mangrove extract
MICA
Pepper
Shellac
Sunn fibre
Talc
Tea
MALAYA
Rubber, natural
Tin
CEYLON
Graphite
Rubber, natural
Tea
AUSTRALIA
GREASE WOOL
Hyoscine
RUTILE
Sheep skins
Zinc
ZIRCON
AUSTRALIA
NEW ZEALAND
GREASE WOOL
60
80
100
120
140
160

MAINLAND SOUTHEAST ASIA AND PERIPHERAL NON-COMMUNIST AREAS:
COMPARATIVE LINES OF SEA COMMUNICATIONS
NEW YO TO BOMBAY
via Suez 8176
via Good pe 11356
SAN FRANCISCO TO BOMBAY
via Yokohama and Singapore 9894
via Celebes Sea, Macassar Straits, and Lombok Straits 10574
via Torres Strait 11209
via Sydney and Fremantle 12634
YOKOHAMA TO BOMBAY
via Singapore 5335
via Macassar Straits 6361
via Torres Straits 8611
via Sydney 10444
CONFIDENTIAL

(Continued...)

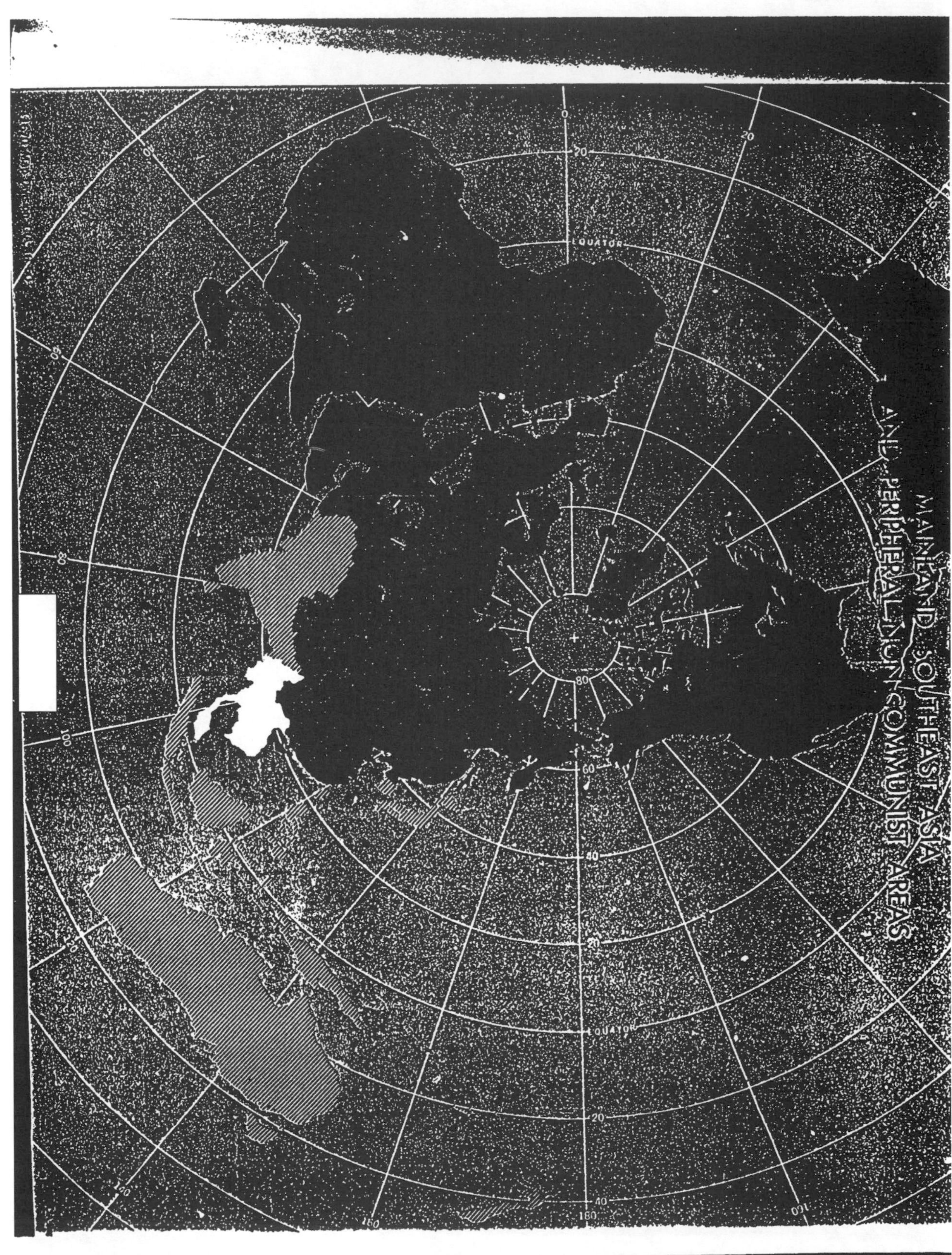
MAINLAND SOUTHEAST ASIA
AND PERIPHERAL NON-COMMUNIST AREAS
EQUATOR
EQUATOR

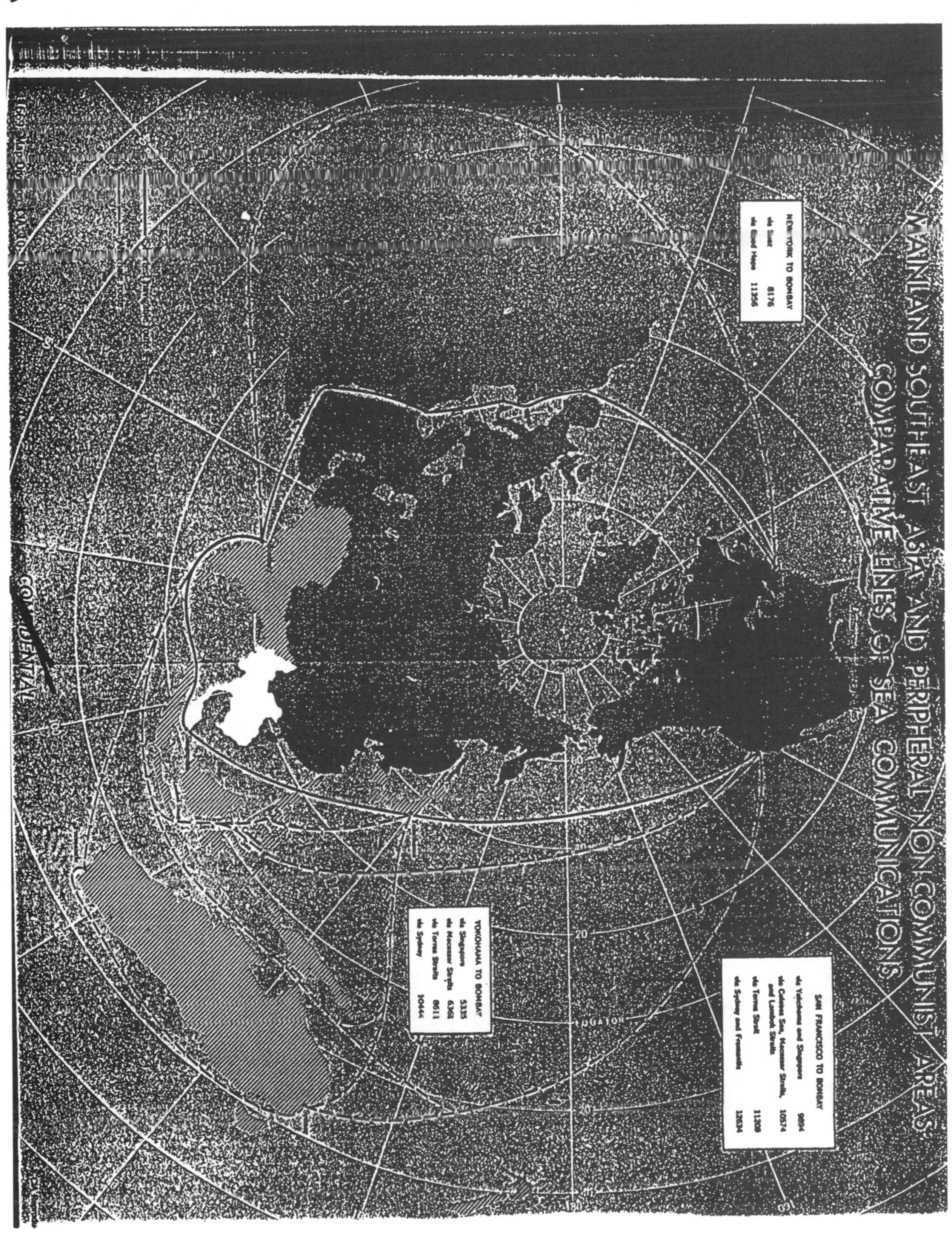
MAINLAND SOUTHEAST ASIA AND PERIPHERAL NON-COMMUNIST AREAS
COMPARATIVE LINES OF SEA COMMUNICATIONS

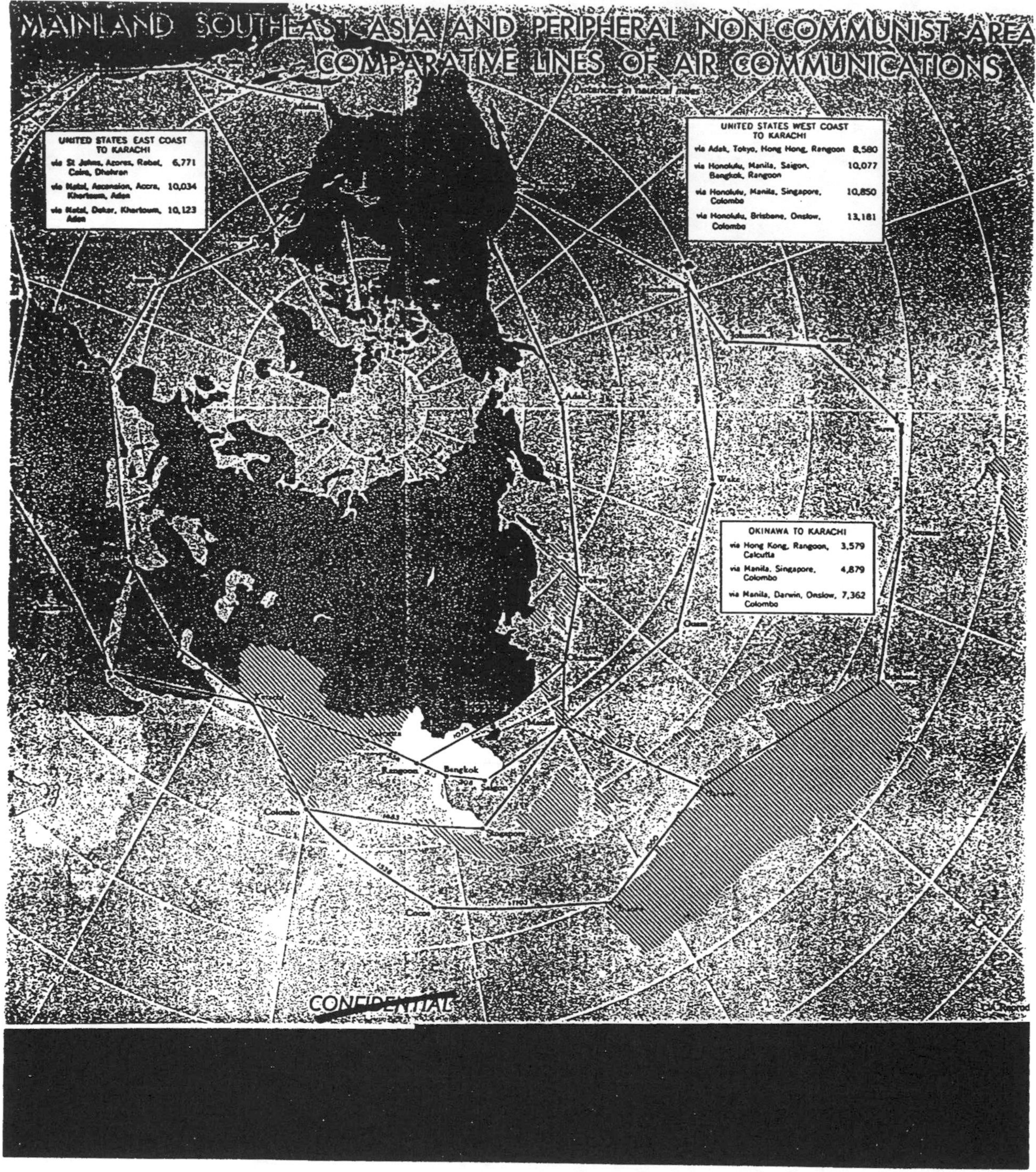
MAINLAND SOUTHEAST ASIA AND PERIPHERAL NON-COMMUNIST AREA
COMPARATIVE LINES OF AIR COMMUNICATIONS
Distances in nautical miles
UNITED STATES EAST COAST TO KARACHI
via St Johns, Azores, Rabat, Cairo, Dhahran 6,771
via Natal, Ascension, Accra, Khartoum, Aden 10,034
via Natal, Dakar, Khartoum, Aden 10,123
UNITED STATES WEST COAST TO KARACHI
via Adak, Tokyo, Hong Hong, Rangoon 8,580
via Honolulu, Manila, Saigon, Bangkok, Rangoon 10,077
via Honolulu, Manila, Singapore, Colombo 10,850
via Honolulu, Brisbane, Onslow, Colombo 13,181
OKINAWA TO KARACHI
via Hong Kong, Rangoon, Calcutta 3,579
via Manila, Singapore, Colombo 4,879
via Manila, Darwin, Onslow, Colombo 7,362
Wake
Tokyo
Rangoon
Bangkok
Colombo
Singapore
Cocos
CONFIDENTIAL

Memo

Critical Developments in French Policy Toward Indochina

10 January 1952

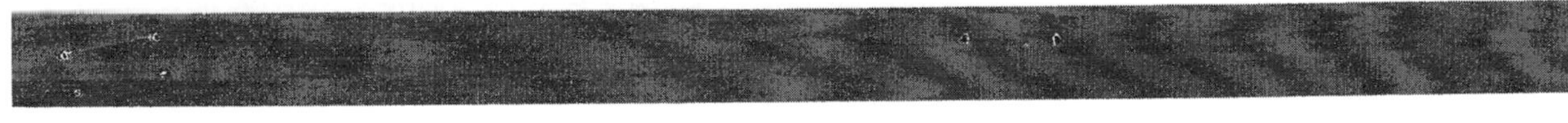

TOP ~~SECRET~~ #53880-a

APPROVED FOR RELEASE
DATE: JAN 2005

CENTRAL INTELLIGENCE AGENCY

(b)(3)

OFFICE OF NATIONAL ESTIMATES

10 January 1952

Memorandum for the Director of Central Intelligence

Subject: Critical Developments in French Policy toward Indochina

As the result of the current French cabinet and budgetary crisis, a critical French reappraisal of their Indochina policy appears imminent and may have major implications for the US. Plagued by continued inflation and limited financial capabilities, all levels of French official and public opinion are rapidly gravitating toward the opinion that France itself cannot simultaneously support two major military efforts, one in NATO and the other in the Far East.

Postwar French military policy has reflected preoccupation with two needs: (a) not to be overshadowed militarily by a resurgent Germany; and (b) not to abandon the French position overseas. The French calculate that, even with projected US aid of all kinds, the cost to France of meeting these two requirements is likely to rise in 1952 to over $4 billion -- roughly $1 billion in Indochina and $3 billion for NATO. They calculate, however, that their maximum practicable military budget will fall short of this figure by over $500 million.

Since French interests in Western Europe are paramount, it appears that any retrenchment must come in the Far East. Among the signs are (a) General de Lattre's recent remarks on

13969 TOP ~~SECRET~~

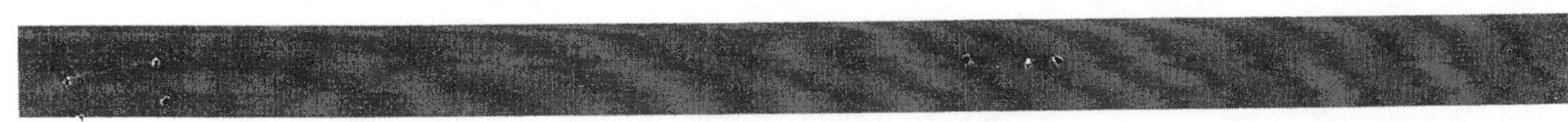

the disproportion between the expense of the war in Indochina and the French stake there; (b) Premier Pleven's recent request for early high-level conversations on Indochina in the context of the whole Far Eastern problem; and (c) indications that many French politicans are becoming converted to the belief that French withdrawal from Indochina is inevitable and should not be too long postponed. Embassy Paris estimates that the "snowball has started to form" and that, in the absence either of some form of internationalization of the Indochina problem or of substantial additional US aid, public sentiment for withdrawal will gain steadily and perhaps accelerate.

Under these circumstances the French Government has apparently concluded that the only chance of solving its problem short of retrenchment lies in convincing the US that France itself can no longer support the major burden of the Indochina war. The French have consistently argued that the Indochina struggle must not be regarded as a purely national interest but as an integral part of the over-all containment effort of the West. Consequently present French policy appears directed toward: (a) securing substantial additional US aid to relieve the French financial burden; (b) securing some form of internationalization of the Indochina war, i.e., a US-UK commitment to defend Indochina, thus acting as a warning to the Chinese Communists, plus a concerting of joint defense measures as recommended by the Singapore Conference; and (c) achieving , if possible, an armistice in Indochina on the Korean model. It appears likely that France intends to press for early decision on these issues, despite their grave implications for French colonial policy. The French Government may well consider that it must act along these lines sooner or later anyway and that it cannot afford to wait until a Chinese invasion is imminent or German rearmament is well underway.

SHERMAN KENT
Assistant Director
National Estimates

Memo

Probable Communist Strategy and Tactics at Geneva

19 April 1954

APPROVED FOR RELEASE
DATE: JAN 2005

(b)(3)

19 April 1954

MEMORANDUM FOR THE DIRECTOR OF CENTRAL INTELLIGENCE

SUBJECT: Probable Communist Strategy and Tactics at Geneva

1. In our view, the Communists see in the forthcoming negotiations at Geneva abundant opportunities to improve their position both in Asia and in Europe. They are almost certainly confident that their negotiating position regarding Indochina will be both stronger and more unified than that of the West. They also are aware that the British and French attitude toward Communist China is more flexible than that of the US and probably consider that this divergence of attitude can be exploited, particularly if discussions of China's status as a world power can be tied to the possibilities of a settlement in Indochina. They probably also believe that the establishment of a Korean armistice has created a receptivity among Western nations for a general Far Eastern settlement and that this receptivity broadens their area for maneuver.

2. The chief Communist objectives for the Geneva conference are probably to weaken or disrupt the Western alliance and to establish Communist China as an acknowledged member of the "big

APR 20 1954
NE-2

SECRET

Memo for DCI

five." The achievements of settlements in Korea and in Indochina, ostensibly the chief purposes of the conference, probably have only secondary importance in the Communist scale of values. The Communists probably see no pressing necessity in either of these local situations for reaching an immediate settlement and are almost certainly not prepared to give up any of the substantial advantages they now enjoy in these areas. On the other hand, the Communists almost certainly do not want the Indochina war expanded, and they probably also will not wish the conference to lead to intervention of the US in the war, either alone or with allies.

3. The Communists probably consider the Indochina question pivotal in the Geneva conference. The Communists almost certainly consider that the keen desire of the French to get out of the Indochina war is the weakest point in the Western facade and offers many opportunities for tactical maneuver. They will therefore seek to exploit the weakness of the French regarding Indochina in order to test the unity and flexibility of the Western bloc. If the Western bloc as a whole demonstrates an inflexibility regarding negotiations for some kind of settlement in Indochina, they will probably undertake largely to create division within the Western bloc through a series of propositions calculated to make France's western partners, particularly the US, appear

- 2 -

SECRET

intransigent and determined to reach a military solution in Indochina. On the other hand, if the Western bloc displays some willingness to bargain, the Communists will probably offer propositions involving minor Communist concessions which could lead to an agreement of narrow proportions in Indochina.

4. Specific Communist tactics during the Indochina discussions are difficult to anticipate. We consider it likely, however, that the Communists will either initiate or be immediately receptive to a proposal for a cease-fire in Indochina. The Communists may link the possibility of a cease-fire to Western concessions of considerable magnitude, such as the establishment of a coalition Vietnam-Vietminh government which would subsequently hold an election, or a division of Indochina at the 16th Parallel. They might include as conditions the withdrawal of French forces from Indochina or recognition of the Ho Chi-minh regime as the sovereign government of Vietnam. On the other hand, the Communists may merely offer a cease fire, with no conditions other than that further conferences be held for arriving at a political solution.

5. We believe that the Communists would be willing to have a cease-fire established in Indochina. Although the three Communist powers - the USSR, Communist China, and the Ho Chi-minh

regime - view Indochina in different perspectives, none of the three would lose by a cessation of the fighting at the present time. The USSR would thereby advance its present world-wide strategy of lessening tensions and would hope to profit, both in Asia and Europe, by reducing Western vigilance and preparedness. Communist China would thereby reduce the diversion of its energy from its primary interest in domestic economic and industrial expansion. Also, from the Chinese viewpoint a cease-fire of indefinite duration would eliminate the possibility that the Indochina war might become another Korean war, thus involving much heavier diversion of effort, the presence of US forces on China's southern flank, and the risk of expansion of the fighting to China itself. For the Ho Chi-minh regime, a cease-fire would mean a shift in emphasis from "armed liberation" tactics to political warfare tactics in furthering the Communist movement in Indochina. The Viet Minh probably consider that they have attained considerable military prestige among the Indochinese people during the past two fighting seasons and may feel that the time is now ripe to place heavier reliance on political tactics.

6. We believe that the Communists do not consider themselves under immediate pressure to make concessions of any considerable significance during the Indochina discussions. However, if the

SECRET

Communists become convinced that direct US participation in the Indochina war is a strong likelihood, their willingness to make concessions will be greater. They might, for example, be willing to make terms for a cease-fire which would permit the French to consolidate their position in the Delta. We believe they will not, however, make concessions representing an abandonment of the Ho Chi-minh regime or the Indochinese Communist movement.

7. Immediate Communist objectives for the Korean discussions at Geneva are probably moderate. They probably hope to bring about a reduction of Western strength in Korea but not to alter the present political division. They will probably attempt to make the Korean discussions revolve around the question of troop withdrawal, and they will almost certainly press vigorously for the withdrawal of all foreign forces from Korea, Chinese Communist forces included. If agreement on this point is reached, the Communists will probably be prepared actually to withdraw Chinese forces, believing that North Korean military strength matches South Korean strength and that such withdrawals will bring considerable political advantages to them. The Communists will probably raise or agree to proposals on certain minor matters such as commercial exchange, postal service, and limited movement of persons.

SECRET

8. Throughout the conference, the Communists will attempt to achieve at Geneva what they were unable to achieve at Berlin: Western acknowledgement of Communist China as one of the world's "big five." They will employ a variety of tactics, on both substantive and procedural issues, to establish that the Geneva conference is a five power conference, that China has equal status at Geneva with the US, the USSR, the UK, and France, and that China has the right to participate also in "big five" decisions on non-Asian questions. The USSR may attempt to enhance the status of China by assuming a less prominent role in the meetings while allowing the Chinese to come to the fore.

9. Consistent with their declared desire to make Geneva a big power conference on lessening world tensions, the Communists will almost certainly introduce issues extraneous to Korea and Indochina. Such issues may include: "normalization" of East-West diplomatic relations, expansion of East-West trade, reduction of armaments, outlawing of thermonuclear weapons, a proposed Asian Security arrangement similar to that currently being hawked by the USSR in Europe, and the future status of Formosa. Moreover, these issues, together with issues concerning Indochina, Korea, and the status of Communist China, may be packaged by the Communists at Geneva in any of a number of "attractive" combinations.

FOR THE BOARD OF NATIONAL ESTIMATES:

SECRET

HAROLD R. BULL
Lt. Gen., USA (Ret.)
Acting Chairman

NIE 63-54

Consequences Within Indochina of the Fall of Dien Bien Phu

30 April 1954

SECRET Return to ONE

COPY NO. 179
ASSISTANT DIRECTOR, ONE
9271 R. Am.

NATIONAL INTELLIGENCE ESTIMATE

CONSEQUENCES WITHIN INDOCHINA OF THE FALL OF DIEN BIEN PHU

APPROVED FOR RELEASE
DATE: JAN 2005

(b)(3)

NIE 63–54
Approved 28 April 1954
Published 30 April 1954

The Intelligence Advisory Committee concurred in this estimate on 28 April 1954. The AEC and FBI abstained, the subject being outside of their jurisdiction.

The following member organizations of the Intelligence Advisory Committee participated with the Central Intelligence Agency in the preparation of this estimate: The intelligence organizations of the Departments of State, the Army, the Navy, the Air Force, and The Joint Staff.

CENTRAL INTELLIGENCE AGENCY

SECRET

(Continued...)

CONSEQUENCES WITHIN INDOCHINA OF THE FALL OF DIEN BIEN PHU

THE PROBLEM

To estimate the probable consequences within Indochina during the next two or three months of the fall of Dien Bien Phu within the near future.

SCOPE

The consequences of the fall of Dien Bien Phu on the political situation in France, and the repercussions of major decisions in France or Geneva on the situation in Indochina, are excluded from the scope of this estimate.

CONCLUSIONS

1. The fall of Dien Bien Phu would have far-reaching and adverse repercussions, but it would not signal the immediate collapse of the French Union political and military situation in Indochina. As a consequence of the fall of Dien Bien Phu, the morale of French Union forces would receive a severe blow. A crucial factor in the military situation thereafter would be the reliability of native units, particularly the Vietnamese. There would almost certainly be increased desertions, and the possibility cannot be excluded that the native components of French Union forces might disintegrate. However, we believe that such disintegration would be unlikely during the ensuing two or three months, and that for at least this period the major part of the native troops would probably remain loyal.

2. Assuming no such disintegration, the fall of Dien Bien Phu would not in itself substantially alter the relative military capabilities of French Union and Viet Minh forces in Indochina during the next two or three months. The French stand at Dien Bien Phu has produced certain compensatory military results. It has prevented an overrunning of Laos and has resulted in the inflicting of casualties upon the Viet Minh comparable in number to the total French force committed at Dien Bien Phu. The bulk of Viet Minh forces released by the fall of Dien Bien Phu would probably not be able to move, regroup, and re-equip in time to be employed in new major operations during the next two or three months, although some lightly equipped infantry battalions might be made available more rapidly for operations in the Delta region.

3. Although the Viet Minh have a substantial capability to organize demonstrations and carry out sabotage and terrorist activities in the major cities of Indochina, we believe that French Union forces could maintain control in those cities.

4. The political consequences in Indochina of the fall of Dien Bien Phu would be considerably more adverse than the strictly military consequences and would increase the tempo of deterioration in the over-all French Union position in Indochina, particularly in Vietnam. There would probably be a serious decline in the Vietnamese will to continue the war and to support the Vietnamese military programs. However, we believe that general collapse of French and native governmental authority during the next two or three months would be prevented by the continued existence of organized French Union forces and the hope among Indochinese that the US might intervene in Indochina.

5. We believe that although the fall of Dien Bien Phu would not immediately lead to collapse of the French Union position in Indochina, it would accelerate the deterioration already evident in the French Union military and political position there. If this trend were not checked, it could bring about a collapse of the French Union position during the latter half of 1954. It should be emphasized that this estimate does not consider the repercussion of major decisions in France or Geneva and elsewhere, which could have a decisive effect on the situation in Indochina.

DISCUSSION

6. We believe that the fall of Dien Bien Phu, if it occurred as assumed in the problem, would result from: (a) French capitulation; or (b) an overwhelming of the French either by assault or by gradual constriction of the French position.

7. If the French were to capitulate without further heavy fighting, the adverse military and political consequences would be essentially similar in kind, though possibly of greater intensity, to those accompanying the fall of the fortress through heavy fighting. Viet Minh losses in the event of capitulation would be less than those which would be incurred during further heavy fighting.

8. In any event, the Viet Minh would have suffered heavy losses in the prolonged fighting at Dien Bien Phu. Estimated Viet Minh casualties in the fighting there to date are approximately 13,000; roughly 50 percent of this number have been killed or rendered permanently ineffective. Although a few experienced units have been sent as reinforcements, individual replacements for the most part have consisted of partially trained personnel. As a result of the Dien Bien Phu operation, the effectiveness of the Viet Minh offensive striking force will be greatly reduced during the next two or three months.

9. French Union casualties at Dien Bien Phu to date have been approximately 5,500. The defeat of the force now at Dien Bien Phu would add another 11,000, thus bringing the total French Union losses to roughly 17,000. At least two-thirds of these troops are experienced, professional units from Algerian, colonial and foreign legion forces. Moreover, six of the thirteen parachute battalions in the French Union forces in Indochina are at Dien Bien Phu. The loss of these elite French Union troops would reduce the French Union offensive striking force by approximately one-

(Continued...)

quarter, thus markedly reducing over-all French Union capabilities for offensive operations in Indochina.

10. As a consequence of the fall of Dien Bien Phu, the morale of the French Union forces would receive a severe blow. Their will to win would be diminished, largely because of a widespread belief that military victory was no longer possible. The loss of morale would probably not be sufficient to reduce the effectiveness of the professional soldiers of the French Expeditionary force. However, a crucial factor in the military situation thereafter would be the reliability of native units, particularly the Vietnamese. There would almost certainly be an increase in Vietnam desertions, and the possibility cannot be excluded that the native components of French Union forces might disintegrate. However, we believe that such disintegration would be unlikely during the ensuing two or three months, and that for at least this period the major part of the native troops would probably remain loyal. Therefore, we estimate that the impact upon the morale of the French Union forces would be severe, but not of such severity as to preclude their employment as an effective military force during the next two or three months.

11. The fall of Dien Bien Phu would not in itself substantially alter the relative military capabilities of French Union and Viet Minh forces in Indochina during the next two or three months unless there were large-scale desertions from the French Union forces. The victorious Viet Minh troops at Dien Bien Phu would have suffered heavy casualties and their efficiency would be reduced. In order to bring these forces up to full strength, the Viet Minh would probably move them from Dien Bien Phu to their main supply and training areas adjacent to the Red River delta. Prior to the rainy season, this redeployment would require at least three to four weeks. After the full onset of the rainy season, which is unlikely before mid-May, the movement would take between two and three months to complete. We therefore estimate that the bulk of the Viet Minh troops at Dien Bien Phu would not be available for major operations elsewhere in Indochina during the next two or three months, although some lightly-equipped infantry battalions might be made available more rapidly for operations in the Delta region.

12. Although the over-all capabilities of the Viet Minh would be reduced as a consequence of the losses inflicted upon their main striking force, Viet Minh forces elsewhere in Indochina would have the capability during the rainy season to maintain and in some instances increase military pressure against French Union forces. In the Red River delta, they could intensify efforts to sever land communications between Hanoi and Haiphong, ambush French detachments, attack villages, air bases, and other installations, and lay siege to isolated French delta strong points. The scale of Viet Minh operations in the Delta, however, would be restricted by the adverse effects of heavy rains on maneuverability. The Viet Minh could use their force concentrated in the Pleiku region in southern Annam to launch fairly large-scale attacks against French forces engaged in the "Atlante" operation. They could also use units from this force for raiding operations in the Mekong River area or to reinforce the Viet Minh battalions now in Cambodia. Combat operations in southern Annam, the Mekong valley, and in Cambodia would be restricted by the tenuous nature of resupply of ammunition and other military equipment for these units. The Viet Minh could at the same time organize demonstrations and carry out sabotage and terrorist activities in the major cities of Indochina. The Viet Minh capability in this regard is probably substantial.

13. French Union forces, assuming no major Vietnamese defections, would have the capability to maintain their present major fortified positions in the Delta, and elsewhere, maintain control in the major cities, prevent the permanent severing of land communications between Hanoi and Haiphong, repulse Viet Minh attacks in southern Annam and the Mekong River area, and retain the area liberated in the "Atlante" operation. If the Viet Minh were to undertake a major military

TROOP STRENGTHS AND DISPOSITIONS

FRENCH UNION		VIET MINH	
Regular and Light Bns 274	402,000	Regular and Regional Bns 155	185,000
Semi-Military	203,500	Semi-Military	106,000
Total	605,500	Total	291,000

MAJOR CONCENTRATIONS [1]

French Union	Region	Viet Minh
65 Regular Bns (35 Fr. Ex. Force) 19 Light Bns 83,000 semi-military	DELTA	22 Regular Bns 10 Regional Bns 35,000 semi-military
16 Regular Bns (15 Fr. Ex. Force)	DIEN BIEN PHU	28 Regular Bns 2 Regional Bns
	NORTHERN TONKIN (Less DB Phu Area)	13 Regional Bns
14 Regular Bns (10 Fr. Ex. Force) 2 Light Bns	NORTHERN LAOS	3 Regular Bns 2 Regional Bns
17 Regular Bns (13 Fr. Ex. Force) 3 Light Bns	THAKHEK-SAVANNAKHET	8 Regular Bns 4 Regional Bns
35 Regular Bns (10 Fr. Ex. Force) 16 Light Bns	CENTRAL VIETNAM	14 Regular Bns 7 Regional Bns
17 Regular Bns (3 Fr. Ex. Force) 20 Light Bns	COCHIN CHINA	10 Regular Bns 2 Regional Bns
8 Regular Bns (3 Fr. Ex. Force)	SOUTHERN LAOS and NORTHEASTERN CAMBODIA	4 Regular Bns
11 Regular Bns (0 Fr. Ex. Force) 3 Light Bns	WESTERN CAMBODIA	Elements

[1] These dispositions cover only infantry units. The regional breakdown does not include the total number of Viet Minh and French bns.

operation against Cambodia, the defense of Cambodia would require troops from other areas. French Union forces would retain the capability to launch limited offensive operations before the full onset of the rainy season, either in the Red River delta region or on the coast of Annam.

14. The political consequences in Indochina of the fall of Dien Bien Phu would be considerably more adverse than the strictly military consequences, although the two are interrelated. The defeat would increase the tempo of deterioration in the over-all French Union position in Indochina, particularly in Vietnam. The principal political consequences would be: (a) a major blow to French prestige among the Indochinese, and an increased conviction on their part that the French were unable to protect them against the Viet Minh; (b) a serious decline in French and Indochinese will to continue the war, and in particular a further decline in popular support in Vietnam for Vietnamese military programs; (c) exacerbation of French-Indochinese relations, partly as a result of increased Indochinese suspicions that the French will "sell out" to the Viet Minh; (d) a sharp increase of "fense sitting" among politically conscious groups previously disposed to support the Vietnam Government; and (e) a sharp increase, particularly among Vietnamese, of covert support of the Viet Minh. However, we believe that a general collapse of French and native governmental authority during the next two or three months would be prevented by the continued existence of organized French Union forces and the hope that the US might intervene in Indochina.

15. The political effect in Laos would probably be similar to that of Vietnam. However, the Laotians would probably display a greater disposition than the Vietnamese to stand by the French and to continue the war effort.

16. The political effect on Cambodia would be extremely uncertain. The internal security of Cambodia and a certain minimum stability might be maintained, but Cambodia's vulnerability to future Viet Minh pressure would increase.

17. The Viet Minh would make every effort to make political capital of their victory at Dien Bien Phu. They would concentrate on increasing the sense of hopelessness in the Associated States, and would seek to convince the Indochinese that the triumph at Dien Bien Phu signalled their imminent "deliverance" from colonial rule by fellow countrymen. They would intensify current efforts to enhance the status of the so-called "People's Governments" of Laos and Cambodia.

18. We believe that although the fall of Dien Bien Phu would not immediately lead to collapse of the French Union position in Indochina, it would accelerate the deterioration already evident in the French Union military and political position there. If this trend were not checked, it could bring about a collapse of the French Union position during the latter half of 1954. It should be emphasized that this estimate does not consider the repercussion of major decisions in France or Geneva and elsewhere which are likely to have a decisive effect on the situation in Indochina.

NIE 63-3-54

Probable Military and Political Developments in Indochina Over the Next 30 Days

21 May 1954

179
COPY NO.
9495 ASSISTANT DIRECTOR, ONE

NATIONAL INTELLIGENCE ESTIMATE

PROBABLE MILITARY AND POLITICAL DEVELOPMENTS IN INDOCHINA OVER THE NEXT 30 DAYS

APPROVED FOR RELEASE
DATE: JAN 2005

(b)(3)

NIE 63-3-54
(Supersedes NIE 63-54)
Approved 20 May 1954
Published 21 May 1954

The Intelligence Advisory Committee concurred in this estimate on 20 May 1954. The AEC and FBI abstained, the subject being outside of their jurisdiction.

The following member organizations of the Intelligence Advisory Committee participated with the Central Intelligence Agency in the preparation of this estimate: The intelligence organizations of the Departments of State, the Army, the Navy, the Air Force, and The Joint Staff.

CENTRAL INTELLIGENCE AGENCY

SECRET

SECRET

PROBABLE MILITARY AND POLITICAL DEVELOPMENTS IN INDOCHINA OVER THE NEXT 30 DAYS

THE PROBLEM

To estimate the probable military and political developments in Indochina over the next 30 days.

ASSUMPTIONS

1. That no cease-fire agreement is reached at the Geneva Conference during the period of this estimate.

2. That French policy with respect to Indochina will not undergo a radical change for the worse within the next 30 days.

THE ESTIMATE

I. MILITARY DEVELOPMENTS

1. The fall of Dien Bien Phu has not precipitated a collapse of the French and Vietnamese military position in Indochina, but it has had a significant impact upon the attitudes toward the war of all participants. From the Viet Minh viewpoint, the fall of Dien Bien Phu has created a climate of victory which offers possibilities for further advances. We believe that the Viet Minh will raise their present level of operations, seeking to reduce further the French and Vietnamese will to continue the war, to improve the Communist basis for bargaining at Geneva, to prevent major redeployments of French Union forces, to prepare for major campaigns, and to exploit any opportunities for early victory. From the French Union viewpoint, the defeat at Dien Bien Phu has underscored the fact that the war cannot be won by French efforts alone. Accordingly, the main French effort appears at present to be directed toward maintaining and in any case preventing a collapse of the French Union military position before a cease-fire is negotiated at Geneva or the conflict is internationalized.

Military Developments Within the Next Two Weeks

2. Without redeployment of major units, the Viet Minh will have during the next two weeks the capability to increase the present level of their military operations throughout Indochina. In the Delta, the Viet Minh over the next two weeks will probably continue to mount attacks against French strong points and to cut temporarily the lines of communications between Hanoi and Haiphong. In addition, they will probably continue to augment their capabilities for sabotage and terrorist activities in Hanoi and Haiphong. However, while the scale of these activities will increase, they will probably not exercise these capabilities for sabotage and terrorism to the full during the next two weeks except in the event of large-scale military operations in this area. Outside the Delta, the Viet Minh will probably launch attacks in central Vietnam, conduct raiding operations in Laos, and increase guerrilla operations in Cambodia.

3. We consider that, despite the defeat at Dien Bien Phu, the French Union forces still

retain the will to defend key points. In the Delta, the French almost certainly will possess for at least the next two weeks the capability to hold major positions. They have redeployed one mobile group from Laos to the Delta, and they apparently intend to regroup forces already within the Delta even though this may require the abandonment of some outlying Delta strong points. Outside the Delta region, the French will probably have the capability to hold most positions during the next two weeks although they may abandon certain positions in order to concentrate their troops in critical areas elsewhere.

Military Developments Within the Next 30 Days

4. If major units now at Dien Bien Phu are redeployed as rapidly as possible, the Viet Minh can within the next 30 days attain a capability for launching a heavy assault against French positions in the Delta. Preparations are now being made for moving the bulk of the Viet Minh units from Dien Bien Phu toward their bases in the Delta area, and there are indications that redeployment, has begun. We believe that approximately one division will remain initially in the vicinity of Dien Bien Phu. The major portion of the forces at Dien Bien Phu with their heavy equipment could not assemble in the Delta area before 7–15 June, although it is believed that their lightly-equipped units could complete the movement by 31 May. However, the gradual increase in intensity of rains during the month of June, combined with French aerial attacks on Route 41, may slow down the movement.

5. In addition to the force at Dien Bien Phu, the concentration of 17 battalions at Thai Nguyen, a point approximately 35 miles north of Hanoi, may be used to augment the Viet Minh capability for major attacks against the Delta. These units, 13 of which are regional battalions, appear to be undergoing advanced training. It is unlikely that these troops will be independently committed in major attacks on Delta strong points during the next 30 days. However, they might be used to attack French static defense units or to fill out a major attacking force made up of units now at Dien Bien Phu.

6. If military considerations alone dictate, we estimate that the Viet Minh will not launch an all-out assault against the Delta during the next 30 days. The major factors militating against such an assault are: the requirement for reorganization and recuperation of the main striking force from Dien Bien Phu, the limited period of time to prepare for major assaults against fortified positions, the possibilities of delay in movement of artillery units into position, the onset of the rainy season with resultant supply difficulties, and the flooding of areas within the Delta which restrict routes for troop movements and areas of maneuver. The most important deterrent, however, is the French strength in manpower, firepower, and airpower. However, the Viet Minh might undertake an assault on the Delta because of political requirements in relation to Geneva, or on the basis of their estimate that French Union forces had become demoralized and that Viet Minh capabilities for assault combined with sabotage, terrorism, and insurrection might prove decisive in the Delta. Barring a serious deterioration of the will to fight of the French Union forces as a result of political developments in Indochina or elsewhere, we believe that the French would be able to counter or blunt such an assault within the next 30 days.

7. On the other hand, we anticipate that, short of mounting an all-out assault on the Delta, the Viet Minh during the next 30 days will increase their present level of operations and will attack French strong points in the Delta and elsewhere. Although we consider it likely that the French will suffer some reverses from attacks on this scale, we believe that they will be able to retain possession of most of their key strong points throughout Indochina, and will be able to keep open the lines of communications between Hanoi and Haiphong except for frequent but temporary interruptions.

8. It is possible that defections by Vietnamese units will occur during the next 30 days and will thus reduce the capabilities of French

Union forces. Some Vietnamese from militia units are believed to have defected recently to the Viet Minh with their arms. On the other hand, since the fall of Dien Bien Phu, French and Vietnamese units have been engaged with no indication of impaired morale or will to fight. We estimate that, unless the Vietnamese become convinced that the French intend to sell out in Indochina or unless the Viet Minh achieve substantial military successes, the fighting capabilities of the French Union forces during the next 30 days will not deteriorate so severely as to preclude their employment as an effective military force. There is always the possibility, however, that some spectacular Viet Minh successes in the Delta would convince the native population and Vietnamese troops there that victory in the Delta was imminent, in which case an extremely rapid deterioration of the situation in north Vietnam would ensue.

Political Developments

9. Barring the unlikely event of a large-scale Viet Minh invasion or of a coup d'état, Laos and Cambodia will probably retain their present uncertain political stability during the next 30 days. The Laotian Government will almost certainly remain in power if the French continue to provide it with support. The Cambodian Government will probably retain control and will continue its efforts to solicit direct US aid.

10. Political stability in Vietnam will probably continue to deteriorate during this period. In the absence of both Bao Dai and Buu Loc, factionalism has become extreme, and the Vietnamese central government is virtually paralyzed. It is possible that the Vietnam central government will disintegrate during the next 30 days. It is also possible that a coup may be attempted by General Hinh, who has obvious dictatorial ambitions. If the Vietnam central government should disintegrate, the French could almost certainly maintain civil control temporarily in the regions they occupy by working through Vietnamese regional governors and local officials. A large part of the Vietnamese troops in the French Union forces probably would continue at least temporarily to be responsive to the French High Command. Thus disintegration of the Vietnam central government, while it would complicate negotiations at Geneva, would almost certainly not cause an immediate collapse of French control in Indochina unless it were accompanied or preceded by a collapse of the French military position.

NIE 63-5-54

Post-Geneva Outlook in Indochina

3 August 1954

APPROVED FOR RELEASE
DATE: JAN 2005

COPY NO. 242

NIE 63-5-54
3 August 1954

~~SECRET~~

(b)(3)

NATIONAL INTELLIGENCE ESTIMATE
NIE 63-5-54

POST-GENEVA OUTLOOK IN INDOCHINA

Submitted by the

DIRECTOR OF CENTRAL INTELLIGENCE

The following intelligence organizations participated in the preparation of this estimate: The Central Intelligence Agency and the intelligence organizations of the Departments of State, the Army, the Navy, the Air Force, and The Joint Staff.

Concurred in by the

INTELLIGENCE ADVISORY COMMITTEE

on 3 August 1954. Concurring were the Special Assistant, Intelligence, Department of State; the Assistant Chief of Staff, G-2, Department of the Army; the Director of Naval Intelligence; the Director of Intelligence, USAF; the Deputy Director for Intelligence, The Joint Staff. The Director of Intelligence, AEC, and the Assistant to the Director, Federal Bureau of Investigation, abstained, the subject being outside of their jurisdiction.

(Continued...)

POST-GENEVA OUTLOOK IN INDOCHINA

THE PROBLEM

To assess the probable outlook in Indochina in the light of the agreements reached at the Geneva conference.

CONCLUSIONS

1. The signing of the agreements at Geneva has accorded international recognition to Communist military and political power in Indochina and has given that power a defined geographic base.

2. We believe that the Communists will not give up their objective of securing control of all Indochina but will, without violating the armistice to the extent of launching an armed invasion to the south or west, pursue their objective by political, psychological, and paramilitary means.

3. We believe the Communists will consolidate control over North Vietnam with little difficulty. Present indications are that the Viet Minh will pursue a moderate political program, which together with its strong military posture, will be calculated to make that regime appeal to the nationalist feelings of the Vietnamese population generally. It is possible, however, that the Viet Minh may find it desirable or necessary to adopt a strongly repressive domestic program which would diminish its appeal in South Vietnam. In any event, from its new territorial base, the Viet Minh will intensify Communist activities throughout Indochina.

4. Although it is possible that the French and Vietnamese, even with firm support from the US and other powers, may be able to establish a strong regime in South Vietnam, we believe that the chances for this development are poor and, moreover, that the situation is more likely to continue to deteriorate progressively over the next year. It is even possible that, at some time during the next two years, the South Vietnam Government could be taken over by elements that would seek unification with the North even at the expense of Communist domination. If the scheduled national elections are held in July 1956, and if the Viet Minh does not prejudice its political prospects, the Viet Minh will almost certainly win.

5. The ability of the Laotian Government to retain control in Laos will depend upon developments in South Vietnam and upon the receipt of French military and other assistance. Even with such assistance, however, Laos will be faced by a growing Communist threat which might result in the overthrow of the present government through subversion or elections, and in any case would be greatly intensified if all

Vietnam were to fall under Communist control.

6. We believe that if adequate outside assistance is made available, the Cambodian Government will probably increase its effectiveness and the effectiveness of its internal security forces and will be able to suppress Communist guerrilla activity and to counter Communist political activity. The situation in Cambodia would probably deteriorate, however, if a Communist government should emerge in Loas or South Vietnam.

DISCUSSION

I. THE CURRENT SITUATION

General

7. The signing of the agreements at Geneva has ended large-scale warfare in Indochina and has affirmed the independence of Laos and Cambodia. It has, on the other hand, accorded international recognition to Communist military and political power in Indochina and has given that power a defined geographic base. Finally, the agreements have dealt a blow to the prestige of the Western Powers and particularly of France.

North Vietnam

8. The Viet Minh has emerged from Geneva with international recognition and with greatly enhanced power and prestige in Indochina. The Viet Minh leaders, while admitting that their ultimate objectives may have been temporarily compromised "for the sake of peace," are acclaiming the agreements as denoting a major victory and ensuring the eventual reunification of all Vietnam under Communist aegis. Ho Chi-Minh is generally regarded as the man who liberated Tonkin from 70 years of French rule. The Viet Minh has initiated a program to absorb presently French-controlled areas in the Tonkin Delta.

South Vietnam

9. In South Vietnam, the agreements and the fact of the imposed partition have engendered an atmosphere of frustration and disillusionment, which has been compounded by widespread uncertainty as to French and US intentions. The present political leadership appears to retain the passive support of the more important nationalist organizations and individuals. However, the government's already weak administrative base has been further dislocated, and it has only uncertain assurances of continued outside military and financial support. Mutual jealousies and a lack of a single policy continue to divide Vietnamese politicians. Moreover, certain pro-French elements are seeking the overthrow of the Diem government with the apparent support of French colonial interests anxious to retain their control.

10. The North Vietnam population is somewhat greater than the South Vietnam population and, in any event, the loss of the Tonkin Delta has deprived South Vietnam of the most energetic and nationalist segment of the population. Although South Vietnam has the capability for agricultural self-sufficiency, the principal industrial establishments and fuel and mineral resources are located in North Vietnam.

11. Provided that the terms of the cease-fire agreement are observed, the combined French-Vietnamese forces in South Vietnam now have the capability of maintaining internal security.

Laos

12. The relatively stable internal situation in Laos, which in the past has depended upon French support, remains essentially unchanged. The Laotian Army is poorly armed and trained and, without the support of French forces and advisers, does not have the capability to maintain internal security. Moreover, "Pathet Lao" Communists continue to have *de facto* control of two northern

provinces adjoining the Communist-controlled areas of Northern Vietnam. Furthermore, the Geneva agreements give members of the "Pathet Lao" movement freedom of political action throughout Laos.

Cambodia

13. The internal Cambodian situation, except for sharp political rivalries among leading Cambodians, is at present relatively stable. Non-Communist dissidence appears to have abated and the principal dissident leader, Son Ngoc Thanh, no longer poses any real threat to the government. The King retains widespread popular support for having obtained a large degree of effective independence from the French and for having safeguarded Cambodia's integrity at Genevá. Although the Communists are permitted freedom of political action in Cambodia, they have only a minimum appeal. The Cambodian forces, although somewhat weakened by the withdrawal of French forces, have the capability of dealing with current Communist subversive action.

II. OUTLOOK IN INDOCHINA

General Considerations

14. The Geneva agreements, although precise and detailed concerning the time and place of troop redeployments and related matters, are imprecise about matters pertaining to future military aid and training. Moreover, the agreements are vague with respect to political matters. Details on the implementation of national elections are left for the interested parties to determine. Except for such influence as may be exerted by the presence of supervisory teams from India, Canada, and Poland, there is no provision for forcing the parties concerned to implement or adhere to the agreements.

15. The course of future developments will be determined less by the Geneva agreements than by the relative capabilities and actions of the Communist and non-Communist entities in Indochina, and of interested outside powers.

16. *Communist policy.* Communist willingness to reach agreement for an armistice in Indochina, at a time when prolongation of the conflict could have produced a steadily deteriorating situation in Indochina, was probably derived in substantial part from the Communist estimate that: (a) an effort to win a total military victory in Indochina might precipitate US military intervention, and (b) the objective of gaining political control over all Indochina could be achieved as a result of the armistice agreement. The Communists also apparently believed that an attitude of "reasonableness" and the acceptance of an armistice in Indochina would contribute to the realization of their objective to undermine western efforts to develop an effective military coalition. They probably consider, therefore, that a deliberate resumption of large-scale military operations from their zone in the north would negate the political and psychological advantages the Communists have gained by negotiating a settlement and could involve grave risk of expanded war.

17. In the light of these considerations, we believe that the broad outlines of Communist policy in Indochina will be to: (a) refrain from deliberately taking major military action to break the armistice agreement while seeking to gain every advantage in the implementation of the agreements; (b) consolidate the Communist political, military, and economic position in North Vietnam; (c) conduct intensive political warfare against non-Communist Indochinese governments and people; (d) work for the ultimate removal of all Western influence, particularly French and US, from Indochina; and (e) emphasize and exploit issues in Indochina which will create and intensify divisions among non-Communist countries. In sum, we believe that the Communists will not give up their objective of securing control of all Indochina but will, without violating the armistice to the extent of launching an armed invasion to the south or west, pursue their objective by political, psychological, and paramilitary means.

18. *French policy.* It is impossible at this time to predict even the broad outlines of French policy in Indochina. The following appear to be the main alternatives:

a. Grant of complete political independence to the Indochina states, accompanied by an attempt to organize strong political regimes in those states. We believe that the French might be persuaded to adopt this policy by strong US–UK pressure, together with economic and military assistance to France and a guarantee of the defense of the free areas of Indochina against further Communist military attack.

b. Continuation of French Union ties with the non-Communist Indochinese states, with indirect French political controls and French economic domination. We believe that French policy may proceed along these lines if the French estimate that: (1) the Communists will follow a conciliatory policy in Indochina; (2) the non-Communist leadership will offer very little difficulty; and (3) the US and UK will not exert pressure toward a grant of full independence to the Indochinese states.

c. Some form of agreement with the Viet Minh providing for expediting elections and achieving a unification of Vietnam. The French might be inclined to follow this line if the Viet Minh held out promises of the maintenance of French economic and cultural interests, and of the continuance of some form of association of the unified Vietnamese state with France.

d. Withdrawal of all French military, administrative, and economic support from Indochina. We believe that this would occur only in the event of a hopeless deterioration of political, military, and economic conditions in the area.

19. *International policies.* The political survival of the Indochinese states is endangered not only by the threat of external Communist attack and internal Communist subversion, but also by their own inherent inexperience, immaturity, and weakness. We believe that without outside support the Indochinese states cannot become strong enough to withstand Communist pressures. The course of developments in Indochina will be largely influenced by the attitudes and policies of other powers. In general, we believe that in the absence of firm support from the US, the non-Communist states of Indochina cannot long remain non-Communist. If they are given opportunity, guidance, and material help in building national states, they may be able to attain viability. We believe that the energy and resourcefulness necessary for this achievement will not arise spontaneously among the non-Communist Indochinese but will have to be sponsored and nurtured from without.

Outlook in Vietnam

20. *Outlook in North Vietnam.* Communist activities in North Vietnam will be concentrated upon consolidation of Communist control, with their efforts in this respect probably appearing moderate at the outset. The Viet Minh will probably emphasize social and economic reforms and the participation of all political, economic, and religious groups in state activity. At the same time, Viet Minh cadres will establish themselves throughout the Delta, will begin the process of neutralizing all effective opposition groups, will undertake the usual Communist program of popular indoctrination, and will prepare for the election scheduled in July 1956. We believe the Communists will be able to achieve the consolidation of North Vietnam with little difficulty.

21. We believe that the Viet Minh will continue to develop their armed forces. Although the armistice provisions forbid the Viet Minh from increasing their supply of arms, we believe they will covertly strengthen and possibly expand their armed forces with Chinese Communist aid. Viet Minh forces will almost certainly continue to receive training in China.

22. Thus established firmly in North Vietnam, the Viet Minh regime will probably retain and may increase its symbolic attraction as the base of Vietnamese national independence. Its methods of consolidating control will probably continue for some time to be moderate, and, its internal program together with its military power, will be calculated to make the regime attractive to the remaining peoples of Indochina. It is possible, however, that the Viet Minh may find it desirable or necessary

to adopt a strongly repressive domestic program which would prejudice its psychological appeal and political prospects. Barring such repressive Viet Minh policies, the unification issue will continue to be exploited to Communist advantage throughout Vietnam. Meanwhile, the Viet Minh regime will continue to strengthen the Communist underground apparatus in South Vietnam, Laos, and Cambodia, aware that significant Communist gains in any one of these countries will strengthen the Communist movement in the others. It will seek to develop strong overt Communist political groups where possible and will generally use all available means towards the eventual unification of the country under Communist control.

23. *Outlook in South Vietnam.* We believe that the Viet Minh will seek to retain sizeable military and political assets in South Vietnam. Although the agreements provide for the removal to the north of all Viet Minh forces, many of the regular and irregular Viet Minh soldiers now in the south are natives of the area, and large numbers of them will probably cache their arms and remain in South Vietnam. In addition, Viet Minh administrative cadres have been in firm control of several large areas in central and south Vietnam for several years. These cadres will probably remain in place. French and Vietnamese efforts to deal with "stay-behind" military and administrative units and personnel will be greatly hampered by armistice provisions guaranteeing the security of pre-armistice dissidents from reprisals.

24. The severe problem of establishing and maintaining security in South Vietnam will probably be increased by certain provisions of the Geneva agreements which prohibit the import of arms and military equipment, except as replacements, and the introduction of additional foreign military personnel, the establishment of new military bases, and military alliances. These provisions limit the development of a Vietnamese national army to such numbers as may be equipped by stocks evacuated from Tonkin, plus stocks now held in Saigon. However, in the last analysis, Vietnamese security will be determined by the degree of French protection and assistance in the development of a national army, the energy with which the Vietnamese themselves attack the problem, and by the will of the non-Communist powers to provide South Vietnam with effective guarantees.

25. In addition to the activities of stay-behind military and administrative groups, the Viet Minh will make a major effort to discredit any South Vietnam administration, and to exacerbate French-Vietnamese relations, and appeal to the feeling for national unification which will almost certainly continue strong among the South Vietnamese population. The Communist goal will be to cause the collapse of any non-Communist efforts to stabilize the situation in South Vietnam, and thus to leave North Vietnam the only visible foundation on which to re-establish Vietnamese unity. French and anti-Communist Vietnamese efforts to counter the Viet Minh unity appeal and Communist subversive activities will be complicated at the outset by the strong resentment of Vietnamese nationalists over the partitioning of Vietnam and the abandoning of Tonkin to Communist control. It may be difficult to convince many Vietnamese troops, political leaders, and administrative personnel in Tonkin to go south, let alone to assist actively in the development of an effective administration in South Vietnam.

26. Developments in South Vietnam will also depend in large part on French courses of action. Prospects for stability in South Vietnam would be considerably enhanced if the French acted swiftly to insure Vietnam full independence and to encourage strong nationalist leadership. If this were done, anti-French nationalist activity might be lessened. With French military and economic assistance — backed by US aid — the Vietnamese could proceed to develop gradually an effective security force, local government organization, and a long-range program for economic and social reform. Nevertheless, it will be very difficult for the French to furnish the degree of assistance which will be required without at the same time reviving anti-French feeling to the point of endangering the whole effort.

27. On the basis of the evidence we have at this early date, however, we believe that a favorable development of the situation in South Vietnam is unlikely. Unless Mendes-France is able to overcome the force of French traditional interests and emotions which have in the past governed the implementation of policy in Indochina, we do not believe there will be the dramatic transformation in French policy necessary to win the active loyalty and support of the local population for a South Vietnam Government. At the present time, it appears more likely that the situation will deteriorate in South Vietnam and that the withdrawal from Tonkin will involve recriminations, distrust, and possibly violence. There will be delays in the development of effective administration in the south; the French military will probably be forced to retain a large measure of control for reasons of "security"; and efforts by French colonial interests to develop a puppet Cochin-China state will persist. It is even possible that at some point during the next two years the South Vietnam Government could be taken over by elements that would seek unification with the Viet Minh in the North even at the expense of Communist domination. Even if a stable government could be established, we estimate that the national elections scheduled for July 1956 would almost certainly give the Viet Minh control of South Vietnam.

28. In the interim, Viet Minh propaganda will find ample opportunities to influence Vietnamese attitudes. Within a year, Viet Minh stay-behind units will probably be active politically, and possibly involved in open guerrilla fighting. In these circumstances, the French will probably be able to maintain their "presence" in South Vietnam through mid-1956, but their influence will probably become increasingly restricted to major cities and the perimeters of military installations and bases. The French might be willing to resolve this situation by an arrangement with the Communists which seemed to offer a chance of saving some remnant of the French economic and cultural position in Vietnam. Such an arrangement might include an agreement to hold early elections, even with the virtual certainty of Viet Minh victory. Only if such an arrangement proved impossible, and the situation deteriorated to the point of hopelessness, would the French withdraw completely from the country.

Outlook in Laos

29. Providing the French maintain the 5,000 troops in Laos which the Geneva agreements permit them, and continue to develop the Laotian forces, the Royal Laotian Government should be able to improve its security forces and, excluding the two northern provinces, to deal with isolated, small-scale Communist guerrilla actions. Also, providing the Laotians continue to receive French and US technical and financial assistance, they probably will be able to maintain an adequate government administration. There is nothing in the Geneva agreements to prevent Laos from becoming a member of a defense arrangement so long as no foreign troops other than specified French personnel are based in Laos.

30. However, if the French for any reason decide not to maintain their troops nor to continue military training in Laos, it will be impossible for the non-Communist powers to provide effective aid to the Laotians without breaching the Geneva agreement. At the same time, Laos will be faced with a growing Communist threat, and the freedom of political action permitted members of the Pathet Lao movement, strengthened by support from the Viet Minh, may result in the overthrow of the present government through subversion or elections. Finally, further successes for the Viet Minh in Vietnam will have an immediate adverse effect on the situation in Laos.

Outlook in Cambodia

31. We believe that the Communists, in withdrawing organized units from Cambodia, will leave behind organizers, guerrilla leaders, and weapons. Initially, the Communists will probably minimize guerrilla action in order to concentrate on building their political potential in Cambodia.

32. Providing the withdrawal of the Communists is substantially in accord with the agree-

ment, the development of stability in Cambodia during the next year or so will depend largely on two interrelated factors: (a) the ability of the Cambodians to develop effective government and internal security forces; and (b) the ability of the Cambodians to obtain external technical and financial assistance. There is no prohibition in the Geneva agreements against Cambodia's obtaining outside assistance to develop its defense forces or on joining a defensive alliance, providing the latter is in consonance with the UN Charter and that no foreign troops are based in Cambodia in the absence of a threat to Cambodian security. If adequate outside assistance is made available, the Cambodians will probably increase the effectiveness both of their government and their internal security forces, and will be able to suppress Communist guerrilla activity and to counter Communist political activity. The efforts of the Cambodians to strengthen their position would probably be more energetic if their independence were guaranteed by some regional defense arrangement. The situation in Cambodia would deteriorate gravely, however, if a Communist government should emerge in Laos or South Vietnam.

NIE 63.1-55

Probable Developments in North Vietnam to July 1956

19 July 1955

NATIONAL INTELLIGENCE ESTIMATE NUMBER 63.1-55

(Supersedes Portions of NIE 63-7-54 on North Vietnam)

PROBABLE DEVELOPMENTS IN NORTH VIETNAM TO JULY 1956

Submitted by the

DIRECTOR OF CENTRAL INTELLIGENCE

The following intelligence organizations participated in the preparation of this estimate: The Central Intelligence Agency and the intelligence organizations of the Departments of State, the Army, the Navy, the Air Force, and The Joint Staff.

Concurred in by the

INTELLIGENCE ADVISORY COMMITTEE

on 19 July 1955. Concurring were the Special Assistant, Intelligence, Department of State; the Assistant Chief of Staff, G-2, Department of the Army; the Director of Naval Intelligence; the Director of Intelligence, USAF; and the Deputy Director for Intelligence, The Joint Staff. The Atomic Energy Commission Representative to the IAC, and the Assistant to the Director, Federal Bureau of Investigation, abstained, the subject being outside of their jurisdiction.

217
COPY NO.
ASSISTANT DIRECTOR, ONE

SECRET

PROBABLE DEVELOPMENTS IN NORTH VIETNAM TO JULY 1956

(Supersedes Portions of NIE 63–7–54 on North Vietnam)

THE PROBLEM

To analyze the present strengths and weaknesses of North Vietnam and to estimate probable future developments and trends to July 1956.

CONCLUSIONS

1. The immediate concern of the "Democratic Republic of Vietnam" (DRV) is to consolidate its control in the area north of the 17th Parallel and to gain control of South Vietnam. *(Para. 14)*

2. We believe that the DRV will experience no great difficulty in maintaining effective control of North Vietnam during the period of this estimate and will probably retain a considerable measure of prestige and general acceptance. However, passive resistance and discontent resulting from harsh control measures and poor economic conditions may increase toward the end of the period. If the situation in the South does not deteriorate, the nationalist appeal of Ho Chi Minh and the DRV will probably be reduced throughout Vietnam. *(Para. 23)*

3. The DRV is confronted by serious economic problems of which the current rice shortage is the most critical. Its present export potential falls far short of providing sufficient funds to pay for necessary imports. However, the Sino-Soviet Bloc will almost certainly provide sufficient economic and technical assistance to meet minimum requirements for stability and control. With such assistance the DRV will probably make gradual progress in gaining control of the economy and in rehabilitating transportation, irrigation, and industrial facilities. *(Paras. 24–30)*

4. Since the Geneva Conference, the strength of the DRV regular army has been increased substantially by drawing on regional forces to form new units and by the receipt of new and heavier military equipment from Communist China. DRV forces are capable of defeating all military forces, including the French, now located in South Vietnam, Laos, and Cambodia. *(Paras. 31–35)*

5. The present DRV tactic with respect to South Vietnam is to pose as the champion of Vietnamese independence and unification, and as the defender of

the provisions of the Geneva Agreement.[1] The DRV probably still believes that it could emerge from free nationwide elections with control of all Vietnam. It will attempt to appear reasonable in any negotiations concerning procedures for elections. While the Communists almost certainly would not agree to complex and elaborate safeguards and guarantees, they probably would agree to some form of "neutral" (but not UN) supervision. They would probably estimate that such election controls would work to their advantage in the South and, as manipulated, would not adversely affect their position in the North. *(Paras. 44–45)*

6. In the meantime, the DRV will continue its efforts, through subversion, intimidation, and propaganda, to weaken the Diem government, and to bring to power in the South men prepared to accept a coalition with the DRV. *(Para. 46)*

7. The Communists in their propaganda have revealed sensitivity to the implication of the Manila Pact which incorporated Vietnam, Cambodia, and Laos in its area of protection. We believe that concern for Western, and particularly US reactions, together with general considerations arising from over-all Bloc policy, will prevent the DRV from openly invading the South during the period of this estimate. Similarly, the resumption of widespread guerrilla activities appears unlikely prior to the election deadline, unless the DRV should come to the conclusion that South Vietnam can be won only by force. Such a conclusion would become more likely should the Diem government persist in refusing to enter the election discussions, should election discussions not proceed favorably for the DRV, or should the Diem government succeed, with US assistance, in consolidating its strength to the point of becoming a nationalist alternative to the Ho regime. Moreover, if during the period of this estimate little progress is made towards relaxing tensions, Peiping and Moscow might permit the DRV greater freedom of action. Should the DRV decide to use force short of open invasion, it would probably attempt to undermine the Saigon government by initiating a campaign of sabotage and terror, seeking to formation of a new government more amenable to demands for a national coalition. These tactics are likely to include the activation of DRV guerrilla units now in South Vietnam and their reinforcement by the infiltration in small units of regulars from the North. *(Para. 47)*

8. The DRV will probably refrain from launching an attack with its own forces to seize Laos during the period of this estimate.[2] It will probably continue efforts to convince the Royal Laotian government of the propriety of the DRV attitude toward Laos, while covertly strengthening the rebel Pathct Lao movement. The DRV would probably infiltrate armed units into Laos to assist the Pathet Lao if Royal government military action should seriously threaten the

[1] For an estimate of probable developments in South Vietnam, see NIE 63.1–3–55, "Probable Developments in South Vietnam Through July 1956," to be published in August 1955.

[2] For an estimate of probable developments in Laos, see NIE 63.3–55, "Probable Developments in Laos Through July 1956," to be published in July 1955.

Pathet Lao position in the northern provinces. *(Paras. 48–49)*

9. The Communists now have few assets in Cambodia and will probably be unable to develop a significant internal threat in that country until their position is greatly strengthened in Laos or South Vietnam.[3] In the meantime, the DRV will probably continue its efforts to promote friendly relations and to secure Cambodia neutrality. *(Para. 50)*

10. We believe the DRV will be willing to continue political and economic contacts with the French. However, it almost certainly will be unwilling to make any agreement which in fact would permit the French to retain an economic and cultural position in North Vietnam. *(Paras. 51–56)*

DISCUSSION

I. INTRODUCTION

11. Under the terms of the Geneva Accords, and with the final withdrawal of French forces from the Haiphong area on 18 May 1955, a Communist regime known as the "Democratic Republic of Vietnam" (DRV) has assumed full responsibility for the administration of the territory of Vietnam north of the 17th Parallel, pending a political settlement and the unification of the country.

12. The DRV, known also as the Viet Minh, was established at the end of the Second World War when a coalition of Vietnamese of all political leanings drew together under the leadership of the veteran Communist, Ho Chi Minh, and proclaimed Vietnamese independence. The DRV openly and frequently professed its solidarity with the Sino-Soviet Bloc after 1949. Since then any loss by the DRV of its Vietnamese support has been offset by a considerable increase in organizational and material strength and by the prestige of victories over French forces.

13. Although the recent assumption of responsibility over 13 million people and several large cities has confronted the DRV with major problems, these problems are not entirely new or unrelated to previous DRV experience. During its years of resistance, which was conducted until 1950 with little or no external assistance and under conditions of severe physical hardship and austerity, the DRV leadership was able to weed out the weak and timid, build an effective army, train a substantial number of experienced cadres and local administators, and obtain considerable experience in the techniques of political control. Thus, when the DRV assumed control of all North Vietnam in 1954, it possessed considerable advantages over the Diem government in terms of military strength and experience, organization and sense of unity and purpose.

14. While the immediate concern of the DRV is to consolidate its control in the North and to gain control of South Vietnam, its longer run objectives almost certainly are to build a strong Communist state in all Vietnam and to assist in the extension of Communist control throughout Southeast Asia.

II. INTERNAL SITUATION AND TRENDS

Stability and Effectiveness of the Regime

15. The DRV is organized on the normal pattern of all Communist "peoples democracies." Although the government of the DRV ostensibly represents all elements in a "united front" grouping (the Lien Viet), actual power resides in the Communist party (the Lao Dong or Workers Party). Out of a total population in North Vietnam of some 13 million, the Lien Viet is estimated to have approximately 8 million members, including the Lao Dong, which

[3] For an estimate of probable developments in Cambodia, see NIE 63.2–55, "Probable Developments in Cambodia Through July 1956," to be published in August 1955.

claims a membership of approximately one million.

16. The regime is undergoing many administrative modifications in order to cope with the changed situation resulting from the ending of the war. The clandestine shadow government in the Red River delta region, whose organization was probably begun in1946 following the collapse of French-Viet Minh negotiations, is being converted into a normal bureaucracy with overt lines of authority and channels of communication. Although still rather primitive in a technological sense, the government appears effective. Its operations are characterized by close copying of typical Communist planning and organization.

DRV Leadership

17. The DRV owes its success to date in large measure to a cohesive, adaptable, and skilled leadership possessing long experience in the Communist movement and to the prestige acquired in its early years as the focus of the anticolonialist struggle. The greatest deficiencies in the leadership, as in the population at large, are in technological and management skills.

18. Ho Chi Minh, President of the DRV, is probably the ultimate authority within the regime. No other Vietnamese currently possesses his great popular appeal among the Vietnamese as the symbol of nationalism. He also has considerable prestige in Asia and long years of contact with European as well as Asian Communist movements. The other principal DRV leaders appear to be: Vo Nguyen Giap, the capable Commander-in-Chief of the "Vietnam People's Army," apparently second to Ho Chi Minh in national popularity; Truong Chinh, party secretary-general, leading theoretician, and probably second to Ho in the party hierarchy; and Pham Van Dong, DRV Vice-President and Foreign Minister. All of these individuals are members of the Central Committee of the Lao Dong Party.

19. There is no reliable evidence of factionalism at present. However, "normal" competition for personal power is almost certainly present within the top leadership and there exists a potential for disputes over such matters as internal domestic policy, courses of action with respect to South Vietnam, and relations with Communist China. The DRV leadership will probably remain unified throughout the period of this estimate.

Control Policies and Popular Appeal

20. Since the Geneva Conference the regime has been generally successful in imposing its authority throughout North Vietnam. It has employed well-known Communist control methods, including secret police operations, "peoples courts," and large-scale indoctrination. DRV armed forces are far larger than necessary to maintain order and they are supplemented by experienced internal security and intelligence organizations.

21. Extension of the DRV's control has probably been facilitated by the prestige and popular support which accrued to the regime from its victories over the French and by its promises of an improved life for the people in the future. The flight of over 600,000 civilians — mainly Roman Catholics — to the south removed a large portion of those people most inclined to resist Communist indoctrination. Despite shortages of food and consumer goods, the general attitude among the population is probably one of relief that the war is over and of passive acceptance of stern DRV control as the normal pattern of existence.

22. However, the regime will probably face difficulties in obtaining the cooperation of some segments of the population. The remaining Catholic population of approximately 1,000,000 may resist DRV efforts to "nationalize" the church. The substantial ethnic minorities, who live outside the river deltas, have an ingrained dislike for all Vietnamese. In addition, landlords and merchants resent the Communist regime.

23. Nevertheless, we believe that the regime will experience no great difficulty in maintaining effective control in North Vietnam during the period of the estimate, and will probably retain a considerable measure of prestige and general acceptance. Although the DRV will

use harsh measures where necessary, it will probably place emphasis on subtle and widely advertised appeals for public support through the activities of the National United Front, "patriotic" religious conferences, "autonomous area" governments, and other programs composed primarily of nationalist slogans and appeals. However, passive resistance and discontent due to harsh control measures and poor economic conditions may increase toward the end of the period. Providing the situation in the South has not deteriorated, the Nationalist appeal of Ho Chi Minh and the DRV will probably be reduced throughout Vietnam.

Economic Policies and Courses of Action

24. The DRV is confronted by serious economic problems of which the current rice shortage is the most critical. Prior to 1954, the annual rice deficit of North Vietnam averaged about 200,000 metric tons. As a result of serious crop failures the shortfall of rice in the crop year 1954–1955 increased to an estimated 700,000 metric tons. The DRV has obtained only a few small shipments of rice from South Vietnam, formerly its principal source of supplementary supply, and at least 10,000 tons from Communist China. Despite rationing and other control measures, rice prices in Hanoi have doubled since the Communist occupation, and current reserves are low. Since the spring harvest appears to have been poor, a large portion of the population in North Vietnam may face conditions approaching famine this summer and fall unless substantial quantities of rice are imported.

25. The DRV must also deal with a deficit in its balance of payments position, a situation which has been chronic to the North Vietnam area. The regime must import substantial quantities of textiles, capital goods, military equipment, and petroleum. Supplies of locally manufactured goods will probably be less than in 1954 because the regime lacks trained manpower to operate efficiently the textile mills at Nam Dinh and Haiphong, the cement plant at Haiphong, and other enterprises formerly operated by the French. In view of rehabilitation requirements import needs are unlikely to be less than before the Geneva Agreements when annual imports into the area now held by the Communists totaled about US $100,000,000. The DRV, however, is incapable of financing large-scale imports from its own resources. Maximum exports — including possible 500,000 metric tons of coal, lesser amounts of cement and raw materials — could earn only about US $20,000,000 in 1955.

26. To assist in meeting this problem, the DRV has been negotiating with the Sino-Soviet Bloc for technical and economic assistance. In December 1954, Communist China agreed to supply the necessary equipment and trained personnel to assist in the restoration of railroads, highways, telecommunications, meteorological services, and water conservation projects. Transportation, manufacturing, and other fields of activity in North Vietnam will probably receive long-term support from Communist China. The Chinese Communists have recenty announced a grant of roughly US $300,000,000 although a portion of this may cover assistance already provided. East Germany, Poland, and the Soviet Union have also promised to send needed equipment, machinery, and technicians to assist in training DRV personnel. The USSR has negotiated with Burma for surplus rice which may be shipped to the DRV. We believe that the Bloc will, in any event, provide emergency economic assistance sufficient to avert any serious threat to the stability of the DRV.

27. Although the DRV appears to be developing its trading relations mainly with the Bloc, it has made overtures to South Vietnam for the resumption of economic relations and has attempted to convince the French that mutually profitable trade is possible. Although political considerations predominated in these instances, the DRV certainly realized that it could obtain economic benefits from trade with South Vietnam and France.

28. The rapid rehabilitation of transportation and irrigation facilities, which has been the principal accomplishments of the regime in recent months, demonstrated the DRV's ability to mobilize large pools of unskilled manpower. It also indicates the receipt of fairly substantial economic and technical assistance

from Bloc countries. The most significant achievement was the restoration in only four months of the 150 mile Hanoi-Dong Dang narrow-gauge railroad line which connects with the Chinese Communist rail net. Rehabilitation of the Hanoi-Lao Kay and Hanoi-Nam Dinh lines, now underway and scheduled for completion in 1955, will further facilitate the distribution of military and economic supplies received from Communist China. If the relatively rapid rehabilitation of irrigation facilities is sustained, food output should be substantially raised within a few years.

29. The DRV has instituted a series of economic measures designed to enhance its over-all control. To increase peasant support for the regime, the DRV has pressed its program of land confiscation and rent reductions. Nevertheless, paddy taxes have not been lowered and continue to absorb about 40 percent of the output. Heavy new sales and inventory taxes have been levied on merchants. The scope of private trade has also been diminished through the establishment of wholesale and retail outlets operated by the regime, and further limitations are in prospect.

30. The DRV probably will continue to make gradual economic progress during the period of this estimate. With continued assistance from the Sino-Soviet Bloc, which will almost certainly be forthcoming the DRV will probably be able to meet minimum requirements for foodstuffs and cloth. They will also be able to rehabilitate further their transportation and industrial facilities. Therefore, we believe that economic deficiencies will not seriously threaten the stability of the DRV during the period of this estimate.

Trends in Military Strength

31. Since Geneva, the Viet Minh army has undergone considerable reorganization and its firepower has been greatly increased. The regular army is estimated to total 240,000 troops, the bulk of which are organized into 10 infantry divisions, 2 artillery divisions, 1 AAA groupment, and 25 infantry regiments. Of these at least 4 infantry divisions, 1 artillery division, and 15 infantry regiments have been activated since the summer of 1954. Although regular army strength has increased some 60,000 over the total of a year ago, the over-all strength of the armed forces remains about the same, since the regular forces were built up by drawing men from Regional and Popular units. Regional and Popular troop strengths are estimated to be 37,000 and 75,000 respectively, a decline of some 35 percent from pre-Geneva strengths of each organization.

32. The substantial increase in firepower and mobility of DRV units is primarily the result of large-scale shipments of new arms, ammunition, and other military equipment from Communist China. The volume of these shipments increased markedly in May 1954 and continued at a high rate until last November. Little information is available on the flow of supplies since November. Since July 1954, many of the shipments have violated the Geneva Agreements. There is no firm evidence that the Viet Minh have received armored vehicles.

33. There is no evidence that the DRV has developed a navy or an air force. At present, the DRV "navy" consists of some 100 men with 3 to 5 motorboats operating as a component of the army. There are unconfirmed reports that the Chinese Communists are training DRV personnel preliminary to the creation of a DRV air force, but we have no evidence that the DRV possesses any aircraft or air organization.

34. Since the cessation of hostilities, the DRV has embarked on an extensive training program designed to improve the military effectiveness of units and individuals, and to assure their loyalty to the regime. Although there have been occasional desertions and defections, these have not assumed significant proportions.

35. DRV armed forces currently are capable of maintaining control over the area north of the 17th Parallel, and of defeating the military forces, including the French, now located south of the 17th Parallel. They are also capable of overrunning Laos in a conventional military operation or of providing sufficient logistic support and guerrilla units to enable

(Continued...)

the Communist military forces in Laos to control the northern provinces and other parts of the country remote from main lines of communication.

36. The DRV almost certainly will maintain the superiority of its armed forces in Indochina during the period of this estimate. There will probably be no significant increase in DRV armed numerical strength during the next 12 months, but continuation of the reorganization and training program will increase its over-all military potential.

37. We believe that there may be as many as 10,000 armed Viet Minh personnel remaining in South Vietnam. They are probably organized as cadres and skeletal units. The effectiveness of these units and their ability to expand through local recruitment will depend in large measure on the political appeal of Diem and the effectiveness of his government.

III. EXTERNAL RELATIONS AND POLICIES

38. Since the 1954 Geneva Conference, the DRV's foreign policy appears to have had the following major objectives: (a) increasing the international stature of the DRV; (b) strengthening ties with the World Communist Bloc; (c) accomplishing the unification of South and North Vietnam; (d) retaining the Pathet Lao strongholds in two Laotian provinces, and expanding Communist influence in both Laos and Cambodia with the eventual aim of absorbing both these countries into the Communist Bloc; and (e) establishing friendly relations with the Asian "neutralist" nations on the basis of the "Five Principles" of peaceful coexistence.

39. In the past few months, the DRV has increased its international stature in the non-Communist world. Three non-Communist nations — India, Indonesia, and Pakistan — have granted it *de facto* diplomatic recognition. In addition, since mid-1954, the French have maintained Jean Sainteny as "special representative" to the DRV, and India and Great Britain have established consulates in Hanoi. Prime Minister Nehru of India made a goodwill stop in Hanoi in October 1954, and Vice President Pham Van Dong of the DRV returned Nehru's visit in April 1955. In late November 1954, Prime Minister U Nu of Burma made a goodwill trip to the DRV. DRV participation in the Bandung Conference was further evidence of its status as an independent state.

Relations with the Sino-Soviet Bloc

40. We believe that the DRV is firmly committed to the policies of the Sino-Soviet Bloc, even to the extent of subordinating or postponing the pursuit of its local or regional objectives in the interest of over-all Bloc tactics and strategy. The attitude of DRV leadership follows from its Communist world outlook and from the fact that DRV objectives can only be realized with Sino-Soviet Bloc support.

41. To date both Peiping and Moscow have participated in formulating DRV policies. The DRV has publicly acknowledged that the Soviet Union is the leading power in the international Communist movement. Official declarations have also acknowledged dependence on the Chinese Communists in the fields of ideology and military strategy. Important DRV legislation such as the basic agrarian reform law is modeled closely after early Chinese Communist measures. DRV leaders have frequently compared their own progress with various stages in Communist China's development.

42. Contacts between the DRV and the Chinese Communists have become significant only since the Communist Chinese troops reached the Indochinese border in December 1949. Beginning in 1950, the Chinese Communists assisted the Viet Minh by furnishing military supplies in increasing quantities, training thousands of military personnel in South China, and providing advisors on military, political, and economic matters. At the present time, large numbers of Chinese Communist technicians are in North Vietnam to assist the DRV in improving transportation and communication facilities. It is probable that economic assistance from both the Soviet Union and Communist China will be maintained and perhaps increased.

43. Despite its close ties with and dependence on Peiping and Moscow, the DRV appears to have greater latitude in its actions than the European Satellites. A number of considerations account for this special status. The Viet Minh fought its own fight against French colonialism. The DRV possesses an army and security organization developed independently of Sino-Soviet material assistance prior to 1950. Finally, the DRV can play an important role in furthering Bloc interests in SEA, particularly if permitted the appearance of independence.

Policies Toward Vietnam

44. Since the Geneva Agreement, DRV policy toward South Vietnam has aimed primarily at preventing the formation of an effective nationalist Vietnamese government and at extending Communist control through "coalition," elections, subversion, or other means short of open invasion. The DRV is attempting to pose as the champion of Vietnamese independence and unification. It has made a show of adhering to the Geneva Agreement, and has attempted in various ways to insure French support for the election provisions of the Agreement. The DRV endorsed the actions of the Binh Xuyen-controlled "United Front of the Sects" which the Viet Minh radio blessed as "working with the people" for the overthrow of Diem. In addition, the DRV has called for the resumption of "normal and peaceful" relations between the two zones of Vietnam as rapidly as possible. This campaign for normal relations, which the DRV probably hope will lead to a coalition government for the whole of Vietnam even prior to elections in 1956, was intensified in March and April with repeated concrete proposals to the Vietnamese government for economic and cultural exchanges.

45. Throughout the period of this estimate DRV policies with respect to South Vietnam and national elections will be conditioned by the requirements of Bloc strategy in Asia and by DRV estimates of the prospects for peaceful unification under a Communist-controlled regime. The DRV probably still believes that it could emerge from free nationwide elections with control of all Vietnam. The DRV, with Bloc support, has been insisting that consultations concerning elections begin on 20 July as specified in the Geneva Agreement. If the consultations get underway the DRV will attempt to appear reasonable with respect to election procedures. It will seek to develop Indian, French, and UK pressures for holding elections. The Communists almost certainly would not agree to complex and elaborate safeguards and guarantees, including neutral supervision over the movements of police and military forces for a considerable time prior to and after the elections. Nevertheless, they probably would agree to some form of "free elections" under "neutral" but not UN supervision. Their willingness to consent to some guarantees for "free elections" would probably be reinforced by an estimate that such controls would work to their advantage in the South and, as manipulated, would not adversely affect their position in the North.

46. The DRV's ostensibly peaceful role probably will not prevent continued efforts to infiltrate and subvert the Vietnamese government, political organizations, and sects. The Communists will seek to bring to power in South Vietnam a government which would be willing to join with the North in establishing a national government prior to general elections. Failing this, they will seek to prevent the development of a strong and effective government in the South which could offer the Vietnamese people an attractive nationalist alternative to the Ho regime.

47. The Communists in their propaganda have revealed sensitivity to the implication of the Manila Pact which incorporated Vietnam, Cambodia, and Laos in its area of protection. We believe that concern for Western, and particularly US reactions, together with general considerations arising from over-all Bloc policy, will prevent the DRV from openly invading the South during the period of this estimate. Similarly the resumption of widespread guerrilla activities appears unlikely prior to the election deadline, unless the DRV should come to the conclusion that South Vietnam can be won only by force. Such a conclusion would become more likely should the Diem

government persist in refusing to enter the election discussions, should election discussions not proceed favorably for the DRV, or should the Diem government succeed with US assistance, in consolidating its strength to the point of becoming a nationalist alternative to the Ho regime. Moreover, if during the period of this estimate little progress is made towards relaxing tensions, Peiping and Moscow might permit the DRV greater freedom of action. Should the DRV decide to use force short of open invasion, it would probably attempt to undermine the Saigon government by initiating a campaign of sabotage and terror, seeking the formation of a new government more amenable to demands for a national coalition. These tactics are likely to include the activation of DRV guerrilla units now in South Vietnam and their reinforcement by the infiltration in small units of regulars from the North.

Policies Toward Laos

48. High on the list of DRV objectives is the establishment of a Communist government in Laos. Control of this area would greatly facilitate Communist penetrations of South Vietnam, Cambodia, and Thailand. DRV operations in Laos are facilitated by the presence of a Communist movement, the Pathet Lao, which is largely the creation and puppet of the Viet Minh. The DRV has covertly contributed material and technical assistance to the Pathet Lao "regime." It has supported the Pathet Lao claim that the Geneva Agreements granted it administrative control over the Laotian provinces of Sam Neua and Phong Saly. It has also supported the Pathet Lao proposal for the establishment of a "joint consultative council" composed of representatives of the Royal Laotian government and of the Pathet Lao "regime." Its objective probably is the creation of a coalition government under terms favorable to the Pathet Lao. At the same time, the DRV has sought to convince the Royal Laotian government that the Pathet Lao is not a puppet of the Viet Minh. To this end, DRV Foreign Minister Dong assured the Laotian Prime Minister, while at Bandung, that the DRV considered the Pathet Lao an internal Laotian problem which should be settled by the Laotians themselves.

49. During the period of this estimate, the Viet Minh will probably continue their present tactics of officially seeking to develop friendly relations with the Royal Laotian government while continuing their covert efforts to strengthen the Pathet Lao. The DRV almost certainly will not launch an attack with its own forces to seize Laos, and it probably will not initiate a major Pathet Lao guerrilla offensive against the Laotian government. However, if the Royal Laotian government should undertake military action which seriously threatened the position of the Pathet Lao in the two northern provinces the DRV would probably infiltrate Viet Minh units to assist the Pathet Lao.

Policies Toward Cambodia

50. Pending the achievement of objectives in Vietnam and Laos and pending the development of a stronger Communist organization in Cambodia, the Viet Minh will probably concentrate on fostering Cambodian neutrality. The DRV has professed friendship for the Royal Cambodian government, and has claimed to have withdrawn all DRV armed forces from Cambodia. It has ceased its propaganda attacks against the Royal government, and apparently has sought a mutual declaration of support of the "Five Principles" by the two governments. Nevertheless, the DRV is probably continuing its efforts to develop Communist strength in Cambodia, although to date it appears to have made little progress.

Relations with France

51. DRV policy towards France has apparently been designed to encourage the French to give full support for holding elections in 1956, to reduce French support for a non-Communist government in Vietnam, and to create conflicts between French and US policy. The DRV, while almost certainly aiming at the eventual elimination of French influence in all of Vietnam, has played upon the French desire to retain an economic and cultural role in that area.

52. The Communist apparently impressed the French at the Geneva Conference by

their moderation. In an exchange of letters between Viet Minh Prime Minister Pham Van Dong and Premier Mendes-France, the DRV indicated agreement in principle to the maintenance of French economic and cultural establishments north of the 17th Parallel. Many French believed that the DRV, because of its difficult economic situation and its supposed reluctance to rely solely on China, might be sincere in its desire to see the French maintain their economic and cultural institutions in the country. Some French officials also believed that a conciliatory policy would lead the Viet Minh to loosen its ties with the Sino-Soviet Bloc.

53. However, the French have had little success in retaining their economic position in North Vietnam and there are no indications of any significant expansion of trade between France and North Vietnam. French business enterprises were reluctant to maintain their capital investment in the area without guarantees from their government. Sainteny and his government endeavored to push through a plan for the establishment of jointly owned companies in which the French government would provide capital and control of management. This plan was subsequently abandoned because of strong US opposition and probably because of the DRV's refusal to leave management in French hands. As a result, the *Charbonnages du Tonkin,* which was being used as a test case, was sold to the DRV for one million tons of coal, (presently worth about 5 billion francs) payable over 15 years by annual allocations. The French, moreover, agreed to maintain 30 or 40 technicians in the DRV-owned company to assist production.

54. The French now appear aware that there is little possibility of maintaining investments and cultural establishments in North Vietnam. The French government has expressed disappointment with the results of the Sainteny mission and have hinted that it will be discontinued in the event that Sainteny himself should relinquish the assignment. Nevertheless, it has felt compelled to continue negotiations with the DRV because of domestic political pressures and because it believes that such a course offers additional guarantees against the recurrence of hostilities while the French Expeditionary Forces are still in Indochina.

55. However, in their dealings with the DRV, the French have been careful to avoid giving the appearance of political support to the regime. They appear to have resisted DRV attempts to accredit a delegate-general to Paris. They have worked to facilitate the emigration of non-Communist elements to South Vietnam and have supported requests for an extension of the time limit allowed for North Vietnam refugees to move to the South. Finally, they have been careful to avoid alienating the US and in such matters as the removal of US equipment from the *Charbonnages du Tonkin* and abandonment of plans for government participation in mixed companies, and they have placed greater emphasis on maintaining their ties with the US than on supporting their economic ambitions in North Vietnam.

56. The DRV almost certainly will be willing to continue to negotiate with France, hoping thereby to exacerbate US-French relations and to prevent all-out French support for the non Communist Vietnamese government in the South. However, the DRV almost certainly will be unwilling to make any agreement which in fact would permit the French to retain an economic and cultural position in North Vietnam.

57. In regard to elections, the primary concern of the French government will be to avoid the development of an impasse that would result in renewed hostilities and the involvement of its forces. It will probably insist that elections be held as scheduled but is likely to strive for arrangements that will at least delay direct DRV control over the South.

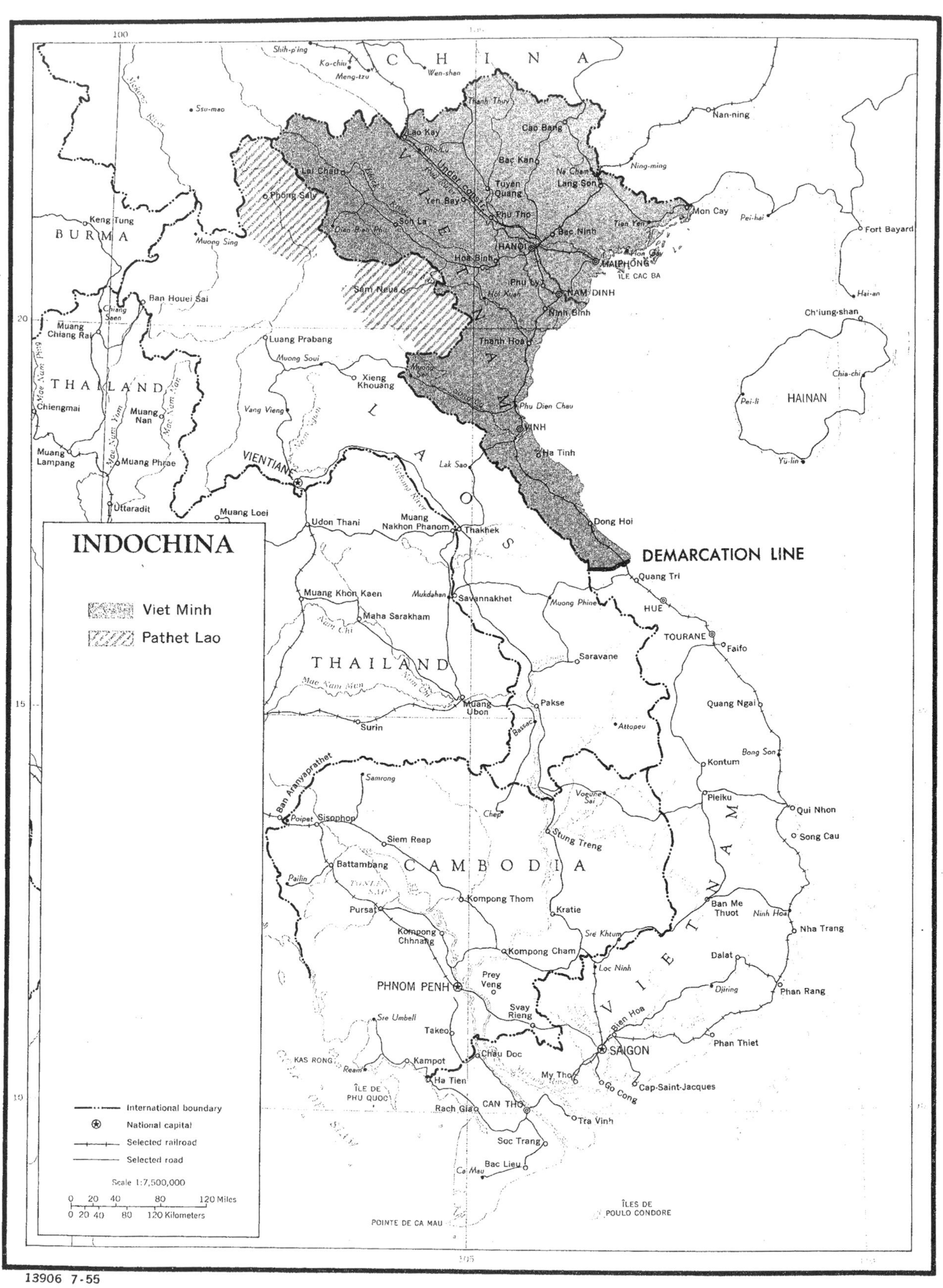
INDOCHINA
Viet Minh
Pathet Lao
International boundary
National capital
Selected railroad
Selected road
Scale 1:7,500,000
0 20 40 80 120 Miles
0 20 40 80 120 Kilometers
DEMARCATION LINE
CHINA
BURMA
THAILAND
LAOS
VIETNAM
CAMBODIA
HAINAN
HANOI
HAIPHONG
NAM DINH
VIENTIANE
PHNOM PENH
SAIGON
HUE
TOURANE
CAN THO
Lao Kay
Cao Bang
Lang Son
Mon Cay
Dien Bien Phu
Lai Chau
Phong Saly
Sam Neua
Luang Prabang
Xieng Khouang
Thanh Hoa
Vinh
Ha Tinh
Dong Hoi
Quang Tri
Savannakhet
Thakhek
Pakse
Saravane
Faifo
Quang Ngai
Kontum
Pleiku
Qui Nhon
Song Cau
Ban Me Thuot
Nha Trang
Dalat
Phan Rang
Phan Thiet
Cap-Saint-Jacques
Siem Reap
Battambang
Kompong Thom
Kratie
Kompong Cham
Kampot
Ha Tien
Rach Gia
Soc Trang
Bac Lieu
Tra Vinh
My Tho
Udon Thani
Surin
Nan-ning
Fort Bayard
Ch'iung-shan
13906 7-55

NIE 63-56

Probable Developments in North and South Vietnam Through Mid-1957

17 July 1956

APPROVED FOR RELEASE
DATE: JAN 2005

NIE 63–56
17 July 1956

4415

(b)(3)

SECRET

NATIONAL INTELLIGENCE ESTIMATE

NUMBER 63–56

(Supersedes NIE 63.1–3–55 and NIE 63.1–55)

PROBABLE DEVELOPMENTS IN NORTH AND SOUTH VIETNAM THROUGH MID-1957

Submitted by the

DIRECTOR OF CENTRAL INTELLIGENCE

The following intelligence organizations participated in the preparation of this estimate: The Central Intelligence Agency and the intelligence organizations of the Departments of State, the Army, the Navy, the Air Force, and The Joint Staff.

Concurred in by the

INTELLIGENCE ADVISORY COMMITTEE

on 17 July 1956. Concurring were the Special Assistant, Intelligence, Department of State; the Assistant Chief of Staff, Intelligence, Department of the Army; the Director of Naval Intelligence; the Director of Intelligence, USAF; and the Deputy Director for Intelligence, The Joint Staff. The Atomic Energy Commission Representative to the IAC and the Assistant Director, Federal Bureau of Investigation, abstained, the subject being outside of their jurisdiction.

COPY NO. 257
ASSISTANT DIRECTOR ONE

SECRET

PROBABLE DEVELOPMENTS IN NORTH AND SOUTH VIETNAM THROUGH MID-1957

THE PROBLEM

To analyze the current political, economic, and military situation in North and South Vietnam and to estimate probable developments through mid-1957.

CONCLUSIONS

1. We believe that the Communist "Democratic Republic of Vietnam" (DRV) will not attempt an open invasion of South Vietnam or a large scale guerrilla warfare effort during the period of this estimate because of the danger of US or possibly SEATO counteraction and because such action would prejudice Bloc emphasis on peaceful coexistence elsewhere. The Communist regime will almost certainly remain in firm political control throughout the period of this estimate, despite some passive resistance and serious economic difficulties. It will require continued large scale Bloc aid to make even limited progress toward developing a self-supporting economy. The DRV army will retain the capability of defeating the total forces of South Vietnam, Laos, and Cambodia. *(Paras. 7–11, 13–16, 18–21, 64–68)*

2. In South Vietnam, the trend toward political stability and popular confidence in the government will probably continue, barring a DRV invasion, large scale guerrilla action, or the death of Diem. Nevertheless, such contingent developments as intensified Bloc support for DRV objectives or reduction in Diem's international support could stimulate greater Communist subversive pressure, weaken the South Vietnam government's confidence, cause some loss of its public support, and revive opposition efforts for reconciliation with the north. *(Paras. 35–39, 69–72)*

3. Progress toward resolving basic economic problems will probably continue slow, but economic conditions in South Vietnam are not likely to have serious adverse political effects during the next year, as rice production, rubber exports, and large scale US aid provide reasonable living standards. *(Paras. 40–46)*

4. All significant sect resistance in South Vietnam has been eliminated, but some 8,000–10,000 armed Communists and a Communist political network scattered through the villages continue to pose a serious internal security problem. The effectiveness of the South Vietnam army will probably improve gradually as more units are released from security missions for training, but by mid-1957 it will still be unable to contain a DRV attack for a prolonged period. *(Paras. 47–56)*

(Continued...)

DISCUSSION

I. INTRODUCTION

5. Under the terms of the 1954 Geneva Accords on Indochina, the area of Vietnam north of the 17th parallel was placed under the administration of the Vietnamese Communists. The French assumed responsibility for implementation of the Armistice provisions in the area south of the 17th parallel, but neither the French nor the Diem government has acknowledged responsibility for implementing the political settlement envisaged in the Final Declaration of the conference.

6. The UK and the USSR, as co-chairmen of the Geneva conference, met in London in April and May 1956 and reaffirmed support for the political settlement foreseen at Geneva but implicitly approved postponement of its implementation, including the nationwide elections. The co-chairman called upon all parties to preserve the status quo and requested the International Supervisory and Control Commission (ICC) to continue supervising the Armistice. Thus no steps have been taken to bring about unification or a political settlement in Vietnam, and the partitioning of Vietnam has been tacitly accepted by the Geneva conference powers for an indefinite period of time. In the meantime, the Communist regime in the north and the Diem government in the south have been developing their own institutions and preparing for an extended period of struggle for control of Vietnam.

II. NORTH VIETNAM — CURRENT SITUATION AND TRENDS

7. The Communist Party of Vietnam (commonly called the Viet Minh) and its governmental apparatus, the "Democratic Republic of Vietnam" (DRV) continue to exercise firm and effective control over the estimated 13 million inhabitants of North Vietnam. Although critically lacking in technically trained personnel, the Communist regime possesses a large number of experienced political workers and has made considerable progress in developing an effective administrative machine. It has strengthened its control despite severe food shortages, continued passive resistance to its internal policies, and the gradual reduction of its prospects for early domination of all Vietnam.

8. Ho Chi Minh continues to occupy a preeminent position among Vietnamese Communist leaders, despite some de-emphasis of his public role. His prestige as a nationalist leader is still a significant factor in the attitude of many people in South Vietnam and Southeast Asia toward the Vietnamese Communist regime. Power relationships at the level below Ho are not clear, but party Secretary Truong Chinh, Premier and Foreign Minister Pham Van Dong, and army commander Vo Nguyen Giap appear to share top level responsibilities. We have no evidence of policy or personal differences among these three men or of the existence of "pro-Chinese" and "pro-Soviet" factions in the party.

9. The regime's primary concern in the past year has been to develop more effective controls over the people and the economy and to deal with such immediate problems as rehabilitation, malnutrition, widespread disease, famine, tightening of the party apparatus, and the development of the armed forces. Although violence and intimidation have been employed selectively, the Communists have so far refrained from the publicized, widespread terror employed in Communist China during the consolidation period in 1951–1952. Strenuous efforts are still being made to rally popular support behind front groups on the basis of nationalist and unification slogans. The most important of these is The Fatherland Front which is designed not only to mobilize support in the north for immediate reconstruction tasks but also to attract support in South Vietnam for Communist efforts to unify the country.

10. The Catholic population of approximately 750,000 appears to be the main center of passive resistance to Communist indoctrination and DRV control. The Communists appear to have recognized the special nature of the Catholic problem and, probably with an eye both to reducing opposition and impressing the evacuees in the south, have moved slowly to restrict church activities. At the same time, they are attempting to weaken the hold of the clergy over the communicants by various means including visits of "puppet" priests from Eastern Europe. To date the Vietnamese Catholic hierarchy appears to have been fairly successful in maintaining its position among the Catholic population.

11. The substantial ethnic minorities, who live outside the river deltas, have an ingrained dislike for all Vietnamese and there have been some instances of armed opposition by the tribal groups of north and northwest Tonkin. To integrate these minorities politically and to lessen their opposition to Communist leadership, the DRV has established "autonomous administrative areas" nominally controlled by tribal dignitaries loyal to the Communists. In any event, Communist military and security forces are capable of eliminating any active resistance in the north.

Economic Policies and Courses of Action

12. The regime is moving gradually to extend its control over all aspects of the economy, but it has not yet attempted detailed over-all planning, the nationalization of small productive units and domestic trade, or the collectivization of agriculture. At present, the regime is attempting to deal with immediate problems on the following priority: (a) increasing agricultural production; (b) restoring the transportation network; and (c) rehabilitating export industries, e. g., coal, cement, phosphates, and textile and other light industries. Thus far the regime has not begun to stress heavy industrial development and is concentrating a major portion of its industrial production on consumer goods.

13. The regime's major economic problem is to meet the minimum consumption needs of the population while developing a self-supporting economy. Prior to 1954 the annual rice deficit of North Vietnam averaged about 200,000 metric tons. As a result of wartime damage to irrigation facilities and an unprecedented series of floods, droughts, and insect scourges, the rice deficit in each of the past two years has amounted to at least 500,000 metric tons. With shipments from South Vietnam cut to a trickle since 1954, the DRV appealed to the Bloc for relief. However, imports through April 1956, consisting of token shipments from Communist China and some 200,000 tons of Burmese rice purchased by the USSR, have fallen far short of minimum requirements. In December 1955 the DRV announced that the per capita food consumption in that year had dropped at times to as low as 500 calories per day.

14. There will probably be some improvement in the food situation in 1956–1957. The USSR has agreed to accept up to 400,000 tons of Burmese rice each year through 1959. It is likely that the Burmese will actually ship a high percentage of this figure and that the DRV will receive a major share of this rice. Although the spring crop in 1956 will probably again fall below normal because of continued adverse weather, the extensive efforts of the regime to mobilize all segments of the population for irrigation repair, reclamation of abandoned land, cultivation of new land, and planting of subsidiary crops should lead to a gradual increase in domestic output.

15. However, North Vietnam will not achieve self-sufficiency in rice in the next few years even with optimum weather conditions. Planned investment to increase the supply of fertilizers, pumps, improved seeds, and agricultural implements appears insufficient to achieve a substantial increase in output in the near future. Moreover, the current program for redistribution of land will probably depress production.

16. Rehabilitation of modern industries has gone slowly due to a lack of raw materials, technicians, and equipment. Coal production in 1955 is estimated to have been about 700,000 tons compared to 900,000 tons under the French in 1953 and the pre-World War II peak of 2,600,000 tons. The rate may reach

800,000 to 1,000,000 tons in 1956, permitting an export of 300,000–500,000 tons. By the end of 1956 cement production may reach its former annual rate of [illegible]00,000 tons. The large textile plant at Nam Dinh returned to limited production in December 1955 but even when operating at full capacity it will provide only about half of North Vietnam's requirements and it is dependent on imported cotton.

17. With Chinese Communist technical and manpower assistance, rapid progress has been made in restoring transportation and communication facilities. The rail link from Hanoi to the Chinese border at Nam Quan has been restored and the Haiphong-Kunming line will probably be fully restored this year. This construction will link southwest China with sea transport at Haiphong and the main Chinese rail system at Nam Quan. The line from Hanoi to the 17th parallel is also being rehabilitated and it is possible that service south to Vinh will be established by the end of the year. With Chinese assistance, the DRV has also made rapid progress in rehabilitating North Vietnam's highway system. A bridge building program for 1956 is aimed at eliminating most of the ferries on primary roads. Rehabilitation of the Hanoi-Lai Chau route and of roads south from Hanoi toward the 17th parallel will facilitate the movement of troops and supplies to any point along the borders of Laos and South Vietnam. Soviet assistance is making possible the improvement of port facilities at Haiphong which will further expedite the distribution of Bloc military and economic supplies.

18. The chronic deficit in the balance of payments position of the North Vietnam area has been deepened by the failure to restore agricultural and industrial production and by the abnormal requirements for foreign goods and technical aid. The foreign exchange position has also been worsened by the break in complementary trade relations with the south. A measure of the deficit and of the critical economic situation is suggested by the magnitude of Bloc grants to the DRV. In July 1955, Communist China granted the sum of 800,000,000 yuan (about $330,000,000 at official rates) and the USSR promised 400,000,000 rubles ($100,000,000 at official rates). Smaller grants have been extended by several of the European Satellites. A substantial portion of the aid received has been in the form of consumer goods.

19. We believe that during the period of this estimate the DRV will continue to concentrate with moderate success, on efforts to increase agricultural, mineral, and light industry production. The DRV has the resources to increase exports and to support a modest industrial development. However, at least for several years, it will require substantial Bloc assistance to support even a minimum standard of living and there appears little prospect for substantial forced saving to support rapid industrialization in the near future.

DRV Military Strength

20. The "Vietnam People's Army" (VPA) now has a total strength of about 266,000 men organized in 16 infantry divisions, 2 artillery divisions, 1 AAA groupment, 10 separate infantry regiments, and 5 border and coastal security regiments. As the VPA continues its evolution toward a modern force, several more divisions may be organized using existing separate regiments. Although further substantial increases in the numerical strength of the army appear unlikely, a ready pool of semitrained manpower exists among the 117,000 men now in regional and popular troop units. The recent announcement by the DRV of a troop reduction probably reflects the release of unfit personnel since the Armistice.

21. More extensive training was probably made possible by reduced commitments to internal security missions and reconstruction projects, and multidivisional maneuvers were reported in late 1955. We believe that about half of the major combat units are combat-ready and the remainder probably will reach that status during 1956. Even at its present level of training, the VPA is capable of defeating the total military forces of South Vietnam, Cambodia, and Laos.

22. There were no significant changes in the dispositions of VPA units during the past

year and the largest concentration remains in the Delta region, approximately 300 miles from the 17th parallel. However, clandestine guerrilla operations, including infiltration of small units, could be conducted against South Vietnam and Laos without major troop movements.

23. The Vietnamese Communists have no combat air capabilities at the present time, but some air training probably is underway in Communist China. It is possible that the DRV will have one or two regiments of piston fighters operational in 1957. There are 26 former French air fields in North Vietnam, five of which could be used with little or no development to support sustained operations by Communist jet fighters, and one of which could probably support sustained jet light bomber operations. The DRV has no separate naval organization and coastal defense depends on small armed craft and ground patrols.

DRV External Relations and Policies

24. *Relations with the Bloc.* We believe that the DRV is firmly committed to the policies of the Sino-Soviet Bloc, even to the extent of subordinating or postponing the pursuit of its local or regional objectives in the interest of over-all Bloc tactics and strategy. The attitude of DRV leadership follows from its Communist world outlook and from the fact that DRV objectives can only be realized with Sino-Soviet Bloc support.

25. Despite its close ties with and dependence on Peiping and Moscow, the DRV on occasion acts in less conformity with the Bloc than the European Satellites. A number of considerations account for this special status. The Vietnamese Communists fought their own fight against French colonialism. The DRV possesses an army and security organization which was developed prior to 1950 independently of Sino-Soviet material assistance. The appearance of relative independence created by some DRV actions may, nevertheless, serve to further Bloc interests elsewhere in Southeast Asia.

26. Over the past year, Bloc economic and diplomatic support may not have met DRV expectations. Bloc deliveries of rice have been far below levels necessary to prevent widespread debility in North Vietnam. Mikoyan's visit to Hanoi in April 1956, the first by a major Soviet official, was made a great public occasion and DRV propaganda suggested some expectation that new aid or economic agreements might result. No new Soviet-DRV arrangements were announced, however, and in fact Mikoyan departed without issuance of the usual joint communique. The USSR also failed to press DRV demands either for the "strict implementation" of the Geneva Agreements with respect to north-south consultations and elections, or for reconvening the Geneva conference. The Soviet position, as it developed at the April-May Geneva co-chairmen talks, accepts maintenance of the status quo for the time being. Although the Chinese Communists have been more forthright in supporting the stated DRV position, the Soviet Union has shown no disposition to support the DRV's basic objective of securing control of all Vietnam at the risk of jeopardizing Soviet policy objectives in other areas or the Bloc's campaign of emphasizing "friendship" and reducing tensions.

27. The rather aloof position of the USSR, which increases the dependence of the Vietnamese Communists on Communist China, may be disappointing to the DRV. Some element of the traditional Vietnamese distrust of the Chinese probably survives among Vietnamese Communist leaders, despite the bond of Marxism, and the DRV may well wish that it could counter Chinese influence with closer Soviet ties.

28. Substantial differences over policy toward South Vietnam, and possibly Laos, may develop between the DRV and the USSR and Communist China if prospects for an early extension of Communist control to South Vietnam continue to decline. Even in this event, however, and despite the DRV's potential capacity for independent action, we believe that other considerations would prevail to cause the DRV to continue its loyal adherence to the Bloc.

29. *Policies Toward South Vietnam.* Lacking full Bloc support for its reunification demands and recognizing that the July 1956 deadline for elections would not be met, the DRV is now adjusting its policies for the longer pull. The regime's public position that the Geneva provisions must be fulfilled and that nationwide elections must be held remains unchanged. However, the DRV is now playing down the demand for early reconvening of the Geneva conference and increasing its demands for direct north-south consultations. The DRV has accepted the position taken by the Soviet Union at the London talks that the ICC and Joint Armistice Commission should continue their functions despite the dissolution of the French High Command. The DRV has also enlarged the scope of its diplomatic activity to enhance its international prestige and position and to secure the broadest possible foreign support for eventual implementation of the Geneva Agreements.

30. At the same time, the DRV has maintained its network of political and paramilitary cadres in the south. It has continued its efforts to penetrate the government of South Vietnam and probably is maintaining contact with non-Communist but anti-Diem Vietnamese, chiefly those now in exile, who favor conciliation with the north. Through use of nationalist themes and front organizations, it is attempting to retain popular following in the south. Ninety-five thousand men were evacuated from the south in the first few months following the Armistice. The DRV probably views this group as a possible instrument for subversive activity in South Vietnam and some may have been retrained, reindoctrinated, and perhaps even reinfiltrated.

31. *Policies Toward Laos and Cambodia.* The Communist rebel movement in Laos, the Pathet Lao, is completely dependent on DRV support and assistance to maintain its position in the northern provinces. Although the DRV continues to support the Pathet Lao, it has begun to soften its line toward the Royal Lao government. In place of its earlier criticism of the Lao government, the DRV now praises the Lao government's professed adherence to the "five principles of coexistence," encourages Laos to adopt a neutral foreign policy and to enter into direct consultations with the Pathet Lao to resolve their differences.

32. DRV policy toward Cambodia encourages neutralism and the establishment of wider contacts between the Cambodian government and the Communist world. The Hanoi radio has virtually eliminated its previously bitter condemnation of the Cambodian government and is now extravagant in its praise of Cambodian foreign policy and its "resistance" to alleged US "plots" to undermine Cambodian independence. Future DRV policies with respect to Laos and Cambodia will probably reflect the guidance of Moscow and Peiping.

33. *Policies Toward Other Countries.* In its relations with other states in Asia, the DRV has attempted to increase support for its position on unification, to further the general Bloc peace campaign, and to obtain diplomatic contacts and recognition. At present, North Vietnam is recognized by all Bloc countries, but no non-Bloc country has extended full diplomatic recognition. India and Indonesia have exchanged consular representatives with both North and South Vietnam and Burma has permitted the DRV to maintain an Information Office in Rangoon. The DRV has taken special pains to woo the Indian delegates to the ICC.

34. The DRV has severely curtailed remaining French cultural activities in North Vietnam and the much publicized commercial arrangements have been too restrictive to hold or attract any significant economic activity by the French. However, the DRV has won French agreement to the establishment of a commercial and cultural mission in Paris. Its presence will complicate French relations with Diem and facilitate the maintenance of DRV influence among Vietnamese resident in France.

III. SOUTH VIETNAM — CURRENT SITUATION AND TRENDS

Political

35. During the past year President Ngo Dinh Diem's government has greatly strengthened

its internal political position in South Vietnam, a country with an estimated population of 12 million. The national referendum in October 1955 established the legitimacy of the Government of Vietnam (GVN), and completed the elimination of Bao Dai as Chief of State and as a major political factor in South Vietnam. By the end of March 1956, Diem reduced the Cao Dai and Hoa Hao groups to political impotence by a series of moves which culminated in the elimination of the Cao Dai army as an independent military force and the capture, trial, and execution of Ba Cut, the last important active Hoa Hao resistance leader.

36. On 4 March 1956, in South Vietnam's first national elections, 80 percent of the eligible voters participated in electing 123 deputies from 405 candidates for the Constituent Assembly. The returns gave pro-Diem forces a substantial majority. Although nearly one-third of the government-favored candidates were defeated, no openly anti-Diem deputy was elected. This was due in part to government manipulation of the election campaign and in part to a boycott of the elections by most of the opposition parties. Despite efforts by the Vietnamese Communists and other resistance groups to disrupt and sabotage the voting, the elections generally were calm and orderly. The Constituent Assembly will sit for a four-year term as the first National Assembly.

37. The deputies in the Constituent Assembly, which convened 15 March, are divided among political parties as follows: National Revolutionary Movement (NRM), 61; Revolutionary Workers Party (RWP), 15; Citizens Rally (CR), 26; Movement of Struggle for Freedom (MSF), 6; and Independents (including one Dai Viet), 15. The NRM is the Diem government's primary source of organized political power. Although Information Minister Tran Chanh Thanh is its titular head, a large part of the party is controlled by Diem's brother, Ngo Dinh Can, who controls Central Vietnam. The RWP, also a government party, is led by Diem's brother, Ngo Dinh Nhu. While the CR, MSF, and most Independents now support Diem, they contain some members who have reservations about some of Diem's methods and are potential centers of parliamentary opposition.

38. Diem will probably maintain his dominant political position in South Vietnam during the period of this estimate. The constitution, which has been drafted under Diem's supervision, gives the President wide powers including the right to appoint the first Vice President and to suspend civil rights during the life of the first Assembly. Diem's personal prestige will probably be enhanced by improvement in internal security and by continued frustration of Vietnamese Communist objectives. However, he will continue to face serious problems in attracting additional active support for his government, in part because of his reliance on a small circle of relatives and trusted friends. While Diem's control of the Assembly during the period of this estimate will probably be adequate to insure adoption of any important measure he wishes enacted, his inclination to hold a tight rein on the legislature may accelerate the development of an active opposition.

39. The appointment of a Vice President by Diem, now 55, will remove much uncertainty over presidential successorship. Nevertheless, Diem's death, whether by natural causes or assassination, could result in serious factional disputes in the government and among the major political parties which could strain the new governmental institutions. Ngo Dinh Nhu and Tran Chanh Thanh, key figures in the RWP and NRM, have a great deal of political power and would play important roles in any redistribution of power, but neither of these men has a wide popular following. To some government critics and government supporters Thanh symbolizes the more regressive features of the Diem regime. At the moment, Secretary to the President and Acting Minister of the Interior Nguyen Huu Chau appears to enjoy Diem's favor and has grown rapidly in stature and power, but he has no organized political backing apart from his support by Diem and Nhu. Ngo Dinh Can would probably play an important behind-the-scenes role in any redistribution of power, but his lack of national stature and poor

health would almost certainly rule him out as a leading contender for leadership. Tran Van Lam, leader of the CR, is ambitious and enjoys considerable popularity in the southern provinces, but his political position is weak. Although the army high command has been trying to keep the army out of politics, the prestige and strength of the army would almost certainly play a major and possibly decisive role in the redistribution of political power. The numerous anti-Diem nationalists in South Vietnam and France would probably attempt to re-enter the picture and their maneuvers would add to the confusion. However, many of these men are discredited because of their past relations with Bao Dai, the French, or the Communists, and it is doubtful that any of them could muster sufficient backing to gain control.

Economic

40. South Vietnam is normally an agricultural surplus area, exporting rice and rubber. During World War II and the civil war periods large portions of cultivated land were abandoned and the transportation and irrigation systems deteriorated. Current rice production is less than two-thirds the pre-World War II levels, and exports in 1955 were only about 100,000 tons as compared with the prewar annual total of more than one million tons. Current rubber output of 54,000 tons exceeds the prewar level by about 10,000 tons and rubber has replaced rice as South Vietnam's leading foreign exchange earner. In 1955, high market prices raised the value of South Vietnam's rubber exports almost 80 percent above 1954 and to more than half the value of all exports.

41. Because of the decline in rice exports and the large imports of consumer goods and, to a lesser extent, capital goods for rehabilitation, South Vietnam is running a large deficit in its balance of payments. In 1954 exports covered 17 percent of imports while in 1955, even with unusually high rubber prices, exports covered only 25 percent of imports. At present, US aid is filling the gap and is an important factor in the relatively high standards of living prevalent in much of South Vietnam. For the fiscal years 1955 and 1956 the planned level of US economic and military aid for South Vietnam totaled approximately $520 million (not including the value of US equipment already in Vietnam and transferred to the GVN). At present the US is financing about 90 percent of the GVN military budget, 65 percent of the combined military-civilian budget, and 75 percent of all South Vietnam's imports.

42. The withdrawal of French military forces, the termination of France's preferential trade status, and the loosening of French-Vietnamese political ties have combined to curtail the scale of French industrial and commercial activity in South Vietnam. French business interests are withdrawing about as rapidly as Vietnamese restrictions on currency transfers permit. South Vietnam's import trade is moving away from France toward Japan and the US. In 1953 and 1954, France supplied about 80 percent of South Vietnam's imports. In 1955 the figure dropped to 50 percent and the downward trend is continuing. In the same two-year period, Japan's share of South Vietnam's imports has increased from three to 12 percent.

43. The GVN has not yet effectively come to grips with its economic problems. President Diem has stated that 1956 will be a year of economic consolidation, but through the first six months of the year, GVN attention continued to be focused on security and political issues. Only the most pressing economic problems have received serious government attention and those have generally been dealt with by *ad hoc* methods or authoritarian decrees. For example the government has attempted to cope with a serious threat of inflation by a series of decrees controlling prices and inventories for many items and establishing high fines and even the death penalty for attempts to corner the market. These measures have contributed little to preventing inflation and have aroused the resentment of the important Chinese community. Inflationary pressures have been held in check primarily because the government has been able, with US aid, to maintain a fairly high level of imports of consumer goods.

44. Progress has been slow in the resettlement of refugees and in the implementation of other measures to increase agricultural production. The limited land reform program inaugurated in 1953 is unattractive to the peasant in comparison with extravagant Communist promises. Landlords are objecting to the low rents provided for in the program and their opposition plus the general lack of official determination and administrative competence has led to the stagnation of land reform.

45. Nevertheless, the GVN has made some progress in building the organizational structure necessary to replace institutions of the French colonial period. The GVN has created an independent national bank, a foreign exchange office, an investment fund, a government-owned commercial bank, and an independent currency. President Diem has proposed establishment of a High Economic Council to guide the country's economic development and he has made informal reference to the possibility of a four or five year plan for economic rehabilitation and development. In addition, government officials now administer a substantial import program and the application of a substantial US foreign aid program. Although these new institutions and economic activities provide an essential beginning for further economic progress, they are not yet fully operative or effective.

46. Though South Vietnam cannot become economically self-supporting so long as it must maintain armed forces of the present size, its economic position could be substantially improved by economic and fiscal reforms. However, during the period of this estimate there is little prospect for marked development of South Vietnam's economy or for a significant reduction in its balance of trade and budget deficits. Inflationary pressures are almost certain to continue. However, the food supply, a critical political factor, is likely to be more than adequate for domestic needs. Provided security conditions continue to improve, the GVN will probably give economic problems increased attention during the coming year and will probably be able to make some progress toward solution of several specific economic problems. A program to resettle 100,000 refugees on abandoned land has been developed and some 40,000 of these have already been relocated. This project will probably be followed by further resettlement projects which are likely to reduce substantially the refugee problem during the estimate period. Additional land will probably be brought under cultivation. Some improvement is likely in tax collection and in handling the problem of French disinvestment. By mid-1957, economic development planning will probably be well advanced, but concrete results are unlikely within the period.

Military

47. Current strength of the Vietnamese National Army (VNA) is approximately 145,000 troops. The VNA is organized into 4 field infantry divisions (8,500), 6 light infantry divisions (5,225), 1 airborne groupment (4,000), 13 territorial regiments, 5 separate sect regiments, and 15 assorted combat battalions. Although some progress has been made during the past year, the extensive plans for training and reorganizing the VNA have fallen behind schedule because most major units have been dispersed with many of them engaged in security operations. Principal VNA weaknesses are an inadequate logistical and technical support system, an ineffective chain of command, and inexperience at the command and staff levels. At least six months of uninterrupted training will be necessary to bring the VNA to minimum operational effectiveness at division level. VNA loyalty to President Diem and his policies seems assured. The army's self-confidence and morale are generally good.

48. When the French High Command was inactivated on 23 April 1956, all previous French-Vietnamese military agreements were terminated. All French combat units have been withdrawn from Vietnam. After 1 July, only a few French army personnel remained in South Vietnam, in addition to a 1,000-man French military support group for the ICC. The Vietnamese and the French are now negotiating concerning French support for the ICC and the French role in training the Vietnamese forces, particularly air and naval

forces. The primary US-directed effort has been the training of a Vietnamese instructor corps and the development of training programs throughout the Vietnamese army. US personnel are detailed to VNA training centers, to units at division level, and to major territorial commands to supervise progress and implementation of the training program. The US military group in South Vietnam has been held to its pre-Geneva size despite the near complete withdrawal of the French mission, which totaled about 2,500 personnel prior to the Armistice. However, a 350-man US Temporary Equipment Recovery Mission (TERM) is being established in South Vietnam.

49. South Vietnam's embryonic air force (VNAF) has grown only slightly during the past year. Its current strength of 3,336 includes 103 trained officer and enlisted pilots and 100 pilot trainees. VNAF aircraft inventory is 143 planes, mostly trainer/liaison and transport types. Although the air force is receiving F8F piston fighter-type planes, it is unable to maintain even limited flight operations because of a lack of qualified maintenance personnel. The VNAF has a limited capability to provide air support to ground troops, artillery observation, air evacuation, liaison, and air lift for paratroop operations. No significant increase in VNAF capabilities appears likely during the next two to three years.

50. South Vietnam's navy is under operational control of the Chief of Staff of the VNA and under the administrative command of a senior naval officer. Personnel strength is 142 officers and 1,755 men, with a Marine Corps of 44 officers and 1,775 men. The forces afloat, which have been augmented over the past year by additions from the withdrawing French forces, include 3 submarine chasers (PC), 3 coastal minesweepers (MSC (O)), 14 amphibious vessels (2 LSM, 2 LSSL, 5 LSIL, 5 LCU), and 170 smaller amphibious and patrol craft. The Vietnamese navy has limited effectiveness, but it is capable of undertaking river patrol and minor coastal and amphibious operations. Capabilities should improve substantially in the near future because of continued US aid and intensive training programs which include technical training in the US and France.

51. We believe South Vietnam's military and security forces are capable of maintaining the government in power against any potential armed opposition now located south of the 17th parallel. In the event of large scale, concerted guerrilla warfare supported by infiltration of men and supplies from the north, relatively large areas of rural Vietnam probably would be lost to government control. In the event of full scale invasion, the Vietnamese forces at present probably could not delay for more than 60 days a Vietnamese Communist advance to the Ban Me Thout-Nha Trang line. If the trend toward improved internal security and increased effectiveness of the Civil Guard continues, it will be possible to step up training and reorganization of the VNA, thereby improving its capabilities during the period of this estimate. However, by mid-1957 Vietnamese forces will still be incapable of delaying for more than 90 days an advance by DRV forces beyond the Ban Me Thout-Nha Trang line.

Internal Security

52. The internal security situation in South Vietnam has improved substantially during the past year. The sects are no longer a major security problem for the GVN. Most of the important non-Communist sect leaders of a year ago have either fled the country, been killed or captured, lost control of their forces, or rallied to the government. Remaining sect armed bands are scattered and disorganized and probably total no more than 2,000. Although various bandit groups will probably continue to cause local disturbances, it is likely that organized non-Communist resistance will virtually disappear during the period of this estimate.

53. With the sect problem basically under control, the Communist underground represents the only serious threat to internal security in South Vietnam. Reports on Communist armed strength in the south over the past year have ranged from 5,000 to 10,000. Our best estimate of current strength is 8,000 to

10,000 with approximately 5,000 organized in skeletal company and battalion sized units which could be expanded through recruitment. These armed forces are generally scattered through the mountains paralleling the Annam coast and the remote swampy regions of Cochin-China. They are capable of harassing actions against VNA outposts and of widespread intimidation, assassination, sabotage, and terrorism, especially in rural areas. They could disrupt north-south traffic throughout Central Vietnam and interfere seriously with provincial and local administration. However, any sustained guerrilla operations would require a flow of reinforcements and supply from the north.

54. The Communists have an unknown number of political cadres in the south engaged in subversive and propaganda activities. Although Communist cadres probably exercise effective control over some remote communities where the GVN has not yet attempted to establish its authority, and have some influence in villages through much of South Vietnam, over-all Vietnamese Communist political influence in the south appears to have diminished during the past year. However, if the Communists decide to exercise their capability for armed intimidation and terror they could quickly reassert political control or influence, at least in some rural areas where GVN authority is tenuous.

55. During the past year the Communists in South Vietnam have remained generally quiescent. They have passed by a number of opportunities to embarrass the Diem regime. Although some cadres and supplies are being infiltrated across the 17th parallel, the DRV probably has not sent any large scale reinforcement or supply to the south. Communist activity in the south appears to concentrate on protecting vital bases and supply caches, developing clandestine paramilitary organizations, and implementing a broad program of infiltration and subversion. While seeking to maintain intact as much of their armed strength as possible, their main activity seems to be an effort to weaken the Diem government by subversive and political tactics. Communist directives indicate that penetration and subversion of the GVN military and security forces is a major objective. Although there is little specific evidence, they probably have penetrated lower echelons of the VNA, especially the integrated sect forces, and probably hold positions of influence in some provincial governments and village councils. Local Communist groups probably gave some assistance to the Cao Dai and Hoa Hao forces opposing the government. Since the collapse of sect armed resistance it is possible that the Communists are seeking to take over the remnants of the sect forces.

56. The GVN has organized a Civil Guard to relieve the VNA of many static internal security duties. Current strength of the Civil Guard is approximately 48,000 men organized in lightly-armed mobile companies. Its mission is to maintain law and order, collect intelligence, and conduct countersubversion operations at the provincial level in areas pacified by the army. Although considerable progress and refinement in its training and organization will be necessary before the Civil Guard can fully discharge its responsibilities, it has shown considerable potential as an instrument for maintaining internal security. A 60,000-man village Self-Defense Corps (Dan Ve Doan) is being organized to provide security at the local level.

Foreign Relations

57. GVN foreign policy objectives are to win recognition as the legitimate government of all Vietnam, to obtain maximum foreign military and economic aid and guarantees of foreign assistance in the event of Communist aggression, and to develop foreign support for its position with respect to the Geneva Agreements. Forty-one nations have recognized the GVN. In addition, India and Indonesia maintain consular relations with the GVN.

58. President Diem consistently has maintained that South Vietnam is not bound by the 1954 Geneva Accords and has no legal responsibility for their implementation. He has refused to deal directly with the DRV on any issue and has been steadfast in his rejection of all-Vietnam elections until "democratic processes can be assured in North Vietnam." He believes that any consultations or implied recognition of the DRV would have

adverse political effects in the south and could lead to increased internal and international pressure for reunification of Vietnam under a coalition government with the Communists.

59. His refusal to permit nationwide elections and to assume responsibilities under the Geneva Accords raised the possibility of a withdrawal of the ICC following the deactivation of the French High Command in April. To deal with this situation, representatives of the Geneva co-chairmen (the UK and the USSR) met in London during April and May 1956. The USSR failed to press DRV demands that the co-chairmen reopen the Geneva conference. Instead, the co-chairmen finally agreed upon identical letters to the DRV and GVN requesting them to prevent any violation of military clauses of the Geneva Accords, to insure implementation of the political terms, to submit at the earliest possible time a convenient deadline for direct consultations and for holding all-Vietnam elections, and to give every assistance to the ICC. The co-chairmen requested the ICC to continue supervising the Armistice. They requested the French government to continue its good offices in support of the ICC, to reach agreement with the GVN to facilitate the task of the ICC and the Joint Armistice Commission (French-DRV), and to preserve the status quo until such new arrangements could be put into effect.

60. Despite his past refusals to assume responsibilities under the Geneva Accords, in his response to the co-chairmen's message Diem agreed to respect the Armistice and to provide security for ICC members. He recognizes the deterrent value inherent in the presence of the ICC, and appears willing to take action necessary to continue its function but continues to avoid the acceptance of any legal obligation under the Geneva Accords.

61. Franco-Vietnamese relations continue to reflect considerable ill-will and distrust on both sides. Recent causes of friction include disagreements concerning the future status and role of French military training missions, residual military base rights in South Vietnam, and the equivocal French attitude toward the Communist regime in the north. The French now exercise little influence in Vietnamese affairs and there is little prospect for any improvement in relations in the near future.

62. South Vietnam-US relations have remained close and friendly during the past year. There have been few evidences of Vietnamese resentment of increasing US influence and activity in South Vietnam despite continual efforts by the Communists and some local French to stir up dissatisfaction on that score. The GVN would like the US to raise the mutually agreed ceiling on VNA force levels and desires greater autonomy in administering the foreign aid program. Diem would also like the US to exercise maximum political pressure, especially on the UK, India, and France, to enable the GVN to avoid any responsibility for the Geneva Accords.

63. Relations between South Vietnam and Cambodia have been strained by activities of resistance groups in border areas, by treatment of minority groups, by boundary disputes, and most seriously by disagreements relating to trade arrangements. A trade stoppage early in 1956 was removed through informal mediation by the US, and by the terms of settlement official representatives have been exchanged for the first time. The basic causes of friction remain, however. Vietnam does not desire full diplomatic relations with Cambodia because it fears such action would lead to Cambodian recognition of the DRV as well. There are no pressing problems in Lao-Vietnamese relations and South Vietnam's relations with the Philippines and Thailand are generally good.

IV. THE OUTLOOK IN VIETNAM

Probable Communist Courses of Action Toward South Vietnam

64. The DRV probably estimates that its chances for securing control of South Vietnam by means short of open attack or large scale guerrilla action supported from the north will gradually diminish with the passage of time. As indicated by Soviet and Chinese Communist performance in the past

several months, the DRV probably cannot expect strong support from the Bloc for the "strict implementation" of the Geneva Agreements. The lack of strong Bloc pressure strengthens international acceptance of the status quo in Vietnam and increases confidence in the future in South Vietnam. Although the DRV may still believe that it could obtain control of all Vietnam through ICC supervised nationwide elections, Vietnamese Communist leaders are probably increasingly doubtful on this point because of their own internal difficulties and the growing nationalist stature of Diem. The DRV probably also believes that its covert assets in South Vietnam will gradually decline if the Diem government is permitted to concentrate on internal security and economic problems free of external harassment.

65. Despite the declining prospects for the "peaceful" take-over of South Vietnam, we believe that the USSR and Communist China will almost certainly continue unwilling to support open DRV military action against South Vietnam during the period of this estimate. They are probably unwilling to risk the chance of US or SEATO intervention which would make it difficult to limit the conflict to Vietnam, and probably believe that overt DRV military action would seriously undercut the worldwide effort of the Bloc to win friends and supporters. Although the DRV retains the capability to launch an independent military action against South Vietnam, the chances of such action in the absence of assured Bloc support appear to be extremely small.

66. The only remaining course of action holding out some promise for the early achievement of Communist control in South Vietnam appears to be the development of large scale guerrilla warfare in the south. In recent weeks a number of reports from sources of untested reliability have indicated that the Communists may have started preparations in both South Vietnam and in the north to begin guerrilla action. DRV allegations of Vietnamese violations of the demilitarized zone along the 17th parallel and Communist claims of US-Diem plans to violate the Armistice could be propaganda cover for the initiation of guerrilla action against the south.

67. However, the possible indications of armed action appear inconsistent with the DRV's insistence on the continued functioning of the ICC — which is in a position to make at least limited observations of DRV activities. Moreover, guerrilla action in South Vietnam, if it were to be sustained and not to result simply in the identification and gradual elimination of Communist cadres, would require large scale support from the north. This would involve some risk of detection by the ICC and of intervention by the US and possibly SEATO. It would also tend to prejudice current Communist maneuvers elsewhere in Asia. For these reasons, we believe that the DRV will refrain from instituting large scale guerrilla action within South Vietnam during the period of this estimate. Communist capabilities for guerrilla warfare in South Vietnam will exist for some time, however, and the chances of their being employed would probably increase in the event of any substantial deterioration in the domestic situation in South Vietnam — such as might conceivably occur on the death of Diem. The chances of Communist guerrilla warfare would also be increased by deterioration of the international aspects of the situation, such as a withdrawal of the ICC under circumstances which would permit the Communists to place the blame for this event on the GVN.

68. The DRV will continue to seek maximum Bloc support for its objectives and will seek, within the limits of Bloc strategy, to harass and undermine the government in South Vietnam. It will continue to seek direct contacts with South Vietnam, offering economic and cultural exchanges while castigating Diem for "blocking" unification. It will continue efforts to penetrate the government of South Vietnam and to improve its covert organization throughout the area. It may attempt to increase pressures for a reconvening of the Geneva conference and to unsettle the Diem government by fabricating or provoking incidents along the demarcation line and by demonstrations of armed strength within South Vietnam.

Trends in South Vietnam

69. Barring a major Communist effort to disrupt the Diem regime by renewal of large scale guerrilla operations, the over-all prospects for improved security of South Vietnam are good. The VNA, as its training progresses and as more units are released from static security duties, probably will be able to pacify and extend government authority into many areas of present Communist influence. Diem's success in by-passing the July 1956 election date without evoking large scale Communist military reaction will reassure many Vietnamese and encourage them to cooperate with GVN programs to expose and root out Communists. Continued improvement in internal security will depend in some measure on the government's ability to deal with economic and social problems and on the effectiveness of the administrative apparatus.

70. If the Communists were to undertake large scale guerrilla action in South Vietnam, they probably would not be able to develop widespread popular support, especially if the VNA were to register some early military success. The GVN is being increasingly accepted as a nationalist alternative to Communist leadership. Public confidence in the GVN, combined with general war-weariness, may have already reached the point where any effort to upset the government by force would lead to a strong popular reaction against the guerrillas.

71. The trend toward increased political stability in South Vietnam will probably continue during the period of this estimate and President Diem will probably continue to exercise effective political control. The trend toward authoritarian rule through the political parties led by Diem's relatives and small circle of trusted associates will probably continue. Isolation and neutralization of government critics and men disliked or distrusted by Diem will also continue. Diem and his associates are likely to exert strong pressures against any opposition in the Assembly. Thus it is not likely that Diem or his government will meet any serious opposition in the National Assembly during the period of this estimate; however, over a longer period the accumulation of grievances among various groups and individuals may lead to development of a national opposition movement. The major economic problems will undoubtedly continue and over the longer run may handicap South Vietnam in competition with the Communist north, but economic conditions are unlikely to affect political stability during the period of this estimate.

72. Despite the moderately favorable outlook projected for South Vietnam, the situation contains many elements of instability, and progress will continue to depend on firm US support. A number of contingent developments could create new tensions among the foreign powers concerned as well as between the GVN and the DRV. For example, the steps which Diem is willing to take toward facilitating the operations of the ICC may not be adequate to satisfy India whose representative serves as chairman of the Commission. Should the Commission withdraw, DRV agitation might well be intensified and international Communist pressures on the diplomatic level would probably increase. The UK might become less firm in its support of Diem's position. Weakening of international support for Diem, a marked increase in Bloc support for the DRV, or a substantial increase in Communist activity within South Vietnam would probably weaken the government's confidence in its position, cause some loss of public support, and lead to renewed efforts by opponents of the regime in the direction of reconciliation with the north.

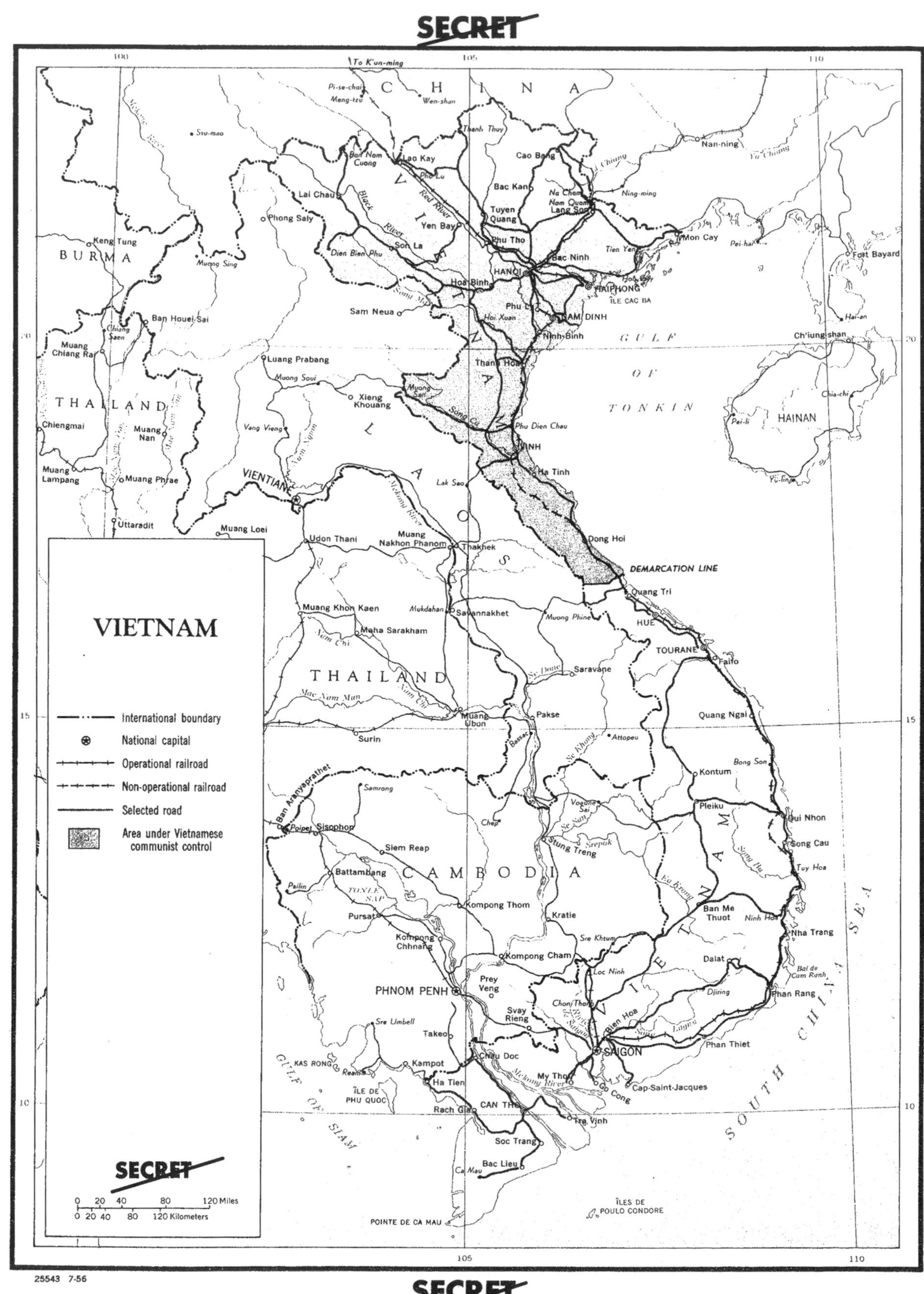

25543 7-56

SECRET

NIE 63.2-57

The Prospects for North Vietnam

14 May 1957

APPROVED FOR RELEASE
DATE: JAN 2005

NIE 63.2–57
14 May 1957

3254

(b) (3)

Nº 280

NATIONAL INTELLIGENCE ESTIMATE

NUMBER 63.2–57

(Supersedes relevant portions of NIE 63–56)

THE PROSPECTS FOR NORTH VIETNAM

Submitted by the

DIRECTOR OF CENTRAL INTELLIGENCE

The following intelligence organizations participated in the preparation of this estimate: The Central Intelligence Agency and the intelligence organizations of the Departments of State, the Army, the Navy, the Air Force, and The Joint Staff.

Concurred in by the

INTELLIGENCE ADVISORY COMMITTEE

on 14 May 1957. Concurring were the Special Assistant, Intelligence, Department of State; the Assistant Chief of Staff, Intelligence, Department of the Army; the Director of Naval Intelligence; the Director of Intelligence, USAF; and the Deputy Director for Intelligence, The Joint Staff. The Atomic Energy Commission Representative to the IAC, and the Assistant Director, Federal Bureau of Investigation, abstained, the subject being outside of their jurisdiction.

(Continued...)

THE PROSPECTS FOR NORTH VIETNAM

THE PROBLEM

To analyze the current political, economic, and military situations and to estimate the prospects for North Vietnam over the next year or so.

CONCLUSIONS

1. Although the Communist regime in North Vietnam (DRV) has probably lost a considerable measure of its original popular support and has been faced with sporadic outbursts of violence, it remains in firm control largely because of the loyalty and effectiveness of the army. Moreover, with substantial help from the Bloc, it has apparently made significant progress toward economic restoration, particularly in agriculture. *(Paras. 13–16, 20–21)*

2. The DRV has undertaken to "correct its mistakes" which it admits caused popular resentment, and it will probably be able to regain some of the popular support which it lost. If the party organization is sufficiently strengthened and if crop prospects are good, steps toward further socialization of agriculture may come as soon as the fall or winter of 1957. Local disturbances may recur but for the foreseeable future the DRV will be capable of maintaining effective control. *(Paras. 17, 23–26)*

3. The DRV is generally isolated from the outside world except for close ties with the Bloc, on which it depends for aid and support. However, the DRV has probably been disappointed by the lack of effective Bloc support for its objective of unifying all Vietnam under DRV rule. The DRV, with Bloc logistical support, could easily overrun South Vietnam, Cambodia, and Laos if opposed only by indigenous forces. However, the Bloc would support such an attack only if Moscow and Peiping were to estimate that such action carried little risk of US military intervention. *(Paras. 29–34)*

4. The DRV will probably continue its tactics of "peaceful competition" with South Vietnam for the support of the Vietnamese, although it will continue its efforts to infiltrate and to subvert official and nonofficial organizations and to exploit dissident and dissatisfied groups in South Vietnam. In Laos, we believe that the DRV will continue to support Pathet Lao efforts to negotiate a political agreement with the Royal Lao Government, with the ultimate objective of Communist control, and may encourage local Pathet Lao military action in order to bring pressure to this end. The DRV will probably not, in the immediate future, play a primary role in Cambodia. *(Paras. 34–36)*

DISCUSSION

5. Since the Geneva Agreements in 1954, the Lao Dong (Workers) Party — the Communist Party of Vietnam — has sought to lay the foundations for the transformation of North Vietnam into a Communist society. Its most important immediate tasks have been to establish an effective system of administration and control over the population and to rehabilitate the economy which had suffered extensive damage during the long years of war.

6. The Lao Dong was in a relatively favorable situation at the time it assumed control in North Vietnam. Its victory over the French had engendered considerable popular support, and its leader, Ho Chi Minh, was considered even by many non-Communist nationalists as the only person who could drive the French from the rest of Vietnam. It controlled and had the loyalty of a large, battle tested, and effective army. Nevertheless, from the Communist point of view the party itself had two major weaknesses. There was a shortage of well-trained cadres, and many members of the party were motivated more by anti-French and nationalist sentiments than by Communist dogma.

7. During the past year these fundamental weaknesses were exposed as the regime attempted to impose its control on the peasantry too rapidly and too crudely. Much of the popular support which the regime once enjoyed as a nationalist force appears to have been dissipated. The regime now confronts the task of rebuilding sufficient popular acceptance of its programs to permit the implementation of further steps toward socialization and increased production without the direct and constant application of force and coercion.

8. While supremacy over all Vietnam remains a basic Communist objective, the success of President Ngo Dinh Diem in South Vietnam and the apparent unwillingness of the Bloc to permit a military invasion have substantially reduced the likelihood of a take-over of South Vietnam in the near future. The Lao Dong has accordingly given increasing emphasis to the less direct tactics of peaceful competition and subversion.

I. THE INTERNAL SITUATION

Current Status

9. The Lao Dong has organized the "Democratic Republic of Vietnam" (DRV) along the lines of other "peoples democracies" and it controls directly the government apparatus and the Vietnam Peoples Army (VPA). Power and leadership are exercised by members of the Politburo who hold positions simultaneously in the party and government. We believe that Ho Chi Minh is the ultimate authority in the regime. He is Chairman of the party, President of the DRV, and, since October 1956, the Secretary General of the Central Committee of the Lao Dong. Other important leaders who hold both party and government positions are Vo Nguyen Giap, member of the Politburo and Minister of Defense and Commander of the Army, and Pham Van Dong, also a member of the Politburo and Prime Minister and Foreign Minister. Truong Chinh, although recently removed from the office of party Secretary General, remains a member of the Politburo and still holds the post of Vice Chairman of the Central Agrarian Reform Committee.

10. Below the top level, the party still suffers from a serious shortage of experienced technicians, administrators, and managers. The government's administrative apparatus and the party's lines of control have proved inadequate to carry out some major aspects of the regime's program. On at least one occasion the party has had to use the army to restore order.

11. The army with a strength of about 268,000 remains the main source of DRV strength. It is a relatively well paid elite enjoying special privileges, and most of its officers are members of the Lao Dong party. The less able and less reliable members are being

weeded out, various categories of militia and regional troops are being integrated into the VPA, and the regime has been seeking to improve the relations between the army and the peasants.[1]

12. As the economy of North Vietnam is basically agricultural, the principal problems facing the regime involved organizing and controlling the peasantry and increasing agricultural production. Land reform cadres, drawn from politically reliable but otherwise poorly trained personnel, have been the regime's principal instrument both for organizing the peasants and for purging and rebuilding the party in the rural areas. These cadres have been largely successful in destroying the landlords as a class and in distributing the land among middle and lower class peasants. As the land was redistributed, the cadres began to introduce rudimentary socialist forms by organizing the peasants into mutual aid teams in which the peasants cooperate to plant and to harvest each other's land. The regime claimed that by mid-1956 some 190,000 mutual aid teams, which included almost 60 percent of the peasant households, had been established. Concurrent with the land reform, these cadres purged from the party a substantial number of members believed to be politically unreliable and recruited replacements primarily from the poorer peasants.

13. The DRV has conceded that the operations of the land reform cadres were so crude and arbitrary that widespread disaffection developed which in some cases broke into open resistance. The regime has admitted that the cadres classified as landlords many peasants who were merely slightly better off than the average peasant. They also victimized landlords who had supported the regime during the war, had sons in the army, or had relatives among the poor peasants. Estimates of the number of landlords put to death by decisions of land reform "people's courts" range from 30,000 to 100,000. Others were imprisoned, suffered expropriation, or were cast out of the community.

14. The cadres further disturbed the normal life of the communities by forcing local peasant organizations to disband. Even some of the peasants who ostensibly profited from the redistribution of land were dissatisfied because the land reform cadres made excessive estimates of the crop yield and, consequently, of the taxes to be paid. Catholic peasants were further alienated when the land reform cadres requisitioned their churches for use as storehouses, distributed church land to individuals, and intimidated worshippers. The concurrent purge of party members involved abuses, guilt by association controversies, and arbitrary rulings, so that by mid-1956 the morale of the party was shaken and the official line changed to a criticism of the manner in which the purge had been administered.

15. The application of controls has probably also caused some loss of popular support in urban areas. Many factory workers, shopkeepers, and small businessmen have reacted adversely to the Communist system of controls and to the shortages of food and other consumer goods. The non-Communist intellectuals, who initially supported the DRV, also became dissatisfied and when the regime gave them some freedom in the fall of 1956, they severely criticized DRV policies in nonparty publications.

16. The DRV has also had the problem of establishing control over the minority groups who inhabit the mountainous regions of North Vietnam and who provided some of the best native troops in the French Union forces during the war. To this end the regime has established some autonomous zones. However, there is a traditional hostility between the mountain tribes and the Vietnamese, and dissidence will almost certainly remain a problem for the regime.

17. Communist China's experience in communization undoubtedly prepared the DRV for the development of opposition to the regime's program, but the vehemence of the opposition apparently exceeded its expectations. During the fall of 1956, the regime's concern over unrest led it to take measures to remove the causes of discontent. In announcing the over-all policy of "correction of our mistakes"

[1] See Appendix A: The Military.

the DRV acknowledged the profound influence of the 20th Congress of the CPSU and the Eighth Congress of the CCP, and some aspects of the regime's program paralleled those in other Communist states. The regime was probably also influenced by awareness that informed Vietnamese on both sides of the 17th parallel were comparing developments in the North unfavorably with those in the South.

18. The most significant corrections have involved the land reform program. The party accepted the resignation of Truong Chinh as its Secretary General, and demoted several other party leaders responsible for agrarian reform and party reorganization programs including the Vice Ministers of Agriculture and Interior. In addition, the central and local agrarian reform committees were shorn of their executive power and reduced to advisory organs, and the regime announced the abolition of land reform "people's courts." The DRV also undertook to indemnify relatives of those wrongly condemned to death, release prisoners, restore some property mistakenly expropriated, reinstate expelled party members and cadres, return churches and church property to the parishes, and reduce crop estimates and tax levies. The DRV promised corrections in other fields including increased "democracy" and improved living conditions.

19. The admission of errors at the top level of the party and government and the promise of reforms and greater "democracy" encouraged the expression of antiregime sentiment. DRV leaders reacted quickly and made it clear that there were narrow limits within which the liberalization program would function, and that the regime would not relinquish any important controls. In early November 1956, the army was placed on alert status throughout North Vietnam. Furthermore, troops were more conspicuous in some cities, probably as a show of force to discourage any possible outbreaks of violence.

20. In mid-November the army suppressed an uprising in Nghe An province. This is the only known major incident in which regular army units were committed. Even in this instance regular troops were probably required more because of the ineffectiveness of the local militia than because of the extent and organization of the uprising. The likelihood of further violent outbreaks declined, largely as a result of the strength exhibited by the army in its operations to restore order. The army alert appears to have been terminated in January 1957.

21. Our knowledge of economic conditions in the DRV is largely derived from Communist statements. However, it has been possible in a number of instances to test these announcements against other evidence. Based on such analysis, we believe that the regime has achieved significant progress toward the restoration of the economy.[2] This has been made possible by the availability of grant aid and technical assistance from the Bloc. The regime appears to have raised rice output substantially, largely by expanding acreage and rehabilitating irrigation and flood control systems. Although 1954 and 1955 were bad rice crop years, in 1956 the cumulative effects of DRV efforts combined with good weather resulted in production of rice nearly sufficient to meet minimum food requirements. This permitted a substantial reduction in rice imports, and some rice was exported. We believe that the regime has been less successful in expanding the production of subsidiary food crops, and rather unsuccessful in its efforts to obtain a major expansion of cotton. The regime has probably completed the restoration of most of the prewar highway and rail systems, except for the line south from Ninh Binh to the 17th parallel. Many mining and industrial installations are back in production. Coal exports in 1956 were more than double those in 1955. However, output of coal, cotton textiles, and other major commodities is still substantially below peak output under the French.

22. There is little likelihood that the North Vietnamese economy will become self-sustaining in the foreseeable future. It has traditionally been a food deficit area, present consumption levels are austere, and reserves for poor crop years are probably nonexistent.

[2] See Appendix B: The Economy.

Although foreign trade has increased, the regime will not be able to cover its chronic trade deficit from its own resources unless there is a substantial increase in domestic production of consumer goods and in the production and export of coal, minerals, and cement. Meanwhile, it will continue to require large scale economic support from the Bloc.

Probable Developments

23. Although local disturbances may recur, the DRV will continue for the foreseeable future to have the capability to maintain effective control in North Vietnam. The army, the principal source of DRV power, will almost certainly remain loyal and retain its offensive capabilities. (See Appendix A.) Its coastal and river patrol forces and its air arm are not likely, during the next year, to increase significantly in size and effectiveness.

24. During the next few months the regime will probably continue its efforts to regain popular support, particularly among the peasants, and at the same time to strengthen the party organization. It will probably continue its "correction of errors" in the land reform program by such measures as readjusting the distribution of land, revising crop collection quotas and tax levies, rehabilitating those wrongly accused or convicted, reinstating party members and cadres mistakenly expelled, and restoring some property to religious organizations. It may also seek to make a display of "democracy" in order to improve the popular attitude, particularly that of the intellectuals. Further effort will probably be made to give the National Assembly the appearance of an instrument of popular will. But despite these steps, the regime will not relinquish its essential controls over the population.

25. The DRV will probably be able to regain some of the popular support which it lost unless its "correction" campaign is as badly managed as the agrarian reform. In any event, the period of consolidation and concern for popular opinion is not likely to continue indefinitely. The regime will probably become impatient to get forward with the socialization of agriculture in the Chinese Communist pattern, since the leaders as Marxists believe that collectivization leads to both better control and increased output. Moreover, they may have completed many of the more obvious "corrections" by the fall or winter of 1957. If so, they are likely to push forward with the socialization of agriculture, handicraft industries, and small commercial firms. They will probably move slowly at first and attempt to obtain compliance by "persuasion."

26. The regime's internal actions during the next year or so will be conditioned by a series of factors outside its control. Its decisions regarding the pace of agricultural socialization will depend not only on the effectiveness of its party apparatus in rural areas but also on the weather, since the regime is less likely to push rapid socialization, at least in the early stages, during a period of bad crops. The regime will also probably seek to avoid courses of action, such as the blatant use of force, which would put the DRV in a bad light in South Vietnam, and will probably continue to emphasize in its propaganda the operations of the National Assembly and other "democratic" procedures. Finally, the rapidity with which internal economic development can be pushed will be determined in part by the willingness of Bloc countries to extend additional credits.

27. Though the death or disability of Ho Chi Minh would weaken the government temporarily, it probably would not have a significant effect on DRV policies or governmental stability. A collective leadership appears a possibility. The regime's success in demoting Truong Chinh while retaining him in important party and governmental offices indicates considerable basic harmony and equilibrium in top leadership. Factionalism might develop, possibly ranging General Giap against Truong Chinh, but it probably would not reach the point of endangering the stability of the regime. In any event, Communist China and the Soviet Union would use their influence to prevent an overt struggle for power.

28. In the next year or so, the restoration of the economy to the prewar (1939) level prob-

(Continued...)

ably will be completed and preparations made for a modest start on new development. However, progress will depend to a large extent on foreign aid, favorable weather, and the ability of the regime to contain peasant discontent. Expansion of foreign trade is also a necessity. The 1957 State Plan calls for the restoration of the economy to the 1939 level, with emphasis on production of consumers goods, plus minerals and other products for export. If external aid is continued at current levels and agricultural production is not adversely affected by climatic conditions, the DRV should be able to provide a modest improvement in the over-all standard of living within the next year or so.

II. RELATIONS WITH THE BLOC

29. Not only are the DRV leaders bound to the Bloc by strong ideological ties, but the very existence of the Communist regime in North Vietnam is dependent on continued Bloc diplomatic, military, and economic support. The Chinese Communists seem to exercise somewhat greater influence than the USSR and have given the DRV greater economic and diplomatic support. In large measure this is probably the logical result of geographic contiguity and the type of initial assistance the DRV has required, i.e., in the military, agricultural, and transportation fields. Finally, the Chinese Communist experience in the application of Communist doctrines appears to be more appropriate then that of the USSR to the situation in North Vietnam. However, there is no evidence that Soviet and Chinese Communists are at odds over North Vietnam.

30. In its public statements concerning intra-Bloc politics, the DRV has tended to follow the line set by the Chinese Communists. It supported the Soviet action in Hungary and welcomed the reforms in Poland. Despite the coldness of current Soviet-Yugoslav relations, the DRV has moved toward establishing more cordial ties with Yugoslavia, and in March 1957 it was announced that ambassadors will be exchanged.

31. The Bloc has recently given less than full support to Vietnamese reunification, to the perceptible discomfort of the DRV. At the May 1956 meeting of the Geneva co-chairmen, the Soviet Union tacitly accepted the status quo in Vietnam for an indefinite period. In January 1957 the USSR further recognized the long term nature of the division of Vietnam when it proposed, as a countermove to Western proposals for the admission of South Vietnam and South Korea, that both North and South Vietnam and North and South Korea should be admitted to the United Nations. Nevertheless, the DRV will almost certainly continue to be guided in its external course of action by the general policy set down by Moscow and Peiping, although it will continue to advocate a stronger policy on reunification.

III. DRV ACTIVITIES IN SOUTH VIETNAM, LAOS, AND CAMBODIA

32. The DRV continues to maintain its apparatus for subversion within South Vietnam and has the capability to infiltrate fairly large numbers of military and political personnel into South Vietnam. Although the Communists in the South have been largely quiescent, some trained military personnel remain, loosely organized in small units that presumably could be reactivated for missions of assassination, sabotage, or limited guerrilla activity. South Vietnamese security forces intermittently discover cached Communist arms.

33. Because the country-wide elections envisaged by the Geneva Agreements have not been held and because military action has been prevented, the DRV has been frustrated in its hopes of gaining control of South Vietnam. This has caused some discontent among cadres evacuated from the South in the expectation that they would soon return. Unification of the country remains a principal objective of the DRV regime, and it continues to seek support for its pretentions to emerge as the government of the whole of Vietnam. Its "liberalization" measures are designed to appeal to the population of the South as well as the North. The DRV has maintained its pose of adherence to the terms of the cease-fire agreement concluded at Geneva while accusing the Republic of Vietnam and the US of violations. It is seeking to enhance its

international prestige and position, and to secure the broadest possible support for the political settlement envisaged at the Geneva conference which it still insists must eventually be implemented.

34. The DRV will probably continue for the next year or two to restrict its campaign for reunification to "peaceful" means. However, the DRV will continue its efforts to infiltrate and to subvert official and nonofficial organizations and to exploit dissident and dissatisfied groups in South Vietnam. It would probably not use its paramilitary forces in South Vietnam to initiate widespread guerrilla activity unless it estimated that the situation in South Vietnam had so deteriorated that such action could overthrow the government. The DRV will continue to have the capability to overrun South Vietnam in a relatively short time if opposed only by South Vietnamese forces, but it would only launch such an attack if the DRV together with Moscow and Peiping were to estimate that such action carried little risk of military intervention by the US.

35. The Communist movement in Laos, the Pathet Lao, continues to be dependent on DRV support and assistance to maintain its position in the northern provinces. However, the Communist Bloc apparently believes that its objective of gaining control of Laos can best be served by political rather than military courses of action. Because of US support to the Royal Lao Government (RLG) and because of the existence of the SEATO protocol, the Communists probably estimate that an attack against Laos would involve risk of intervention of US forces. On the other hand, the Lao government is weak and potentially vulnerable to a political assault by a well-organized, legal Communist party. Consequently, for the past year the Pathet Lao has been seeking to obtain participation in the RLG and recognition as a legal political party. Simultaneously, the USSR, Communist China, and the DRV have sought to establish diplomatic, economic, and cultural relations with the RLG. Although these efforts have failed to date, we do not believe that the Communist Bloc will throw over the political approach completely and launch an attack on the RLG. However, during the next few months the DRV may support local Pathet Lao military action in order to bring pressure on the RLG to conclude a political agreement.

36. During the past year the DRV has praised the Cambodians for their policy of neutrality which involved closer relations with Communist governments while accusing the West of undue pressure to induce Cambodia to take a more pro-Western line. The DRV has been unsuccessful in cautious attempts to secure formal diplomatic relations with Cambodia. However, in 1956, Cambodia entered into an economic aid agreement with Communist China and permitted the USSR to open an embassy in Phnom Penh. For the immediate future we believe that Communist objectives in Cambodia will be pursued primarily by Peiping and Moscow.

IV. RELATIONS WITH OTHER COUNTRIES

37. Except for conclusion of a new trade agreement with Indonesia in January, the DRV has made no substantial recent progress in its continuing drive to develop closer relations with the countries of South and Southeast Asia. The DRV continues to maintain a semiofficial mission in Rangoon (ostensibly a branch of the Vietnam News Agency), and is represented by Consuls General in Djakarta and New Delhi. Although there is a British consular establishment in Hanoi, DRV relations with the UK are slight. The DRV is dissatisfied with French refusal to accept a political mission in Paris. The drying up of French-DRV relations is reflected in the limited implementation of French-DRV trade accords, the progressive withdrawal of French cultural institutions from the Communist zone, and the failure of the Sainteny mission which was established in Hanoi at the time of the French withdrawal to develop French-DRV ties.

APPENDIX A

THE MILITARY

A1. Since July 1954, the DRV has placed a major emphasis on reorganizing and strengthening its army (the VPA). Substantial quantities of arms and equipment have probably been received from the Chinese Communists and these have made possible the augmentation of unit firepower, the development of new specialized and technical components, and the improvement of tactical organizations. We believe that the VPA, given external logistical support, has the capability of defeating the total military forces of South Vietnam, Cambodia, and Laos simultaneously.

A2. The VPA is estimated to total about 268,000 troops, organized into 14 infantry divisions, one artillery division, one AAA groupment, 11 separate infantry regiments, 5 border and coastal security regiments, and 5 separate battalions. In addition, there are Regional Troops and Armed Popular Troops with strengths estimated at 35,500 and 75,000 men respectively; these are assigned an internal security mission under the over-all control of the VPA. VPA units continue to be deployed in a generally defensive posture. The largest concentration almost certainly is in the Red River Delta region. We also believe that major units are located in Thanh Hoa and Vinh and that smaller forces are deployed near the 17th parallel, in the west, and in the northeast.

A3. The DRV naval force is not an independent organization but a maritime adjunct of the VPA. Currently the 25 to 30 small, lightly armed, motor-launch-type patrol craft and 12 to 15 motor junks which comprise this force are based principally in the Haiphong area. The patrol craft, mostly of Chinese origin, are employed in coastal and inland waterway patrol while the junks are used exclusively for training. The DRV naval force could not cope with the South Vietnam navy if the latter sought to deny them the use of the Gulf of Tonkin in the event of hostilities. DRV naval forces will probably not expand beyond their present strength or assume a role of broader scope as long as the International Control Commission (ICC) remains in Vietnam.

A4. Up to the present the DRV has demonstrated no combat air capabilities, and the DRV is not expected to present any serious air threat for the next several years. Presently the DRV has an estimated 10 liaison-type aircraft used in a semimilitary role. The personnel of this quasi-air force number about 250. Operational training direction and maintenance probably are provided by Communist China, and it is possible that a real air force is being created covertly in Communist China. There are 26 former French airfields in North Vietnam, one of which could probably support sustained jet light bomber operations. Four other airfields are suitable for limited jet fighter operations and could support sustained jet fighter operations if developed. (See Map.)

A5. In an important and lengthy speech to the National Assembly in January 1957, army Commander-in-Chief General Giap outlined plans for continuing the transformation of the VPA into a balanced, modern force, and also emphasized the political aspects of its mission. In addition to its "defensive" mission, General Giap said that the VPA as combat arm of the Lao Dong party has the duty of maintaining internal security, and of supporting the "peaceful struggle for the reunification of Vietnam." General Giap called for an intensified training in "political-mindedness" in the VPA, and for the adoption of a compulsory military service system for developing a "reserve force which includes all the people."

A6. General Giap implied that the strength of the VPA might be reduced, and cited the following as factors which have placed limitations on the buildup of the VPA's effective strength: the DRV's "peace policy," the VPA's

"defensive mission," the manpower shortage, and budget possibilities. In June 1956 the DRV announced with great fanfare, intended to prove the peaceful policy of the regime, that 80,000 troops were being demobilized. (Probably with some justification, local civilian Communist leaders have regarded these ex-soldiers as having been discharged because they were politically unreliable, and apparently treated them accordingly. As a result many of these veterans have become associated with the disaffected groups.) We believe that to the extent these discharges actually took place, they have been offset by new recruitment and by integration of other elements into the VPA.

A7. Chinese Communist military advisors and technicians have been assisting in the development of the VPA since 1950, but we have little information on either the number of advisors or the current extent of Chinese (or Soviet) military assistance to the DRV. It is reported that in late 1956 a joint Sino-DRV military headquarters was established in the Kunming area of Yunnan Province in Communist China. This could be used both for coordinating logistic and training activities and for developing joint operational plans to meet future military contingencies in the Indochina area. It might permit the Chinese Communists to exercise considerable influence in the VPA and thus in the DRV itself.

APPENDIX B

THE ECONOMY

B1. North Vietnam traditionally has been a food deficit area and prior to the division of Vietnam was dependent on imports largely from South Vietnam. Hence a major problem of the regime is to raise the production of foodstuffs to meet the minimum needs of the population while developing a self-supporting economy. Despite progress in restoring the economy North Vietnam continues to have a low standard of living and to be dependent on foreign aid to cover the trade deficit in its balance of payments. The DRV since 1955 has received credits and grants, to be used over a period of years, in the amount of $100 million from the USSR, $330 million from Communist China, and small amounts from European Satellites (all conversions at official rates).

B2. The DRV had intended 1955 to be the first of two years of planned economic rehabilitation after which a larger scale plan of longer duration would be launched. But the combination of unfavorable weather, the government's lack of experience in economic administration and planning, and the delay in obtaining Bloc technical aid and equipment resulted in a year of trial and error, and probably of acute distress in large parts of the country. Up to the end of 1955 very little progress had been achieved in developing production in the established industries of coal, cement, electric power, ferrous and nonferrous metals, and textiles. Only in the fields of transportation and telecommunications, where Chinese Communist aid was most readily available, and in irrigation and flood control, was there significant progress.

B3. The formation of a National Planning Board in October 1955, the creation of a statistical service in November 1955, and the arrival of Bloc advisors enabled the regime by early 1956 to inaugurate planned economic development and to utilize effectively the Sino-Soviet Bloc aid which began to arrive in the second quarter of the year. The DRV in 1956 operated under a one-year plan aimed generally at rehabilitating the economy and laying the foundations for the transition to socialism. The plan was formulated along the lines of the Chinese Communist experience of the period from 1949 to 1952. No absolute figures were announced for the 1956 budget, but the regime indicated the amounts to be spent for economic and social projects would be allocated as follows.

20 percent – agriculture and irrigation
38 percent – industrial construction
23 percent – transport and communications
19 percent – culture, health, education, and miscellaneous.

The regime has claimed fulfillment of most of the specific goals of the 1956 economic plan.

B4. Agricultural rehabilitation is fundamental to the recovery and development of all sectors of the North Vietnamese economy and it has been the most important program of the regime. Emphasis has been given to expansion of rice acreage, and there have been striking achievements in irrigation and flood control. These coupled with favorable weather conditions have resulted in 1956 rice production significantly above 1955. Imports of rice, which had been sizable during 1955 and early 1956, were negligible during the latter half of 1956 when the regime was able to export small quantities of rice. In order to increase the availability of rice the government has maintained strict rationing of rice and is pushing a program for raising of secondary agricultural crops. The regime is also emphasizing the development of cotton cultivation, with the aim of insuring self-sufficiency in raw cotton. Although this program is promising for the long run, 1956 production was disappointing and even if 1957 plans are fulfilled, only one-third of North Vietnam's raw cotton requirements will be furnished by domestic production.

B5. Rehabilitation of modern industries has proceeded rapidly with the extensive aid from the Soviet Bloc, and most major mining and industrial installations are now back in production, although output is generally well below prewar levels. Emphasis is being given to development of exportable minerals and industrial products and to production of consumer goods. The DRV claims that production in 1956 reached 75–80 percent of the peak in the period of French control. Although evidence is scanty, we believe that these claims in most cases are high and that in 1956 coal output reached about 1.2 million tons compared with 2.6 million in 1939, and cotton yarn output 3,000 tons compared with 12,100 in 1940. Cement production was about 300,000 tons against 312,000 in 1939. The Tinh Tuc tin mine, where a tin-processing plant has been installed, is being exploited apparently under the direction of Soviet technicians. The DRV has claimed that the tin resources are far larger than previously believed and that gold, tungsten, chrome, uranium, and iron ores are also present. Mineral surveys throughout North Vietnam are reported by the DRV to have revealed more than 50 exploitable mineral deposits previously unknown.

B6. Cotton textile plants and phosphate crushing plants, as well as other factories serving the domestic economy, have returned to production, and production from small industry and handicrafts has increased markedly. In spite of this progress in industrial reconstruction, the regime is still far from being able to provide either a satisfactory supply of goods for home consumption, or sufficient exports to balance the large quantities of imported material and equipment necessary for further economic development.

B7. In 1956 North Vietnam's foreign trade was more than double that of 1955. The regime continues to be primarily dependent on trade with the Bloc, but trade with non-Bloc areas has also increased, principally with Japan. Exports of coal, the principal export item, increased from about 300,000 tons in 1955 to about 700,000 tons in 1956, including 300,000 tons to Japan and 130,000 tons to Western Europe. It is estimated that by 1960 coal exports will have doubled, and that moderate increases will be made in the export of cement and other basic commodities.

B8. North Vietnam's seaborne trade has comprised mainly the export of coal to Japan, Western Europe, and China, the importation of limited quantities of material and equipment from the European Satellites and the Soviet Union, and the importation from Burma of Soviet-purchased rice. The only discernible trends are the rapid increase in coal exports since the third quarter of 1955 and the reduction of rice imports in 1956.

B9. Socialization is in its early stages. Major industrial plants and construction projects are operated by the state, but most small scale industry and handicraft production is still in private hands. In the interest of efficient operation, the regime has announced that state factories will be given autonomous status with the management assuming responsibility for the capital and property and operating on a profit and loss basis. The regime apparently intends, at least for the time being, to control small industry indirectly through taxation and marketing and supply mechanisms while attempting to organize artisan craftsmen gradually for cooperative production. State control of domestic and foreign trade was expanded greatly during 1956. In agriculture, the regime is proceeding along the Chinese Communist road to collectivization. By mid-1956 the regime claimed there were some 190,000 "mutual aid teams" in North Vietnam involving almost 60 percent of the peasant households. Most of these were seasonal arrangements for sharing labor and equipment, but they almost certainly will become more permanent as pressure from the party cadres increases. A stepped up program for agricultural producers cooperatives as well as marketing and credit cooperatives will probably follow as soon as the regime considers this move feasible.

B10. With Chinese Communist technical and manpower assistance, rapid progress has been made in restoring transportation and communications facilities. Rail lines have largely been reconstructed (see map) with the ex-

(Continued...)

ception of the line south from Ninh Binh to the 17th parallel. North Vietnam's highway system has been restored generally to its prewar status and in some areas improved. Major emphasis is being directed toward bridging numerous streams in order to eliminate ferries on the primary roads. The Hanoi-Lai Chau route and roads south from Hanoi toward the 17th parallel have been significantly improved, thereby facilitating the movement of troops and supplies to many points along the Lao and South Vietnamese borders. Soviet Bloc assistance is facilitating the improvement of port facilities which will further expedite the increase of trade.

B11. Planning goals for 1957 have been reported in general terms. These goals carry on the same line as those for 1956. Agricultural production will continue to be basic. Priority will be given to light industry for the manufacture of consumer goods and to those industries which process goods for export. The state-owned sector is to be constantly expanded, although for the present the regime is apparently counting on private enterprise to supply an important portion of locally-produced consumer goods and various tax and price adjustments have been suggested to encourage such private production.

B12. There have been no announcements of long range economic plans. The regime has presumably looked on the years 1955–1957 as a period in which it would reconstruct the economy and gain planning experience before launching a long range plan. We believe that the DRV is likely to formulate such a plan by 1958, but the plan almost certainly will require revisions in later years.

B13. In trying to attain a position of relative economic independence, North Vietnam will continue to face difficult problems. Production of food must be greatly increased, exports must be raised substantially, and a body of skilled technical and administrative personnel must be built up. Even if Sino-Soviet Bloc aid is continued at its present high level, achievement of a self-supporting economy will take some time, and will place a heavy burden on the mass of the population.

B14. We believe that during the next year or so the DRV will continue to concentrate on efforts to increase agricultural, mineral, and light industrial production. The unusual emphasis placed by the DRV on light industry may be due in part to a desire to attain consumption standards comparable to those in South Vietnam. The DRV has a resource base capable of supporting increased exports and modest industrial development and it will probably have moderate success in its economic efforts. If external aid is continued at current levels and agricultural production is not adversely affected by weather, the DRV should be able to provide a modest improvement in the over-all standard of living within the next year or so.

SECRET

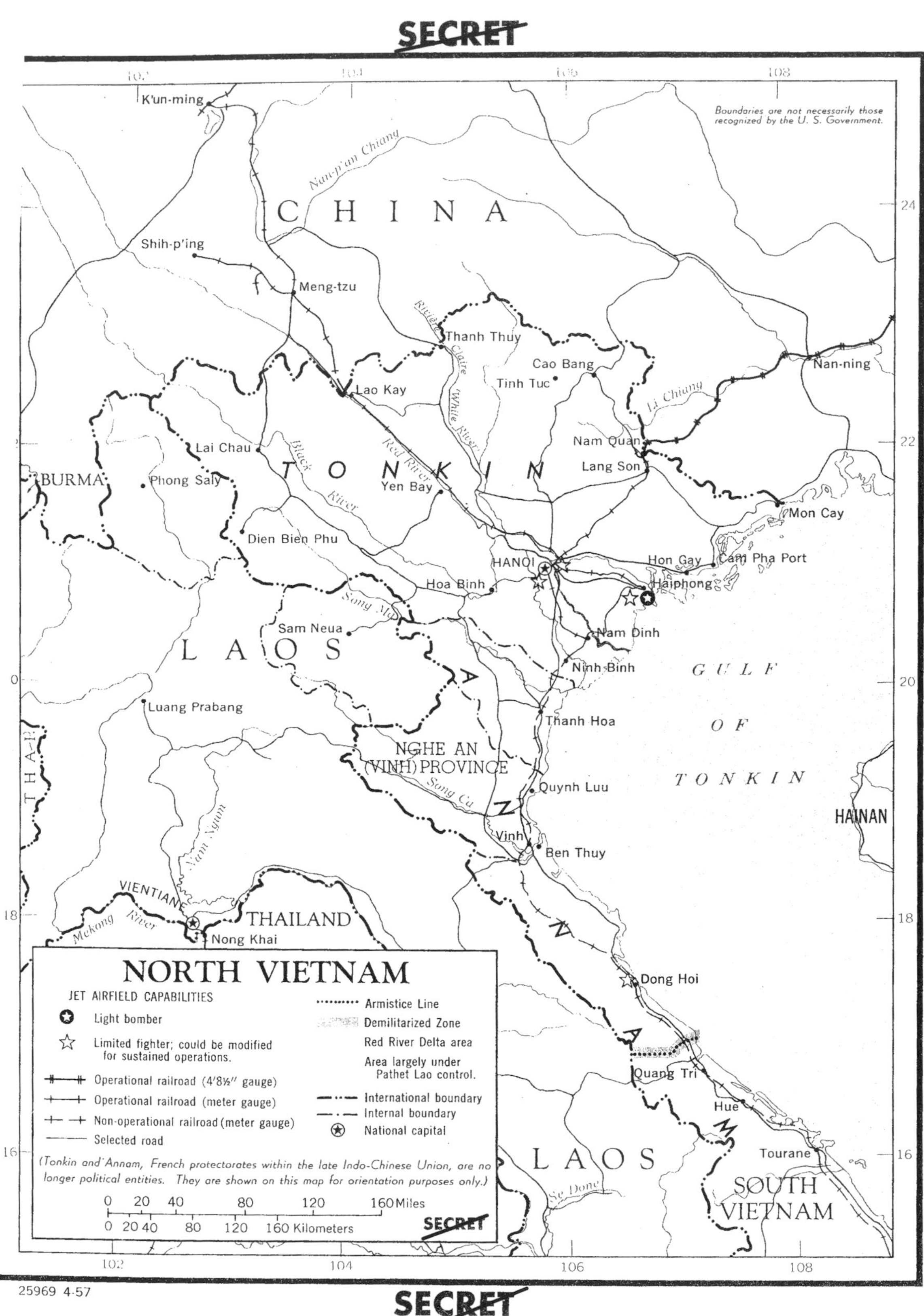

SECRET

NIE 63-59

Prospects for North and South Vietnam

26 May 1959

APPROVED FOR RELEASE
DATE: JAN 2005

NIE 63-59
26 May 1959

(b) (3)

SECRET

NATIONAL INTELLIGENCE ESTIMATE NUMBER 63-59

PROSPECTS FOR NORTH AND SOUTH VIETNAM

Submitted by the

DIRECTOR OF CENTRAL INTELLIGENCE

The following intelligence organizations participated in the preparation of this estimate: The Central Intelligence Agency and the intelligence organizations of the Departments of State, the Army, the Navy, the Air Force, and The Joint Staff.

Concurred in by the

UNITED STATES INTELLIGENCE BOARD

on 26 May 1959. Concurring were The Director of Intelligence and Research, Department of State; the Assistant Chief of Staff for Intelligence, Department of the Army; the Assistant Chief of Naval Operations for Intelligence, Department of the Navy; the Assistant Chief of Staff, Intelligence, USAF; and the Director for Intelligence, The Joint Staff. The Atomic Energy Commission Representative to the USIB, the Assistant to the Secretary of Defense, Special Operations, the Director of the National Security Agency, and the Assistant Director, Federal Bureau of Investigation, abstained, the subject being outside of their jurisdiction.

SECRET

Nº 351

PROSPECTS FOR NORTH AND SOUTH VIETNAM

THE PROBLEM

To analyze the current situations in North and South Vietnam and to estimate probable developments over the next two or three years.

CONCLUSIONS

1. The prospect of reunification of Communist North Vietnam (DRV) and western-oriented South Vietnam (GVN) remains remote. In the DRV the full range of Communist techniques is used to control the population, socialize the economy, impose austerity and direct investment to economic rehabilitation and development. The DRV maintains large armed forces. In South Vietnam, despite the authoritarian nature of the regime, there is far more freedom. Local resources and US aid are devoted to developing the armed forces, maintaining internal security, and supporting a relatively high standard of living, with lesser emphasis on economic development. (*Para. 9*)

2. In South Vietnam political stability depends heavily upon President Diem and his continued control of the instruments of power, including the army and police. Diem will almost certainly be President for many years. The regime will continue to repress potential opposition elements and depend increasingly upon the effectiveness of the Can Lao, the regime's political apparatus, which is run by Diem's brothers Nhu and Can. (*Paras. 11–14, 29–31*)

3. The capabilities of the GVN armed forces will improve given continued US materiel support and training. Continuance of the present level of training is threatened by a recent finding of the International Control Commission (ICC) that the US Temporary Equipment Recovery Mission (TERM) should end its activities by mid-1959. In any event, GVN forces will remain incapable of withstanding more than temporarily the larger DRV forces. The internal security forces will not be able to eradicate DRV supported guerrilla or subversive activity in the foreseeable future. Army units will probably have to be diverted to special internal security assignments. (*Paras. 15–17, 33–34*)

4. The GVN is preoccupied with the threat to national security and the maintenance of large military and security

(Continued...)

forces. It will probably remain unwilling to devote a significantly greater share of resources and attention to longer range economic development. Assuming continued US aid at about present levels, modest improvement in South Vietnam's economic position is likely. However, development will lag behind that in the North, and the GVN will continue to rely heavily upon US support to close the gap between its own resources and its requirements. (*Paras. 19–22, 32*)

5. There is little prospect of a significant improvement in relations between South Vietnam and Cambodia so long as the present leaders of the two countries remain in power. Relations with Laos will probably remain generally friendly. Continued suspicion that the French are intriguing in the area to recapture a position of major influence will probably prevent an improvement of Franco-GVN relations. (*Paras. 25–27, 35*)

6. Despite widespread popular discontent, the Government of the DRV is in full control of the country and no significant internal threat to the regime is likely. With large-scale Bloc aid, considerable progress has been made in rehabilitating and developing the economy with major emphasis on agriculture, raw materials and light industry. The regime will probably soon have laid the foundations for considerable economic expansion. (*Paras. 37–38, 42, 44*)

7. The DRV has no diplomatic relations with any country outside the Bloc and its foreign policy is subservient to the Bloc. We believe that it will continue its harassment of the GVN and of Laos, though a military invasion of either is unlikely. (*Paras. 46, 48–49*)

INTRODUCTION

8. The 1954 "provisional military demarcation line" dividing Vietnam at the 17th parallel has become a fixed boundary separating two entrenched and hostile governments, the Government of Vietnam (GVN) in the south and the Communist Democratic Republic of Vietnam (DRV) in the north. The all-Vietnam elections called for under the Geneva Agreements of 1954 have not been held, and the divergent conditions demanded by both governments preclude the holding of such elections. To date the GVN has been preoccupied with the threat to internal security posed by DRV subversion and guerrilla warfare and with the threat that the Communists' numerically superior armed forces will one day invade the south. However, there are no indications that the DRV is willing to assume the risks of US intervention and attempt to conquer South Vietnam by military invasion. Such a decision would probably be made by Peiping and Moscow rather than by Hanoi.

9. Meanwhile life on the two sides of the boundary is marked by an increasing disparity. The north is organized along strict Communist lines. The standard of living is low; life is grim and regimented; and the national effort is concentrated on building for the future. The DRV claims it has reduced its reliance on Bloc aid to about one-third of its national budget. Its large army is almost entirely financed domestically, except for arms delivered by the Bloc. Both its foreign aid and its Spartanly acquired domestic capital are devoted to restoring and increasing productive capacity in agriculture and industry. In the south the standard of living is much higher and there is far more freedom and gaiety. However, South Vietnam's economic development is still at an early and uncertain

stage, and basic economic growth has been slower than that of the north. The GVN still depends upon US aid to finance about two-thirds of its national budget, including most of the support for the armed forces.

I. MAJOR TRENDS IN SOUTH VIETNAM

A. Political Trends

10. President Diem continues to be the undisputed ruler of South Vietnam; all important and many minor decisions are referred to him. Although he professes to believe in representative government and democracy, Diem is convinced that the Vietnamese are not ready for such a political system and that he must rule with a firm hand, at least so long as national security is threatened. He also believes that the country cannot afford a political opposition which could obstruct or dilute the government's efforts to establish a strong and secure state. Although respected for his courage, dedication, and integrity, Diem has remained a somewhat austere and remote figure to most Vietnamese and has not generated widespread popular enthusiasm.

11. Diem's regime reflects his ideas. A facade of representative government is maintained, but the government is in fact essentially authoritarian. The legislative powers of the National Assembly are strictly circumscribed; the judiciary is undeveloped and subordinate to the executive; and the members of the executive branch are little more than the personal agents of Diem. No organized opposition, loyal or otherwise, is tolerated, and critics of the regime are often repressed. This highly centralized regime has provided resolute and stable direction to national affairs, but it has alienated many of the country's educated elite and has inhibited the growth of governmental and political institutions which could carry on in Diem's absence. The exercise of power and responsibility is limited to Diem and a very small circle mainly composed of his relatives, the most important being his brothers Nhu and Can. Nhu is particularly influential in international affairs and in matters relative to the southern half of the country. Can is more concerned with internal security and the northern half of the country.

12. An increasingly important and effective mechanism employed by the Diem regime to maintain control over the affairs of South Vietnam is the Can Lao, a semicovert political apparatus. Its structure, like that of the Kuomintang or a Communist party, is based on the cell and cadre system. The Can Lao is organized on a regional basis. The southern region is run by Nhu, an articulate, pragmatic activist. It is loosely organized and administered. The northern region is ruled with an iron hand by Can, a withdrawn eccentric feared by most Vietnamese, who seldom ventures from his headquarters in Hue. Although there is considerable rivalry and tension between the two brothers, there is no evidence that either is less than completely loyal to Diem. Diem apparently finds it advantageous to continue the division of authority as a means of controlling the ambitions of Nhu and Can.

13. Can Lao members are active at virtually every level of Vietnamese political life. Membership is becoming increasingly important for professional advancement. One-third of the cabinet members and over one-half of the National Assembly deputies are probably Can Lao men; the actual figure may be higher. The Can Lao controls the regime's mass political party, the National Revolutionary Movement. It apparently has its hand in most important business transactions in South Vietnam and is engaged in dubious business practices. Recently the Can Lao has stepped up its campaign to recruit key officers in the GVN military establishment, probably to establish a control mechanism within the only organization in South Vietnam strong enough to challenge the Diem regime.

14. Although the popular enthusiasm attendant on the achieving of independence and the end of colonial rule has subsided and some disillusion has arisen, particularly among the educated elite, there appears to be little identifiable public unrest. There is some dissatisfaction among military officers largely because of increasing Can Lao meddling in military affairs. The growth of dissatisfaction is inhibited by South Vietnam's continuing high standard of living relative to that of its neigh-

bors, the paternalistic attitude of Diem's government towards the people and the lack of any feasible alternative to the present regime.

D. Internal Security

15. The Communist apparatus in South Vietnam is essentially an operating arm of the North Vietnamese Communist Party (Lao Dong), but there have been recent indications of Chinese Communist participation in its operations. It is estimated that there are about 2,000 active guerrillas. They are in small units scattered along the Cambodian border, the south coast, and in the remote plateau region of the north. There are probably several thousand others, now inactive, who have access to arms and would participate in guerrilla activities if so ordered. The guerrillas are able to marshall a force of several hundred men for major hit-and-run raids, as they demonstrated twice during 1958. They have recently stepped up their intimidation campaign, assassinating local officials in remote areas, terrorizing local populations and disrupting government operations. The dissident armed remnants of the religious sects are largely broken up. About 2,000 such dissidents surrendered to the government during 1958 and the few hundred remaining in the jungle are probably now absorbed or dominated by the Communists.

16. The government has been able to restrict but not eliminate the subversive and espionage activities of clandestine Communist agents. It is probable that Communists have penetrated some local army and security units, village councils, and local branches of the government. There is no evidence, however, that such penetration is sufficient to hamper government operations seriously or that it extends to the higher echelons of the government. There is probably a widespread Communist underground in the urban areas, especially Saigon, and Communist intelligence of GVN plans and activities is probably good. Communist agents are also stimulating unrest among the tribal minorities in the central highlands, a relatively inaccessible and sparsely populated area which the government is attempting to settle and develop, primarily for security reasons.

17. South Vietnam's 136,000-man army,[1] supported by the Civil Guard, the Self-Defense Corps and the police services, is capable of maintaining effective internal security except in the most remote jungle and mountain areas. Until mid-1957, the army had the primary responsibility for internal security, and had considerable success. By that time major responsibility for internal security had been given to the provincial Civil Guard (48,000) and the village Self-Defense Corps (47,000). These organizations have proven to be inadequately trained and equipped for the job, and units from the armed forces have continued to be called in to meet special situations. The size and scattered distribution of the Civil Guard and Self-Defense Corps add to the problems of training and equipping them and of coordinating their activities. In some regions, they are infiltrated by Communists. The police services, which include the 7,500-man Vietnamese Bureau of Investigation and 10,500-man police force stationed in the main cities, have had considerable success in tracking down subversives and terrorists and are developing into efficient organizations.

C. Economic Trends in South Vietnam

18. South Vietnam has made only limited progress toward basic long-term economic development in the five years since independence. US aid during that period, excluding military equipment and training, has totaled over one billion dollars. The bulk of this aid has been provided to finance imports of commodities which have been sold domestically. Most of the local currency accruing to the government has been used to support the armed forces and to finance the resettlement of over 700,000 refugees from the north. The GVN meets, out of its own limited resources, about one-third of the total civilian-military budget, including about 15 percent of the military budget. The GVN does not have the necessary additional financial resources to undertake a significant economic development program.

---

[1] See Military Annex.

19. Basic economic development is also inhibited by the GVN's preoccupation with South Vietnam's problems of internal security and military preparedness. It continues to regard programs for long-range economic growth as of lower priority than the building of defense strength. Moreover, for political reasons, it is reluctant to take any measures which might reduce the country's relatively high standard of living. Consequently, the GVN devotes only a small part of available resources to long-range economic development. Diem is hopeful, however, that resources for development will be provided from external sources, principally the US and the Japanese reparations settlement. There is little prospect for private foreign investment, primarily because of the unsettled security situation, uncertainty regarding GVN economic policy, and other factors creating an unattractive economic climate.

20. Another aspect of the economic situation has political as well as economic ramifications. A considerable amount of US aid is in the form of grants of dollars which are used to import commodities. This practice has tended to inhibit the development of local consumer goods industries, although steps are now being taken to encourage domestic industries. It has supported a standard of living higher than the country could maintain on its own resources. A significant cutback in the standard of living would probably create serious political problems for the government. The present slow pace of economic development holds little promise that the gap between the present living standard and the capacity of the economy will be closed in the foreseeable future.

21. Nevertheless, South Vietnam is making some economic progress. The heavily damaged transportation network is being repaired. After an initial period of frustration and delay, considerable progress is being made in a modest agrarian reform program. In addition, almost 100,000 persons from crowded urban and coastal areas have been relocated on land development projects in the Mekong delta area and in the sparsely populated central highlands. The economic viability of these last mentioned projects has not yet been proved. The resettlement of refugees from the north is about completed. Rice production is approaching 1939 levels, but increased domestic consumption has kept rice exports far below prewar levels. Rubber has surpassed 1939 levels and has replaced rice as the nation's major export.

22. Some constructive long-range measures are being taken. The GVN is attempting to increase internal revenues by strengthening its tax system and is trying to restrict domestic consumption and total imports to about present amounts. If the main part of the defense burden is carried by the US, it is probable that over the next few years the steps taken and planned by the GVN will enable domestic production to expand and thus reduce the balance of payments deficit on goods and services, which was about $190 million in 1958. The planned development of manufacturing would make possible over the next five years the lowering of import requirements by about $25 million a year. In the same period the trade gap should narrow by another $30 to $40 million if land development and rice productivity programs produce the planned results. Even if these results are achieved, however, South Vietnam will still have large foreign trade and internal budget deficits and continue to depend upon US aid.

D. South Vietnam's Foreign Relations

23. South Vietnam's foreign policy is based upon fear of and rigid opposition to communism, and upon a conscious dependence on the US as its major source of assistance and protection and as its principal international sponsor. The GVN leaders desire to maintain and to assert their nation's independence, which they believe to be endangered most directly by the activities and military strength of North Vietnam. They are also concerned over what they consider the weakness and pro-Chinese Communist orientation of Cambodia, and the machinations of the French.

24. *DRV:* In responding to persistent DRV bids to "regularize" relations, GVN policy is to impose conditions it is sure will be unacceptable. By this means the GVN seeks to improve its propaganda position, while main-

taining intact its opposition to closer contact with the DRV. Although the GVN may agree to limited discussions with DRV representatives, such as the proposed negotiation regarding administrative problems of the Demilitarized Zone, it is not likely to enter into any broader discussions (whether or not held under the auspices of the International Control Commission (ICC)), and even less likely to agree to the establishment of regular official contacts with the north.

25. *Cambodia:* Relations between the GVN and Cambodia have become acutely strained. Diem is convinced that Cambodia's Prince Sihanouk is untrustworthy and is tolerating, if not supporting, anti-GVN operations on the Cambodian border area by both Communists and non-Communists. The GVN leaders have little confidence in the ability of Cambodia to resist Communist pressures and they are convinced that Cambodia's recent recognition of Communist China shows that there is little will to resist. The GVN is fearful of a Communist takeover in Cambodia which would provide a base for subversive operations or attack. GVN leaders were closely involved in recent anti-Sihanouk plots, and probably will continue activities designed to stir up anti-Sihanouk feeling both inside and outside of Cambodia and to lead to Sihanouk's downfall.

26. *Laos:* South Vietnam's relations with Laos are on a generally friendly basis, especially since the Lao Government has indicated greater awareness of the Communist threat and has become more outspokenly pro-West in its foreign policy statements. The GVN has undertaken to advise the Lao Government on an anti-Communist program, has offered to train some Lao troops, and in other ways is seeking to stiffen the anti-Communist position of the Lao Government. However, GVN worries have been only partially relieved by recent Lao Government measures to check Lao Communist political activity; the GVN continues to feel considerable disquiet because of North Vietnamese pressures along the DRV-Laos border.

27. *France:* The GVN leaders continue to suspect the French of intriguing to overthrow the Diem government and to increase their influence in South Vietnam. French businessmen and officials in South Vietnam are carefully watched and the scope of French commercial, cultural, and educational activities is restricted. The GVN leaders also believe that the French are at least partially to blame for Cambodia's apparent drift towards Communist China and for the failure of recent anti-Sihanouk plots. Although many South Vietnamese leaders have a cultural affinity for France, GVN-French relations are likely to remain cool.

28. *US:* Although we do not expect the present close GVN-US relationship to be undermined, the GVN's sensitivity to its dependence on the US is likely to grow and to complicate our dealings with it. Nhu and some other leaders have expressed resentment at what they consider US attempts to dictate to them and to restrict their freedom of action at home and abroad. Diem has indicated that South Vietnam expects the maintenance of large US aid and special consideration from the US as a reward for its steadfast support. Failure to receive such special consideration could lead Diem to assume a stance of greater independence *vis-a-vis* the US. However, in light of Diem's strong aversion to the French and in the absence of any acceptable alternative source of support, he will almost certainly avoid jeopardizing basic US-South Vietnamese ties during the period of this estimate.

E. Outlook for South Vietnam

29. The prospects for continued political stability in South Vietnam depend heavily upon President Diem and his ability to maintain firm control of the army and police. The regime's efforts to assure internal security and its belief that an authoritarian government is necessary to handle the country's problems will result in a continued repression of potential opposition elements. This policy of repression will inhibit the growth of popularity of the regime, and we believe that dissatisfaction will grow, particularly among those who are politically conscious. The power and unscrupulousness of the Can Lao, if unchecked, will probably prejudice the prestige of the gov-

ernment and of Diem himself. However, the controls available to the government, including its apparatus the Can Lao, will probably enable it to prevent dissatisfaction in the country from erupting into a serious threat to the regime at least during the next few years.

30. It seems almost certain that if Diem, now 58, remains alive and active, he will continue as President for many years to come. The National Assemly elections will probably be held in the fall of 1959, and elections for President and Vice President in 1961, as scheduled. Neither election is likely to produce any significant change. Diem will probably remain unreceptive to proposals to widen participation in the top councils of government.

31. In the event of Diem's death, Vice President Nguyen Ngoc Tho would probably assume the presidency; real political power, however, would probably remain in the hands of the Ngo family, particularly Can and Nhu. We believe that the strength of family ties and the advantages of cooperation would prevent an open struggle between Nhu and Can. Neither of these two men shares Diem's paternalistic and humanistic outlook to any great extent, and with either or both of them in positions of top power the GVN's reliance upon authoritarian methods would probably be accentuated. If a struggle for power were to develop between Can and Nhu a period of political instability would follow. The support of the army would probably be the decisive factor. Although the army might split badly, the major part of it would probably back Nhu.

32. If armed forces of the present size are maintained, there is little likelihood of any substantial reduction in the need for US aid over the next few years. Assuming continued US aid at about present levels, modest improvement in South Vietnam's basic economic position is likely. However, Diem will probably not be willing to devote a significantly greater share of resources to long-range economic development. Diem will continue to oppose any significant cutback in the standard of living, largely for political reasons. Economic development will lag behind that in the north, and the GVN will continue to rely heavily upon US support to close the gap between its own resources and its requirements.

33. The capabilities of the armed forces will improve, given continued US materiel support and training. Training activities are carried out by both MAAG and the US Temporary Equipment Recovery Mission (TERM), which are of about equal size. The continuance of TERM is threatened by a recent finding of the ICC that TERM should end its activity by mid-1959. Developments in Laos, such as difficulties with the former Pathet Lao troops or disagreements as to the role of the US military mission in Laos, could bring the Geneva Accords and the ICC into prominence and have a prejudicial effect on the maintenance of TERM. Any significant reduction in the number of US military instructors would have an adverse effect on the GVN armed forces.

34. In any event, the GVN forces will not become a match for the much-larger North Vietnamese forces within the period of this estimate. In a war between the two parts of Vietnam, the GVN forces would be capable only of conducting a delaying action. However, barring a more widespread war in the Far East, we do not believe that relative capabilities of the two armed forces are likely to be tested over the next two or three years at least. The Communist armed action against the GVN will probably continue to be limited to irregular forces and unconventional warfare.

35. The GVN will not be able to eradicate Communist guerrilla or subversive activity in the foreseeable future. Indeed the DRV is capable of stepping up such activity in the south, and will probably do so from time to time, such as during the national election campaign. The Self-Defense Corps and Civil Guard will probably increase gradually in effectiveness, but not to the point of being capable of efficiently assuming full responsibility for internal security. From time to time army units, occasionally up to regimental size, will probably have to be diverted from their training programs for special internal security assignments. This might disrupt training schedules, but it will have the ad-

vantage of keeping the military in close touch with the most immediate threat to the security of South Vietnam—Communist infiltration, subversion, and guerrilla warfare.

36. There is little prospect of a significant improvement of relations between South Vietnam and Cambodia so long as the present leaders of the two countries remain in power. Relations between the two are now so delicate that a break could occur at any time. Even if both sides should decide to attempt to reduce tensions and improve relations, as is suggested by recent reports, mutual suspicion and basic antagonism are so great that any trivial incident could lead to a renewal of recrimination and hostile acts.

II. MAJOR TRENDS IN NORTH VIETNAM

A. Political

37. The Communist regime in North Vietnam has had little success in generating public enthusiasm. The regime retains some prestige from having won military victories over the French and having attained independence. However, there is dissatisfaction among the tribal minorities, the several hundred thousand Catholics, the intellectuals, and the peasant population. They resent their drab and harried existence and the regime's repressive controls. Although widespread, this dissatisfaction is unorganized and not channeled into any known resistance movement. The population is, in general, passive and apathetic in the face of the regime's widespread and effective system of controls. Public unrest or dissatisfaction, while not forcing the regime to alter its basic programs, has undoubtedly been a factor influencing the regime's timetable, particularly in the socialization of agriculture.

38. The development of significant internal opposition to the regime is unlikely. Although Catholic and tribal minorities will probably continue to be centers of disaffection, their ability to undertake organized resistance is very limited at present and is likely to decline as the regime further perfects its controls. Disaffection among the peasantry will probably continue to trouble the regime but is unlikely to prevent the regime from carrying out its basic program.

39. The leaders of the party and government are all veteran Communists with considerable experience both as revolutionaries and as administrators. There is no firm evidence of any serious antagonism between cliques or persons within the leadership group. Ho Chi Minh as President of the government and Secretary General of the Lao Dong (Communist Party) is unchallenged as top man. Ho is apparently in good health, and makes many public appearances. Despite the general public dissatisfaction with life in North Vietnam, Ho apparently continues to enjoy considerable personal popularity.

40. There is no clear successor to Ho Chi Minh. If Ho should die, control would probably initially be exercised by some form of collective leadership. The three strongest leaders in the second echelon are Premier Pham Van Dong, Vice Premier Truong Chinh and party secretary Le Duan. The latter two have effective apparatus of their own within the party, and one of them would probably rise eventually to the top of the hierarchy. General Vo Nguyen Giap, military hero of the revolution, appears to have little political strength, but as Commander-in-Chief of the armed forces he would probably have considerable influence in the selection of a successor to Ho. A change in the top leadership would almost certainly not result in any change in the nature of the regime or its orientation.

B. Economic

41. North Vietnam's economic planning appears to be generally realistic and well adapted to the economic potential of the country. In contrast to South Vietnam, the emphasis is on present sacrifice for promised future benefits, and the standard of living is being kept very low in order to squeeze out capital for investment. In contrast to both the USSR and Communist China, the Hanoi leaders seem to have begun their planning with full attention to the basic importance of agriculture in their economy. As a result they are emphasizing investment in irrigation and the production of fertilizer and agricultural implements and the processing of agricultural crops. By controlling consumption

and increasing production, North Vietnam has ended its rice imports and has even exported small amounts. Plans for industrialization tend to emphasize mining, light industry, and the production of consumer goods.

42. The period from the signing of the Geneva Agreements in 1954 through 1957 was devoted to rehabilitation of the prewar economic plant. At the end of this period the First Three-Year Plan (1958–1960) was introduced. In the first year of the plan (1958) production was already well above prewar (1939) levels in electric power, cotton cloth, and a number of food-crops, including rice, but the output of coal had recovered only about 60 percent.[2] The 1960 production goals[3] for industry do not appear unattainable, but the agricultural goals are much more ambitious and less likely to be achieved. In fact the output of grains has tended to level off during the past three years, and a major increase in production must be achieved if orderly economic progress is to be continued. In light of the relatively large amount of capital and labor currently being devoted to agriculture, we believe that the DRV will achieve adequate success and that by the end of 1960 it will have established a firm base for considerable economic expansion.

[2] The principal source for economic data on North Vietnam is the DRV. The relatively small amount of information from other sources tends in most cases to support the official DRV claims. Comparisons of present figures with prewar figures, however, are exaggerated in favor of the former, because prewar statistics omitted an unknown amount of locally produced and consumed goods.

[3] See Charts A and B.

43. Hanoi is following Peiping's pattern of socialization fairly closely. By early 1959, about half the peasant households of North Vietnam had been organized into labor-exchange teams and about five percent had moved beyond this stage into cooperatives. This is about parallel with the development in Communist China in 1952. The Three-Year Plan requires that by the end of 1960 all peasants be organized into cooperatives of at least an elementary form. This speedup in agricultural socialization will be resented by the peasantry and is likely to be met with at least some passive resistance, but the controls available to the party and government will probably enable the goal to be met. Despite the regime's statements that they do not intend to institute Chinese-style communes now, their general adherence to the Chinese pattern as well as some of their recent theoretical writings indicate that they may do so in a few years. The general trend of North Vietnam's economic development is toward closer economic integration with Communist China, producing food, raw materials, and consumer goods and exchanging with China for the products of heavy industry.

44. Since 1954 the economy of North Vietnam has been bolstered by over $500 million worth of aid from the rest of the Bloc. About 70 percent of this has come as outright grants, and of the total, roughly 55 percent has come from Communist China, 30 percent from the USSR, and the rest from the Satellites. Annually this aid has amounted to more than one-third of the total budget, and it has consisted mainly of capital equipment, raw materials for light industry, and the services of advisors and technicians. Whatever military

CHART A

NORTH VIETNAM: OUTPUT OF SELECTED AGRICULTURAL PRODUCTS (FROM DRV SOURCES)

In thousands of metric tons

	1939	1955	1956	1957	1958	1959 (Annual Plan)	1960 (Three-Year Plan Goal)
Rice	2,400	3,600	4,132	3,950	4,576.9	6,200	7,600
Maize	140	187	259	197	197	N.A.	280
Potatoes	N.A.	534	1,062	540	540	N.A.	910
Cotton	1	N.A.	6	6	6	7	9
Sugar Cane	109	N.A.	168	333	492	674	623

CHART B

NORTH VIETNAM: OUTPUT OF SELECTED INDUSTRIAL PRODUCTS (FROM DRV SOURCES)

	Unit	1939	1955	1956	1957	1958	1959 (Annual Plan)	1960 (Three-Year Plan Goal)
Electric Power	Million kwh	120	53	94	123.5	162.3	204.3	271
Coal	Thousand metric tons	2,615	460	1,214	1,088	1,500	2,100	2,700
Cement	Thousand metric tons	305	8.5	197	165	302	385	450
Phosphate	Thousand metric tons	35.7	8.4	34.1	22.5	32.1	52.3	65.0
Chromite	Thousand metric tons	2.9 (1943)	Nil	1.2	3.7	5.7	N.A.	32.0

aid has been received has been in addition to these economic aid figures. Economic aid at about the present levels will be needed for the next few years and will almost certainly be forthcoming. More than three-quarters of North Vietnam's foreign trade is with the Bloc, Communist China being the chief trading partner.

45. It is certain that military aid is being received from the rest of the Bloc in violation of the Geneva Agreements, but precise information on types and amounts is not available. Some Bloc military aid will almost certainly continue to arrive each year, and, in the event of large-scale hostilities, the North Vietnamese would almost certainly be supplied by the Bloc with logistical support as needed.

C. Foreign Relations

46. *Sino-Soviet Bloc:* The DRV relies heavily upon Communist China for support and guidance, but there is considerable Soviet influence within the top ranks of the Vietnamese Communist Party and Soviet advisors are active in the DRV's mining and industrial programs. There is no evidence of any significant Sino-Soviet competition for influence in the DRV. On the contrary, the entire Bloc seems to be contributing aid and advice in the areas most appropriate to the capabilities of the contributing nations.

47. *Non-Communist Countries:* No non-Communist nation has as yet formally recognized the DRV. However, the UK, India, and Indonesia maintain consulates and the French have a small mission in Hanoi. The few officials who staff the Western missions have been subjected to petty harassment, the scope of their activity is very limited, and in May 1958 their right to transmit radio messages was rescinded. The DRV has made efforts to expand its contacts abroad and has had some success particularly through the trips of Ho to India and Indonesia.

48. *GVN:* Hanoi appears to have abandoned for the present its hopes of unifying all Vietnam under a Communist regime by overt means. Although it has the military capability to overrun all the states of former Indochina against indigenous resistance,[4] the DRV probably is convinced that this would mean war with the US. In any case, the ultimate decision for such a venture almost certainly rests with Moscow and Peiping. For the next few years, at least, the DRV is likely to continue to rely on propaganda, subversion, and paramilitary action to promote its aims in South Vietnam.

49. *Laos:* The DRV is taking an increasingly aggressive stand toward Laos. It is applying pressure on the Lao Government by military probing of the ill-defined border areas, by de-

[4] See Military Annex.

mands for reconvening the ICC in Laos, and by a threatening propaganda barrage in the DRV press and over Radio Hanoi. Inside Laos, the DRV has a major asset in the Neo Lao Hak Zat (NLHZ), the legal political party which replaced the Communist dominated guerrilla army, the Pathet Lao. The DRV gives basic policy direction to the NLHZ and almost certainly continues to support and direct a Communist underground apparatus in Laos and a guerrilla force on the DRV side of the border. If the Lao Government makes substantial inroads against the NLHZ, the DRV may direct the Lao Communists to return to guerrilla tactics. We think it very unlikely, however, that within the period of this estimate the DRV or its Sino-Soviet mentors will attempt to seize Laos by an overt DRV military invasion.

50. *Cambodia:* Relations with Cambodia have been amicable, especially since Sihanouk's recognition of Communist China in June of 1958. There are indications that Peiping's embassy in Phnom Penh is providing some guidance and advice to DRV agents in Cambodia, and the DRV news representative in Cambodia promotes Lao Dong interests and provides a legal address for communications. This base facilitates DRV subversive work among the approximately 400,000 Vietnamese residents in Cambodia. The jungle areas of eastern Cambodia have been useful as a primary route for Communist cadres dispatched to South Vietnam and have served as a base and sanctuary for guerrilla penetrations by Vietnamese dissidents (nearly all under the guidance of the DRV) into South Vietnam.

51. *Thailand:* The Government of Thailand has been a target of abuse by the DRV propagandists, in line with general Communist policy. A major issue among Thailand and North and South Vietnam is the 90,000 Vietnamese community in Thailand. About 50,000 of these are North Vietnamese refugees from the Indochina War, most of whom tend to be sympathetic to the Hanoi regime. Thailand is anxious to remove this potentially subversive group from the area of its northeastern frontier and seems willing to negotiate indirectly (through the Red Cross societies) with the DRV to this end. However, it is highly improbable that Thailand would agree to direct negotiations with the DRV on this or any other issue.

MILITARY ANNEX

SOUTH VIETNAM

ARMY: 136,000 regulars
48,000 Civil Guard
47,000 Self-Defense Corps

NAVY: 4,750 personnel (including 1,430 marines)
5 subchasers (PC)
2 small subchasers (SC)
3 old coastal minesweepers (MEC(O))
11 landing ships (LSM, LSSL, LSIL)
7 landing craft (LCU)
1 small cargo ship (AKL)
23 service craft

AIR FORCE: 4,600 personnel (including 175 pilots)
151 piston-engined aircraft

NORTH VIETNAM

ARMY: 270,000 regulars
35,000 provincial forces
75,000 militia

NAVY: 2,000 personnel (est.)
30 wooden-hulled patrol craft (est.)

AIR FORCE: No reliable figures available—appears to be in incipient stage of organization.

ANNEX

SOUTH VIETNAM

52. The South Vietnamese Army has been relieved of many of its police and internal security duties although it is still called upon for special anti-Communist operations. With more time available for training and reorganization, the army's capabilities for regular combat have been improved. A large number of its officers and NCO's have had considerable combat experience. There have been reports of dissatisfaction in the armed services, particularly among higher officers, as a result of the increasing influence of the Can Lao in military affairs and the rapid rise of certain younger officers with greater political than military talents. However, such dissatisfaction is probably not widespread nor of serious proportions. There has been some Communist infiltration of the lower ranks, and the conscription program, which has created certain problems of discipline and morale, will probably increase the opportunities for Communist subversion.

53. The South Vietnamese Air Force is a small, untried force, currently in a training phase and possessing only a limited military capability. Its primary military value lies in its capability to support ground forces. South Vietnam has 34 airfields with runways of over 2,000 feet, including two capable of supporting limited operations by jet medium bombers, and two others capable of supporting jet light bomber and precentury jet fighter operations. The South Vietnamese Air Force is prohibited from having jets by the terms of the Geneva Agreements.

54. The South Vietnamese Navy is composed of obsolescent ships and maintenance of equipment is deficient by US Navy standards. On the other hand, training has improved over the past several years and prospects are good for the continued improvement of training and of over-all capabilities. The South Vietnamese Navy is considerably larger than the naval forces of North Vietnam and training is superior. The river forces of the navy are capable of supporting amphibious operations of ground forces against dissidents. They are experienced in this type of warfare and have been quite successful.

NORTH VIETNAM

55. The North Vietnamese Army is the largest and most powerful military force in Southeast Asia and it has the capability to overrun all of former Indochina if opposed only by existing indigenous forces. Hanoi has recently begun to build up its trained reserve forces and to regularize the flow of manpower to its armed forces through national conscription. We believe that, as the trained reserve forces are increased in size and potential, the size of the regular army will gradually be reduced. This will add manpower to the labor force and make good "peace" propaganda.

56. The North Vietnamese Navy is a small force with only local capabilities. Recent evidence, including the sighting of air force uniforms, suggests that an air force has also been formed, but we know nothing of its combat capabilities, if any.

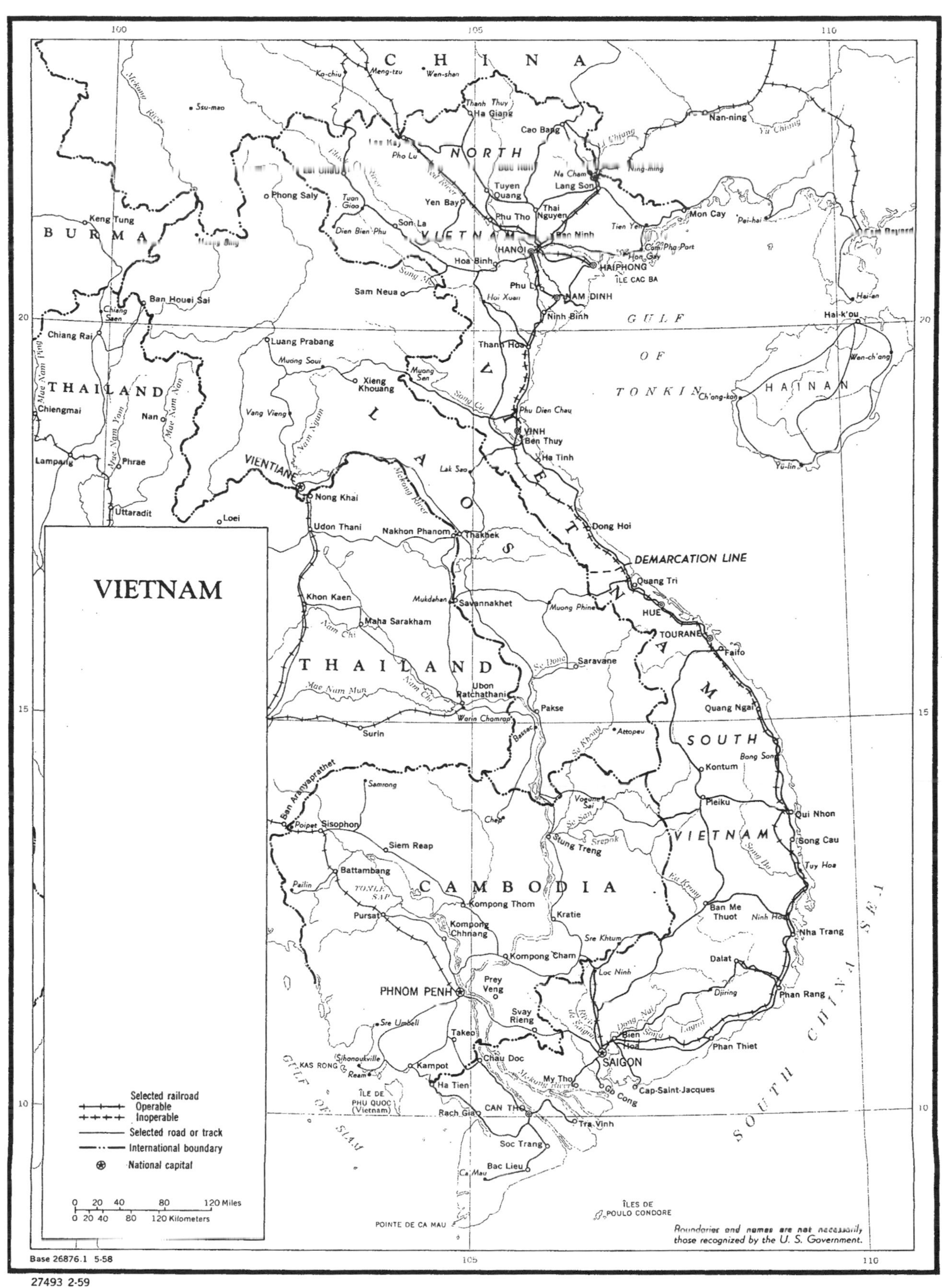
VIETNAM
C H I N A
B U R M A
T H A I L A N D
L A O S
NORTH VIETNAM
SOUTH VIETNAM
C A M B O D I A
H A I N A N
GULF OF TONKIN
SOUTH CHINA SEA
GULF OF SIAM
DEMARCATION LINE
HANOI
HAIPHONG
NAM DINH
VINH
HUE
TOURANE
SAIGON
PHNOM PENH
VIENTIANE
Luang Prabang
Dong Hoi
Quang Tri
Quang Ngai
Qui Nhon
Nha Trang
Dalat
Phan Rang
Phan Thiet
Ban Me Thuot
Pleiku
Kontum
Savannakhet
Thakhek
Pakse
Saravane
Kratie
Kompong Cham
Kompong Thom
Siem Reap
Battambang
Sisophon
Kampot
Ha Tien
Chau Doc
My Tho
Can Tho
Rach Gia
Soc Trang
Bac Lieu
Tra Vinh
Cap-Saint-Jacques
Nong Khai
Udon Thani
Khon Kaen
Nakhon Phanom
Ubon Ratchathani
Chiang Rai
Chiengmai
Nan-ning
Hai-k'ou
Selected railroad
Operable
Inoperable
Selected road or track
International boundary
National capital
0 20 40 80 120 Miles
0 20 40 80 120 Kilometers
Boundaries and names are not necessarily those recognized by the U. S. Government.
Base 26876.1 5-58
27493 2-59

SNIE 63.1-60

Short-Term Trends in South Vietnam

23 August 1960

SPECIAL

NATIONAL INTELLIGENCE ESTIMATE

NUMBER 63.1-60

SHORT-TERM TRENDS IN SOUTH VIETNAM

Submitted by the

DIRECTOR OF CENTRAL INTELLIGENCE

The following intelligence organizations participated in the preparation of this estimate: The Central Intelligence Agency and the intelligence organizations of the Departments of State, the Army, the Navy, the Air Force, and The Joint Staff.

Concurred in by the

UNITED STATES INTELLIGENCE BOARD

on 23 August 1960. Concurring were the Director of Intelligence and Research, Department of State; the Assistant Chief of Staff for Intelligence, Department of the Army; the Assistant Chief of Naval Operations (Intelligence), Department of the Navy; the Assistant Chief of Staff, Intelligence, USAF; the Director for Intelligence, Joint Staff; the Assistant to the Secretary of Defense, Special Operations; and the Director of the National Security Agency. The Atomic Energy Commission Representative to the USIB, and the Assistant Director, Federal Bureau of Investigation, abstained, the subject being outside of their jurisdiction.

SECRET

SHORT-TERM TRENDS IN SOUTH VIETNAM

THE PROBLEM

To assess political and security problems and probable trends in South Vietnam over the next year or so.

CONCLUSIONS

1. Developments within South Vietnam over the past six months indicate a trend adverse to the stability and effectiveness of President Diem's government. Criticism of Diem's leadership within urban groups and government circles has been mounting. More immediately important, the Communist Viet Cong, with support and guidance from Hanoi, has markedly increased subversive operations, terrorist activities, and guerrilla warfare. (*Paras. 4–13*)

2. Although Diem's personal position and that of his government are probably not now in danger, the marked deterioration since January of this year is disturbing. These adverse trends are not irreversible, but if they remain unchecked, they will almost certainly in time cause the collapse of Diem's regime. We do not anticipate that this will occur within the period of this estimate. However, if Diem is not able to alter present trends and the situation deteriorates substantially, it is possible during the period of this estimate that the government will lose control over much of the countryside and a political crisis will ensue. (*Para. 17*)

DISCUSSION

3. Since the beginning of 1960, there has been a general decline in the political and security situations in South Vietnam. The Communist Viet Cong[1] has stepped up terrorist activities and guerrilla warfare. At the same time, grievances against the government, which have long been accumulating, have become increasingly urgent and articulate.

The Political Situation

4. Discontent with the Diem government has been prevalent for some time among intellectuals and elite circles and, to a lesser extent, in labor and urban business groups. Criticism by these elements focusses on Ngo family rule, especially the roles of the President's brother, Ngo Dinh Nhu, and Madame Nhu; the

[1] The Viet Cong insurgents represent the paramilitary arm of the North Vietnam Communist Party. The Viet Cong is estimated to have in South Vietnam between 3,000 and 5,000 regular armed cadres and about 3,000 irregulars organized as underground troops. Main areas of Viet Cong activity lie south and west of Saigon and along the Cambodian border. North Vietnam furnishes guidance, personnel reinforcements, and logistical support to the insurgents.

pervasive influence of the Can Lao,[2] the semi-clandestine apparatus of the regime; Diem's virtual one-man rule; and the growing evidence of corruption in high places. In late April, 18 prominent Vietnamese publicly petitioned Diem to "liberalize the regime, expand democracy, grant minimum civil rights, (and) recognize the opposition in order to let the people speak without fear." This unprecedented public attack on Diem by a non-Communist group may embolden other urban elements to become more vocal.

5. A new and even more important element in the political situation is the growing criticism of Diem's leadership within government circles, including the official bureaucracy and military; this criticism has become more intense than at any time since 1956. Since the early part of this year, Vice President Tho, other members of the cabinet, and middle echelon officials have made known their serious concern over Diem's handling of the internal security problem and have privately criticized the power and influence exerted by Nhu and his entourage. In addition, there is considerable uneasiness concerning the operations and activities of the Can Lao organization.

6. Although most of the Vietnamese peasants are politically apathetic, they also have their grievances against the government. These include the ineptitude and arrogance of many local and provincial officials, the lack of effective protection from Viet Cong demands in many parts of the country, the harshness with which many peasants have been forced to contribute their labor to government programs, and the unsettling economic and social effects of the agroville (government-sponsored settlements) program. As a consequence, Diem's government is lacking in positive support among the people in the countryside.

7. The members of Diem's immediate entourage have attempted, with some success, to keep him insulated from unpleasant developments and trends. However, he has become concerned over the deteriorating internal security situation, although he still tends to discount the amount of discontent both in the countryside and among urban elements. Although he has taken some steps to meet the internal security problem, he tends to view it almost entirely in military terms. He believes that increased military activity against the Viet Cong, along with an expansion of the agroville program, will greatly improve internal security. He has been openly contemptuous of the views of oppositionists in Saigon and regards them as uninformed and dupes of the Communists. Diem also has failed to take any major steps against corruption and arbitrary conduct on the part of the Can Lao organization.

The Security Situation

8. Aggravating many of the government's problems is the active campaign of the Viet Cong to discredit Diem and weaken the government's authority through political subversion as well as paramilitary action. The Viet Cong has had some success in exploiting discontented intellectuals, sowing disaffection among the populace, and disrupting the effective administration of government. This campaign has been well organized and skillfully executed, with the result that Diem has been confronted not merely with the armed threat of guerrilla operations but with a comprehensive subversive program.

9. Between mid-1957 and the end of 1959, the Viet Cong conducted a steady but low key campaign of propaganda, subversion, and terrorism in the South Vietnamese countryside. Since January, there has been a significant increase in the number and size of Viet Cong attacks in several areas, particularly in the southwest. Civilian travel on public roads more than 15 miles outside Saigon has become hazardous. Attacking units,

[2] The Can Lao organization is based on the cell and cadre system, similar to that of the Kuomintang or a Communist party. It is controlled by Diem's brothers, Nhu and Can. Can Lao members are active at virtually every level of Vietnamese political life. One-third of the cabinet members and over half of the National Assembly deputies probably belong to the Can Lao. The organization also controls the regime's mass political party, the National Revolutionary Movement. It is deeply involved in Vietnamese business affairs and has a program to recruit key officers in the Vietnamese military establishment.

estimated to number at times in the hundreds, have operated over wider areas than at any time since 1954 and have assaulted Vietnamese Army installations. Since the beginning of the rainy season in April and the launching of Vietnamese Army counteroperations, Viet Cong operations have abated somewhat but terrorist activity, such as assassination and kidnapping of provincial officials and government sympathizers, has continued at high levels.[3] Support from North Vietnam appears to have increased over the past several months. In particular, senior cadres and military supplies such as communications equipment are believed to be moving south through Laos and Cambodia and by junk along the eastern coastline.

10. The upsurge in Viet Cong activity, accompanied by a stepped up propaganda campaign from Hanoi, probably reflects a recent Communist decision to increase pressures on the South Vietnamese Government. The indications of increasing dissatisfaction with the Diem government have probably encouraged the Hanoi regime, supported and guided by the Chinese Communists, to take stronger action at this time. The Chinese Communists probably regard South Vietnam as a promising area for weakening the US position in Southeast Asia at little cost or risk. From the Chinese point of view, many favorable elements are present: a sizable and effective indigenous guerrilla apparatus responsive to Communist control; a government lacking in positive support from its people; and the widely recognized political commitment the US has in South Vietnam.

11. In countering the Viet Cong challenge, Diem faces many of the same problems which confronted the French during the Indo-China War. Viet Cong guerrilla units have succeeded in exploiting their natural advantages of surprise, mobility, and initiative. In many of their areas of operations, they have exploited the tendency of the largely passive population to accommodate to their presence and thereby avoid reprisals. In some areas of operations, however, they have obtained the active cooperation of the local population.

12. In contrast to the French strategy in the Indo-China War, however, the Vietnamese Government is attempting not only to control the populated areas and main lines of communications but also to group the peasantry into more defensible units through its agroville program. Special measures in organization and training have been implemented enabling the army to react more quickly and effectively against guerrilla hit-and-run tactics. The civil guard is forming "commando" units and new stress is being placed on the building of a youth corps, 10,000 strong, for patrol and reconnaissance purposes in the villages and towns.

13. The most effective government measure against the Viet Cong, however, remains the active participation of the army, with air force support. Until recently, the army's commitment to internal security operations has been limited by the deployment of major elements in defense against an overt attack from North Vietnam and by training activities in support of this mission. Some improvement in the army's effectiveness and capabilities can be expected with the increased emphasis on antiguerrilla training, improved organization, and better combat intelligence. We believe it unlikely, however, that the army will be able to do more than contain the Viet Cong threat, at least over the short run.

The Outlook

14. The Viet Cong will probably maintain its pressure on provincial officials and government installations at the present high level, and, with the end of the wet season in October, return to large-scale guerrilla actions aimed at nullifying the government's authority in the rural areas. Hanoi could step up the weight and pace of the Viet Cong activities in South Vietnam. In the absence of more effective government measures to protect the peasants and to win their positive cooperation, the prospect is for expansion of the areas of Viet

[3] In the first five months of 1960, 780 government officials and sympathizers were assassinated by insurgents. The total number of assassinations in 1958 was 193 and in 1959, 239. Kidnappings this year through May total 282, as compared with 236 in 1958 and 344 in 1959.

Cong control in the countryside, particularly in the southwestern provinces.

15. Dissatisfaction and discontent with the government will probably continue to rise unless the security situation improves and unless Diem can be brought to reduce the corruption and excesses of his regime. Although there have been no popular demonstrations so far, we believe that the possibilities for antiregime disturbances are increasing. The Viet Cong will attempt to capture and control major demonstrations that occur. Existing police and civil guard strength is capable of controlling small-scale disorders in major population centers, but army support would be required if rioting became widespread.

16. The position of the army in the Vietnamese political scene is not entirely clear. The regime has taken pains to insure that no one army figure could acquire such personal standing or prestige that he could range himself and the army against the government. However, there is some discontent among officers over Can Lao influence in promotions and assignments, and concern over corruption and nepotism in the army has increased. If unrest in official circles and urban elements became extreme and attempts were made to organize an antiregime opposition, the attitude of the army would become a vital political factor. But it is not clear what the army's action would be in these circumstances.

17. Although Diem's personal position and that of his government are probably not now in danger, the marked deterioration since January of this year is disturbing. These adverse trends are not irreversible, but if they remain unchecked, they will almost certainly in time cause the collapse of Diem's regime. We do not anticipate that this will occur within the period of this estimate. However, if Diem is not able to alter present trends and the situation deteriorates substantially, it is possible during the period of this estimate that the government will lose control over much of the countryside and political crisis will ensue.

SNIE 10-4-61

Probable Communist Reactions to Certain US Actions in South Vietnam

7 November 1961

APPROVED FOR RELEASE
DATE: JAN 2005

TS 142424-d

59

SNIE 10-4-61
7 November 1961

(b) (3)

SPECIAL NATIONAL INTELLIGENCE ESTIMATE

PROBABLE COMMUNIST REACTIONS TO CERTAIN US ACTIONS IN SOUTH VIETNAM

- **Communist interests**
- **Probable reactions**

NOTE: This is the final version of the estimate and additional text will not be circulated.

Central Intelligence Agency

TS# 142424-d

C E N T R A L   I N T E L L I G E N C E   A G E N C Y

7 November 1961

SUBJECT: SNIE 10-4-61: PROBABLE COMMUNIST REACTIONS TO CERTAIN US ACTIONS IN SOUTH VIETNAM

SCOPE

The purpose of this estimate is to assess Communist (Soviet, Chinese, and North Vietnamese) reactions and, where significant, non-Communist reactions to certain US military actions intended to assist the Government of Vietnam cope with the Communist threat.[1/]

1/ Other National Intelligence Estimates pertinent to this problem are SNIE 10-2-61, "Likelihood of Major Communist Military Intervention in Mainland Southeast Asia," dated 27 June 1961; SNIE 58-2-61, "Probable Reactions to Certain Courses of Action Concerning Laos," dated 5 July 1961; NIE 14.3/53-61, "Prospects for North and South Vietnam," dated 15 August 1961; and SNIE 53-2-61, "Bloc Support of the Communist Effort Against the Government of Vietnam," dated 5 October 1961; SNIE 10-3-61, "Probable Communist Reactions to Certain SEATO Undertakings in South Vietnam," dated 10 October 1961.

TOP SECRET

The courses of action here considered were given to the intelligence community for the purposes of this estimate and were not intended to represent the full range of possible courses of action. The given courses of action are:

A. The introduction of a US airlift into and within South Vietnam, increased logistics support, and an increase in MAAG strength to provide US advisers down to battalion level;

B. The introduction into South Vietnam of a US force of about 8,000-10,000 troops, mostly engineers with some combat support, in response to an appeal from President Diem for assistance in flood relief;

C. The introduction into the area of a US combat force of 25,000 to 40,000 to engage with South Vietnamese forces in ground, air, and naval operations against the Viet Cong; and

D. An announcement by the US of its determination to hold South Vietnam and a warning, either private or public, that North Vietnamese support of the Viet Cong must cease or the US would launch air attacks against North Vietnam. This action would be taken in conjunction with Course A, B, or C.

THE ESTIMATE

I. INTRODUCTION

1. The interests of the Soviet Union, Communist China, and Communist North Vietnam overlap at many points but they vary considerably in intensity and urgency. To Hanoi, the ouster of President Diem and the reunification of Vietnam under Communist rule are basic objectives. Both objectives were accorded high priority at the North Vietnamese Communist Party Congress in 1960. The announcement of these objectives ended a preparatory phase and marked the beginning of a sharp increase in Viet Cong guerrilla, subversive, and political warfare. During the past year, North Vietnam has made a substantial investment in the campaign against Diem, and Hanoi is probably determined to press for an early victory in South Vietnam. The North Vietnamese leaders are convinced that they defeated the French in the Indochina War but were deprived of the fruits of their victory at the conference table in 1954-1955. Recent events in Laos have encouraged the North Vietnamese leaders and given them increased confidence in their "national liberation" tactics. They almost certainly believe that, by these tactics, they can in time upset the

Diem government and take over South Vietnam. They probably believe that they could, provided that the war would be confined within the boundaries of South Vietnam, render ineffective a level of US military support to South Vietnam substantially in excess of that postulated in Course C.

2. Chinese Communist interests are more directly involved in the Indochina states than are those of the USSR. Peiping's leaders appear impatient for concrete Communist advances, particularly in areas of substantial US interest. Moreover, Communist China would regard any increase in the US commitment in South Vietnam, and in particular any introduction of US troops into the area, as a serious challenge. The USSR, while sharing the desire of North Vietnam and Communist China to bring South Vietnam into the Communist Bloc, almost certainly does not regard this as justifying the assumption of serious risk.

3. Thus, we believe that the USSR would be inclined to a less militant response than Communist China or North Vietnam to any of the given US courses of action except possibly in the case of Course D. Moscow would seek to maintain control

of the situation and to restrain both Peiping and Hanoi from any responses likely, in Moscow's view, to run serious risk of expanded hostilities and the involvement of Soviet forces. The Soviet leaders would probably believe that, while the US commitment under Course A, B, or C would temporarily strengthen South Vietnam, it would only slow down, not reverse, the trends favoring the Communists in that country. Thus they would probably seek to avoid substantial escalation of the fighting.

4. The Chinese, in our view, would be much more sensitive than the Soviets to the arrival of US forces in South Vietnam. They also place a higher priority upon the early victory of the Communist cause in Southeast Asia, and would be considerably less concerned about the possible impact on Communist interests in Europe. While they are almost certainly more sensitive to the consequences of general war than some of their more radical statements indicate, their concern over this possibility does appear to be less acute than that of their Soviet partner. They would probably be more inclined than the Soviets to believe that the US would not undertake a further escalation. Thus we believe that they would argue for a rapid buildup of local Communist capabilities and the vigorous engagement of US forces.

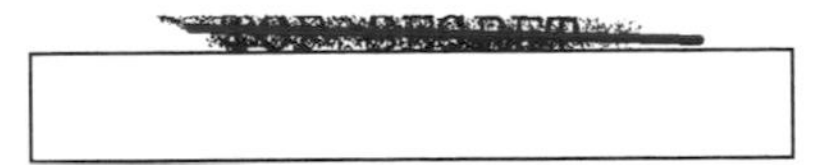

5. Communist China is presently faced with serious internal problems: the aftermath of a period of gross economic mismanagement; three successive bad harvests; and a substantial disruption of the economic development plan. Moreover, tension in relations with the USSR has reached a new high. Nevertheless, these developments are not likely to substantially alter Communist China's attitudes toward military commitment in Southeast Asia.

6. If the Chinese and the Soviets reacted in these ways, some further strain would be placed upon Sino-Soviet relations already aggravated by Khrushchev's indirect but strong attacks at the XXII Congress in Moscow. The Soviets would not wish to give Peiping additional reasons to charge them with insufficient militancy and boldness. Also they would be reluctant to back away from Khrushchev's oft-repeated promise of support for wars of "national liberation." At the same time the Soviet are deeply dubious of Chinese prudence and would be reluctant to give them a free rein. These strains would be acutely felt by the North Vietnamese, who have thus far attempted to avoid aggravating either side and preserve for themselves a maximum freedom of maneuver.

II. PROBABLE COMMUNIST REACTIONS

7. In response to either Course A, B, or C the Bloc would initiate a major political and propaganda campaign in the UN and worldwide to highlight and condemn the US action and to brand the US as an aggressor. The US would be denounced for violating the 1954 Geneva Agreements and torpedoing the present Geneva Conference on Laos. The intensity of this campaign would increase as the US involvement increased. Its purpose would be to generate international pressure to force a US withdrawal. The Bloc, particularly the USSR, would consider that substantial political and propaganda gains could be made from exploiting non-Communist criticism of these actions.

8. It is likely that Courses C and D in particular would lead to widespread demands for a conference -- for "negotiations" to diminish the tensions and "settle" the crisis. The Communist powers, and particularly the USSR, would almost certainly promote this demand, and signify their willingness to negotiate. They would do so in the conviction that such a procedure would provide a period of time in which they could pursue their efforts in South Vietnam, perhaps on a somewhat diminished scale, but still

with fair success and lessened risk. Any they would probably also calculate that, conditions being what they are in the area, almost any form of negotiated settlement would leave them with substantial opportunities to continue the "liberation" struggle.

> Course A. The introduction of a US airlift into and within South Vietnam, increased logistics support, and an increase in MAAG strength to provide US advisers down to battalion level.

9. We do not believe that this course of action would evoke a significant military response by Moscow or Peiping. Hanoi would probably press forward with its Viet Cong campaign, infiltrating cadres and logistic support to South Vietnam through the mountain routes of eastern Laos, across the Cambodian-Vietnamese border, and by sea from North Vietnam. Additional regular North Vietnamese Army units probably would be infiltrated into South Vietnam and southern Laos. The Viet Cong would probably step up its exploitation of South Vietnam's weaknesses in the plateau areas of South Vietnam seeking to establish a logistics base from which larger scale (regimental level) operations could

be mounted. The Communists probably would augment their efforts to build up the eastern part of south Laos as a major supply channel for the introduction of Bloc equipment into northern and central South Vietnam. US supply and communications lines would be harassed and the Communists would increase terrorist and sabotage attacks against US personnel and installations. In certain areas US aircraft would probably be subjected to antiaircraft fire. The Communist airlift would probably be expanded and extended to include airdrops and airlanding of supplies in South Vietnam as well as in southern Laos.

Course B. The introduction into South Vietnam of a US force of about 8,000-10,000 troops, mostly engineers with some combat support, in response to an appeal from President Diem for assistance in flood relief.

10. The announcement that US troops were being sent to South Vietnam for purposes of flood relief would not be convincing to the Communist states or to non-Communist governments. This would be so even if the troops confined their activity strictly to flood relief work. Nevertheless, most governments would consider that the flood relief

announcement provided opportunities for disengagement. However, later disengagement by the US would have serious adverse effects in Southeast Asia.

11. Moscow, Peiping, and Hanoi would regard this US course of action as a significant new indication of US intention to support the Diem government and to defend South Vietnam. However, they almost certainly would not respond by overtly committing regular North Vietnamese or Chinese Communist forces to a military attack against South Vietnam or Laos.

12. They would, nevertheless, probably build up their readiness posture in the general Southeast Asia area. The Bloc capitals would issue strong threats against the US to withdraw its forces. The Communists would probably accept increased risk of exposure and introduce additional North Vietnamese forces, similar to those mentioned under Course A, into South Vietnam and southern Laos to stiffen Communist forces there and to protect communications routes. Within South Vietnam, Communist-directed operations would probably be intensified throughout the countryside. The US forces would probably be subjected to harassment and ambush, the

intensity and scope of such action depending upon the extent to which the US forces were threatening Communist-controlled areas. The Chinese Communists would probably increase their ground and air forces in south China and would possibly introduce air units into North Vietnam.

> Course C. The introduction into the area of a US combat force of 25,000-40,000 men to engage with the South Vietnamese forces in ground, air, and naval operations against the Viet Cong.

13. The three Communist governments would probably estimate that the Viet Cong, with increased support, could successfully harass the US troops, avoid major defeats, and continue to hold the initiative and to score victories in many areas of South Vietnam. At the same time, however, all three would recognize that this commitment had greatly increased the involvement of US prestige in the South Vietnamese cause and was a strong indication that at a later stage the US might go further if necessary to prevent the defeat of that cause. The North Vietnamese and the Chinese Communists would view the US military force as a threat to their interests in Southeast Asia and the reinforced US presence as a potential threat to their security. The objective of all

three Communist powers would be to maintain Communist bases and strength in South Vietnam and, eventually, to terminate the US intervention. The Chinese and North Vietnamese Communists would probably be keener on the latter point since their interests are more directly involved; the Soviets would prefer to do it in a more gradual way, through attrition of US forces in the area and diplomatic-political pressures elsewhere.

14. Although an extreme military response might follow this US course of action, we believe it more likely that the Communist military reaction in South Vietnam would be a compromise -- somewhat stronger than the Soviets would wish but still limited enough to keep the risks under tolerable control. The USSR would almost certainly try to take the lead in supplying whatever outside military assistance was necessary, in order to maximize its control over the situation. The North Vietnamese would support this effort in order to ward off an increase in Chinese influence within their country. In any event, we believe that such a compromise would be unstable, that the three partners would continue to argue among themselves, and that the subsequent development of the crisis might result in Peiping's assuming a more independent role.

15. However, on balance we believe that the initial Communist reactions would be directed toward a holding operation in South Vietnam. In addition to an intensification of the types of Communist response we have estimated would ensue from the initiation of either Course A or B, we believe that Course C would evoke the following actions: strong and specific Soviet and Chinese Communist declarations of their intention to maintain the security of North Vietnam and sustain the "revolutionary struggle" in South Vietnam; an increase in the scale of Viet Cong guerrilla efforts against the US forces; and possibly the introduction of Chinese Communist or Soviet air units into North Vietnam.

16. We believe that the Communists would have considerable confidence that these measures would in the long term render ineffective US armed assistance to South Vietnam. If, however, the US action appeared to be seriously threatening the Communist movement in South Vietnam and establishing a strong military position in the country, the Communists would seriously consider providing more direct armed support. In these circumstances, the Communists might commit major North Vietnamese regular units in South Vietnam and introduce Chinese Communist support units into North Vietnam, although

they would recognize that this action would raise the risks of broadening the war. It is possible on the other hand that they would lower the tempo of military activity in South Vietnam with a view to raising it at another time or at another place in Southeast Asia.

> Course D. An announcement by the US of its determination to hold South Vietnam and a warning, either private or public, that North Vietnamese support of the Viet Cong must cease or the US would launch air attacks against North Vietnam. This course would be taken in conjunction with Course A, B, or C.

17. A specific warning of air attacks against North Vietnam, whether conveyed privately or publicly, would evoke very serious concern among all three Communist powers. A warning of air attacks on North Vietnam would be taken particularly seriously if it were issued in conjunction with the commitment of substantial US troop strength, as under Course C. Moscow and Peiping would regard the defense of North Vietnam against such an attack as imperative. They would seek to forestall such an attack to prevent military damage to North Vietnam and also to avoid the risk of expanded

hostilities. If the US warning were given privately, the Communist powers would probably feel that their interests could best be served by making public the warning and castigating it as a threat to world peace. They would probably see considerable advantage in this course and in bringing the case before the UN even if they did not believe that the US was prepared to make good on its threat.

18. Moscow and Peiping would probably announce their determination to defend North Vietnam against attack and stress that any such action would carry the risk of general war. The Communist powers would probably also take certain military measures not only to make credible their position but also to provide for improved air defense of North Vietnam. These measures would probably include the stationing of Soviet and/or Chinese Communist aircraft and antiaircraft units in North Vietnam. It is also possible that a "North Vietnamese" Air Force, complete with jet fighters, might suddenly be unveiled. The Soviet leaders would probably calculate that they could, by such political and military measures, generate sufficient worldwide pressures to dissuade the US from its threat, particularly if it could be depicted as a threat to use nuclear weapons. While not

desiring to precipitate a major military incident, the USSR and Communist China would be determined to avoid conducting themselves in such a manner as to let the US conclude that it had found a way to stop Communist support of "national liberation" movements.

19. If the US did subject North Vietnam to air attacks, the USSR and Communist China would commit air power to defend North Vietnam. They would probably undertake retaliatory attacks against targets in South Vietnam and against the bases or carriers from which the attacks on North Vietnam had been launched. These retaliatory attacks would probably be made by a "North Vietnamese" Air Force which would, in fact, be a mixed force. Similarly, a nuclear attack by the US would probably elicit some nuclear response.

20. The postulated courses of US action in South Vietnam would have an impact upon Communist tactics in Laos. The Communists would probably interpret the US action (except possibly Course A) as evidence of a stiffening US attitude in Southeast Asia. They would probably drag their feet in the negotiations at Geneva and step up their efforts to consolidate and expand their military and political position in Laos.

III. NON-COMMUNIST REACTIONS

21. South Vietnam. Most South Vietnamese would strongly welcome Courses A or B. In view of the seriousness of the security situation and its adverse impact on national morale, we do not believe that a substantial increase in the number of Americans in Vietnam would generate any appreciable concern that the country was coming under US domination. While supporting the introduction of larger numbers of troops such as envisaged under Course C, the South Vietnamese Government would probably desire that they be used, at least initially, as a static defense force freeing South Vietnamese military units for combat operations. The introduction of such a US force might precipitate some unfavorable reaction within middle and lower echelons of the government and within certain intellectual elements in Saigon.

22. The people of South Vietnam would also strongly welcome a US announcement of determination to defend South Vietnam, but would be apprehensive of Communist retaliation against South Vietnamese cities should the US attack the cities of North Vietnam.

TOP SECRET

23. Laos. Phoumi and Boun Oum would probably interpret Courses B, C, or D as a US decision to harden its position in Southeast Asia and as raising the likelihood of US support of their position in Laos, especially if hostilities were resumed in that country. Souvanna Phouma would probably feel that his position had become impossible to maintain and he would probably either swing fully to the side of Hanoi or abandon the field to the Pathet Lao.

24. Cambodia. Sihanouk would be highly concerned by any increase in US military activity in South Vietnam, fearing that it might lead to an expansion of hostilities in which Cambodia would become involved. His traditional fear and suspicion of Thailand and South Vietnam would color his views as to US intentions. He would continue to be susceptible to Soviet or Chinese Communist pressures to accommodate Cambodian policy to Bloc purposes in Southeast Asia. Sihanouk would, however, seek to keep the North Vietnamese regime at arms length.

25. SEATO. With the exception of the UK and France, the SEATO members would welcome Courses A, B, and C as evidence of US determination to defend its allies in Southeast

Asia. The SEATO members would be in varying degrees apprehensive of any US threat to carry the war to North Vietnam. France would almost certainly refuse to take part in any military activity in South Vietnam and would probably oppose such US action.

26. Neutrals. Burma, India, and Indonesia would all take a very alarmed view of Course B, C, or D. Burma in particular is acutely conscious of Chinese Communist power and would be particularly susceptible to pressures from Peiping. India's criticism would center primarily upon the violations of the 1954 Geneva Accords which would be involved in any of the given courses of US action. The ICC would file reports of the US violations and its members (particularly Poland and India) would seek an international conference to resolve the conflict.

SNIE 10-62

Communist Objectives, Capabilities, and Intentions in Southeast Asia

21 February 1962

APPROVED FOR RELEASE
DATE: JAN 2005

~~SECRET~~

SNIE 10-62
21 February 1962

1 MAR 1962 957

(b)(3)

SPECIAL

NATIONAL INTELLIGENCE ESTIMATE

Number 10-62

Communist Objectives, Capabilities, and Intentions in Southeast Asia

Submitted by the

DIRECTOR OF CENTRAL INTELLIGENCE

Concurred in by the

UNITED STATES INTELLIGENCE BOARD

As indicated overleaf

21 February 1962

~~SECRET~~

Nº 352

COMMUNIST OBJECTIVES, CAPABILITIES, AND INTENTIONS IN SOUTHEAST ASIA

THE PROBLEM

To estimate Communist objectives, military and subversive capabilities, and short-term intentions in continental Southeast Asia.[1]

CONCLUSIONS

1. The long-range Communist Bloc objectives in Southeast Asia are to eliminate US influence and presence and to establish Communist regimes throughout the area. Although the Communist powers have some differences of view as to tactics and priorities and the risks to be run in pursuing their objectives, they have thus far maintained a basic unity of ultimate objectives and a high degree of policy coordination with respect to Southeast Asia. If the current differences between Moscow and Peiping continue to grow, a major split on Southeast Asia policy could ensue. In this event, Peiping and Hanoi, which have special interests in Southeast Asia, might resort to more militant tactics. (*Paras. 6–9*)

2. Communist China, with the largest land army in the world, has the capability to overrun Southeast Asia and defeat the combined indigenous armed forces of the area. The North Vietnamese forces are superior to those of any other mainland Southeast Asia state. We do not believe,

[1] The following estimates also bear upon the problem: SNIE 13–3–61, "Chinese Communist Capabilities and Intentions in the Far East," dated 30 November 1961; SNIE 10–2–61, "Likelihood of Major Communist Military Intervention in Mainland Southeast Asia," dated 27 June 1961.

however, that the Communist powers intend to attempt to achieve their objectives in Southeast Asia by large-scale military aggression. We believe that they intend to continue to pursue these objectives primarily through subversion, political action, and support of "national liberation" struggles, so as to minimize the risks of Western, particularly US, military intervention. Over the past several years there has been a clear pattern of increasing Communist military, paramilitary, and political capabilities for pursuing Communist objectives in Southeast Asia. The development of these capabilities is particularly advanced in Laos and South Vietnam. (*Para. 11*)

3. We do not believe that Communist efforts in Southeast Asia follow a predetermined timetable or priority listing. Laos and South Vietnam are now their priority targets. We continue to believe that the Communists do not intend to initiate an all-out military effort to seize Laos. If, however, a military showdown between the Laotian Government forces and the Communists does develop, we believe that the Communist side would win out, bringing additional forces from North Vietnam if necessary. Nevertheless, the Communists are unlikely to pursue actions involving substantial risk of direct US military involvement so long as they continue to believe that they have a good chance of achieving their objectives in Laos by legal, political means. (*Paras. 12, 15–16*)

4. In South Vietnam, we believe that there will be no significant change over the short run in the current pattern of Viet Cong activity, although the scope and tempo of the Communist military and political campaigns will probably be increased. The Viet Cong will probably again resort to large-scale attacks, seeking to dramatize the weakness of the Diem forces and to reduce both civilian and military morale, in an effort to bring about Diem's downfall under circumstances which could be exploited to Communist advantage. (*Para. 21*)

5. In Thailand, the initial effort of Communist China and North Vietnam will probably be to increase their subversive potential, particularly in the northeastern frontier area.

Concurrently, the Soviets will continue to employ a combination of political pressures, military threats, and economic inducements to persuade the Thai Government to seek accommodation with the Bloc and adopt a more neutral policy. The Communists almost certainly believe that by sapping the independence of Laos they will be advancing their interests in Thailand as well. The neutralist positions of Cambodia and Burma are acceptable to the Communists for the time being. Communist activity in both countries will, therefore, probably be kept at low key. (*Paras. 12, 24, 26, 28*)

DISCUSSION

I. COMMUNIST OBJECTIVES

6. The Communist Bloc long-range objectives in Southeast Asia are to remove all vestiges of US influence and presence and to establish Communist regimes throughout the area. As an intermediate step, the Communists are seeking to move Laos into a strongly Communist influenced, if nominally "neutralist" position. In South Vietnam, the struggle is probably so sharply drawn that the Communists look for only a brief neutralist stage, if any, in the progression toward communism. In Thailand, the Communist effort has not yet reached major proportions, and emphasis is upon pressures at the government level to move Thailand away from its ties with the West into a neutralist position. However, there are differences of view among the Communist powers immediately concerned—the USSR, Communist China, and North Vietnam—as to tactics and priorities and the risks to be run in seeking their long-range objectives in the area. There are also differences between Moscow and Peiping over certain fundamental matters of ideology and policy.[2]

7. The national interests of the USSR, Communist China, and North Vietnam in Southeast Asia differ. The Soviets are not linked with the area in terms of geography, history, or economics, and they feel no threat to their national security emanating from the area. Moscow's interests in Southeast Asia appear to be mainly political and strategic, and its tactics tend to be less militant than desired by Peiping and Hanoi. Thus, the Soviets, while supporting "wars of national liberation," as in Laos, are more cautious than the Chinese and more concerned with the risk of local wars in the Far East spreading into general war.

8. Communist China and North Vietnam, on the other hand, have special interests in Southeast Asia derived from their geographic position, historical associations, and economic needs. Peiping considers continental Southeast Asia to be part of its sphere of influence. Hanoi regards Laos and South Vietnam as within its special purview. Both have been involved in ambitious economic development plans and would stand to gain economically from domination of Southeast Asia. In addition, they are, at present, more militantly revolutionary than the Soviets and less reluctant to risk local war in order to achieve the early establishment of Communist regimes in the area.

9. Despite these differing interests and viewpoints, the Communist powers appear to have maintained a basic unity of ultimate objectives and a high degree of policy collaboration with respect to Southeast Asia. Laos provides the only apparent exception to this generalization, but as yet the Communist powers do not appear to be seriously at cross purposes. If, however, the differences between Moscow and Peiping continue to grow, a major split on Southeast Asia policy could ensue. In this case, Peiping and Hanoi might resort to more militant tactics.

II. COMMUNIST CAPABILITIES

10. Every country in continental Southeast Asia is vulnerable in some degree to Communist subversion, political and economic pressures, and military aggression. The governments of the area all feel threatened and exposed. Most have tended to overemphasize

[2] For an analysis of the differences between the USSR and Communist China see NIE 11-5-62, "Political Developments in the USSR and the Communist World," dated 21 February 1962.

the threat of military aggression by Communist China and/or Communist North Vietnam and to underemphasize the threat from internal subversion and Communist "national liberation" tactics. Whether neutralist or pro-Western in orientation, the governments of Southeast Asia gear their policies to their assessment of the balance of force between the Communist and non-Communist powers in the Far East and of the willingness of the West to intervene militarily.

11. Communist China, with the largest land army in the world, has the capability to overrun mainland Southeast Asia and defeat the combined indigenous armed forces of the area. The armed forces of Communist North Vietnam are superior to those of any other mainland Southeast Asia state. We do not believe, however, that the Communist powers intend to attempt to achieve their objectives in Southeast Asia by large-scale military aggression. We believe that they intend to continue to pursue these objectives primarily through subversion, political action, and support of "national liberation" struggles, so as to minimize the risks of Western, particularly US, military intervention. Over the past several years there has been a clear pattern of increasing Communist military, paramilitary, and political capabilities for pursuing Communist objectives in Southeast Asia. The development of these capabilities is particularly advanced in Laos and South Vietnam.[3]

III. COMMUNIST SHORT-TERM INTENTIONS

12. We do not believe that the Communists have developed a firm timetable for achieving their objectives in Southeast Asia, or that their efforts follow a precise priority listing. It is clear that Laos and South Vietnam are now receiving priority attention. We believe that the neutralist positions of Cambodia and Burma are acceptable to the Communists for the time being, and that Thailand is likely to become an increasingly active arena for Communist political pressures, infiltration, and subversion.

A. Laos [4]

13. The minimum short-term Communist objectives in Laos had probably been satisfied, in general, at the time of the cease-fire in May 1961. Communist-held territory in Laos permitted the overland movement of personnel and supplies into South Vietnam by way of the secure, if difficult, maze of connecting mountain trails in Laos. Moreover, the Lao Army was disorganized, disheartened, and ineffective. Movement by Communist personnel into and across Laos was virtually unchallenged even where nominal government control remained in effect. Hence it was unnecessary for the Communists to risk the possibility of armed intervention by the US, by seeking to achieve the complete domination of Laos by military means. At the same time, developments of the past few months have probably caused the Communists to revise downward their estimate of the chances of US military intervention in Laos.

14. The delays in negotiations for establishing a coalition government in Laos, the substantial buildup of the Laotian armed forces during the cease-fire, and the pattern of limited Lao Army offensive action, particularly since mid-December 1961, probably caused considerable annoyance and some concern to the Communist Pathet Lao and to the North Vietnamese leaders who control and direct the Communist effort in Laos. These considerations probably account for the limited Communist counterattacks of recent

[3] For details concerning Communist activity and strength in Laos and South Vietnam see Annex and maps.

[4] See also SNIE 58-62, "Relative Military Capabilities of Opposing Forces in Laos," dated 11 January 1962, and SNIE 58/1-62, "Relative Military Capabilities of Opposing Forces in Laos," dated 31 January 1962.

weeks. We do not believe that the pattern of military activity thus far indicates preparations for an offensive designed to take the major Mekong cities by assault.

15. We continue to believe that the Communist powers do not wish to become deeply involved militarily in Laos, and that to the extent possible they prefer to keep their military involvement clandestine. Thus, so long as they see a reasonable chance to achieve a political settlement which would not in practice preclude continued use of southern Laos as a base for operations against South Vietnam, the Communists are unlikely to adopt a course of action which would involve substantial risk of direct US military involvement. Moreover, the Communist side probably considers that their chances of winning control of Laos by legal, political means are good.

16. However, if the Laotian Government increases the scale of its military activity, the Communists will respond with counter military action, and a general military showdown between the two sides could ensue. Such a showdown might also develop from continued Communist military pressures designed to force the government to return to negotiations. In case of a test of military strength, we believe that the Communist side would win out, bringing additional forces from North Vietnam, if necessary.

B. South Vietnam [5]

17. The primary Communist objective in South Vietnam is its reunification with North Vietnam under Communist domination. The tactics being used are a combination of political and guerrilla warfare which have been developed to a high degree of proficiency by the Vietnamese Communists over a long period of time. The Communists operating in South Vietnam (the Viet Cong) are directly controlled and provided with political and strategic guidance by the Communist Party of North Vietnam (the Lao Dong). The North Vietnamese regular army provides military guidance, and some cadres, technicians, and logistical support.

18. The major strengths of the Viet Cong include their superior intelligence service, the extent of their control of the countryside and the peasantry, their thorough knowledge of the local terrain, and their mobility and their ability to achieve surprise, all of which are characteristic of a well organized guerrilla force. The Viet Cong are not capable of defeating the South Vietnamese armed forces in conventional type warfare. On the other hand, the government forces are able to concentrate their efforts against a given area only by exposing other areas to Viet Cong attack.

19. The Viet Cong's progression from guerrilla to conventional warfare tactics, if it occurs, will probably vary in different areas and will depend on a number of factors, including their success achieved in lowering the South Vietnamese Army's morale, the consolidation of their control in the countryside, and their introduction of new weapons and materiel. In the meantime, they will probably continue their current campaign of concentrating upon the government's paramilitary forces and attacking regular army units only when they have sufficient numerical superiority to inflict decisive defeats. Isolated outposts, patrols, and vehicle convoys will be the principal military targets, with a concurrent major political and economic effort in the rural areas to reduce governmental authority and further disrupt the Vietnamese economy.

[5] See also NIE 14.3/53-61, "Prospects for North and South Vietnam," dated 15 August 1961; SNIE 10-3-61, "Probable Communist Reactions to Certain SEATO Undertakings in South Vietnam," dated 10 October 1961; SNIE 53-2-61, "Bloc Support of the Communist Effort Against the Government of Vietnam," dated 5 October 1961; and SNIE 10-4-61, "Probable Communist Reactions to Certain US Actions in South Vietnam," dated 7 November 1961.

Further attacks can be expected against the capitals of provinces, particularly those in areas under considerable Communist control.

20. The North Vietnamese leaders may still hope to achieve the reunification of North and South Vietnam through the medium of the countrywide elections stipulated in the 1954 Geneva Accords. North Vietnam seeks to remove President Diem and eliminate US influence in South Vietnam through military and political pressures. There is a continuing possibility that Hanoi may attempt to establish a "rival government" in South Vietnam. Statements by Radio Hanoi on the internal and external activities of its "National Front for the Liberation of South Vietnam," as well as the Front's recent initiation of its own broadcasting operations, suggest that Hanoi may be preparing for such a move.

21. For the short run, however, we believe that there will be no significant change in the current pattern of Viet Cong activity in South Vietnam, although the scope and tempo of the military and political campaigns will probably be increased. The Viet Cong will probably again resort to large-scale attacks, seeking to dramatize the weakness of the Diem forces and to reduce both civilian and military morale, in an effort to bring about Diem's downfall under circumstances which could be exploited to Communist advantage.

C. Thailand[6]

22. Communism has never been attractive to the Thai people. However, neutralism has certain historical roots in Thailand and considerable immediate appeal to the Thai people. The USSR has been pressing the Thai Government to disengage from SEATO, expand relations with the Soviet Union, and move toward neutrality. At the same time, the Thai leaders feel increasingly exposed to attack and infiltration from Communist China and North Vietnam as a result of developments in Laos.

23. In the northeast Thai provinces, which historically have been economically depressed, the people are ethnically close to the Laotians. The area also has a special vulnerability to Communist penetration as a result of the presence of more than 50,000 Vietnamese refugees of the Indochina War, most of whom frankly admit their allegiance to Ho Chi Minh. North Vietnamese and Lao Communists are probably maintaining liaison with cadre elements among this Vietnamese refugee community and providing them with small arms and guerrilla warfare training. Thailand's long, poorly-defended border with Laos facilitates Communist infiltration.

24. The Communists are unlikely to initiate an overt attack against Thailand in the foreseeable future. The Asian Communist states probably believe that their base of subversive activities in Thailand must be substantially strengthened before a major guerrilla-supported national liberation movement could be attempted. At present, no widespread indigenous Communist movement exists in Thailand, and the small, illegal Thai and Chinese Communist parties are relatively ineffective. Communist Chinese and North Vietnamese tactics, therefore, probably will be employed initially to increase the subversive potential in Thailand, particularly in the northeastern frontier area. Concurrently, the USSR will continue to employ a combination of political pressures, military threats, and economic inducements to persuade the Thai Government to seek accommodation with the Bloc and adopt a more neutral policy. The Communists almost certainly believe that by sapping the independence of Laos they will be advancing their interests in Thailand as well.

[6] See also SNIE 52-61, "Thailand's Security Problems and Prospects," dated 13 December 1961.

D. Burma

25. The objectives of the USSR and Communist China in Burma appear to be directed toward achieving gradual control over that country under the guise of friendly cooperation. Communist China has made considerable progress during the last year in exploiting the good will created by the Sino-Burmese border settlement and generally has increased its influence among key Burmese political and military leaders. Burmese military leaders during 1960–1961 accepted Chinese Communist offers of troop assistance in operations against the anti-Communist Chinese irregulars based in Burma, and additional Chinese military assistance may be utilized against other dissident groups along the Sino-Burmese border.

26. In view of the foregoing successes, the Chinese Communists probably see little necessity for projecting a takeover of Burma by force or even by fostering a pro-Communist revolutionary movement among indigenous Communist political and insurgent groups.

E. Cambodia

27. Communist tactics in Cambodia generally have de-emphasized any appearance of force or intimidation. Cambodia's Chinese and Vietnamese minorities, each numbering about 300,000, are targets for Communist Chinese and North Vietnamese subversive efforts and are a potential insurgent factor. The expanding student and teacher groups in Cambodia have shown considerable susceptibility to Communist propaganda and appear to be special Communist targets.

28. However, the Communists will probably continue to display friendship and generosity toward Cambodia, and especially toward Prince Sihanouk, to demonstrate the advantages of "peaceful coexistence" and continue to take advantage of Cambodia's friendly neutrality to increase their influence in Cambodia by peaceful means. Communist China continues to lead the Communist Bloc countries in overtures to Cambodia; the Soviet Union has played a relatively minor role. Cambodia's Communist front party, known as the Pracheachon Group, wields little overt influence. It numbers about 1,000 active members and possibly as many as 30,000 sympathizers. It is tolerated by Prince Sihanouk, probably as a gesture of neutrality, but its activities are stringently curtailed. There has been contact between the Communist embassies in Cambodia and the Pracheachon, but no evidence of Communist control.

ANNEX

A. Laos

1. The combat effectiveness of the Pathet Lao and other antigovernment forces is considerably lower than that of the North Vietnamese units. The combat capability of the North Vietnam troops is high. Many of them are regulars and combat-proven veterans who participated in the decisive defeat of the French forces in the Indochina War. The use of North Vietnamese cadres and technicians, and more recently units, in critical tactical situations has been an important factor in the success of Communist military operations in Laos.

2. Antigovernment military forces in Laos are now estimated to total about 38,000, comprised of about 6,000 Kong Le, 4,000 Kham Ouane, 19,000 Pathet Lao, and 9,000 North Vietnamese regular armed forces (the latter includes a minimum of 10 understrength infantry battalions and support troops of engineer, artillery, antiaircraft artillery, and armor).

3. Although outnumbered by the Lao armed forces, the antigovernment forces now in Laos have a superiority in artillery and armor. They are generally capable of maintaining their main forward positions and of conducting local operations to counter aggressive actions by the government forces. Without further external reinforcements, they could, by concentrating their forces, seize and hold certain key positions now held by government troops. If reinforced by additional combat units from North Vietnam, they could quickly overrun the remainder of Laos.

B. South Vietnam

4. The territory currently controlled by the Viet Cong gives them access to at least 25 percent of the 2 million militarily fit males between the ages of 15 and 49. There are now estimated to be on full-time antigovernment operations at least 25,000 Viet Cong organized into 22 battalions, 109 separate companies, and 210 separate platoons, of varying strengths. Supporting these forces are an estimated 100,000 part-time, partially armed, trained local militia who serve as village self-defense forces. Some of these are as well armed and trained as the full-time forces. In addition to providing replacements for the full-time regular units, the militia perform other support functions, such as collecting intelligence, providing guides for operational units, and supply services.

5. The Viet Cong receive coordinated directions from high level political and military headquarters in North Vietnam and operate from political bases in South Vietnam under their control. They have divided South Vietnam into two operational regions. Each region is further divided into interprovincial commands, provincial commands, districts, and villages. Each command has troop units available to it, generally on the basis of battalions in the region and interprovincial commands, and companies in the provinces.

6. The Viet Cong are equipped with an assortment of US, French, and locally-produced weapons. Generally, the "regular" units are armed with US weapons up to and including medium mortars. The principal source of these weapons in the past has been the South Vietnamese military and paramili-

tary units, but reports indicate that additional weapons are being infiltrated to the Viet Cong from North Vietnam. North Vietnam undoubtedly has a considerable stockpile of US weapons captured from the French during the Indochina War and, more recently, from the government forces in Laos.

7. Several divisions of the North Vietnamese Army (PAVN) located in the southern portion of North Vietnam have been linked with the support and training of Viet Cong personnel. These divisions are organized from former South Vietnamese who fought against the French and withdrew to North Vietnam in 1954–1955. These approximately 50,000 combat-experienced personnel form a ready pool of trained PAVN soldiers, and they generally provide the commanders, cadres, technicians, and specialists for the Viet Cong forces. If needed, personnel from these divisions could be made available for guerrilla operations in South Vietnam.

8. The number of PAVN personnel with the Viet Cong in South Vietnam is believed to be at least 800. These officers and NCO's serve as cadres for the various Viet Cong battalions and companies. In addition, they probably also act as instructors or technicians to operate communications systems and the more complex equipment in the Viet Cong arsenal.

9. The Viet Cong utilize both land and sea routes to infiltrate cadres and limited supplies into South Vietnam. The sea route is used primarily to transport couriers and technical equipment while the longer and more difficult overland route is used for personnel and other supplies.

(Continued...)

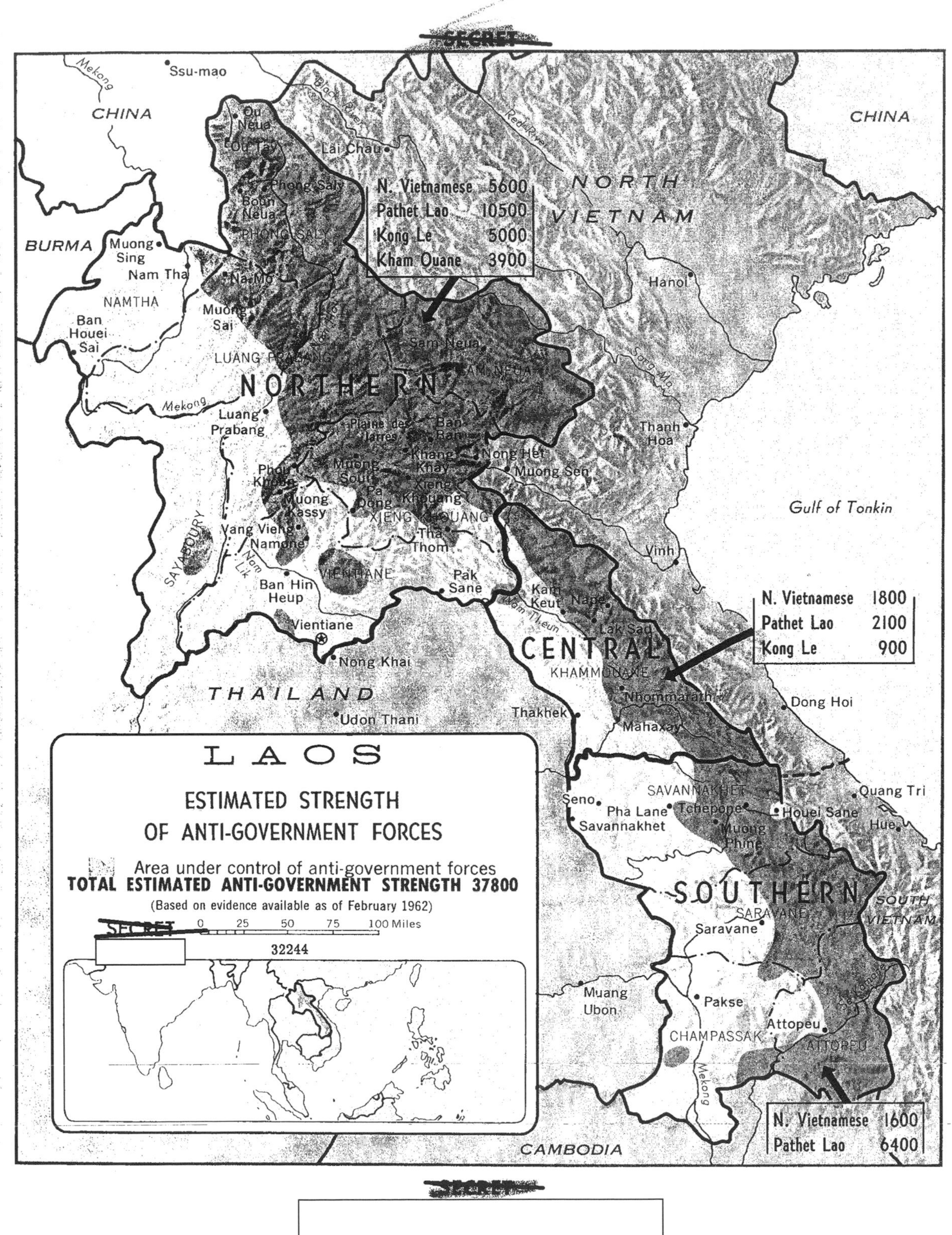
SECRET
CHINA
BURMA
NORTH VIETNAM
THAILAND
CAMBODIA
SOUTH VIETNAM
Gulf of Tonkin
NORTHERN
CENTRAL
SOUTHERN
N. Vietnamese 5600
Pathet Lao 10500
Kong Le 5000
Kham Ouane 3900
N. Vietnamese 1800
Pathet Lao 2100
Kong Le 900
N. Vietnamese 1600
Pathet Lao 6400
LAOS
ESTIMATED STRENGTH
OF ANTI-GOVERNMENT FORCES
Area under control of anti-government forces
TOTAL ESTIMATED ANTI-GOVERNMENT STRENGTH 37800
(Based on evidence available as of February 1962)
0 25 50 75 100 Miles
32244
SECRET

SECRET

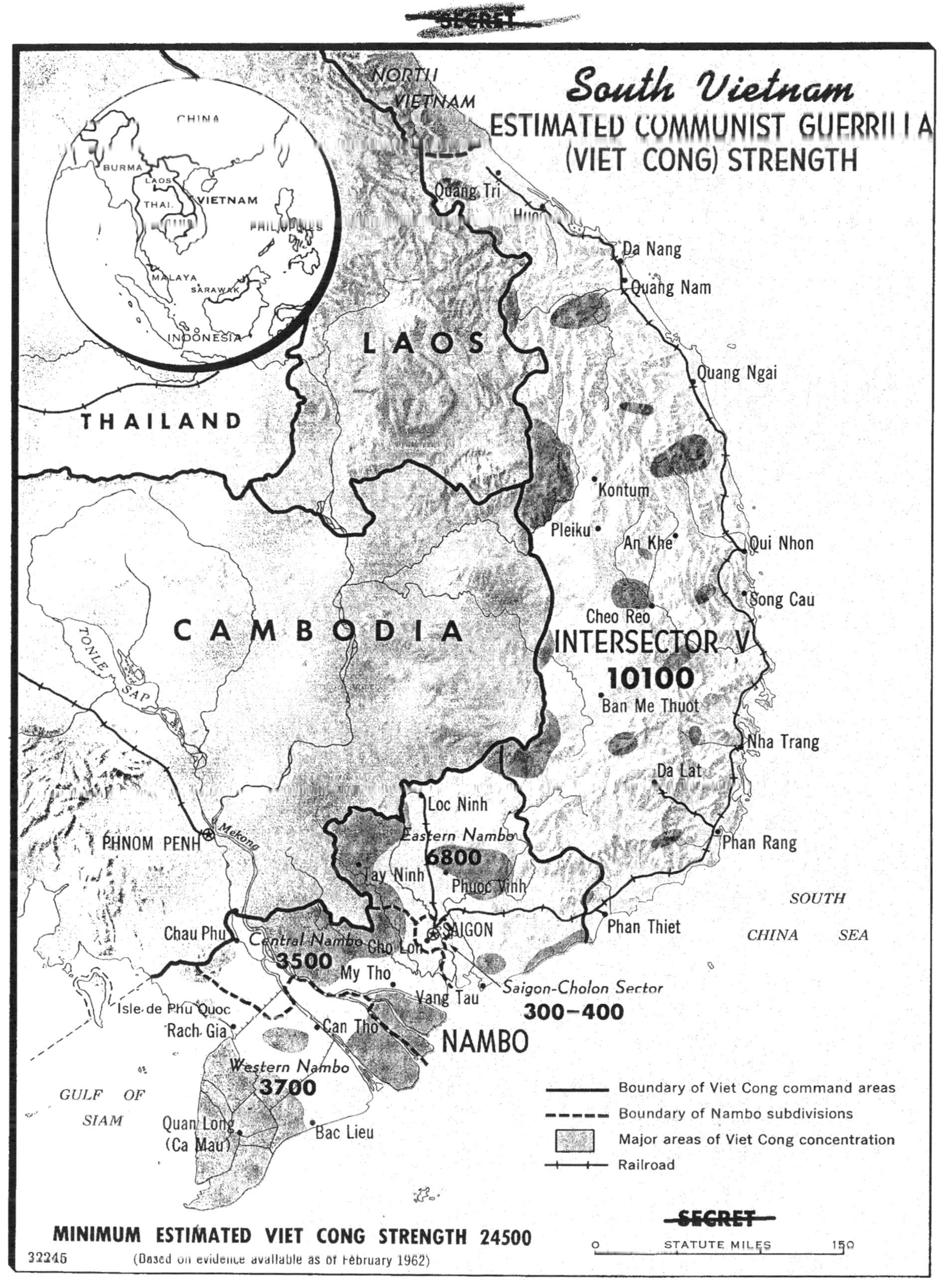

SECRET

NIE 53-63

Prospects in South Vietnam

17 April 1963

APPROVED FOR RELEASE
DATE: JAN 2005

(b)(3)

SECRET

1243 23 APR

NIE 53–63
17 April 1963

NATIONAL INTELLIGENCE ESTIMATE

NUMBER 53–63

(Supersedes NIE 14.3/53–61)

Prospects in South Vietnam

Submitted by the
DIRECTOR OF CENTRAL INTELLIGENCE
Concurred in by the
UNITED STATES INTELLIGENCE BOARD
As indicated overleaf
17 APRIL 1963

SECRET

Nº 361

(Continued...)

~~SECRET~~

PROSPECTS IN SOUTH VIETNAM

THE PROBLEM

To assess the situation and prospects in South Vietnam, with special emphasis upon the military and political factors most likely to affect the counterinsurgency effort.

CONCLUSIONS

A. We believe that Communist progress has been blunted and that the situation is improving. Strengthened South Vietnamese capabilities and effectiveness, and particularly US involvement, are causing the Viet Cong increased difficulty, although there are as yet no persuasive indications that the Communists have been grievously hurt. (*Paras. 27–28*)

B. We believe the Communists will continue to wage a war of attrition, hoping for some break in the situation which will lead to victory. They evidently hope that a combination of military pressure and political deterioration will in time create favorable circumstances either for delivering a *coup de grâce* or for a political settlement which will enable them to continue the struggle on more favorable terms. We believe it unlikely, especially in view of the open US commitment, that the North Vietnamese regime will either resort to overt military attack or introduce acknowledged North Vietnamese military units into the south in an effort to win a quick victory. (*Paras. 29–31*)

C. Assuming no great increase in external support to the Viet Cong, changes and improvements which have occurred during the past year now indicate that the Viet Cong can be contained militarily and that further progress can be made in expanding the area of government control and in creating greater security in the countryside. However, we do not believe that it is pos-

sible at this time to project the future course of the war with any confidence. Decisive campaigns have yet to be fought and no quick and easy end to the war is in sight. Despite South Vietnamese progress, the situation remains fragile. (*Para. 32*)

D. Developments during the last year or two also show some promise of resolving the political weaknesses, particularly that of insecurity in the countryside, upon which the insurgency has fed. However, the government's capacity to embark upon the broader measures required to translate military success into lasting political stability is questionable. (*Paras. 33–35*)

(Continued...)

DISCUSSION

I. NATURE OF THE CONFLICT

1. The Communists have been struggling to win control of Indo-China ever since the Indo-Chinese Communist Party was organized in the 1920's. This struggle has passed through several stages, including operations against the Japanese in the later years of World War II and a major war against the French from 1946–1954. After the French withdrawal, the Communists were apparently confident that the South Vietnamese Government (GVN) would collapse, or that in any event, the nationwide elections called for in the Geneva Accords would soon deliver all of Vietnam into their hands. Although guerrilla bands were left behind when the country was partitioned, the Communists did not engage in armed operations against the GVN, but attempted to undermine it by other means. Contrary to Communist expectations, however, the GVN, under President Ngo Dinh Diem, not only survived but developed sufficient strength, partly as a consequence of Western political and economic support, to enable it to ignore the 1956 election deadline and to make appreciable progress.

2. These developments confronted the Vietnamese Communists with a new situation. They had developed substantial ground forces in North Vietnam, but South Vietnam also, with US assistance, had substantially improved its military capabilities. Open invasion, therefore, could not be a walk-in, and in any case the strong US commitment, not only to South Vietnam but to southeast Asia as a whole, made such a course an undesirable one. The Vietnamese Communists thereupon resumed guerrilla warfare combined with intensified terrorism, subversion, and enticement. They evidently concluded that, by winning converts and sympathizers in the countryside, by depriving the government of effective control, and by causing loss of morale and will within the government cadres, they would pave the way for a final political victory. This campaign was sharply stepped up in late 1959.

3. South Vietnam was and remains highly vulnerable to rural terrorism and guerrilla warfare. Its people have no tradition of loyalty to a government in Saigon. The Vietnamese peasant has always accommodated himself to whatever force was best able to protect or to punish him—or offer him a vision, however illusory, of a better life. The "government" meant the local officials with whom he was in contact, many of whom tended to be ineffective and often venal. Various forms of minor corruption and petty bureaucratic tyranny have long been rife in the provinces, and the offenders were seldom disciplined by their superiors. Most peasants are primarily interested in peace and do not care who wins the military victories. Security is significant to the peasant largely in terms of how it affects him personally.

4. From 1954 to about 1957, major steps were taken by the Diem regime to create a viable South Vietnamese state. The government completed the resettlement of about one million refugees from North Vietnam, developed promising Civic Action and public information programs in the countryside, extended governmental authority throughout most of the country, substantially improved internal security, established governmental institutions more responsible and representative than had existed before, and brought into the bureaucracy an appreciable number of young and capable civil and military personnel. However, after 1957 Diem failed to expand this social, political, and economic base. Perhaps most important of all, the government failed to develop a capability to protect the peasant and the villager. Partly on US advice, the Vietnamese Army had been organized, trained, and deployed primarily as a defense against open attack from the north. It proved ill-qualified to protect the population against guerrilla attack and terrorism.

5. With Diem's consolidation of his personal control over the bureaucracy and the military establishment, he became increasingly reluctant to delegate authority or take other measures to improve the efficiency and morale of the military and civil services. Close operational control from Saigon not only generated serious discontent within all levels of the government but also inhibited the effectiveness of government actions, particularly in the countryside. The launching of a full-scale Communist insurgency in late 1959, finally led the Diem regime, partly out of necessity and partly as a result of the substantially increased US commitment to South Vietnam, to initiate broad measures to rectify these conditions.

6. The Communist effort in South Vietnam is essentially one of political subversion in which extensive military activity presently plays the predominant role. The primary aim of the Communists is to secure the support of the rural population—support buttressed, where possible, by positive loyalty. By various forms of military and terrorist action, they endeavor to cow the recalcitrant, demonstrate that the government cannot protect its adherents, and create a general atmosphere of insecurity. They also endeavor to weaken the government's position in the countryside by assassinating its officials, defeating its forces, sapping the morale of its cadres and supporters and, generally, tarnishing its image in every way possible. They make extensive use of guerrilla base areas and safe havens which they seek to protect, although they seldom attempt to hold ground against appreciably superior government forces. In addition, the Communists are continually developing the capabilities of their "regular" units, with the apparent hope of ultimately becoming able to engage government troops in at least quasi-conventional combat.

(Continued...)

7. To counter the impact of increased US assistance, the Communists are gearing for a long struggle and have reorganized their military and political apparatus accordingly. They claim to be fighting in the cause of the "National Front for the Liberation of South Vietnam," organized late in 1960. This organization currently has little following in Vietnam, is clearly a front for the Communists, and its ostensible leaders are political nonentities. It is designed to provide the framework of a governmental apparatus, if and when more significant gains are made in the current struggle, and to serve meanwhile as a vehicle for seeking international neutralist support.

II. COMMUNIST CAPABILITIES

8. Hanoi directs the Communist campaign against the GVN, although it permits the Viet Cong commanders considerable tactical discretion. The Sino-Soviet quarrel apparently has not affected the Communist war effort. North Vietnam is being courted by both sides, but there is no evidence that either Moscow or Peiping has offered to underwrite a substantial intensification of the Viet Cong effort or that Hanoi has sought greatly increased aid from either. In pursuing their interests in southeast Asia and maintaining their independence, the North Vietnamese probably feel that they need the support of both Moscow and Peiping, and will probably continue therefore to attempt to avoid commitment to either side.

9. *Military Strength.* We estimate that there are now about 22,000–25,000 full-time Viet Cong military personnel organized into identifiable units of up to battalion size. A substantial portion of these forces is well trained, well disciplined, and well led. Their armament consists of light infantry weapons, machine guns, bazookas, mortars, and a few 57-mm recoilless rifles. Viet Cong forces are not known to have artillery or antiaircraft artillery weapons, though in recent months they have become quite adept at using small arms and machine guns against South Vietnamese and US aircraft.

10. Viet Cong regular units are supplemented by a large pool of lightly armed, semitrained local guerrillas and militia who probably number about 100,000. The guerrillas and militia sometimes are used with regular units as a first or shock wave of an attack in their locality. At other times, operating under local district committee supervision, they are employed for terrorism, armed propaganda, and small ambushes. The militia are charged with protecting Viet Cong areas when other units are absent. Both militia and guerrillas constitute a training and replacement pool for the regular forces. The bulk of the Viet Cong regular troops consists of locally recruited or impressed South Vietnamese peasants promoted as needed to regular units on the basis of their previous experience and performance in militia and local guerrilla groups.

(Continued...)

11. *Logistics.* For weapons, ammunition, and related supplies, the Viet Cong forces rely primarily upon capture from government forces. Some stocks were left behind when the Communists withdrew northward in 1954, some arms are brought in by infiltrators, and some are fabricated by the Viet Cong themselves. They also rely upon indigenous sources for food, shelter, and other nonmilitary supplies. Supplies are frequently purchased, although they are seized if necessary. In areas where the Viet Cong have established firm control, they operate as a government, levying taxes and providing some services. Since most of the cadres sent from North Vietnam are of southern origin and are normally returned to their own provinces, they are able to draw local support for the Viet Cong effort.

12. The limited evidence available indicates that some equipment, such as recoilless rifles, mortar fuses, and medical supplies, together with selected cadres, have for some time been infiltrated from the north. As the scale of Viet Cong operations has increased over the last two years, the amount of materiel and numbers of personnel brought in from North Vietnam have probably also increased. While the basic guerrilla effort could continue without outside support, this support probably has been essential to the higher levels of effort which have been achieved in the last year or so.

13. Men and materiel are evidently being infiltrated through Laos, and to a lesser extent through Cambodia and by sea. The Laotian corridor, which is controlled by Communist forces, is an important military asset. Due to the nature of the terrain, however, the Vietnamese infiltrators could almost certainly continue to make some use of the area even if it were not under Communist control. Use of the corridor would probably significantly increase if the Viet Cong decided to substantially step up the level of military activity.

14. *Tactics and Effectiveness.* The Viet Cong have proved themselves a formidable enemy and an effective guerrilla force. Despite some setbacks, they have generally proved adept at the classic tactics of surprise, constant movement, concentration for attack, withdrawal and dispersal. They have also demonstrated flexibility in modifying their tactics to counter new South Vietnamese operational concepts. They have shown themselves capable of company, and even battalion, size attacks and of carrying out strikes against widely dispersed targets at about the same time. One important factor in their success is their effective intelligence system. Informants and sympathizers exist throughout the countryside, and the Viet Cong evidently have been able to maintain intelligence coverage of virtually every level in the South Vietnamese military and civil establishment. This has enabled them to avoid some government counteractions and effectively to combat others.

15. *Nonmilitary Capabilities.* The Viet Cong possess two important capabilities which they have not yet fully exercised—terrorism in the cities and harassment of economic life. Although the Viet Cong almost certainly have many adherents in urban areas, their terrorist activities have been few and generally unsuccessful. Commercial road and water transport continues to function, and rubber—the principal earner of foreign exchange—continues to be produced and moved to market. One reason the Viet Cong have not attempted to interdict these activities is that they receive considerable revenue from "taxation" of rubber plantations and transport facilities. Another and perhaps more important reason is that the Viet Cong probably have felt that full exercise of these capabilities would hinder rather than help them attain their objective of winning popular support.

III. THE SOUTH VIETNAMESE RESPONSE

16. *General Approach and Strategy.* The initial South Vietnamese response to the intensified guerrilla activity in the countryside reflected neither a sense of urgency nor an understanding of the nature of the challenge. There was a tendency to regard the strengthened insurgency simply as a threat created and sustained from the outside; there was a general failure to appreciate the internal support which the insurgency generated or the grievances and basic conditions upon which it fed. It was regarded as essentially a military problem to be dealt with by military means. These views have become modified as a consequence of the progress of events and as a consequence of US effort to convince the regime to regard the conflict in broader perspective. During the past year and a half, the government has begun to see the conflict as an internal one requiring socio-political as well as military measures and to view the military problem as one requiring greater flexibility in deployment and tactics. Government recognition of these factors has resulted in the development, with US assistance, of a comprehensive counterinsurgency strategy.

17. *Military Capabilities and Weaknesses.* The South Vietnamese regular military establishment consists of about 215,000 men, of whom almost 200,000 are army. The paramilitary services, consisting of the Civil Guard of about 75,000 men and a Self Defense Corps of about 100,000 men, are responsible for internal security as well as counter-guerrilla operations. Supplementing these are another 40,000 men in Citizens' Irregular Defense Groups, which embrace a wide variety of units, some of which serve part-time.

18. During the past year, force levels have been substantially increased. The various military and paramilitary forces have been retrained and re-equipped and their tactical mobility improved, principally through US helicopter and transport aircraft. As a result of this improvement in tactical mobility, the South Vietnamese forces

are now able to strike more quickly and in greater strength than ever before. The establishment of Citizens' Irregular Defense Groups is creating a paramilitary capability in certain areas not now reached by regular forces. This program has also introduced the government's presence into many hitherto remote areas and enlisted the active support of minority groups. Appreciable progress has also been made in securing the support of ethnic minorities (Montagnards) in the Central Highlands, long courted by the Viet Cong, though traditional sentiments of reciprocal suspicion and disdain between the Vietnamese and the Montagnards still hamper this effort.

19. In recent months, offensive operations have been stepped up significantly, the Viet Cong have been engaged in small-unit actions and caught in ambushes, and efforts have been made to destroy Viet Cong forces rather than to drive them away and allow them to disperse. Night operations and patrolling are increasing. Recent reorganization of the army command structure, together with retraining of army personnel, is bringing about greater participation by the regular establishment in the counterguerrilla effort and more effective coordination with the paramilitary services. Some 5,000–6,000 US-trained Montagnards are now conducting armed patrols designed to provide intelligence and, to some extent, to interdict Viet Cong access routes from Laos.

20. Nevertheless, a number of factors still prevent the South Vietnamese military and security forces from realizing their full potential. The army still makes extensive use of conventional tactics against guerrilla forces. The Civil Guard and Self Defense Corps have borne a major share of the fighting and have suffered heavy casualties. Although the quality of intelligence is improving, there is still a lack of reliable and timely combat intelligence at the provincial and district level and of political intelligence on the Communist apparatus. Also, available combat intelligence is often not exploited operationally. These shortcomings, together with Viet Cong intelligence coverage—including penetration—of the South Vietnamese establishment, reduce the effectiveness of counteraction.

21. A shortage of experienced and aggressive leaders, especially at the company grade and noncommissioned officer level, is one of the GVN's most serious weaknesses. This in part reflects the problem of adapting a conventional force to the requirements of counterinsurgency and simultaneously expanding the size of this force. In part it also reflects political factors. For example, promotions tend to be based upon presumed loyalty to Diem rather than upon professional competence. Senior commanders frequently feel hampered by the fact that some of their subordinates are directly controlled by or have direct access to the Presidency. US support and presence and some increased disposition on the part of the Presidency to allow professional officers greater freedom have tended to improve officer morale and to increase

military initiative in the field. Some officers, however, still question Diem's ability to lead the country to victory, and reports of military coup plotting persist. Morale among the enlisted ranks is harder to determine and varies from unit to unit, but desertions and AWOLs still constitute a serious drain on manpower.

22. The political impact of government military operations has sometimes been diminished by mistakes and offenses committed by government forces. Although such incidents are difficult to prevent, South Vietnamese leaders generally recognize this problem and are trying to correct it.

23. *Politico-Military Programs and Their Effectiveness.* In concert with its military endeavors, the GVN is engaged in a number of social, economic, and political programs. Especially important are two interrelated politico-military programs: clear-and-hold operations and the strategic hamlets. Both of these programs are designed to provide the peasantry with protection from Viet Cong depredations and, concomitantly, to deny the Viet Cong continued access to the peasantry. Clear-and-hold operations are integrated pacification projects in which priority areas are cleared by military force; political control is then consolidated by building strategic hamlets and sending in Civic Action teams to set up governmental services and help the villagers help themselves. The strategic hamlet program involves grouping the peasant population in fortified, defensible settlements and undertaking various measures within these settlements to weed out Viet Cong sympathizers, improve the villager's lot, enhance the government's image, and give the peasant grounds for identifying himself with the government's fight against the Viet Cong. The Citizens' Irregular Defense effort is a related program also designed to separate the populace from the Viet Cong. Its armed groups, for example, are designed to penetrate insecure areas and establish enclaves of security; these, in turn, are to be expanded and eventually linked with areas where strategic hamlets are already established.

24. The strategic hamlet program is an undertaking of major importance. It has enlarged the area under effective government control, and there are many indications that the Communists consider it a threat of considerable magnitude. If effectively implemented it can strike at the roots of Viet Cong strength. Most South Vietnamese leaders regard the program as a key element in the counterinsurgency effort. Some of them—principally Ngo Dinh Nhu—also regard the program as a major step in the social reconstruction of rural Vietnam and as a means of consolidating their political control over it.

25. The government claims to have completed more than 5,000 strategic hamlets and to have about 2,000 others under construction. The "completed" hamlets vary widely in the quality of their physical defenses

and the effectiveness of their political programs. The most successful have been ones set up in areas where integrated and systematic pacification has been undertaken; however, in many instances, hamlets have been set up without the necessary basis for their continuing defense having been established. Administrative deficiencies have also hampered the execution of the program; excessive exactions have frequently been levied on local resources, peasants have often not been compensated for materials or labor furnished, and officials have tended to show more interest in controlling the hamlet population than in improving its living conditions.

26. Results of clear-and-hold operations conducted in a few provinces last year were encouraging, and plans for similar operations have been drawn up for all provinces. However, there is evidence that the government is becoming impatient with the time and effort such integrated operations demand. Diem is apparently coming to feel that his armed forces have improved to the point where they may now be able to mount quick, "leap-frog" military strikes against the Viet Cong throughout the country without worrying about the political consolidation of such military gains.

IV. PROGRESS AND PROSPECTS

27. *Current Military Situation.* Although there is no satisfactory objective means of determining how the war is going, we believe that—all factors considered—Communist progress has been blunted and the situation is improving. Strengthened South Vietnamese capabilities and effectiveness, and particularly US involvement, are causing the Viet Cong increased difficulty. There are some indications that the Viet Cong are suffering from local shortages of supplies and a decline in morale. There have been few desertions by Viet Cong regular personnel, but there has been some increase in desertions from the Viet Cong militia and guerrilla forces. Although statistics of casualties and figures on the numbers of villages under government control are not very reliable or very helpful indicators, a greater degree of security in the countryside has apparently been achieved and the government's control of important population areas has expanded somewhat during the past several months.

28. There are as yet no persuasive indications, however, that the Viet Cong have been grievously hurt. They continue to operate in most sections of South Vietnam, and much of the countryside remains in their hands. Although the number of Viet Cong incidents and attacks is below 1962 levels, this number has increased in the past few weeks. Government military capabilities have increased markedly during the past year, but so have those of the Viet Cong.

29. *Communist Intentions.* The magnitude of the US commitment and the increasing effectiveness of the South Vietnamese counterinsurgency effort are almost certainly causing Hanoi and its Viet Cong subordinates increasing concern. Although we believe that the Communists have in no way relaxed their determination to win control of South Vietnam, they must realize that their task is becoming increasingly difficult, and they may be reappraising their general policy. We believe it unlikely, especially in view of the open US commitment, that the North Vietnamese regime will either resort to overt military attack or introduce acknowledged North Vietnamese military units into the south in an effort to win a quick victory.

30. For the present, at least, we believe that the Communists will continue to wage a war of attrition, hoping for some break in the situation which will lead to victory. They must be aware, for example, of the disaffection engendered by the political methods of the regime, and they are probably also aware of the dissatisfaction among many Americans over the policies and practices of the GVN. They probably hope for political deterioration which will make their task easier, or that the US will tire of costly and frustrating guerrilla warfare and accept some facesaving way out. At some point the Communists might launch a serious effort to convene an international conference to consider the neutralization of South Vietnam.

31. Any non-Communist coup effort would probably be regarded as providing an opportunity for exploitation. We believe that at present the Communists have neither the capability themselves to lead a successful *coup d'état* nor the ties with the non-Communist opposition which would enable them to participate in a coup led by non-Communists. Nevertheless, they might be able in an unstable situation resulting from either a successful or unsuccessful coup to gain some politically strategic position. In any event, the Communists evidently hope that a combination of military pressure and political deterioration will in time create favorable circumstances either for delivering a *coup de grâce* or for a political settlement, say on the model of Laos, which would enable them to continue the struggle on more favorable terms.

32. *The Outlook.* Whether the Communists are correct in their appraisal will, of course, depend in some measure upon the extent and nature of US involvement, but primarily upon the South Vietnamese response to the developing situation. We do not believe that it is possible at this time to project the future course of the war with any confidence. Despite GVN progress, the situation remains fragile. A series of major Viet Cong successes, should they occur, might have a shattering psychological effect. Nevertheless, the heavy US involvement and close working relationships between US and Vietnamese personnel have fundamentally altered the outlook. Changes and improvements have occurred during the past year which for the first time

(Continued...)

indicate that the Viet Cong can be contained militarily and that further progress can be made in expanding the area of government control and in creating greater security in the countryside. However, some areas of Viet Cong control, such as the Mekong delta, will be very difficult to pacify, decisive campaigns have yet to be fought, and no quick and easy end to the war is in sight.

33. Developments in the last year or two have also gone some distance in establishing a basis for winning over the peasantry and in improving the efficiency of the military establishment and the civilian bureaucracy. It can, of course, be argued that only a highly centralized regime, single-mindedly dedicated to independence, and placing a heavy emphasis on personal loyalty can cope with the problems of guerrilla warfare. However, we believe that a greater willingness on the part of the regime to enlist the active support of those who have become disaffected or discouraged in the face of Diem's techniques of government would considerably speed the reduction of the Viet Cong insurgency.

34. Substantial reduction of Viet Cong military power, however, would probably intensify rather than reduce the need for changes in the philosophy and practice of the Diem regime, if revived insurgency were to be precluded and military victory translated into political consolidation. The achievement of physical security in the countryside would in itself satisfy a major political requirement in convincing the peasants of the government's ability to protect them. But the government must be both willing and able to expand its efforts to bring social, political, and economic improvements to the countryside if the peasant is to recognize a stake in the survival of the government and to be fortified against Communist blandishments. Effective action in this and other fields, particularly with the removal of a substantial US presence at all levels of the government, would almost certainly require a wider participation in the development and implementation of policy and a considerable reduction in the tight, personal control of the bureaucracy.

35. On the basis of its past performance, the ability of the Diem regime to move willingly and effectively in these directions is questionable, and may become even more so should military victory come within sight. With the removal of the inhibiting effects of an immediate and overwhelming military danger, political stability would be greatly threatened if disappointment with the regime's performance mounted among important sectors of the population and the conviction deepened that legal avenues to change remained blocked.

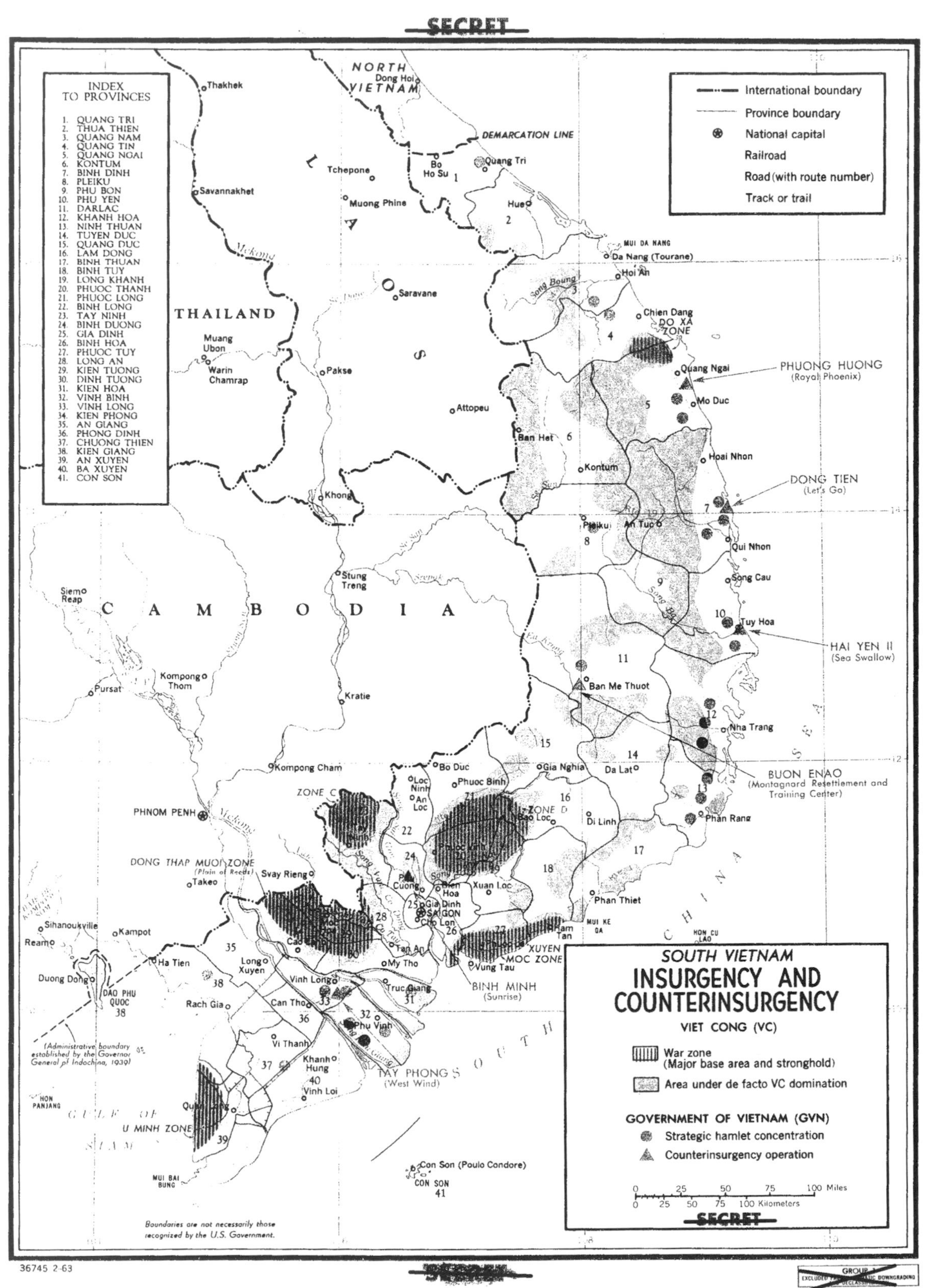
SECRET
INDEX TO PROVINCES
1. QUANG TRI
2. THUA THIEN
3. QUANG NAM
4. QUANG TIN
5. QUANG NGAI
6. KONTUM
7. BINH DINH
8. PLEIKU
9. PHU BON
10. PHU YEN
11. DARLAC
12. KHANH HOA
13. NINH THUAN
14. TUYEN DUC
15. QUANG DUC
16. LAM DONG
17. BINH THUAN
18. BINH TUY
19. LONG KHANH
20. PHUOC THANH
21. PHUOC LONG
22. BINH LONG
23. TAY NINH
24. BINH DUONG
25. GIA DINH
26. BINH HOA
27. PHUOC TUY
28. LONG AN
29. KIEN TUONG
30. DINH TUONG
31. KIEN HOA
32. VINH BINH
33. VINH LONG
34. KIEN PHONG
35. AN GIANG
36. PHONG DINH
37. CHUONG THIEN
38. KIEN GIANG
39. AN XUYEN
40. BA XUYEN
41. CON SON
International boundary
Province boundary
National capital
Railroad
Road (with route number)
Track or trail
NORTH VIETNAM
DEMARCATION LINE
THAILAND
CAMBODIA
PHUONG HUONG (Royal Phoenix)
DONG TIEN (Let's Go)
HAI YEN II (Sea Swallow)
BUON ENAO (Montagnard Resettlement and Training Center)
BINH MINH (Sunrise)
TAY PHONG (West Wind)
DO XA ZONE
ZONE C
ZONE D
DONG THAP MUOI ZONE (Plain of Reeds)
MOC ZONE
U MINH ZONE
PHNOM PENH
SAIGON
SOUTH CHINA SEA
GULF OF SIAM
(Administrative boundary established by the Governor General of Indochina, 1939)
Boundaries are not necessarily those recognized by the U.S. Government.
SOUTH VIETNAM
INSURGENCY AND COUNTERINSURGENCY
VIET CONG (VC)
War zone (Major base area and stronghold)
Area under de facto VC domination
GOVERNMENT OF VIETNAM (GVN)
Strategic hamlet concentration
Counterinsurgency operation
0 25 50 75 100 Miles
0 25 50 75 100 Kilometers
SECRET
36745 2-63

SNIE 50-2-64

Probable Consequences of Certain US Actions with Respect to Vietnam and Laos

25 May 1964

APPROVED FOR RELEASE
DATE: JAN 2005
(b)(3)

~~TOP SECRET~~

SNIE 50-2-64
25 May 1964
TS #0038277

SPECIAL
NATIONAL INTELLIGENCE ESTIMATE
NUMBER 50-2-64

Probable Consequences of Certain US Actions with Respect to Vietnam and Laos

Submitted by the
DIRECTOR OF CENTRAL INTELLIGENCE
Concurred in by the
UNITED STATES INTELLIGENCE BOARD
As indicated overleaf
25 MAY 1964

~~TOP SECRET~~

Nº 55

PROBABLE CONSEQUENCES OF CERTAIN US ACTIONS WITH RESPECT TO VIETNAM AND LAOS

THE PROBLEM

To estimate the consequences of certain US and US-sponsored actions against North Vietnam (DRV) and Communist-held Laos, the objectives of which would be to induce the DRV to bring about a major reduction of Viet Cong insurrectionary activity in South Vietnam and to respect the 1962 Geneva agreement on Laos.

ASSUMPTIONS [1]

I. The actions to be taken, primarily air and naval, would begin with GVN (US-assisted) operations against the DRV and Communist-held Laos, and might subsequently involve overt US military actions. They would be on a graduated scale of intensity, ranging from reconnaissance, threats, cross-border operations, and limited strikes on logistical targets supporting DRV efforts in South Vietnam and Laos, to strikes (if necessary) on a growing number of military and economic targets in the DRV. In the absence of all-out attacks by the DRV or Communist China, the measures foreseen would not involve attacks on population centers or resort to nuclear weapons.

---

[1] These assumptions have been given to the intelligence community for the purpose of this estimate and are not meant to represent the full range of options open to the US. The intelligence community is not asked to assess the consequences either (1) of undertaking other broad courses, or (2) of not undertaking the general course discussed in this estimate.

~~TOP SECRET~~

II. That these actions would be accompanied by these US moves:

A. Through various channels, conveying the limited nature of US intentions to Hanoi, Peiping, and Moscow.

B. Stationing initially some 5,000 US combat troops and certain additional air elements in northeastern Thailand, with a possible increase at a later stage.

C. Giving the enemy tangible evidence of US seriousness of purpose by readying and deploying strong US strike units—naval, air, and ground assault—to the Western Pacific and the South China Sea.

D. Providing increased military support, including air defenses, to South Vietnam. Further, stiffening overall GVN military and administrative capabilities by the infusion of substantial additional US personnel.

E. Acting diplomatically to avert a new Geneva conference, at least until it was judged that the above actions had improved the bargaining position of the US and its associates.

CONCLUSIONS

A. In response to US preparatory and low-scale actions—force deployments, serious threats, or GVN/Farmgate attacks on outlying targets in Communist-held Laos or North Vietnam—Hanoi would probably agitate world opinion against the US, hoping that a new Geneva conference or UN action would result, and bring a cessation of attacks. We think that North Vietnam, while taking various precautionary measures, would order the Viet Cong and Pathet Lao to refrain from dramatic new attacks, and might reduce the level of the insurrections for the moment. Communist China and the USSR would both support these courses. The Communists' line would probably be that the outcome of a conference should be to stabilize the situation in South Vietnam and Laos. Their intention, however, would be to preserve Communist gains and assets in these two countries and to resume the insurrectionary campaigns at a later date.

~~TOP SECRET~~

~~TOP SECRET~~

B. If these initial responses did not succeed, and attacks on North Vietnam continued, it is likely that the Communists would intensify their political action efforts against the US course. Hanoi might intermittently step up the tempo of the insurrections in South Vietnam and Laos, while still seeking a negotiated settlement. If these tactics, too, failed, the scale of attacks broadened, and North Vietnam began to suffer considerable destruction, Hanoi's leaders would have to ask themselves whether the tactics they were pursuing were worth the destruction of their country. We are unable to set any meaningful odds for the course North Vietnam's leaders would adopt at this juncture, though we incline to the view that they would lower their terms for a negotiated outcome; they would do so in the interests of preserving their regime and in the expectation of being able to renew the insurrections in South Vietnam and Laos at a later date. There would nevertheless be a significant danger that they would fight, believing that the US would still not be willing to undertake a major ground war, or that if it was, it could ultimately be defeated by the methods which were successful against the French.

C. Communist China almost certainly would not wish to become involved in hostilities with US forces. It would accordingly proceed with caution, though it would make various threatening gestures. There would probably not be high risk of Chinese Communist ground intervention unless major US/GVN ground units had moved well into the DRV or Communist-held areas of northern Laos, or possibly, the Chinese had committed their air and had subsequently suffered attack on CCAF bases in China. The USSR would make strenuous propaganda and political efforts in Hanoi's behalf, and would probably offer various weapons and air defense equipment. We believe, however, that the USSR would refrain from military actions in the area, and would not provoke a crisis with the US elsewhere which would bring a direct US–USSR confrontation. Its primary concern would be to exert its influence in a manner to insure a negotiated settlement, though without prejudicing its future relations with Hanoi.

~~TOP SECRET~~

D. Clear-cut achievement of the US objectives as stated in the Problem would signify not that the Communist threat in Southeast Asia was removed, but simply that time had been gained for further constructive action to deal with the threat. The US commitment would in itself improve anti-Communist morale and improve the chances for such action. On the other hand, to the degree that the consequences of the US action were ambiguous or unsuccessful, there would almost certainly be a strong tendency for morale and discipline in South Vietnam and Laos to deteriorate rapidly—perhaps more rapidly than if the US had not begun its intensified effort. Such deterioration would be felt generally through non-Communist Asia.

~~TOP SECRET~~

DISCUSSION

I. THE NATURE OF THE PROBLEM

1. The ability of the US to compel the DRV to turn off the VC insurrection rests principally upon the effect of US sanctions on the *will* of DRV leadership to continue and to enlarge that insurrection. The measures envisaged would not seriously affect Communist *capabilities* to continue that insurrection. Despite the direction, personnel, and material support which the DRV gives the VC, the primary sources of Communist strength in South Vietnam are indigenous: peasant grievances and war-weariness; VC terror, arms capture, disciplined organization, and highly developed intelligence systems; and the fact that the VC enjoys some status as a nationalist movement. Provided DRV direction continued, from either Hanoi or the bush, such indigenous support would continue to constitute a substantial threat until and unless the GVN developed hamlet security and overcame the political misrule and uncertainty of the past two years.

2. The situation is different in the case of Laos; indeed, the PL would deteriorate rapidly if the substantial stiffening now provided by the DRV were withdrawn.

II. PRINCIPAL FACTORS INFLUENCING REACTIONS TO US AND US-SPONSORED ACTIONS

3. *Hanoi's Comprehension of GVN and US Intentions.* If the Communists are to respond in the desired way, they must understand that although the US is not seeking the destruction of the DRV regime, the US is fully prepared to bring ascending pressures to bear to persuade Hanoi to reduce the insurrections in South Vietnam and Laos. We believe that the leaders in Hanoi would almost certainly comprehend US purposes in the early phase of the actions proposed. Hitherto they have evidently understood and played on the reluctance of the US to become deeply engaged on the Asia mainland, and they would count on domestic pressures in an election year to sustain this reluctance. The means for communicating US intentions seem likely to be effective, and the advice given by the USSR and Communist China would probably support a correct interpretation.

4. As the scale of GVN and US attacks mounted, however, especially if the US seemed adamant against entering negotiation, Hanoi would tend increasingly to doubt the limited character of US aims. Similarly, the retaliatory measures which Hanoi might take in Laos and South Vietnam might make it increasingly difficult for the US to regard its

~~TOP SECRET~~

TOP SECRET

objectives as attainable by limited means. Thus difficulties of comprehension might increase on both sides as the scale of action mounted.

5. *The DRV View of its Stake in South Vietnam and Laos.* The DRV has been patient and cautious in pursuing the war in Laos and South Vietnam. It has been careful to avoid the costs and risks of direct involvement, and, to date at least, has pulled back whenever it appeared that its tactics might provoke a major US response. It has been willing to use time to wear down the morale of the South Vietnamese and Laotian governments and populations, to convince them that victory for the DRV, the VC, and the PL is inevitable, and to persuade them that the US will prove an unreliable and ineffective ally. Further, the DRV runs the insurrections very much on the cheap, without any major drain on its economy or military establishment. Nevertheless, the DRV is intensely committed to the final aim of bringing South Vietnam, and at some stage Laos, under Hanoi's control, an outcome which would for Hanoi's leaders mark the completion of their revolution.

6. There is evidence that confidence has been growing in Hanoi that the final phase in the struggle in South Vietnam is approaching. Evidently there has been a belief that disintegration was under way in South Vietnam, and that the pace of VC activity could be intensified. Nevertheless, we believe that Hanoi is not presently committed to a rapid push for final victory, is prepared to accept further delay and even temporary setbacks, confident that Communist or pro-Communist regimes responsive to Hanoi will eventually be established in Saigon and Vientiane. Further, the degree of Hanoi's control over the insurrections in South Vietnam and Laos is sufficient to insure that it could raise or lower the level of action there.

7. *DRV Capability to React Militarily in South Vietnam and Laos.* VC forces in South Vietnam include about 25,000 regulars (full-time troops in identifiable district, provincial, and regional units), plus 60–80,000 troops (most of whom are part-time) in local self-defense and guerrilla elements. Regular troops have been employed in combat, and we know of no units being "hoarded" for commitment at some decisive future time. Nevertheless, regular forces generally see action only one or two days a month. Further, many larger regular formations are normally broken up into smaller units (platoons and squads) which serve with local, part-time elements. Consequently, the VC would probably be able to mount a concentrated, fairly short-term attack considerably more intense than any it has to date. Against some single objective—of key psychological importance—they could probably coalesce and concentrate normally dispersed regular units to mount a much larger action than has yet been attempted. We are fairly confident that the VC could not gather more than a few battalions without

TOP SECRET

giving some prior indication. There are almost certainly VC terrorist cells in urban areas which have not yet been committed or discovered; thus the VC probably have the capability significantly to increase urban terrorism, particularly in Saigon, should they so decide.

8. Should the DRV wish to respond by augmenting VC capabilities with regular North Vietnamese forces, we believe that in about a month the DRV could infiltrate the equivalent of about one regular DRV brigade (on the order of 7,500 men) into South Vietnam. If, instead, the DRV undertook to react immediately with an overt invasion, they could probably attack across the DMZ with about two divisions in approximately two weeks time from making the decision to move, but they would have great logistical difficulty in sustaining such a force in combat in South Vietnam. Given more time, they could of course commit a considerably larger force.

9. Under present circumstances, PL/DRV forces now in Laos probably have the capability of overrunning most of the country. Should US or allied units be introduced, present Communist forces would probably have only a harassing capability. However, two North Vietnamese army brigades are believed to be positioned near the Laotian border (one at Dien Bien Phu, the other opposite Sam Neua) and elements of two additional brigades are deployed at various points near the frontier along the main routes leading into Laos. Consequently, Communist strength in Laos could be quickly augmented by at least two fully armed and equipped North Vietnamese regular brigades (about 15,000 men).

10. *DRV Capabilities for Defending Itself Against Attack.* The DRV could certainly concentrate sufficient troops to protect any major installation against ground attack by South Vietnamese forces, whether infiltrated overland, put in by sea, or air-dropped. Present DRV defense capabilities against aerial bombardment, however, are minimal. Its capabilities in anti-aircraft artillery have improved over the past several years to the point where the DRV could probably cope with helicopters and propeller aircraft, but North Vietnamese defenses would be relatively ineffective against high speed jets. It has a radar net of about 29 early warning and fire control installations situated throughout the country, but the equipment is obsolete. Mainland Chinese radar also covers North Vietnam, but so far as we know it is not now coordinated with the DRV net. North Vietnam is not known to have any surface-to-air missile capability. It has no combat aircraft at the present time, though the foundations for the creation of an air arm have been laid: headquarters, maintenance, and support organizations have been at least partially developed, and much work has been done on airfield improvement and construction. China could of course

provide fighter aircraft (probably MIG 17s) for a small "North Vietnamese" air force on short notice.

11. *DRV Ability and Willingness to Sustain Damage.* We have many indications that the Hanoi leadership is acutely and nervously aware of the extent to which North Vietnam's transportation system and industrial plant is vulnerable to attack. On the other hand, North Vietnam's economy is overwhelmingly agricultural and, to a large extent, decentralized in a myriad of more or less economically self-sufficient villages. Interdiction of imports and extensive destruction of transportation facilities and industrial plants would cripple DRV industry. These actions would also seriously restrict DRV military capabilities, and would degrade, though to a lesser extent, Hanoi's capabilities to support guerrilla warfare in South Vietnam and Laos. We do not believe that such actions would have a crucial effect on the daily lives of the overwhelming majority of the North Vietnamese population. We do not believe that attacks on industrial targets would so greatly exacerbate current economic difficulties as to create unmanageable control problems.

12. It is reasonable to infer that the DRV leaders have a psychological investment in the work of reconstruction they have accomplished over the last decade. Nevertheless, they would probably be willing to suffer some damage to the country in the course of a test of wills with the US over the course of events in South Vietnam.

13. *DRV Appraisal of the Value and Hazards of Chinese Communist Rescue.* An important concern of the DRV leaders would be to avoid having to be rescued at the price of Chinese dominance. DRV leaders seek to run their own show in Indochina, however often certain of them may voice support of Chinese debating positions against the Soviets. The considerable material support they have received from Communist states has not derogated DRV freedom of action. Moreover, they are chiefly dependent for economic and technical assistance upon the USSR and Eastern Europe. DRV leaders would probably consider that the introduction of Chinese and Soviet-supplied air defense means might have a deterrent effect on US intentions, and might provide some military offset to GVN measures against the North; we doubt, however, that Hanoi would have much confidence that such defense means could effectively protect the DRV from either overt US or Farmgate air attacks. Though DRV leaders would doubtless differ sharply on the question, Hanoi would almost certainly refrain from requesting such Chinese assistance as might endanger DRV independence, for example, large-scale ground force "volunteer" intervention. This hesitancy would of course be overcome if DRV leaders considered the existence of their regime to be at stake.

~~TOP SECRET~~

14. *DRV Judgment of the Weight to Attach to World Pressures (Communist and non-Communist) Against the US Actions.* In the early stages at least, Hanoi would probably rely heavily on a belief that considerable pressure would develop in the world against the US action and that this would compel the US to relax its pressures. DRV leaders probably would be confident that the VC and the PL could continue to undermine non-Communist authority in South Vietnam and Laos while the DRV and its Communist allies were spinning things out interminably at Geneva. Hanoi's leaders would also probably count on significant opposition to the US course developing within the US, especially in the event the US action were not quickly successful and a major world crisis had developed.

15. *The Interests and Capabilities of Communist China in the Area.* Peiping appears to be more-or-less content with the present scheme of things in Laos and South Vietnam. These situations have served as a convenient "national liberation" club with which to flail the Soviets, and Peiping doubtless considers that South Vietnam and Laos will ultimately be Communist, and even though DRV-dominated, fairly responsive to China. Moreover, it is increasingly clear that Peiping is taking advantage of the vacuum in northern Laos to increase its own, Chinese, presence there.

16. The Chinese leaders are, however, in no hurry, and almost certainly wish to avoid major hostilities with the US. Despite their brave talk, they have been niggardly with tangible support of the Vietnam war. Their military cautiousness of the past few years strongly suggests that they are painfully aware of the wide disparity which exists between modern US combat aircraft and their own obsolescent and deteriorating CCAF. They are concerned over GRC and even Indian intentions toward mainland China. These considerations, added to their vast domestic problems and their difficulties with Moscow, almost certainly impel the Chinese to caution.

17. *The Interests and Capabilities of the USSR in the Area.* The USSR has little effective control or influence over the immediate situations in Laos or South Vietnam, though its roles as Geneva co-Chairman and potential provider of support against US military actions make the Soviet position a highly important one. Current Soviet objectives in the area appear to be to preserve some semblance of unity with North Vietnam, to contain the growing influence of China in Hanoi, and to prevent escalation of local situations into a direct conflict involving US forces. For some time, the Soviets have been disengaging from their obligations in Laos and avoiding attitudes or positions which would antagonize North Vietnam. In order to forestall any more direct US intervention and obtain some means of influencing Hanoi, the Soviet

leaders evidently see a new conference as the best path. They probably appreciate, however, that should a major crisis develop in the area, they would be under great pressure not to be backed down by US firmness of purpose.

18. *The Interests of Other Principally Concerned Parties.* World opinions vary greatly concerning the South Vietnam and Laos situations. The GRC is always in favor of a more forceful US course. Certain states in the area friendly to the US—Thailand, the Philippines, Malaysia, Japan, and Australia—have rather ambiguous views: on the one hand, fear that the US will not prove staunch, and, on the other, fear that US staunchness might provoke extreme enemy reactions. The prevailing opinion among many observers in much of Western Europe seems to be that the Indochina and Laos situations are not susceptible of military solution, and that any American efforts to expand the war to the North would probably be ineffective and not worth the risk. The governments of America's various allies of course recognize that US success or failure in Indochina will in varying degree affect their countries accordingly. We doubt, however, that such considerations outweigh fears and uncertainties concerning US expansion of the war.

III. PROBABLE CONSEQUENCES OF THE US AND US-SPONSORED COURSES OF ACTION

A. Reactions of the DRV

19. In response to US preparatory and low-scale actions—force deployments, serious threats, or GVN/Farmgate attacks on outlying targets in Communist-held Laos or North Vietnam—Hanoi would probably agitate world opinion against the US, hoping that a new Geneva conference or UN action would result, and bring a cessation of attacks. We think that the DRV, while taking various precautionary measures, would order the VC and PL to refrain from dramatic new attacks, and might reduce the level of the insurrections for the moment. Communist China and the USSR would both support these courses. The Communists' line would probably be that the outcome of a conference should be to stabilize the situation in South Vietnam and Laos. Their intention, however, would be to preserve Communist gains and assets in these two countries and to resume the insurrectionary campaigns at a later date.

20. Although Hanoi leadership would doubtless be divided on the question, the DRV at this initial juncture would probably incline to the view that US reluctance to assume larger risks had been overcome only by the fact of deteriorating situations in Laos and South Vietnam. Hanoi would probably assume that US resort to GVN cover for its attacks

indicated an unwillingness to become deeply entangled itself, and that the basic US intent was perhaps limited to holding the South Vietnam and Laos situations together until after the US national elections. Accordingly, the DRV tactics of feigning compliance and of spinning out negotiations would be based on an expectation that VC and PL pressures in the area, and world pressures on the US, would oblige the US to call a halt.

21. Should this initial DRV course not succeed—especially if the level of punishment being suffered by North Vietnam were rising or the US were beginning overt attacks on North Vietnamese targets—Hanoi would probably make an all-out propaganda and diplomatic drive for negotiations. In such negotiations, Hanoi would probably still seek to avoid an outcome which would, for example through strict inspection procedures, effectively deny it the opportunity to continue support for the insurrections in South Vietnam and Laos. Hanoi might intermittently turn up the scale and level of the insurrections in order to improve its bargaining position and intensify international concern. Though we doubt that the DRV would attempt any overt invasion of Laos or South Vietnam, Hanoi might try for some psychologically spectacular victories in Laos and in South Vietnam (e.g., the seizure and sack of a provincial capital such as Quang Ngai). By this stage, DRV leaders would certainly have appealed for Soviet and Chinese Communist air defense support (radars, anti-aircraft artillery, SAMs, and possibly even CCAF aircraft), but we doubt that Hanoi would request Chinese Communist ground troops.

22. If the scale of the attacks broadened, approached Hanoi, and destroyed more and more valuable targets, the DRV leaders would have to ask themselves whether the tactics they were pursuing were worth the destruction of their country. Their confidence in their ability to achieve an acceptable outcome at the negotiating table would decline, and they might conclude that the US was after all aiming at the destruction of their regime. At this point, they might believe that their only choices were ostensible capitulation to the US demand to halt all action in South Vietnam and Laos, or an all-out attack with their own forces in one or both of these areas. We are unable to set any meaningful odds for their choice between these alternatives. On balance, we incline to the view that they would still seek a negotiated outcome in the interest of preserving their regime and in the hope of a future opportunity to resume the struggles in South Vietnam and Laos. There would nevertheless be a significant danger that they would fight, believing that the US would still not be willing to undertake a major ground war, or that if it was, it could ultimately be defeated by the methods which were successful against the French.

B. Communist China's Role in the Crisis

23. Peiping would almost certainly threaten intervention as the action mounted and take a number of moves intended to deter further US attacks on the DRV. Nevertheless, we believe that the Chinese would in fact be cautious about becoming involved in hostilities with US forces. Peiping would probably respond to stepped-up punishment of the DRV by deploying sizable numbers of its forces to areas bordering Vietnam and Laos. It would probably offer Hanoi anti-aircraft units, and might make some combat aircraft available to the DRV. We do not believe that it would offer to commit the CCAF[2] at this stage, although this cannot be ruled out. There would be a possibility that unacknowledged Chinese Communist units might make deep incursions into Laos and, possibly, Thailand and Burma. The Chinese Communists might also resume HE shelling in the Taiwan Straits. We doubt, however, that they would undertake any significant military activity elsewhere in Asia. There would probably not be high risk of Chinese Communist ground intervention unless major US/GVN ground units had moved well into the DRV or Communist-held areas of northern Laos, or possibly, the Chinese had committed their air and had subsequently suffered attack on CCAF bases in China.

C. The Soviet Role in the Crisis

24. The Soviets would probably not take any extreme action in the Indochina area. They probably now expect some increase in US pressures against the DRV, and it is likely that they have already warned Hanoi that its present course could create a dangerous military confrontation. The USSR would make strenuous propaganda and political efforts in Hanoi's behalf, and would probably offer various weapons and air defense equipment. As the crisis deepened the Soviets would probably engage in some vague missile diplomacy and otherwise seek to bring strong pressure on the US to find some political settlement. They would meanwhile exert pressure on Hanoi to make concessions sufficient to insure the opening of negotiations. We do not believe that the Soviets, in the interests of supporting Hanoi, would provoke a crisis with the US elsewhere which would bring a direct US–USSR confrontation.

25. The Sino-Soviet dispute has not to date had any major effect on the situations in Laos or South Vietnam. Moscow probably would on the one hand be happy to see a neutralist barrier sustained in Laos and

[2] The CCAF probably could deploy about 420 jet fighters (MIG–15s, 17s, 19s) about 160 jet light bombers (IL–28), and about 40 piston light bombers to airfields in South China where they would be within operational range of Vietnam.

South Vietnam. On the other, because it could not afford to alienate the DRV and the PL, or to lay itself open to Chinese accusations of selling out the Communist revolutionary cause in the area, Moscow could not avoid giving at least political support to the Peiping-leaning DRV, PL, and VC. On balance, Moscow, like Peiping, would probably be guided primarily by regard for its own security interests; thus the fact of the Sino-Soviet dispute, *per se,* would probably not have great impact on developments in Southeast Asia. We believe that the interests of Moscow and Peiping conflict on so many vital scores that anything short of Sino-US hostilities or a threat to the existence of the DRV would do little to alter the Sino-Soviet relationship in any crucial fashion.

D. Probable Development in South Vietnam

26. The encadrement of a substantial number of American personnel into the military and civil sectors of the GVN would, in the DRV view, lend credence to US statements of its intent to increase its support to South Vietnam. Hanoi would, of course, not miss the opportunity to charge that the US was "taking over" South Vietnam. In addition there might be a stepped up campaign of anti-American terrorism in Saigon and in the field. These actions of the US, together with its new course against the North, would hearten the GVN and large segments of the military and civil population, as clear evidence of increased US commitment and involvement.

E. Reactions by US Allies and Others

27. Except in the case of a few of our most staunchly anti-Communist allies, initial world reactions to the US course would tend to be adverse in direct proportion to the intensity of US actions against the DRV: low-scale indications of disapproval in the case of lesser sanctions, rising, in many cases, to condemnation as the crisis fever rose. Even in the latter case, these reactions would generally not so much be pro-Communist as they would be critical of US "brinkmanship." Once US attacks on North Vietnam occurred, and especially if the US resisted a cease-fire and negotiations, a General Assembly majority for condemnation, on the pattern of Suez, would be probable. Subsequent world reactions would of course hinge fairly directly on success of the US sanctions: if they halted Communist expansion in Indochina and led to an easing of tensions, US firmness would be retrospectively admired, as in the Cuban missile showdown; if they ended in failure and retreat, US "maturity" and world leadership would again be questioned.

28. The role of France deserves special mention. We believe it altogether likely that de Gaulle would from the outset associate himself with Communist demands for a return to Geneva without preconditions.

in such a conference the French would seek to play an independent role in the interest of pushing de Gaulle's well-known but ill-defined proposals for neutralization of the area. This French line would no doubt encourage the Communists to keep their concessions to a minimum, and would limit the support the US and GVN might receive from others. If no outcome acceptable to the US could be obtained, and especially if the US became directly involved in a major military effort in South Vietnam, the strains already present in Franco-American relations and in the NATO alliance would be severely exacerbated.

F. General Consequences

29. Clear-cut achievement of the US objectives as stated in the Problem would signify not that the Communist threat in Southeast Asia was removed, but simply that time had been gained for further constructive action to deal with the threat. The US commitment would in itself improve anti-Communist morale and improve the chances for such action. On the other hand, to the degree that the consequences of the US action were ambiguous or unsuccessful, there would almost certainly be a strong tendency for morale and discipline in South Vietnam and Laos to deteriorate rapidly—perhaps more rapidly than if the US had not begun its intensified effort. Such deterioration would be felt generally through non-Communist Asia.

Memo

Would the Loss of South Vietnam and Laos Precipitate a "Domino Effect" in the Far East?

9 June 1964

APPROVED FOR RELEASE
DATE: JAN 2005 ~~SECRET~~

9 June 1964

MEMORANDUM FOR THE DIRECTOR

SUBJECT: Would the Loss of South Vietnam and Laos Precipitate a "Domino Effect" in the Far East?

1. The "domino effect" appears to mean that when one nation falls to communism the impact is such as to weaken the resistance of other countries and facilitate, if not cause, their fall to communism. Most literally taken, it would imply the successive and speedy collapse of neighboring countries, as a row of dominoes falls when the first is toppled--we presume that this degree of literalness is not essential to the concept. Most specifically it means that the loss of South Vietnam and Laos would lead almost inevitably to the communization of other states in the area, and perhaps beyond the area.

2. We do not believe that the loss of South Vietnam and Laos would be followed by the rapid, successive communization of the other states of the Far East. Instead of a shock wave passing from one nation to the next, there would be a simultaneous, direct effect on all Far Eastern countries. With the possible exception of Cambodia, it is likely that no nation in the area would quickly succumb to communism as a result of the fall of Laos and South Vietnam. Furthermore, a continuation of the spread of communism in the area would not be inexorable, and any spread which did occur would take time--time in which the total situation

~~SECRET~~

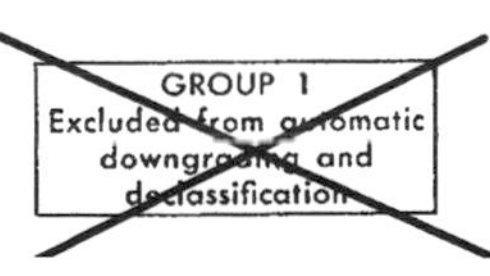

~~SECRET~~

might change in any of a number of ways unfavorable to the Communist cause.

3. The loss of South Vietnam and Laos to the Communists* would be profoundly damaging to the US position in the Far East, most especially because the US has committed itself persistently, emphatically, and publicly to preventing Communist takeover of the two countries. Failure here would be damaging to US prestige, and would seriously debase the credibility of US will and capability to contain the spread of communism elsewhere in the areas. Our enemies would be encouraged and there would be an increased tendency among other states to move toward a greater degree of accommodation with the Communists. However, the extent to which individual countries would move away from the US towards the Communists would be significantly affected by the substance and manner of US policy in the period following the loss of Laos and South Vietnam.

4. Southeast Asia. In the remaining piece of Indochina, Sihanouk would probably accelerate his movement toward accommodation with the Communists, in anticipation of a Communist victory he considers inevitable. Thailand would almost certainly shift toward a neutralist position, hoping thus to forestall any vigorous Communist move against

---

* This memorandum assumes a clear-cut Communist victory in these countries, i.e., a withdrawal of US forces and virtual elimination of US presence in Indochina, either preceeded or soon followed by the establishment of Communist regimes in Laos and South Vietnam. The results of a fuzzier, piecemeal victory, such as one staged through a "neutralist" phase, would probably be similar, though somewhat less sharp and severe.

-2-

~~SECRET~~

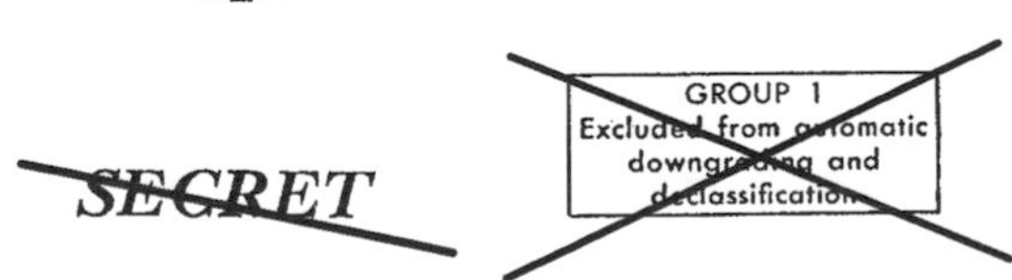

~~SECRET~~

the regime for as long as possible. Cooperation with the US would be reduced. Already, Thai leaders have made clear their worries about the firmness of US commitments in the area and their doubts about the wisdom of ready responsiveness to Washington's immediate policy desires. Burma would be less affected, having already virtually severed its ties with the US. Ne Win would see the ouster of the US from Indochina as confirming the wisdom of the isolationist, somewhat pro-Peiping course he has already embarked upon.

5. London, Canberra, and Kuala Lumpur have been counting ultimately upon US support for Malaysia against Indonesian aggression. They would be badly disconcerted by a US failure in Indochina, and would almost certainly seek some clear US commitment to help them defend Malaysia. Indonesia, for its part, would be emboldened in its efforts to crush Malaysia.

6. US Western Pacific Bases. US military strength in the Far East is based on the chain of islands from the Philippines to Japan, not on the Asian mainland. As long as the US can effectively operate from these bases, it will probably still be able to deter Peiping and Hanoi from overt military aggression. Furthermore, the protection of these island countries from Communist subversive efforts is a different problem from that of protecting countries on the mainland. In the Philippines, there would be some impetus to the tendency of ultra-nationalists, such as former Foreign Minister Lopez, to press for reduced cooperation with the US and a softening of the Philippines' anti-Peiping stand. They would also seek restrictions on US bases

-3-

~~SECRET~~

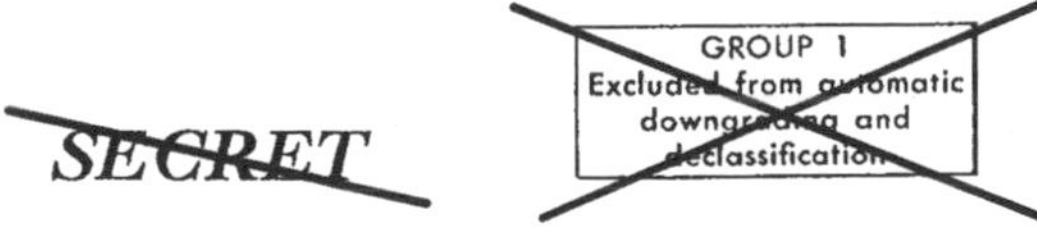

~~SECRET~~

similar to those presently enforced in Japan. We do not think this would affect Philippine government policy, at least as long as the present administration is in power in Manila.

7. On Taiwan, Chiang Kai-shek and his followers would be greately disheartened, but they would not be likely to seek an accommodation with the Communists. As in the case of the Philippines, the Nationalist Chinese leaders appreciate the efficacy of US sea and air power, and their nation has proved among the least vulnerable in the Far East to Communist infiltration and subversion.

8. In Japan, the loss of South Vietnam and Laos would almost certainly produce some increase of neutralist sentiment. There would be more questioning of the desirablity of remaining committed to the US side and continuing to be made a prime Communist target by the presence of US bases. The mutual defense treaty and the US bases in Japan and Okinawa would come under even greater attack than at present. At a minimum, political pressures for further restrictions on the use of these bases would be greatly intensified, and the government would probably make a few concessions to these pressures. We do not believe that there would be major changes in Japanese policy.

9. Communist Asia. Aside from the immediate joy in the DRV over achievement of its national goals, the chief effect would be upon Communist China, both is boosting its already remarkable self-confidence and in raising its prestige as a leader of World Communism. Peiping has already begun to advertise South Vietnam as proof of its thesis that the underdeveloped world is ripe for

-4-

~~SECRET~~

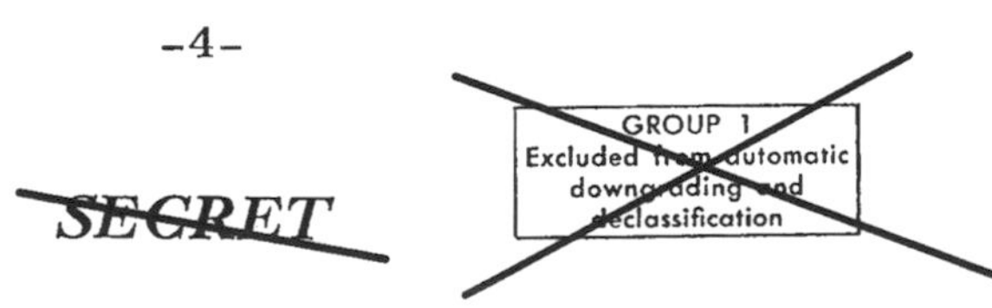

SECRET

revolution, that the US is a paper tiger, and that local insurgency can be carried through to victory without undue risk of precipitating a major international war. The outcome in South Vietnam and Laos would conspicuously support the aggressive tactical contentions of Peiping as contrasted with the more cautious position of the USSR. To some degree this will tend to encourage and strengthen the more activist revolutionary movements in various parts of the underdeveloped world.

FOR THE BOARD OF NATIONAL ESTIMATES:

SHERMAN KENT
Chairman

-5-

SECRET

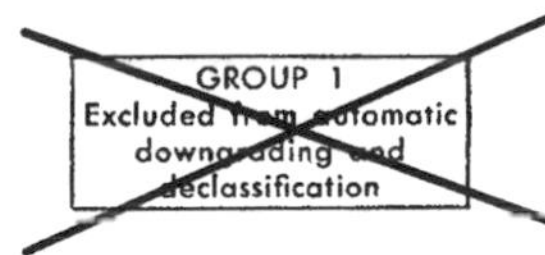

SNIE 53-2-64

The Situation in South Vietnam

1 October 1964

~~SECRET~~

SNIE 53-2-64
1 October 1964

SPECIAL NATIONAL INTELLIGENCE ESTIMATE
53-2-64

APPROVED FOR RELEASE
DATE: JAN 2005

(b)(3)

THE SITUATION IN SOUTH VIETNAM

NOTE: This is an estimate as approved by the United States Intelligence Board. No further distribution will be made.

Submitted by the
DIRECTOR OF CENTRAL INTELLIGENCE

Concurred in by the
UNITED STATES INTELLIGENCE BOARD

As indicated overleaf
1 October 1964

~~SECRET~~

(Continued...)

~~S-E-C-R-E-T~~

C E N T R A L   I N T E L L I G E N C E   A G E N C Y

1 October 1964

SUBJECT: SNIE 53-2-64: THE SITUATION IN SOUTH VIETNAM

THE PROBLEM

To examine the situation as it has developed since early September, and to assess its implications for the US.

CONCLUSIONS

A. Since our estimate of 8 September 1964* the situation in South Vietnam has continued to deteriorate. A coup by disgruntled South Vietnam military figures could occur at any time. In any case, we believe that the conditions favor a further decay of GVN will and effectiveness. The likely pattern of this decay will be increasing defeatism, paralysis of leadership, friction with Americans, exploration of possible lines of political accommoda-tion with the other side, and a general petering out of the war effort. It

* SNIE 53-64, "Chances for a Stable Government in South Vietnam," dated 8 September 1964, ~~SECRET~~.

~~S-E-C-R-E-T~~

GROUP 1
~~Excluded from automatic downgrading and declassification~~

is possible that the civilian government promised for the end of October could improve GVN esprit and effectiveness, but on the basis of present indications, this is unlikely.

B. We do not believe that the Viet Cong will make any early effort to seize power by force of arms; indeed, we doubt that they have the capability for such a takeover. They will continue to exploit and encourage the trend toward anarchy, looking for the emergence of a neutralist coalition government which they can dominate.

DISCUSSION

The GVN

1. Continued Political Deterioration. Political conditions in South Vietnam have continued to deteriorate since our estimate of early September.* Despite efforts by Prime Minister Nguyen Khanh to stabilize the situation, he has been faced with an attempted coup, rioting and demonstrations in the northern provinces, a massive labor strike in Saigon, and an armed revolt by Montagnard elements among the Special Forces. Khanh's authority, already weakened by the Buddhist-student crisis in August, has been further diminshed, and the degree of his support within the military establishment is increasingly

* SNIE 53-64 "Chances for a Stable Government in South Vietnam," dated 8 September 1964, ~~SECRET~~.

S-E-C-R-E-T

in question. Most of the non-Communist power elements appear to be marking time, pending their assessment of the civilian government which Khanh has promised will be formed by the end of October.

2. The Picture in Saigon. South Vietnam is almost leaderless at the present time. General Khanh has retained his position by making concessions to various interest groups -- political, religious, students, military, and labor -- which have pressed their demands upon him. In turn, these groups still seem bent on pursuing self interest and factional quarrels almost to the point of anarchy. A lack of sense of purpose and an absence of direction from above have seriously affected morale and created passiveness and apathy within the civil law enforcement agencies. Government ministries in Saigon are close to a standstill, with only the most routine operations going on. Cabinet ministers, as well as second-level bureaucrats, freely express their pessimism, and even though US and GVN officials are again meeting on pacification and other joint planning, these meetings are not being followed by action from the Vietnamese side.

3. GVN Military Morale and Effectiveness. The continuing disarray of the Saigon government, power struggles within the military leadership, and the activities of self-seeking politicians and religious leaders have adversely affected morale within the military establishment. However, the

S-E-C-R-E-T

the existing level of effectiveness of combat operations does not seem to have been seriously affected as yet. Nevertheless, continuing political instability would almost certainly aggravate such longstanding deficiencies in the Vietnamese military effort as inadequate motivation, initiative, and aggressiveness. A continuing lack of firm direction, and further squabbling among senior officers in particular, could depress the morale of the troops and junior officers to the critical point. Although the GVN armed forces have long had a high rate of desertion by individuals, there have been no important unit desertions or defections. If military morale continues to decline, however, desertion and defections within both the military and paramilitary services may occur on a larger scale, perhaps even by organized units.

4. Signs of Defeatism in GVN Leadership. High-ranking ARVN officers have confessed to US officers deep discouragement at the lack of leadership and direction. The J-3 of the Joint General Staff has indicated that he feels little reason even to discuss further pacification planning; various high-ranking field commanders have expressed similar pessimism; and General Khanh himself has shown signs of being overwhelmed by his responsibilities.

5. The Situation in the Countryside. The near paralysis of government initiative in Saigon appears to be spreading rapidly to outlying areas. Although the southern areas still appear relatively unaffected by the crises of the past several weeks, governmental authority has declined seriously in the northern coastal provinces where provincial and police officials are apparently receiving little guidance from Saigon. In such urban centers as

Hue, Danang, Qui Nhon, and Nha Trang, Vietnamese commanders have repeatedly failed to intervene in civil disturbances and rioting on the grounds they lacked precise orders; in some instances, actual authority has passed by default to extremist "vigilante" groups, such as the "People's Salvation (or Revolutionary) Council" (PRC). The nature of the provincial bureaucracy is such that it can rock along for considerable time, carrying out existing programs despite political deterioration in Saigon. Nevertheless, continued confusion and inaction in Saigon, or another coup, could rapidly produce a critical deterioration in government in the countryside. A slippage in morale and in programs among provincial administrations, at least in the central provinces, has already begun.

6. The Peoples Revolutionary Council (PRC). The PRC has established local councils in many coastal cities and may seek to form a chapter in Saigon, where two PRC leaders have recently been named to the new 17-men High National Council. The aims of the PRC are not clear, but the local councils seem vulnerable to Viet Cong penetration, and the fact that they have assumed government powers in some provincial cities tends to undermine Saigon's control and to damage the morale of civil servants.

7. The Montagnard Problem. The Rhade revolt of 20 September and the continuing possibility of further and more general uprisings by the Montagnards pose an immediate and very serious problem for the GVN. The Montagnards have

a violent dislike for and distrust of the lowland Vietnamese, and have sought autonomy for years. The Vietnamese on their part look down on the Montagnards; until recently, the GVN has usually acted in a manner which has widened rather than lessened the breach between the two. The problem has been further compounded by constant and rather intensive Viet Cong political and psychological agitation among the Montagnards, playing on their aspirations and their dislike of the ethnic Vietnamese. Resentment over the killing of some 70 Vietnamese by tribesmen during their revolt will make it extremely difficult for the GVN to offer settlement terms acceptable to the Montagnards. Thus, there will probably be continuing disorders in the Highland areas, diminishing cooperation with the GVN, and increasing Viet Cong influence.

8. Offsetting Considerations. Although the signs of deterioration are many and clear, there are offsetting considerations that reduce the likelihood of sudden collapse and afford some very slim hope that the trend can be arrested. The Vietnamese people have a long record of resilience in the face of adversity; the ability of the peasants and even of urban elements to continue normal patterns of life despite political disorder makes for some degree of basic stability. The routine functions of government still work fairly normally; business does go on; and the streets are not places of constant terror. Discouragement over the absence of leadership and the progress of the war has not yet led to calls for ending the fighting. Few if any of the many groups now seeking to enlarge their powers regard an accommodation with the Communists

as consistent with their interests. Finally, the military instrumentalities of pacification still exist and retain significant capabilities.

9. Tensions in US-GVN Relations. In the last month or so, there has been a disturbing increase in anti-American sentiment at various levels of Vietnamese society. Recent demonstrations in Hue, Da Nang, Qui Nhom, and Nha Trang have had definite anti-American overtones. These were probably attributable in part to Viet Cong agitation and incitement, but in some measure they seem also to have reflected a genuine irritation at the Americans for various reasons having no direct connection with Viet Cong activity. For its part, the Buddhist leadership, whether anti-Communist or not, is imbued with intense nationalism which has at times manifested itself in opposition to US policies and actions. Suspicion of US motives and concern over US involvement in internal policy is growing among the top echelons of the GVN, and, most importantly, on the part of Khanh himself.

10. GVN Contacts with the Communists. The principal GVN leaders have not to our knowledge been in recent contact with the Communists, but there has been at least one instance of informal contact between a lesser governmental official and members of the "National Liberation Front," which is a creation of Hanoi. Moreover, there are numerous potential channels of communication between the present GVN leadership and the DRV authorities, and these could very likely be used without US knowledge.

~~S-E-C-R-E-T~~

11. Coup Possibilities. Although no definite coup plans are known to be afoot at the moment, we believe that further coup attempts are likely, given the ambitions, discouragement, and bitterness prevalent among certain key South Vietnamese military and civilian figures -- and the comparative ease of mounting a coup attempt in the present deteriorating scene.

12. Alternatives to Present GVN Leadership. Present plans call for the establishment of a new, broadly-based, and predominantly civilian government by the end of October. Such a government might do better than the present one, but the odds are against its having the cohesion and effectiveness necessary to arrest the current decline. No visible alternative seems any more promising. Indeed, we cannot presently see any likely source of real leadership; no Magsaysay has yet appeared. None of the military personalities and factions seems capable of commanding a sufficiently broad spectrum of support. Of nonmilitary figures, the Buddhist leader Tri Quang is the strongest political personality and has demonstrated talents for leadership and organization. But he apparently desires to avoid such responsibility, and a Tri Quang government would face strong opposition from militant Catholics, some of the military, and certain other groups. Not least, it would be a difficult government for the US to work with, and some of its major policies would almost certainly not be consonant with US interests.

~~S-E-C-R-E-T~~

The Viet Cong

13. Viet Cong Policy. There are numerous signs that Viet Cong agents have played a role in helping sustain the level of civil disorder which has recently prevailed in the cities of South Vietnam; they have also affected the tone and direction taken by some recent protest demonstrations. Their hand was evident in the recent riots in the capital of Binh Dinh Province, and they may have already penetrated the PRC. Viet Cong propaganda throughout September has increasingly called upon the people to take advantage of the government's confusion by pressing on all fronts. This capitalizing on unrest is an old policy; what is new is the rich opportunity presented by the collapsing of GVN authority. The Viet Cong have apparently decided that heightened efforts on their part will reduce the country to near anarchy and the government to impotence, bringing an early victory in the form of a negotiated truce and a "neutralist" government dominated by their National Liberation Front. Although these heightened efforts may include some battalion-sized, or larger attacks, we do not believe that the Viet Cong are trying to force a military decision at this stage. Rather, they will continue stressing small-scale terrorist activity aimed at furthering the breakdown of administration and the decline of faith in the government.

14. Viet Cong Capabilities in the Cities. Viet Cong strength in the cities has almost certainly increased substantially in recent months. We

base this conclusion on our general reading of the present situation rather than on specific knowledge of current Viet Cong assets. In the closing days of the Diem regime, Vietnamese police and security agencies had a fairly good reading on the nature and extent of the Viet Cong apparatus in the capital area, and it did not constitute a serious threat at that time. Immediately following the November 1963 coup, however, Colonel Tran Ba Thanh became Deputy Director of National Police. There are strong grounds for believing that Thanh may be a Communist agent; in any event he released some key Viet Cong prisoners, destroyed Viet Cong dossiers in police archives, and placed at least one known Viet Cong agent in a key position within the police structure. Although Thanh was ousted when Khanh seized power, the Saigon police and security services have not recovered their anti-Communist capabilities. The fact that Communist agitation still remains under careful cover, however, suggests that the Viet Cong intend still to husband these assets and not risk them in a premature takeover attempt.

SNIE 10-6-65

Probable Communist Reactions to Certain US Actions

2 June 1965

~~TOP SECRET~~

107

SNIE 10-6-65
TS 185858
2 June 1965

APPROVED FOR RELEASE
DATE: JAN 2005

(b)(3)

SPECIAL NATIONAL INTELLIGENCE ESTIMATE

PROBABLE COMMUNIST REACTIONS TO CERTAIN US ACTIONS

This is the final version, no further distribution will be made

Submitted by the
DIRECTOR OF CENTRAL INTELLIGENCE

Concurred in by the
UNITED STATES INTELLIGENCE BOARD

As indicated overleaf
2 June 1965

~~TOP SECRET~~

~~T-O-P S-E-C-R-E-T~~

TS # 185858

CENTRAL INTELLIGENCE AGENCY

2 June 1965

SNIE 10-6-65: PROBABLE COMMUNIST REACTIONS TO CERTAIN US ACTIONS

THE PROBLEM

To estimate the reactions of the USSR, Communist China, and North Vietnam to US air strikes, including the use of heavy bombers, aimed at destroying fighter and bomber aircraft and surface-to-air missiles in North Vietnam.

THE ESTIMATE

1. Present Communist Reading of the Situation. In failing to make any meaningful response to the "pause," the DRV has plainly indicated that it is prepared to accept not only a continuation of US air attacks on military and transportation targets south of the 20th parallel, but also a considerable risk that the US will extend such attacks northward. The USSR, by supplying limited numbers of fighters, SAMs, and light bombers to the DRV, probably hopes to deter the US from air attacks in the Hanoi-Haiphong

~~T-O-P S-E-C-R-E-T~~

~~GROUP 1
Excluded from automatic downgrading and declassification~~

area. The Soviets would not consider the actual combat capabilities of these weapons to be the primary deterrent factor; the deterrent effect would rest more in the recognition by the US that to attack this element of Soviet support for the DRV would risk involving Moscow even more deeply. "In addition, the Communists may be testing US determination through introduction of offensive bombers into the Hanoi 'sanctuary', and, if this provokes no reaction, it may well be the Soviet/DRV intention to proceed with creating a sizable offensive air threat capable of supporting a major DRV thrust into South Vietman and/or Laos." Peiping's apprehensions regarding an extension of US air attacks northward are evident in its propaganda, its civil defense measures, and its public and private statements to outsiders, but it is evidently prepared to accept this risk.

Probable DRV Reactions

2. In light of these circumstances, attacks on North Vietnam's jet-capable airfields and SAM sites would be read by Hanoi to mean that military targets anywhere in the DRV were not safe from US attacks and that the chances of future attacks on urban centers and/or industrial targets were greatly increased. The DRV leaders would almost certainly believe that the US was ready to apply substantially greater force if needed to attain its stated objective of stopping DRV intervention in South Vietnam. It would also reinforce their concern that US objectives

may not be as limited in scope as the US has avowed. They recognize the vulnerability of their cities and industry to US or US-aided aerial bombardment and realize that their laborious efforts at industrialization over the past decade could be wiped out in short order.

3. Hanoi's decisions, however, probably have been and will continue to be influenced by its estimate of the likely course of the war in the South bolstered by the memory of the Viet Minh victory over the French and by its doctrinal conviction that its determination to sustain a prolonged and grinding struggle will prove stronger than that of the US. It probably thinks that, given present VC military strength and the political fragility of the Saigon regime, Communist forces in South Vietnam are moving toward victories which could crack their adversaries' will to continue the struggle. If so, Hanoi might feel that punishment from the air would be an acceptable price to pay for the achievement of its political objectives, and the vindication of its doctrinal belief in the inevitable success of a "People's War."

4. The present Problem postulates specified vehicles of attack, i.e., B-52s, and precisely specified targets, i.e., the Soviet-supplied SAMs and jet fighter and light jet bomber aircraft (IL-28s), the former located close in to Hanoi, the latter located in the northerly areas of North Vietnam, and asks our estimate of probable reactions under the

current political and military conditions. Our present estimate is that the odds are against the postulated US attacks' leading the DRV to make conciliatory gestures to secure a respite from the bombing; rather, we believe that the DRV would persevere in supporting the insurgency in the South. *

* The Assistant Chief of Staff, Intelligence, USAF disagrees with the judgment made in this paragraph. He would substitute the following for the last sentence:

"Our present estimate is that the odds on the DRV making conciliatory gestures to secure a respite from further bombing will be markedly enhanced by successful accomplishment of the postulated US attacks, which by eliminating any concept of an area 'sanctuary' in North Vietnam will pose the added threat that urban/industrial targets might be next. The selective and limited nature of US bombing target selections to date may well have led Hanoi seriously to underestimate the extent of US determination to exert the necessary power to force discontinuance of DRV support for the insurgency in the south. A Moscow/Hanoi agreement on the requirement for a respite could provide both countries an acceptable 'out' which they could justify for 'tactical' purposes within the tenets of Communist doctrine."

5. If Hanoi did persevere, it would be unlikely to revise its military strategy or basic timetable in response to the US strikes. Nevertheless, for psychological effect on both Communists and anti-Communists, Hanoi might order retaliatory Viet Cong raids, sabotage, or sneak attacks on major bases or installations in South Vietnam. For similar reasons, Hanoi -- perhaps encouraged by Peiping -- would almost certainly re-examine the possibility of striking at the US carrier force in the Tonkin Gulf by sea or from the air and would certainly study the feasibility of an air strike against US installations in South Vietnam. Though Hanoi would probably estimate that the chances of seriously damaging US forces were not great, the effect of a successful attack would by psychologically so advantageous that Hanoi might make the attempt if it had the capability.

6. If the US strikes had destroyed their air offensive capabilities, the North Vietnamese might consider an overt invasion of South Vietnam. Because of the great risks of such an action, however, we believe they would not do so. Hanoi would certainly continue and, to the extent possible, step up its support of the Viet Cong and would almost certainly seek to inject an increasing number of North Vietnamese line units into Viet Cong forces with little or no effort at concealment. The fears engendered by the US bombings would probably not destroy Hanoi's determination or loosen its control of the country. Indeed, it might have the opposite effect of rallying the population behind the regime.

~~T-O-P S-E-C-R-E-T~~

7. Probable Chinese Communist Reactions. Although the Chinese Communists have professed to believe all along that the US would expand its air strikes, the bombing of SAM sites and airfields north of the 20th parallel would still be regarded in Peiping as a major and serious development. However, the Chinese leaders probably are more optimistic than Hanoi, and certainly more so than Moscow, that the US is nearing a humiliating defeat in the South, and will urge Hanoi to stand firm whatever the cost. The use of SAC bombers would increase Peiping's concern that eventually these strategic forces might be used against targets in China, particularly in nuclear attacks against advanced weapons facilities. Nevertheless, the Chinese would feel a strong need to do something more to help the North Vietnamese, and to prevent Moscow from gaining more influence in Hanoi and in the Vietnamese situation in general. They would also seek to exploit the situation to further weaken Moscow's influence in the international Communist movement and in the underdeveloped world.

8. It is likely that Hanoi would request -- and that the Chinese would provide -- additional support, e.g., ground equipment and personnel for air defense purposes or engineering help for constructing and repairing airfields. The Chinese probably would also supply fighter aircraft units on request, providing

~~T-O-P S-E-C-R-E-T~~

they could be based in North Vietnam. They would not wish to use bases in China because of the risk of US retaliatory strikes against these bases.* The Chinese might offer to send ground combat troops to North Vietnam as an earnest of their commitment to defend their ally, but we do not believe bombing of airfields and SAM sites would bring Hanoi to the point of accepting such an offer by Peiping. Unless and until Peiping concluded that the existence of the Hanoi regime was in danger, it would probably not unilaterally send a "rescue mission" into North Vietnam. Peiping might, however, make threatening troop movements and additional air deployments in South China with the objective of deterring the US from further bombings.

Probable Soviet Reactions

9. US bombings or airfields and SAM sites, especially by bombers from the Strategic Air Command, would provoke a crisis for Soviet policy. So far the Soviets have been pursuing three somewhat inconsistent objectives -- to compete with Peiping for influence over the DRV, to contribute to deterring US pressures against Hanoi, and at the same

* The Director of Intelligence and Research, Department of State, believes that the assumed vigorous US air attacks on major DRV targets would probably evoke the employment over North Vietnam of Chinese air defense from bases in China. Current deployment of Chinese aircraft to South China, the apparent completion of an airfield just north of the DRV border, and explicit Chinese statements alleging willingness to accept US bombing of China, suggest Chinese readiness to test US assertions that no sanctuary will necessarily exist should Peiping provide important support to Hanoi.

time to avoid becoming overly involved in the present US-DRV confrontation. As noted in paragraph 1, the Soviets may also be testing US determination and be prepared, in the absence of a US response, to further increase the DRV's offensive capability They have apparently hoped that, in view of the situation in South Vietnam, the US would sooner or later have to negotiate its way out of the war. The postulated US actions would strike a blow at such calculations and would probably convince the Soviets that the risks and costs of their involvement would be greater than they had assumed. In particular, there would be a greater loss of prestige in ignoring any casualties among Soviet personnel than might have been the case only a month ago.

10. The Soviets would almost certainly feel compelled to comply promptly with DRV requests to provide substitutes for those weapons systems destroyed by the US attack, though they might not again provide bomber aircraft. It is also probable that more Soviet personnel would be supplied to man such equipment. Moscow might even acknowledge a Soviet presence in the hope of deterring the US from further attacks, though this would risk a further loss of prestige if deterrence again failed.

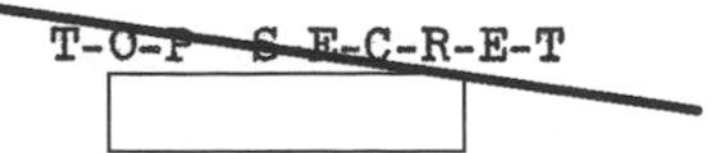

11. The Soviets would clearly recognize the danger of continued escalation, particularly since SAC had been employed. Hence, they would probably urge Hanoi to open up political avenues for controlling the conflict and would put pressure on the US to stop bombing and to negotiate. Soviet pressures would be exerted in a variety of forums, but the DRV's demonstrated unwillingness to involve the UN in Vietnam makes it unlikely that that organ would become a major political battle ground. US-Soviet relations would further deteriorate. If the crisis deepened and Hanoi chose to continue the struggle, the Soviets would face their most serious dilemma since the Cuban missile crisis.

12. If Hanoi stood adamant against negotiation, it is possible that the Soviets, recognizing the growing chances of being forced to confront the US in Indochina, would break with Peiping and Hanoi and back away from any deeper commitments. Moscow almost certainly realizes that the US enjoys a local military advantage vis-a-vis the USSR in the area. Nevertheless, we doubt that the Soviets would pay the political price of backing down and thereby handing China a major political victory and weakening its own prestige and influence throughout the world.*

---

* See Assistant Chief of Staff, Intelligence, USAF footnote to paragraph 4, page 4.

13. Thus in the aftermath of the US attacks, we think the Soviets would probably conclude that they had little choice but to increase aid to the DRV. If the war continued without the prospect of US-DRV negotiations, the Soviets would probably extend new commitments to Hanoi and level new pressures and threats against the US. What precise moves Moscow would make in this direction would depend greatly on Hanoi's demands, on the nature and degree of Chinese involvement, and on how the Soviets interpreted US actions and estimated US intentions.

Memo

Reactions to a Further US Buildup in South Vietnam

10 June 1965

APPROVED FOR RELEASE
DATE: JAN 2005

(b)(3)

TS# 185904 b

10 June 1965

MEMORANDUM

SUBJECT: Reactions to a Further US Buildup in South Vietnam

1. In this memorandum we consider foreign reactions to an assumed US buildup to 150,000 troops in Vietnam as compared with the 50,000 now present and the 70,000 level due to be reached in August. We assume that no comprehensive public announcement of force goals would be made, and that foreign opinion would be reacting to a gradual perception of the US course of action.

2. Our main conclusions are that this strengthening of the US commitment would make some impression on the Communists, and would raise some dangers in our relations with the South Vietnamese, but that the important reactions would come later, when the effectiveness of the total US effort was tested in combat. These considerations are discussed in the following paragraphs.

Reactions in South Vietnam

3. The initial reactions of the South Vietnamese would be somewhat ambivalent: encouragement over the reinforcement,

GROUP 1
Excluded from automatic downgrading and declassification

accompanied by some tendency to relax and let the US do the fighting. Much would depend upon the way in which US troops were employed. If used to clear and hold large areas, particularly heavily populated areas, the US forces would tend to acquire both the responsibility for the war and the stigma of an army of occupation with colonialist ambitions. This tendency would be less if the US forces were used in a mobile fashion to assist ARVN units, and shared in the most difficult fighting.

4. Ultimately, of course, the key determinant would be the effectiveness of the total US effort, political, economic, and diplomatic, as well as military. If this produced a slackening of VC pressures, US-South Vietnamese working relations would be fairly smooth. If, on the contrary, the war dragged on without respite, war weariness and anti-Americanism would probably begin to threaten the US political base in South Vietnam.

Communist Reactions

5. Viet Cong and DRV. We believe that a US buildup itself, on the scale considered here, would not alter VC/DRV determination to prosecute the struggle. The Communists would recognize that, in military terms, their task had become harder. They would recognize that, in political terms, the US action reaffirmed

~~TOP SECRET~~

its determination not to accept military defeat. But the arrival of US forces in these numbers would not change the Communists' basic calculation that their staying power is inherently superior to that of Saigon and Washington.

6. The real test, then, would be that of combat. The Viet Cong would respond, as it has to past injections of US forces, by stepping up the insurgency, and the DRV would reinforce it as necessary with men and equipment, including further line units of the PAVN. In this effort, the Communists would probably hold to their present strategy of attrition and subversion, although on a significantly increased scale. They would still seek to defeat the GVN through exhaustion and internal collapse without letting US/GVN forces engage them in decisive battle.

7. We do not know how the test of combat would come out at the level of US involvement now being considered. If, at this or some higher level, the tide of battle runs against the Viet Cong for a substantial period, the Communists would probably consider a large-scale ground offensive by DRV troops. They would recognize, however, that the enlarged US forces had made this more difficult. They would also fear that the US, with a very heavy stake in the war, would not accept defeat in that new

- 3 -

~~TOP SECRET~~

kind of war without expanding it to the DRV and China. In these circumstances, they would probably prefer to resort to negotiations or simply to let the fighting subside while conserving their own forces. They would be particularly likely to react in this way if they had become convinced that in any enlarged war, the US would use nuclear weapons.

8. China. Peiping would react to the assumed US buildup by urging the VC and the DRV to continue the struggle. It would promise to come to Hanoi's aid if the US involvement reached the point of an invasion of North Vietnam. It might also make some troop movements in South China to underscore this commitment. We believe that as the fighting continued, China would be even less ready than the DRV to conclude that larger US ground forces could turn the tide.

9. The USSR. As the US commitment grew, the Soviet Union would find its problems growing more acute. Moscow would recognize that its own military assistance, and its general shift to a hard, anti-US line, had failed to turn the US from its course. We believe that the Soviets would see no alternative to continued support for the DRV. In time, however, the risks of a prolonged

- 4 -

~~TOP SECRET~~

and intensified war in Vietnam might press hard on the new collective leadership and face Moscow with the choice of further deepening its commitments and aid or moving toward withdrawal.

Non-Communist Reactions

10. A wide sector of non-Communist world opinion doubts that the US can avoid eventual defeat in Vietnam. In this sector, an increasing injection of US forces would be seen as a prolongation of the agony and an increase in the risks of future escalation. Governments which now support the US course, such as the British, Italians, and Japanese, would come under renewed domestic criticism. Governments which oppose the US, such as France and India, would step up their pressures for negotiations. In general, however, these world reactions would not have as much force as would reactions to more dramatic events, such as a change in the scope of the air war. The ultimate effect upon the US position would continue to be determined by the eventual success or failure of US policy in the Vietnamese war.

Reactions to Use of ROK Forces

11. The South Vietnamese would not be unreservedly receptive to increased ROK contingents in their midst. Greater ROK troop

- 5 -

~~TOP SECRET~~

commitments probably would not cause serious repercussions in South Korea, though some mutterings would be heard. In the event of major ROK troop losses, it is likely that public sentiment in South Korea -- stimulated by Pyongyang radio and domestic oppositionists -- would begin to question the judgment of President Pak, thereby contributing to the endemic political instability in South Korea. North Korea, through propaganda and troop movements and, possibly, contrived incidents in the Korean DMZ area would attempt to heighten any insecurity among South Koreans that developed as a result of troop shifts to Southeast Asia.

SNIE 10-9-65

Communist and Free World Reactions to a Possible US Course of Action

23 July 1965

53

~~TOP~~ SECRET

SNIE 10-9-65
TS 185875
23 July 1965

APPROVED FOR RELEASE
DATE: JUN 2005

SPECIAL NATIONAL INTELLIGENCE ESTIMATE

(b) (3)

COMMUNIST AND FREE WORLD REACTIONS TO A POSSIBLE US COURSE OF ACTION

This is the estimate. No further versions will be published.

Submitted by the
DIRECTOR OF CENTRAL INTELLIGENCE

Concurred in by the
UNITED STATES INTELLIGENCE BOARD
as indicated overleaf
23 July 1965

~~TOP~~ SECRET

~~TOP~~ ~~S-E-C-R-E-T~~

TS 185875

CENTRAL INTELLIGENCE AGENCY

23 July 1965

SNIE 10-9-65: COMMUNIST AND FREE WORLD REACTIONS TO A POSSIBLE US COURSE OF ACTION

THE PROBLEM

To estimate foreign reactions, particularly those of the Communist powers, to a specified US course of action with respect to Vietnam.

ASSUMPTIONS

For purposes of this estimate, we assume that the US decides to increase its forces in South Vietnam to about 175,000 by 1 November. We further assume related decisions to call up about 225,000 reserves, to extend tours of duty at the rate of 20,000 a month, to increase the regular strength of the armed services by 400,000 over the next year, and to double draft calls.

~~TOP S-E-C-R-E-T~~

~~GROUP 1
Excluded from automatic downgrading and declassification~~

We further assume (a) that the increase in forces would be accompanied by statements reiterating our objectives and our readiness for unconditional discussions, (b) that US forces would be deployed so that no major grouping threatened or appeared to threaten the 17th Parallel, and (c) that we might either continue present policy with regard to air strikes or extend these strikes in North Vietnam to include attacks on land (but not sea) lines of communication from South China* and military targets in the Hanoi-Haiphong area.

THE ESTIMATE

1. Communists and non-Communists alike would see in the increased US military involvement in Vietnam a strong indication that the US saw little hope of early negotiations. This would be particularly true if, at the same time, the US extended its air operations in North Vietnam.

---

* See Annex for a discussion and map of both land and current sea routes from China to North Vietnam.

(Continued...)

TOP S-E-C-R-E-T

I. VIET CONG AND DRV REACTIONS

2. At present the Viet Cong (VC) and North Vietnamese (DRV) leaders appear confident that their course in South Vietnam promises ultimate and possibly early success without important concessions on their part. They seem to believe that they can achieve a series of local military successes which, sooner or later, will bring victory through a combination of a deteriorating South Vietnamese army (ARVN) morale and effectiveness, a collapse of anti-Communist government in Saigon, and an exhaustion of the US will to persist.

3. We do not believe that inauguration of the US actions here assumed would basically alter these expectations. The VC and the DRV probably have come to expect increased US commitments, and they probably believe that the VC, with increased North Vietnamese assistance, can find ways to offset the effect of larger US forces. Nor do we think that the extension of air attacks to military targets in the Hanoi and Haiphong area would significantly injure the VC ability to persevere in the South

TOP S-E-C-R-E-T

or persuade the Hanoi Government that the price of persisting was unacceptably high.*

4. If the extension of air attacks were to include sustained interdiction of land lines of communication leading from South China, these actions would obviously make the delivery of Soviet and Chinese aid more difficult and costly, and would have a

---

* The Assistant Chief of Staff, Intelligence, USAF, disagrees with the judgment made in this paragraph and would substitute the following: "3. We believe that inauguration of the US actions here assumed, which emphasize US willingness and determination to become more deeply involved in combat operations in the South and eliminate the concept of an area 'sanctuary' in North Vietnam, has a reasonable chance of basically altering the Communists' short-term expectations. While the VC and the DRV probably have come to expect some additional US commitments, and they probably believe that the VC, with increased North Vietnamese assistance, can find ways to offset the effect of larger US forces, such confidence could be quite quickly undermined by effectively expanded US combat operations. Extension of air attacks to military targets in the Hanoi and Haiphong areas would pose the added threat that urban/industrial targets might be next. The selective and limited nature of US bombing target selections to date may have led Hanoi seriously to underestimate the extent of US determination to exert the power necessary to force discontinuance of DRV support for the VC. US military actions resulting from the assumed program could well persuade the Hanoi Government that the price of persisting was becoming unacceptably high."

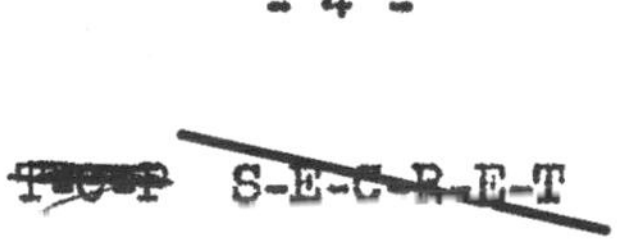

TOP S-E-C-R-E-T

serious impact on the limited industrial sector of the DRV general economy. It would still not have a critical impact on the Communist determination to persevere and would not, at least for the short term, seriously impair VC capabilities in South Vietnam.

5. If, in addition, POL targets in the Hanoi-Haiphong area were destroyed by air attacks, the DRV's ability to provide transpotation for the general economy would be severely reduced. It would also complicate their military logistics. If additional PAVN forces were employed in South Vietnam on a scale sufficient to counter increased US troop strength, this would substantially increase the amount of supplies needed in the South. The VC also depend on supplies from the North to maintain their present level of large-scale operations. The accumulated strains of a prolonged curtailment of supplies received from North Vietnam would obviously have an impact on the Communist effort in the South. They would certainly inhibit and might even prevent an increase in large-scale VC military activity, though they would probably not force any significant reduction in VC terrorist tactics of harassment and sabotage. These strains, particularly if they produced a serious check in the development of VC capabilities for large-scale (multi-battalion) operations might lead the DRV to consider

negotiations.* But the final decision on whether to seek negotiations would depend to a great extent on political developments in the Indochina area and elsewhere, and on the actual course of combat in South Vietnam.

6. In response to the US program, the Communists would almost certainly undertake measures to increase their own strength in South Vietnam for a higher level of struggle. They are already augmenting VC units and dispatching additional PAVN forces to South Vietnam; the assumed US actions would probably result in a speeding up of this process. By the end of 1965, the total of PAVN regulars in organized units in South Vietnam could reach 20,000 to 30,000 men. Although the Communists are aware of the dangers of concentrating their troops in large numbers, they might, during the next few months, attempt major assaults against GVN forces and positions, seeking to shatter ARVN before the increased weight of US strength could be brought to bear.

* The Director of Intelligence and Research, for the Department of State, and the Assistant Chief of Staff for Intelligence, Department of the Army, believe that in spite of greater damage and harassment caused by sustained air attack on lines of communication (LOC) and other targets, the capacities of DRV and Laos LOC are sufficient to permit support of the war in South Vietnam at the scale envisaged in this estimate. Other significant factors supporting this position are the impossibility of doing irreparable damage to LOC capacity; demonstrated Communist logistic resourcefulness and ability to move large amounts of war material long distances over difficult terrain by primitive means; and the difficulty of detecting, let alone stopping, sea infiltration.

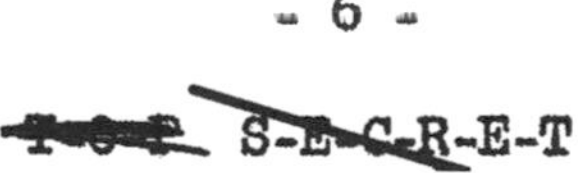

7. In coping with larger US forces employed in a more aggressive fashion, we believe that the Viet Cong would seek to avoid the kind of engagements which risked a serious Communist defeat. Instead, they would probably concentrate on harassments intended to bleed and humiliate US forces, trapping and destroying isolated units where possible. At a minimum, the Communists would almost certainly continue present efforts to cut land communication lines and would step up the dispatch of small, expendable teams on sabotage and assassination missions designed to make the US look impotent or foolish. The Communists might also seek to increase their activities in Laos.

8. Over the longer run, the Communists' strategy will depend upon the actual course of combat and their estimates of South Vietnamese stability and US will to persist. They are predisposed to attach great weight to signs of disintegration in Saigon and to manifestations of domestic US opposition to Administration policies. These boost popular morale on the Communist side and reinforce the leadership's conviction that Communist staying power is inherently superior.

9. Should future military and political developments bring this conviction into serious doubt, the DRV might express

increased interest in negotiations. However, they would endeavor to preserve their own freedom of action while laying inhibitions on US/GVN military operations, hoping to promote disarray in Saigon and encourage US opinion in favor of withdrawal.

10. Faced with the buildup outlined in our assumptions, the DRV would probably request more air defense equipment from the USSR, including SAMs, fighters, technicians, and perhaps pilots, particularly if US air attacks were expanded. From the Chinese, Hanoi would probably request more radar equipment, anti-aircraft artillery, and technicians in addition to a further increase in shipments of infantry arms and ammunition. Hanoi might also request China (and, perhaps, North Korea) to furnish aircraft and pilots. In general, however, we believe that Hanoi would wish to maintain some limits on, and a rough balance between, Soviet and Chinese personnel.

11. Deployments on the scale here assumed would cause the DRV some concern about US invasion. This would be true even if US forces took up positions which were not suggestive of an invasion. We believe, however, that the DRV would not react to this concern by requesting the introduction of Chinese combat forces. It probably would make such a request only if actual invasion seemed clearly imminent.

II. CHINESE COMMUNIST REACTIONS

12. The Chinese are probably even more convinced than the Vietnamese Communists that if the DRV/VC remain firm, in the end the US will be wholly defeated in Vietnam. Renewed US determination, evidenced by the buildup assumed in this estimate, would give the Chinese some pause but, in our view, not much. They would believe that the US measures were sufficient only to postpone defeat while magnifying its eventual effect.

13. We do not believe that the Chinese would react to the assumed US moves including the present level of air attacks, by overtly intervening in the military struggle with combat forces. They are already stepping up their military assistance, including the introduction of some rear service elements into North Vietnam, and would give more aid if requested by the DRV. Moreover, they would try to increase alarm among non-Communists, especially the US public, by intensifying their propaganda and reiterating their willingness to accept hostilities if attacked by the US. They would probably continue to strengthen their forces in South China and might take some further overt steps toward mobilization.

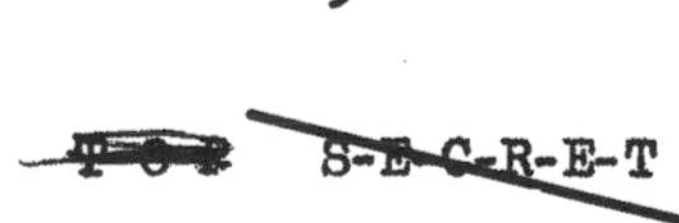

14. If air strikes were extended to the Hanoi-Haiphong area and particularly to lines of communication from South China, the chances of Chinese Communist air intervention from Chinese bases would increase. This would particularly be true if the air strikes were effective in cutting the main roads and rail lines over which the principal supplies are moving. While we believe the Chinese would be reluctant to engage the US in an air war or to risk US retaliation against Chinese military installations, we consider the chances are about even that Chinese aircraft would deliberately engage the US over North Vietnam from bases within China. We do not believe, however, that this would lead to greatly increased Chinese Communist participation in the conflict. In any case, if large numbers of US aircraft were operating close to the frontiers of China the likelihood of hostile encounters would be high.*

15. If, in the circumstances described in paragraph 9, the Viet Cong and the DRV at some point wished to move toward negotiations, an important divergence might open up between Hanoi and Peiping. The Chinese are themselves not suffering direct military damage and they fear that negotiations would give the USSR a chance to increase its role in Vietnam. Thus they would exert strong pressures to dissuade the DRV from entering into negotiations.

* Footnotes of dissent from this paragraph appear on the next page.

---

* The Director, Defense Intelligence Agency; Assistant Chief of Staff for Intelligence, Department of the Army; Assistant Chief of Naval Operations (Intelligence); Assistant Chief of Staff, Intelligence, USAF; and the Director of NSA, do not agree with the judgment expressed in this paragraph. They believe that it should read as follows: "If air strikes were extended to the Hanoi-Haiphong area and particularly to lines of communication from South China, the chances of Chinese Communist air intervention from Chinese bases would increase. Nevertheless, we believe the Chinese would be reluctant to engage the US in an air war or to risk US retaliation against Chinese military installations. We therefore consider it unlikely that Chinese aircraft would deliberately engage the US over North Vietnam from bases within China."

The Director of Intelligence and Research, Department of State, believes that the chances are better than even that Chinese aircraft would deliberately engage the US under these circumstances. Even if air engagements were accidental they would have extremely dangerous repercussions and if they were deliberate they could not fail to lead to a wider war.

III. SOVIET REACTIONS

16. The USSR hopes for an eventual Communist victory in South Vietnam, but it is more conscious than Peiping and Hanoi of the larger military risks. Moreover, the USSR wants to maintain or improve its influence over the DRV and in the world Communist movement generally; it does not wish the kind of Communist victory which would magnify the prestige and power of China. Unlike Peiping and Hanoi, Moscow is concerned with minimizing damage to East-West relations. In this situation, the USSR prefers a course of negotiations, but it cannot afford to appear laggard in supporting the DRV, and it is deepening its commitment to Hanoi's cause.

17. In the circumstances outlined in our assumptions, we believe that the USSR would see no alternative to continued support of the DRV and further expansion of its military aid. It would thus be likely to grant a DRV request for additional air defense equipment and personnel. It would probably feel compelled to comply promptly with DRV requests to replace air defense equipment destroyed by US attacks in the Hanoi area. The Soviet aid program might be hampered by Chinese restrictions on transit rights.

18. The USSR would probably indicate that, if the US remains unyielding in Vietnam, it faces trouble elsewhere in the world, as, for example, in Berlin. We do not think, however, that Moscow would confront us with a major challenge. Nor do we believe that the Soviets would wish to foreclose the possibility of negotiations at some future stage; indeed, they would probably work to keep this possibility alive on both sides.

19. We believe that the US decisions considered here would produce important reactions in general Soviet policy. Moscow would almost certainly harden its general stance toward the US. For example, although the Soviets have agreed to renewed disarmament talks, partly in order to check the deterioration in East-West relations, the assumed US course in Vietnam would probably lead them to devote the talks entirely to attacks on the US or even to break them off.

20. The assumed moves would carry total US military manpower above the 2.8-2.9 million total which we estimate for the USSR; they would also imply a reversal of the downward trend in US military spending which Kosygin cited in justifying the 1965 reduction in the overt Soviet military budget. We believe that

the USSR's declared policy of restraining or even reducing military expenditures has been under attack by military spokesmen in recent months and is the subject of debate within the collective leadership. It is likely that the US moves, plus the worsening of general Soviet-US relations, would strengthen the position of those arguing for additional military appropriations. In these circumstances, the USSR probably would respond with an overt increase in its own military spending.

IV. NON-COMMUNIST REACTIONS

21. Most non-Communist nations have already realized that the US, already heavily engaged in South Vietnam, is likely to increase its commitment if necessary. The measures here considered would nevertheless cause rising alarm because, in combination with Communist statements in response, they would revive and fortify fears of increased cold-war tensions and even of a much larger war. This might make some governments more reluctant to give public support to US policy, particularly governments in political difficulty, e.g., the UK, Canada, and Norway. Significant extension of bombing in North Vietnam would increase apprehension in these countries. Over the longer run, however, the more important reactions will depend on the subsequent course of the conflict.

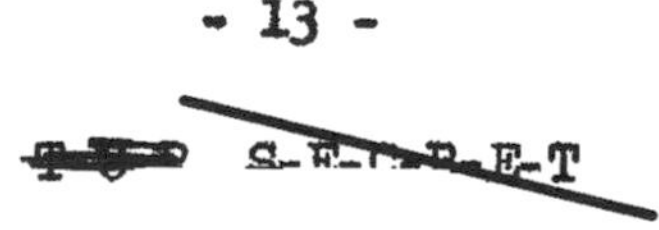

22. In non-Communist Asia, Japan offers the most serious problem. We believe the Sato government would maintain its policy of supporting US policy in spite of howls from the press and opposition forces. Sato's position would be made much more difficult, however, if Okinawa or especially Japan were to become a greatly expanded conduit for support of US forces in Vietnam, or if it appeared that China was about to become involved in the fighting. India would deplore increased bombing of the DRV but would otherwise continue its position of public questioning and private acquiescence in US actions in South Vietnam. Pakistan, hoping to continue to receive American aid while remaining on good terms with China, would reaffirm its neutrality and its noninvolvement in Vietnam.

V. REACTIONS TO THE MODE OF ANNOUNCEMENT

23. If the announcements were made in piecemeal fashion and with no more high level emphasis than necessary, the development of a crisis atmosphere might be mitigated. It is also possible that private assurances to the USSR that the US increase in overall military strength was directed solely toward the situation in Vietnam, and not meant to improve the US position vis-a-vis

the Soviets, might soften the tone of the Soviet response. This avoidance of strident recriminations might in turn decrease somewhat the negative reaction of non-Communist countries. We believe, however, that the reactions of the Communist powers, particularly in the military field, would not be basically changed by the method of announcement. We also believe that there would still be increased apprehension among non-Communist countries.

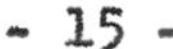

ANNEX

LAND TRANSPORTATION: RAIL

1. The North Vietnamese rail system is meter gauge. The two rail lines which connect the railroads of North Vietnam with those of Communist China are the most important logistic links for the movement of military supplies from Communist China to North Vietnam. The main route -- Hanoi to Dong Dang -- connects with the Chinese standard-gauge network at Ping-hsiang in Kwangsi Province, where cargo is then transloaded. The Hanoi-Lao Cai route continues as a meter-gauge line into China's Yunnan Province terminating near Kunming. This is Kunming's only rail connection with the main rail system of China. The railroad from Haiphong to Hanoi is important because Haiphong is the main port of North Vietnam.

2. North Vietnam is short of rolling stock, with about 120 locomotives and 1,800 freight cars, and a small number of petroleum tank cars. Additional meter-gauge rolling stock and locomotives could be obtained quickly only from Yunnan Province where the supply is not large.

GROUP 1
Excluded from automatic downgrading and declassification

TOP S-E-C-R-E-T

ANNEX

3. The maximum capacity of each of the rail routes to China is about 3,000 metric tons per day each way, but the Hanoi-Dong Dang line is the more important for the movement of military supplies because it provides a link with the rail system of all of China. Some of the vulnerable points on this line are the bridge over the Song Cau about 20 miles northeast of Hanoi, the bridge over the Red River in Hanoi itself, and the bridge over the Canal des Rapides about 6 miles northeast of Hanoi. Some of the vulnerable points on the Hanoi-Lao Cai rail route are the bridge over the Song Lo (Claire) River about 50 miles northwest of Hanoi, the bridge about 7 miles southeast of Vinh Yen, and a bridge over the Nam Si River at the border with Communist China.

LAND TRANSPORTATION: ROAD

4. The capacity of all roads leading to Hanoi from Kwangsi Province is about 2,300 metric tons a day during the dry season and 650 metric tons a day during the wet season. The most important is highway Route 1A, which runs generally parallel to the Hanoi-Dong Dang railroad line. The limiting section of this road has a capacity of about 1,000 metric tons per day during the dry season and about 300 metric tons during the wet season. There are alternate, but longer, road systems through Mong Cai and

Cao Bang. There is only one through road between Hanoi and Lao Cai. This road has a limiting section with a capacity of only 500 metric tons per day during the dry season and is not capable of supporting truck traffic during the wet season. Another road west of the Hanoi-Lao Cai rail line also connects Yunnan Province with Hanoi. The capacity of the limiting section of this road is about 550 metric tons per day during the dry season and 100 metric tons during the wet season. The most important single target for disrupting road traffic is the Daumer bridge across the Red River in Hanoi.

INLAND WATER ROUTES

5. The Red River could be used to supplement other means of transport from Yunnan Province, particularly during the wet season when road capacities are reduced.

SEA ROUTES

6. North Vietnam's only major port, at Haiphong, is rail served and has relatively modern cargo-handling facilities. Two secondary ports at Cam Pha and Hon Gai are well equipped to handle the export of coal from nearby mines, but have very limited facilities for handling other types of cargo and are not connected to North Vietnam's rail system.

7. The bulk of ocean-going traffic from China to North Vietnam originates at Canton, Swatow, Fort Bayard, and ports on Hainan Island. In addition, there are approximately 900 motor-powered and 4,800 sailing junks operating in the coastal waters of southern China and the adjacent northern coasts of North Vietnam. If one-third of the available junks were devoted to supplying goods to North Vietnam, they would be capable of transporting an estimated 570,000 tons annually. These shallow-draft craft would not require port facilities for off-loading, but could discharge cargoes over the beach. This type of traffic, which could move close to shore, would be difficult to detect and intercept. Such cargoes would, of course, be limited to items which could be easily handled by these methods.

(Continued...)

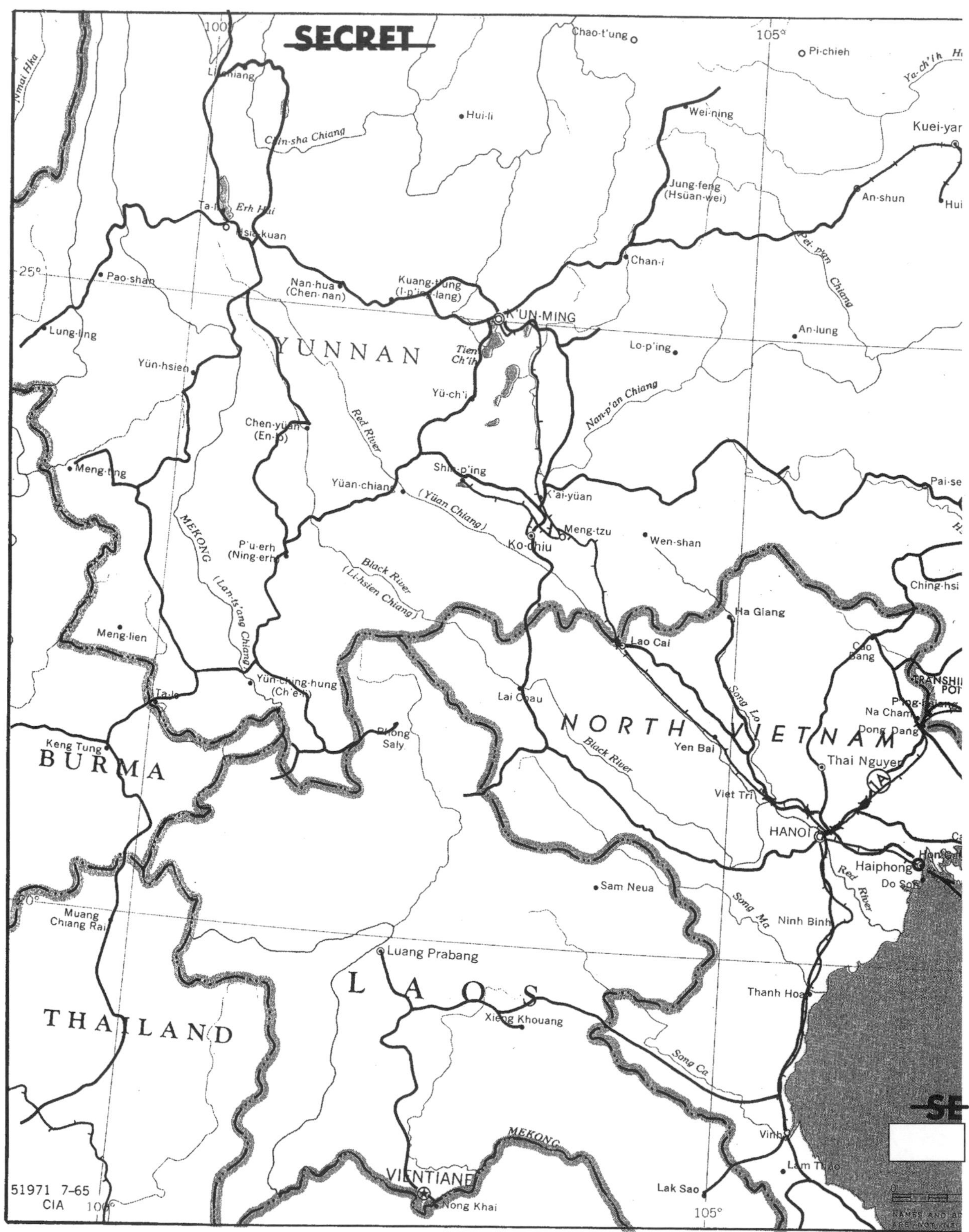
SECRET
YUNNAN
K'UN-MING
NORTH VIETNAM
HANOI
Haiphong
BURMA
LAOS
THAILAND
VIENTIANE
Luang Prabang
Sam Neua
Lao Cai
Ha Giang
Lai Chau
Yen Bai
Viet Tri
Thai Nguyen
Ninh Binh
Thanh Hoa
Vinh
Ko-chiu
Meng-tzu
Wen-shan
Chan-i
An-shun
An-lung
Lo-p'ing
Red River
Black River
Song Ma
Song Ca
Nong Khai
Lak Sao
Keng Tung
Muang Chiang Rai
105°
51971 7-65
CIA

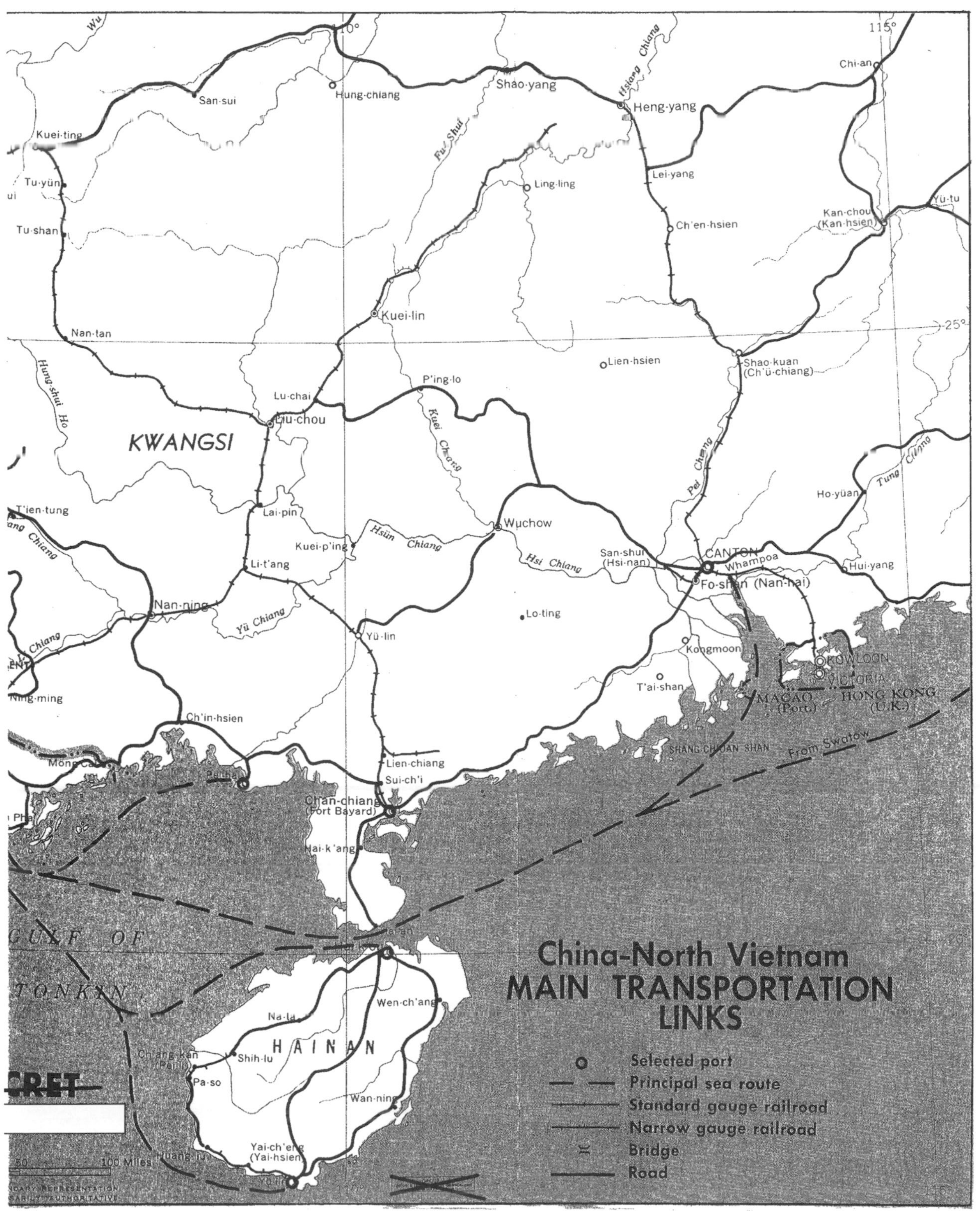
China-North Vietnam
MAIN TRANSPORTATION LINKS
Selected port
Principal sea route
Standard gauge railroad
Narrow gauge railroad
Bridge
Road
KWANGSI
HAINAN
GULF OF TONKIN
CANTON
Whampoa
Fo-shan (Nan-hai)
MACAO (Port.)
HONG KONG (U.K.)
KOWLOON
VICTORIA
Heng-yang
Shao-yang
Kuei-lin
Liu-chou
Wuchow
Nan-ning
Yü-lin
Lien-chiang
Sui-ch'i
Chan-chiang (Fort Bayard)
Shao-kuan (Ch'ü-chiang)
Kan-chou (Kan-hsien)
Lei-yang
Ch'en-hsien
Ling-ling
Hung-chiang
San-sui
Kuei-ting
Tu-yün
Tu-shan
Nan-tan
Lu-chai
P'ing-lo
Lai-pin
Kuei-p'ing
Li-t'ang
Lien-hsien
Lo-ting
San-shui (Hsi-nan)
Kongmoon
T'ai-shan
Ho-yüan
Hui-yang
Chi-an
Yü-tu
T'ien-tung
Ch'in-hsien
Hai-k'ang
Wen-ch'ang
Wan-ning
Shih-lu
Pa-so
Yai-ch'eng (Yai-hsien)
Hsi Chiang
Yü Chiang
Hsün Chiang
Kuei Chiang
Pei Chiang
Tung Chiang
Hsiang Chiang
Fu Shui
Hung-shui Ho
From Swatow
115°
25°
100 Miles

SNIE 10-11-65

Probable Communist Reactions to a US Course of Action

22 September 1965

APPROVED FOR RELEASE
DATE: JAN 2005

(b)(3)

TOP SECRET

SNIE 10-11-65
TS 185884
22 September 1965

SPECIAL NATIONAL INTELLIGENCE ESTIMATE

SNIE 10-11-65

PROBABLE COMMUNIST REACTIONS TO A US COURSE OF ACTION

NOTE: This is the estimate

Submitted by the
DIRECTOR OF CENTRAL INTELLIGENCE

Concurred in by the
UNITED STATES INTELLIGENCE BOARD

As indicated overleaf
22 September 1965

TOP SECRET

~~T-O-P S-E-C-R-E-T~~

TS# 185884

C E N T R A L   I N T E L L I G E N C E   A G E N C Y

22 September 1965

SUBJECT: SNIE 10-11-65: PROBABLE COMMUNIST REACTIONS TO A US COURSE OF ACTION

THE PROBLEM[1]

To estimate probable Communist reactions to a US program of air attacks on certain new targets in North Vietnam.

ASSUMPTIONS

For the purposes of this estimate we assume air strikes against Phuc Yen and four other airfields near Hanoi and Haiphong; against rail and highway routes and traffic between Hanoi and Haiphong and between Hanoi-Haiphong and China; against four major thermal power plants; and against SAM installations defending these areas. We further assume that attacks on all these targets are begun within the next few weeks

1/ The Director of INR, Department of State, dissents from this entire estimate. His reasons are set forth at the end of the estimate.

~~T-O-P S-E-C-R-E-T~~

GROUP 1
~~Excluded from automatic downgrading and declassification~~

and in a roughly simultaneous fashion. We also assume restrikes as necessary and subsequent armed reconnaissance against the rail and highway targets.

THE ESTIMATE

1. For many months our estimates have emphasized the crucial importance of the fact that the Communists, especially the DRV and China, believed they were winning the war in South Vietnam and needed only to maintain their momentum until the GVN collapsed and the US was forced to abandon the struggle. In this confidence Hanoi has been willing to endure bombings of the DRV, to accept the increasing US commitment, and to refuse any negotiations. Moreover, the Communists have counted on international and domestic pressures on the US, as well as on the growing capabilities of air defense around the critical Hanoi-Haiphong area, to deter further escalation. Finally, they probably have had strong doubts about US determination to face a protracted war, and these feelings have probably been strengthened by repeated US soundings and overtures for negotiations.

2. We think, however, that recently this general confidence has been weakened both by US/GVN military successes and by tangible evidence that the US is willing to increase its commitment. The situation has

come to seem more dangerous and discouraging than they probably had expected, and victory must seem to them much further off than it did a few months ago. Thus, we think that the assumed US action would come at a time when DRV doubts may be growing.

3. Public Communist declarations and commitments to continue the struggle, however, remain as firm as ever. Recently, the DRV has once again vigorously rejected negotiations on any terms except its own, apparently in response to approaches from various intermediaries. The Chinese have been vehement in denouncing negotiations altogether; they have even warned the DRV more or less openly against them. Their warnings may indicate Chinese worry that the DRV is weakening; indeed, there are a few indications, private and tentative, that Hanoi may not be quite as adamant in its position as its public declarations assert.

Immediate Reactions

4. The Communists, while they have hoped that the US would continue to exempt the Hanoi-Haiphong area from attack, probably have rated as fairly high the chances of the kind of US attacks assumed here. Their reactions, therefore, would probably not be greatly affected by shock or surprise.

5. The North Vietnamese would, of course, defend as best they could against the attacks. Beyond this, they might retaliate quickly. It is possible that the DRV has contingency plans for surviving aircraft to attack American bases in the South or US carriers. There is no evidence of training for this type of mission. They would probably expect such strikes to provoke wider and heavier US attacks. Thus, we think that the chances would be against such retaliation, though it cannot be ruled out.

6. A second immediate danger would be Chinese air intervention -- either over the DRV or against South Vietnam or US carriers. It is possible that Hanoi and Peking already have an agreed plan for the Chinese to intervene from their own bases in response to the kind of US attack assumed in this estimate. We doubt this; the Chinese are not likely to have made a firm or unqualified commitment. They would wish to weigh the effectiveness of the initial US attack and to receive the DRV reaction before making any move likely to invite a US attack on South China. However, the danger of accidental encounters would be particularly high if US aircraft were operating close to the border.

7. Thus in the first few days, during and immediately following the onset of the US attacks, there would be a chance of an attack on US bases or ships and a chance of Chinese air intervention. But we think these unlikely.

8. Of course, there would also be a great hue and cry from the Communist side, and the usual stream of protests, threats and warnings. We would also expect new acts of terrorism and sabotage inside South Vietnam, particularly against US forces. Viet Cong capabilities in these fields are considerably greater than they have yet chosen to demonstrate. The principal Communist reactions however, would come in later weeks and months, and they would of necessity be greatly affected by the ongoing course of military and political events as well as by the US actions we consider in this estimate.

Subsequent Reactions

9. China. The Chinese would strongly urge the DRV to continue the fight; to this end they would probably promise more equipment and personnel to build up air defenses, and particularly to defend and repair the interdicted lines of communication to South China. The Chinese might agree to send their own aircraft and pilots to the DRV, but on balance we think this unlikely in the wake of the demonstrated vulnerability of DRV airfields.[2] Almost certainly the Chinese would oppose negotiating, and they might warn the DRV not to count on Chinese support if it moved toward a cease-fire or a diplomatic settlement. We think Chinese views carry great weight in Hanoi, particularly if the DRV leaders were divided over future policy.

2/ The Director, NSA, for the National Security Agency, considers the chances of the Chinese sending their own aircraft and pilots to the DRV despite the demonstrated vulnerability of its airfields as being about even.

10. It may be that these US attacks would tip the balance and cause Chinese intervention. The Chinese might believe that the war had passed the point of no return and that a US-Chinese confrontation was the inevitable price of continuing the war in South Vietnam. The Chinese have made this war the test case for their doctrine of "peoples war" against the US; they have staked much prestige on it. We cannot be very confident that the Chinese would continue to refrain from intervening in the air from their own bases as the US continued attacks near the Chinese border and against a weakened DRV. But on balance we think it unlikely that they would so intervene.3/ With somewhat more confidence, we estimate that the US attacks would not provoke large-scale Chinese intervention with ground combat forces; Peking would almost certainly believe that this would run very high risks of war with the US.

11. The USSR. The Soviets would increase their efforts to halt the conflict. They would put pressure on the US and urge negotiations on Hanoi. There are some recent indications that the Soviets are now more willing to put some pressure on the DRV, perhaps because they believe their military assistance and the trend of the guerrilla war gives their view greater authority. The Soviets would almost certainly agree to DRV

3/ The Director, NSA, National Security Agency, considers the chances that the Chinese will intervene in the air from their own bases as the US continues attacks near the Chinese border as being about even.

requests to replace air defense equipment, although they would do so more to retain their influence with the DRV than in the expectation that they could furnish an adequate defense against US operations.

12. The Soviets could try to relieve pressures on the DRV by moving against the US in Berlin. We continue to believe there are strong inhibitions against a double crisis. Carefully controlled harassments and occasionally provocative demonstrations of US vulnerabilities are always possible, however. A potentially unstable situation in the Soviet leadership adds an element of uncertainty to the Soviet positions.

13. The DRV. In Hanoi, reactions would probably develop along one of two conflicting lines:

(a) Hanoi might believe that the new US attacks and the subsequent interdiction campaign did not alter the basic situation. The North Vietnamese might stick to their belief that the guerrilla war is, by definition, a prolonged struggle against heavy odds, that there will be setbacks and defeats, but that the ultimate gain is worth it. They might feel that damping down the war in the wake of US attacks would appear as capitulation. They might feel that if the war were interrupted the Viet Cong movement could not long maintain its morale and cohesion. Along this line of reasoning they might also conclude that the US escalation of bombings would still not do intolerable damage and would probably not be extended to attacks on urban population. They might decide that the US was desperate in the face of a long war involving US troops in the South, and that further struggle, perhaps involving the dispatch of PAVN units to the South on an increased scale, was the best course to crack the Saigon Government and US resolve.

(b) On the other hand, the DRV might estimate the situation quite differently. The growing US commitment in the South might persuade them that the guerrilla war could not be prosecuted to final victory. Without such a promise of ultimate success they might believe Viet Cong morale could not be sustained. Moreover, the attacks on the DRV's air defenses and on a wider range of targets might convince them that the US intended to escalate the air war almost indefinitely, if necessary. Thus they might decide that, while their position in the South was still strong and the Viet Cong still intact, it would be more expedient to move toward negotiations or some tacit understanding in order to pursue their objectives through political means, and possibly at some future time to resume guerrilla warfare.

14. We believe that the US course of action assumed here would reinforce the thinking described in subparagraph (b) above. Even so, it is not likely that the North Vietnamese would move immediately to

the conference table; they would probably feel that there was still time to test the effectiveness of the Viet Cong against US forces. They might still hope to strike a critical blow against US and GVN morale, perhaps by engaging US forces somewhere in the hinterland. Failing this, they might next revert to hit and run tactics for a time. And there is still the question of whether China could prevent a switch to political tactics.

15. In general, however, we think it unlikely that in the new situation created by the US attacks assumed here, the DRV would simply continue the war along present lines. We think that this US course of action would be more likely in time to move the North Vietnamese toward political and diplomatic initiatives than to cause them to escalate the war

16. The Viet Cong. As noted above, Viet Cong morale is an important ingredient in DRV estimates of how to prosecute the war. We have little good evidence on the state of Viet Cong morale. And it is difficult to judge the impact of specific US moves, since their effectiveness is a gradual cumulative process. In the assumed instance, the new US air attacks on the DRV would be unlikely to affect Viet Cong capabilities or intentions in the short run. Over the longer term, however, if it became apparent that supply and reinforcement were more and more difficult, it is likely that VC morale would deteriorate, particularly if they suffered setbacks on the order of Chu Lai together with continuing pressure on the ground and from the air.

17. Other Considerations. A current factor which might play some role is the Indo-Pakistani conflict. The Communists might see the new US move in Vietnam as an attempt to take advantage of the diversion of world attention to the Indian subcontinent. The US attack might help to dissuade the Chinese from any major involvement there. Peking would almost certainly be increasingly reluctant to divert resources to support Pakistan in the face of new escalation in Vietnam, its primary area of concern. In general, however, we think that the course of the Indo-Pakistani conflict would not greatly affect Communist reactions to the US course of action considered in this estimate.

The following is the position of the Director of Intelligence and Research, Department of State:

1. The Director, INR, Department of State, dissents fundamentally from the key estimates made above. He believes that the postulated air strikes against the DRV's SAM sites, airfields, thermal plants, and prime rail, road, and traffic targets would be seen by the Communists -- as well as by most other observers -- as marking a fundamental change in the character of our escalation of the Vietnam war. Separated strikes on these targets, carefully spaced over time, would help reduce adverse reactions, although these would be serious in any event. The composite

program assumed here, however, would be regarded as a political and military watershed comparable to that of last February when our bombing of the DRV began.

2. Hanoi, Peking, and Moscow would all view the strikes as initiating -- and in large part executing -- the highest level of militarily significant escalation available in the DRV short of ground invasion. Even assuming precision bombing, the strikes would inextricably involve industrial and civilian losses beyond the objectives deliberately targeted, as well as almost certain Soviet and Chinese casualties. In operation the new program would appear to have exempted only deliberate attacks (of no military significance) on the population itself. Communists and non-Communists alike would consider that this sudden massive action contradicted the many prior official indications, public and private, that we intended to respect the special sensitivity of the Hanoi-Haiphong complex. They would regard these undifferentiated and simultaneous strikes as a gross departure from our past policy of graduated pressure. They would probably conclude that we had decided to forsake further efforts to project a judicious combination of political-military pressures against the infiltration network, and had chosen instead the blunt instrument of a broad military assault on the chief elements of the DRV economy and its self-defense capability. The credibility of our protestations of limited objectives would slump, and our actions would just as plausibly be seen to invite

~~T-O-P S-E-C-R-E-T~~

the capitulation of the DRV under pain of total destruction, raise the specter of an eventual invasion on the ground, and in any case appear to threaten the DRV's ability to survive.

3. Under these circumstances, it is unlikely that Hanoi would choose to move toward negotiations or compromise; it is unlikely that Moscow could afford or would be willing to urge Hanoi to do so; and it is certain that Peking would press Hanoi to persevere. These positions would be mutually reinforcing.

4. The DRV leaders, as the estimate notes, have recently indicated that their terms for negotiation may not be as inflexible as they have sometimes seemed. The assumed attacks, however, would immediately deter Hanoi from any diplomatic overtures it may possibly have been contemplating. It would fear that any sign of compromise under such pressure would be read by friends and enemies as capitulation, would undermine all possible future bargaining positions, would irreparably damage Viet Cong morale, and would predispose the US to renew these pressures at any time and under any conditions it thought appropriate. Whatever hesitancies the DRV may have had would now be resolved in favor of militant prosecution of the war and of more insistent requests for, and far fewer qualms over, Chinese and Soviet aid.

~~T-O-P S-E-C-R-E-T~~

5. Far from seeking a respite from the bombings, the DRV would attempt to retaliate by raising the tempo of the ground war. It would send additional ground forces to Laos and South Vietnam as rapidly as the infiltration routes permit. It probably would surface these efforts, at least to the extent of acknowledging the despatch of "regrouped southerners" and "volunteers," both to raise Viet Cong morale and to discourage the US and its supporters with the prospect of a long jungle war.

6. The DRV would certainly at once press Peking and Moscow vigorously for prompt aid in rebuilding its defenses against air attacks. Inhibitions about additional Soviet and Chinese presence in the DRV would diminish. Hanoi might well drop whatever reservations it may have had against the use of Soviet or Chinese pilots. It would be most impatient with Sino-Soviet disputes about transit rights, but would expect those past hurdles to be overcome in the new atmosphere.

7. Although Hanoi's reaction will continue to be of primary importance, the locus of decision making will shift perceptibly away from Hanoi to Peking and Moscow. Peking will have a major role in determining the overall Communist response to the assumed US actions. Given the preceding estimate of Hanoi's response, these reactions will be consistent. Hence the frustrating dilemma of the main estimate probably will not arise -- Hanoi's switching to a negotiatory track despite giving China's contrary views "great weight." (Compare paragraphs 9 and 15 of the SNIE).

8. It is almost certain that Hanoi and Peking have concerted their preparations and discussed plans for Chinese action in the event of US attacks such as the ones assumed here. The Chinese would strongly urge Hanoi to reject any thought of negotiations, and they will purposefully underwrite the DRV's will to persist. They would furnish the DRV with logistic assistance in prosecuting the war in the south and in making further US air attacks as costly as possible. They would give safe haven to any DRV planes which escaped our strikes and would permit them to operate from Chinese bases. They would probably provide Chinese planes and pilots to operate from the remaining DRV facilities if and when useable.

9. The Chinese would immediately increase their defensive air patrols along their frontier and perhaps over adjacent DRV territory in which their ground forces appear to be active. The danger of accidental encounters with US planes will be high and will increase as US planes approach the border. If the DRV airfields are successfully interdicted, there is a better than even chance that Chinese air will intervene from Chinese bases.

10. The Chinese would probably in any case increase their presence on the ground in North Vietnam, furnishing anti-aircraft, engineer, and supply units and, if asked, providing combat forces to defend against a

possible US invasion of the north, thus freeing DRV forces to go southward. With the destruction of the rail line into China, the logistical problem of supplying the DRV would increase. To the degree that the US program is successful and South China must become the operational and infrastructure base for further air defense of the DRV, the Chinese will need Soviet support and protection. Greater Soviet involvement might reluctantly be desired to deter the US. This is an additional factor likely to promote a constructive resolution of previous Sino-Soviet frictions over the speed, scope, and method of aiding Hanoi and bolstering South China bases.

11. We do not believe that the Pakistan-India war is likely to place any limitation on Peking's willingness and ability to carry out the foregoing responses. Peking has prepared its forces and its population for some time to face the eventuality of the US actions assumed in this estimate. Its likely actions against India, outlined in SNIE 13-10-65, will probably not be deterred by such US actions, nor will the Indian theater require the diversion of Chinese air or ground forces available to support North Vietnam and to defend South China.

12. Indeed in addition to the general increase in pressures generated by the interacting nature of the two Asian theaters of war, Peking would be aware of certain comparative advantages in an escalatory response to the American move in North Vietnam. Peking knows that the Vietnam theater tends to bring the US into confrontation with both China and the USSR,

while the Indian theater tends to bring the US into confrontation only with China. Therefore Peking would hope to breach US-USSR relations on the matter of Vietnam, reducing thereby the freedom of both the USSR and the US to respond against Chinese pressures in the Subcontinent.

13. The Soviets would be specifically affronted by the assumed US course of action in Vietnam. They would almost certainly interpret it as an assault on the viability of North Vietnam, whose security they have committed themselves to defend. They would be likely to regard the US action as a direct challenge to themselves, the more so since it would probably result in Soviet casualties. They would be unlikely to place any credence in assurances that US intentions were still limited (something they have been prepared to do thus far). The sensational nature of the American initiative and the obstinacy of the Chinese and DRV reaction to it would harden the Soviet response.

14. Under these circumstances Moscow would be less likely than ever to press Hanoi to negotiate, and it would redouble its effort to participate meaningfully in the defense of the DRV. Moscow would renew its earlier offers of additional aircraft and pilots and would attempt to increase the flow of SAMs and technicians to man them. The Soviets would renew their proposals of last spring for a cooperative effort with the Chinese to aid Hanoi. The Chinese, for their part, would find it

more difficult than previously to refuse reasonable cooperation in expediting Soviet aid, especially in view of the assumed destruction of DRV-Chinese rail lines. Despite the continuing hostility between Chinese and Soviets, their respective stakes in the struggle are likely to lead to competition to see who can help Hanoi most effectively.

15. Unfortunately for them, Soviet problems in providing rapid and effective aid would be serious. DRV airfields and associated installations would be unusable, heavily damaged, or under continuing attack. Previously prepared SAM sites would likewise be difficult to replenish, and the US would presumably not abstain from attacking sites in preparation, as it did during the installation of the present Soviet-supplied SAM capability. Under these conditions, it is likely that the Soviets would make a strong attempt to mount an air defense effort from Chinese territory and we believe that, despite haggling, some arrangement to this end would be consummated. As a bargaining factor with Moscow, Peking will probably request -- and Moscow provide -- sophisticated Soviet air defense equipment (MIG 21s and SAMs) to protect bases and logistical lines in South China.

16. We believe that fundamentally the Soviets would nevertheless remain interested in an end to the conflict. While under the stepped up military assistance effort which we believe they would be bound to make

the Soviets would be prepared to run the risk of direct engagements with US forces in Vietnam, we believe that they would not contemplate these risks with any equanimity and would still attempt to prevent escalation from running out of control. Accordingly, even in addition to its greater military involvement, Moscow can be expected to resort to various forms of political pressures to deter the US, including a further substantial worsening in bilateral relations.

Memo

Reactions to Continuation or Termination of the Pause in Air Attacks on the DRV

19 January 1966

APPROVED FOR RELEASE
DATE: JAN 2005

S-E-C-R-E-T

(b)(3)

CENTRAL INTELLIGENCE AGENCY

OFFICE OF NATIONAL ESTIMATES

19 January 1966

MEMORANDUM

SUBJECT: Reactions to Continuation or Termination of the Pause in Air Attacks on the DRV

THE PROBLEM

To estimate the reactions of Communist and important non-Communist nations to:

I. A continuation of the bombing pause;

II. A resumption of bombing in the DRV:

A. On the pre-pause pattern, with LOCs bombed to within defined limits from the Chinese border and no strikes within the Hanoi and Haiphong perimeters;

B. Extension of bombing to POL facilities, power plants, and other military associated targets including those within the Hanoi and Haiphong perimeters, where this could be done without major civilian casualties;

S-E-C-R-E-T

GROUP 1
Excluded from automatic downgrading and declassification

(Continued...)

S-E-C-R-E-T

C. As in A and B, plus mining of Haiphong harbor and the two lesser ports to the north.

For all three cases, it is assumed that SAM sites would be struck as necessary to carry out the program without unacceptable losses, and that airfields would be struck if, but only if, hostile air action became a significant impediment to the carrying out of the program.

We assume that, whether or not bombing is resumed, there will be a continued buildup of US forces in the South.

I. INTRODUCTION

1. The great bulk of present evidence indicates that Hanoi is not prepared to make significant concessions in order to negotiate a settlement in Vietnam or to gain a prolonged cessation of US air attacks. This would not rule out private or public moves by Hanoi to test US terms for a settlement. Such efforts would, from their point of view, serve both to test US determination, now possibly under doubt in their minds, and also to encourage the US to prolong the pause. In our view, however, Hanoi's general attitude toward the pause and the US diplomatic efforts indicates that the DRV leaders intend to continue the insurrection in the South, even though they expect that if they do the US will eventually resume bombings, probably on an augmented scale.

- 2 -

S-E-C-R-E-T

S-E-C-R-E-T

2. There are a number of possible reasons for this attitude, including Chinese pressures and concern over Viet Cong cohesion during any possible negotiations. Moreover, behind these tactical considerations lie basic judgments by the North Vietnamese that they can absorb a great deal more bombing if necessary, and that they have political and military advantages which still promise ultimate success or at least a far more favorable settlement than the US appears willing to accept at this time. Thus, their hopes and morale ride almost entirely on the course of events in the South.

3. The Chinese make similar judgments. In addition, they believe that larger stakes are involved. They greatly fear that a negotiating phase in the Vietnam war would reinforce what they see as a Soviet-US collaboration to isolate China and stifle the world revolutionary movement. They have almost certainly urged a hard line on Hanoi during the pause, and have publicly warned against entering into any dealings with the US.

4. The Soviets probably take a more complicated view. They have reaffirmed their commitments to Hanoi in the face of the continued US buildup and the chances of renewed bombing. At the same time, they have made some effort to bring the US and the DRV into political contact in hopes of blocking further escalation.

S-E-C-R-E-T

We doubt that they have put much pressure on Hanoi to enter negotiations, but they have probably made clear Moscow's preference for primarily political tactics at this stage of the struggle. Their efforts have apparently failed, and they probably see no choice now but to persevere in supporting Hanoi while awaiting another opportunity for diplomacy.

5. The Non-Communist Countries. Most opinion, both governmental and private, is relieved that US air attacks have been suspended and hopes that negotiations can be arranged. In the middle ground between staunch US supporters and those alienated from US purposes, the contrast between US initiatives and the DRV's inflexibility has shifted onto Hanoi and Peking a larger share of the blame for an unpopular war. Except for certain US allies in Asia, most governments hope that escalation can be prevented, and several states are making or plan to make mediation efforts which, in their view, would be nullified by an early renewal of bombing.

II. REACTIONS TO CONTINUATION OF THE PAUSE

6. The DRV. It is possible that Hanoi intends to make some meaningful approach to the US. If so, the most logical time would be in the near future, at a point it calculated to be the last moment before the anticipated resumption of US bombing. Almost certainly it would not do so after bombing was resumed -- at least for some time.

7. Given Hanoi's attitudes as we now estimate them to be, however, an indefinite continuation of the bombing pause would almost certainly encourage the DRV to believe that continued struggle was on the right course. It would probably attribute prolongation to heavy foreign and domestic pressures on the US government. It might from time to time make minor political moves designed to encourage the US to extend the pause. But we do not believe that a prolonged pause would lead the DRV leaders to reduce their terms for a settlement so long as they still expected to prevail in the South.

8. Communist China. Peking would be encouraged by a continued bombing pause. The Chinese leaders would feel that the continued standdown has greatly reduced the chances of a Sino-US war and the risks of any call upon their air forces to try to defend the DRV. They would urge upon Hanoi that the failure to resume bombing was a sign of US weakness, and would claim that the policies they have advocated were being justified. They would still be concerned that the pause was related to diplomatic probings, and would continue to warn Hanoi against negotiations.

S-E-C-R-E-T

9. The USSR. The Soviets would not share the view that a continuation of the pause betrayed a fundamental US irresolution. They would probably still regard the US as committed to a long war in SVN, but they would be gratified that the pause limited the risks of their own involvement and relieved them of pressures to protect DRV airspace. Soviet policy toward Vietnam probably would not change much. The USSR would continue to supply military aid, but it would probably seek to keep alive the possibility of negotiations, hoping in this way to ward off future escalation and achieve a resolution which assured a continued Soviet presence in the area. If the pause were prolonged, the Soviets would feel somewhat freer to improve their relations with the US in other areas as opportunity and interest dictated.

10. Non-Communist World. Asian governments allied with the US, except Japan, would be distressed by prolongation of the bombing pause. In the GVN especially, morale would be lowered and doubts as to US constancy would grow. However, the continuing rapid buildup of US forces in the South would do much to relieve these feelings. In Japan, where the bombing of the North has been the major element in growing public opposition to the US course in Vietnam, continuation of the pause would be generally welcomed. As a result, the Sato government would be strengthened against leftist attacks on its handling of Southeast Asian policy.

- 6 -

S-E-C-R-E-T

S-E-C-R-E-T

11. The European allies of the US would in general be glad to see an indefinite prolongation of the pause in bombing. They would be relieved that the prospect of a widened war seemed thereby to be diminished. The uncommitted nations would probably give the US some credit for good intentions, but on the whole the effect among these nations would be not to win them to the US side but to diminish the degree of their opposition to the general US course in Vietnam.

III. REACTIONS TO RESUMPTION OF BOMBING

12. The DRV. Hanoi almost certainly expects the US to resume bombing in the absence of any conciliatory moves on their own part. If anyone in Hanoi seriously thought that the pause indicated an intention of the US to yield its position, he would be disabused. Hanoi might be confirmed in its declared view that the pause was no more than a device to strengthen the US political standing and justify an intensification of the war. There is a possibility that Hanoi would have misjudged the pause, miscalculated the intentions of the US, and be surprised by the resumption of bombing. In the unlikely event that this was true, a gradual renewal which began with targets related to the movement of men and supplies to the South, might cause the DRV to make some political moves to avert an expansion of the attack. We think it far more likely that Hanoi has discounted in advance the renewal of bombing and would be prepared to accept it.

- 7 -

S-E-C-R-E-T

13. As a general proposition, we believe that variations in the scope of the bombing would not produce significantly different responses from the DRV. Courses B and C would present them with greater physical difficulties than Course A. But in all of these contingencies we believe that Hanoi would continue to support the insurgency in the South and to defend its air space as best it could. At some point it might elaborate on the hint, planted by General Tolubko's visit, that continued escalation could bring Soviet surface-to-surface missiles into North Vietnam.

14. Communist China. Renewed bombing, even on the expanded scale of B and C, would not be likely to diminish the confidence of the Chinese in eventual victory through the techniques of "people's war." Indeed, though they would prefer a continued pause, they would even derive some satisfaction, in the event of renewal, from the obvious failure of the US and the Soviets to move the struggle to the negotiating table, from the increasing political and military costs to the US of the effort, from the hardening of the DRV attitude which bombing would produce, and from the continuing heavy dependence of the DRV on China.

15. On the other hand, renewed bombing, especially Courses B and C, would raise problems for the Chinese. They would feel that their boasted readiness to aid their small partner was being

tested in the eyes of the world. At the same time, they would be deeply worried that the war might spread to Chinese territory. It is likely that they would respond to enlarged air attacks on the DRV with greatly increased logistic support, including large additional numbers of engineer and supply troops and, possibly, anti-aircraft units. We think it unlikely that Peking would intervene in combat with aircraft or infantry. Nevertheless, the increase of their logistical presence in North Vietnam and the strengthening of their military position in South China improves their capabilities for such intervention should they decide to undertake it.

16. The USSR. The Soviets would belabor the US in public, would send more military aid to the DRV, and would make other gestures of support. We continue to believe, however, that the odds are against their intervening in radical new ways which would expose them to serious risks -- e.g., by introducing surface-to-surface ballistic missiles. The chances are somewhat greater that they would contribute KOMAR boats or cruise missiles. Moscow would also try to keep up US hopes for a peaceful settlement, working to achieve another pause in the future as a prelude to such a settlement.

S-E-C-R-E-T

17. The Non-Communist World. Resumption of air attacks would produce popular disappointment, much of which would be directed against the US. Nevertheless, the contrast between US efforts to get negotiations started and DRV inflexibility would cause a large share of the blame to fall on Hanoi and Peking. We believe that no states that now support the US policy would cease to do so. However, states which conceive of themselves as active mediators would feel that their efforts had been slighted. The most significant effect would probably be in Japan, where there would be renewed apprehension over Chinese involvement and pressures on Sato for a more neutral stance on Vietnam would grow.

18. The timing and manner of resumption would probably have some effect on initial non-Communist reactions. The tendency to blame the US would be appreciably strengthened if bombing were resumed immediately after Tet and if it were renewed on the scale of Course B or C. Conversely, Hanoi would bear a greater burden if major post-Tet offensives by VC/PAVN forces preceded the renewal of air attacks upon the North. Even in these circumstances, however, much of world opinion would tend, in time, to forget the particulars and to urge the US again to make concessions.

S-E-C-R-E-T

19. Special Considerations of Course B. Destruction of the main POL facilities and electric power plants would deprive the modern sector of the North Vietnamese economy of its main sources of power. However, this modern sector is not essential to the viability of the DRV. About 85 percent of the people live in rural areas and depend little if any on the modern sector. Traditional means of transport could provide the rather limited necessary circulation of food and clothing. The fundamental needs of the people would continue to be met. Nevertheless, many people would undergo great inconvenience; some would suffer serious hardships and personal losses; and civilian casualties would be higher than heretofore. These things would arouse protests in various parts of the world, especially among those who already oppose US policies. But we think that this kind of bombing would not create serious problems of popular morale in the DRV or weaken the regime's determination to resist.

20. Reactions Peculiar to Course C, Mining the Ports. During the past six months, calls at North Vietnamese ports by Free World ships, primarily vessels of British registry chartered by the Communists, have ranged between 11 and 21 a month. We believe that mining the main harbors, even with adequate warning to avoid unintentional damage to shipping, would bring increased attacks on

US policy throughout the Free World. The Norwegian and British governments, especially, would be under added domestic pressure to oppose the US actions. The UK government would indicate reservations about the mining, but would probably not vigorously press its case on the US nor oppose the action in public.

21. The Soviet Union would be presented with a particular dilemma. The difficulty of clearing such mine fields and the ease of resowing would virtually rule out efforts to reopen the ports. The Soviets would certainly protest vigorously and might try for some kind of action in the UN. We do not believe, however, that the Soviets would risk their ships in mined Vietnamese harbors. Peking and Hanoi would try to keep the necessary supplies moving by shallow-draft coastal shipping and overland transport.

Impact on the Military Situation in the South

22. In the preceding paragraphs we have discussed our conclusion that renewed aerial attacks at A, B, or C levels would probably not produce a significant change in Communist policy with respect to Vietnam. We have stressed that Hanoi would be likely to be discouraged only if Communist forces were taking a consistent beating in the South. We must, therefore, consider what effect renewed bombing in the North would be likely to have on Communist military capabilities in the South.

S-E-C-R-E-T

23. Resumption of pre-pause levels (Course A) would not have an appreciably different impact from that of the past few months, during which the Communists have been able to increase the level of their military activity in the South.

24. Course B attacks, if prosecuted vigorously enough, could knock out most of the DRV's modern industrial sector and substantially reduce its modern transport capability. However, this modern sector is not essential to the support of the insurgency in the South. DRV industry provides only a small part of the weapons and munitions sent South -- grenades, land mines, and some small-arms munitions -- and these could be replaced from Chinese sources.

25. Destruction of the major POL facilities would deprive the DRV of most of its stored POL. About 10,000 tons, or two-thirds of a normal month's supply, is estimated to be dispersed in drums and small tanks. Closing of Haiphong by mines would cut off the means by which most POL has been entering the country. Such losses would initially disorganize the Communist logistic effort, but they would probably resort to rail shipment to P'ing-hsiang on the Sino-Vietnamese border and truck shipment from there on (often moving at night), augmented by coastal shipping, to continue

S-E-C-R-E-T

S-E-C-R-E-T

essential supplies. Carts and wagons drawn by animals and humans could continue logistic support where POL was lacking. This was done in Vietnam during the war against the French and in Korea by the Chinese and North Koreans. Supply of the Communist troops in South Vietnam would be much more difficult than at present, but they could not be prevented from moving the relatively small amounts required even for an expansion of the levels of conflict in the South.* Thus we do not believe that even the maximum (Course C) level of air attack on the DRV would, in itself, have a critical impact on the combat ability of the Communist forces in South Vietnam.

FOR THE BOARD OF NATIONAL ESTIMATES:

SHERMAN KENT
Chairman

* The requirement for outside supply of the Communist forces in South Vietnam at recent levels of combat is estimated to average about 12 tons a day. Even with the Communist force increases projected by MACV for the end of 1966, and at greatly intensified levels of combat, requirements would average only about 165 tons a day. The weakest part of the lines of communication, the Lao corridor, is estimated to have a capacity of about 400 tons a day even under present levels of bombing.

- 14 -

S-E-C-R-E-T

SNIE 10-1-66

Possible Effects of a Proposed US Course of Action on DRV Capability to Support the Insurgency in South Vietnam

4 February 1966

APPROVED FOR RELEASE
DATE: JAN 2005

~~TOP SECRET~~

TS 185926
SNIE 10-1-66
4 February 1966

(b) (3)

SPECIAL NATIONAL INTELLIGENCE ESTIMATE

POSSIBLE EFFECTS OF A PROPOSED US COURSE OF ACTION ON DRV CAPABILITY TO SUPPORT THE INSURGENCY IN SOUTH VIETNAM

Submitted by

W.F. Raborn

DIRECTOR OF CENTRAL INTELLIGENCE

Concurred in by the

UNITED STATES INTELLIGENCE BOARD

As indicated overleaf

4 February 1966

DATE

Authenticated:

James S. Lay, Jr.

EXECUTIVE SECRETARY, USIB

~~TOP SECRET~~

C E N T R A L   I N T E L L I G E N C E   A G E N C Y

4 February 1966

SUBJECT: SNIE 10-1-66: POSSIBLE EFFECTS OF PROPOSED US COURSES OF ACTION ON DRV CAPABILITY TO SUPPORT THE INSURGENCY IN SOUTH VIETNAM

THE PROBLEM

To estimate how DRV capabilities to support the insurgency in the South would be affected by increasing the scope and intensity of the bombing of North Vietnam, and how long it would take for the impact to be felt in the South.

CONCEPT OF THE COURSES OF ACTION

The immediate aims of the bombing would be:

1. To destroy those resources already in North Vietnam that contribute most to support of Communist forces in the South;

2. To block external assistance to the DRV;

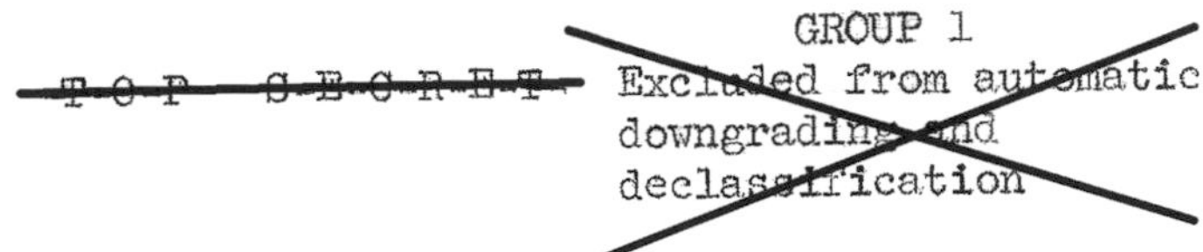

3. To harass, disrupt, and impede the movement of men and material through the southern DRV into Laos and South Vietnam.

Course A: The enlarged bombing program would include aerial attacks designed to:

1. Destroy all known POL facilities in the northern DRV;
2. Destroy all large military facilities in the northern DRV, except airfields and SAM sites;[1/]
3. Interdict the land LOCs from China and close DRV ports by various means including mining;
4. Put and keep electric power facilities out of action;
5. Carry out armed reconnaissance against land and water LOCs and all identified military facilities. South of the 20th parallel, such reconnaissance would be particularly intensive and carried out day and night.

Course B: The program as above, but without closing DRV ports by mining or otherwise.

1/ Constant surveillance of the airfields would be maintained and their destruction undertaken whenever interference with our planned air operations, or any offensive air actions against our military forces in SVN, might be initiated. Any SAM installations threatening to interfere with these operations would be attacked.

NOTE

This estimate considers only how DRV physical capabilities to support the insurgency in South Vietnam would be affected by certain assumed US bombing attacks on North Vietnam; it does not deal with the possible effect of these attacks on DRV <u>will</u> to continue the war.

CONCLUSIONS

A. The combined impact of destroying in-country stockpiles, restricting import capabilities, and attacking the southward LOCs would greatly complicate the DRV war effort. The cumulative drain on material resources and human energy would be severe. The postulated bombing and interdiction campaign would harass, disrupt, and impede the movement of men and material into South Vietnam and impose great overall difficulty on the DRV. However, we believe that, with a determined effort, the DRV could still move substantially greater amounts than in 1965.[2/]

2/ Major General Jack E. Thomas, Assistant Chief of Staff, Intelligence, United States Air Force, believes that this conclusion and the tone of the estimate reflect an under-estimation of the overall impact of the postulated bombing program and closing of the DRV ports. He believes that the cumulative interacting effect of such bombing and port closure on the economy, the military structure and the political and psychological fabric of North Vietnam would degrade the DRV capabilities to support the war in the south to a greater extent than this estimate indicates. By excluding consideration of the North Vietnamese will to continue the war, a very important effect of the postulated bombing and port closing has been eliminated.

B. However, the cumulative effect of the campaign would almost certainly set a limit to the expansion of PAVN and VC mainforce units and activities in South Vietnam. There are too many uncertainties to permit an estimate of just where that limit would be set.

C. If the main ports were not closed, supply of DRV needs from the outside would be greatly simplified, and the problem of moving goods within the DRV would be eased.

DISCUSSION

I. INTRODUCTION

1. The two key elements in this problem are the logistic requirements of the Communist forces in South Vietnam and the capability of the DRV to acquire and move supplies to those forces, while at the same time meeting essential requirements in North Vietnam and Laos. Presently available intelligence permits assigning only rough orders of magnitude to either the requirements or the capability.

2. Requirements for external supply of the Communist military forces in South Vietnam have thus far been small. Petroleum products (POL) and food for these forces come almost entirely from within South Vietnam. Supplies received from the DRV in 1965 almost certainly totalled well under 10,000 tons, possibly less than 5,000; some portion of these imports probably went into stockpiles. Because of the numbers of PAVN

troops infiltrated during the year, increased standardization on the 7.62 mm. family of weapons, and the introduction of heavier weapons, the call on outside supply rose greatly during the latter part of the year; the total 1966 requirement is likely to be substantially higher than that of 1965. The main requirement is for arms and ammunition, the remainder being communications equipment, quartermaster goods, medical supplies, and small amounts of other items. Only minor quantities of all these items originate in the DRV; most come from Communist China.

3. Intelligence on actual movement of supplies shows that existing lines of communication (LOCs), under the levels of aerial attack carried out prior to the bombing pause, were not used at anywhere near their estimated capacities. Nevertheless, the Communists have been making major efforts to increase these capacities. We believe this is done partly in anticipation of increased requirements and partly to provide a maximum margin of excess capacity to absorb reductions which might be caused by intensified aerial attack.

II. IMPACT OF COURSE A

4. Destruction of In-Country Resources. Successful implementation of the campaign against in-country resources, especially the destruction of most of the electric power facilities, would practically paralyze the small modern industrial sector of the DRV's economy. However, this would

not critically weaken the traditional subsistence economy upon which the majority of the population depends. And, because so little of what is sent south is produced in the DRV, an industrial shutdown would not very seriously reduce the regime's capability to support the insurgency, though it would complicate maintenance and repair of transport and other equipment.

5. Destruction of the nine major remaining POL storage facilities would deprive the regime of some 168,000 tons of bulk storage capacity and whatever POL is now stored there. This would leave probably less than a month's normal consumption (about 15,000 tons in 1965) in distribution facilities and dispersed storage -- drums and small buried tanks. Destruction of the major military facilities in the DRV would mean the loss of some stockpiled munitions, although most such storage is now well dispersed and concealed. In general, the regime would respond to the loss of stored reserves by tightening the priority system, and resorting to substitutes where possible. Nevertheless, the loss of these reserves, especially POL, would force the DRV to almost complete dependence on current imports to sustain its operations.

6. Cutting the LOCs for Outside Supplies. In 1965 the DRV received about a million tons of imports, two-thirds by sea and nearly one-third by rail, the small remainder coming by road, trail, and river. Closing the main seaports to normal shipping, whether by bombing, mining, or both, would necessitate a reduction in imports and diversion to railroad, highway,

small-craft, and coastal shipping. An industrial shutdown in the DRV would remove some strain from the rail system, as about half of the 300,000 tons imported by rail in 1965 was coal for the Thai Nguyen blast furnaces, and other raw materials accounted for further tonnage. About 100,000 tons of military equipment are estimated to have arrived by rail in 1965, mostly for DRV air defense.

7. The effectiveness of the interdiction campaign would not be the same for all means of transport. While ocean shipping would be stopped from using the ports, some supplies could be offloaded by lighters and other small craft. The use of shallow-draft coastal shipping could probably be increased over present levels even if harassed by a fairly high intensity of armed reconnaissance. Rail transport south of the Chinese border could be reduced drastically, but the experience of World War II and Korea indicates that a 100 percent shutdown is most unlikely. Road transport, which now plays only a small part in the import trade, could be expanded.

8. The effect of the postulated US course of action would be to reduce substantially the level of imports into the DRV. But a substantial portion of current imports are for supporting the modern sector of the economy and other uses not critical to the survival of the regime or the support of essential military tasks. We believe that sufficient supplies for these vital purposes could be brought in. This would include the small quantities necessary for transshipment to South Vietnam. Importation

of POL would be a key problem, but would be surmountable in a comparatively short time, probably a few weeks, since quantities involved would not be large, even if increased somewhat over previous levels. Soviet POL could be unloaded from tankers at Chan-chiang in South China, moved thence by rail to the DRV border and from there to the Hanoi area by truck. It could also move from the USSR by rail directly across China, or down the coast from Chan-chiang in shallow-draft shipping.

9. Restricting the LOCs in North Vietnam South of the Hanoi Region. Over these routes -- both sea and land -- must move: (a) the relatively small amounts of materiel that are forwarded to South Vietnam; and (b) the considerably larger amounts required for the North Vietnamese Military Region IV (roughly, that part of the DRV south of the 20th parallel). The crucial problem would almost certainly be POL; at the end of 1965 the forces in Military Region IV were consuming POL at the rate of about 1,500 short tons a month. This supported three main activities: (a) maintenance of LOCs and local transport within the Military Region itself; (b) operation of the Region as a training and staging area; and (c) actual movement of men and supplies into Laos and on to South Vietnam. We believe that despite air attacks, a combination of trucks, shallow-draft coastal shipping, and other means of transport, moving at night and hiding by day, could bring into the region 1,500 tons of POL a month plus other essential supplies.

~~TOP SECRET~~

Overall Impact in North Vietnam

10. Obviously the combined impact of destroying in-country stockpiles, restricting import capabilities, and attacking the southward LOCs would greatly complicate the DRV war effort. Life in North Vietnam would be on a stringent wartime footing. Supply and maintenance of air defense, PAVN, and coastal defense installations, supply of Communist units in Laos, and maintenance of internal LOCs would be given the highest priorities. All these activities would involve a great expenditure of time and effort, and the cumulative drain on material resources, human energy, and morale would be severe. But so long as the regime was determined to continue, Communist China and the USSR would almost certainly feel compelled to make the necessary material support available. We believe also that China, at least, would if necessary send in additional personnel to aid in maintenance of LOCs and equipment and in the movement of supplies within North Vietnam. The experience of previous wars, as well as our analysis of the situation in Vietnam itself, leads us to believe that the DRV would be able to move essential supplies to the places needed for a prolonged period of time.

11. Specifically, while the bombing and interdiction campaign assumed in this paper would harass, disrupt, and impede the movement of men and material into South Vietnam and impose great overall difficulties on the DRV, we believe that, with a determined effort, the DRV could move substantially greater amounts than it did in 1965.

~~TOP SECRET~~

~~T-O-P S-E-C-R-E-T~~

Impact On The War In The South

12. Especially in the first few weeks of the intensified aerial campaign, the supply operation would almost certainly suffer dislocations and disruptions. The deliveries would probably be irregular and there might be considerable uncertainty as to whether key materiel destined for particular military units would arrive as scheduled. Considering the VC/PAVN penchant for long and detailed planning of offensive operations, the irregularity of deliveries and doubt as to the reliability of resupply might lead to the postponement or cancellation of some large-unit offensive operations. However, tactics could be adjusted to meet the problem of irregular supply.

13. Beyond these tactical consequences, the cumulative effect of the postulated aerial campaign would almost certainly set some limit to the expansion of PAVN and VC mainforce units and activities in South Vietnam. During the past year, the requirements of these forces have already gone up considerably. We believe that the Communists intend to expand them further and provide them with heavier weapons. If so, logistic requirements would rise, not in proportion to the numbers of additional troops infiltrated, but much faster, for several reasons. For one thing, PAVN regular forces almost certainly require greater amounts and more diversified

~~T-O-P S-E-C-R-E-T~~

kinds of external supply than do VC forces. The introduction of heavier mortars (120 mm) has already begun and some light antiaircraft artillery may be moving in. The latter is increasingly needed to counter the effect of US/VNAF close air support. These weapons create heavier logistic demands.

14. During the last year, the Communists have lost stockpiles of food, weapons, and other stores in South Vietnam to ground action and bombing. Moreover, to the extent the Communist forces try to intensify hostilities in the South or are compelled to meet expanded US/GVN offensive operations, they will use up supplies at a higher rate. This effect would be particularly noticeable in the category of ammunition. In the categories of food and weapons, we do not know enough about the amounts and distribution of stockpiles to estimate what reserves the Communist forces still have, but they can probably continue to obtain their essential POL and food from sources within South Vietnam.

15. All these factors taken together indicate that an attempt by the Communists to increase their strength in South Vietnam might raise supply requirements to a level beyond the practical ceiling imposed on their logistic capabilities by the bombing campaign. In short, whereas the proposed US course of action would probably not force reduction of present levels of support, it would probably place an effective ceiling on

Communist capabilities to expand their military effort in the South. We believe that the level of reinforcement previously projected for 1966[3/] -- i.e., about 4,500 men per month with necessary supplies -- would still be possible despite the postulated bombing program. There are, however, too many uncertainties to permit estimating at just what level the limit on expansion would be. Among these uncertainties are the extent to which the Communists might infiltrate men and materiel into the South by sea, through Cambodia, or by alternate LOCs.

16. As for the time at which the impact of these effects would be felt in South Vietnam, we cannot on the basis of the above considerations estimate that we could detect any impact in the sense of a consistent and appreciable diminution of previous general levels of activity.

3/ Reference SNIE 10-12-65, "Probable Communist Reactions to a US Course of Action," Annex A, paragraph 6, which reads as follows: "There are an estimated 38 infantry regiments in the North Vietnamese army, of which 15 would probably be reserved for home defense. Of the remainder, about half could be used to train new units and replacements for infiltration to South Vietnam. With a force of this size available to furnish instruction and training, about 36 new PAVN regiments or regimental equivalents of approximately 1,500 men each could be trained and infiltrated into South Vietnam during 1966. This would amount to an average of 9 battalion equivalents a month.

III. IMPACT OF COURSE B -- i.e., THE SAME PROGRAM, BUT WITHOUT CLOSING NORTH VIETNAMESE PORTS

17. During the past year about two-thirds of total imports into North Vietnam came by sea. If the main ports were not closed, these or larger amounts could continue to arrive, though foreign shipping would almost certainly be somewhat inhibited by doubts as to whether the US would continue to leave the ports unmolested. The problem of improvising land transport from the China border to the Hanoi area would scarcely arise at all if necessary supplies could come by sea into Haiphong. Additional trucks would then be available for use in other parts of the DRV. The difficulties of importing POL would be greatly alleviated, even though bulk storage facilities were destroyed. The problems of distribution within North Vietnam and of forwarding supplies to South Vietnam would be eased, but they would remain substantial. In general, supply of DRV requirements from outside sources would be easier and more effective, and much of the impact of the previously considered course of action would be diminished.

SNIE 13-66

Current Chinese Communist Intentions in the Vietnam Situation

4 August 1966

APPROVED FOR RELEASE
DATE: JAN 2005

SECRET

(b) (1)
(b) (3)

SNIE 13-66
4 August 1966

SPECIAL NATIONAL INTELLIGENCE ESTIMATE

CURRENT CHINESE COMMUNIST INTENTIONS IN THE VIETNAM SITUATION

Submitted by

[signature]

DIRECTOR OF CENTRAL INTELLIGENCE

Concurred in by the

UNITED STATES INTELLIGENCE BOARD

As indicated overleaf

4 August 1966

DATE

Authenticated:

James S. Lay, Jr.

EXECUTIVE SECRETARY, USIB

SECRET

SECRET

CENTRAL INTELLIGENCE AGENCY

4 August 1966

SUBJECT: SNIE 13-66: CURRENT CHINESE COMMUNIST INTENTIONS IN THE VIETNAM SITUATION

CONCLUSION

The Chinese Communists have responded to recent US air action against North Vietnamese POL facilities and to Ho Chi Minh's July 17 appeal for more aid with massive propaganda demonstrations all over China. These occasions were used to renew pledges of complete support for Hanoi and to reiterate the Chinese view that the war must be continued to final victory. At the same time, the Chinese seem likely to provide more manpower for logistical and engineering functions in North Vietnam, and, for the first time, they may move some infantry troops into North Vietnam as a precautionary step against the contingency of invasion.

GROUP 1
Excluded from automatic downgrading and declassification

SECRET

We do not conclude, however, that the Chinese have changed their basic policy because of the recent air strikes. We have estimated that Peking would almost certainly intervene if North Vietnam were invaded or if the collapse of the Communist regime seemed likely. But we continue to believe that, at present levels of US action against NVN, China will not commit its ground forces to the war, nor its air force to deliberate and sustained action against US forces.

DISCUSSION

1. Peking has responded to the US air strikes on POL facilities in North Vietnam and to Ho Chi Minh's July 17 appeal for more aid with massive propaganda demonstrations all over China. The burden of the declarations made on these occasions is for the most part not new: that China is no longer bound by any restrictions in aiding North Vietnam, that China is a great "rear area" in the struggle, and that Peking and Hanoi are now ready to deal "joint blows" against the US. In addition, the Chinese have warned against underestimating their willingness to support Hanoi and have stated that China was prepared to make the greatest "national sacrifice" in this effort.

the Chinese Foreign Minister indicated that increased bombing of Hanoi and Haiphong and an invasion of North Vietnam would bring China into the war. Chen Yi argued that the US was following a course which would lead to heavier bombings, then to an invasion of North Vietnam, and finally to an attack on China.

2. It may be that Peking intended these various warnings to presage a more direct involvement in Vietnam. In again asserting a right to take action at any time and in any place, and in adding to this a total denunciation of the Geneva agreements, the Chinese could be laying the political and legal foundation for certain open military steps. It is possible, moreover, that they are unfolding new courses of action worked out with Ho Chi Minh more than a month ago when he is thought to have visited Peking.

3. On the other hand, the Chinese clearly had to take a hard line in response to the Hanoi-Haiphong bombings, particularly if they were not to be outdone by the Warsaw Pact declaration sponsored by the USSR. And the North Vietnamese mobilization order, which preceded the more significant of the Chinese declarations, called for "still more vigorous support" from all Communist countries.

4. Taking Chinese statements as a whole, we note that Peking has been careful to hedge any commitment to direct action and has purposely tried to portray China in a supporting rather than a direct role. It is significant that the Chinese have reiterated the Maoist doctrine that outside aid cannot "replace" the people's struggle and that the Vietnamese people "should and can rely on themselves" to prosecute the war. It seems

likely that if China planned some direct participation in the war, it would adopt a less negative position on the value of outside assistance. Such a gratuitous reminder of the limits to outside aid may also have been intended to discourage Hanoi from accepting the Warsaw Pact offer of volunteers.

5. A complicating factor in judging Chinese intentions is the recent internal crisis. This situation has been confusing and we are far from certain as to its meaning and implications. It could be that after a period of turmoil, the Chinese leadership is now speaking with a new assurance and developing a bolder line on the Vietnam war. On the other hand, the "cultural revolution" must be creating considerable disarray in China, perhaps even within the armed forces, and this would seem to argue against a decision to go to war in Vietnam. Indeed, one theme of the campaign has been that the main enemies are inside China. Compared to the situation six months ago, there is apparently less emphasis in domestic propaganda on preparing the population for war with the US, by stressing civil defense, for example.

6. As to recent military indicators, there is no evidence thus far of significant movements of ground or air forces to South China. Nor are there other indicators of the sort that might be expected, if the Chinese leadership intended to commit ground forces to combat at an early date. Furthermore, there have been no movements indicating an intention to threaten military action in other areas such as Laos, Taiwan, or Korea.

(Continued...)

SECRET

7. It seems probable, therefore, that the current Chinese line on Vietnam is designed mainly to serve a number of political purposes. Peking wants to provide a dramatic reassurance to North Vietnam, now that Hanoi has again rejected all overtures for negotiations and reaffirmed its intention to fight a long war. Since Chinese actions have been cautious, Peking also probably feels that some strong words are needed to augment concern in the US and elsewhere that China's intervention is becoming more imminent. The hoped for effect would be to deter a still further increase in the scale of attack on NVN. Finally, the Chinese seem intent on destroying any lingering hopes that a negotiated settlement can be arranged. To this end Peking, unlike Hanoi, has emphasized that the Geneva agreements are dead and can no longer be thought of as a basis for negotiations.

8. We conclude that the Chinese have not changed their basic policy because of the recent air strikes. We have estimated that Peking would almost certainly intervene if North Vietnam were invaded or if the collapse of the Communist regime seemed likely. But at present levels of US action against NVN we continue to believe that China will not commit its ground or air forces to sustained combat against the US. In our view, neither the Chinese nor the North Vietnamese regard the present situation as critical enough to justify outside intervention with its attendant risks of a much wider war, including ultimately the threat of nuclear war, which the Chinese must now reckon they would have to face without assurance

of Soviet support. Hanoi still has considerable freedom of action vis a vis both Moscow and Peking, and Ho Chi Minh's polite refusal of Communist "volunteers" strongly suggests that North Vietnam is not moving to expand the war in this way.

9. This is not to say that Chinese involvement in the war will not grow, or that the Chinese will confine themselves to resounding phrases. Peking and Hanoi probably estimate that the war has entered a new and more intense phase with the Hanoi-Haiphong bombings and the rapid commitment of NVA troops to SVN. They anticipate a further US buildup, and Hanoi apparently intends to continue a heavy rate of infiltration into SVN. They probably also estimate that US air strikes against NVN will become more intense and widespread.

10. For some time Chinese military personnel have been present in North Vietnam; current strength is estimated at 25,000 to 45,000.* They include AAA troops, engineers, construction crews, and various other logistical support groups. More assistance of this nature is almost certain.

11. Hanoi and Peking may now believe that the time has come to move ahead with plans for greater Chinese support against the contingency of invasion. The Chinese are already apparently participating in the construction of a large base, perhaps including an airstrip, located some

* Lieutenant General Marshall S. Carter, Director of the National Security Agency, does not believe there is sufficient intelligence to support a numerical estimate of Chinese Communist troop strength in the DRV.

75 miles northwest of Hanoi. The ultimate purpose of this base is unknown. Beyond this, it is possible the Chinese will move some infantry troops into North Vietnam.

12. Altogether, there is some reason to believe that the Chinese presence, and consequently influence in North Vietnam may grow, consonant with Hanoi's apparent resolution to continue the war for some time. We do not believe however, that recent Chinese behavior indicates that Peking has made a decision to enlarge the war by overt involvement of their forces against the US.

Memo

The Vietnamese Communists' Will to Persist—Summary and Principal Findings only

26 August 1966

TOP SECRET
CENTRAL INTELLIGENCE AGENCY
UNITED STATES OF AMERICA
APPROVED FOR RELEASE
DATE: JAN 2005
(b)(1)
(b)(3)
Memorandum
THE
VIETNAMESE COMMUNISTS
WILL
TO PERSIST
DIRECTORATE OF INTELLIGENCE
TOP SECRET
GROUP 1
Excluded from automatic downgrading and declassification
10

~~TOP SECRET~~

An Analysis of the Vietnamese Communists' Strengths, Capabilities, and Will to Persist in Their Present Strategy in Vietnam.

26 AUGUST 1966

This memorandum has been produced by the Directorate of Intelligence of the Central Intelligence Agency. It was jointly prepared by the Office of Current Intelligence, the Office of Research and Reports, the Office of National Estimates, and the Special Assistant for Vietnamese Affairs in the Office of the Director of Central Intelligence.

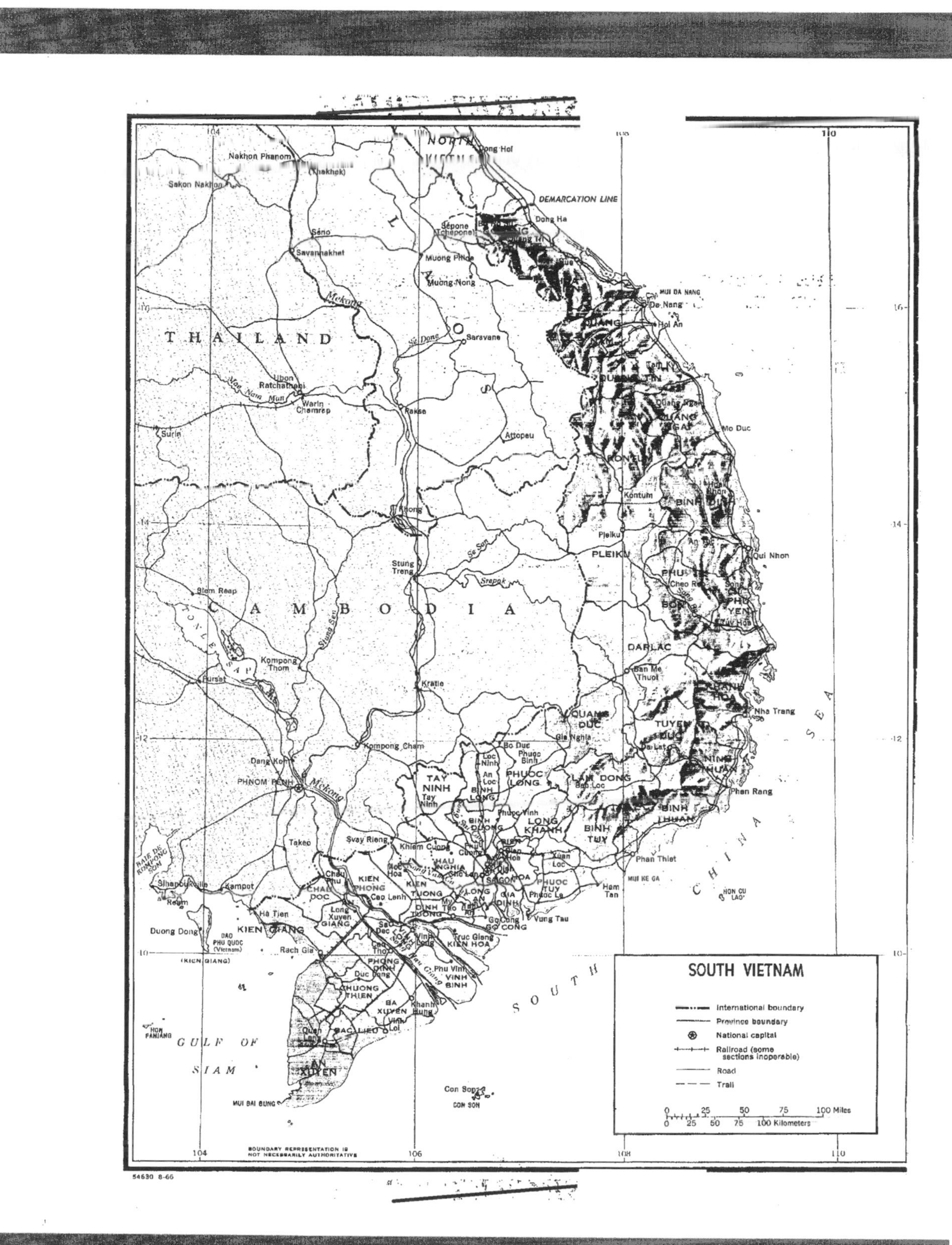
SOUTH VIETNAM
International boundary
Province boundary
National capital
Railroad (some sections inoperable)
Road
Trail
0 25 50 75 100 Miles
0 25 50 75 100 Kilometers
THAILAND
CAMBODIA
DEMARCATION LINE
Nakhon Phanom
Sakon Nakhon
Savannakhet
Seno
Muong Nong
Saravane
Ubon Ratchathani
Warin Chamrap
Pakse
Attopeu
Surin
Siem Reap
Kompong Thom
Pursat
Stung Treng
Kratie
Kompong Cham
PHNOM PENH
Takeo
Svay Rieng
Kampot
Ha Tien
Rach Gia
Duong Dong
Dong Ha
Da Nang
Hoi An
Mo Duc
Kontum
Pleiku
PLEIKU
Qui Nhon
DARLAC
Ban Me Thuot
Nha Trang
QUANG DUC
TUYEN DUC
LAM DONG
Phan Rang
Phan Thiet
BINH TUY
LONG KHANH
TAY NINH
PHUOC LONG
SAIGON
Vung Tau
KIEN GIANG
KIEN PHONG
KIEN HOA
VINH BINH
BA XUYEN
Con Son
GULF OF SIAM
SOUTH CHINA SEA
BOUNDARY REPRESENTATION IS NOT NECESSARILY AUTHORITATIVE
54630 8-66

TOP SECRET

SUMMARY DISCUSSION

I. Introduction

1. For thirty-six years the Vietnamese Communist Party has struggled unrelentingly to acquire political control of Vietnam. During this period the Vietnamese Communists have often altered their strategy but never their objective, which remains today what it was when the Party was founded in 1930. Since 1959 their strategy has focused on a "War of National Liberation"--a blend of military and political action in South Vietnam designed to erode non-Communist political authority, to create an aura of Communist invincibility, and, eventually, destroy the South Vietnamese and U.S. will to resist.

2. The Lao Dong (i.e., Vietnamese Communist) Party now controls only the government of North Vietnam (the DRV), but it is national in scope, even though, for cover purposes, its members in the South operate under the name of the "People's Revolutionary Party." It instigated the present insurgency and has controlled it from its inception. In every significant respect the Communist movement throughout Vietnam is a single political entity whose strengths, capabilities and strategic intentions cannot be properly assessed unless it is analyzed as such.*

II. The Vietnamese Communists' Investment in the Struggle

3. During the early years of insurgency, the Vietnamese Communists fought at negligible cost to the DRV itself. The Viet Cong's political apparatus and its military forces were almost entirely composed of ethnic southerners. Even cadre and technicians infiltrated from North Vietnam were primarily Southerners who had gone north in the post-1954 regroupment. The insurgents

*Additional details on Vietnamese Communist organization are given in Annex III.

TOP SECRET

lived off the land and obtained a large proportion of their supplies, including weapons and ammunition, from pre-1954 caches or capture from GVN forces. While the war ravaged the South, North Vietnam's own territory and economy were untouched. All of this, of course, has changed since 1961, and particularly since 1964. Hanoi's continued expansion of the insurgent effort has altered the complexion of the struggle and the ground rules under which it is waged.

4. This has required a drastic increase in the Communist investment. On a population base of around 18 million, North Vietnam now is supporting a military establishment of at least 400,000 men. By mid-1966 Hanoi was maintaining a force of at least 38,000 North Vietnamese troops to fight in the South. We estimate that this figure will rise to 60,000 by the end of 1966 and to 75,000 by mid-1967. Furthermore, to sustain its commitment in the struggle, North Vietnam has undergone partial mobilization and has had to divert at least 350,000 laborers to military or war-related tasks. North Vietnam's economy has been dislocated, its transportation system disrupted and the personal lives of its citizens adversely affected. To facilitate the dispatch of troops to South Vietnam and the external supplies they now require, Hanoi has had to develop and maintain an elaborate road and trail network through Laos in the face of continued interdiction and harassment.*

5. In South Vietnam, the Communists have developed an insurgent structure which includes an armed force estimated to be around 232,000 in addition to the 38,000 North Vietnamese troops already mentioned. This figure includes Viet Cong Main and Local Force troops, political cadre and combat support elements, and Southern Communist irregulars. Recently acquired documentary evidence, now being studied in detail,

*See Annex I for further details on North Vietnamese resources and capabilities.

suggests that our holdings on the numerical strength of these irregulars (now carried at around 110,000) may require drastic upward revision.* To direct the execution of their insurgent campaign, the Communists have developed a party apparatus in the South estimated to number around 100,000 members, supported by a somewhat smaller youth auxiliary.** The Communists have also probably enrolled around 700,000 people in some component of their front organization, the "National Front for the Liberation of South Vietnam." This total apparatus must be controlled, funded and supplied, although most of its requirements may be met from resources within South Vietnam.

6. Casualties the Communists have incurred and are incurring in ever increasing numbers represent another major element of human cost. We estimate that total Communist losses in South Vietnam alone--killed in action, captured, seriously wounded and deserted--ranged from 80,000 to 90,000 during 1965, counting both North and South Vietnamese.*** We estimate that during 1966 these losses may range from 105,000 to 120,000. We further estimate that the Communists may incur an additional 65,000 to 75,000 losses during the first six months of 1967, if current rates of combat are maintained and presently projected troop strengths are achieved.

---

*Details on Communist military forces in South Vietnam are given in Annex IV.

**Around 25,000 party members and somewhere between 15,000 to 20,000 members of the youth auxiliary are thought to be serving in the Communist armed forces. They would be included in the military strength totals already cited. If our estimate of the number of Communist irregulars proves to require upward revision, our estimate of the size of the party apparatus in the South and of its youth auxiliary will also require compensating adjustments. Details on the Communist organization in South Vietnam are given in Annex III.

***See Annex IV.

TOP SECRET

III. Vietnamese Communist Capabilities for Persisting in Their Present Strategy

7. The Northern Base: North Vietnam's role in the present insurgency is that of a command and control center, a source of manpower and a channel of supplies. The command and control function is something relatively invulnerable to physical pressure or external assault. Present Communist strategy is imposing some strains on North Vietnam's manpower reserves, but the strains are more qualitative than quantitative, and they are not likely to become insurmountable. The major pressures on manpower have resulted from the Hanoi regime's inability to manage manpower effectively, a relative scarcity of technicians and skilled laborers, and an excessive drain on the agricultural labor force. Over the next 12 months North Vietnam should be able to meet the manpower requirements generated by its internal needs, as well as those generated by projected further deployments of troops to the South, but these needs will be met at increasing costs in the economic, educational and social fields.

8. North Vietnam's own industrial plant makes only the most marginal contribution to Vietnamese Communist military strength. With minor exceptions (e.g., a modest small arms ammunition manufacturing capability) the Vietnamese Communists' military hardware is entirely supplied from external sources. Thus Hanoi's ability to provide continued materiel assistance to Communist forces in South Vietnam is largely dependent on North Vietnam's continued receipt of materiel support from China, the Soviet Union and East European Communist countries.* So far, the US aerial pressure program has not appreciably impeded North Vietnam's receipt of materiel support from abroad and its dispatch to South Vietnam. Despite the disruptions inflicted, the North Vietnamese transport and logistic system is now functioning more effectively after almost 18 months of bombing than it did when the

*This aspect of Vietnamese Communist capability is discussed in detail in Annex II.

TOP SECRET

Rolling Thunder program started. Both internal transportation and infiltration traffic in 1966 were carried on at higher levels than in 1965. So long as the US air offensive remains at present levels, it is unlikely to diminish North Vietnam's continued ability to provide materiel support to the war in the South.

9. The Logistic Supply Network: Communist forces in South Vietnam are supplied with manpower and materiel primarily over the Communist-developed and -maintained network of about 650 miles of roads and trails through southern Laos, and to a lesser extent by sea or through Cambodia. Allied harassment and interdiction certainly complicate the Communist supply system. The volume of traffic now moving through Laos, however, is so much below route capacity that it is unlikely that conventional attack can ever reduce the capacity of the Laos trail network below the level required to sustain Communist efforts in South Vietnam. Communist forces use Cambodia with almost complete immunity from allied countermeasures and with minimal interference from the Cambodian government. US and South Vietnamese naval patrols have probably curtailed Communist sea infiltration, but given the extent and nature of South Vietnam's coastline and the amount of small boat traffic in South Vietnamese waters, even this channel can never be completely closed.

10. The Southern Apparatus: The buildup of both VC/NVN and allied forces in South Vietnam and the rising tempo of combat are placing appreciable strains on the Viet Cong's ability to support the war. The distribution of needed supplies, particularly foodstuffs, within South Vietnam has become extremely difficult. This problem has been aggravated by the concentration of VC forces in food-deficient areas.* Furthermore, the manpower squeeze on Viet Cong resources is becoming serious. The Viet Cong have borne the brunt of Communist personnel losses in South Vietnam and have also had to compensate for losses of North Vietnamese personnel. We believe that the Viet Cong capability to recruit and train manpower is adequate to cover losses estimated

*See Annex V.

TOP SECRET

for 1966 but will probably be inadequate to compensate for casualties and losses in 1967. During 1967 the North Vietnamese will have to assume most of the burden of expanding force levels, and an increasing role in replacing losses. These manpower requirements can almost certainly be met from North Vietnamese resources, but they will impose additional strains on North Vietnam's limited supply of skilled personnel and leadership cadre.

11. Apart from military manpower requirements, documentary evidence indicates that the Communist political apparatus in South Vietnam is already stretched thin and is not considered by the Communists themselves as fully adequate to their needs, particularly in urban areas. Cadre and leadership shortages will almost certainly increase in the months ahead. Although these shortages can be ameliorated by additional personnel dispatched from North Vietnam, the injection of an increasing number of northerners into the Southern apparatus will of itself produce some measure of discord within the Communist movement. Although the Viet Cong personnel needs are not likely to prevent the Vietnamese Communists from persisting in their present strategy, they almost certainly represent the weakest link in the Communists' capability chain.

12. Net Capability Assessment: The Communists' present strategy is costly in both human and economic terms and is taxing Communist resources in some areas, particularly within South Vietnam itself. Allied actions are complicating Communist efforts and raising the costs of their execution. However, neither internal resource shortages nor allied actions within present political parameters are likely to render the Vietnamese Communists physically incapable of persisting in their present strategy.

IV. The Vietnamese Communists' Probable Estimate of The Current State of the Struggle

13. The Communists' evaluation of the war and estimate of its future course will involve interlocked judgments on a variety of key factors, some of which are discussed below.

TOP SECRET

TOP SECRET

14. The Communists' "Time Table": The Communists almost certainly do not have any fixed or rigid time table for victory. Their consideration of where they stand now, however, must in some measure be influenced by earlier estimates of where they had expected to be in mid-1966. Analysis of available documentary evidence suggests that in the 1959-1960 era, Hanoi's rulers thought it would take at least five years of all-out military and political action to gain control over South Vietnam. Until about 1962, the Communists appear to have been reasonably satisfied with the progress of their insurgent movement and to have felt that things were going more or less as planned. The counterinsurgency efforts of the Diem regime after 1962, however, and the expanded US advisory/support program confronted the Communists with unwelcome obstacles and led them to conclude that the conquest of South Vietnam would take longer than they had originally estimated.*

15. During 1964, as the Communists watched the continuing political disarray in Saigon, and devised tactics to cope with the increased U.S. assistance, Communist documents discussing the war grew progressively more optimistic. Communist optimism apparently reached its apex in the spring of 1965. They still carefully refrained from tying "victory" to a definite calendar date, but the Communists appear to have believed that they were then perhaps within a year or two of achieving a major part of their objectives. They had every reason to be optimistic in the spring of 1965; the GVN's strategic reserve was stretched to the breaking point, and the Communists were scoring tactical military successes with considerable cumulative political impact.

16. The massive infusion of US combat strength which began in mid-1965 probably saved the GVN from defeat and certainly disabused the Communists of any hopes of early victory. Their propaganda began to shift away from the theme of early victory to its present theme of inevitable victory. During 1966, Communist documents and public pronouncements have indicated that the Communists

*See Annex VIII.

-7-

TOP SECRET

TOP SECRET

expect a long war. The Communists must be disappointed in comparing the present situation with that which existed in the spring of 1965. At least indirectly, they have acknowledged that the infusion of US and Allied combat forces has created new problems which must be overcome before victory can be won. Yet Communist realism is presently tinged more with defiance than pessimism; the Communists may be disappointed, but they do not yet seem to be discouraged.

17. The Lessons of the Franco - Viet Minh War: Present Vietnamese Communist strategy is appreciably influenced by the 1946-1954 struggle in which the Communist-controlled Viet Minh forced the French to withdraw from Vietnam. In Communist eyes, probably the most significant feature of this earlier successful campaign was the fact it was won without inflicting a strategic defeat on the French Military Forces.* During their nine-year struggle, the Communists successfully used military pressure as a political abrasive. They worked more on French will than on French strategic capabilities, and eventually succeeded in making the struggle a politically unsaleable commodity in metropolitan France. Communist strategy, in short, succeeded in creating a climate in which the government in Paris lost its will to fight even though the French Expeditionary Corps remained effective and largely intact as a military force. The Communists suffered horrendous casualties and went through periods of severe setback, but their persistence eventually paid off.

18. Soviet and Chinese Support** There is substantial evidence that the political positions of the Soviet Union and Communist China vis-a-vis the Vietnam struggle, and the amount of military assistance they both provide, are major influences on Vietnamese Communist policy. A cessation of bloc war aid would probably make

---

*The battle of Dienbienphu was a major tactical--rather than strategic--reverse for the French. It certainly did not destroy the French Expeditionary Corps as an effective military entity.

**See Annex II.

TOP SECRET

TOP SECRET

it impossible for the Vietnamese Communists to sustain their struggle at its present level of intensity. Hanoi recognizes, however, that contemporary international Communist politics make such a cessation highly unlikely. Hanoi views bloc support as valuable in sustaining, and in some ways increasing, the military pressure which the Communists can bring to bear in South Vietnam and also sees it as a factor which at least partially inhibits and offsets the military pressure which allied forces can impose directly on North Vietnam. So long as bloc aid continues at least at its present levels, however, it will probably not be a critical factor in any basic determination the Vietnamese Communists might make on whether to continue the conflict. North Vietnamese assertions that, in the final analysis, they must rely mainly on their own resources to prosecute the revolution appear to reflect a genuine and deeply-held belief. Hanoi apparently believes that there are distinct limits to the amount of political and material support which it can count on from Peking and Moscow. Furthermore, the Vietnamese would not want to receive a degree of external (i.e., Chinese) aid that would jeopardize their control of the war, unless such aid were required to prevent the extinction of the Communist regime in North Vietnam.

19. Despite Peking's willingness to pressure Hanoi, the Chinese probably could not force the Vietnamese Communists to stay in the war if they decided of their own volition to end the fighting. The Vietnamese probably estimate that, in view of the limitations on the Chinese commitment, Peking would do little more than complain if the conflict were terminated short of an insurgent victory. The Chinese, in fact, seem to recognize this, for they have repeatedly left themselves an out by emphasizing that all decisions on the war are "strictly" up to the Vietnamese.

20. On the basis of Moscow's assistance so far, the Vietnamese probably judge that the Soviet commitment in the war is considerably more restrained than that of the Chinese. Hanoi is fully aware that Moscow, like Peking, is anxious to avoid steps which might lead to a direct military confrontation with the U.S. It is also doubtless clear to the Vietnamese that the Soviets

TOP SECRET

TOP SECRET

would welcome an early end to the war. On balance, however, it is probable that Soviet backing has the effect of buttressing the Vietnamese Communist will to persist in the conflict. The Vietnamese probably judge that they can continue to count indefinitely on Moscow's assistance along present lines so long as the war continues in its present context. They probably believe, in fact, that the Soviets now are locked into a struggle in view of Moscow's desire to retain leadership of the Communist camp.

21. The Course of the Military Struggle in the South: Any objective assessment the Communists make of the course of the military struggle in South Vietnam will acknowledge that although they may not be losing the war at the present time, they are certainly not winning it. They have gone for months without a major tactical success. They are suffering severe and increasing casualties. They no longer enjoy a virtual monopoly of the initiative. Their base areas are no longer virtually sacrosanct; instead they are increasingly subject not only to aerial harassment but also to penetration by allied troops. Their plans are constantly being disrupted by allied spoiling actions, to which Communists must react either by fleeing or by fighting an unplanned engagement. The absolute strength of the forces with which the Communists must contend is steadily increasing. The time-honored guerrilla principle of ensuring numerical superiority at the point of attack has been undercut by the mobility of allied forces who cover ground by helicopter instead of by road. The Communists are far from being defeated, but they are faced with problems greater than any they have had to contend with before in this struggle. Furthermore, for the time being at least, Communist forces have lost the aura of invincibility which in days past (and in the Franco - Viet Minh war) was one of the Communists' most potent political assets.

22. The Price Being Paid in the North:* The air strikes against North Vietnam have created problems for

*See Annex I

TOP SECRET

the Communists, but in both military and economic terms, the damage inflicted so far has probably not exceeded what the Communists regard as acceptable levels. In most cases the reconstruction or repair of damaged facilities can be postponed or effectively achieved by cheap and temporary expedients. In both financial and material terms, the cost inflicted on North Vietnam by allied aerial attack is more than covered by the military and economic aid and technical assistance provided by other Communist countries. Although economic growth has stagnated and will probably deteriorate further in the coming year, air attacks conducted under present rules of engagement almost certainly cannot stop North Vietnamese activities essential to the support of the Communist war effort. In short, North Vietnam is taking punishment in its own territory, but a price it can afford and one it probably considers acceptable in light of the political objectives it hopes to achieve.

23. Communist Capabilities For Additional Force Commitment: In absolute numerical terms the Communists cannot hope to match present and projected allied force commitments. However, it is extremely unlikely that they feel any need to do so. An analysis of relative force levels shows that the apparent present free world superiority of six to one over VC/NVA Forces is largely eliminated when one compares the relative ratios of actual maneuver battalions--i.e., tactical combat troops available for commitment to offensive ground operations.* The present ratio of allied to Communist maneuver battalions is nearly one to one. If present estimates of allied and Communist force projections are accurate, by mid-1967 the Communists will have a slight advantage in this critical ratio. The Communists almost certainly feel that if they can maintain a maneuver battalion ratio in this range, they will be able to prolong the struggle indefinitely and wear down U.S. will to persist.

24. The Calculation of International Attitudes:** There is considerable evidence that the Vietnamese

*Maneuver battalion ratios are analyzed in detail in Annex IV.

**See Annex X.

-11-

TOP SECRET

(Continued...)

TOP SECRET

Communists believe popular opposition throughout the Western world to U.S. policy in Vietnam can be an important political factor in the ultimate outcome of the struggle. Even though Hanoi appears to be concerned with the Vietnamese Communists' relatively limited ability to spur Western agitation against the allied policy by dint of their own propaganda apparatus, they obviously welcome the widespread belief that the struggle in South Vietnam has its roots in what is essentially a southern civil war and not, as Washington claims, in North Vietnamese aggression. Consideration of world popular opposition to U.S. policy would certainly enter into any eventual Vietnamese Communist decision on whether to revise present strategy but would almost certainly not be a decisive factor.

25. The Calculation of U.S. Domestic Attitudes: The Vietnamese Communists pay close attention to evidence of opposition to current U.S. policy arising within the United States itself. Despite some occasional signs of realism about the actual political force of such opposition, by and large the Vietnamese Communists almost certainly overestimate its present strength. Detailed knowledge of the realities of U.S. domestic politics is a fairly scarce commodity in Hanoi. Furthermore, not only do the Communists want to believe that there is strong American domestic opposition to current U.S. policy, but the course and eventual outcome of their previous struggle with the French almost certainly predisposes them to draw invalid parallels to French domestic opposition in the Indochina war and to look for signs of American domestic political pressures capable of forcing policy changes on Washington.

26. The Communists also appear to believe that the U.S. cannot match the continued input of North Vietnamese forces into the struggle (particularly in light of the maneuver battalion comparison outlined above) without going on a virtual wartime footing. They believe this would involve at least partial mobilization and create economic pressures which would drastically increase American opposition to the war, particularly as casualties continue. The Communists may hope that all of these pressures would be sufficiently unpopular within the U.S. to make the war politically unsaleable.

TOP SECRET

27. Morale in North Vietnam:* The wearing effects of the war are causing some decline of civilian morale in North Vietnam, and there are indications the regime fears there may be a further deterioration. The decline, however, has not had any meaningful impact upon the determination of the regime to continue with the war or the policy options it may elect to achieve its objectives.

28. Communist Morale in South Vietnam:** Morale within Communist military forces and the political apparatus in South Vietnam has declined since mid-1965. It is conceivable that at some future point, the prospect of indefinite struggle if not defeat could break the morale of key elements of the Communist southern apparatus. Although Communist morale is obviously fraying badly in some parts of the insurgent structure, nowhere has it yet deteriorated to the point where the battle performance of Communist units is adversely affected. It has certainly not declined to a point presently sufficient to force any major revision in the basic Communist strategy.

29. Attitudes Among the People in Viet Cong Areas:*** There is a substantial body of evidence that morale and, consequently, support for the Communist cause, is dropping in Viet Cong - controlled areas of South Vietnam. The flow of refugees from such areas has increased drastically, and even if a desire for safety is the main motive for this exodus, the exodus itself attests to popular realization that no Viet Cong region is now immune from attack. Furthermore, there are indications that the refugee flow is caused not only by a quest for safety but also by a desire to escape increasingly onerous Communist levies of taxation, forced labor and

---

*See Annex I.

**The critical subject of morale in Communist Forces is the subject of Annex VI.

***This subject is examined in detail in Annex VII.

TOP SECRET

TOP SECRET

conscription. Even though distaste for the Viet Cong is not necessarily positive support for Saigon, this shift in popular attitude could eventually cause the Communists serious problems.

30. The Course of South Vietnamese Political Development: Communist prospects obviously brighten perceptibly during periods of political turmoil within South Vietnam. Conversely, the development of a popularly rooted, viable non-Communist South Vietnamese state is the thing which, over the longer term, the Communists have the greatest reason to fear. Hanoi cannot ignore the fact that although the present Saigon regime is fragile, is far from effective or genuinely popular, and is beset with internal stress, it has nonetheless successfully weathered storms which several of its predecessors were unable to survive. The Communists must also recognize that the events of last spring made painfully manifest how weak they were in urban areas and how limited were their capabilities for capitalizing on political strife among contending non-Communist factions. While the present Saigon government would probably stand no chance of unaided survival in a contest with the Viet Cong, even if all North Vietnamese troops were withdrawn from South Vietnam, there are trends in South Vietnamese political life which are probably a source of disquiet to the Communists. Furthermore, they must recognize that the type of political activity represented by the Rural Development program, even if it is only moderately successful, strikes at the roots of their insurgency's indigenous strength and alters one of the necessary conditions for a successful "war of national liberation" strategy.

V. Probable Communist Near-Term Military and Political Strategy*

31. If they are objective, the Communists must acknowledge that during the past year their insurgent campaign has lost momentum in both the military and political fields. There are signs that the Communists have indeed recognized that developments of the past year have created problems which they must solve,

*Discussed in further detail in Annex XI.

-14-

TOP SECRET

TOP SECRET

along with a situation quite different from that which they faced in fighting the French. Acknowledgment of the existence of these problems does seem to have provoked debates over strategy within the Communist hierarchy, but there is no present sign of any Communist intent to abandon or significantly alter the Communists' present strategy.

32. This strategy in the near term will probably revolve around two major efforts: (1) to keep intact, as far as possible, Main Force units in South Vietnam, and (2) to build up the Main Force strength, both in quantity and in quality, in order to be able to counter allied power when US forces in Vietnam have built up to the level of 400,000 expected by the Communists at the end of 1966. The North Vietnamese leaders probably believe that if they can go into 1967 with an ability to field a Main Force strength of about 125,000, as compared to a US strength of 400,000, they will be able to continue the war. Hanoi probably estimates that a four-to-one absolute military manpower advantage in favor of the US will not be enough for the US to defeat the insurgents; even under these conditions the Communists will be able to match allied forces in maneuver battalions.

33. Analysis of Communist materials indicates that the military strategy of the Communists during the coming months will be largely a continuation of their operational concepts of 1964 and 1965. They will concentrate mainly on opening simultaneous campaigns in the highlands and the area northwest of Saigon, combined with occasional other major actions in the northern coastal provinces. The latter may accelerate as the northeast monsoons begin. Their primary aim will be to stretch the allied forces as thin as possible and inflict as many casualties as possible on allied units. The primary target of the Communists during the coming months will probably be U.S. forces, rather than South Vietnamese. The Communists will continue their attempts to reduce American military mobility and striking power by harassment and by concentration of Communist forces around U.S. base areas to tie down as many Americans as possible in static defense tasks.

TOP SECRET

TOP SECRET

34. To keep U.S. and other allied forces from hitting and hurting large Communist units, the insurgents will probably stick primarily to ambushes, hit-and-run strikes, and guerrilla harassment in situations where they believe the odds of success are decidedly in their favor. Should favorable conditions arise, however, they will almost certainly attempt to conduct operations in regimental strength and greater. The Communists will be working in the meantime on efforts at better concealment of the locations of their main force units in order to counter the improved allied intelligence on the tactical disposition of Communist elements. When large-scale battles occur, the Communists may attempt to devolve them into a series of skirmishes in which Communist ambush and hit-and-run tactics can be used more effectively against small-sized elements of the allied attacking force.

35. On the political side, Communist strategy and goals for the remainder of 1966 and early 1967 will have to take account of recent insurgent setbacks. Captured documents indicate that the Communists will give priority to strengthening and improving their political apparatus, notably by trying to improve the quality of political cadres down to the village level, and by continued emphasis on the recruitment of party members and sympathizers in both rural and urban areas. They will probably continue to concentrate their subversive efforts on the South Vietnamese army and civil service. Laboring class elements may also attract increasing attention in the hope that economic discontent with the inflation spiral in South Vietnam can be exploited to the insurgents' advantage.

36. There is an increasing number of reports that the Communists will make serious efforts to disrupt the constitutional assembly election on 11 September. It is doubtful at this time that the Communists themselves have any significant number of followers among the candidates who have filed, though many of the candidates are relative unknowns even to local government officials. Communist propaganda statements have vigorously denounced the coming election as a farce and a trick. The Communists may feel impelled to take an active role through covert campaigning against candidates, or through terrorism and other direct sabotage efforts.

TOP SECRET

TOP SECRET

VI. Key Trends and Factors

37. In addition to their own logistic, manpower and morale problems, future Communist strategic decisions will probably be primarily influenced by developments in three areas: the course of South Vietnam's political evolution, the course of the military struggle in South Vietnam, and the attitude of the United States--or, more accurately, their estimate of American will and the US Government's political ability to persevere. The Communists, for example, will be paying particular attention to the outcome of the September elections in Vietnam and their resultant effect on South Vietnamese political stability and strength; Communist success or failure in matching allied maneuver battalion strength and achieving at least some tactical successes; and the outcome and import--or what the Communists believe to be the import --of next November's elections in the United States.

VII. The Day of Decision

38. The timing of any Vietnamese Communist decision on altering basic strategy--and the nature of such a decision--will be greatly affected by a variety of considerations including those outlined in the preceding paragraph. We estimate that none of the pressures upon the Communists which we can now identify is severe enough to force a major change in Communist strategy over the next eight to nine months. The Communists would be even less inclined to alter their strategy if they should find political and military developments during this period running in their favor--for example, serious political deterioration in South Vietnam, a series of major Viet Cong military successes, or what they construe as a significant rise of anti-war sentiment in the United States. If on the other hand pressures on them are maintained, and the course of events gives them no grounds for encouragement, they will probably feel compelled by late spring of 1967 to take stock and consider a change in their basic strategy.

TOP SECRET

TOP SECRET

VIII. Alternate Communist Strategic Options

39. Should the Vietnamese Communists decide at this point that continuation of their insurgency along current lines would not be profitable, they would have three basic policy options. They could: (1) convert the struggle into a major war by inviting massive Chinese Communist military intervention; (2) relax Communist pressure and withdraw some North Vietnamese troops, in the hope that the appearance of tranquility would eventually impel the US to disengage the better part of its forces without any formal commitments from the Communists in return; or (3) enter into some form of negotiations.

40. We believe Option (1) is the option the Vietnamese Communists would consider least in their long-term interests. Option (2), despite some advantages, would entail major problems for the Communists. It carries no guarantee that the U.S. would in fact disengage, and puts the Communists in a position of bidding by successive increments to bring this about. It would engender serious morale problems for the Communists during a protracted stand-down without simultaneous U.S. response. It would be hard to explain as anything but acknowledgement of a serious reverse for long-range Communist objectives.

41. In our view, the Vietnamese Communists would be most likely to try some variant of Option (3)--negotiation. They would hope initially to achieve a reduction of allied offensive pressure, including a suspension of bombing in the North.* They would probably work to keep the talks going in order to prolong such a respite. During the course of the negotiations, they would probably determine whether they would seriously explore the possibilities of an acceptable political solution, or examine the alternative courses still open to them.

---

*Communist behavior in periods of negotiation is examined in Annex XII.

-18-

TOP SECRET

TOP SECRET

PRINCIPAL FINDINGS

1. So long as the U.S. air offensive remains at present levels, it is unlikely to diminish North Vietnam's continued ability to provide materiel support to the war in the South. North Vietnam is taking punishment on its own territory, but at a price it can afford and one it probably considers acceptable in light of the political objectives it hopes to achieve.

2. The Viet Cong have borne the brunt of Communist personnel losses in South Vietnam and have also had to compensate for losses of North Vietnamese personnel. We believe that the Viet Cong capability to recruit and train manpower is adequate to cover losses estimated for 1966 but will probably be inadequate to compensate for casualties and losses in 1967. During 1967 the North Vietnamese will have to assume most of the burden of expanding force levels, and an increasing role in replacing losses. These manpower requirements can almost certainly be met from North Vietnamese resources, but they will impose additional strains on North Vietnam's limited supply of skilled personnel and leadership cadre.

3. The Communists' present strategy is costly in both human and economic terms and is taxing Communist resources in some areas, particularly within South Vietnam itself. Allied actions are complicating Communist efforts and raising the costs of their execution. However, neither internal resource shortages nor allied actions within present political parameters are likely to render the Vietnamese Communists physically incapable of persisting in their present strategy.

4. In absolute numerical terms the Communists cannot hope to match present and projected Allied force commitments. However, if present estimates of Allied and Communist force projections are accurate, by mid-1967 the Communists will have a slight advantage in maneuver battalions--i.e., tactical combat troops available for commitment to offensive ground operations.

5. Nevertheless, if they are objective, the Communists must acknowledge that during the past year their

TOP SECRET

TOP SECRET

insurgent campaign has lost momentum in both the military and political fields. Although they may not be losing the war at the present time, they are certainly not winning it. The Communists are far from being defeated; but they are faced with problems greater than any they have had to contend with before in this struggle. Furthermore, Communist forces have at least temporarily lost the aura of invincibility which was one of their most potent political assets.

6. Morale within Communist military forces and the political apparatus in South Vietnam has declined since mid-1965 but not to a point presently sufficient to force any major revision in basic Communist strategy.

7. The Communists must be disappointed in comparing the present situation with that which existed in the spring of 1965. At least indirectly, they have acknowledged that the infusion of U.S. and Allied combat forces has created new problems which must be overcome before victory can be won. Yet Communist realism is presently tinged more with defiance than pessimism; the Communists may be disappointed, but they do not yet seem to be discouraged.

8. Consideration of world popular opposition to U.S. policy would certainly enter into any eventual Vietnamese Communist decision on whether to revise present strategy but would most certainly not be a decisive factor.

9. The Vietnamese Communists pay close attention to evidence of opposition to current U.S. policy arising within the United States itself. The outcome of their previous struggle with the French almost certainly predisposes them to draw invalid parallels to French domestic opposition in the Indochina war and to look for signs of American domestic political pressures capable of forcing policy changes on Washington.

10. The timing of any Vietnamese Communist decision on altering basic strategy--and the nature of such a decision--will be greatly affected by a variety of considerations, including those outlined in this paper. We estimate that none of the pressures upon the Communists

TOP SECRET

~~TOP SECRET~~

which we can now identify is severe enough to force a major change in Communist strategy over the next eight to nine months. The Communists would be even less inclined to alter their strategy if they should find political and military developments during this period running in their favor--for example, serious political deterioration in South Vietnam, a series of major Viet Cong military successes, or what they construe as a significant rise of anti-war sentiment in the United States. If on the other hand pressures on them are maintained and the course of events gives them no grounds for encouragement, by late spring of 1967 they will probably feel compelled to take stock and consider a change in their basic strategy.

~~TOP SECRET~~

SNIE 11-11-67

Soviet Attitudes and Intentions Toward the Vietnam War

4 May 1967

APPROVED FOR RELEASE
DATE: JAN 2005

SECRET

SNIE 11-11-67
4 May 1967

(b)(3)

SPECIAL

NATIONAL INTELLIGENCE ESTIMATE

NUMBER 11-11-67

Soviet Attitudes and Intentions Toward the Vietnam War

Submitted by

Rufus Taylor

DEPUTY DIRECTOR OF CENTRAL INTELLIGENCE

Concurred in by the

UNITED STATES INTELLIGENCE BOARD

As indicated overleaf

4 May 1967

Authenticated:

James S. Lay, Jr.

EXECUTIVE SECRETARY, USIB

Nº 461

SECRET

(Continued...)

~~SECRET~~

SOVIET ATTITUDES AND INTENTIONS TOWARD THE VIETNAM WAR

THE PROBLEM

To examine the USSR's policies toward the Vietnam war and its views of relevant US policies, and to estimate Soviet intentions in relation to that conflict.

CONCLUSIONS

A. While the Soviet leaders see the war as advantageous to them in many ways, they also see disadvantages which make their options unpromising and hazardous. They probably believe that there is no prospect of movement toward a political solution for several months at best and appear to have concluded that for the time being they have no alternative but to help Hanoi to carry on the war, hoping that changes of attitude in either Hanoi or Washington, or both, will make a political solution possible later.

B. The Soviet leaders fear that the US, in its impatience to get the war over, will escalate the conflict in a way which will increase the risks and costs for the USSR; in an effort to forestall this they are currently stressing their intention to move to more vigorous support of North Vietnam. We believe that during the coming months they will continue to supply equipment designed to strengthen air and coastal defenses in North Vietnam and to increase the firepower of both the regular North Vietnamese forces and the Communist forces fighting in the South.

C. Whether or not there are formal arrangements covering the transit of Soviet supplies across China, we believe that Peking will not pose serious obstacles to such transit. But the relations between

(Continued...)

Moscow and Peking are still fundamentally hostile, and their attitudes toward major issues of war and peace in Vietnam will continue to differ profoundly.

D. The North Vietnamese at some point will probably press the Soviets for more sophisticated equipment than those types now arriving on the scene or in the pipeline. These might include cruise missiles and tactical rockets which could be used to support North Vietnamese operations in the DMZ area and against US warships. The USSR might believe it had to respond to such pressure, although it would be concerned that the use of such weapons would provoke a still more dangerous US response.

E. If the intensity of the conflict were to be increased by the US, we believe that at some point the USSR would create an atmosphere of heightened tension with the US. The Soviets might take certain actions designed to bolster North Vietnam and to warn the US, such as the provision of limited numbers of volunteers or crews for defense equipment or possibly aircraft. They might also break off negotiations with the US on various subjects and suspend certain agreements now in effect. The mining or the blockade of the North Vietnamese coast would be most likely to provoke these responses, since this would constitute a direct challenge to the Soviets, and there would be little they could do on the scene. We do not think the Soviets are prepared to resort to strong and direct threats of general war as a means to protect North Vietnam or to preserve Soviet face.

F. There would also be a good chance that at some juncture the Soviets would exert strong efforts toward a political solution, but they would probably not make Hanoi's acceptance of talks an explicit condition of continued material support.

(Continued...)

DISCUSSION

I. SOVIET POLICY

1. The USSR's initial post-Khrushchev commitment to North Vietnam in late 1964 was almost certainly based on what proved to be a miscalculation: in all probability, the Soviet leaders did not then expect the US to step up its involvement in the conflict and they foresaw a relatively quick and easy Communist victory in the South. They wanted to be associated with that victory and—more concerned than Khrushchev with the problems and issues of the Communist world—were especially anxious to disprove Chinese charges that they were soft on imperialism. Initiation of the US air campaign in February 1965 caught them by surprise (and Kosygin in Hanoi), and their actions ever since have reflected their determination to maintain their commitment to Hanoi, but at the same time to control the risks of doing so, especially vis-a-vis the US.

2. There is within this broad context a wide area of uncertainty in the USSR's attitude toward the war. The Soviets surely see the war as advantageous to them in many ways. It diverts US political and strategic attention away from areas of primary interest to the USSR, it imposes burdens on US resources, and it employs a substantial portion of US military forces-in-being. Moreover, it has deeply troubled many US allies and associates, especially in Europe, and it is a divisive factor within the US itself. Finally, the war—and their important role in it—allows the Soviets to score further gains against the Chinese, both in Hanoi and in the Communist movement as a whole.

3. On the other hand, the conflict, as seen from Moscow, has its adverse aspects as well. The bombing of North Vietnam constitutes a continuing reproach to the Soviet Union, unable as it is to protect a small ally. The war is taking place far from the USSR and is being waged by a state which is unwilling to accept Soviet political guidance on the conduct of the war and is suspicious even of Soviet counsel. The buildup of US forces, and their engagement in combat, increases pressures on the Soviet leaders to expand their own forces, and this, in turn, may impose some additional strains on the economy and further complicate long-range economic planning. Perhaps most important, the US may undertake new courses of action which would force the Soviets to choose between confronting the US or backing down. Moscow is also almost certainly concerned that a Korean-type war could develop, leading to Chinese involvement and all the complications and dangers which the USSR desires to avoid.

4. The pro's and con's of this situation tend to make alternative Soviet options unpromising or hazardous. If they attempted to force Hanoi into negotiations—e.g., by threatening to stop supplies—they might fail, for Hanoi, even without Soviet aid, could fight on if it wished, though the nature and the level of the conflict would necessarily change. Such a failure would effectively end Soviet

influence in Hanoi, throw North Vietnam entirely back on China, and diminish Soviet prestige in the Communist world as well as in many "uncommitted" countries. The same calamities would follow if Moscow simply withdrew its support of Hanoi in order to escape the risks of deeper involvement. On the other hand, Moscow cannot feasibly undertake any serious military participation in the war, with its own combat forces, far from the sources of Soviet power, and at the end of lines of communication passing through the dubiously friendly territory of China or risking US counteraction at sea. Finally, if Moscow tried to influence the US by heavy pressures elsewhere in the world, it would risk provoking a partial US mobilization and a major international crisis.

5. As for the war itself, the Soviet leaders have probably concluded that a military victory by the Viet Cong and the North Vietnamese is not possible. They probably also believe that a clear-cut military victory by the US-Vietnamese forces is also impossible, unless the US steps up its war against North Vietnam to a very substantial degree or is prepared to engage in a long and costly struggle. In addition, the Soviet leaders have probably concluded, as a consequence of the events of the past two to three months, that there is no prospect of movement toward a political solution, at least by negotiation, for several months at best. Especially since Kosygin's visit to London in February, it must appear to the Soviets that both sides are determined not to accept the other's terms for the opening of negotiations. The Soviet leaders thus appear to have concluded that for a time they have no alternative but to help Hanoi to carry on the war, hoping that changes of attitude in either Hanoi or Washington, or both, will make a political solution possible later.

6. The Soviet leaders probably recognize that a substantial majority in the US supports the President in his wish to terminate the war by a political settlement and that US withdrawal without meaningful concessions from the Communists in Vietnam is an unrealistic hope. But they fear that, in its anxiety to get the war over and finished, the US will escalate the conflict in a way which would pose those serious dangers we have noted above.

7. In its efforts to prevent the US from escalating the conflict and to accept terms also acceptable to Hanoi for moving toward a political settlement, the Soviet leaders have engaged in a variety of stratagems. For a period they sought to warn the US of the harmful effect upon US-Soviet relations of the continued rise in the US commitment. Although they have continued to pursue this theme, they have since last summer also used another route; they permitted some tangible progress in US-Soviet relations, partly in order to persuade the US that such progress should not be jeopardized by new US actions in Vietnam. Finally, they took steps, which culminated in the Wilson-Kosygin talks, designed to convince the US leaders that there was a real prospect for political settlement. At the moment, because of their fear of imminent escalation, they are trying to convince the US of the hazards of escalation, this time by stressing that they intend to meet US moves with even more vigorous support of North Vietnam.

II. SOVIET REACTIONS TO ESCALATION

8. We believe that both Hanoi and Moscow have expected a higher level of US military operations against North Vietnam, and it seems likely that the Soviets will respond to the current expanded bombing program by providing additional quantities and perhaps new types of weapons and equipment. Indeed, they may already have decided to do so.

9. We believe that the attitude of China will not pose serious obstacles to the continued transit of Soviet military supplies. We have no evidence that shipments have been significantly disrupted in the past, despite Soviet charges to the contrary and despite some degree of Chinese harassment. Early this year, at the height of the anti-Soviet demonstrations in Peking, the Soviets and the North Vietnamese apparently made some new arrangements under which the North Vietnamese would accept Soviet cargo at the Sino-Soviet border and assume responsibility for its onward movement.[1] Such an arrangement would lessen still further the chances of Chinese meddling with Soviet supplies, but it would seem to have little bearing on Sino-Soviet relations. These relations remain fundamentally hostile, and Chinese and Soviet attitudes toward major issues of war and peace in Vietnam will continue to differ profoundly.

10. In general, we believe that the types of weaponry the Soviets are likely to supply during the coming months will be intended to strengthen the air and coastal defenses of North Vietnam and to increase the firepower of both the regular North Vietnamese forces and the Communist forces fighting in the South.[2] To bolster air defense, the Soviets will probably supply more jet fighters with air-to-air missiles, more surface-to-air missiles, and improved antiaircraft artillery (e.g., the ZU-23). We think it somewhat less likely that they would introduce an improved surface-to-air missile system with a somewhat better capability against low altitude attacks than the SA-2's now in North Vietnam. To meet US naval attacks on coastal shipping, there is a good chance that the Soviets will provide coastal defense missiles with conventional warheads (the Samlet and perhaps even the coastal defense version of the Shaddock). They will also probably supply more patrol boats, perhaps even the Komar or OSA guided missile patrol boats. For the ground forces, the Soviets will probably provide additional multiple rocket launchers, heavier artillery and mortars, better antiaircraft and antitank weapons, and a variety of antipersonnel devices. Some of the lighter, more mobile equipment would be sent forward by Hanoi to South Vietnam for use against US personnel and bases. Indeed, some has already appeared there.

11. The North Vietnamese would probably at some point press the Soviets for more sophisticated equipment, and this would pose a serious problem for the Soviets. They might believe they had to respond to such pressure,

---

[1] A critical change in Chinese internal affairs, should it come, could of course significantly alter existing transit arrangements.

[2] See ANNEX for the characteristics of selected weapons and weapons systems.

especially if hard pressed by North Vietnam and if no break appeared on the political horizon. They might provide nonnuclear weapons with additional range and firepower, hoping that the new military situation thus created would bring about a change in the US position. But the Soviets would also be concerned that the introduction of new types of weapons and especially their use in South Vietnam would provoke further US retaliation, which they would like to avoid, or even create a situation which would invite a US invasion of North Vietnam. We believe nevertheless that there is a good chance that they would provide some of these weapons systems.

12. If the Soviets did decide to embark on this course, some of the weapons involved might be the Salish short-range ground-support cruise missile or the Frog tactical rocket. Both are road mobile, require little in the way of permanent support facilities, and would not present a ready target for US bombing. Vietnamese could be trained to man them in a few months. They could be used from sites in North Vietnam against US forces in the DMZ area, but probably would not be transported South. The 150 n.m. Scud and the 300 n.m. Shaddock would also meet these general criteria for mobility and Vietnamese manning. The latter however, is a relatively new and complex system never deployed outside the USSR, and, in any case, both the Scud and Shaddock are too cumbersome and complicated for use in the South. If the Soviets were prepared to provide a weapon for attacks upon the South Vietnamese population or US bases, they might consider MRBMs with conventional warheads. Such weapons would create logistical problems and have marginal military value; if provided, their use would be primarily for political and psychological reasons. In any event, the Soviets would probably believe that the emplacement of such weapons would provoke an unacceptable level of US retaliation, and we consider their provision unlikely.

13. Beyond supplying equipment, the Soviets could take certain other actions to bolster the North Vietnamese and warn the US. They might believe, for example, that the provision of limited numbers of volunteers, or of crews for defense equipment or possibly aircraft, would serve as a warning without leading to a serious confrontation.

14. In any event, a steady increase in the level of combat and especially in the level of US air attacks would make the Soviet leaders increasingly nervous, and each new step would bring them closer to responses which would seriously impair US-Soviet relations. They might, for example, break off various negotiations and contacts with the US, and perhaps suspend certain agreements of recent months. We cannot say precisely what would be the Soviet response to particular actions. Much would depend upon what had gone before and how dangerous the situation of North Vietnam had become. But we are persuaded that at some point the USSR would create an atmosphere of heightened tension with the US.

15. The mining or the blockade of the North Vietnamese coast would be most likely to produce this result, since such action would constitute a direct challenge to the Soviets. At a minimum they would try to mobilize world opinion

against the US on this issue, and, depending on the attitude of North Vietnam, would consider taking the matter to the UN.

16. There is little that the Soviets could do on the scene if confronted with this kind of situation. They do not have the strength in the area to force a blockade or to confront the US with a major military challange, and we do not believe they would wish to run large risks simply in order to harass US forces or gain temporary respite. In the case of mining, for example, the Soviets could try to reopen shipping routes by bringing in minesweepers, other naval ships for protection, and air cover from North Vietnam. But this would be a hazardous venture, since the US could continue to sow mines by air and the Soviets could not prevent it unless they were prepared to begin a major naval and air war. We believe they would not risk their shipping in mined waters and would attempt the necessary supply by other means, e.g., through China or by lighterage. Most important, we do not think that the Soviets are prepared to resort to strong and direct threats of general war as a means to protect North Vietnam or to preserve Soviet face.

17. Regardless of the precise action taken by the US, the Soviets might at some point exert pressures on the US outside of Southeast Asia. Heightened tensions in Korea, new troubles in the Middle East are possibilities. But Berlin is the most plausible pressure point; US interests there are directly engaged and vulnerable, and the USSR could be surer of controlling the action. They might consider that only minor pressure on access routes would be enough to create the impression of an impending crisis. But we think it unlikely that the Soviets would want to take the risk of provoking by such pressures a major and generalized crisis which would not only undercut their policies in Western Europe but could also lead to a US-Soviet confrontation.

18. There would be a good chance that the Soviets would at some juncture exert strong efforts toward a political solution of the Vietnam problem. They would have to weigh the risks of some level of confrontation with the US against their reluctance to put real pressure on Hanoi for such a solution. They would almost certainly urge the course of negotiation more vigorously than they have heretofore. But they would probably not be willing to make Hanoi's acceptance of talks an explicit condition of continued material support. If negotiations did get underway, they would, of course, still bend every effort to obtain terms which gave Hanoi hope of eventually achieving its aims.

(Continued...)

ANNEX

CHARACTERISTICS OF CERTAIN SOVIET WEAPONS MENTIONED IN THE TEXT

I. GROUND FORCES

Scud A or B (SS-1b or c)

- Type: single-stage, tactical ballistic with storable liquid propellant
- Range: 150 n.m.
- Warhead: 1,500 to 2,000 lbs. HE or CW (intended primarily for nuclear option)
- Accuracy: 0.5 n.m. CEP
- Refire time: 1½ to 2½ hours
- Remarks: the Scud launcher is mounted on a modified tank chassis; it has been deployed in the USSR and some East European countries

Salish (SSC-2a)

- Type: surface-to-surface version of the Kennel air-to-surface, turbo-jet cruise missile
- Range: 60 n.m.
- Warhead: 2,200 lbs. HE (nuclear possible)
- Accuracy: 300-500 feet CEP
- Refire time: unknown
- Remarks: the Salish is transported on a wheeled launcher; it is deployed in the USSR, Cuba and with Soviet forces in East Germany

Shaddock (SSC-1a)

- Type: tactical ground forces version of the SS-N-3 naval cruise missile
- Range: 300 n.m.
- Warhead: 1,000 to 2,000 lbs. HE (nuclear option)
- Accuracy: 0.5 n.m. CEP at 150 n.m. range
- Refire time: unknown
- Remarks: the Shaddock is transported in a launch tube on a wheeled vehicle; it has not been made available to non-Soviet forces

~~SECRET~~

Frog

Type: solid propellant, surface-to-surface, unguided rocket available in several versions
Range: 18 to 37 n.m. with conventional warhead
Warhead: 820 to 1,300 lbs. HE (nuclear option)
Accuracy: 500-800 meter CEP at ⅔ maximum range
Reaction time: 15-30 minutes
Remarks: the Frog is mounted on a light tank chassis and can support ground forces in a variety of climatic and terrain conditions; variants have been deployed in the USSR, East Europe and Cuba

II. COASTAL DEFENSE

Samlet (SSC-2b)

Type: coastal defense version of the Kennel air-to-surface, turbo-jet cruise missile
Range: 45 n.m.
Warhead: 2,200 lbs. HE or CW
Overall system reliability: 60-70 percent
Refire time: 15 minutes
Remarks: two, wheeled Samlet launchers are deployed per launch site; the system has been deployed in the USSR, Cuba, Communist China, North Korea, and East Europe

Shaddock (SSC-1b)

Type: coastal defense version of the SSC-1a ground forces cruise missile
Range: 270 n.m.
Warhead: 1,000 to 2,000 lbs. HE or CW (nuclear option)
Overall system reliability: 60 percent
Refire time: no refire
Remarks: the Shaddock has not been made available to non-Soviet forces.

Styx (SS-N-2)

Type: liquid-fuel, antiship cruise missile launched from Osa and Komar-class guided missile patrol boats
Range: 20 n.m.
Warhead: 500-2,000 lbs. HE
Overall system reliability: 50 to 75 percent depending on homing mode
Refire time: no refire

~~SECRET~~

Remarks: carried by Komar (2 launchers) and Osa-class (4 launchers) guided missile patrol boats; deployed in the USSR, Cuba, China, North Korea, Egypt, Indonesia, Algeria, and East Europe

III. ANTIAIRCRAFT

ZU-23

Type: 23 mm twin antiaircraft gun mounted on a towed, two-wheel chassis

Range: 8,200 yards horizontal; 19,000 feet vertical; 6,600 feet effective antiaircraft range

Rate of fire: 60 rounds per minute per gun

Muzzle velocity: 3,050

Weight: 2,060 lbs. overall

Remarks: the ZU-23 is a dual-purpose weapon suitable for AA use as well as direct-fire ground use against personnel and light armor; it is standard issue in the USSR and has been delivered to several other countries

IV. MEDIUM RANGE BALLISTIC MISSILES

Shyster (SS-3)

Type: single stage MRBM employing radio-inertial guidance and nonstorable liquid propellant

Range: 630 n.m.

Warhead: 2,700 lbs. nuclear (conventional possible)

Accuracy: 1.0 to 1.75 n.m. CEP

Refire time: 2 to 5 hours

Remarks: the SS-3 is now obsolete; it has never been deployed outside the USSR

Sandal (SS-4)

Type: single stage MRBM employing inertial guidance and storable liquid propellant

Range: 1,020 n.m.

Warhead: 1,900-2,500 lbs. nuclear (conventional possible)

Accuracy: 1.25 n.m. CEP

Refire time: 2 to 4 hours

Remarks: the SS-4 is deployed in both soft and hard sites, primarily in the European USSR; a much larger conventional warhead could be delivered to shorter ranges (e.g., 4,000 lbs. to about 800 n.m.); this system was deployed to Cuba and withdrawn in 1962

Memo

Implications of an Unfavorable Outcome in Vietnam

11 September 1967

APPROVED FOR RELEASE
DATE: JAN 2005

(b)(3)

IMPLICATIONS OF AN UNFAVORABLE OUTCOME IN VIETNAM

11 September 1967

000027

IMPLICATIONS OF AN UNFAVORABLE OUTCOME IN VIETNAM

PROBLEM AND ASSUMPTIONS

1. At some stage in most debates about the Vietnam war, questions like the following emerge: What would it actually mean for the US if it failed to achieve its stated objectives in Vietnam? Are our vital interests in fact involved? Would abandonment of the effort really generate other serious dangers? Naturally, those who oppose the war tend to minimize the costs of failures, while those who support the war point ominously to far-reaching negative effects which they allege would follow such a setback. This aspect of the Vietnam argument has lacked clear and detailed definition on both sides, even though it is crucial to the Why and Wherefore of our whole involvement there.

2. What we are attempting in this paper is to provide some greater precision about the probable costs, for American policy and interests as a whole, of an unfavorable outcome in Vietnam. It is not assumed in this inquiry that such an outcome is now likely; it has been demonstrated, in fact, that the Communists

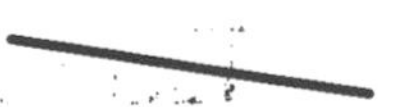

cannot win if the US is determined to prevent it. But the question of what it would mean for the US if its own objectives are not achieved is relevant and fair. The debate itself shows the need for a sounder basis by which to measure the costs of an unfavorable outcome against the exertions which would presumably still be required to achieve a favorable one.

3. What we mean by an "unfavorable outcome" needs to be defined with some realism. We are not discussing the entirely implausible hypothesis of a political-military collapse, say, the precipitate withdrawal of American forces or sweeping political concessions tantamount to granting Hanoi outright achievement of its aims in the South. It seems realistic to believe, given the present scale of US involvement and the sacrifices already made, that this government would approach a settlement short of its aims only by a series of steps involving gradual adjustment of our present political-military posture. Apart from the domestic political pressures that would cause this to be so, the very concern to minimize unfavorable effects on other relationships and on the American world position would argue strongly for such a course.

4. We assume, therefore, that an outcome favorable to the Communists would come about as the result of a process of negotiation,

probably fairly prolonged. A resulting political settlement, whether or not it looked at first like a "compromise," would in the end lead to the establishment of Communist power in South Vietnam. Insofar as the broader repercussions of this development are concerned, a critical variable would be the time the process took. If it took 10 years, obviously the significance of US acceptance of such a settlement would tend to be lost in the new context produced by interim events. We are assuming for purposes of this discussion that the period would be short enough to make it impossible to blur the fact that American policy had met with a serious reverse; it would appear in fact that the US had deliberately accepted a faulty settlement rather than pay the price of trying longer to avert it. This seems a realistic assumption for two reasons: the Communists would probably try to turn a shaky settlement to early advantage and would be little concerned to delay their triumph for a long period in order to save face for the US; and, the divided non-Communist political forces in South Vietnam, if left to their own devices under such a settlement, would probably not be able to put up effective political resistance for very long.

5. If all this went off peacefully, it would constitute the best rather than the worst case, or rather a successful US effort

to achieve the best case, given a decision to place priority on ending hostilities rather than on achievement of the aims we have so far pursued. It is possible, however, that events would be precipitated in such a manner that the outcome -- the taking of power by the Communists -- would emerge very rapidly and in conditions of breakdown and disorder on the non-Communist side. There could be a spectacle of panic flight from the country, suicidal resistance by isolated groups, and Communist terror and vengeance. Clearly, if this worst case came about, the discredit the US would earn, which would be seen by many as not merely political but also as moral discredit, would be far greater. The following discussion assumes a negotiated settlement applied in reasonably orderly circumstances, but which nevertheless works out to Communist advantage within a relatively brief period, say, a year or so.

SOME GENERAL PROPOSITIONS

6. Viewed purely as an intellectual problem, the question posed can have no complete and wholly satisfactory answer. One is asked to assume a single event, the scenario and context for which cannot be described in detail, and to project its consequences for subsequent developments on the world scene as a whole. In fact,

no single event, even one as important as this one, can be determining for all subsequent developments. In any case, it is impossible to disentangle the effects of a single event from the whole continuum of interacting forces; compensatory motions of unforeseeable magnitude, or even quite unrelated developments, would come into play to alter the sum of interactions. Only historians, after the fact, can have the satisfaction of tracing back orderly chains of causation. The view forward is always both hazy and kaleidoscopic; those who have to act on such a view can have no certainties but must make choices on what appears at the moment to be the margin of advantage.

7. If it is impossible to list and measure all the forces which would be brought into play by the event assumed, it may nevertheless be possible to state some general propositions which would tend to govern the directions in which events might move. Such propositions can at least suggest how to think about the issues posed. Those stated in the immediately following paragraphs will be applied later in the paper in attempting to forecast developments affecting some concrete situations and relationships.

8. The failure of American policy in Vietnam would have repercussions worldwide; it cannot be thought of merely as a local or even as a regional event. This is so, not only because world

(Continued...)

attention has been so intensively focussed on the drama of Vietnam for so long, but even more importantly, because the US is involved and it is a primary power factor on a world scale.

9. There would inevitably be a reappraisal in many quarters of the real weight and reach of US power. In a sense, international politics is the sum of calculations made by all the actors concerning the power and intentions of all others. Since the US has been viewed as the most powerful actor in the game, all parties would feel obliged to reconsider their views of US power, as well as of the will and wisdom of those who wield it.

10. That this should happen at all is a measure of the importance of the event which occasions it. The respect of others for US power and the uses to which it is put is one of the key building blocks for such order and security as obtain in the world. If it were removed from this inherently fragile structure, many unsettling and perhaps dangerous consequences would follow. Those who are responsible for the conduct of American policy cannot in prudence afford to treat this consideration lightly.

11. The contingency we are discussing in this paper would constitute a rather dramatic demonstration that there are certain limits on US power, a discovery which would be unexpected for many,

disconcerting for some, and encouraging to others. To be sure, no one doubts that the US could utterly destroy North Vietnam with nuclear weapons, if it chose to do so. Most would probably agree that the US could achieve its objectives by less drastic methods, if it persisted long enough and paid the cost. But the compelling proposition emerging from the situation would be that the US, acting within the constraints imposed by its traditions and public attitudes, cannot crush a revolutionary movement which is sufficiently large, dedicated, competent, and well-supported. In a narrow sense, this means more simply that the structure of US military power is ill-suited to cope with guerrilla warfare waged by a determined, resourceful, and politically astute opponent. This is not a novel discovery. It has long been suspected. What our postulated situation would do is to reveal it dramatically.

12. On the other hand, the contingency we are discussing in this paper does not involve a reversal of power relations, of the sort that occurred for example, with the defeat of Germany in World War II. The case in question is rather one of a setback for a very great power whose essential strength would remain unimpaired. Historically, great powers have repeatedly absorbed setbacks without permanent diminution of the role which they subsequently played.

(Continued...)

Everyone acknowledges that the USSR has suffered a number of major setbacks in the last 20 years, but few would argue that its power bulks any the less formidable today. Similarly, the view held by others of US power would probably be affected relatively and temporarily, though it is not possible to say with certainty whether new complications and dangers might not be set in train by such a setback.

13. Moreover, the reappraisals of the US made by others would not be uniform; they would be heavily conditioned by the particular perspectives, expectations, and interests of different countries. The fears of some would rise because they would conclude that US power was a less reliable support to their security than they had supposed. Others would be reassured because they would believe that US power was being used with greater responsibility and concern for the general peace than they had thought. Some would fear a tendency for the US to withdraw generally from involvement with the security and development of other areas. Others would rejoice because they would expect the US to reveal a better-balanced concern for other parts of the world than southeast Asia, and still others because they would hope that US resources saved by peace in Vietnam would be applied elsewhere.

- 8 -

14. The reappraisals would also be tentative. Few would conclude that the Vietnam episode gave a firm fix for the future on the content and direction of US policy. Almost all would recognize that, while Vietnam indicated something about the limits of US power and especially about its relevance to that particular situation, the power of the US would remain the weightiest single factor in world politics. The indications that the US gave in subsequent pronouncement and action of how it intended to use its power would increasingly over time efface the impact of the Vietnamese affair. It would not have permanent effect on how others viewed this country since the reappraisal of power relations is a continuing process.

15. A similar tentativeness would affect the attitudes of states which have a particular interest because of US security commitments to them. We think there is none which would withdraw forthwith from its security relationship with the US because of an unfavorable outcome in Vietnam. Some might consider whether they ought not to allow such ties to dissolve and move to a more neutral stance. Some might even draw the lesson that the US would in future be more exacting of reciprocal performance from its alliance partners. Probably all would decide to await further evidence before making a definitive reading of US intentions,

evidence in the form of reassurances or actions bearing directly on themselves. But a trend toward degeneration of some alliance relationships is one of the risks that would be involved.

16. Finally one general proposition towers over all the above in importance; it concerns a factor which probably would have more decisive effect on the net result than any other. This is the appraisal made by the US itself -- its leaders and general opinion -- of the meaning of the Vietnam experience for the future course of US policy. A traumatic reaction, perhaps revealed by a deeply divisive national debate or by a feverish search for "guilty" parties, could greatly compound the damage done. An apparent confusion of counsels, with one set of extremists demanding a more ruthless use of American power and another the renunciation of any world power role, would have similar effect. More than other nations, and far more than any great power known to history, the Americans live with open windows. Especially in the immediate aftermath of the event, a clamor of domestic quarreling and disarray might go far to fix the views of friends and foes abroad in a mistaken and ultimately dangerous mold. Conversely, if American opinion seemed in the main to take a steady and sober line, foreign echoes would tend to be similarly moderated. In fact, American domestic interpretations of a setback in Vietnam, and the

impression others consequently formed of the likely subsequent course of American policy, might finally prove as important as the event itself.

IMPLICATIONS FOR ASIA

17. Turning to some more concrete implications, the most direct and immediate would be evident in the region of Southeast Asia itself. But what happens in this area bears in turn on Chinese policy and the future of Chinese-American relations, and also on the role which the US is to play in the affairs of Asia over the long term.

Southeast Asia

18. In considering Southeast Asia, the first questions are: Does Hanoi have ambitions beyond the extension of Communist power to the whole of Vietnam? Having won that, how would it conduct itself toward other states of the area? There does not seem much doubt that it would aim to establish its ascendancy over Laos and Cambodia; the Vietnamese Communists, partly because they had an organized existence for several decades under the colonial regime, apparently regard themselves as the successors to the French in all of Indo-China. But this does not mean that Hanoi would proceed

at once to wage subversive-guerrilla war against these two countries in order to establish outright Communist regimes. For some period at least, the Communists would be preoccupied with the consolidation of their rule in South Vietnam. Probably Hanoi would be satisfied initially to have well-disposed governments responsive to its influence in Laos and Cambodia. Its primary requirement would be that they not have a military association with the US. If they did, they would become the object of subversive attack, though probably not of formal invasion. Sooner or later, of course, Hanoi would expect these two countries to be governed by subordinate branches of the Vietnamese Communist Party.

19. The situation of Thailand would be perilous and complicated. Sooner or later, both Hanoi and Peking would bring pressure in an attempt to force Bangkok into a "cooperative" relationship. The test would be the latter's willingness to dissociate itself from the US, and, presumably, new political leadership would be required as an earnest of this change. We have no sound basis for estimating how the Thais would respond to such pressure. Our best guess is that, despite the discredit the US would suffer because of the outcome in Vietnam, the present Thai leadership would continue to seek US support. The Communist powers would then press the subversive effort already in being in northeast Thailand,

using it as a lever on the Bangkok government. Its dilemma would be whether to try to buy off Communist pressure by realigning its policies, or whether to give resistance with US aid, assuming this was offered. With such aid, the Thais' chances of beating off a subversive campaign would probably be good, though the pressures for accommodation generated by leftist political forces, which would no doubt gain strength in the wake of a Communist success in Vietnam, might be great. We see no way of anticipating how the internal political struggle generated in Thailand by these events would fall out. Obviously, the stance adopted by the US, and Thai appraisal of it, would be crucial.

20. Similarly, in other countries of the region, judgments made about the further intentions of the US in the area would decisively affect the balance of internal political forces and, therefore, the policies adopted toward the Communist powers. In Malaysia, Burma, the Philippines, and Indonesia, non-Communist political forces now have a clear ascendancy. The will of the present ruling groups to maintain themselves in power, to assert full national independence, and to resist internal subversion would persist despite Communist success in Vietnam. None of these four states would be destined inevitably to fall under Communist control or to be pressured into a vassal relationship with China.

But clearly their will and capacity to resist internal and external pressures would be greatly strengthened if the US demonstrated convincingly that its backing would continue to be available to them. What the US did about supporting the Thais, who would be most immediately exposed to Communist pressures, would greatly affect judgments of political leaders in the other states about US intentions.

21. The outlook would be very much darker if leaders in these countries concluded that they had to write off the US as a power factor in the region. A strong regime in China determined to press a campaign of subversion against the mainland states has considerable assets with which to work. Burma is vulnerable because of its long border and its dissident minorities; its political weakness and stagnation may make it a target for the Communists regardless of the outcome in Vietnam. In Malaysia and Singapore, the Communist parties, largely Chinese, are responsive to Peking's direction and have a demonstrated capacity for terrorist activity. With new pressures on these governments, leftist fronts agitating for accommodation with the Communist powers would gain in strength. Even if not inevitable, it is possible, especially assuming the absence of effective US support, that political realignments would occur in one or another of these countries.

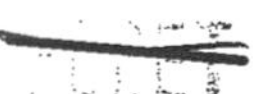

At a minimum, internal instability and a setback to economic development would be a danger.

22. Indonesia and the Philippines would be very much less vulnerable, in part because their island situations make external support to guerrilla forces far more difficult. It seems unlikely that the present Indonesian leaders would, because of Communist success in Vietnam, falter in their determination to cope with their own internal Communist problem. Given continuation of the economic aid programs in which the US, Japan, and others are involved, their will to move ahead with orderly development would remain. If, however, Communist gains eventually took place in Thailand and other mainland states, leftist nationalist forces, which have been repressed along with the Communists in the last two years, might revive; the result could be a new phase of severe instability. In the Philippines, the outlook for stability and sound development is not good in any case. US failure in Vietnam would give encouragement to Communist and anti-American forces, but the problem of subversion would probably still be manageable. As in Indonesia, of course, if Communist gains were extended beyond Vietnam, there would probably be a tendency for the internal situation of the Philippines to deteriorate also.

(Continued...)

23. Thus the eventual repercussions of failure in Vietnam are potentially serious in Southeast Asia as a whole, but that failure alone would not necessarily unhinge the entire area. Other factors which would come into play subsequently would be far more important. The primary one is the role the US would decide to play in the area, and its success in convincing leaders there of its will and capacity to continue backing them. Next in importance would be the outcome in Thailand. If the Thais, with US backing, successfully held off the pressures which would be brought to bear against them, the whole region would probably remain reasonably stable. If they did not, deteriorating situations in Burma and Malaysia would probably develop, and the political balance in Indonesia and the Philippines could eventually be affected also. Finally, much in all this hangs on the situation in China; restored unity there, if combined with a reinvigoration of expansionist policies, would obviously worsen the odds against stability in Southeast Asia.

China

24. In view of the present internal turmoil in China, it is impossible to say whether and in what degree it will be a significant factor in Asian power alignments during the next few years. The discussion here assumes that order will ultimately be restored

under the authority of a central government, and that such a government will aspire to great-power dominance in the Asian region. This means that it will strive to limit or displace US influence and to bring lesser states of the area into a dependent or at least reliable relationship with itself. This will be true whatever faction wins the internal power struggle, though the manner in which a future Chinese regime pursues such aims clearly depends on its political complexion and on its strength. In any case, we would not think that Communist success in Vietnam would make overt Chinese aggression in Southeast Asia any more likely. Like Hanoi, Peking would try to follow up by increasing pressure on states of that area to dissociate themselves from the US. Probably on the political plane, though surely not in power terms, a unified Communist Vietnam could become something of a competitor to China in that region.

25. It seems unlikely that Communist success in Vietnam would itself have any important bearing on the internal struggle in China. No doubt the Maoists would claim the event as a triumph of the leader's doctrines, but the Vietnamese war is apparently not at issue between the Chinese factions; other contentions over internal power and policy are dominating. Whether in the long run

the fact that the US was no longer militarily present in a border country would improve the prospects of Chinese-American relations seems doubtful. These relations will depend far more fundamentally on other issues, notably Taiwan, and on the general political disposition of the leadership in China which succeeds Mao.

The US Role in Asia

26. Not only the states of Southeast Asia, but all the non-Communist states in the Far East would feel obliged to ask themselves what the failure of US policy in Vietnam meant for the future role of the US in that part of the world. There would surely be a shock to all these states, and a period of some uncertainty while they re-examined their relations with the US and made frantic efforts to get a new reading on US intentions.

27. Eventual reactions would vary with the particular situations of individual states. Those which feel themselves most immediately threatened by Communist forces -- Thailand, South Korea, Taiwan -- would be the most alarmed. The latter two would demand concrete reassurance, recognizing that they had no possibility of accommodation with their enemies. As indicated above, Thailand's case would be more complex. And, also as argued above, other states in Southeast Asia would be very much affected

eventually by whether Vietnam seemed to set a limit to Communist advance, by the fate of Thailand, and by what the US demonstrated there that it was prepared to do in future. Broadly speaking, we think that all these states would want the US to continue to play a major role in support of Asian security and development, but they would expect it to demonstrate anew that it had the will to do so. For some, the lesson of Vietnam might be that US support could not be effective without greater effort by them on their own behalf. The outcome in Vietnam might also give some impulse to regional association in Asia, though this would be unlikely to be significant from a security point of view.

28. In Japan, one would not expect any sudden retreat from the security relationship with the US, but stronger neutralist opinion would be heard and the future of the US-Japanese security treaty would be more uncertain. For the Japanese, however, the relationship with the US would be weighed primarily against the long-term threat posed by a nuclear China, and if developments in China did not seem likely to promise a diminution of this threat, Japan would probably want to preserve its present ties with the US. But the alternative of seeking security by becoming a nuclear power herself would probably also gain wider support.

- 19 -

(Continued...)

29. The way in which US leadership defined the future American role in Asia, and the extent to which such utterances appeared to command political support in this country, would be by all odds the most important determinants for Asian attitudes. This means that if the US persuasively conveyed the intention to continue to be present in the Far East as a security factor, and also to continue supporting the moves toward regional institutional development which have begun there, then it seems unlikely that in the end an unfavorable outcome in Vietnam would greatly alter the present pattern of relationships. There would no doubt be a troubled and uncertain phase in the immediate aftermath of the event, but it should not be beyond the capacity of our leadership and diplomacy to negotiate this passage, provided again that our domestic politics did not give such a picture of confusion and disarray that Asians felt it necessary to discount the US as a power factor in that area.

30. Thus we do not conclude that other states in Asia would inevitably fall under Communist control in the wake of Communist success in Vietnam. The ensuing period would be marked by increased political instability, especially in Southeast Asia, and the slow process of political-economic development and regional association which we have sought to promote would surely be set

back. If one or more states in Southeast Asia did in fact fall under Communist control, the outlook for these goals would be even dimmer; the region could be in a turbulent and regressive condition for a long time. This would mean a major frustration of US policy aims, but we think would not bring any major threats to US security.

SOVIET-AMERICAN RELATIONS

31. We turn next to Soviet-American relations because these constitute the central power conflict in the world, because only the USSR can seriously threaten US security, and because the conclusions the Soviets might draw from a US failure in Vietnam could affect American policy problems in many areas other than Asia.

32. The Soviets did not stimulate Hanoi's aggression; had their influence been dominant, the Vietnamese Communists would probably have pursued a more cautious and less costly course toward their goal of winning power in all of Vietnam. Since 1964, however, Moscow has given full political and material support, partly to counter Chinese influence in Vietnam and in the Communist movement generally, and partly because the Soviet leadership came to believe Hanoi had a good chance for success. The USSR's interests as leader of the Communist world and as a great power demanded that it be associated with this success. The anticipated setback for US arms and policy would serve both kinds of interests.

(Continued...)

33. How would Soviet conduct be affected by the outcome in Vietnam that we are assuming? One hypothesis that can be dismissed, the one promoted currently by Soviet propaganda, is that the way would be opened toward a number of constructive developments which would greatly advance Soviet-American detente. Surely the so-called "American aggression in Vietnam" has contributed to the hardening of Soviet-American relations over the last several years, but Vietnam has been as much pretext as cause. The Soviets have not tried seriously to promote a settlement there, among other reasons, because they wanted to use the political liabilities the war has imposed on the US to undermine American influence in other areas and to advance their own. They would use a setback for US policy in Vietnam to the same end, pointing out to others the limitations and unreliability of US power, and the dangers of being aligned with it against "progressive" forces. Against this background, no very significant progress in bilateral relations would be likely, though the Soviets might initially favor an improvement in atmospherics in order to push settlement of some issues on what they would call "a more realistic basis." In sum, the Soviet-American conflict is too broad and basic, involving a power contention in other areas far more crucial than Southeast Asia, to be turned around toward detente merely by the end of the war in Vietnam.

34. A more challenging question is whether the Soviets might not make a reappraisal of American power and will which would tempt them into rashly aggressive moves. We know their preoccupation with the psychology of power. While they would realize that objectively American capabilities were undiminished, they might speculate on the disorientation of American leadership and on a loss of nerve. We think there is some chance that the Soviets would wish to try on some such hypothesis. It is impossible to say where and how they might move to test American will. If they did so, it would probably be in a tentative manner; any really dangerous probe would be ended as soon as they were satisfied that the US did not accept that any general change in the relations of power had occurred. Moreover, they would be conscious that particularly strong American reactions were possible precisely in order to demonstrate that the outcome in Vietnam had no general significance. They would also be aware that a reversion by them to aggressive behavior would prejudice political tendencies they have been trying to nourish, notably in Europe. We think, therefore, that while the Soviets would certainly entertain moves toward policies of pressure, they would actually undertake these only with their usual caution, and would draw back when they were satisfied that the results were likely to be counterproductive.

This adds up to saying that Soviet conduct in the wake of an unfavorable outcome in Vietnam might present problems, but that these would probably be manageable if the US played a steady hand and conveyed to others that it was doing so.

THE INSURGENCY PROBLEM

35. Since the beginning of this decade "national liberation warfare" has been celebrated by Soviet doctrine and policy as the key to overcoming "imperialism," advancing "socialism," and thus, impliedly, to extending the Soviet imperium. Would the Soviets see a Communist success in South Vietnam as validating their theses about national liberation struggle, and thus be disposed to sponsor similar tactics more widely? There is reason to doubt this. Surely Soviet propaganda would in a general way make much of the heroic exploits of the liberation fighters in Vietnam, and might in selected areas urge that their example be followed. But Moscow would be unlikely to advocate their methods as a general prescription for Communist parties and "progressive" forces, or pledge Soviet support indiscriminately to such ventures. The Soviets probably realize that the case of Vietnam is sui generis, that the Communists there had the luck to capture a broadly-based nationalist movement directed genuinely against foreign colonial rule. They know that

almost everywhere else in the Third World the colonial oppressors have been long gone, and that the conditions for armed action by Communists are more complicated and less favorable. Accordingly, they would continue to weigh the balance of forces obtaining in each national arena separately, counseling their clients to avoid "adventurism," and to resort to armed violence only when the prospects for success were good. One of the criteria for judging this would still be the likelihood of external aid to the regime being attacked, especially US aid. Therefore, any change in this aspect of Soviet policy would reflect Moscow's judgment that US counterinsurgency intervention had become less likely.

36. Moscow is not in a position to orchestrate all insurgency activity, however, and nowadays even in the Communist movement its advice may go unheeded. It seems likely that, in some Communist parties and in some other leftist groups, armed violence as the way to power would acquire greater appeal. Some, stirred by the romantic revolutionary aura which might seem to surround the Vietnamese in victory, might actually try to imitate them. Manifestations of this sort would be most likely to occur in Southeast Asia itself, and perhaps in Latin America. In certain of the Latin American Communist movements there are minority factions which are

- 25 -

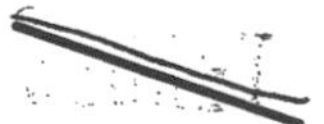

now, under Castro's influence, wholly committed to armed violence. Such groups would see the failure of US counterinsurgency action in Vietnam as a particularly favorable omen for them, and would be encouraged to enlarge their efforts.

37. We doubt, however, that such impulses would result in a much more widespread and serious Communist insurgency problem than would obtain in any case, either in Latin America or elsewhere. If Communists in some countries temporarily acquired more will to fight, the odds for or against success for such ventures in any particular national setting would remain essentially the same. It is possible, in fact, that threatened governments would draw the lesson that more vigorous efforts on their own behalf were indicated, a result which would contain insurgency far more effectively than aid by the US could ever do.

38. The effect on organized international Communism of more reckless resort to insurgency by some parties would probably be divisive. The great majority of the Communist parties would continue to adhere to the traditional Soviet view that impetuous resort to armed violence heedless of local circumstances manifests the deviation of "petit bourgeois adventurism." Those who defied this view would find themselves isolated and without effective support

- 26 -

from the main body of the movement. Thus, there would almost certainly not be a tendency for the Communist movement to regain its unity by coalescing around a general line of greater reliance on armed violence. The divisions fomented by Chinese, Castroites, or others who believe that "the primary duty of revolutionaries is to make revolution" might even be intensified. Moreover, there will continue to be numerous other grounds for splits within international communism.

39. Wherever a fresh impulse might in fact be given to revolutionary insurgency in certain less developed countries, there would be a setback to political stability and economic development. This, rather than the likelihood of new Vietnams, is the cost to measure. Even in these terms, the cost seems likely to be limited. Perhaps it could be argued that US capacity to give leadership to Third World development would be compromised, but such an effect is not measurable and would be temporary, especially if the US continued to make significant resources available for military and development aid.

THE US AND THE THIRD WORLD

40. By and large, the US involvement in Vietnam has had little sympathy in the Third World. The reactions to US failure

(Continued...)

would probably be as varied and conflicting as the political colorations and interests which obtain there. For many states, preoccupied with their own national and regional concerns, the Vietnam outcome would be a matter of indifference. Some would be pleased because of a general commitment to "anti-imperialism" as a cause. Others would hope for a more generous outpouring of US aid with the drain of the war stopped. A few might revise their view of the account that had to be taken of US power, and this might be damaging in international forums like the UN.

41. Certain states which, formally or informally, have linked their security to reliance on US power would be the most troubled. Some have done so in the belief that ties with the US were necessary to deter aggression by the USSR or, just as often, for support against their regional adversaries. This applies especially in the Middle East among the moderate Arab states and among states on the southern borders of the USSR. There might be some tendency among these to believe that US power had been overrated or was on the wane, so that accommodation to a new shape of things to come was indicated. On the whole, it seems unlikely that the Vietnam affair alone would cause any radical changes of alignment. There would probably be time and opportunity for US policy to offset

- 28 -

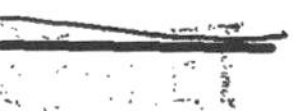

such tendencies, though there would be a price to pay in reassurances and aid.

42. Nevertheless, allowance should be made for special uncertainties in the Third World. Many governments there have an unstable view of power relations in the world, and are faced by equally excitable oppositions. For some, a setback for US power, which may have seemed more imposing and invulnerable to them than to us, will come as a severe shock. Thus, there is the possibility that one or another government, or its opposition, would over-interpret the significance of what happened in Vietnam, with unpredictable effects on its stability and aligment.

THE ATLANTIC ALLIANCE

43. Allied governments and general opinion in Europe have had mixed views of the American involvement in Vietnam, but on the whole there has been a tepid reception of the American rationale for the effort made there. Some opinion has been actively opposed, seeing Vietnam as an American aberration owing to a continuing addiction to cold war. Most governments have thought the US mistaken, but have recognized that once the Americans were committed, it was best to give some passive support, provided there was no

European involvement. These attitudes reflect a current European mood of reluctance to be involved in affairs entailing cost or risk which do not seem to have a direct bearing on national interests.

44. Concern about an unfavorable outcome in Vietnam would not, therefore, be related so much to the event itself or to what it might mean for that part of the world, as it would to possible effects on American policy and attitudes. Of course, those who hearken to Gaullist doctrine would consider such a setback for American power to be a desirable development, but these would be few. Some, especially in Germany, would ask questions about the reliability of American commitments to Europe's security, but it is unlikely that mistrust on this score would be widespread or take on a morbid character. Most would understand that the American stake in Europe's security is of a far different order of importance, and would not be disposed to make false analogies. However, the output of opinion-makers, especially that of journalistic intellectuals given to sensational and pseudo-sociological interpretations, ricochets with exceptional velocity within the Atlantic world. There would thus be some danger, and especially if there were serious political ructions here, that European opinion would be led to doubt American capacity to lead the Alliance. But on the whole, despite some alarums and excursions, the basic security relationship with Europe would survive.

45. Of course, there is more to the Atlantic relationship than the security tie. The US has thought of it also as a coalition of the advanced Western nations committed to certain constructive enterprises, especially in the struggle for order and development in the Third World. The credibility of American leadership for such purposes might be adversely affected, despite the fact that most European governments have wanted us to shed the Vietnam involvement and would not mind very much the manner of our doing so. This would be a cost to be borne, in the hope that time would efface it, as it probably would.

CONCLUSION

46. The foregoing discussion has roamed widely over many areas and possibilities. Any very precise or confident conclusions would misrepresent what has been said and exceed what sober judgment would allow. The following are the broad and essential impressions which this paper has intended to convey:

a. An unfavorable outcome in Vietnam would be a major setback to the reputation of US power which would limit US influence and prejudice our other interests in some degree which cannot be reliably foreseen.

- 31 -

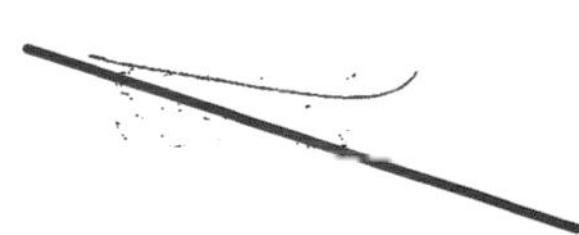

b. Probably the net effects would not be permanently damaging to this country's capacity to play its part as a world power working for order and security in many areas.

c. The worst potential damage would be of the self-inflicted kind: internal dissension which would limit our future ability to use our power and resources wisely and to full effect, and lead to a loss of confidence by others in the American capacity for leadership.

d. The destabilizing effects would be greatest in the immediate area of Southeast Asia where some states would probably face internal turmoil and heightened external pressures, and where some realignments might occur; similar effects would be unlikely elsewhere or could be more easily contained.

47. As indicated at the outset of this paper, no single analysis of this subject can be entirely adequate. The uncertainties and imponderables involved in projecting the consequences of the contingency discussed are so great that other implications can legitimately be drawn. If they were either more comforting or more ominous, they could not be disproved.

48. But any honest and dispassionate analysis must conclude that, if the US accepts failure in Vietnam, it will pay <u>some</u>

price in the form of new risks which success there would preclude. The frustration of a world power, once it has committed vast resources and much prestige to a military enterprise, must be in some degree damaging to the general security system it upholds. In the case of Vietnam, there does not seem to be a common denominator which permits such eventual risks to be measured reliably against the obvious and immediate costs of continuing war. Presumably those who have to make the agonizing choices were aware of that already. If the analysis here advances the discussion at all, it is in the direction of suggesting that such risks are probably more limited and controllable than most previous argument has indicated.

- 33 -

SNIE 14.3-67

Capabilties of the Vietnamese Communists for Fighting in South Vietnam

13 November 1967

APPROVED FOR RELEASE
DATE: JAN 2006

(b)(3)

~~TOP SECRET~~

TS 186035
SNIE 14.3-67
13 November 1967

SPECIAL
NATIONAL INTELLIGENCE ESTIMATE
NUMBER 14.3-67

Capabilities of the Vietnamese Communists for Fighting in South Vietnam

Submitted by

DIRECTOR OF CENTRAL INTELLIGENCE

Concurred in by the

UNITED STATES INTELLIGENCE BOARD

As indicated overleaf

13 November 1967

Authenticated:

EXECUTIVE SECRETARY, USIB

Pages 27

Copy No. 58

~~TOP SECRET~~

(Continued...)

CHINA
NORTH VIETNAM
LAOS
THAILAND
CAMBODIA
SOUTH VIETNAM
BURMA
HAINAN
GULF OF TONKIN
INDOCHINA
North Vietnam military region boundary
Railroad
Road
Hanoi
Haiphong
VIENTIANE
BANGKOK
PHNOM PENH
SAIGON
Demilitarized Zone
VINH LINH SPECIAL ZONE
Da Nang
Hue
Kontum
Pleiku
Ban Me Thuot
Da Lat
Phan Thiet
Vung Tau
My Tho
Can Tho
Bac Lieu
Quan Long
CON SON
DAO PHU QUOC (Vietnam)
Sihanoukville
NAMES AND BOUNDARY REPRESENTATION ARE NOT NECESSARILY AUTHORITATIVE

CAPABILITIES OF THE VIETNAMESE COMMUNISTS FOR FIGHTING IN SOUTH VIETNAM[1]

THE PROBLEM

To estimate the capabilities of the Vietnamese Communists to conduct military operations in South Vietnam over the next year or so.[2]

INTRODUCTORY NOTE

Our earlier understanding of overall Communist capabilities in Vietnam had, of necessity, to rely heavily on data provided by the GVN. Much of this turned out to be unreliable, and in many instances our numerical estimates of Communist forces, other than for the Regular units, were too low. Our information has improved substantially in the past year or two, but the unconventional nature of the war poses difficult intelligence problems, the more so in a social environment where basic data is incomplete and often untrustworthy.

Manpower, for example, is a key element for the Communists but we lack precise basic data on population size, rates of growth, and age distribution for both North and South Vietnam. Assessing Communist capabilities also involves an understanding of the organization and effectiveness of the various components in the Communist military and political apparatus in South Vietnam. Much of the evidence on these components is obtained from a variety of sources, including captured documents, of varying reliability and timeliness. The analysis of this data, as well as that concerning North Vietnamese support to the South and all manpower questions requires complex methodological approaches which cannot rise above the uncertain data inputs.

[1] This estimate supersedes NIE 14.3-66, "North Vietnamese Military Potential for Fighting in South Vietnam," dated 7 July 1966, TOP SECRET.

[2] The figures in this estimate are current as of 1 October 1967.

Our data and conclusions are therefore subject to continuing review and revision, especially since capabilities do not remain static. In this estimate we have concentrated on reaching the best judgments of the current strength of the Communist forces and, because of incomplete and unreliable basic data, we have not attempted to reconstruct Communist strength retrospectively.

Reservations with respect to evidence are explained where appropriate in the individual sections of the estimate. The main conclusions which follow, however, allow for such uncertainties in the supporting intelligence, represent our best appreciation of the overall situation as it now stands, and are based on the assumption that there is no radical change in the scale and nature of the war.

CONCLUSIONS

A. During the past year, Hanoi's direct control and share of the burden of the war in South Vietnam has grown substantially. This trend will continue.

B. Manpower is a major problem confronting the Communists. Losses have been increasing and recruitment in South Vietnam is becoming more difficult. Despite heavy infiltration from North Vietnam, the strength of the Communist military forces and political organizations in South Vietnam declined in the last year.

C. The major portion of this decline has probably been felt at the lower levels, reflecting a deliberate policy of sacrificing these levels to maintain the structure of political cadres and the strength of the Regular military forces. In particular the guerrillas, now estimated to total some 70,000-90,000, have suffered a substantial reduction since the estimated peak of about early 1966. Regular force strength, now estimated at 118,000, has declined only slightly, but Viet Cong (VC) units are increasingly dependent upon North Vietnamese replacements.

D. Given current Communist strategy, and levels of operations, a major effort will be necessary if the Regular forces and the guerrillas are to be maintained at or near present levels. To do so will require both a level of infiltration much higher than that observed in 1967 and intensive VC recruitment as well. Considering all the relevant factors, however, we believe there is a fairly good chance that the

overall strength and effectiveness of the military forces and the political infrastructure will continue to decline.

E. The Communist leadership is already having problems in maintaining morale and quality. These problems have not yet impaired overall military effectiveness, but they are likely to become more difficult.

F. Difficulties in internal distribution will continue to cause local shortages and interfere with Communist operations from time to time. But we believe that the Communists will be able to continue to meet at least their essential supply requirement for the level of forces and activities in South Vietnam described in this estimate.

G. Communist strategy is to sustain a protracted war of attrition and to persuade the US that it must pull out or settle on Hanoi's terms. Our judgment is that the Communists still retain adequate capabilities to support this strategy for at least another year. Whether or not Hanoi does in fact persist with this strategy depends not only on its capabilities to do so, but on a number of political and international considerations not treated in this estimate.

DISCUSSION

1. It has become increasingly obvious that Hanoi's share of the burden of war in South Vietnam has grown substantially. Infiltration of personnel in 1966, particularly into the northern provinces, was more than twice that of 1965. Hanoi's direct control of military and political operations has become more evident. The supply of weapons from the North has continued, and new weapons of greater firepower have been introduced. The logistical systems within North Vietnam and in Laos and Cambodia have been expanded since 1965 to provide a greater flexibility to cope with the effects of air interdiction, thereby enabling the Communists to meet higher levels of combat and support the growth of their forces to at least their present levels.

I. CAPABILITIES OF NORTH VIETNAM

A. Manpower and Mobilization Potential

2. The growing intensity of the war in the South and more than two years of US air strikes against the North have made manpower an increasingly important aspect in estimating Communist capabilities. Since mid-1965 the North Vietnamese Armed Forces have expanded from an estimated 250,000 men to at least 470,000. This expansion includes those troops in Laos and South Vietnam. The bulk of the physically fit draft age class of 17-year-olds (about 100,000 each year) is being taken into military service. The war in general and the bombing in particular have forced Hanoi to divert from 500,000 to 600,000 civilians (men and women, young and old) to full-time and part-time war-related activities.

3. Nevertheless, it does not appear that North Vietnam is encountering insurmountable problems in obtaining sufficient able-bodied men to support the war in South Vietnam. Of North Vietnam's total population of over 18 million, about 4 million or so are males between 15 and 49, and about half of these are probably physically fit for military service.[3] At present, the North Vietnamese Armed Forces have taken less than one-quarter of the fit males aged 15 to 49 and less than two-fifths of the approximately 1.2 million fit males in the prime military ages of 17 to 35. Though there is some evidence of lowering of draft standards and extending of age limits, it appears that, with a few local exceptions, Hanoi is still drafting only those between the ages of 17 and 35.

4. The number of physically fit males above and beyond the annual increment of those reaching age 17 and who are not yet in the armed forces is substantial. The most obvious source of manpower is agriculture, where there are almost 3 million men of all ages, and where per capita production is low. There are also about half a million men in the service sector of the economy, including

[3] These figures are based on US Census Bureau estimates of North Vietnam's population, which do not accept entirely the figures of North Vietnam's 1960 census and subsequent demographic statistics published through 1963.

170,000 in consumer services; almost half a million men in industry, over half of whom are in handicrafts; and some 60,000 male students of military age.

5. There is of course no fixed percentage of these men who can be spared for military duty. Hanoi has already drawn men from the civilian economy for military and war-related tasks, replacing them where possible with women. Taking large additional numbers of men would obviously involve some additional costs to the civilian economy, but this would be a question of priorities in Hanoi. Losses in agricultural and industrial production can be made up by imports to the extent necessary to maintain essential subsistence levels of consumption; consumer services are to some degree expendable and education can be postponed. Thus we believe that the manpower problem, while growing more serious, is still manageable in North Vietnam. At a conservative estimate we believe there are some 100,000 to 200,000 men who could be called into military service, in addition to the annual draft class.

B. The Armed Forces

6. The North Vietnamese Armed Forces expanded last year and are now estimated to total about 470,000. Despite better evidence on their strength, there are still some uncertainties concerning the actual strength of units, the number of North Vietnamese Army (NVA) troops in Laos, and the size of the Armed Public Security Forces. The following table should be regarded as a conservative estimate.

TABLE 1

ESTIMATED NORTH VIETNAMESE ARMED FORCES

1 October 1967

SUMMARY

Army	447,500
Air Force	4,500
Navy	2,500
Armed Public Security Forces	16,500
TOTAL Armed Forces	471,000
North Vietnamese Army Breakdown	
Out-of-Country	
South Vietnam	54,000
Laos	18,000
TOTAL	72,000
In-Country	
Infantry	171,500
Air Defense [a]	93,000
Other [b]	111,000
TOTAL	375,500

[a] This includes only regular army personnel in AAA units, radar, and SAM battalions. It does not include part-time air defense personnel such as militia, or logistical troops supporting air defense.

[b] This includes artillery, armor, high command, logistics, engineers, and transportation.

7. If the recruitment of men for replacements and for unit infiltration into the South should become a critical problem for Hanoi, as a last resort it could draw down its standing military establishment in North Vietnam. The number of troops which could be released for out-of-country duty would be influenced greatly by Hanoi's concern to retain a sizable force for defense against a possible invasion. If, for example, Hanoi should want to keep some 225,000 troops for the defense of North Vietnam and another 85,000 as a training base and for command and administration, then some 65,000 additional NVA troops could be made available for use outside of North Vietnam.

C. Military Training and Leadership

8. Special preinfiltration training of North Vietnamese recruits has averaged about 3 months, although increasing numbers of prisoners report training of only 1 month prior to infiltration. There is evidence of a growing deficiency of properly trained personnel to fill the ranks of squad leaders, platoon sergeants, and platoon leaders. There are indications that the normal source of platoon leaders, the Infantry Officers' School near Son Tay, has reduced its 2-year course to 8 months. The bulk of the reserve officers and noncommissioned officers have been recalled to active duty. The largest single source of junior officers is now from battlefield commissions.

D. Infiltration

9. North Vietnam has the capability to train 75,000-100,000 men a year for infiltration. By shortening current training cycles or increasing the number of units involved in the training of new recruits, this number could be substantially increased. Training replacements at the rate of 75,000-100,000 annually, however, would not permit organizing all of them into units and providing them with the necessary leadership at the same rate. Theoretically, North Vietnam could train and form 24-36 infantry regiments (48,000-72,000 men) per year, but at this pace there would be a considerable reduction in quality. In any case, actual formation and training of organized units for infiltration has been well short of this theoretical capability.

10. During 1966 at least 55,000 and possibly as many as 86,000 North Vietnamese troops were sent into South Vietnam (see Table 2). Through July 1966, the bulk of the infiltration was accounted for by the introduction of organized infantry regiments, including three regiments that moved directly across the DMZ. After July the pace of infiltration slackened somewhat, and it appeared that the Communist Regular force structure had reached planned levels. Most of the infiltration thereafter was to provide replacements in existing units.

11. During 1967, however, the introduction of organized units resumed—six regiments thus far—and the flow of individual replacements has continued. This mixture of units and individual replacements, plus the special situation along the DMZ, complicates an estimate of total infiltration. Not only is there the usual lag in identifying new units and infiltration groups, but there is less chance

TABLE 2

MONTHLY INFILTRATION: 1966-1967 [a]

(Data as of 30 September 1967)

		Accepted				Monthly
		Confirmed	Probable	TOTAL	Possible	TOTALS
1966	Jan	4,200	1,800	6,000	3,000	9,000
	Feb	6,900	2,200	9,100	2,100	11,200
	Mar	11,700	1,400	13,100	3,600	16,700
	Apr	100	500	600	600	1,200
	May	1,300	500	1,800	3,600	5,400
	June	12,300	700	13,000	1,700	14,700
	July	4,000	700	4,700	4,100	8,800
	Aug	1,800	400	2,200	3,700	5,900
	Sept	1,400	700	2,100	600	2,700
	Oct	100	600	700	4,700	5,400
	Nov	500	100	600	600	1,200
	Dec	800	600	1,400	2,500	3,900
TOTAL 1966		45,100	10,200	55,300	30,800	86,100
1967	Jan	1,000	800	1,800	3,600	5,400
	Feb	1,700	2,000	3,700	1,300	5,000
	Mar	3,600	400	4,000	4,600	8,600
	Apr	3,700	600	4,300	300	4,600
	May	2,700	1,500	4,200	1,600	5,800
	June	3,300	—	3,300	300	3,600
	July	—	400	400	—	400
	Aug	1,100	—	1,100	700	1,800
	Sept	—	—	—	—	—

[a] Infiltration includes only arrivals in South Vietnam. Statistics for 1967 are subject to retroactive updating because of the continuing receipt of new information. In particular, the figures for the last 6 months or so are incomplete, and inadequate to determine trends. These figures include the following categories:

ACCEPTED: *Accepted Confirmed:* A confirmed infiltration unit/group is one which is accepted in South Vietnam on the basis of information provided by a minimum of two POW's or returnees from the unit/group, or two captured documents from the unit, or a combination of personnel and documents.

Accepted Probable: A probable infiltration unit/group is one which is accepted in South Vietnam on the basis of information provided by one POW or returnee from the unit/group, or a captured document, supported by information from other sources which can be evaluated as probably true.

POSSIBLE: A *possible* infiltration unit/group is one which may be in South Vietnam on the basis of information which can be evaluated as possibly true even though no POW, returnee, or document is available to verify the reports.

of capturing personnel or documents from each of the numerous small replacement groups. There is also the problem of the units that suffer casualties in the DMZ area and return to North Vietnamese territory for replacements; these latter cannot always be identified as new infiltrators when the units return to South Vietnamese territory. A similar problem applies to other border areas.

12. Infiltration thus far in 1967 totals about 35,000 in all categories (accepted and possible). Allowing for the probability that later information will raise these figures, and extrapolating, it now appears that total infiltration for 1967 will be no more than last year's and possibly somewhat less. We estimate that some 65 to 75 percent of the infiltration will probably consist of replacement personnel for existing units. The remainder will probably include seven to nine organized regiments which will add to the Communist force structure but not necessarily their total military strength, because losses have resulted in generally lower unit strengths. There still appears to be no clear-cut seasonal pattern in infiltration or any significant indication that Hanoi is unwilling to dispatch additional men and units to South Vietnam.

E. LOCs[4]

13. Supplies for Communist forces move into South Vietnam by various means. In North Vietnam, truck, rail, and water transport are used to bring supplies through Military Region 4 (MR-4). From MR-4, most supplies are trucked through Laos, although some use of waterways is also made in Laos. Some supplies move directly across the DMZ, and some are moved by sea. In addition, some supplies from Cambodia enter South Vietnam directly while others are routed through Laos.

14. *Roads.* The Communist logistical roadnet in MR-4 in North Vietnam and in Laos was improved over the past year. Though the improvements have increased tonnage capacities somewhat, they were intended primarily to provide additional flexibility for the system and better year-round movement. One development was the extension of a new motorable road from Laos directly into the A Shau Valley of South Vietnam. In addition, the administration and operational control of the LOCs have been improved and expanded. The capacity of the entire system for delivery of supplies to South Vietnam through Laos continues to be limited by the capacities of the routes in Laos rather than by those of North Vietnam.

15. *Trucks.* We estimate that at the end of 1965 the North Vietnamese had an inventory of between 11,000 and 12,000 trucks. Losses from air attack have been substantial, and North Vietnam has been forced to increase its imports to counter this attrition. Imports from Eastern Europe, the USSR, and China have enabled North Vietnam roughly to maintain the size of its inventory.

16. Maintenance problems have increased, and as many as 30 percent of the trucks may not be operable on a daily basis. There is a lack of well-equipped,

[4] See centerspread map.

properly manned maintenance facilities, and the variety of truck imports has resulted in a fleet of over 30 models from at least seven different countries. POL imports into North Vietnam during the first half of 1967 have been at record levels, and we have had no evidence of any serious POL shortages affecting the movement of supplies to South Vietnam.

17. *Waterways* The coastal and inland waterway system in North Vietnam provides a useful supplement to the road and rail system and has been used extensively, particularly since the start of the US bombing program. Although the mining of some North Vietnamese waterways has reduced the movement of large craft, small boat traffic continues. Increasing imports of barges and barge sections into North Vietnam and a program of waterway improvement indicate that the Communists intend to exploit further the potentialities of these water routes. In Laos, there has been increased use of small pirogues and motorboats on rivers over the last year. The use of these waterways will probably continue to increase.

18. *Rail.* The North Vietnamese also use the rail line south of Hanoi for movement of supplies into MR-4. Despite repeated US air attacks, the North Vietnamese have been able to construct bypasses and keep sections of the line serviceable from Hanoi to Vinh. South of Vinh the rail line is not operable for regular rail equipment. The North Vietnamese can only use light gear, principally trucks with converted wheels, to transport supplies over the remaining rail segment in this area.

19. *Impact of Air Attacks.* Air attacks in North Vietnam, Laos, and the DMZ have destroyed trucks, railroad rolling stock, and watercraft, have damaged the highway and rail systems, and have restricted the movement of cargo and personnel particularly during daylight hours. They have created construction problems and delays, caused interruptions in the flow of men and supplies, caused a great loss of work-hours, and forced North Vietnam to tie up large numbers of people in air defense and in the repair of LOCs. Communist countermeasures in North Vietnam and Laos have included diversification of the means of transport to include greater use of inland waterways and porter trails, construction of alternate roads, and of multiple bypasses at important bridges. A number of truck parks and vehicle pulloffs for quick convoy dispersal have been built. These measures have increased the ability of the Communists to cope with the effects of air attacks, although at a considerable cost and effort. Units and personnel moving to South Vietnam have been forced to move under cover of darkness, slowing their movement and subjecting them to the rigors of the trail for longer periods.

20. *Cambodia.* The importance of Cambodia as a sanctuary and a source of supply (principally rice) to the Communist war effort is substantial and growing.[5] Recently captured documents indicate that some Communist units in Tay Ninh

[5] For a more detailed discussion of this subject, see SNIE 57-67, "Significance of Cambodia to the Vietnamese Communist War Effort," dated 19 January 1967, SECRET. We believe the conclusions are still valid.

Province have substantially increased their purchases in Cambodia since March 1966. The movement of supplies in Cambodia to Communist forces along the border, particularly on the Se San and Tonle Kong Rivers in the northeast and along Route 110 in Laos, has increased in the past year. Indications are that Communist units along the Cambodian border have been stockpiling some of the food and other materials obtained from Cambodia.

21. There is still no good evidence, however, that substantial amounts of weapons or ammunition are being obtained by the Communists from Cambodian stocks or through Cambodian ports. On the other hand, there is evidence that Communist units, particularly in the border area, receive arms and ammunition from stockpiles maintained on Cambodian territory. These munitions probably were moved south through Laos. Should infiltration of arms into South Vietnam through Laos be substantially reduced, Cambodia could be an alternative route for the Communists.

22. *Sea Infiltration.* We are unable to estimate the extent of the infiltration of supplies by sea into South Vietnam. We believe, however, that such infiltration has been greatly reduced by US counterefforts. Much of the Communists' use of sea routes, at present, is for the movement of supplies along the South Vietnamese coast. We believe that when a pressing need exists North Vietnam will increase attempts to move some supplies by sea, primarily arms and ammunition.

II. THE MILITARY SITUATION IN THE SOUTH

A. Communist Forces

23. For the purpose of this estimate, we consider the following elements of the Communist organization in South Vietnam: the Regular forces (NVA and VC Main and Local forces), the administrative service units which support them, the VC guerrilla forces, the political cadres, the self-defense forces, the secret self-defense forces, and the "Assault Youth." The contribution of these diverse elements to the Communist effort in South Vietnam differs widely in value. Their capabilities and missions are set forth in the following paragraphs.

24. We believe that, with the exception of the Regular forces, we have previously underestimated the strength of these elements. The figures carried in this estimate for these elements reflect new information and analysis rather than an increase in actual Communist strength. Furthermore, our information on the strength and organization of the different elements varies widely. For the Regular forces it is good; for other components it is much less reliable, less current, and less detailed. The resulting uncertainties are explained in the following paragraphs and are reflected by the use of ranges in the estimates we present.

25. *Regular Forces.* We are reasonably confident that the Communist Regular forces in South Vietnam now total about 118,000 troops who are generally well-armed (see Table 3). This strength has fluctuated over the past 12 months; it is now somewhat less than it was at this time last year. During this period,

however, an increasing number of NVA replacements have been introduced into VC Main force units.

TABLE 3

ESTIMATED STRENGTH OF REGULAR COMMUNIST FORCES IN SOUTH VIETNAM
(As of 1 October 1967)

Type	Number	Organization
Regular NVA Forces	54,000	3 Front Headquarters[a]
		7 Division Headquarters[b] [c]
		26 Regiments (18 divisional and 8 separate)
		106 Battalions (76 regimental and 30 separate)
VC Main and Local Forces	64,000[d]	2 Division Headquarters[b]
		11 Regiments (7 divisional and 4 separate)
		96 Battalions (34 regimental and 62 separate)
		234 Separate Companies
		54 Separate Platoons
TOTAL	118,000	

[a] A Front is a military organization designed to perform tactical and administrative functions and to control a number of units in a specific area. A Front is intentionally flexible, its military force composition changes as operational requirements dictate. Vietnamese Communist Fronts currently operating against South Vietnam are the B-3 Front, the DMZ Front, and the Northern Front or Subregion (now called the Tri-Thien-Hue Military Region). (See map on page 17.)

[b] NVA/VC divisions in South Vietnam are considered as light infantry divisions tailored specifically for operation in South Vietnam. These divisions are highly foot-mobile and are flexible in force structure, organization, and strength. They normally are composed of three regiments (of about 1,500-2,000 per regiment) with varying technical and fire support elements. They lack wheeled transport and the type of artillery normally associated with NVA conventional divisions.

[c] In addition to the seven NVA divisions in South Vietnam, elements of the 341st division in North Vietnam have been committed from time to time to operations south of the DMZ under control of the DMZ Front.

[d] This total includes some NVA replacements; see paragraph 56.

26. *Administrative Service Units.* There is an extensive system for the administrative support of both NVA and VC Regular forces. It operates throughout South Vietnam and extends into Laos and Cambodia as well as the area immediately north of the DMZ. In South Vietnam it includes the military personnel in the staff and service elements (e.g., medics, ordnance, logistics, etc.) comprising the central, regional, provincial and district military headquarters, and in rear service technical units of all types directly subordinate to these headquarters. The need for administrative service forces, and hence their size, varies widely from province to province.

27. We cannot be confident of the total size of the administrative service forces at any given time. Information on the current strength of the administrative services at the various echelons is insufficient to establish a firm estimate. This force has almost certainly suffered attrition and has probably been drawn down to provide some combat replacements. Moreover, we do not estimate

(Continued...)

LAOS PANHANDLE AREA COMMUNIST ROADNET

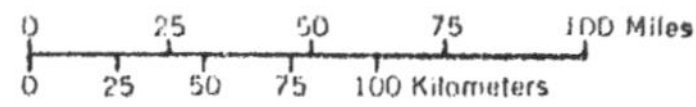

EXPANSION OF THE COMMUNIST ROADNET

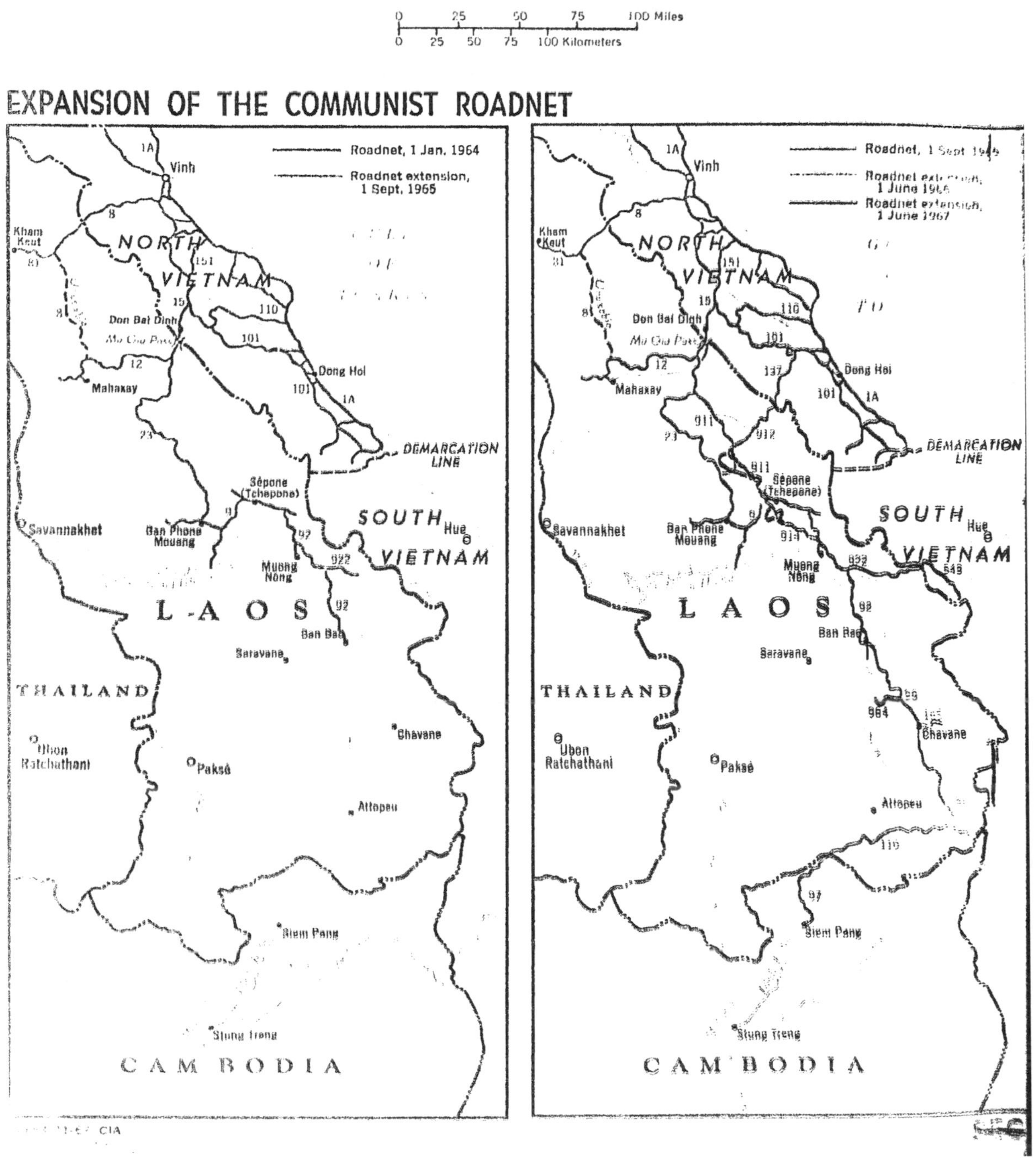

Roadnet, 1 Jan. 1964
Roadnet extension, 1 Sept. 1965
1A
Vinh
8
Kham Keut
NORTH VIETNAM
151
15
110
101
Don Bai Dinh
Mu Gia Pass
12
Mahaxay
Dong Hoi
1A
23
DEMARCATION LINE
Sépone (Tchepone)
9
Savannakhet
Ban Phone Mouang
SOUTH VIETNAM
Hue
92
922
Muong Nong
LAOS
Ban Bac
Saravane
THAILAND
Ubon Ratchathani
Paksé
Chavane
Attopeu
Siem Pang
Stung Treng
CAMBODIA
CIA

Roadnet, 1 Sept. 1965
Roadnet extension, 1 June 1966
Roadnet extension, 1 June 1967
1A
Vinh
8
Kham Keut
81
NORTH VIETNAM
151
15
110
101
Don Bai Dinh
Mu Gia Pass
12
137
Mahaxay
Dong Hoi
101
1A
911
912
23
DEMARCATION LINE
911
Sépone (Tchepone)
9
Savannakhet
Ban Phone Mouang
914
SOUTH VIETNAM
Hue
922
548
Muong Nong
LAOS
92
Ban Bac
Saravane
THAILAND
96
964
Chavane
Ubon Ratchathani
Paksé
Attopeu
110
97
Siem Pang
Stung Treng
CAMBODIA

INFILTRATION AND ROAD CAPACITIES

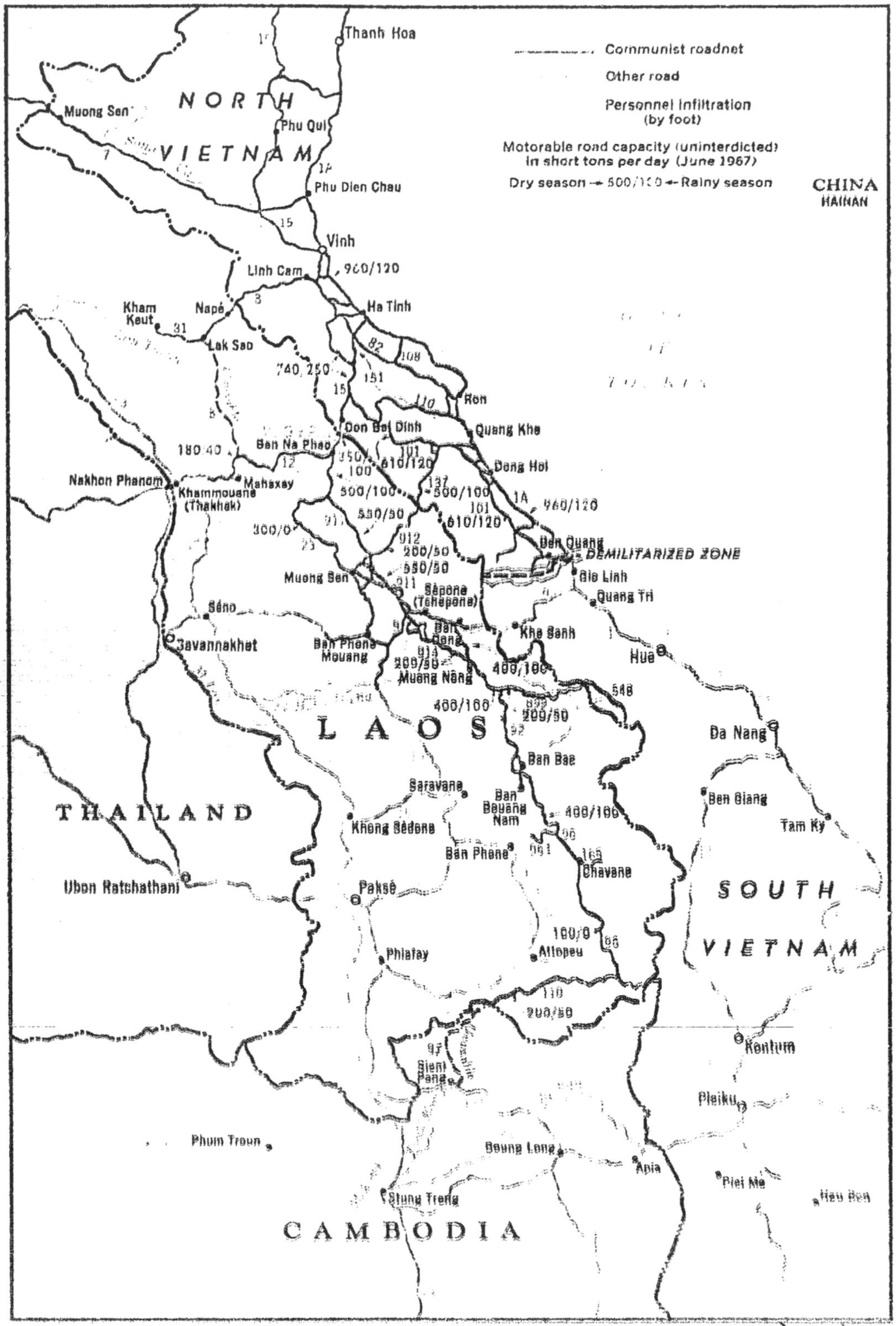

Communist roadnet

Other road

Personnel infiltration (by foot)

Motorable road capacity (uninterdicted) in short tons per day (June 1967)

Dry season → 500/100 ← Rainy season

the size of the administrative service units located outside the boundaries of South Vietnam which support the forces in the DMZ and the western highlands. In light of these considerations, we estimate that there are now at least 35,000-40,000 administrative service personnel in South Vietnam who are performing essential administrative support functions. In addition, almost anyone under VC control can be and is impressed into service to perform specific administrative or support tasks as local conditions require.

28. *Guerrillas.* The guerrillas provide an essential element of the VC combat capability. They are organized into squads and platoons which are not necessarily restricted to their home village or hamlet. Typical missions for guerrillas are terrorist and sabotage activities, protection of villages and hamlets, provision of assistance to VC Main and Local force units as well as NVA, and the creation of local threats in order to divert allied forces to local security missions.

29. The guerrilla force has been subject to conflicting pressures. On the one hand, increasing numbers of guerrillas have been drawn upon to provide replacements for the VC Main and Local forces, because these have suffered heavy casualties as a result of more intense combat. At the same time, numerous captured documents as well as VC propaganda indicate a concern to increase the guerrilla force substantially. There is evidence which suggests that the leadership set very high force goals for the guerrillas but had, by mid-1966, fallen far short of its aims.

30. Information from captured documents leads us to believe that we have previously underestimated the guerrilla strength. Certain Communist documents which date from early 1966 assert that there were then about 170,000-180,000 guerrillas. This figure was almost certainly exaggerated. There is evidence which suggests that the Communists sometimes consider other groups part of the guerrilla force and therefore carry a larger number of guerrillas on their rolls. There is also considerable uncertainty over the accuracy of VC reporting at the lower levels. We believe that guerrilla strength has declined over the past year or so because of losses, upgrading of some personnel to Main and Local force units, and recruiting difficulties. We are unable to substantiate the extent to which the VC have been able to replace guerrilla losses. Considering all the available evidence and allowing for some uncertainties, we estimate that the current strength of the guerrilla force is 70,000-90,000.

31. *The Political Organization.* Presiding over the Communist effort is the political apparatus. This includes the leadership and administration of the National Liberation Front (NLF) and the People's Revolutionary Party (the name under which the North Vietnamese Communist Party operates in South Vietnam), both of which extend down to the hamlet level. The apparatus not only acts as a government in VC-controlled areas but also has major responsibilities for maintaining morale and for mobilizing manpower and other resources in support of the war effort. Its functions are not primarily military and it is therefore not included in the military order of battle. Nevertheless, it does represent a continuing potential for organizing and motivating the military forces. Through this apparatus the Communists seek to control the people of

South Vietnam. It is, therefore, a key element which ultimately will have to be overcome along with the military and guerrilla forces. Its numbers are large—with a hard core estimated at about 75,000-85,000—but more important is the wide geographical extent of its power and the dedication and effectiveness of its personnel.

32. *Other Communist Organizations.* The Communists make a deliberate effort to organize most of the people under their control into various work forces and semimilitary organizations. Among the more significant of these organizations are the self-defense forces, secret self-defense forces, and groups such as the "Assault Youth." Moreover, when occasion demands, almost every able-bodied person under VC control may be called upon to support the war effort.

33. The self-defense force is described by the Communists as a military organization. It is clear, however, that its organization and mission differ from that of village and hamlet guerrillas. Self-defense forces include people of all ages and a substantial percentage of them are females. They are largely unarmed and only partially trained. The duties of self-defense units include the maintenance of law and order, the construction of bunkers and strong points, warning against the approach of allied forces, and the defense of villages and hamlets in VC-controlled territory. Self-defense forces do not leave their home areas, and members generally perform their duties part-time. Their existence poses an impediment to allied sweeps and pacification, however, and in their defensive role, they inflict casualties on allied forces.

34. Another element, the secret self-defense forces, operates in government-controlled and contested areas. They provide a residual Communist presence in such areas and support the Communist effort primarily by clandestine intelligence activities.

35. During the past year we have learned more about a VC organization called "Assault Youth." They serve full time at district level and above, and they are organized into companies and platoons. Although some are armed, the Communists do not consider them a combat force; their primary mission appears to be logistical, frequently in battlefield areas. This organization also serves as a manpower pool and provides a training program for youth who later go into the VC Main and Local forces. Little information is available to indicate the strength or distribution of the "Assault Youth."

36. Our current evidence does not enable us to estimate the present size of these groups (self-defense, secret self-defense, the "Assault Youth," or other similar VC organizations) with any measure of confidence. Some documents suggest that in early 1966 the aggregate size of the self-defense force was on the order of 150,000. This force and the other groups, however, have unquestionably suffered substantial attrition since that time, as well as an appreciable decline in quality, because of losses, recruiting of some of their members into the guer-

rillas or other VC military components and, particularly, the shrinkage in VC control of populated areas. Though in aggregate numbers these groups are still large and constitute a part of the overall Communist effort, they are not offensive military forces. Hence, they are not included in the military order of battle total. Nevertheless, some of their members account for a part of the total Communist military losses.

37. In sum, the Communist military and political organization is complex, and its aggregate numerical size cannot be estimated with confidence. Moreover, any such aggregate total would be misleading since it would involve adding components that have widely different missions and degrees of skill or dedication. The VC/NVA Military Force (Main and Local forces, administrative service elements and guerrillas) can be meaningfully presented in numerical totals and, as indicated above, we estimate that this Military Force is now at least 223,000-248,000. It must be recognized, however, that this Military Force constitutes but one component of the total Communist organization. Any comprehensive judgment of Communist capabilities in South Vietnam must embrace the effectiveness of all the elements which comprise that organization, the total size of which is of course considerably greater than the figure given for the Military Force.

B. The Command Structure

38. The Communists have continued to modify their command apparatus, and, in particular, Hanoi has significantly increased its direct control. This is most apparent in the DMZ and central highlands areas where Hanoi increasingly bypasses both COSVN and Military Region 5 (MR-5) Headquarters. With the exception of two VC divisions and one NVA division, all division headquarters and all the confirmed Fronts are in MR-5 or the DMZ area.[6] In addition to the creation of the DMZ Front, which is controlled directly by Hanoi, it appears almost certain that MR-5 has been divided into three operational areas: The Tri-Thien-Hue Military Region (formerly the Northern Front or Subregion), the B-3 or Western Highlands Front, and the remaining coastal provinces of the region.[7] There is substantial evidence that Hanoi also exercises direct military control over the Tri-Thien-Hue Military Region and the B-3 Front.

C. Logistical Support

39. During the past year captured documents and POW interrogations have provided a better basis for estimating how much of each class of supplies was needed and consumed by the Communist forces. Table 4 shows the estimated total daily Communist requirement in South Vietnam for Regular and Administrative Service Forces and that portion of it which comes from external sources.

40. About one-quarter of the daily requirement for both 1966 and 1967 was drawn from sources outside of South Vietnam. There is a growing dependence

[6] The remainder of the command structure consists of provincial commands and of separate units, both directly subordinate to the respective VC military regions.

[7] See map on opposite page for provinces included in these areas.

(Continued...)

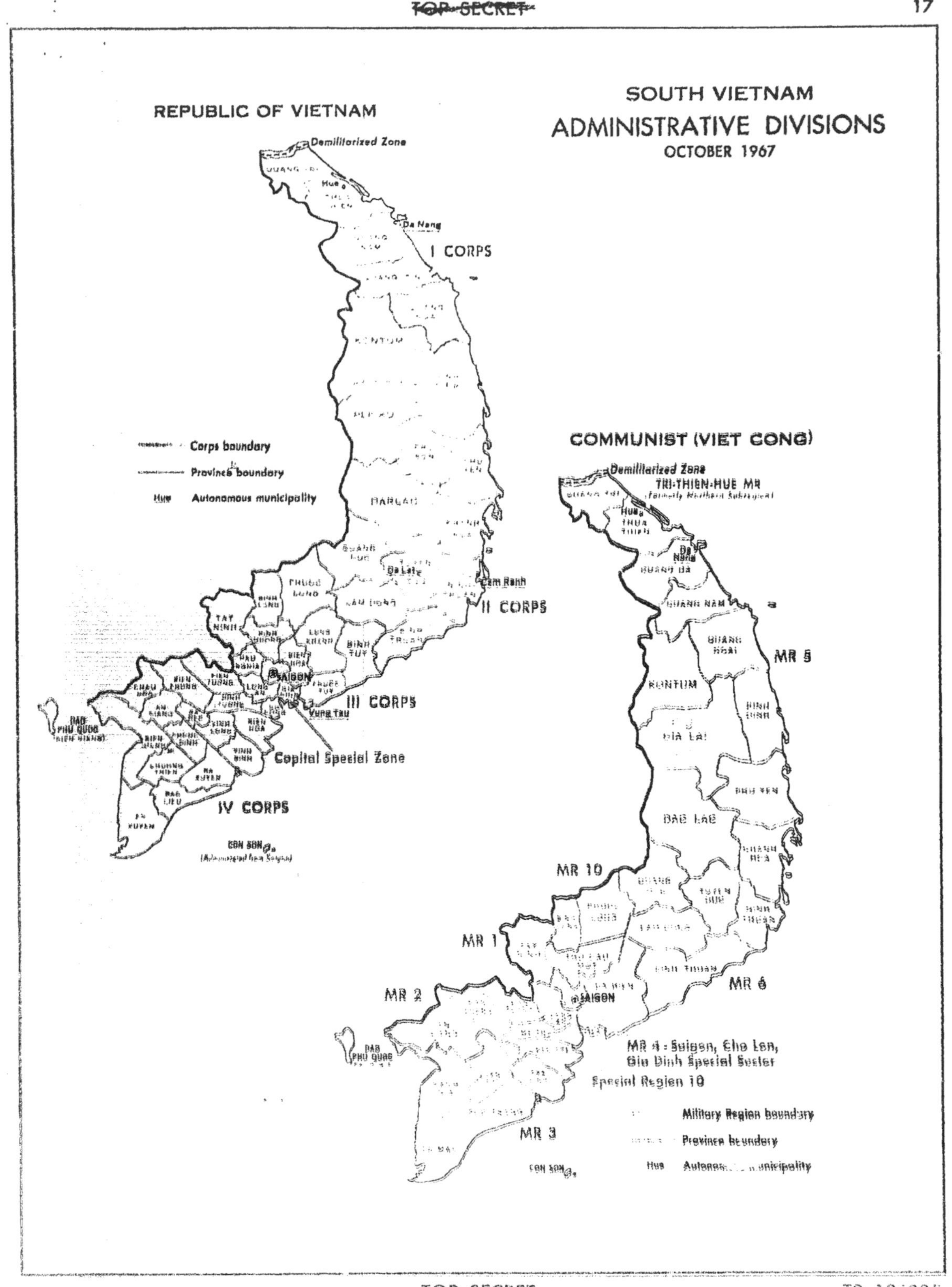
TOP SECRET
17
SOUTH VIETNAM
ADMINISTRATIVE DIVISIONS
OCTOBER 1967
REPUBLIC OF VIETNAM
Demilitarized Zone
Da Nang
I CORPS
KONTUM
DARLAC
Corps boundary
Province boundary
Hue Autonomous municipality
Da Lat
Cam Ranh
II CORPS
TAY NINH
SAIGON
III CORPS
Vung Tau
Capital Special Zone
IV CORPS
CON SON
COMMUNIST (VIET CONG)
Demilitarized Zone
TRI-THIEN-HUE MR
Hue
Da Nang
QUANG NAM
MR 5
KONTUM
GIA LAI
DAC LAC
MR 10
MR 1
MR 2
SAIGON
MR 6
MR 4: Saigon, Cho Lon, Gia Dinh Special Sector
Special Region 10
Military Region boundary
Province boundary
MR 3
TOP SECRET
TS 186035

on external sources, not only for Classes II and IV (weapons and equipment), Class V (ammunition), but also for Class I (food). This is partly because of allied denial efforts and partly a result of the growing proportion of North Vietnamese forces in South Vietnam, especially since these are generally deployed in food deficit areas. VC guerrilla forces probably require a small amount of food and ammunition from external sources, but the bulk of their supplies is obtained from local sources within South Vietnam. We have not included guerrilla forces in the logistical computations.

TABLE 4

ESTIMATED DAILY LOGISTICAL RESUPPLY REQUIREMENTS FOR NVA AND VC REGULAR AND ADMINISTRATIVE SUPPORT FORCES IN SOUTH VIETNAM[a]
(As of 30 September 1967)

Class	Short Tons Per Day External	Total
I (Food)[b]	38-40	177-183
II & IV (Weapons, Quartermaster, Engineer, Medical, Signal, Chemical, etc.)	6-7	23-24
III (POL)	Negl.	Negl.
V (Ammunition)[c]	10	11
TOTAL	54-57	211-218

[a] Based on 118,000 NVA and VC Main and Local force troops, and 35,000-40,000 administrative support troops. Requirements are computed on the basis of actual strength, which is about 70 percent of full TO&E strength. In estimating weapons requirements, losses due to capture or destruction were considered, as were losses due to normal attrition. In addition, an allowance was made to provide for the reequipping of those forces who are not presently equipped with the new family of weapons. These requirements, of course, will change as weapons losses fluctuate over time. Ammunition requirements are based upon estimates of actual ammunition expenditures in combat, and may be subject to a considerable margin of error.

[b] Includes a 15 percent factor for spoilage, but does not include replacement of food captured or destroyed by friendly forces.

[c] One-third of the weight of the external requirement represents a packaging factor; two-thirds of the weight is actual ammunition. No packaging factor is included in estimating internal ammunition requirements. The total ammunition requirement does include the external packaging factor.

41. Communist logistical requirements from external sources vary considerably in both amounts and class in the different areas of South Vietnam. In the northern provinces, for example, the requirement is probably higher per soldier than elsewhere in South Vietnam because the rate of combat there has been higher, and the troops are predominantly NVA and are better equipped. In the rice-deficit highlands, the external requirement for food is high. On the other hand, in the Delta and the Saigon area, Communist troops probably have no external requirement for food.

42. While we cannot estimate with confidence what proportions of external logistic resupply requirements are met by the respective routes into South Viet-

nam, some generalizations can be made about the logistical systems involved. The road network through the Laotian Panhandle is used primarily to supply weapons, equipment, and ammunition. A portion of the food requirement for Communist forces in the northern provinces is infiltrated through or around the DMZ along with some other supplies. Cambodia is primarily a source for food (probably over 80 percent of the Communists' external requirement) and some items such as medical supplies and radios. Within South Vietnam, the Communist procurement and distribution system is usually organized under the Communist military regional headquarters.

43. *Food Supply.* The Communists continue to have problems with food supplies in certain areas, because of local shortages, distribution bottlenecks, and the effects of allied military operations which have increasingly intruded into Communist base areas and disrupted the supply network. The amount of Communist food supplies captured or destroyed by allied forces in 1967 is substantial. From 1 January through 30 August it amounted to an average of 55 to 75 tons per day, which is more than one-fourth the Communist Regular and Administrative Forces' daily requirement, and greater than their external requirement. But despite some severe local difficulties, the overall effectiveness of the Communist military forces has not yet been seriously impaired by these problems. The food requirements for the Communists in many areas are met from internal sources through taxation, purchase, and coercion. However, the Communist military forces in the DMZ area and in the rice-deficient areas in the highlands are largely dependent on imports from North Vietnam and Cambodia.

44. On balance, we believe that food supply problems for the Communists are likely to become more burdensome, and in some areas will impede military operations. Nevertheless, we do not believe that food shortages will greatly restrict overall Communist operations in the near future as long as the Communists have access to Cambodian rice.

45. *Impact of New and Heavier Weapons.* Communist forces in South Vietnam have increased their mortar, rocket, and artillery attacks. Over a year ago, 120 mm mortars and 70 mm and 75 mm howitzers began to be used. Other types of weapons have been employed since early 1967. These include Chinese Communists 102 mm rockets, Soviet 122 mm and 140 mm rockets, and RPG-7 antitank grenade launchers. In addition, the NVA has fired light and medium artillery into South Vietnam from positions within or north of the DMZ. The use of these heavier weapons in the DMZ area has increased substantially in 1967, and during periods of peak fire in September it is estimated that Communist forces in that area were expending mortar, rocket, and artillery ammunition at a rate of close to 4 tons per day.

46. The estimated ammunition expenditure for all mortar, artillery, and rocket weapons of the Communist forces in South Vietnam for the first 8 months of

1967, not including that fired against allied forces just south of the DMZ averaged less than 1 ton per day. While logistic problems would inhibit increased use of these heavier weapons throughout South Vietnam on the scale they have been used near the DMZ, it is likely the Communists will increase their capabilities for mortar, rocket, and artillery attack against selected fixed targets.

47. Hanoi has recently concluded a new agreement with the USSR for military aid. It is possible that Hanoi has sought more sophisticated types of equipment than those now arriving on the scene. These might include cruise missiles and tactical rockets which could be used to support North Vietnamese operations in the DMZ area and against US warships.[8] A continuing and intensive watch has been maintained for any indications of the presence of these or larger missiles in North Vietnam. So far, no deliveries have been detected.

48. The North Vietnamese already have some SA-2s in the vicinity of the DMZ and we think it likely they might increase the numbers of SA-2s there. It is also possible, but less likely, that they would deploy SA-2s in Laos. They would almost certainly not introduce them into South Vietnam. It is possible that Hanoi would use aircraft against South Vietnam but we think this unlikely. In general, we believe that during the coming months the Soviets will continue to supply equipment designed to strengthen air and coastal defenses in North Vietnam and to increase the firepower of both the regular North Vietnamese forces and the Communist forces fighting in the South.

D. Communist Manpower in the South

49. *Communist Losses.* Total Communist losses have been rising sharply over the past 2 years. On the basis of the latest data, we estimate that total losses for 1967 will amount to about 170,000—an increase of about two-thirds compared with 1966. The bulk of these losses are killed-in-action as reported from body count. Our estimate of permanent losses from wounds is based on evidence indicating that for every 100 killed there would probably be 150 wounded, and that, of these, at least 35 die or are permanently disabled. Obviously, these figures involve a margin for error, but since they cannot take into account all casualties from air attacks or from artillery fire, or losses from sickness and accident, the killed and wounded estimates are probably not overstated. Figures for military returnees and prisoners are firm. But the number of deserters is an estimate based on a study that suggests there is likely to be one permanent desertion for every military returnee. If the overall totals do err, it is likely to be on the low side.

[8] For more detailed information on the types of weapons which the Soviets might supply the North Vietnamese, and the likelihood of their doing so, see SNIE 11-11-67, "Soviet Attitudes and Intentions Toward the Vietnam War," dated 4 May 1967, SECRET. We believe the conclusions are still valid.

TABLE 5

ESTIMATED COMMUNIST LOSSES IN SOUTH VIETNAM

	1966	1967 (Estimated Total)[a]
Killed-in-Action	55,500	90,000
Permanently Lost from Wounds	19,000	31,000
Military Returnees	13,000	21,000
Prisoners	2,500	7,000
Deserters	13,000	21,000
TOTAL	103,000[b]	170,000[b]

[a] The 1967 estimated totals are the projections of averages of Communist losses during the first 9 months of 1967.

[b] These totals include not only losses for Regular and Administrative Service Forces and guerrillas, but also losses for an unknown number of other Communist elements such as self-defense, secret self-defense forces, and "Assault Youth," etc.

50. A major problem in assessing the significance of these Communist losses is that we are unable to determine what proportion are suffered by the fighting forces and what proportion by such elements as the self-defense forces, "Assault Youth," conscripted laborers and other civilians caught up in combat areas. What is clear is that not all of the killed and wounded are members of primary fighting units (NVA Regular forces, VC Main and Local forces, and guerrillas). Consequently, we cannot estimate the loss to these Communist military forces for any given year.

51. *VC Manpower Inputs.* In the face of these increasingly heavy losses, the manpower resources available to the VC and the actual rate of recruitment are critical elements in an estimate of Communist capabilities to continue military operations. A calculatic , of manpower available to the VC for recruitment is difficult because of the absence of trustworthy population statistics. But even if such statistics were fairly accurate, major assumptions have to be made concerning what percentage of able-bodied males are available to the VC recruitment apparatus in their own areas, in the contested areas, and in GVN-controlled areas.

52. Bearing in mind these caveats, we estimate that the VC may have access to approximately 1.4 million males between the ages of 15 and 45. From this total, we believe that the VC could recruit from a manpower pool of some 700,000-800,000 men, though less than half of this total are in VC-controlled areas.

53. It is difficult to reconcile this apparently large block of manpower derived from limited demographic data, with the increasing evidence over the past year of VC problems in obtaining recruits. One reason for this discrepancy is that the manpower in VC areas is already subject to other important requirements which are related to the war effort, such as food production, and some of these tasks are increasing. A second reason for VC difficulties is that losses of all types have probably reduced the real, as opposed to the theoretical manpower

available to the VC. The third, and perhaps most important reason is the declining ability of the VC to obtain recruits because of allied forays into contested areas, the mounting flow of refugees out of these areas, and the likelihood that individuals are more reluctant to enlist in the VC movement than in 1964-1965 when the Communists appeared to be riding a crest of success.

54. These increasing recruitment problems are least evident in the Regular forces and most conspicuous among the guerrillas and self-defense forces, and have resulted in unfilled recruitment quotas, reduced standards (as to age, physical condition, and political reliability), and greater employment of women and youth. They have been particularly severe in areas of intense allied military pressure, but have not been totally absent elsewhere. Moreover, the Revolutionary Development (RD) program poses a threat to Communist access to the population, and is undoubtedly one of the reasons the VC have decided to exert heavy pressure against it.

55. We estimated that during 1966 the VC were probably able to recruit about 7,000 men per month. A reevaluation of recruitment for early 1967, however, shows that this performance has fallen off. We estimate that the average monthly recruitment probably falls within the range of 3,000 to 5,000 men per month for the Main forces, the Local forces, and the guerrillas. In addition, however, the VC commonly upgrade personnel from the lower to the higher echelons of the Communist organization. For example, a Local force unit will receive replacements from village guerrillas in the area; and these guerrillas in turn may be replaced by hamlet guerrillas, self-defense forces, or "Assault Youth." Some recent evidence suggests that in IV Corps, hamlet guerrillas and hamlet self-defense forces are being consolidated.

56. In any case, a persuasive indication of growing manpower problems for the VC is the increasing number of individual NVA soldiers serving as replacements in VC Main forces units. A study in late 1966 of a number of VC units in III Corps area indicated that at least 23 percent of the men in VC Main force units were NVA replacements, and the percentage is probably higher now. VC units in I and II Corps probably contain a higher percentage of NVA personnel, but we have not found NVA personnel in VC units in the Delta.

57. *Quality and Morale.* The rapid manpower turnover caused by increasing casualties has lowered the quality of all the VC fighting forces, but it is not yet apparent that this has seriously impaired their military effectiveness. The Communists have been forced to rely more and more on coercion to obtain recruits, have made greater use of women to free men for combat, and have reduced their recruitment and training standards. The decline in quality has been greatest at the lower levels, where personnel have repeatedly been siphoned off for higher echelons. More important, though probably not so pronounced, is the decline in the quality of the cadres—the cement of the VC organization.

58. In an endeavor to rectify this situation the Communists are resorting to several expedients to overcome weaknesses in their political operations. These

include intensive reindoctrination sessions and the infusion of North Vietnamese cadre into the VC organization. Since mid-1966, the VC have also been shifting some experienced cadre down to the lower levels to improve the quality of leadership and to eliminate the overdependence of village and hamlet party chapters on higher echelons. Some administrative reorganizations have also been instituted in an attempt to strengthen local responsibility and initiative. The effects of such measures are not yet evident, but could somewhat improve VC efficiency at lower levels.

59. Captured documents and evidence from prisoners amply demonstrate that morale problems are becoming serious and are likely to become worse as the war continues. But there have been no mass defections. This year's returnee rate, a statistical indicator of morale, is well above last year's rate. Captured documents have repeatedly noted this trend as one of the Communists' major shortcomings. Since the bulk of the returnees come from the lower levels of the VC structure, the immediate effect of these losses has not been critical. The troops continue to fight well, and the VC infrastructure remains generally strong. Over the longer term, however, such losses not only deprive the Communists of manpower, but, more important, they erode the base of the VC infrastructure.

III. THE OUTLOOK FOR COMMUNIST FORCES

60. In early 1965, prior to the commitment of sizable US forces, the Communists apparently expected to administer a knockout blow. After a period of some uncertainty and hesitation created by the US intervention in 1965, and certain tactical setbacks to the Communist forces, a general political-military strategy was worked out at the 12th Plenum of the North Vietnamese Communist Party in December 1965. This spelled out how to fight the war and manage its international aspects under the altered circumstances.

61. The essence of these decisions was to maintain sufficient forces in being to support a prolonged and aggressive war of attrition. Their objective in pursuing this strategy was and is to persuade the US that it cannot win; that it must eventually pull out or settle on terms favorable to Hanoi's further pursuit of its political goals. As part of this strategy, the war would be conducted without specific timetables; negotiations would be avoided unless from a position of significant military successes; and an effort would be made to limit the risks of an expanded war in the North or throughout Southeast Asia. This strategy aimed at maintaining a continuous threat by Regular forces, avoiding combat under unfavorable conditions, sustaining a high level of guerrilla activity, and undertaking limited objective offensives when favorable opportunities arise.

62. During 1966 and thus far in 1967, the Communists have apparently adhered to these basic decisions. For example, a new debate arose in late 1966 over the role of the guerrillas with some officials advocating a greater role for these forces at the expense of the Main forces. This proposition has apparently been rejected as tantamount to accepting a "strategic" reversal. Nevertheless, it is clear that debates over military-political tactics are continuing.

63. Perhaps the most important problem for Hanoi during the last year has been how to maintain military pressure in the face of the superior firepower and mobility of the Allied forces. Its answer to this problem has been to emphasize artillery, rocket, and mortar attacks, especially on I Corps, and to develop substantial threats by large units in border areas in such a way as to spread thin the Allied forces, open opportunities for localized "victories," and create better conditions for attacks against the RD program. Over the past year the Communists have used elements of at least three and possibly four divisions in the DMZ area plus artillery and some air defense units. Another buildup of Communist forces has taken place in the highlands along the Cambodian border. Such threats tie down large US forces in these areas, thereby lessening Allied military pressures elsewhere.

64. *Future Force Levels.* Regardless of their previous policy decisions, the Communists will assess the actual situation as it evolves. Their decisions as to force structure and strengths over the next year will be affected in part by the level of combat, their casualty rates, the extent of any further buildup of Allied forces in the South, and the overall impact of the war effort against the North. Another factor which complicates estimates of future force structure and strength levels is that North Vietnam retains the capability to move division size forces across the DMZ. Should they exercise this option, then the total force structure in South Vietnam could be expanded relatively quickly by introducing one or two divisions into Quang Tri Province. Regardless of whether they introduce these divisions in the DMZ area, we feel the NVA will still try to expand its Regular forces in South Vietnam, by the deployment of some new combat infantry regiments. However, this may not result in any net increase in the numerical strength of Regular forces since continuing losses may further reduce the average unit strength.

65. Taking into consideration the estimated rates of infiltration, and allowing for the downward trend in population control by the VC, the rising Communist casualties, and VC recruiting problems, we conclude that the strength of the Communist military forces and political organizations in South Vietnam declined in the last year. The major portion of this decline has probably been felt at the lowest levels, reflecting a deliberate policy of sacrificing this level to maintain the structure of political cadres and the strength of the Regular military forces. Whether this trend will continue is difficult to estimate. There are still important unknowns and variables involved in measuring total losses against inputs from recruiting and infiltration. Moreover, there are alternative strategies, such as avoiding combat for prolonged periods, which the Communists might adopt to reduce casualties and conserve their forces. Another option, though less likely, would be for the Communists deliberately to reduce the strength of the Regular forces, in order to preserve guerrilla forces and strengthen the political apparatus. The locale and effectiveness of all allied operations will also have an important bearing on future Communist force levels; losses in the northern provinces and western highlands could be made up more readily through infiltration than losses in the Delta, where the burden is on VC recruitment.

66. In any case, we believe that a major effort will be required to maintain the Regular forces and guerrillas at or near present levels. To do so will call for both a level of infiltration much higher than that observed in 1967 and intensive VC recruitment as well. Considering all the relevant factors, however, we believe that there is a fairly good chance that the overall strength and effectiveness of the military forces and the political infrastructure will continue to decline.

67. *Logistical Support.* The Communists will continue to have difficulties with internal distribution of supplies in South Vietnam that will cause local shortages and interfere with Communist operations from time to time. Their dependence on supplies from external sources is growing and could increase further over the next year, even if their strength declines somewhat. Nevertheless, we believe that the Communists will be able to continue to meet at least their essential supply requirements for the level of forces and activities in South Vietnam described in this estimate.

68. *Future Strategy.* The Communists apparently recognize that the chances of a complete military victory have disappeared, and they aim instead at a protracted war. Their objectives in this phase of the war are to immobilize and wear down the Allied military forces, to maintain base areas, expand their political agitation and control in contested and GVN areas, and defeat the RD program. In pursuit of these objectives, their tactics are to combine and coordinate closely their military operations and political activity.

69. Our judgment is that the Communists still retain adequate capabilities to support this strategy for at least another year. Whether or not Hanoi does in fact persist with this strategy depends not only on its capabilities to do so, but on a number of political and international considerations not treated in this estimate, such as the state of Sino-Soviet relations, conditions inside China, and Hanoi's view of US will and determination. Even if some combination of circumstances should make it impossible or undesirable for Hanoi to continue employing large conventional forces, the Communists would still have the capability to continue some forms of struggle—though at greatly reduced levels.

IM 0587/68

Hanoi's Negotiating Position and Concept of Negotiations

6 May 1968

APPROVED FOR RELEASE
DATE: JAN 2005

(b)(3)

~~Secret~~

INTELLIGENCE MEMORANDUM

Hanoi's Negotiating Position and Concept of Negotiations

~~Secret~~

1

6 May 1968
No. 0587/68

(Continued...)

SECRET

NO. 0587/68

CENTRAL INTELLIGENCE AGENCY
6 May 1968

INTELLIGENCE MEMORANDUM

Hanoi's Negotiating Position and Concept of Negotiations

Summary

Hanoi's negotiators will come to Paris reasonably confident that the negotiations can be used to advance Hanoi's basic objectives in Vietnam. The Communists see themselves more as revolutionaries opening a second front than as negotiators exploring the possibilities for compromise. Given their conviction that little can be gained at the bargaining table that has not been won on the ground, the North Vietnamese position in Paris will be governed largely by events in South Vietnam. Thus Hanoi almost certainly intends to intensify and maintain as much military pressure as possible, for psychological impact as well as for tactical reasons.

Hanoi sees itself leading from strength, even though it probably recognizes that its over-all position is not as strong as it had hoped it would be at this point in the struggle. Both military and political achievements in the South have fallen well short of Hanoi's stated objectives since the opening of its major offensive last fall. Although pressures for peace may bear more heavily on the US, North Vietnam will also be constrained by internal and external pressures.

Hanoi is likely to yield little on the bombing issue. Its negotiators will insist on a unilateral cessation of all hostile action by the US. Although the North Vietnamese are likely to reject, officially and openly, any variant of the San Antonio formula, they might acquiesce in some tacit understanding not to take advantage of a halt in the air strikes in order to keep the discussions going. We would not

SECRET

expect any significant de-escalation of the Communist military effort at this stage.

More formal negotiations probably will hinge on the question of Communist representation from South Vietnam. In this phase Hanoi will focus on its four points and the program of the National Liberation Front (NFL) as the basis of a political solution. Its immediate aim would be to determine how far the US is prepared to go in accepting a new coalition government with Communist representation.

Hanoi probably is not certain in its own mind just how the play will unfold and precisely what its positions will be on every issue. It probably is prepared, however, for a long and arduous campaign of fighting and talking, carrying perhaps through the US elections and possibly into a new American administration.

-2-

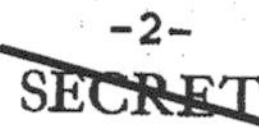

General Considerations

1. Four fundamental considerations shape Hanoi's attitude toward negotiations and will materially influence the way Hanoi's negotiators play their hand in Paris:

(a) Hanoi is much more interested in victory than settlement, hence its purpose in entering discussions is to further North Vietnam's basic objectives more than to work out a compromise acceptable to all parties engaged in the Vietnam struggle.

(b) Hanoi's leaders presently believe that the widespread desire for peace and opposition to the Vietnam war, particularly within the US, places more political pressure on Washington than on Hanoi to be "forthcoming" in any talks.

(c) Hanoi does not believe that diplomacy alone can achieve significant gains not securable or already secured by military and political struggle in South Vietnam itself.

(d) Hanoi's view of the actual result of the settlements negotiated in 1954 and 1962 has made the Lao Dong's leaders chary of negotiations and, particularly, of less than optimum negotiated solutions.

Political Strategy

2. Hanoi's negotiators will be coming to Paris primarily to open another front of revolutionary struggle. They will be much more interested in exploiting this front's potential contribution to the success of the revolution--i.e., the acquisition or imposition of

(Continued...)

~~SECRET~~

Communist control over South Vietnam--than engaging in a serious effort to de-escalate the war or negotiate a mutually agreeable solution. Hanoi is almost certainly suspicious of US intentions and determined not to yield on any significant point at least until the US position has been fully disclosed and US firmness thoroughly probed. Hanoi's initial intent, therefore, will be to "use" the talks aggressively to further its declared aims in South Vietnam. North Vietnam's leaders probably believe the US was "compelled" to restrict the bombing and enter into talks by mounting domestic political pressures and because Washington felt the tide was running against the allied position in South Vietnam. Hanoi hopes both trends can be intensified during the course of the Paris discussions. Hanoi will endeavor to turn the mere process of talking to its advantage by increasing pressure on the US to end the war without sticking on the terms of settlement, by exacerbating relations between Saiogn and Washington, by undermining the Saigon government's confidence in the constancy of its principal ally, and by undermining the confidence of all non-Communist South Vietnamese in their government and their future. Hanoi's initial position and tactics will be tailored to a great extent by these aims.

Propaganda Considerations

3. Most of what Hanoi says and does in Paris will be aimed as much at the US and world press as at the American negotiators. Hanoi believes that peace sentiment in the US is widespread and politically potent. The North Vietnamese may exaggerate this factor but certainly intend to take full advantage of it. They probably calculate that once actual diplomatic contacts are opened, war-weariness (and opposition) will increase in the US and peace will become a matter of increasing political urgency as the casualties continue and the US election campaign develops. Hanoi probably expects that such consideration will ultimately lead to American concessions. To this end, Hanoi will endeavor to isolate the bombing issue and create the impression that complete termination of the bombing is all that stands in the way of serious negotiation on a peaceful settlement.

SECRET

The Talks and the Battlefield

4. The behavior of Hanoi's negotiators in Paris will be materially influenced and in certain aspects actually dictated by the course of events in South Vietnam. It is no accident that Hanoi's statement of 3 May proposing the Paris talks was shortly followed by country-wide attacks in South Vietnam. Throughout any talks there will be a closely coordinated correlation between action at the negotiating table and action on the battlefield. The current series of attacks illustrates Hanoi's obvious intention to use its military and political action potential in South Vietnam in a manner and with a timing designed to enhance its bargaining position. Hanoi will orchestrate military pressures as much for psychological and propaganda impact as for concrete or tactical considerations. The North Vietnamese will almost certainly believe that any apparent Communist gains or apparent allied reverses will probably be reflected in a weakening of the American negotiating position. In this context, the Communists will consider appearance at least as important as substantive reality, and hence they will almost certainly exert every effort (and accept severe casualties) to prevent any apparent manifestation of allied progress.

The Lessons of History

5. Hanoi's leaders have twice before ventured down the negotiation track--in 1954 and in 1962. In their opinion, both times they were euchred by events which developed in a manner contrary to all reasonable expectation. In 1954, under Russian and Chinese pressure, the Lao Dong politburo settled for half a loaf, confident that Diem's fledgling and beleaguered government was certain to collapse and hence South Vietnam would be theirs either through the 1956 elections or the simple absence of any effective non-Communist opposition. Reality's confounding of this near-certain calculation has forced Hanoi's leaders to embark upon and wage an eleven-year struggle for something they saw within their grasp fourteen years ago. In 1962 they bought a "settlement" in Laos in the confident belief that Souvanna was in their

-5-

SECRET

pocket. His subsequent behavior as a truly independent neutralist confounded Hanoi's eminently reasonable calculations.

6. Recent Vietnamese history, in short, has made Hanoi's leaders extremely chary of negotiations or of settlements that leave anything to the vagaries of chance. Hanoi's reading of this history will almost certainly influence its willingness to entertain any current settlement propositions that do not virtually guarantee Communist control over South Vietnam in a very short time frame.

Communist Strengths and Weaknesses

7. Hanoi's negotiators will come to the table reasonably confident of obtaining most of the objectives outlined above. Hanoi sees itself in a strong position, though its position is not one of unblemished confidence or unalloyed strength. On the contrary, in our view the over-all prospects for the Communists in South Vietnam have become more uncertain in recent months. Currently, their position is not at all what they thought it would be, let alone hoped for, when they conceived the winter-spring campaign last year. The GVN/ARVN have not only survived the Tet onslaught, but have proved more resilient than many thought possible. The military initiative has passed again to the US in many areas, even though the North Vietnamese have every intention of attempting to regain it. That Hanoi now counts on the early disintegration of the GVN and ARVN under new pressures is at least open to serious question. And the political atmosphere in the US, which must have been an important factor in Hanoi's calculations, has probably become more uncertain and ambiguous than it appeared in the period from the Tet attacks through President Johnson's address of 31 March.

8. Moreover, Hanoi is not entering into the upcoming phase with the support and encouragement of one of its principal allies--China. For this reason alone it must proceed carefully and avoid making its conduct at the talks a new subject of Sino-Soviet confrontation. The net effect of this fact probably is that Hanoi's flexibility is somewhat circumscribed, and the potential influence of the USSR is further

SECRET

limited. China's influence and leverage over Hanoi is also limited, however, though an early collapse of the talks would appear to justify China's reservations and objections, and probably open a new round of charges against the USSR for collusion with the US.

The Overview

9. In sum, Hanoi's negotiators will come to Paris believing that their position is a good one and that at a minimum the talks offer opportunities for political warfare. But they probably also realize that they do not yet hold all the high cards and probably cannot impose their terms. If they fail to achieve the significant gains they hope to register in South Vietnam during the course of the talks, they will then confront the hard choice of whether to stonewall in the face of adversity on the battlefield or settle for something short of their oft-stated objectives.

Objectives and Tactics

10. We think it realistic to accept Hanoi's declared objectives more or less at face value. Hanoi will open by seeking a full halt to the bombing and all other "acts of war" against the North. Unless it makes a presently unlikely major concession, only when all the bombing has stopped will Hanoi proceed to a second phase to deal with "related questions." These will almost certainly center around the essentials of its four points": a negotiated US withdrawal from Vietnam, the formation of a new government in Saigon as specified in the program of the NLF, the neutralization of South Vietnam, and a governmental structure built around the NLF or, at least, an NLF-dominated "alliance."

11. The major questions for speculation are how these objectives and phases relate and what flexibility Hanoi will display in their tactical development. Hanoi has probably already devised a fairly clear scenario but, as indicated above, many of the basic decisions will still depend on developments on the ground in South Vietnam as well as on the response and reaction of the US in the course of the discussions.

SECRET

SECRET

The Bombing Issue

12. As an opener Hanoi will insist that the only purpose of preliminary contacts is to determine the date for a cessation of all bombing, naval gunfire, artillery shelling, and reconnaissance against North Vietnam. Moreover, Hanoi's negotiators will insist that this be accomplished unilaterally and without reciprocity, and that US failure to accept these demands will mean an end to further discussion. North Vietnam will refuse to acknowledge any participation of its own forces in the South Vietnam struggle and thus will probably not officially or openly accept any variant of the San Antonio formula.

13. For several reasons, we do not believe, however, that Hanoi intends for the discussions to break down on the bombing issue. To begin with, Hanoi wants the present bombing restriction maintained and wants an end to all bombing. Furthermore, the statement of 3 May agreeing to talk in Paris and the appointment of Xuan Thuy as the negotiator suggest Hanoi has deliberately blurred the distinction between contacts and formal talks. Finally, Hanoi has a strong incentive to move the discussions on to some of the more critical substantive issues, that can affect the mood and outlook in Saigon and further unsettle the South Vietnamese (i.e., the formation of a coalition regime and a US withdrawal).

14. We think it likely, therefore, that the bargaining will be hard, but that Hanoi will find a way out of any impasse over the bombing issue. The North Vietnamese leaders probably now believe that the US position in this entire matter is not firm or fixed, and that Hanoi need not go beyond some kind of vague indication that it will not take advantage of a complete halt in air strikes. Assurances through third parties or in behind-the-scenes contacts would be one way. The North Vietnamese might also tacitly accept some continuing US reconnaissance, say below the 20th parallel, to verify that Hanoi is not accelerating its movement of men and materiel. In short, while avoiding overt commitments, Hanoi may try to create the impression that the US would be justified in "assuming" Hanoi will not take advantage to an end of all bombing.

-8-

SECRET

SECRET

15. As an alternative route around this potential impasse, Hanoi might eventually settle for an agreement "in principle" to an end of the bombing, once an agreement had been reached on the place, level, and agenda of the next phase of talks. In this way, Hanoi could, if it desired, slide into "formal talks" without technically abandoning its initial position.

16. Whatever the agreement on the bombing, we would not expect any significant de-escalation of the Communist military effort at this juncture. Hanoi almost certainly believes the US is vulnerable on the bombing question and that there will be great public pressure in the US and the world at large not to allow the discussions to break down on this issue. Thus, unless extremely hard pressed in the South, Hanoi is not going to pay much of a price to end the bombing. The way the bombing issue is resolved will be read by Hanoi as a key indicator of the relative hardness or weakness of the entire US negotiating position.

Formal Talks

17. It is more difficult to look beyond the initial encounter over the bombing issue to the next stage of talks. In the formal talks Hanoi could develop any of three broad courses: it could proceed forthwith to discuss the full range of issues involved in Vietnam, but will probably not do so promptly unless the NLF participates and the GVN is excluded. Alternatively, Hanoi could insist on narrow discussions of bilateral issues--reparation for the bombing, prisoner exchange, etc. Except as a stalling device this holds no special advantage from Hanoi's standpoint. More likely, Hanoi would probably see the formal talks as focusing on US acceptance of North Vietnam's four points and the program of the NLF as the "basis" for a political solution of the Vietnamese war.

18. In the course of this debate, and perhaps at the very outset, Hanoi's negotiators would probably fix on the issue of political representation

SECRET

from South Vietnam and are certain to take a very adamant line in refusing to accept any participation by the present GVN. The North Vietnamese will probably insist that no discussion of a settlement can proceed very far without the formation of a new government in Saigon, representing all political forces, and its participation in the negotiations. As an ostensible concession, they might abandon the old position that only the NLF was the legitimate voice of the "people," and propose a new government be formed by representatives from the NLF, the new "Alliance for Peace," members of the present GVN (except Thieu or Ky) and perhaps even groupings currently in exile.

19. They might also propose adjourning the Paris talks while these South Vietnamese elements negotiated among themselves, or Hanoi might propose inviting them to join with the US and DRV. In either case, here is the fundamental issue at stake in Vietnam: who will hold real power in Saigon? In Hanoi's view the purpose of the formal talks with the US at this juncture will be to determine whether the US will, in fact, agree to the formation of a new government (and hence to scuttling the present constitutional structure) and how far the US will be prepared to go in accepting Communist influence in such a government.

20. There are a number of variants on this issue. For example, Hanoi might press for direct negotiations between the NLF and the US, or inclusion of the NLF in the Paris talks. In any case, this is likely to be the critical juncture of the talks and Hanoi's toughest position. Hanoi will hope that any discussions on Communist representation in Saigon will help precipitate the collapse of the Thieu-Ky government and one of Hanoi's primary objectives throughout the talks will be to exert political pressure on South Vietnam.

Other Issues

21. It is at this point that Hanoi would want to intensify military pressure. But it may also be inclined to make some concessions if it believed

they would facilitate negotiations toward a government of "national union" in Saigon. Hanoi might hint that a cease-fire could be quickly arranged with establishment of a new government. And of course Hanoi's interest in a cease-fire would increase if its military position in the South seemed likely to deteriorate. Hanoi might slow down certain military operations in certain areas, especially along the DMZ. And it might hint that the US could retain some limited presence in Vietnam, or at least that a US withdrawal could be extended over a fairly long period. Probably, these questions would come up off-stage, since Hanoi will insist that questions directly related to the war in the South must be discussed with some representation by the NLF. The issue of a US withdrawal, however, could conceivably be discussed under the rubric of "aggression" against Vietnam, which is one of Hanoi's four points. It might even be discussed simultaneously with the question of formation of a coalition government.

22. Beyond this it is difficult to estimate Hanoi's position on such issues as Laos, a new Geneva conference, international guarantees, supervision, reunification, etc. Moreover, there are side issues which can always arise--the level of the talks, new sites, agenda. Hanoi could, if it chose, find a number of ways to becloud the issues and draw out the discussions at any phase, if the situation in South Vietnam warrants it.

23. In any case, it is unlikely that Hanoi has decided how to handle every issue or procedure or what outcome would ultimately be acceptable. Hanoi probably is preparing, however, for a lengthy and difficult process of fighting and talking subject to interruptions and breakdowns, lasting perhaps through the elections and the installation of a new American administration.

SNIE 14.3-69

Capabilties of the Vietnamese Communists for Fighting in South Vietnam

17 July 1969

APPROVED FOR RELEASE
DATE: JAN 2005

~~TOP SECRET~~

SNIE 14.3-69
17 July 1969

(b)(1)
(b)(3)

SPECIAL

NATIONAL INTELLIGENCE ESTIMATE

NUMBER 14.3-69

(Supersedes SNIE 14.3-67)

Capabilities of the Vietnamese Communists for Fighting in South Vietnam

Submitted by

DIRECTOR OF CENTRAL INTELLIGENCE

Concurred in by the

UNITED STATES INTELLIGENCE BOARD

As indicated overleaf

17 July 1969

Authenticated:

EXECUTIVE SECRETARY, USIB

~~TOP SECRET~~

Nº 100

INDOCHINA
MILITARY REGIONS
Military region or corps boundary
Railroad
Road
0 50 100 150 Miles
0 50 100 150 Kilometers
NAMES AND BOUNDARY REPRESENTATION ARE NOT NECESSARILY AUTHORITATIVE
CHINA
BURMA
THAILAND
LAOS
CAMBODIA
NORTH VIETNAM
SOUTH VIETNAM
HAINAN
NORTH-WEST
VIET BAC
MR LEFT BANK
MR RIGHT BANK
VINH LINH SPECIAL ZONE
Demarcation Line
CAPITAL SPECIAL ZONE
HEADQUARTERS
CAPITAL
Ko-chiu
Meng-tzu
P'u-erh
Ha Giang
Cao Bang
Lao Cai
Nan-ning
Yü-lin
Ta-lo
Tuyen Quang
Lang Son
Saly
Dien Bien Phu
Son La
Mong Cai
Muang Luong Nam Tha
Son Tay
Hanoi
Hon Gai
Haiphong
Houei Sai
Samneua
Hai-an
Chiang Rai
Louangphrabang
Thanh Hoa
Sala Phou Khoun
Muong Sen
Tung-fang-hsien
Nan
Vinh
Huang-liu
Paksane
VIENTIANE
Nong Khai
Udon Thani
Dong Hoi
Khammouane (Thakhek)
Quang Tri
Phitsanulok
Seno
Sepone
Savannakhet
Hue
Khon Kaen
Da Nang
Nakhon Sawan
Saravane
Ubon Ratchathani
Nakhon Ratchasima
Warin Chamrap
Pakse
Attopeu
Kontum
Pleiku
Prachin Buri
BANGKOK
Chachoengsao
An Nhon
Samut Songkhram
Sisophon
Siem Reap
Stung Treng
Battambang
Pursat
Kratie
Ban Me Thuot
Kompong Cham
Da Lat
PHNOM PENH
Kompong Speu
Svay Rieng
Bien Hoa
SAIGON
Phan Thiet
Sihanoukville
Kampot
My Tho
Vung Tau
Long Xuyen
Vinh Long
DAO PHU QUOC (Vietnam)
Can Tho
Bac Lieu
Quan Long
CON SON
I
II
III
IV
V
76478 6-69

CAPABILITIES OF THE VIETNAMESE COMMUNISTS FOR FIGHTING IN SOUTH VIETNAM

THE PROBLEM

To estimate Vietnamese Communist capabilities to sustain military operations over the next year or so.

CONCLUSIONS

A. The military capabilities of Communist forces in the field in South Vietnam have declined over the past year, and the overall intensity of their military effort probably fell below intended levels. GVN/Allied operations have caused heavy casualties and logistic problems for Communist forces and, overall, have impaired their operational effectiveness. Despite their success over the past year in maintaining the numerical strength of their forces and a relatively high level of military operations, the Communists are suffering an erosion of their position in South Vietnam.

B. Nonetheless, the Communists retain a substantial capability to sustain military operations. The Viet Cong infrastructure, which plays a vital role in supporting the war effort, continues to function effectively despite some attrition and reduced access to the population and resources of the South.

C. Communist manpower losses reached record levels in 1968 and have continued high through June 1969. These losses are almost certainly a matter of serious concern to Hanoi, in part because of the longer term social and economic implications. But given the will, Hanoi could continue through 1970, at least, to supply replacements at the high rates of the past 18 months.

D. The overall logistic system functions adequately in local procurement in South Vietnam and in the movement of arms and ammunition, some food, and other supplies from North Vietnam and Cambodia to the borders of South Vietnam. We nevertheless believe that the system has begun to feel the strain of the more intensive tempo of the war. There are many difficulties in movement through Laos due to the air interdiction campaign. Within South Vietnam, there are difficulties in pre-positioning and protecting supplies for contemplated operations. On balance, however, we conclude that the overall system can continue to support military operations at the average levels of the past 12 months.[1]

E. We believe that Communist capabilities will support the following options, at least through 1970:

1. to escalate military pressures substantially for a short period;
2. to reduce military operations well below average levels of the past year;
3. to undertake military operations at substantially the same average levels as over the past year.

F. Option (1) appears unlikely without a considerable decline in the strength or morale of Allied forces, since under present circumstances large-scale attacks would be extremely costly for the Communists and could not be sustained. A maximum effort with the forces available in South Vietnam might be launched as a prelude to proposing a general cease-fire and shifting the struggle almost entirely to the political/psychological arena.

G. Option (2) would conserve Communist manpower and might be adopted for some months to test its political effect in the US and in Saigon. But a prolonged stand-down would risk rapid loss of position in the countryside, deterioration of Communist morale, and a probable reduction of domestic pressures in the US to withdraw US forces.

H. Option (3), the course pursued by the Communists over the past year, would be relatively costly to Hanoi and would add to strains and pressures in North Vietnam which have become increasingly apparent. Yet so long as political issues are not resolved in negotiations

[1] For the views of Major Gen. Jammie M. Philpott, Assistant Chief of Staff, Intelligence, USAF, see his comments in his footnote to paragraph 51.

and the fighting continues, Hanoi may feel it necessary to stay in the field with forces which will enable them to conduct periodic offensives, some of which may be fairly large and costly, and to maintain pressures on the GVN presence in the countryside.

I. As indicated above, we believe Hanoi has the capability to pursue this military course through 1970 at levels approximating those of the past 12 months. Whether it considers such an effort feasible or worthwhile depends, of course, on its judgment with respect to US and GVN resolve, subjects beyond the scope of this estimate. In any case, political action and maneuver will probably be intensified within South Vietnam and on the international scene as the Communists continue efforts to undermine the GVN and isolate its leaders from the US.

DISCUSSION

I. INTRODUCTION

1. In the aftermath of Tet 1968, if not before, the Vietnamese Communists recognized that they could not achieve decisive military results on the battlefield in South Vietnam against the combined strengths of GVN and allied forces. The alacrity with which the Communists responded to the March 1968 cutback in the bombing and the US offer to begin talks demonstrated their own readiness to enter a negotiating phase of the struggle.

2. The move to the conference table was followed by some adjustments in military tactics. Since the costly offensives of Tet and May 1968, there have been virtually no large-scale assaults on major cities; rather the Communists have attempted to maintain military pressures by standoff attacks on some cities and military installations, and by ambushes, sapper activity, and occasional frontal assaults on allied military positions. Meanwhile assassinations, kidnappings and other terrorist acts directed at pacification and other local officials have continued.

3. Despite the resort to "economy of force" tactics, the human and material costs to the Communists of sustaining military pressures have not been substantially reduced from the peak levels of January-June 1968. Casualties have been running at a high rate, necessitating continued inputs of North Vietnamese manpower to maintain force levels in the South, and logistic requirements are undiminished. In short, the Communists have felt it necessary to sustain a relatively high level of military operations in South Vietnam in support of their current objectives—undermining the position of the GVN and persuading the US to pull out or to settle generally on terms acceptable to Hanoi.

4. In the following sections of this paper, we examine Communist capabilities in terms of manpower and logistics to sustain the average level of fighting over

the past year, and some of the considerations that might influence the Communists to intensify or de-escalate the level of combat.

5. We are aware, however that the capabilities of Communist forces in South Vietnam are not a simple function of the availability of men and arms. Qualitative factors directly affecting the performance of Communist forces in the field and the will and morale of the population and the regime in North Vietnam, are important. Communist capabilities to prolong the war are also directly affected by the effectiveness and performance of the GVN and Allied forces. Finally, given the heavy dependence of the Communist effort on the active or passive support of several million people in South Vietnam, psychological and political factors affecting their allegiance bear heavily on Communist military capabilities. To the extent possible, we will deal with some of these additional elements in this estimate, but it is not our purpose here to "war game" or "net" Communist capabilities against the allies.

II. COMMUNIST FORCES

A. The Organization and Strength of Communist Forces in South Vietnam

6. Under Hanoi's direction, a large, well-organized, political-administrative apparatus motivates and manages the overall Communist effort in South Vietnam. This apparatus has existed throughout Vietnam since 1945; its control element is the Vietnam Workers Party (Lao Dong) and the southern wing is publicly called the Peoples Revolutionary Party (PRP). Front groups controlled by the Party include the newly formed Provisional Revolutionary Government (PRG), the National Liberation Front (NLF), and the Alliance of National Democratic and Peace Forces. This organization acts not only as a government in Viet Cong-controlled areas, but maintains an important clandestine presence elsewhere, collecting intelligence and undertaking various subversive efforts. Its primary responsibilities, however, are to maintain discipline and morale, and to mobilize manpower and other resources in support of the overall effort. Because of these functions and the leading political role it would also play for the Communists should combat cease, this apparatus is the key element of the Communist presence in South Vietnam.

7. The current estimate of hard-core members of the infrastructure—totaling 80,000 to 100,000—is a projection based on sketchy and dated evidence. The widespread geographical distribution of the infrastructure and the dedication and effectiveness of its personnel are as significant as its numbers. A co-ordinated allied effort directed specifically against the political-administrative apparatus has gotten under way within the past year. It is difficult to assess the results of this effort thus far. It is clearly causing the Communists some concern but, despite some attrition and disruption, the infrastructure remains basically intact and capable of engaging in roughly the same magnitude of operations as it has during the past four years of the war.

8. *Military Forces.* Overall control of military operations in South Vietnam is exercised by the High Command in Hanoi. The Central Office for South Vietnam

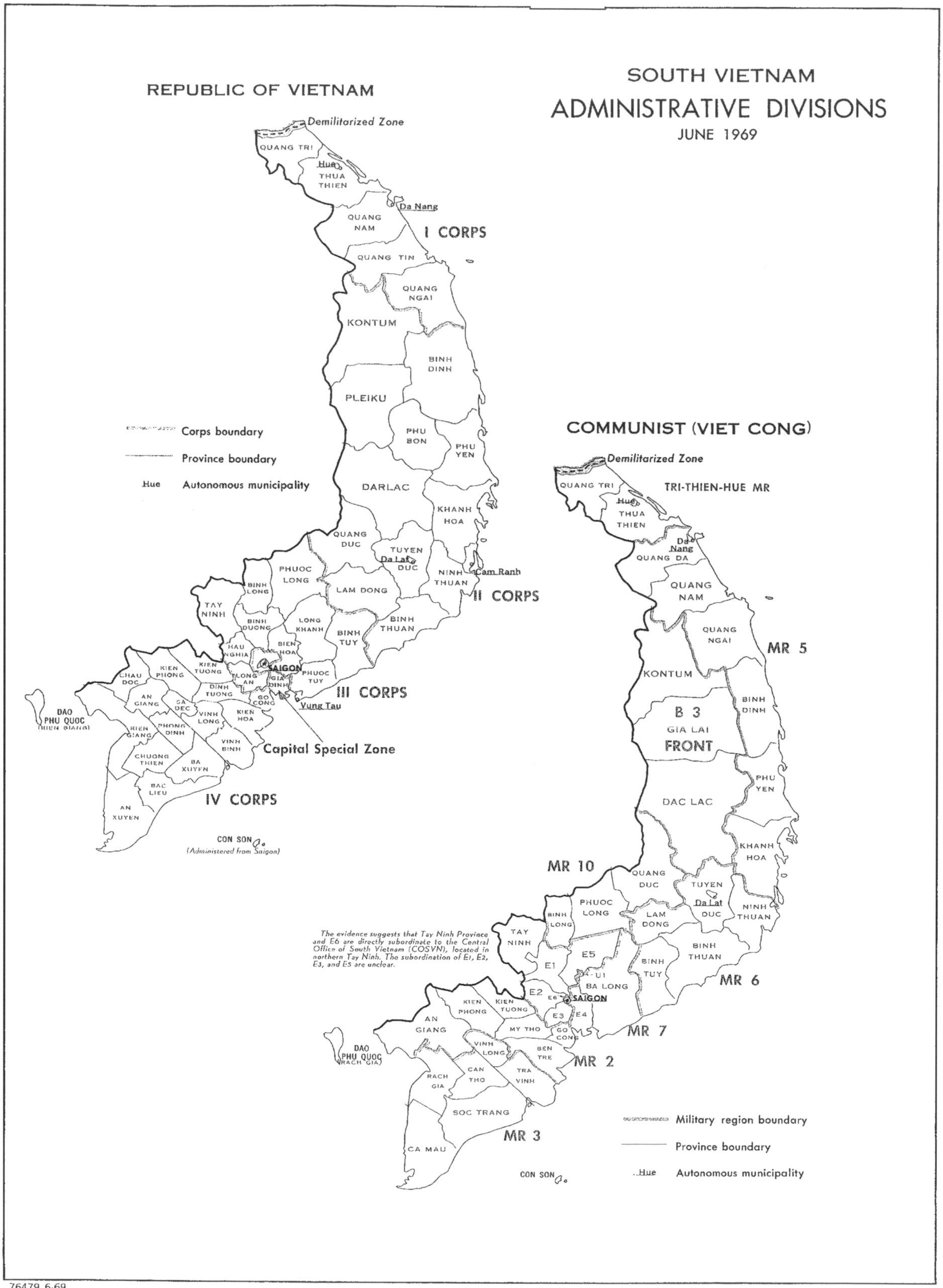

SOUTH VIETNAM

ADMINISTRATIVE DIVISIONS

JUNE 1969

REPUBLIC OF VIETNAM

Corps boundary

Province boundary

Hue Autonomous municipality

Capital Special Zone

CON SON (Administered from Saigon)

COMMUNIST (VIET CONG)

The evidence suggests that Tay Ninh Province and E6 are directly subordinate to the Central Office of South Vietnam (COSVN), located in northern Tay Ninh. The subordination of E1, E2, E3, and E5 are unclear.

Military region boundary

Province boundary

Hue Autonomous municipality

76479 6-69

TOP SECRET

(COSVN)—the Vietnam Workers Party headquarters in the south—has a military affairs office which exercises tactical control over those military forces located in the southern half of South Vietnam. Elsewhere, Communist military forces are tactically controlled by Hanoi, either directly or through the military affairs sections of appropriate regional party headquarters. Hanoi and COSVN maintain effective links with the district and small-unit levels through a hierarchy of regional, subregional, and provincial commands.

9. Communist military forces are organized into three complementary structures or levels: the Main Forces, including North Vietnamese Army (NVA) units; the Local Forces; and the Guerrilla/Militia. Main Forces are battalion and larger units, supported by appropriate staffs, which are subordinate to military commands above the provincial level. Local Forces are battalion, company, and platoon-size organizations, also supported by appropriate staffs, which are subordinate to the provinces and districts. Guerrilla units are platoon and squad-size units which are subordinate to villages and hamlets.

10. Our latest estimate of the personnel strength of Communist military forces in the South is listed in Table I.

11. Organizationally, the Communists have increased their manuever forces by a number of additional battalions, thus adding to their tactical flexibility. The intensity of combat has caused a wide fluctuation in the actual personnel

TABLE I

ESTIMATED VIET CONG/NORTH VIETNAMESE ARMY PERSONNEL STRENGTH IN SOUTH VIETNAM AND ADJACENT AREAS
(As of 31 March 1969)

REGULAR COMBAT FORCES	
North Vietnamese Army	120,000-130,000 [a]
Viet Cong (Main and Local Force)	50,000- 65,000
Subtotal	(170,000-195,000)
ADMINISTRATIVE SERVICES [b]	
North Vietnamese Army	25,000- 30,000 [c]
Viet Cong	40,000- 50,000
Subtotal	65,000- 80,000
GUERRILLAS	50,000-100,000 [d]
Total	285,000-375,000

[a] In addition to those troops deployed in South Vietnam, this figure includes two divisions and other forces in adjacent areas of Laos, Cambodia, and North Vietnam, and an estimated 25,000 NVA fillers in Viet Cong Main and Local Force units.

[b] Within the Communist military organizations, administrative services personnel are included among NVA, Main Force, and Local Force troops.

[c] This includes up to 10,000 personnel of the 559th Transportation Group who may be deployed in South Vietnam at any given time.

[d] We believe that the military threat represented by the Guerrilla forces is not on a parity with that of the Main and Local Forces. The number of guerrillas who are well-trained, organized, and motivated is somewhere near the lower end of the range given above.

strength of these units, and overall has led to a lower average strength. The major change in the general positioning of enemy forces during the past year or so has occurred in III Corps, where a significant buildup has taken place.

12. Trends relating to the size and mix of Communist forces are extremely difficult to discern. In general, however, it appears that Viet Cong Main Force and NVA strength has increased slightly since the end of 1967; the proportion of North Vietnamese troops in the regular forces has also increased somewhat during this period. Viet Cong Local Forces have probably declined in numbers despite a growing number of NVA replacements, while guerrilla strength has declined numerically and qualitatively during the past year and one-half. Generally, all of these trends appear to have involved only moderate shifts, and overall, we believe that total Communist military personnel strength as of 31 March 1969 was about the same as in the months prior to the dramatic 1968 Tet offensive. Since then, there may have been some decline due to continuing high losses in combat.

13. *Other Groups.* In addition to the political infrastructure and military forces, the Communist presence in South Vietnam includes other organized paramilitary insurgent groups. Self-Defense Forces, for example, construct fortifications, warn of the approach of allied forces, and defend hamlets and villages in Viet Cong-controlled territory. They are not well-armed, do not leave their home areas, and perform their duties only on a part-time basis. Assault Youth primarily perform rear service functions at the district and province level. They serve full-time, however, and are organized into companies and platoons. We believe that Self-Defense Forces may number between 80,000-120,000 while the Assault Youth total about 10,000-20,000. These estimates are projected from limited data, and are included only to suggest a rough order of magnitude.

B. Communist Manpower Requirements and Availability

14. *Losses.*[2] Our estimate of VC/NVA personnel losses in South Vietnam for 1967 was about 170,000; in 1968, it increased to nearly 300,000, and was running at about the same high level during the first half of this year. Up to now, the Communists have managed to offset these heavy losses by local recruitment in South Vietnam and by the deployment of replacement groups and organized units from North Vietnam. In the following paragraphs we consider Communist capabilities to continue the replacement process.

15. *Recruitment in South Vietnam.* There is no reliable demographic estimate of the manpower pool in South Vietnam. Seemingly slight variations in assump-

[2] These estimates include defectors, prisoners, and allowances for various other types of losses, but depend primarily upon an admittedly imperfect count of those killed in action. Because of the widespread use of allied artillery and air power, the effects of which cannot often be verified, it is likely that our estimates of Communist losses are somewhat understated. In light of the tenuous nature of these estimates and other difficulties, it is not possible to apportion Communist losses among the various types of Communist forces.

tions regarding the age-sex ratio of the population or the percentage of physically fit males can result in differences of many hundreds of thousands of available men. Moreover, the manpower actually available to the Viet Cong varies considerably as the Communist presence expands or contracts in various areas of the country. Nevertheless, it is clear that the manpower supply available to the Viet Cong is growing smaller. It is being reduced by continuing casualties on both sides, by the recently intensified GVN mobilization effort and by the continuing shift of population from rural to urban areas; the latter is especially damaging to Communist recruiting. Our estimates of Communist recruiting in South Vietnam remain tenuous. During the past year and one-half, the estimated monthly recruitment rate has ranged from a few thousand during certain periods to 15,000 for several months following the 1968 Tet offensive. Estimates of total recruitment in 1968 ranged from 60,000 to 100,000.

16. In any event, the growing manpower squeeze has affected the quality of the recruits to some extent. Men of prime military age are becoming more scarce, and there is evidence of a growing number of recent recruits in the 13-17 year age bracket within Viet Cong ranks. The high, rapid turnover has necessitated a shorter training period for recruits, which also detracts from performance. Most important, the growing recruitment problem in the South has forced the Communists for some time to rely primarily on troops from North Vietnam to maintain the strength of their forces.

17. *Manpower Available in North Vietnam.* Heavy troop requirements for the South coupled with increases in the North Vietnamese Armed Forces have been cutting into North Vietnam's pool of able-bodied young men. From 1965 through the first half of 1969, North Vietnam increased its original armed forces of 300,000 by 230,000-255,000 men and infiltrated to the South an estimated 540,000-615,000 men. These figures suggest that close to one million men were mobilized by the armed forces during this period.

18. A precise manpower balance is impossible to construct because of the lack of reliable demographic data on North Vietnam and uncertainty about the number of males physically fit. Nonetheless, we estimate that close to 200,000 North Vietnamese males reach 17 each year, that some 130,000 of these would be physically fit for military service, and that the total number of physically fit males remaining in the 17-35 age group is something less than one million.

19. The men in this pool are variously employed in the agriculture, industry, and services sectors of the economy, or are students. No very precise calculation of the numbers of men that could be drawn from these civilian activities for military service is possible. So long as foreign aid is available to replace losses in material production, military exemptions could be limited primarily to those with special skills in administrative, distributional, transport, and war support activities. In addition, a few men may be excluded from military service for political reasons, including some Catholics, "rightists," and ethnic minorities.

20. There are other indications that North Vietnam is not yet at the bottom of its manpower barrel. During the bombing program, North Vietnam was able to mobilize a considerable civilian labor force to repair bomb damage and, with the help of Chinese troops, to expand its transportation network. With the cessation of the bombing and the improvements in the transportation system, the total demands on the civilian labor force have slackened considerably. Moreover, analysis of North Vietnamese prisoners indicates that North Vietnam has not yet taken significant numbers of draftees from outside the primary draft age group of 18 to 30.

21. However, the mere existence of manpower in a given age group is not the sole determinant of Hanoi's willingness or ability to supply troops to South Vietnam. A continuing drawdown of manpower reserves over the long-term imposes social and economic strains on any society that cannot be ignored. Such social and economic strains could place a more relevant ceiling on the number of men Hanoi could send south than the absolute numbers involved.

22. *North Vietnamese Armed Forces.* The North Vietnamese Armed Forces continued to expand during 1968 and are estimated to total 530,000 to 555,000 as of 31 March 1969.

TABLE II

ESTIMATED NORTH VIETNAMESE ARMED FORCES
(As of 31 March 1969)

SUMMARY

Army	500,000–525,000
Air Force	10,000
Navy	2,500
Armed Public Security Forces	17,500
TOTAL ARMED FORCES	530,000–555,000
Breakdown	
Out-of-Country	
South Vietnam[a]	145,000–160,000
Laos	60,000– 70,000
Total	205,000–230,000
In-Country[b]	
Total	325,000

[a] In addition to those troops deployed in South Vietnam, this figure includes two divisions and other forces in adjacent areas of Laos, Cambodia, and North Vietnam, and an estimated 25,000 NVA fillers in Viet Cong Main and Local Force units.

[b] In-country North Vietnamese forces include the following major units: 6 infantry divisions, 1 artillery division, 1 anti-aircraft artillery division, 3 training divisions, 1 infantry brigade, 6 independent infantry regiments, and 2 armored regiments. These combat elements total some 105,000 men. The remaining 220,000 are in training, air defense, engineer, transportation, administration and other support units including personnel assigned to the High Command.

23. *Military Training in the North.* From 1965 to 1969, demands on North Vietnam's training capability grew as increasing numbers of men were recruited, trained, and infiltrated to South Vietnam. From prisoners and other evidence, we know that Hanoi's regular training establishment now consists of three training divisions plus one training group, with an estimated capacity to train a total of 25,000 recruits in one three-month training cycle, or 100,000 recruits per year. Beyond this, we also know that subordinate units of regular line divisions and independent regiments in North Vietnam are used to perform a training mission. We estimate that the eight infantry and one artillery divisions could train about 60,000 recruits per year using one regiment per division, or 120,000 using two. Similarly, the eight independent regiments could turn out an additional 18,000 recruits per year using one battalion per regiment for training or 36,000 using two. On this basis, we estimate that the North Vietnamese have the capability to train a total of about 180,000 to 250,000 men annually and the upper limit of this range could be raised by shortening the training cycle.

24. In 1968, the infiltration of unprecedented numbers of troops from the North indicates that record numbers of North Vietnamese were trained during that year. A sample of NVA prisoners captured in South Vietnam indicates that about four-fifths of those who were drafted in 1967 and earlier years had received at least three or four months of basic training, while three-fourths of those inducted in 1968 had less than three months. Thus it appears that a reduced training cycle and somewhat less than two-thirds of the line units were used to train the record number of troops trained in 1968. The North Vietnamese have apparently attempted to compensate for the shortened training cycle to some extent by expanding pre-induction militia training for 17-year olds.

25. We believe that the level of training carried out in 1968 represents a near maximum effort, and that it could probably not be sustained without a deteriorating effect on both the caliber of training cadre and the quality of the training received by the infiltrees. This effort, for example, apparently spread thin the available high-caliber training personnel, and this, together with a shorter training cycle, probably contributed to the observed decline in Communist combat performance in the South in recent months.

26. *Infiltration.* Since 1959 the North Vietnamese have dispatched well over half a million men to South Vietnam and adjacent areas. We estimate that about 250,000 and possibly as many as 300,000[3] arrived in 1968. Based on inputs into

[3] Vice Adm. Vernon L. Lowrance, Acting Director, Defense Intelligence Agency; Major Gen. Joseph A. McChristian, Assistant Chief of Staff for Intelligence, Department of the Army; Rear Adm. Frederick J. Harlfinger, II, Assistant Chief of Naval Operations (Intelligence), Department of the Navy; and Major Gen. Jammie M. Philpott, Assistant Chief of Staff, Intelligence, USAF, believe that the best single estimate of infiltration into South Vietnam during 1968 is 250,000. If anything, this figure may be high. Experience has shown that as new information is obtained, the total figure for 1968 has decreased. It is, therefore, considered unlikely that the estimate will go above 250,000.

the system through March 1969, 85,000-100,000 probably arrived during the first half of this year.

27. The picture for additional arrivals in South Vietnam for the remainder of the year is now in doubt. Analysis of available intelligence indicates that since the end of March there has been a sharp reduction in the numbers of new troops put into the infiltration system in North Vietnam.
several groups entering the pipeline in May, and in July

southward
movements of some 11,000 personnel plus five groups of undetermined size over the next few months. We cannot determine the departure dates from North Vietnam for these personnel.

28. In any event, and even if replacement inputs pick up substantially in coming weeks, it appears that there will be a substantial reduction in the numbers of replacements arriving in South Vietnam during the next few months. This reduction might not have a noticeable impact on Communist capabilities until later in the summer since the troops which have already arrived in South Vietnam, those projected to arrive by July, and those recruited in South Vietnam, should largely offset Communist losses during the first half of the year.

29. The rate of infiltration has always been erratic, with no clear pattern apparent, and the totals varying considerably from month to month. While weather and other seasonal factors have occasionally disrupted infiltration, they have never been important in limiting it, or even controlling it in the sense of establishing any seasonal patterns. There are considerable logistic problems in feeding and caring for the troops enroute, but on the basis of actual numbers of troops infiltrated we can only conclude that the Communists have steadily expanded this capability. There is some attrition among troops during infiltration because of sickness, desertions, and hostile actions. The overall loss rate for infiltrators from all causes is estimated at 10 to 15 percent.

30. North Vietnam probably has the capability to sustain even the relatively high 1968 level of infiltration at least through the end of 1970. There is, as explained earlier, sufficent manpower available in North Vietnam. Provision of adequate training for such a large number of recruits over such a prolonged period would be something of a strain, but it probably could be managed. The present logistical facilities along the infiltration pipeline are probably sufficient to support such levels of infiltration.

31. *Availability of Forces for a Major Reinforcement Effort.* If North Vietnam decided to make a maximum effort rapidly to reinforce Communist troops in South Vietnam, it could conceivably deploy eight to nine division equivalents—the bulk of its combat forces in Laos and North Vietnam—to the DMZ area within 90 days. There are, however, a number of considerations militating against such an effort. By removing troops which play an important role in recruit train-

ing, Hanoi would impair its capabilities to provide a continuing flow of replacements. Such a removal would also weaken North Vietnam's internal security and home defenses, probably to an extent not acceptable to Hanoi. In this connection, Hanoi might fear that such a major reinforcement would precipitate renewed bombing of the North. Hanoi could remove its forces from Laos for deployment in South Vietnam, but this would weaken severely the military position of the Pathet Lao. Given these limitations, and depending on Hanoi's view of the risks and opportunities, it might be willing at some point to extract an additional three or four divisions (some 30,000-40,000 men) from its existing forces in North Vietnam and Laos for reinforcement of the South.

III. LOGISTICS

32. To supply their forces in the South at the relatively high level of combat which has developed, the Communists have had to create an extensive and elaborate logistical network within South Vietnam, supported from North Vietnam, Laos, and Cambodia. In addition, they have had to depend increasingly upon military and other supplies received from the USSR, China, and other Communist countries.

A. Logistical Requirements of Communist Forces in South Vietnam and Adjacent Areas

33. In their own planning the Communists almost certainly establish supply requirements based upon the anticipated levels of combat and upon forecasts of losses to allied action. We have insufficient information regarding detailed Communist military planning or their expectations of losses to estimate these requirements, but the normal tendency would be for the planners in the field to cover all contingencies. Moreover, the pattern of actual supply movements in support of the Communist effort in South Vietnam fluctuates considerably. The seasonal weather pattern, changing levels of combat, the requirement to maintain some contingency stockpiles, and the vulnerabilities of the two major external logistical systems all contribute to these fluctuations in traffic. As the external requirement for arms and ammunition has grown since 1965, so has the need for stockpiles. Thus, leaving aside the question of consumption and losses in Laos or elsewhere in the external system, the total tonnages actually moved for use in South Vietnam almost certainly are somewhat greater than would be indicated by the average daily requirements shown in Table III.

34. At this point, however, we are concerned with estimating the actual quantities of supplies needed to sustain military operations at the average levels of the past year or so. For purposes of making this estimate we define these requirements as the total of supplies actually consumed or expended plus losses due to capture or destruction by allied forces. Despite the uncertainties involved in estimating these tonnages, there is no doubt that the Communist logistical burden has increased considerably. Our estimate of their daily consumption

requirements in South Vietnam is now about 276 tons per day,[4] about 25 percent more than estimated requirements in late 1967. About 75 tons of this daily requirement comes from outside South Vietnam—an increase of 35 percent. These increases in requirements over late 1967 are due to the higher rate of combat, to a larger Communist force structure in South Vietnam, and to the equipping of nearly all Communist forces with newer and heavier weapons.

35. *Losses.* The quantities of Communist supplies captured or destroyed by allied ground action have also increased since late 1967. For the past six months or so, these losses have been averaging 40 tons per day, including an estimated 10 tons of arms and ammunition received from external sources. Communist supply losses from allied air operations in South Vietnam are much more difficult to estimate, but they clearly constitute another significant burden on the Communist logistical system which further increases the volume of needed supplies from out-of-country sources. Among the supply categories, the loss of ammunition is the most serious problem for the Communists; overall ammunition losses may total more than three times the current daily Communist consumption requirement. Considering both losses and consumption requirements then, it appears that over the past two years total supplies needed for NVA and Viet Cong regular and administrative support forces in South Vietnam have increased by over 50 percent, while the proportion which must be procured from external sources has almost doubled.

---

[4] See Table III.

TABLE III

ESTIMATED AVERAGE DAILY REQUIREMENTS FOR NVA AND VC REGULAR AND ADMINISTRATIVE SUPPORT FORCES IN SOUTH VIETNAM[a]
(November 1968-April 1969)

	Short Tons Per Day					
	Daily Consumption		Daily Losses		Total Requirements	
Class	Total	External	Total	External	Total	External
I (Food)	235	60	37	2	272	62
II and IV (Weapons and Equipment)	35	10	3	3	38	13
III (POL)	Negl.	Negl.	Negl.	Negl.	Negl.	Negl.
V (Ammunition)	6[b]	5	21	20	27	25[c]
TOTAL	276	75	61	25	337	100

[a] This table does not include the requirements for those forces deployed in and immediately above the DMZ.

[b] For all of 1968, the total consumption of Class V was about 11 tons per day of which about 10 tons came from external sources. The lower requirement in the table reflects the decline in ammunition expenditures that occurred in the last half of 1968 compared to the higher expenditures of the Tet, May, and August 1968 offensives.

[c] One-third of the weight of the external requirement represents a packaging factor; two-thirds of the weight is actual ammunition.

CAMBODIA and SOUTH VIETNAM
MAJOR COMMUNIST BORDER BASE AREAS
Military region boundary
Major Communist border base area
Province boundary
Railroad
Road
Trail
Route number
Canal
Statute Miles
Kilometers
THAILAND
LAOS
CAMBODIA
SOUTH VIETNAM
PHNOM PENH
SAIGON
KONTUM
PLEIKU
DARLAC
QUANG DUC
PHUOC LONG
BINH LONG
TAY NINH
HAU NGHIA
GIA DINH
LONG AN
KIEN PHONG
CHAU DOC
KIEN GIANG
AN XUYEN
CON SON
(Administered from Saigon)
BOUNDARY REPRESENTATION IS NOT NECESSARILY AUTHORITATIVE
76481 6-69 CIA
CONFIDENTIAL

(Continued...)

CONFIDENTIAL

Laos Panhandle-Communist Roadnet Development

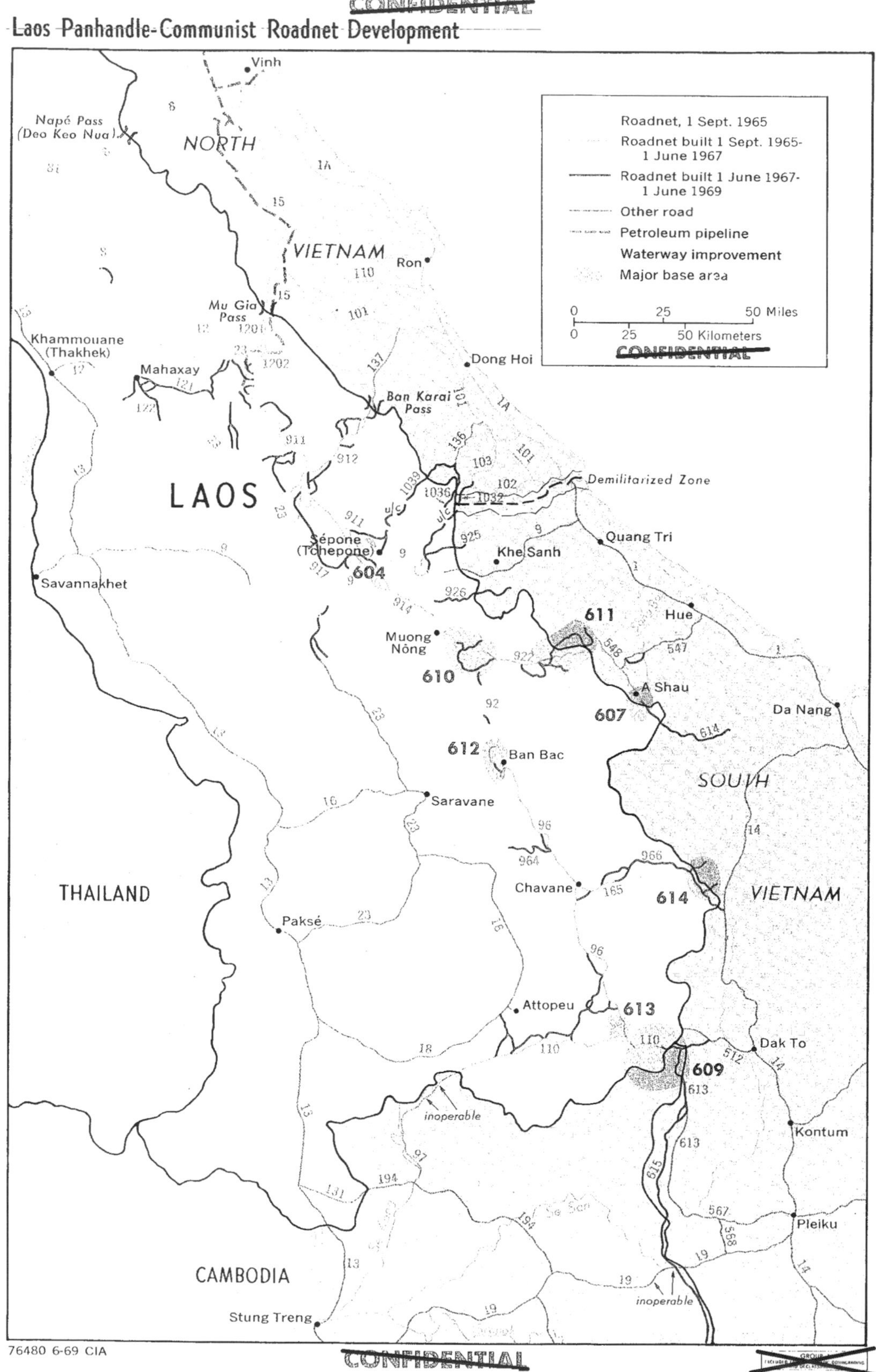

76480 6-69 CIA

CONFIDENTIAL

B. The Logistical System

30. The logistical system consists of a well organized structure within South Vietnam which has both procurement and distribution functions, procurement-transportation arrangements in Cambodia, and supply lines from North Vietnam extending through the DMZ and Laos into South Vietnam.

37. Communist forces in the field do not operate with a "logistics tail"; they depend on prepositioned stocks of food, ammunition, and other necessary supplies. Thus, the entire object of the system is to get supplies to the right places in forward areas, in the necessary quantities, and in advance of planned operations. Given the time-consuming process of moving supplies, it is obvious that requirements must be estimated and submitted well in advance, probably in six-month cycles geared to the seasonal campaigns in South Vietnam (e.g., "winter-spring campaign"). It is also obvious that if the prepositioned stocks are captured, destroyed or otherwise denied, the Communists have to reduce the intensity of operations, or shorten, postpone or cancel them.

38. The nature of the system also places a premium on maintaining major supply stocks reasonably close to the combat zone. The Communists have attempted to do this by establishing numerous base areas in relatively secure districts in South Vietnam, in the sanctuary offered by the Cambodian border region, and in Laos convenient to the exit routes into South Vietnam. These base areas serve other functions; they contain hospitals, troop training facilities, rest areas for combat forces, way stations for infiltrating troops, and secure camps for high-echelon command and administrative authorities.

39. As indicated earlier, a large proportion of the total Communist supply requirement is met from sources within South Vietnam. Much of the food, clothing, and POL used in South Vietnam is purchased, confiscated, or produced by the Communist apparatus in the South. But important quantities of rice come from Cambodia and nearly all arms and ammunition come from sources external to South Vietnam.

C. North Vietnam: The Rear Supply Base

40. Domestic economic conditions do not greatly affect North Vietnam's capabilities to support the war in the South. The principal material contributions of the North Vietnamese to the war have been manpower and the maintenance of a transport system capable of moving men and imported war materiel to the combat zones. The lost domestic output of North Vietnam's rather primitive economy has been compensated for by increasing imports of a wide variety of non-military goods, particularly food. In addition to heavy imports of foodstuffs, North Vietnam receives from the Soviet Union, Communist China, and Eastern Europe virtually all of its requirements for petroleum, machinery, and construction materials. The bulk of the military equipment used by the Communists in both North and South Vietnam is, of course, also imported from the Communist countries. The value of military aid from other Communist countries is estimated

at about $400 million in 1968, down from about $600 million in 1967. The decline in military imports in 1968 probably reflects reduced needs for air defense weapons, particularly ammunition and surface-to-air missiles, since the US bombing cutbacks of 31 March and 31 October 1968. So long as external sources continue to supply North Vietnam's basic domestic requirements and the resources necessary to maintain the flow of war materiel to the South, the deteriorated economy will probably have little effect on the regime's capability to wage war.

41. Since the bombing halt, North Vietnam has restored the essential parts of its transportation system to normal use, and has stepped up the expansion and improvement of selected facilities. The important rail lines have been fully repaired and construction has begun on some new rail segments. Additional berthing facilities and other improvements are being made in the port of Haiphong. The major LOCs running south from Hanoi/Haiphong to the DMZ and the Laos border were quickly restored after the bombing halt, and the three main roads to Laos through the Nape, Mu Gia, and Ban Karai passes have been improved. In addition, the North Vietnamese have been constructing a new supply corridor—consisting of three roads—into Laos along the western edge of the DMZ, which when completed, will provide a shorter and much less exposed means of moving supplies into Laos.

42. These developments now provide Hanoi with the capability to move supplies rapidly toward Laos and the DMZ. Indeed, since the bombing halt, the Communists have undertaken a major supply movement into the southern panhandle of North Vietnam using available rail lines, truck routes, waterways and coastal shipping. This has produced a substantial military supply buildup in the southern panhandle of North Vietnam some of which is visible in open storage. While we have not attempted to quantify this buildup or the overall stockpile level in North Vietnam with any precision, we are confident that the stocks available are more than adequate to support the war in South Vietnam without further imports into North Vietnam for several months.

D. The Laos Panhandle

43. *Communist Forces Involved in Logistic Movements Through Laos.* The responsibility for the establishment, operation, maintenance and protection of Communist infiltration and supply routes in Laos rests with the NVA 559th Transportation Group, headquartered near Tchepone. It is organized into a number of "Binh Trams"—i.e., military way stations—which are assigned specific areas of responsibility and are located along major LOCs extending at least as far south as the Cambodian frontier. They have organic ground security and air defense forces, and the larger stations have engineer forces, civilian laborers, and Assault Youth available to effect road repairs and construction.

44. We estimate that the strength of the NVA 559th Transportation Group, including transportation, engineer, AAA, commo-liaison and infantry elements, is between 25,000-40,000.[5] Normally some of these forces return to North Vietnam

[5] This figure includes 10,000 who may be deployed to South Vietnam at any given time and are also carried in the order of battle for South Vietnam.

from the Laotian Panhandle during the rainy season; such a movement is currently underway.

45. *Road Construction.* Since the North Vietnamese started to build roads on a large scale in the Laos Panhandle in 1965, they have followed a construction schedule influenced primarily by weather. In the dry season (November to June) they construct new roads and improve existing ones; in the rainy season when the roads deteriorate, new construction stops and work is concentrated on maintenance of the existing roadnet. Because of the intensified bombing during the past dry season, the Communists had to devote greater efforts to the repair of existing roads and to the construction of new bypasses. These new bypasses, together with other new road construction, added about 300 miles to the road network in the Laotian Panhandle. Most of this year's work has been devoted to the three new cross-border roads from North Vietnam near the DMZ, and to bypasses around heavily-bombed chokepoints.[6]

TABLE IV

COMMUNIST ROAD CONSTRUCTION IN THE LAO PANHANDLE

Period	Miles constructed
In existence prior to June 1965	300
September 1965-June 1966	363
September 1966-June 1967	118
September 1967-June 1968	280
September 1968-June 1969 (estimated)	300

46. In addition to their road construction and improvement activities, the Communists have constructed a petroleum pipeline and undertaken waterway improvements including dredging. The petroleum pipeline—first noted in July 1968—now extends from the Vinh area in North Vietnam through the Mu Gia pass southward some 30 miles into Laos.[7] The pipeline is undoubtedly intended to lighten the truck traffic on the LOC net, to free truck resources for other cargo, and to aid in better distribution of fuel to the upper panhandle region. The pipeline does not extend the length of the North Vietnam-Laos logistic corridor, however, and trucking operations must still be maintained from the pipeline terminus southward. Finally, in attempting to divert aerial attacks from primary targets, the Communists have increased their use of deception techniques such as building dummy roads and water crossings, lures, extensive camouflage and trellising.

47. Thus, the Communists now have in Laos a more complex year-round logistical system with a higher capacity than ever before, even though truck

[6] See centerspread map of Laos Panhandle.

[7] This pipe is four inches in diameter and has a daily capacity of about 1,000 metric tons. The heaviest demand for petroleum in Laos is in the region between the Mu Gia Pass and Tchepone, and along Route 912. If the pipeline is extended beyond its present terminus to meet this demand, it would release additional trucks for other duties.

traffic falls off sharply during the rainy season. The many new bypasses around interdiction points and other troublespots will assist in diversifying traffic patterns to counter air interdiction efforts. The new cross-border roads just north of the DMZ will offer more options for introducing supplies into the Laotian Panhandle and could become a main route for truck traffic during the forthcoming monsoon season because they have less mileage vulnerable to the weather and air attack than the routes through more northerly passes.

48. *Logistical Movement.*

49. The variance in the information reported from the sources available makes it difficult to make accurate determinations on the quantity of supplies moved into Laos over the dry season.

There are other complicating factors. The average truck load appears to have increased from three to almost four tons, but we are not sure when this change took place. On balance, we believe that the volume of supplies actually moved into Laos from North Vietnam from November 1968 through April 1969 was at least as much as during the same period in the preceding year, and probably slightly higher.

and extrapolating, which provides a lower estimate than other sources, we calculate that about 220 [8] tons per day of supplies moved into the Laos Panhandle during the period as compared with 210 tons per day during the same period last year. This does not include any figure for POL tonnages moving through the pipeline.

50. *Losses from Air Attack.* The air interdiction effort in Laos has been very costly to the Communists. Over the past six months trucks and supplies have been destroyed at a high rate. More manpower has been necessary to construct new roads, to repair damaged roads and trucks, and to man anti-aircraft posi-

[8] A USAF study indicates that this total may be 290 tons per day.

tions. It is difficult to estimate the amount of goods lost in Laos by bombing because of the inherent possibility of error in pilot reports of trucks destroyed and damaged, and assessments of the amounts lost in secondary explosions, which are the main sources of these estimates. Nevertheless, given these caveats and potential for error, we estimate that during the 1968-1969 dry season, enemy supplies lost as a result of trucks effectively destroyed by bombing probably totaled about 15 percent of the tonnages of supplies entering Laos from North Vietnam during the period; secondary explosions and fires resulted in additional losses.

51. *Tonnages Available for South Vietnam.* We estimate that Communist consumption requirements for their forces in the Laos Panhandle together with losses there total about 130 tons per day. Using the estimate of 220 tons per day entering Laos, this leaves a total of about 90 tons per day for stockpiling or movement to South Vietnam. It is estimated that Communist forces in South Vietnam require only 50 tons a day of supplies from North Vietnam via the Laotian Panhandle.[9] If pilot sightings are used as a basis for estimating the flow, the net amount available for onward movement to Communist forces in South Vietnam or stockpiling in Laos would be even greater. In sum, all the available evidence indicates that over the past year the Communists have moved more than enough supplies through Laos to the South Vietnamese border to cover our estimate of their requirements in South Vietnam that are satisfied from the North.[10]

E. Cambodia

52. Cambodia has long been an important source of supplies for the Viet Cong. The Communists obtain some of their medical supplies, chemicals useful in the manufacture of explosives, and communications equipment there, but most of the non-military shipments consist of Cambodian rice. We believe that Cambodian sources supply as much as 15 percent of the daily food requirement of Communist forces in South Vietnam. Cambodian rice is particularly important to

[9] The estimate of total external requirements of Communist forces in South Vietnam is about 100 tons per day (see Table III, page 13). Roughly, it is estimated that some 15 tons of these external requirements come directly across the DMZ, another 35 tons (mainly food) from Cambodian sources, and the remaining 50 tons via Laos.

[10] Major Gen. Jammie M. Philpott, Assistant Chief of Staff, Intelligence, USAF, dissents from the figures quoted in, and the judgment at the end of, this paragraph. While it is useful to tabulate the enemy's estimated consumption and losses in order to gain a better understanding of his logistic system, as was done in Table III, page 13, his actual requirements, of necessity, must be related directly to his intentions and his capabilities. USAF analysis indicates that during the November 1968-April 1969 period, after internal consumption and losses from bombing, the net logistic tonnage available for onward movement to South Vietnam was approximately 60 tons per day. This amount represents a reduction of about 20 tons per day from stockpiles that existed in Laos prior to November 1968. The foregoing, when viewed in conjunction with his supply losses within South Vietnam indicates that the enemy has experienced a logistics shortfall that should result in a reduced level of enemy activities during the last half of 1969.

Communist troops in the rice-deficit highlands of II Corps and northern III Corps, where it probably constitutes their main food source. Most of the food is shipped directly across the Cambodian border; some of it is moved up the Se Kong River to Communist forces located in Laos or in adjacent parts of Vietnam. The Cambodian Government controls the trade in foodstuffs for profit and in order to maintain some political leverage. Recent evidence, for example, indicates that the Cambodians temporarily suspended major shipments to the Communists while working out new arrangements governing the use of Cambodian territory by Communist forces.

53. We have also been convinced for some time, that some of the arms and ammunition arriving in Sihanoukville from Communist China are diverted to the Communists in the III and IV Corps regions of South Vietnam.
have provided a reasonably detailed and consistent picture of an organization within the Cambodian Army,
which controls these arms shipments to the Communists, as well as deliveries of food and other supplies.
two types of contracts exist between Cambodian authorities and the Viet Cong. The first involves the shipment of non-military goods to the Communists; the other concluded between FARK and VC/NVA representatives, governs the shipment of arms and munitions.

54. We have been less successful in obtaining reliable and consistent evidence on the actual tonnages involved in these arms shipments. We lack firm and reliable information on the actual tonnages of arms and ammunition off-loaded at Sihanoukville, and there is considerable doubt over what proportion represents the legitimate military requirements of the Cambodian armed forces.

55. Nonetheless, recent evidence strengthens the case for something more than minor diversions from Cambodian stocks.

We still cannot quantify the flow, but recent evidence suggests that the tonnages involved over the past year or so have constituted an important, and at times a substantial proportion of Communist requirements in III and IV Corps.

56. Perhaps the major limitation on Communist use of the Cambodian route for movement of arms and ammunition—as well as reliance on Cambodian rice—is the dependence on Cambodian co-operation. The entire system is vulnerable

to sudden termination.

Over the past few months there have been numerous instances of Cambodian-initiated military clashes with Vietnamese Communist forces on Cambodian territory. The recent embargo appeared to involve arms and ammunition as well as food It almost certainly was designed to force the Communists to reduce the presence of their troops on Cambodian soil and stop the support they are alleged to give local dissidents. But whatever the reason for this recent Cambodian move it serves to illustrate the limits on the reliability of the Cambodian portion of the Communist logistical system.

57. As for the logistical route leading southward from the Laos Panhandle, we have difficulty estimating the extent of its use over the past year or so. Southbound traffic levels in the vicinity of the tri-border region in 1967 and 1968 suggest that Communist requirements for southern II and all of III Corps could have been met via the Lao Panhandle logistical route. But the direct evidence available on the actual movement of arms and ammunition moved southward from the tri-border area towards III Corps is extremely limited. Nevertheless, there is a long-established and extensive trail network there which is continuously being improved, and Communist forces are present along its entire length. Moreover, personnel are infiltrated via this route. For these reasons, and in view of the small tonnages involved, we believe this trail system is more than adequate to handle all the estimated arms and ammunition requirements of Communist forces in southern II Corps and all of III and IV Corps.

58. In sum, we believe that Communist forces in III Corps now obtain arms from both the Laotian route and the Sihanoukville route. The evidence remains insufficient to prove that one or the other route presently carries the bulk of the required arms and ammunition to IV, III and southern II Corps, although there is little doubt that the importance of the Cambodian route has grown significantly over the past two years or so. Whatever the past or present pattern of movement, however, we believe that Hanoi considers the Laotian route as its most important channel since it is firmly under Communist control, has the necessary capacity, and is not subject to the political vagaries We believe the Communists will continue to defend and improve the Laotian route.

F. Seaborne Infiltration

59. We believe that the Communists no longer rely to any important degree on sea infiltration as a means of obtaining arms from abroad. The last detected attempt at sea infiltration by a steel-hulled trawler was in March 1968. It is highly unlikely that such large craft can evade US patrols and we doubt that attempts to do so are now being made. However, it is possible that small craft

do bring in some supplies from North Vietnam and Cambodia. The principal Communist use of the sea routes is for the local movement of supplies along the coast in small wooden craft within South Vietnam.

G. Principal Supply Problems and Prospects

60. It is evident that the Communist logistic system, through internal procurement in South Vietnam, overland shipments from North Vietnam, and deals with the Cambodian Government, has functioned adequately over the past two years to make supplies available sufficient to sustain a tempo of combat much higher than that prior to mid-1967. The system is well developed and continues to deliver more than the minimum supplies we estimate are necessary to sustain Communist forces in combat at the average levels of the past year.

61. We nevertheless believe that the system has begun to feel the strain of the more intensive tempo of the war. The portion within Laos is encountering many difficulties and strains because of air interdiction. Difficulties in positioning and securing supplies within the actual combat zones in South Vietnam, particularly those far removed from Communist bases, have grown appreciably. Denial of cached supplies, as a result of allied ground operations and allied artillery and air power, frequently upset plans for particular military operations and perhaps in some instances caused the Communist to alter specific campaign objectives and tactics. These difficulties are among the several factors which limited the overall level and intensity of Communist military pressures during 1968 to levels which we believe were below those intended. Logistic problems have also had some influence upon Communist strategy thus far in 1969. The present reduced intensity of combat, however, is not one that imposes severe strains on the Communist logistics system. Thus, so long as Hanoi continues to receive the necessary external supplies, the Communists should be able to provide their forces with the necessary support to continue the war at the average levels of the past 12 months.

IV. OTHER FACTORS AFFECTING COMMUNIST CAPABILITIES

62. *New Weapons.* In certain respects Communist forces in South Vietnam have managed to improve their capabilities. They have re-equipped their forces, including a portion of the guerrillas, with new Chinese Communist and Soviet weapons, including AK-47 automatic rifles, and various caliber mortars, rockets, and recoilless rifles. This has improved the assault capabilities of Communist infantry and enhanced their street fighting and sapper capabilities as well. The new weapons have also increased the Communists' defensive capabilities and, in general, the confidence of their lower level troops. Perhaps most important, these developments have enhanced their capability for standoff attacks. Finally, while the equipping of Communist forces with heavier weapons has increased tonnage requirements from external sources, the standardization of weapons simplifies their logistics.

63. *Intelligence Capabilities.* Communist military capabilities in South Vietnam are considerably enhanced by good tactical and strategic intelligence information. The quality and timeliness of their intelligence is due partly to the nature of the war; there is no front line and Communist sympathizers exist throughout South Vietnamese society. In addition, however, the Communists have a highly developed and professional intelligence effort

64. *The NVA Presence.* The impact of the increased proportion of North Vietnamese troops and units in South Vietnam in recent years is more difficult to assess. This trend may have caused some resentment in Viet Cong units, though there is no evidence that friction has reached serious proportions. Moreover, the North Vietnamese are far less familiar with the terrain. But they are better trained and equipped, and more tightly disciplined than southern recruits of recent years. On balance, the increased NVA presence has probably enhanced Communist capabilities.

65. *Morale.* It is evident from captured documents, ralliers, and prisoners that morale problems among Communist forces in South Vietnam are increasing. The main reasons appear to be the diminishing expectation of clear-cut victory, and the unwillingness to face increasing physical hardships and allied firepower, especially with the Paris talks raising hopes of an early peace. The impact of these concerns is reflected to some extent in the large number of Communists who have rallied under the Chieu Hoi program over the past year and the evidence of increased desertions. Moreover, captured documents and other evidence indicate that Communist leaders are increasingly concerned about troop morale.

66. Any conclusions as to the impact of these morale problems on Communist military capabilities must be tempered by the knowledge that similar evidence of serious morale problems has been available throughout the war, even in late 1967 just prior to the Tet offensive. Moreover, there have been no large-unit defections. Nor are there many medium- or high-level political or military cadre among the ralliers. It is also evident that Communist forces still show considerable aggressiveness and initiative on the battlefield.

67. Communist capabilities are also being adversely affected by signs of increased alienation of the population under Communist control and in contested areas. Disillusionment with the Communist cause, increased Communist demands, and anticipation of an early end to the fighting appear to be the main causative factors. The situation has contributed to increasing migration to areas under GVN control, and greater popular reluctance to co-operate with Communist recruitment and tax collection efforts. However, these trends have existed for some time and their effects have developed in a slow, cumulative manner rather than sharply and suddenly.

68. *Allied Operations.* Allied military activities have imposed major limitations on Communist military operations. The heavy casualties suffered by the Communists in the 1968 Tet and May offensives, when they sent large units against urban centers, undoubtedly contributed to the decision to switch to the more conservative, economy-of-force tactics which have since characterized their offensive operations. Even so, many of these more recent attacks have been blunted by increasingly effective Allied spoiling operations. Allied military action has resulted in the capture and destruction of large quantities of Communist supplies and, along with the GVN's pacification program, has constricted Communist controlled territory and hampered their ability to recruit personnel; it has also limited Communist access to local funds and supplies. In short, Allied forces have not only denied the Communist forces in the field any military progress but have also reduced their overall military capabilities during the past year and a half.

69. *Political/Psychological Factors in the North.* The cohesion and determination of the leadership in Hanoi are among the most important intangibles affecting Communist capabilities. The leadership probably has been strained by increasing opposition to committing more and more of North Vietnam's resources to the war without the clear prospect of early success in the struggle. Debate over the proper extent of involvement by the North has gone on since late 1963 when Hanoi first decided to send regular North Vietnamese troops to the South. We have recently learned, for example, that this debate reached such proportions in the months prior to the 1968 Tet offensive that a number of middle-level officials were arrested.

70. Late last summer, the regime appeared to have reached some new conclusions about the overall effects of its previous policies. These were reflected in a long report by party theoretician Truong Chinh which criticized implicitly the inadequacy of political preparations for the 1968 Tet offensive and expressed deep dissatisfaction with the state of affairs in the North. Not only had the results of Hanoi's efforts in the South failed to match earlier expectations, but the war had adversely affected the all-important "socialist-base" in North Vietnam. Marxist orthodoxy was being eroded, and the country remained dependent on massive doses of foreign aid. Chinh's report left no doubt that the regime was bent on correcting these internal problems and that it was reluctant to to make them worse by launching more large-scale offensives in the South, until adequate political and other preparations had been made.

71. Since last autumn, the leadership has been making a major effort to tidy up affairs in North Vietnam and to counter increasing war-weariness. Its appeals to youth, party cadre, and the military, in particular, reflect growing concern with the long-term corrosive effects of the war on these key elements of the population. They also suggest that the regime finds it increasingly difficult to obtain full support for its policies and the sacrifices they entail.

72. It is possible that all factions in Hanoi now agree that the US will to continue the struggle is declining rapidly, citing the start of US troop reductions

as the most recent evidence of this. But the evidence available suggests that Hanoi remains quite uncertain regarding US intentions, the implications of Vietnamization, and the probable duration of the military conflict. We believe that recent developments have not removed the grounds for debate in Hanoi; indeed the policies of the new US Administration may have served to sharpen and enlarge the area of debate.

73. These political and psychological considerations restrict Hanoi's ability to exercise the capabilities described in this paper. Their influence should not be overrated; we do not believe that they will necessarily force Hanoi to make early concessions in order to bring the war to an end. We certainly see no evidence, for example, which suggests that problems of security, morale, or indecision will cause any early collapse of the Communist war effort. The Vietnamese Communists have proved quite skillful in coping with such problems in the past and they have devised their current military and diplomatic tactics to take account of these weaknesses.

V. THE OUTLOOK FOR COMMUNIST MILITARY STRATEGY AND TACTICS

74. We believe it is fair to say that Communist military effectiveness on the battlefield has suffered a qualitative decline over the past year. In any prolonged conflict at the current level of GVN/Allied commitment, this decline would almost certainly continue and perhaps at an accelerating pace. While Hanoi is almost certainly concerned about these trends and its heavy casualties, it retains a firm and disciplined control over its people and armed forces, and there is little evidence that the infrastructure in South Vietnam is weakening in its dedication and effort, despite long years of struggle.

75. As indicated above, the Communists appear to have sufficient manpower to absorb casualties and to maintain military pressures at the 1969 levels for at least another year or so. The logistic system is also adequate to sustain such efforts, although its maintenance in Laos will involve considerable difficulties so long as air interdiction continues and, within South Vietnam, logistic problems will continue to influence the overall level and intensity of Communist military operations.

76. Within the present level of effort, there are many variations in tactics open to the Communists; they can concentrate their efforts on US forces and bases, on the ARVN, on the pacification organizations, on urban areas, or on some mix of all these. They can attempt relatively low-level but sustained pressure, or they can mount relatively large-scale attacks interspersed with prolonged periods of regroupment to base areas for rest and refit.

77. The Communists could also opt for a substantial escalation of the conflict for a short period. Some might argue, for example, that later this year, or early in 1970, conditions in South Vietnam and the US will be ripe for a major military effort similar to Tet 1968. But given allied military power and the current state of readiness, such attacks would be extremely costly and they

could not be sustained. Particularly in view of past concern in Hanoi over the indecisive results of heavy investments of northern resources, and its desire to retain a capability for protracted war, we doubt that Hanoi would gamble on a desperation campaign to bring decisive results. Hanoi might be more tempted to increase military pressures some time in the future, however, if it concluded as a result of phased US troop reductions that morale in Saigon and the ARVN was declining and that higher US casualties would accelerate the reduction of US forces. Finally, it might launch a maximum effort with the forces available in South Vietnam, as a prelude to proposing a general cease-fire, and shifting the struggle almost entirely to the political/psychological arena.

78. Hanoi could, of course, decide to reduce military pressures to a substantially lower level. If they do this, the North Vietnamese would be likely concurrently to increase efforts in Paris to extract allied concessions, both in terms of a political settlement and in terms of curbs on allied military activity.

79. A prolonged reduction of military pressure, however, would raise several problems for the Communists in the absence of political progress or an obvious reduction in Allied military pressures. It would probably produce a decline in the US casualty rate, and the Communists might consider that this would ease US domestic pressures for an end to the fighting. Furthermore, the Communists might feel that such a reduction in their military effort would appear as a tacit admission of military weakness, shaking the confidence of their troops and political apparatus in the South, and reinforcing that of the GVN. Finally, the Communists might be concerned that such a course would permit allied operations and programs to erode their political and military base.

80. Even at their present force levels and with their present military effort, the Communists are suffering in the South an erosion of their organization and of their control over the population. Nevertheless, if they see the war continuing well into 1970, it seems likely that Communist strategy will call for them to stay in the field with forces which will enable them to conduct periodic offensives, some of which may be fairly large-scale and costly, and to maintain pressure on the GVN presence in the countryside. In any case, political action and maneuver will probably be intensified within South Vietnam and on the international scene as the Communists continue efforts to undermine the GVN and isolate its leaders from the US.

SNIE 14.3-70

The Outlook from Hanoi: Factors Affecting North Vietnam's Policy on the War in Vietnam

5 February 1970

APPROVED FOR RELEASE
DATE: JAN 2005

SECRET

(b)(3)

SNIE 14.3-70
5 February 1970

SPECIAL NATIONAL INTELLIGENCE ESTIMATE

NUMBER 14.3-70

The Outlook from Hanoi: Factors Affecting North Vietnam's Policy on the War in Vietnam

Submitted by

DIRECTOR OF CENTRAL INTELLIGENCE

Concurred in by the

UNITED STATES INTELLIGENCE BOARD

as indicated overleaf

5 February 1970

Authenticated:

James S. Lay, Jr.
EXECUTIVE SECRETARY, USIB

NOTE: This is the Estimate. No further version will be published.

Copy No. 20

SECRET

SECRET

C E N T R A L   I N T E L L I G E N C E   A G E N C Y

5 February 1970

SUBJECT: SNIE 14.3-70: THE OUTLOOK FROM HANOI: FACTORS AFFECTING NORTH VIETNAM'S POLICY ON THE WAR IN VIETNAM

THE PROBLEM

To assess the factors affecting Hanoi's outlook on the war in Vietnam and to estimate its probable course of action during 1970.

CONCLUSIONS

A. Hanoi's primary aims are to develop North Vietnam along "socialist" lines and to extend its control over South Vietnam. Currently, its leaders seem to believe that the first of these goals has been scanted and must be given greater attention. They also believe that the US presence in Vietnam is the major obstacle to the achievement of their objectives.

B. Hanoi still considers that it has the will and basic strengths to prevail. But it also plainly realizes that its position in the

GROUP 1
Excluded from automatic downgrading and declassification

SECRET

South has declined. In particular, it is apprehensive concerning Vietnamization; it fears that the longer the program goes on without effective challenge, the greater the likelihood that the GVN can develop the capability to hold its own without a substantial US military presence.

C. In this state of affairs, Hanoi has essentially three options. The first, to undertake an all-out military effort, would involve heavier losses and greater risks than Hanoi seems willing to contemplate. Moreover, for the next six months at least, the Communists might calculate that such action would slow the US departure rather than hasten it. In time, however, as further US forces depart and as Hanoi has more time to repair existing deficiencies, it might be tempted to seek quick and decisive results in new large offensives.

D. The second and, in our view, the likeliest course for the Communists through 1970 is to pursue a prolonged war much along present lines. Even with this approach, they will wish to inflict setbacks to Vietnamization and pacification, to impose casualties on US troops, and to keep pressure on the South Vietnamese Armed Forces (RVNAF), including possible occasional major tests. Thus, there could be fairly sharp fighting later this spring or thereafter which might produce sizable US and RVNAF losses. The problem with this course from Hanoi's point of view is that it still involves relatively high casualties, prolongs the strains of the war in North Vietnam and on the weakened Communist apparatus in the South, and offers no certain hope of a decisive success in the foreseeable future.

E. The third option, to negotiate an arrangement which would speed US withdrawal, has -- in the past at least -- seemed to the Communists to have more risks than advantages. Hanoi probably fears that any political formula that could win US withdrawal would also undermine the overall Communist position in the South. But given the uncertain prospects in South Vietnam and the current Communist priority on getting US forces out, Hanoi may see some utility in probing the possibility of some arrangement which it calculates would hasten US withdrawal or fix a timetable for such withdrawal. In this process, any concessions that the Communists might make would almost certainly be limited and not aimed at an overall negotiated settlement.

DISCUSSION

1. Hanoi's aims are to develop the North along "socialist" lines and to extend its control to the South, which from its point of view is an integral part of its domain.[1/] Despite years of strenuous effort and sacrifice, neither goal seems close to realization.

1/ When we refer to "Hanoi," we mean the Vietnamese Communist Party, which has always regarded itself as national in scope, not as an entity confined to what is referred to as "North Vietnam." From the date of its founding 40 years ago, the prime objective of the Party has always been the acquisition of political control over all of Vietnam and some form of domination over Laos and Cambodia.

~~SECRET~~

I. HANOI'S VIEW OF THE SITUATION IN SOUTH VIETNAM

2. From our perspective, the Communists are in trouble in South Vietnam. Their casualties still exceed their infiltration and local recruitment rates. The quality of their forces is also declining, and the VC forces continue to depend heavily on NVA support. The morale of Communist cadres and soldiers has declined further. Their already troublesome supply problems are complicated by Cambodia's variable attitude toward the movement of Communist materiel across its territory. Large areas of the South Vietnamese countryside are being denied to them, and this reduces their access to manpower and economic resources. These losses have also reduced Communist capabilities to maintain an effective political apparatus and to proselytize and gain political support. Although the people of South Vietnam remain politically apathetic, they seem less disposed to cooperate with the Communists. But these are our views; the question is whether the Communists see their situation in the same way.

3. We believe that to some extent they do. Though Communist statements and documents normally contain lists of shortcomings, there was a more sombre tone following the 1968 Tet offensive. Communist cadres have been roundly excoriated for their shortcomings, particularly in the political field, have been exhorted to do more, and have then been reproached for failing once again. In mid-1969, COSVN Resolution 9 seemed to admit that Communist capabilities had been considerably reduced. It contained the most explicit catalogue of Communist

~~SECRET~~

liabilities yet to appear in a high-level Communist document. This has continued to be a common theme in captured documents and in the testimony of Communist prisoners and ralliers. Finally, in December, General Giap pointed out that the Communists had ignored many of the cardinal precepts of fighting a "people's war," and declared it imperative to repair these faults even if this meant going on the defensive temporarily.

4. In South Vietnam, Hanoi has taken various actions to cope with its difficulties in the military field. In an effort to avoid the heavy casualties associated with large-scale military actions, the Communists have resorted to tactics designed to conserve manpower. They have increasingly relied on small unit, sapper, and shelling actions directed against South Vietnamese territorial security forces and Allied field positions and military installations. They have sent five main force regiments into the Mekong Delta to bolster their eroding position. At the same time, there is a concerted effort to halt the erosion of guerrilla and local forces; indeed, in some areas it appears that NVA main force units are being broken up and assigned to lower echelons.

5. The Communists seem to fear that they have overemphasized military action and neglected the political and subversive base. They have begun a significant restructuring of their apparatus in South Vietnam, apparently designed to enhance its staying power. This restructuring consists of: (a) the movement of cadres into government-held territory, often under the guise of defectors; (b) the transfer of experienced cadres from military to political bureaucracies; and (c)

the tightening up of the party structure by raising standards and conducting purges. The Communists also have stepped up efforts to subvert the South Vietnamese people and military. And, in a significant departure from past practice, many -- perhaps most -- of the operatives are being assigned strategic or long term responsibilities instead of tactical functions. Finally, the Communists are attempting to refurbish and strengthen their mass organizations.

6. Despite Hanoi's obvious concern with its problems, the Communists almost certainly believe that they enjoy some basic strengths and advantages which will ultimately prove to be decisive. They see themselves as the only valid representatives of Vietnamese nationalism; in their eyes, the Saigon regime could not sustain itself if deprived of US support. The recent GVN military and political gains are probably not considered by Hanoi to have been either crippling or irreversible. Hanoi probably believes that its infrastructure is inherently more durable than that of the GVN, although it must be bothered by the degree of political stability achieved in South Vietnam over the past few years and by the fact that the GVN, whatever its efficiency, has now extended its presence over a greater area and a larger number of people than for several years. Militarily, the Communists attach considerable importance to controlling the adjacent Laotian and Cambodian border areas, which they probably believe can continue to serve as base areas and sanctuaries.[2/]

2/ See SNIE 58-70, "The Communist View of the Situation in Laos," dated 5 February 1970, for our estimate of the situation in Laos.

7. Even if US support is withdrawn only gradually, Hanoi almost certainly believes that the GVN can be undermined sufficiently to enable the Communists to move from their rice roots positions to an eventual seizure of power. The Communists count heavily on their abilities in the areas of guerrilla war, terrorism, and political organization and agitation to exploit basic vulnerabilities in the South Vietnamese situation -- vulnerabilities which they think will become more pronounced as time passes. Hanoi must be heartened by President Thieu's failure to rally greater political support, by the GVN's economic difficulties, and by the general war weariness of the people of South Vietnam. Hanoi probably also draws some encouragement from attempts by oppositionist political figures in Saigon to exploit grievances and popular aspirations for peace, and by their increasing boldness in criticizing the Thieu government. None of these vulnerabilities has proved decisive as long as US troops anchored the military effort and shored up the Thieu regime. But with the US now moving out of Vietnam, Hanoi's leaders probably are counting on better opportunities to develop in the future and are bent on trying to be ready to exploit them.

II. HANOI'S VIEW OF US POLICY AND VIETNAMIZATION

A. US Policy

8. Hanoi's assessment of US policy in Vietnam probably has undergone several shifts in the past 18 months. In the latter part of 1968 and early 1969, the Communists seemed to believe there was a good chance

~~SECRET~~

that the US would choose to extract itself from the conflict on the best terms it could get~~, but extract itself in any event~~. In the first months of the Nixon Administration, this belief seemed to be manifested in two major political moves -- the announcement in May 1969 of a "new" Ten-Point Peace Proposal, and the formation in June of a "Provisional Revolutionary Government of South Vietnam." Both seemed to reflect increased interest in pursuing possible US concessions by exploiting the negotiating track.

9. Around mid-year, however, as it became evident to Hanoi that Washington was not ready to settle for merely a "face-saver" in South Vietnam, a prolonged stalemate ensued in Paris. Hanoi came to realize that, barring additional Communist military pressure or political concessions, the US intended to leave only gradually and under conditions in which the GVN and South Vietnamese Armed Forces (RVNAF) would be strengthened sufficiently to meet the Communist threat with minimal US military support -- the program of Vietnamization.

B. Vietnamization

10. Although Hanoi almost certainly still believes that its will to persist over the long haul remains stronger than that of the US, the Communists see themselves, perhaps for the first time, confronted with an allied strategy designed to challenge this fundamental assumption. Hanoi's view, reflected in practically every public and private Communist statement on the subject, is that Vietnamization is the

device through which the US plans to prolong the war, to maintain large forces in Vietnam for an extended period, and to perpetuate the Thieu regime. The Communists may see the remaining US military presence not only as large enough to constitute a formidable obstacle to future Communist military action but also, by virtue of its essential combat support make-up, as being less vulnerable to heavy casualties. Hanoi probably fears that this may substantially reduce antiwar sentiments in the US, thus giving the administration considerably more flexibility in its timetable for total withdrawal and in its general policy and goals in South Vietnam.

11. Hanoi may calculate that the Vietnamization program is inherently fragile and likely to become increasingly so as additional US troops are withdrawn. But Hanoi probably also recognizes that the program may work well enough and long enough to give the GVN a fair chance of holding its own without a substantial US military presence, and that the longer the program remains unchallenged, the greater the danger that both the South Vietnamese populace and the Communist cadres will consider that it is succeeding. For this reason alone, the Communists are likely to seek out opportunities to inflict setbacks, however minor, to the program.

12. Thus far, the Communists have not subjected the RVNAF to major tests. Hanoi probably considers that developments to date provide insufficient evidence of the US timetable for withdrawal or the RVNAF's

ability to fill the gaps left by departing US units. Hanoi may be waiting until more US units have departed, in the expectation that this will provide better opportunities with lesser risks, and that Communist forces will be better prepared to strike. At some point, however, Hanoi will probably feel compelled either to engage the RVNAF seriously, or to face up to the prospect of a considerably prolonged struggle.

13. Hanoi probably views the GVN's pacification effort as an integral and key element in the Vietnamization strategy. During the past year and one-half, the GVN has sharply reduced the population controlled or influenced by the Communists. As a result, Communist access to local manpower and sources of supply is being restricted, the mobility of many Communist units limited, and local cadre exposed and demoralized. Hanoi may well believe that GVN pacification progress is essentially fragile and can be rolled back once US forces are out of the way. However, it may now feel compelled to recognize that further contraction of Communist-controlled areas, or even a prolonged continuation of the current situation, will limit the ability of its forces to confront the RVNAF, to launch major attacks on population centers, or even to wage a prolonged struggle. Propaganda, prisoners, ralliers, and captured documents indicate that Hanoi does realize this danger and plans to devote increasing resources to countering the pacification effort.

~~SECRET~~

III. DOMESTIC NORTH VIETNAMESE FACTORS

A. The Post-Ho Leadership and Policy

14. The death of Ho Chi Minh was a severe loss to the Communist cause. Ho was widely regarded as a nationalist, and he tried to stand above the terrorism and treachery of the Communist resistance in the preindependence period and the subsequent excesses of the Hanoi government. None of his heirs has his charisma; without Ho, the regime losses some of its appeal as the defender of Vietnamese nationalism. Ho's heirs probably understand that they lack his authority and cannot match his ability to extract the extra sacrifices and effort from the cadre and people in the North.

15. It would be surprising if Ho's death has not introduced some uncertainties within the top leadership. Although his disciples have been working together for common goals for nearly four decades, they almost certainly have held differing views on key issues over the years, and it would be most unusual if they were devoid of personal ambitions. Ho's commanding presence did not stifle debate, but he was an umpire whose rulings were accepted, and his authority served to maintain a basic unity in support of agreed policies. In the absence of a recognized leader within the collective, the achievement of this unity may now become more difficult.

~~SECRET~~

16. As yet, no single individual seems to have emerged as the dominant member of the Politburo. A case can be made that either Le Duan, the Party First Secretary, or Truong Chinh, Chairman of the National Assembly Standing Committee, is first among equals. A rather shadowy figure, rarely emerging except on important occasions, Le Duan was ranked first in published listings of the leadership at Ho's funeral, is frequently quoted (along with Ho) in articles and speeches by other Party Leaders, and gave the keynote speech on the 40th anniversary of the Party earlier this month. On the other hand, Truong Chinh has been seen much more frequently in public since Ho's funeral. Indeed, his star has been on the rise again since mid-1968,[3/] when he made a major speech which implicitly scored the lack of preparation, particularly in the political and organizational fields, in prosecuting the war in the South and in attempting to build socialism in the North. There are, moreover, other potential claimants to the number one position, notably Pham Van Dong who was a long-time personal friend of Ho's and is currently ranked third in the Politburo.

17. In any event, we see no indication that the leadership is immobilized or in a state of disarray over policy differences. The shift in Hanoi's line in respect to the war in the South has not been abrupt -- it has evolved over a considerable period. This has probably

---

3/ Truong Chinh was one of the founders of the Vietnamese Communist Party. In 1956, he was made the scapegoat for the regime's ill-fated land reform policies and removed from his post as Secretary General of the Party.

served to allow more time for accommodation and to mute the impact of Ho's death on the leadership

B. Party Authority and Discipline

18. Even before Ho died, Hanoi seemed concerned that Party authority and discipline had declined and that an unhealthy degree of ideological slippage had taken place. In effect, the regime seems to be admitting that the Party has been slack in exercising its role as the "vanguard" and that this has led to a lack of responsiveness to Party directives across the board. To improve the Party apparatus, the regime is relying on exhortations, self-criticism, some reshuffling of personnel, and an increased emphasis on the first principle of Party organization -- ideological purity. In the recent heavy emphasis on the Party's key role in guiding the military effort, there is also a suggestion of a need to improve morale and tighten discipline in the armed services. These problems are not critical enough to threaten the regime's viability, but they do go to the heart of the Communist system and probably add to the urgency with which the regime is directing its efforts to internal affairs.

C. Economic Conditions

19. The economic situation has improved only slightly since the bombing halt. Distribution bottlenecks are common, shortages of consumer goods are endemic, rice substitutes continue to make up a

substantial part of the normal diet, human and material resources are ill-utilized, and import requirements remain high. Many of these problems are a result of the bombing, some are inherent in the bureaucratic and ideological rigidities associated with Communist states in general, and some have been aggravated by bad weather. A brief report on the 1970 economic plan suggests that emphasis will be put on production of food and other consumer goods, but little improvement is likely to result so long as the war continues. North Vietnam has always been a poor country, however, and the current stringencies are not critical, nor are they likely to become so as long as Moscow and Peking continue to provide assistance to offset shortfalls in production.

D. Manpower Strains

20. North Vietnam clearly has felt the manpower pinch caused by its massive infiltration effort from late 1967 to mid-1969. The country has sufficient manpower to maintain essential economic and security functions in North Vietnam and to increase support to the wars in South Vietnam and Laos should it desire to do so. But the quantitative aspect is only part of the story. Hanoi must consider the longer term impact on the strength and vigor of its society of the death or maiming of its men at rates which in both 1968 and 1969 surpassed the annual total of physically fit males reaching draft age. Such sacrifices would probably be acceptable to Hanoi if they achieved an early and decisive result; but they would almost certainly begin to produce profound social and

political consequences if extended over a long period. More immediately, the war has brought substantial dislocations and strain on the population. Reallocations of manpower have resulted in a decline in efficiency and production, and the effort to replace heavy combat losses has produced a deterioration in the quality of the troops and cadres dispatched to South Vietnam. We believe that concern for this situation helped lead Hanoi in 1968 to adopt tactics designed to conserve manpower and in the latter part of 1969 to reduce its infiltration rate.

E. Popular Attitudes

21. The cumulative dislocations of the war seem to have produced a general domestic letdown within North Vietnam. This letdown has in increased as the direct pressures of the war on the population have lessened. With the bombing halts, the advent of negotiations, and probably some popular hope for a settlement, people have tended to relax. Ho's death probably has led to some further decline in morale. In general, the regime's claims of one success after another probably are wearing thin, particularly in face of the enormous number of youths sent South and never seen again and the increasing number of maimed soldiers who have returned to North Vietnam.

22. A decline in discipline has also shown itself in a variety of ways, none of them overly significant by itself, but collectively of some consequence. Cupidity seems to be on the rise, fed by bureaucratic

inefficiencies. There seems to be a general disposition, extending even into the Party and army, to evade some of the regime's regulations. Black marketeering, hooliganism, and similar breaches of law and order may have increased. Military recruitment is apparently running into some trouble, and as a result the regime has resorted to a propaganda campaign to encourage enlistments.

23. Hanoi has manifested its concern by strengthening its internal security apparatus and procedures, and it has dwelt regularly on the need to heighten "revolutionary vigilance" and to uncover "counter-revolutionary plots." Some of this, of course, is the normal use of exaggeration to make a point. But it appears to run somewhat deeper and to represent a definite effort to root out even latent signs of disquietude in every quarter. In some cases, the regime's approach is simply to tighten the screws, but there also are signs of greater efforts to reduce pent up grievances by giving more attention to the welfare of the people. Such measures will probably be sufficient to keep the problem within bounds. But the leadership has major domestic problems which have caused it to give more of its attention to the North than conditions of recent years have permitted.

IV. IMPACT OF THE SINO-SOVIET CONFLICT

24. The excesses of the Cultural Revolution in China and the attendant worsening of relations between Moscow and Peking raised the

spectre in Hanoi of the termination of vital Soviet munitions shipments via China and the possibility of diminished US restraint in prosecuting the war against North Vietnam. But US bombing has stopped, and supplies have continued to arrive -- albeit with occasional delays -- even during the heightened Sino-Soviet border tensions in mid-1969. And Hanoi has been able throughout to maintain a balanced political position between Moscow and Peking.

25. At this juncture, therefore, the North Vietnamese must be reasonably certain that the USSR and China will continue to provide adequate support for both the economy of the North and the war in the South. Moreover, Hanoi probably believes that even under conditions of heightened tensions, both Moscow and Peking would make every effort to continue deliveries.

26. Even in the event of larger scale and more widespread Sino-Soviet border fighting, Hanoi probably would have adequate amounts of most essential military and civilian supplies to support current levels of consumption for several months while the situation could be assessed. If, however, such fighting were to continue for very many weeks, Hanoi would have grave concern about its supply lines. In these circumstances, the North Vietnamese leaders might deem it prudent further to scale down the level of military operations in the South, or even to move toward a cease-fire.

V. OUTLOOK

27. In Hanoi's view, the US presence in South Vietnam is the major obstacle to the achievement of its goals. In attempting to get around this obstacle, Hanoi has three basic options: (a) undertaking another all-out military effort to break US will by inflicting heavy casualties and exposing GVN military weaknesses; (b) prolonging the struggle in the hope that the South Vietnamese leadership cannot keep up the fight as US force levels diminish; and (c) offering sufficient concessions in negotiations to speed the US withdrawal. The Communists can, of course, shift from one military option to the other, and in Hanoi's view, either could lead eventually to more substantive negotiations.

28. At present, Hanoi does not seem willing to pay the price and assume the risks likely to attend an all-out military effort. In addition to the heavy Communist casualties this would involve, Hanoi probably calculates that, for the next six months at least, such action would slow, rather than hasten, US withdrawal and might lead to an escalation of the US military effort. In time, however, as further US forces depart and as Hanoi has more time to repair existing deficiencies, it might be tempted to seek quick and decisive results in new large offensives.

29. Attempting to wear out US resolve through prolonged war is more or less what the Communists are presently doing. This course puts substantially fewer strains on their capabilities, but it still ties

down Communist manpower and resources in what could be an indecisive struggle for an indefinite period. Hanoi might fear that this would further reduce its popular support among South Vietnamese and further erode its general position in the South. Moreover, though this approach complicates on-going GVN and US programs, including Vietnamization, it is not likely to curtail them significantly.

30. Even if it adopted the option of prolonged struggle, Hanoi would probably believe it necessary to sustain a level of military action sufficient to maintain pressure on the Vietnamization and pacification programs and to inflict casualties on both RVNAF and US forces. Indeed, it is rather clear that the Communists are preparing for an early increase in military activity. While these activities will probably be aimed at selected targets and involve relatively modest objectives and commitment of forces, certain "key" targets might be hit hard. Some RVNAF units might be selected for attack, particularly in the Delta or I Corps as a test of Vietnamization; in addition, the Delta area appears as a likely target for extensive attacks on the pacification program. Attacks by fire will probably increase and even a few coordinated sapper/main force attacks on towns and cities might be attempted. But even in maintaining relatively low levels of warfare, significant losses would be incurred by the Communists; their force levels are likely to decline even further during the next six months, barring a substantial increase in their rate of infiltration and recruitment in South Vietnam.

31. Despite the risks and costs of a prolonged struggle, Hanoi's actions over the past year and the policy statements emanating from the regime's leaders strongly indicate that this is the course the Communists intend to pursue. They seem to have concluded that a more measured and balanced approach to the war is necessary to preserve their military structure, to strengthen their Party apparatus, and to rebuild popular support. This approach apparently stems from two basic judgments on Hanoi's part. First, they see an increasing possibility that the US/GVN effort will continue at effective levels for some indefinite period; second, they believe that somewhere in the evolving situation there will be a possibility of a sudden change or critical opportunity which they must be in position to exploit.

32. While we believe that the Communists are buckling down for the long haul and that they will not try to alter the military situation in South Vietnam decisively in 1970, we also believe that Hanoi is not satisfied with the way the war is going. Given the evident strains of the war in North Vietnam and the decline in the Communist position in the South relative to the GVN, the Communists might be tempted within the year to seek an arrangement at Paris which would hasten US withdrawal within a stated period. So far, at least, the Communists have been unwilling to use negotiations for anything more than tactical purposes. Hanoi probably fears that any political formula which could win US withdrawal would also undermine the overall Communist position

and objectives in the South, and therefore may consider that serious negotiations must await a weakening of the US position and the strengthening of the Communist position in the South.

33. Nonetheless, Hanoi's presence in Paris and Le Duc Tho's recent return there evidence a continuing interest in negotiations. Although Hanoi probably harbors little hope of reaching an overall political settlement, including a coalition government, it may see some utility in probing the possibility of some arrangement which it calculates would hasten US withdrawal or fix a timetable for such withdrawal.

34. At a minimum, Hanoi would of course hope that such action would sharpen US-GVN differences and stimulate antiwar sentiment in the US. Any concessions which Hanoi might make in the coming months will almost certainly be limited, and aimed at speeding US withdrawals rather than toward an overall settlement.

SNIE 57-70

The Outlook For Cambodia

6 August 1970

APPROVED FOR RELEASE

SECRET

SNIE 57-70
6 August 1970

SPECIAL NATIONAL INTELLIGENCE ESTIMATE
57-70

THE OUTLOOK FOR CAMBODIA

Submitted by

R. E. Cushman, Jr.

DEPUTY DIRECTOR OF CENTRAL INTELLIGENCE

Concurred in by the

UNITED STATES INTELLIGENCE BOARD

As indicated overleaf

6 August 1970

Authenticated:

James S. Lay, Jr.

EXECUTIVE SECRETARY, USIB

Note: This is the Estimate. No further dissemination will be made.

Copy No. 1

SECRET

~~SECRET~~

C E N T R A L   I N T E L L I G E N C E   A G E N C Y

6 August 1970

SUBJECT: SNIE 57-70: THE OUTLOOK FOR CAMBODIA

NOTE

Evidence on many aspects of the Cambodian situation is fragmentary and subject to conflicting interpretations. This is true with respect both to the situation within Cambodia and to communist intentions concerning it. Hence, this Estimate devotes more attention than is usual to identifying areas of particular uncertainty and to assessing alternative explanations. The principal conclusions of this Estimate are stated in Section III.

DISCUSSION

1. In the four months since Sihanouk's ouster, the communists have overrun half of Cambodia, taken or threatened 16 of its 19 provincial capitals, and interdicted -- for varying periods --

~~GROUP 1
Excluded from atuomatic
downgrading and
declassification~~

(Continued...)

all road and rail links to the capital, Phnom Penh. In the countryside, VC/NVA forces generally continue to move at will, attacking towns and villages in the south and converting the north into an extension of the Laos corridor and a base for "peoples' war" throughout the country and in South Vietnam as well.

2. This being the situation, survival of the Lon Nol government will depend heavily on the extent of foreign assistance as well as on the will and ability of the people and their leaders to organize themselves for effective military resistance to the communists; on the unity and morale of the country in the face of hardship, destruction, and death; and on the reaction to the divisive political appeals issued in Sihanouk's name. But of equal or greater importance are the capabilities and intentions of the Vietnamese communists; the extent to which they can bring pressures to bear on the Lon Nol government and the degree to which they are willing to allocate available resources to such an effort.

~~SECRET~~

I. THE SITUATION OF THE LON NOL GOVERNMENT

A. Military Strengths and Weaknesses

3. *Manpower.* Prior to Sihanouk's removal the Cambodian Armed Forces (FANK) totaled about 38,000 men, almost all in the army. Their main role was that of a civic action and internal security force; their chief military role was to cope with minor border transgressions and scattered insurgent bands. The army lacked qualified officers, was poorly trained (despite French efforts) and had low morale. Although its fighting units had some new communist equipment, their overall combat effectiveness was low.

4. In their frantic expansion since March, the FANK have more than tripled in size and now number some 135,000 men. Almost all of this increase has been in the army. The infantry, in particular, has grown from some 55 battalions totaling about 20,000 men to 205 battalions with about 100,000 men (as of 30 July). Some of these battalions exist only on paper, however, and it appears that less than half of the units have had any real preparation for battle. The rapid expansion of the army has been accomplished mainly by recruiting raw young volunteers, but reserves and retirees have also been called up

and provincial guard personnel mobilized. Since VC/NVA attacks began in earnest in early April, Cambodian youth have been flocking to enlist in the army and in various auxiliary security forces; they apparently come from all parts of the country and all walks of life, and their morale seems high.

5. The government's ability to use the available manpower is limited by a number of factors. One of the most serious has been the generally poor state of training of the regular forces prior to March. The French Mission in Cambodia did a reasonably good job of assisting in training a number of junior officers and NCOs; in most cases, however, these men were not used effectively. Moreover, the Cambodian Government never permitted the French to conduct unit training. Basic training conducted by the Cambodians themselves was perfunctory and seldom went beyond absolute essentials; most troops for example, fired only a few rounds from their weapons during their entire military career. Unit training was virtually non-existent, the men being assigned to garrison chores and civic action projects rather than to military exercises. There are indications that training deteriorated even further in the aftermath of the communist attacks; in some instances, recruits received only a day of military instruction before being shipped

SECRET

to the "front." The situation now appears to be improving; there is an effort to provide a full six weeks of training at the unit level for all recruits.

6. *Logistics.* Before the recent, rapid expansion of the army, most Cambodian infantry battalions were reasonably well equipped with communist-supplied weapons. Newly-formed units are being equipped from existing stocks of Chinese, US, Soviet, French, and other foreign weapons, as well as light weapons recently supplied by the US and captured communist weapons provided by South Vietnam. Yet many of the weapons in stock are inoperable, and many of the new units are inadequately equipped. Moreover, the heterogeneous nature of the arsenal has created an extremely difficult supply problem. Ammunition reserves have been rapidly depleted, primarily to supply newly-formed units rather than in combat. Weapons losses to the communists have not been as great as initially thought, although some ammunition was left behind by troops evacuated from outposts in the north and northeast; at Kratie, a regional arms and ammunition depot containing an unknown quantity of ordnance was abandoned.[1/] There is a serious shortage of communications equipment throughout the army and a general lack of trucks and other vehicles; even uniforms are in short supply.

1/ *All the weapons at the ordnance depot at Kompong Speu and possibly at Lovek were evacuated before VC/NVA troops attacked these towns.*

~~SECRET~~

7. *Combat Effectiveness.* As might be expected, the performance of Cambodian forces so far has generally been poor. This is due in part to the generally low professional competence of their officers and NCOs. Most of the small number of Cambodian military successes have been the result of timely allied intervention, on the ground or in the air. Patriotic zeal alone has been insufficient to cope with experienced VC/NVA units or even roving communist bands. According to official FANK reports, Cambodian Army casualties from 18 March to 8 July 1970 totaled about 800 killed, 1,700 wounded, 1,500 missing, and 1,600 desertions. These figures are roughly consistent with our own information which indicates that some 18 FANK battalions have either been overrun or dissolved since March. Cambodian military planning is poor and operations are further hampered by inadequate tactical intelligence and communications, and by general inexperience in combat situations.

8. But the picture may not be entirely bleak. There has been some degree of improvement over the months among units consistently engaged, particularly with regard to troop discipline and unit coordination. Cambodian forces have also shown increased ability and determination in defending fixed

positions (Kompong Thom) and in attacks on communist-held positions (Kirirom). Given enough time, the Cambodians probably could become good soldiers. It is clear, however, that a lengthy period of training and re-equipping would be necessary before very many Cambodian units could be a match -- on a unit-for-unit basis -- for the VC/NVA forces operating in the country.

9. *Foreign Assistance.* Obviously, at this stage, Lon Nol's army is counting heavily on allied assistance -- including fighting forces, materiel, and air support. The withdrawal of US ground forces from Cambodia on 30 June was a major disappointment to Phnom Penh. The Cambodians clearly have reservations about relying on their traditional enemies, the Vietnamese, for assistance; they have been angered by the behavior of some ARVN units in eastern Cambodia and they also wonder if ARVN troops would withdraw from Cambodian soil once the communist danger had passed. It is possible that these feelings could increase to the point where they represented a serious hindrance to collaboration between the two countries.

10. For the present, however, Lon Nol seems relieved that ARVN has set up a major combat base at Neak Luong at the junction of the Mekong and Route 1 (Saigon-Svay Rieng-Phnom Penh), and is prepared to keep open those vital supply links from South

Vietnam. He is also reassured by President Thieu's agreement to move troops as necessary deep into Cambodia's eastern border regions and to respond militarily to any major communist assault on important towns in the Phnom Penh region, including any attack on the capital itself. South Vietnamese air is also available for Cambodian defense to the extent deemed appropriate by Saigon; and the South Vietnamese Navy intends to maintain its surveillance of Cambodian coastal waters. Finally, Saigon has agreed to provide facilities for the training of some 10,000 Cambodian recruits on an annual basis, as well as numbers of FANK officers and NCOs.

11. ARVN will probably not, however, undertake significant defensive responsibilities in areas remote from South Vietnam's borders; its capabilities for action in Cambodia are not unlimited, and its actions outside South Vietnam are subject to US-imposed restrictions. Most important, President Thieu appears sensitive to the dangers of overcommitting his forces in Cambodia at the expense of internal security and pacification in South Vietnam.

12. With regard to ground defense in western Cambodia, therefore, Lon Nol has been anxiously soliciting Thai involvement. Despite enthusiasm among some Thai leaders for ambitious military

SECRET

operations in Cambodia, Bangkok has been slow and cautious in extending actual commitments. The Thai are providing some tactical air support from bases in Thailand to FANK units in western Cambodia. Thai border security detachments are patrolling in adjacent Cambodian frontier zones and occasionally have engaged communist units. (The Thai have also occupied the coveted Preah Vihear Temple on Cambodian soil.) Bangkok has provided a number of small river patrol craft to Cambodia and will provide more. There have been shipments of other types of military materiel in small quantities. Finally, the Thai are recruiting two regiments from their ethnic Khmer (i.e., Cambodian) population and have scheduled them for deployment to Cambodia in the fall.

13. Beyond this, the Thai have been constrained by opposition at home and -- more important -- by uncertainty over the availability of US financial support to any Thai military enterprise in Cambodia. If such support is not forthcoming, it seems probable that any commitment of regular Thai troops to Cambodia will be relatively small and limited to defense of areas contiguous to Thailand.

(Continued...)

~~SECRET~~

14. Although the Lon Nol government has been soliciting international support, no other nation is likely to send troops to Cambodia in the foreseeable future. South Korean ardor has cooled because of US unwillingness to pay the bills as it has in South Vietnam. There was never any possibility that any other nation might dispatch troops though a few -- including Australia Indonesia, and Nationalist China -- may provide some military materiel. Sustained US air attacks on communist supply lines and troop concentrations should be of considerable value to the Lon Nol forces. And Cambodia counts on extensive material assistance from the US.

B. The Political Situation

15. *The Government.* When they took control after deposing Sihanouk, the new Cambodian leaders moved quickly to consolidate their position. The Cabinet and both houses of the National Assembly continued to display the same unity and support for Prime Minister Lon Nol and his deputy, Sirik Matak, that they had throughout the months leading up to Sihanouk's ouster. A few administrative figures whose allegiance was questionable

were removed from their posts. For the most part, provincial governors, ambassadors, and the bureaucracy fell into line.

16. As communist military and psychological pressures have increased, however, cracks have begun to appear in the facade of unity. In the main, these result from the resentment of civilian politicians over their lack of influence in the present government. There are also personal criticisms of the two top leaders and stories of rivalries between them. So far, these frictions do not appear to be serious. Lon Nol has responded constructively to most criticisms and recommendations; for example, he has eased pressures from young intellectuals by bringing them into responsible government positions. Lon Nol and Sirik Matak appear to work together well and to complement each other. In general, Lon Nol runs military affairs and Sirik Matak the political sector, although there is some evidence that both are now spending so much time on military matters that other problems receive insufficient attention from them. We have had one report that the two hold differing views regarding the possibility of some kind of deal with either the communists or Sihanouk -- that Sirik Matak would be more inclined than Lon Nol to accept a compromise settlement of the conflict.

(Continued...)

~~SECRET~~

17. The possibility of such an arrangement does, of course, exist. The political unity that followed Sihanouk's ouster and the sense of nationalism (with strong anti-Vietnamese overtones) that was artfully used by Lon Nol and Sirik Matak in their bid for power could weaken over time. If the military situation does not soon improve, for example, Lon Nol's support might begin to dissipate and his policies come under open attack.

18. There is no way of knowing whether Lon Nol and Sirik Matak have the fortitude and the inner resources to meet such a challenge. While they have surmounted many difficult problems, there is a disquieting note in the continuing optimism -- bordering on wishful thinking -- that the two leaders have displayed in private talks. They seem to believe that the Cambodian Army will be able to take the offensive in the relatively near future; and they seem unprepared for the possibility of a long war. If their leadership should falter, the attitudes of Cambodia's Army and the urban elite would be critical.

19. *The Army.* The real power behind the Cambodian Government today is the army. Despite some grumbling, it has remained loyal to Lon Nol through the trying period since Sihanouk's removal and

~~SECRET~~

if this situation persists it is difficult to imagine a successful effort by any group in Phnom Penh to overthrow the government.

20. But we have little basis for judging the depth of the commitment among individual officers to Lon Nol; nor do we know much about political attitudes within the army as a whole. It would be prudent to assume that there are military elements who still are pro-Sihanouk, others who are probably disturbed by the troubles that now beset Cambodia and hold Lon Nol accountable, and some who are simply concerned over their personal interests and safety. At the same time, the rapid expansion of the army has brought increased authority and opportunity to the officer corps, reinforcing longstanding personal bonds to Lon Nol. And there is, no doubt, a strong and genuine sense of nationalist commitment to the government in the face of the foreign threat. On balance, we think the army's loyalty will hold up so long as there appears a reasonable prospect for continued foreign assistance and for the survival of a viable non-communist regime in Cambodia.

21. *The Elite and the Youth.* For years, members of the Cambodian bureaucratic, economic and political elite have complained about Sihanouk's policies of economic nationalization

and his accommodations with the Vietnamese communists, while continuing to serve him. Although the Lon Nol/Sirik Matak regime has made little progress toward fulfilling its promises to rid the country of North Vietnamese, to eradicate corruption, and to establish a republic, major political components are muting their dissatisfaction in view of the military threat posed by the communists. For example, elements within the National Assembly complain about the lack of progress in implementing reforms and appear increasingly dissatisfied with the minor role the government is allowing it to play, but they have confined their reactions to verbal criticisms. The majority of students and young intellectuals, another key group, although they were at the center of left-wing sentiment in the past, also see the present government as an improvement over the past and as the only viable alternative in present circumstances. As a result, at least for the present, the students continue to constitute an element of support for the new regime.

22. *The Buddhists*. Buddhism is an influential force in Cambodian life, particularly in the countryside where the temple is the center of social life and the interpreter of most news. For the most part, Cambodian monks have been

apolitical, unlike those in some other Asian countries. But they played a critical leadership role a century ago in a Cambodian revolt against the Vietnamese and some elements actively opposed the French as part of the post-World War II movement for Cambodian independence. The regime recognizes the political importance of the monks and has made efforts to gain their support. In the villages, however, the monks have been slow in responding to government requests to rally the peasants. In a recent tactic, the government has sought to portray the war as a struggle between Buddhism and the atheistic communists of North Vietnam. Such efforts may be having some success; the government now claims that monks in some areas are providing information about VC/NVA movements and activities.

23. *The Peasantry.* The Cambodian peasantry has no serious problems of land tenancy and its village-oriented way of life has changed little over the centuries. Although governmental authority extends down through the provincial and district capitals into the villages, actual contact with the bureaucracy at local levels is infrequent. And the social and political aspirations of the governing group in Phnom Penh have generally had little in common with those of the villagers. Conservative

~~SECRET~~

and religious in their outlook, the peasantry has traditionally had great respect for royalty and affection for Sihanouk, providing a broad base of support for his leadership. They have been the slowest to demonstrate approval of the new regime. In large part, this may be due to the traditional apathy of the peasants toward events in the capital.

24. Few, if any, government leaders have ventured into rural areas since the coup, and there is some question whether any government services are being provided in the countryside. Indeed, the government appears to have abandoned most outlying areas and withdrawn back to the major towns. Virtually no reliable information is available to indicate the developing attitudes of the peasantry or the depth of its commitment, when made, to either side of the struggle. The government recognizes that more has to be done to establish closer ties with the peasantry and is beginning to develop programs aimed at gaining the loyalty of the rural population and counteracting communist organizational activities.

25. *Imported Khmers.* The introduction of comparatively well-trained ethnic Cambodian troops from South Vietnam -- the so-called

Khmer Krom -- has injected a new factor into the political equation in Phnom Penh. Although they have thus far accepted their military mission, the political character of their parent organizations[2/] may foreshadow political ambitions on the part of Khmer Krom leaders. Lon Nol has dealt with the Khmer Krom through his brother Lon Non, an indication that he understands their political importance. He has also engaged in gingerly bargaining with Son Ngoc Thanh -- the Khmer Serei leader -- in an effort to limit Thanh's future political role while gaining the assistance his recruits can provide. In the fragile consensus which has so far characterized the Lon Nol regime, men like Son Ngoc Thanh with the backing of the Khmer Krom could emerge as political factors of some importance.

2/ *These are the Khmer du Kampuchea Krom (KKK or "White Turbans") and the Khmer Serei. The KKK, a semi-bandit group, was initially supported by Sihanouk as a means of maintaining contact with Khmer and Montagnard elements in South Vietnam and harassing the GVN. The Khmer Serei, an anti-Sihanouk group led by Son Ngoc Thanh, has -- off and on -- enjoyed South Vietnamese and Thai support. Neither group played any significant role in Cambodia while Sihanouk was in power.*

C. The Economic Situation

26. The rising tempo of the war has confronted the Cambodian Government with critical economic problems. Defense costs, of course, have skyrocketed, while wartime destruction and dislocations have greatly reduced governmental revenues and the availability of foreign exchange. Some basic consumer necessities are in short supply in the urban areas, and manufacturing -- such as it is -- has been slowed almost to a halt. Disruptions to transport resulting from communist interdiction of lines of communication and commandeering of civilian trucks by the Cambodian military have contributed heavily to the severe constriction of domestic and foreign trade. Moreover, half a million people or more have been uprooted from their homes, causing serious labor shortages in many regions. In particular, the repatriation of ethnic Vietnamese has removed many skilled workers from the economy.

27. On the other hand, the Cambodian peasant and village economy is still in tolerable shape. There is no shortage of food; rice, sugar, vegetables, and meat are relatively plentiful and should continue so for some months. If severe transport

disruptions continue, however, the urban population, especially those in Phnom Penh who are largely dependent on earnings from trade and industry, will have an increasingly difficult time. As shortages and inflation develop, the urban middle class, which provides the nucleus of Lon Nol's political support, could become increasingly disenchanted.

28. The loss of hard currency export earnings will cause problems for the government, especially because of the impact on the urban middle class, who are highly dependent on imported consumer goods. Estimated earnings from the three major exports -- rice, rubber, and corn -- are down sharply. 3/ Most rubber processing facilities have been destroyed and no

---

3/ *These products normally account for about 85 percent of Cambodia's foreign exchange earnings. Rice exports for 1970 will probably be less than half the 450,000 tons (valued at US $44 million) originally projected; rubber exports will probably be less than one-third the 52,000 tons (valued at about US $20 million) originally projected; and corn exports, derived largely from the war-torn southeastern provinces, will be greatly diminished.*

further production is expected this year. It will probably take at least a year to put facilities back in service once security is established. Moreover, many mature trees have been damaged and their replacement would take much longer. Planting of the rainy season crop of rice and corn has been disrupted by hostilities and the displacement of rural population, and this may cause a significant decline this year in the production of both. Tourism -- i.e., the temples at Angkor -- which had been growing rapidly as a source of foreign exchange for Cambodia, has been all but wiped out. Despite this generally bleak foreign exchange picture, reserves on hand total about US $60 million and are probably sufficient to sustain necessary imports into early 1971.

29. A related problem is in the realm of government operating expenditures. While revenues have been reduced to a trickle, expenses have soared, particularly in the defense sector. The government is already in arrears on its military (and civilian) payroll. Government expenditures this year will be considerably in excess of the US $176 million budgeted; and a deficit of between $60 and $100 million seems likely. The Cambodian Government will probably be forced increasingly to

resort to the printing press. With supplies of imported and domestic goods reduced, an expansion of the money supply will almost certainly produce a major inflation, unless foreign financial assistance is made available.[4/]

30. So far, however, there are few firm commitments for any substantial foreign aid. The French made a commitment in January 1970, before Sihanouk's ouster, for a $22.7 million loan; it is being implemented, but with many strings attached. Cambodian officials have high hopes for substantial aid from Japan, but so far the Japanese have provided only a $2 million grant for refugee relief. Miscellaneous commitments from Australia, New Zealand, and Denmark total only a few million dollars. Aid from communist countries, once an important element in the Cambodian economic picture, has now been cut off.

4/ *One of the most significant indicators of Cambodia's financial difficulties has been the rapid depreciation of the riel. Businessmen, especially Vietnamese and Chinese elements, have been exchanging large riel balances for hard currencies; consequently, the riel, which traded at 65 to US $1 shortly after devaluation a year ago, has been quoted as high as 130 to US $1 in recent weeks. The riel is officially exchanged at a rate of 55 to US $1.*

(Continued...)

~~SECRET~~

II. THE SITUATION OF THE COMMUNISTS IN CAMBODIA

A. Military Capabilities

31. *Available Forces.* According to the latest order of battle estimates based on newly-captured documents, there probably were, in April 1970, some 50,000-60,000 VC/NVA troops operating in the Cambodian/South Vietnamese border region, almost all of them in Cambodia. About 60 percent of these forces are believed to have been in administrative units -- primarily concerned with operating and protecting the various communist command, logistic, and intelligence functions in the region -- and 40 percent in combat units. Virtually all of these troops were deployed deeper into Cambodia at some time over the past few months, though many did not move any further than necessary to avoid confrontations with US and ARVN forces. Indeed, all available evidence indicates that fewer than 10,000 combat troops have been involved in the deeper deployments and wide-ranging attacks against Cambodian towns and cities.

32. Precise determinations of communist deployments are difficult to make.

SECRET

To the extent that we can determine, it appears that communist operations in the northeast were largely the work of one regiment; and that elements of this same regiment, augmented by an undetermined number of troops from southern Laos and some Cambodian recruits, were responsible for the initial communist thrust across northern Cambodia as far west as Siem Reap. As far as we can determine, all the attacks south and southwest of Phnom Penh (in the area of Takeo, Angtassom, Kompong Speu, and Kirirom) were the work of roughly the equivalent of two regiments.

33. In sum,

the communists have ranged over much of Cambodia with what appears to be a relatively small combat force. Thus, if Hanoi should decide to increase the weight of its attacks against the Lon Nol government, it already has additional combat troops in nearby border areas and would not necessarily have to await reinforcements from North Vietnam. Nevertheless, many of these forces are needed to defend supply caches still remaining in the old border base areas, to guard against attacks on supply routes through Laos, and to support the struggle in South Vietnam. Thus, Hanoi might think a considerable

reinforcement from North Vietnam was desirable before making an all-out effort to topple the Lon Nol regime -- an effort which might provoke substantial allied opposition on the ground and in the air.

34. At the moment, it is difficult to see how the communists could effect such a reinforcement -- if they feel they need it -- before the end of the year. The 12,000 infiltrators scheduled to reach COSVN during the May-July period were only sufficient, together with local recruiting, to balance losses suffered by communist units in Cambodia during the May/June allied incursions. And the scheduled arrivals in August and September in the COSVN area number only some 1,500[5/], almost certainly insufficient to cover continuing attrition. To be sure, the communists could, with considerable difficulty, move substantial numbers of troops through the Laos panhandle in the midst of the monsoon (July-October). Even so, it would be two or three months before they would be ready for operations in Cambodia.

5/ [ ]

35. *Logistical Factors.* At this point there is still great uncertainty about the communist supply situation in part because we do not know the extent of supply caches before the allied intervention. In the Cambodian interior, a new theater of operations for communist forces, it seems likely that their system for the distribution of supplies is still rudimentary. Though obviously adequate to support the relatively light combat of the past few months, it is probably not as secure and effective as Hanoi would wish before embarking on any large-scale or sustained combat. The communist forces no longer have assured sanctuaries south of the DMZ; and their former supply route through Sihanoukville is no longer available. Aside from supplies, there is also the problem of evacuating or caring for wounded. And, in the absence of a friendly population and a well-developed infrastructure, the communists in Cambodia could be forced to employ large numbers of combat troops in a support role. The peculiarities ofthe Cambodian situation could require many other modifications of the efficient supply procedures developed in South Vietnam and Laos over the years.

36. *Subversive Capabilities.* The communists, true to their doctrine of "peoples' war," are making a considerable effort to win over the rural population. The north and northeast areas, however, which the government has virtually abandoned to communist

(Continued...)

control, contain relatively few people. The population of the four provinces in the Hanoi-controlled northeast, for example, totals less than 250,000 or only about 4 percent of Cambodia's 6.8 million people.[6/] However, the communists are active in many heavily populated areas of the south as well.

37. Access to the population is only part of the communist problem. The communist movement in Cambodia has always been weak and has suffered in the past from its identification with alien Vietnamese. We have no good estimate of the number of Khmer communists, but at the time of Sihanouk's overthrow there probably were no more than a few hundred in Battambang Province in the far west and some 2,000 in the eastern regions. These Khmer communists will probably have the role of fronting for the Vietnamese in the effort now underway to develop a communist-controlled infrastructure in the Cambodian countryside.

38. Sihanouk's name probably remains something of an asset to the Vietnamese communists in their efforts to rally the rural populace.

6/ *Most of the population in three of the provinces -- Stung Treng, Ratanakiri, and Mondolkiri -- is Lao or Khmer Loeu, not ethnic Cambodian.*

At the same time, his involvement with the Chinese and Vietnamese communists -- particularly the latter -- has hurt him in Cambodia. It won over to the new regime many among the elite, the students, and the army who were fence-sitters when Lon Nol first took over. Moreover, although Sihanouk probably has the sympathies of many peasants and some of the Buddhist monks, there is no political apparatus available to him in Cambodia except that which Hanoi can develop.

39. Whatever the current extent of Sihanouk's appeal, the job of establishing a viable communist infrastructure in Cambodia will not be easy. The Vietnamese are racially, culturally, and linguistically distinct from the Khmer, and they must overcome the burden of longstanding Khmer animosity toward all Vietnamese. But the Vietnamese communists are superb organizers, and they know how to use terrorism to get what they cannot obtain otherwise. The information available on their recruitment effort is meager, and what we do get provides a mixed and confused picture. In some areas, particularly those long subject to communist influence, entire villages are apparently collaborating, and local recruits are being rapidly if superficially trained for military and administrative

(Continued...)

tasks. Elsewhere, while there is undoubtedly a good deal of coercion, the communists have apparently not yet resorted to large-scale terrorism. On past form, particularly in Laos, it seems likely that they will succeed in winning the active loyalty of some peasants to a communist-dominated Khmer resistance front and the passive acquiescence of many more to the presence of such an organization in areas where communist forces predominate.

40. Another potential asset for Hanoi in Cambodia is the community of some 300,000-400,000 Vietnamese. This community did contain a sizable Vietnamese communist apparatus, including a "Rear Services Group" in Phnom Penh which supported the war effort in South Vietnam. But the recent evacuation of close to 150,000 ethnic Vietnamese to South Vietnam has reduced the potential for exploitation of this group in Cambodia.

B. Hanoi's View of the Cambodian Situation

41. Hanoi has given no firm clues as to how it views the situation arising from recent developments in Cambodia. There have been some public and a few private statements, which demonstrate little more than that the communists are neither panicked nor elated by events. There has been some military action which was to be expected, such as that to restructure the supply system, and some which would not necessarily have been expected, such as operations westward as far as Siem Reap and Angkor. These give some small basis for judging Hanoi's attitude, but the following paragraphs actually present no more than some of the pros and cons which, from our own view of the situation, must have occasioned debate or concern among the communists.

42. The overthrow of Sihanouk, the adoption of a strong anticommunist line by the Lon Nol government, and the allied incursions into Cambodia upset a situation which had been highly advantageous to Hanoi in its campaign to take over South Vietnam. And, while communist forces in Cambodia have weathered the May-June phase of allied operations and continue to extend their presence into large portions of the country, Hanoi can scarcely

assume that its troubles are over. It has recognized its problems with statements to the effect that new difficulties and increased demands will have to be met in supporting the Indochina-wide struggle.

43. The obvious immediate problem was to restore and secure as far as possible the channels of supply and infiltration into South Vietnam. Communist forces advanced westward to the Mekong (and beyond) in order to open up alternate routes, and their recent advances in southern Laos are presumably a related move. Pathet Lao approaches to Souvanna Phouma since mid-June may also reflect, at least in part, Hanoi's concern regarding possible allied ground incursions into the Laos corridor. In any event, the immunity from attack formerly enjoyed by supply routes (and sanctuaries) in Cambodia is at an end. For the time being at least, the route through Sihanoukville is wholly closed to the communists.

44. Experience of past years indicates that the communists will be able to maintain a flow of supplies and manpower to southern South Vietnam and Cambodia. This is not to say that they will have all the material they need for any operation they may contemplate, and still less that their logistic operations will be without severe difficulties and setbacks. Such difficulties and setbacks

will of course play an important part in Hanoi's estimate of what it can accomplish, and within what time, and at what cost. All the evidence suggests, however, that the communist leadership is still committed to a long struggle, carried on primarily by relatively small-scale military actions over extensive areas, and that such a struggle will not be rendered infeasible by material or manpower shortages.

45. As respects Cambodia itself, from one point of view Hanoi may perceive tempting opportunities. It has always been clear that its ultimate objective was to control, or at least to establish hegemony over that country. Hanoi-inspired insurgency began on a small scale in Cambodia in 1967, but progress was slow, at least until Sihanouk's ouster in March of this year. Now, with Sihanouk in the communist camp and half of Cambodian territory in communist hands, prospects for a rapid advance toward the ultimate objective might seem to be greatly enhanced.

46. In any effort to gain control of Cambodia, however, the communists would lack some of the advantages they have enjoyed in South Vietnam: a well-established and extensive logistic system; a political base and infrastructure deeply rooted among the people;

(Continued...)

and a claim to legitimacy deriving from identification with nationalist aspirations. Moreover, they cannot be certain of how far the US and its allies may go in attempting to preserve an anticommunist regime in Phnom Penh. Hanoi's fears must have been diminished by the extent of US domestic opposition and by the limitations that the US Government has placed upon its military commitment in Cambodia. Nevertheless, if Hanoi plans to persist in efforts to undermine the Lon Nol government, it must weigh the costs of deploying additional resources -- particularly manpower -- to deal with anticipated US and ARVN air attacks, plus ARVN (and possibly Thai) ground attacks. It must also consider that the opposition offered by Cambodian government forces may grow stronger as allied arms become available and allied training programs are carried out.

47. In the wider context of the whole Indochina conflict, Hanoi may also see both advantages and disadvantages in the extension of the area of fighting into Cambodia. On the one hand, it means a diversion of communist resources into new territory, into protecting and maintaining more lines of communication, probably against increased air attacks, and into organizational and propaganda efforts among a largely unsympathetic people. Yet

it may also give opportunity to tie down South Vietnamese (and possibly Thai) forces in Cambodia without excessive cost or risk and to divert Saigon's attention from the more important struggle in its own country. It may conceivably lead to frictions between the US and its allies over the necessity and the means of keeping the Lon Nol regime in power.

48. Finally, Hanoi has above all to judge the effect of the Cambodian situation upon the will of the US to prosecute the struggle. Obviously it has never doubted the superior physical and material capabilities of the US; its hopes have lain in its ability to outstay the US in a prolonged politico-military contest carried on according to the principles of revolutionary struggle. It has doubtless been impressed by the considerable public outcry against the Cambodian adventure which occurred in the US, and may overestimate its importance. But it must recognize that the contest in Indochina will continue for some time.

C. Courses of Action

49. The full range of communist intentions in Cambodia is difficult to judge. Hanoi clearly intends, at a minimum, to retain

supply and infiltration channels into South Vietnam. But the evidence strongly indicates that its objectives extend beyond this. Communist units have been on the outskirts of Siem Reap, some 250 miles west of the Vietnamese border, for over two months; and Hanoi's attacks in the southerly areas have created serious insecurity almost everywhere and virtually wrecked the national economy. Meanwhile, communist forces and their agents have been working assiduously wherever possible to create a Khmer resistance movement. These developments, and Hanoi's public statements, indicate that the communists have set their sights on the elimination of the Lon Nol government and its replacement by a regime which would be responsive to their wishes.

50. At this point, therefore, the main issue in Hanoi's view is almost certainly one of method and timing: Whether to seek Lon Nol's destruction by early and direct military pressure on Phnom Penh, or by a more prolonged and measured campaign of military, political, and psychological pressures designed to undermine the government's position in stages.

51. There are a number of factors that might incline Hanoi to seek a rapid military victory in Cambodia. The communists

might believe that the quick removal of the anticommunist leadership in Phnom Penh would provide a timely political-psychological triumph of major proportions, one which would further weaken support in the US for the war in South Vietnam. They might be concerned to finish off Lon Nol before substantial numbers of South Vietnamese, Thai or other Asian troops (with US air support) could be marshalled against them -- or before Cambodian government forces could be made effective. They might also be pessimistic about their prospects for building an effective Khmer insurgent movement, even in a matter of years, and therefore think it more practicable to establish a "neutralist" regime in Phnom Penh as soon as possible. And Hanoi might also hope that a military push on the Cambodian capital would tempt ARVN to overextend its forces, thus opening the way for communist gains in South Vietnam itself. The force of these considerations would be increased if Hanoi perceived signs of collapse by the FANK or signs of serious political instability in Phnom Penh.

52. At the present time, there are arguments of at least equal weight against Hanoi's seeking a rapid military solution in Cambodia. With ARVN at the ready, it would probably require a major redeployment of VC/NVA forces within Cambodia, which might lessen the communist threat to southern South Vietnam. It would also draw

heavily on available VC/NVA supplies, probably to the detriment of units in southern South Vietnam already known to be subject to rationing of munitions. In any case, Hanoi could not be sure that its campaign, including an assault on Phnom Penh, would be successful. The monsoon rains present an important obstacle at this time to any major offensive in central Cambodia; the low-lying plains around Phnom Penh are particularly subject to widespread inundation. There would almost certainly be resistance by the Cambodians themselves and, more important, Hanoi would expect that ARVN units with US air support would be available to the defense. At best, the military costs of taking the capital and nearby major towns would probably be high; and Hanoi might be concerned over the loss of prestige if a major assault failed.

53. Hanoi may also see the advantages of an early overthrow of the Lon Nol regime as dubious. Such a development would not automatically end the fighting in Cambodia and reduce communist manpower requirements there; indeed, the possible need for defense of occupied towns might impose a larger military burden. The allies could hardly be expected to cease attacks on supply lines in the east, or even in other parts of the country, or to forego a continuing naval blockade, nor would FANK necessarily give up the struggle.

SECRET

54. More important, probably, would be the problem of securing a reliable successor government. In this connection, Hanoi might be reluctant to bring the unpredictable Sihanouk back to the scene. It would first have to assess his popular appeal and his willingness, under the circumstances, to act in accord with communist wishes. In any event, unless Hanoi were able to base its control of Cambodia on a well-organized indigenous communist movement, the North Vietnamese would have to assume the main burden of running the country.

55. The alternative to a major military campaign is, of course, an attempt to erode Lon Nol's position over time by some combination of military, psychological, and political means. The current pattern of communist military attacks, for example, could be designed to cripple and demoralize the inadequate military force at the disposal of the government; to create serious insecurity in the countryside; to isolate the populace from the central government; and to wreck the national economy. Hanoi may be bent on making it clear to all that the Lon Nol government is weak and ineffective, incapable of defending even its major towns, and utterly dependent on allied support. In this context, Phnom Penh itself might be harassed occasionally by communist forces. Through such tactics, and

accompanying propaganda, Hanoi could hope to discourage the faint of heart among Cambodians and to encourage political opposition to Lon Nol. It might hope, in this case, to encourage the formation of a regime prepared to accept the communist presence in Cambodia. Meanwhile, in pursuance of this course of action, Hanoi could be expanding its indigenous insurgent force for the longer pull in Cambodia, and strengthening its grip on the strategic northeastern quadrant of the country. It could be achieving these objectives in accordance with classic communist doctrines and at relatively low cost or risk.

56. This alternative, as we describe it, clearly implies a continuation of communist operations and pressures in Cambodia at levels approximating those of the past several months. There would, of course, be lulls and peaks in military pressures as forces were rested and resupplied, or diverted to support operations in South Vietnam; but the effort to build an indigenous insurgent movement would continue at a steady pace behind the screen of maneuvering VC/NVA military units. Even if this course were followed, the communists would retain the option of an all-out military assault on the Lon Nol government -- at any time.

III. SUMMARY AND CONCLUSIONS

57. The main points that emerge from the foregoing discussion may be summarized in these propositions:

a. Despite its numerous shortcomings and difficulties, the Lon Nol government is still generally united and in fairly good heart. It has the support of the army, the urban elite, and for the moment at least, the students. The peasantry appear largely apathetic, but certainly there has been no large-scale flocking to the communist cause.

b. The Cambodian Army has with some exceptions performed poorly against communist forces. Its morale is still generally high, but it presently is manifestly incapable of resisting anything more than small-scale attacks, and a lengthy period of training will be necessary before it will be an effective fighting force.

c. Whatever military defense of Cambodia is put up will depend greatly upon assistance from ARVN ground and air forces and on US air support, and (insofar as time is available) on substantial outside help in equipping and training the Cambodian Army. Thai regular forces are unlikely to engage in combat operations

except in areas adjacent to their own borders. No other countries are likely to send combat forces to Cambodia, or provide more than a small amount of economic or material assistance.

d. Hanoi's forces have caused the Cambodian Government to give up much of the north and the entire northeast areas of the country, and are operating with disruptive effect in the south and southeast. This signifies that communist objectives are not limited to the maintenance of supply lines from Laos through Cambodia into South Vietnam, but almost certainly include the collapse of the Lon Nol regime. Yet it is not clear how rapidly or with what weight of effort Hanoi intends to pursue this aim.

58. We are reasonably confident that the Lon Nol government, with continued allied support, has enough strength and determination to withstand likely communist military and political pressures during the current rainy season. Once the rainy season is over, however, sometime in October or November, the prospect opens up of a stronger communist military offensive, possibly against Phnom Penh itself, to get rid of the Lon Nol government rapidly. For the military and political reasons discussed in Sections I and II above, we doubt that Hanoi would think such a course of action worth the cost

and risk. If this were the only threat to the government's survival, we would judge that its chances of lasting through 1970 and into 1971 were good.

59. But all-out attack is not the only circumstance in which the Cambodian Government might fall. Hanoi will assuredly continue and perhaps increase its military pressures and political activities within the country. We doubt that either Lon Nol or his adherents have yet faced up to the prospect of a long and difficult struggle. Once it is borne in upon them that death and destruction inflicted by both sides are likely to be the order of the day for months or years, and that Cambodians will have to do much of their own fighting, against very heavy odds, the mood in Phnom Penh could turn to depression and despair. In such circumstances, the present leadership might seek an accommodation with the communists or it might be challenged by other non-communist elements bent on such an accommodation, or central authority might simply dissolve as individual leaders left the country for refuge abroad.

60. Even in view of these considerations, we think the chances are somewhat better than even that Lon Nol's government will still be in existence at the end of 1970. The fact that it

~~SECRET~~

has survived the major upheavals and disasters of past months suggests that it probably has sufficient stamina and public support to see it through a few more months, and perhaps longer. By year's end, however, its situation is highly unlikely to be improved in any basic way. Thus, the end of the year will not mark any decisive moment of the struggle; the critical period may come in the early months of 1971.

NIE 53-71

South Vietnam: Problems and Prospects

29 April 1971

SECRET/

NATIONAL INTELLIGENCE ESTIMATE

APPROVED FOR RELEASE
DATE: JAN 2005

(b) (3)

South Vietnam: Problems and Prospects

SECRET
NIE 53-71
29 April 1971

№ 116

SECRET

SOUTH VIETNAM: PROBLEMS AND PROSPECTS

NOTE

The US military presence in South Vietnam will be reduced to about 185,000 by the end of 1971 and even further by the end of 1972. But it is assumed in this paper that a US military support effort will be maintained beyond 1972 along with substantial amounts of US economic assistance. As the US disengages militarily, however, the non-communist forces in South Vietnam will face the test of dealing with a variety of challenges largely on their own. This Estimate assesses the major problems which will confront the Saigon government in the future as the US reduces its presence and which, depending on how they are met, will largely determine South Vietnam's prospects through the mid-1970s.

(Continued...)

~~SECRET~~

CONCLUSIONS

A. The outlook in South Vietnam for the remainder of 1971 is reasonably good. The past three years have produced a more stable political situation, a marked improvement in security conditions, and considerable progress in Vietnamization. Meanwhile, communist problems in supporting the insurgency have mounted. Though communist military strength remains substantial, particularly in the northerly provinces, most of the available evidence suggests that—for the next six months or so—they will continue to rely essentially on the basically conservative tactics observed over the past year. While occasional spurts of larger scale military activity seem almost certain, particularly in the north, any such activity in South Vietnam would probably be limited in area and duration.

B. On the political front, the odds in the presidential election of October 1971 appear to favor a Thieu victory. His re-election would, of course, constitute a mandate for continuing to oppose the communists along present lines. But even the election of the more equivocal "Big" Minh would not necessarily lead to any major shift in Saigon's approach to the struggle, if only because the South Vietnamese military would compel Minh to be extremely circumspect in any dealings with the communists. As for Hanoi, the defeat of Thieu would provide a tempting opportunity to feel out South Vietnamese sentiment on continuing the war.

C. Prospects for 1972 are less clear. The approaching US election period, coupled with continued drawdowns of US troop strength in South Vietnam, make it probable that Hanoi will elect to step up its military activity by early 1972. We do not envisage an effort to duplicate in scale or intensity the 1968 Tet offensive. We would expect a general increase in the level of communist activity with sharp focus on a few selected areas, most likely the northern provinces and highland region of South Vietnam. The aim of this strategy would be to score tactical victories likely to impact adversely on the South Vietnamese and US will to persist in the struggle—specifically, to discredit the Vietnamization program and to encourage sentiment in the US for complete disengagement from the war. There are practical limits, however, to what the communists could accomplish militarily next year in South Vietnam, and we do not believe that they will be able to reverse the military balance there.

~~SECRET~~

D. At the same time, there seems little doubt that the communists will continue to maintain an active military and political challenge to the GVN well beyond 1972. The question in their mind is how and at what level the campaign should be prosecuted. Much would depend on Hanoi's view of the remaining US presence and commitment to Saigon, and on what balance Hanoi struck in its willingness to continue investing resources in the struggle. There are risks and practical difficulties in any course which Hanoi might contemplate: an effort to exploit the drawdown of US forces by a return to large-scale military action; to continue a course not unlike that of the past two years; or to pursue a purely guerrilla struggle at a much lower level. In any case, as it views developments in Laos and Cambodia, Hanoi may well calculate that it can maintain forces on South Vietnamese borders as long as necessary to sap Saigon's will to continue the struggle.

E. In attempting to cope with the communist military threat, South Vietnamese forces will probably require substantial US support for many years. ARVN lacks the logistical system and technological and managerial skills required to maintain and support a modern fighting force. There are also serious personnel problems, including a shortage of qualified leaders and a propensity for enlisted ranks to desert. Problems of leadership and morale are even more severe in the territorial forces and village militia, key elements in the campaign to control the countryside.

F. A major element in Hanoi's ability to stay the course in South Vietnam is the apparent durability of the communist party apparatus there. The apparatus has been hurt, severely in some areas, but relatively few high-level communist cadres have been eliminated as a result of direct GVN action against them. The communists have been able to maintain a viable organization, and this is likely to continue to be the case for the foreseeable future.

G. In addition to the threat posed by the communists, the GVN will have to cope with internal problems. These include meeting the increased demands of a society in the process of change. A greatly enlarged urban slum population has been created and is a target for radical agitation, while the rural populace looks increasingly to the government to meet its growing needs. In the economic sphere, the GVN simply will not be able to satisfy the demands of this "revolution

(Continued...)

of rising expectations" from its own resources. The political impact of the changing South Vietnamese society is less easily defined. But the regime is likely to find itself faced with rising nationalism, often manifested as anti-Americanism. In the future, there is also likely to be a shift toward a more traditional Vietnamese pattern of a centralized executive authority, although the major elements of the present constitutional system are likely to be retained. Such a system might result in a more efficient government, but the regime might also rely increasingly on its coercive powers, thereby leading to instability and risking political disintegration.

H. Over the longer term, a critical factor in South Vietnam's survival will be the will of the South Vietnamese as a people and as a nation to sustain the struggle against the communists. As Vietnamization proceeds, the South Vietnamese will have to cope with the communists and face the country's problems largely on their own. Developments thus far suggest that they are responding reasonably well to the challenge. But there is no way to determine how tenacious they will be a few years hence when the US is much further along the road to disengagement.

I. Thus, it is impossible at this time to offer a clear-cut estimate about South Vietnam's prospects through the mid-1970s. There are many formidable problems and no solid assurances over this period of time. In our view, the problems facing the GVN, the uncertainties in South Vietnam about the magnitude, nature, and duration of future US support, doubts concerning the South Vietnamese will to persist, the resiliency of the communist apparatus in South Vietnam, and North Vietnam's demonstrated ability and willingness to pay the price of perseverance are such that the longer term survival of the GVN is by no means yet assured.

DISCUSSION

I. THE PRESENT SITUATION

1. Over the past three years, South Vietnam has made substantial progress. The performance of the army (ARVN) has improved steadily; it has assumed the bulk of the ground fighting responsibility without any appreciable decline in territorial security. Indeed, in this period, the Government of South Vietnam (GVN) has extended its control, or at least its access, to most of the country's territory and almost all of its population. As a result, people's confidence in the government has increased, particularly in the rural areas.

2. A more stable political situation has also evolved in South Vietnam. Political participation has broadened greatly, and all major groups have at least a piece of the action—if not in the executive branch, then in the legislature or at the local level. The regime apparently values the aura of legitimacy that accrues from operating on a constitutional basis, and most political elements, including the key military leaders, show no disposition to challenge the government frontally. To most groups, the gains to be derived from working within the system appear to outweigh the costs and risks of efforts to overturn it. In addition, the government's administrative structure has improved, making possible a more vigorous and effective attack on the country's problems. Overall, there is considerable forward momentum in South Vietnam today, and an air of cautious optimism permeates many sectors of the population.

3. As for the Vietnamese communists, during the past year their military/political position in the countryside has been further eroded, considerably in some areas, and their forces have continued to suffer substantial casualties despite lower levels of combat activity. Captured documents continue to reflect difficulties in the communist effort to strengthen the party's control apparatus. Nor has Hanoi been able to achieve decisive results on the political front. Despite surges in antiwar sentiment in the US, the administration

has been able to pursue Vietnamization at a deliberate pace, thus dimming any hopes that Hanoi may have had of winning concessions from the US in the near term. The turn of events in Cambodia and southern Laos has compounded communist problems in South Vietnam, requiring Hanoi to divert energy and manpower toward reconstituting and expanding logistical routes. The loss of sanctuaries and the widened area of conflict have particularly complicated the communist situation in South Vietnam. Hanoi also has problems on the home front, where economic reconstruction and development continue to be subordinated to the requirements of the war. Morale problems have resulted as manpower losses in the South have increasingly been brought home to the North Vietnamese populace.

4. But the war is far from over. Despite their difficulties, the communists retain important military capabilities throughout Indochina. As their recent performance in southern Laos demonstrates, they can still fight hard when they choose to do so. Meanwhile, the tightly disciplined communist party organization in South Vietnam gives them considerable flexibility in adapting to changing conditions. Finally, as the US withdraws, existing weaknesses in South Vietnamese government and society will tend to surface, requiring increased attention in Saigon to basic problems affecting internal stability and national development.

II. GVN PROBLEMS AND PROSPECTS THROUGH 1971

A. Political Problems—the October Election

5. As the next order of business, the South Vietnamese must settle the question of national leadership for the next several years. This process will come to a head in the presidential election now scheduled for October 1971.[1] The election will test public acceptance of Thieu's stewardship and, to some degree, the strength of the system of government now prevailing in South Vietnam.

6. The Thieu government's image with the electorate is at best gray. Inability to bring peace, the military's large role in government, corruption, economic problems, and the GVN's extensive dependence on US support all will cost Thieu votes. Even so, Thieu seems to be the front runner at this time. He has, first of all, tremendous assets at his disposal. Thieu can utilize available governmental and military personnel and funds to propagandize for his candidacy and to get out the vote. His control of the massive governmental administrative and security apparatus and his personal support within the military establishment probably assure him a large number of votes from these sectors. Finally, he has worked hard in recent years to broaden his appeal to the rural population; the land reform program and the improved security conditions in the countryside should serve to bolster his standing among the peasantry.

7. *Thieu's Opposition.* Thieu's major opponent currently appears to be Duong Van ("Big") Minh, though he may ultimately decide not to run. Minh's appeal has never been tested at the polls, but he is a national figure and appears to have a favorable image throughout much of the country. And despite his ineffective performance during his three months as Chief of State (1963-1964), Minh apparently retains some support within the military and administrative establishments. The An Quang Buddhists, despite certain reservations, are also likely to throw their con-

[1] Elections for the Lower House will take place in August. Although these elections may provide clues to the way the political winds are blowing in South Vietnam, they are more likely to reflect local issues and personalities.

siderable influence behind his candidacy. Although he is neither a "peacenik" nor anti-American, Minh would probably pull a substantial proportion of the pro-peace and anti-US vote. More important, Minh should also gain the bulk of the anti-administration protest vote. Finally, Minh might be the recipient of whatever votes the communists could deliver, though there are no indications that they believe Minh would wittingly serve communist ends.

8. Minh so far has stuck to platitudes about national unity under his leadership; his stand on major issues has been vague. He blames Thieu for inflation in South Vietnam, but has not indicated how he would handle the problem. He has identified himself more or less with groups espousing peace sentiments, but he has not come forth with any specific proposals for settlement of the war. He seems to believe that he could outmaneuver the communists and has adopted a less bellicose stand than Thieu against their participation in the political process, but he has ruled out the possibility of a coalition arrangement. He has been in contact with most major political elements in South Vietnam, but has made no firm commitments to any. Many people, including some of his supporters, have reservations as to whether Minh will run and whether he could provide adequate leadership, especially in the period when the US is withdrawing from South Vietnam.

9. Vice President Nguyen Cao Ky is also a potential candidate. Although he has not officially declared himself in the race, he is casting about for political support and is increasingly vocal in his criticism of Thieu and his policies. Ky, however, does not appear to have a major power base or a large popular following and would appear to have little chance of winning the election. Thus, it is possible that his current maneuvering is designed to enhance his bargaining power and that he will not actually run. But if he does, Ky's candidacy will be a complicating factor in the election. He would probably cut into Thieu's support among the military; since he seems to be trying to project a somewhat "dovish" image, Ky could also draw some support away from Minh.

10. *The Communist Role in the Election.* The communists would certainly like to see Thieu defeated or at least to discredit the election results in South Vietnam. It is doubtful, however, that they have the capability to do very much either to influence the election's outcome or to disrupt the voting process on a countrywide basis. Their past performance in this area has been weak, and captured documents suggest that their shortcomings have not yet been overcome. Thus, while the communists would attempt to exploit any anti-regime demonstration that occurred, it is doubtful that they could spark significant demonstrations on their own. Beyond this, Hanoi might surface a "peace" initiative during the campaign in an effort to complicate Thieu's position.

11. But in general Hanoi seems to assume that Thieu will be re-elected and is already denouncing the elections as a fraud. Even if Minh won, the communists probably would not view his victory as portending a decisive shift in the political climate in their favor. Communist hopes in the event of a Minh victory would probably rest more on an expectation that the GVN would be more inefficient and unstable under his leadership than on a belief that he would be conciliatory. They might feel out Minh's intentions, however, by adopting a less bellicose attitude toward the new government and perhaps by showing a somewhat greater interest in talking with Minh.

12. *Election Prospects.* Uncertainties as to trends in the overall military situation over the next few months complicate an election forecast. If, on top of Lam Son 719, the com-

munists maintain a considerable show of military strength over the next few months, Thieu's election prospects might be affected adversely. On the other hand, a generally low level of communist military action during this period could enhance the regime's claims to progress in the military and security fields, and increase Thieu's support in the election.

13. Another factor in the election campaign will be the South Vietnamese perception of the US posture. Paramount in the minds of many South Vietnamese is the question of whether the election results would significantly affect the level of US support. Most South Vietnamese believe that the US favors Thieu staying in office, and this may incline many voters to opt for him in hopes of ensuring continued US support. Aware of such sentiment, Minh has gone to some lengths to urge a policy of "neutrality" for the US in the election, stating that unless the US demonstrates that it favors no particular candidate, he may not even run since Thieu would be sure to win. In any event, if the South Vietnamese public came to believe that the US was truly neutral or favored someone other than Thieu, his chances of election would probably decline.

14. All things considered, however, Thieu appears to stand a better than even chance of winning the election. His control of the governmental apparatus and the financial resources at his disposal are advantages difficult to overcome. This knowledge should encourage discretion on his part and reduce the possibility of blatantly underhanded election tactics by the regime. For their part, despite a desire to unseat Thieu, most of the noncommunist opposition elements would probably be loath to risk undermining the present system by disruptive actions.

15. If Thieu is re-elected, it will be an obvious mandate for continuing along present lines. But Minh also might not depart significantly from existing policies. He would face the same problems with basically the same assets as Thieu; and, ultimately, he would have to rely on the military as the major prop of his regime. There would be a chance of erosion in governmental effectiveness under Minh as he attempted to put his stamp on the administration, mainly because this would almost certainly entail a shake-up in personnel assigned to key programs. Minh's policies toward the communists, however, would be the key factor in his hold on power once elected. If he began to assume what the military deemed an overly accommodating posture toward the communists, they would probably warn him to desist; a coup would be possible.

16. Previous elections under the Thieu regime have appeared to be relatively honest. But the stakes are higher than ever before. The country's future is likely to be determined by developments during the next four years, a period in which the South Vietnamese will have to demonstrate that they can fend largely for themselves as the US progressively disengages from Indochina. This could increase the regime's nervousness about the Minh candidacy. Ky's appearance on the ballot would increase the uncertainty in Thieu's camp. The regime might conclude that a relatively honest election was too risky and be tempted to rig the voting. If they did so in a blatant manner, it could inflame the political opposition and special interest groups, and the regime might find itself faced with demonstrations and rioting, especially in the cities. Such developments obviously would lessen the prospects for national cohesion over the longer term.

B. Economic Problems

17. With the help of large infusions of US economic assistance, the South Vietnamese economy has responded relatively well to years of war and military mobilization. Per

capita consumption has remained approximately stable, and there has been no serious decline in domestic production despite the massive dislocation of the labor force. In addition, as a result of military construction activities, South Vietnam now possesses a well-developed transportation network and air and port facilities. In the past few years, the agricultural sector has benefited from technological advances, and a revolutionary land reform program has gotten underway.

18. Nevertheless, there are still serious shortcomings in the South Vietnamese economy. It is far from being self-sustaining; large-scale US assistance provides the basic underpinning for the economy and will have to do so for years to come. And GVN economic policies have perforce largely been concerned with the short-term military and political consequences of the war, and have slighted the more basic aspects of economic development.

19. Over the short term, the major problem continues to be the threat of inflation.[2] Although the regime's recent economic reforms contributed to a substantial slowdown in the pace of inflation, it is a persistent and serious problem. At its heart is the massive spending by the Vietnamese and US Governments for war-related purposes. As a result, effective demand has tended to exceed the available supply of goods and services. Only by recourse to a program of massive imports, financed almost totally by the US, has the GVN been able to keep inflation from skyrocketing.[3] The availability of imported consumer goods has improved the GVN's image at home, but at the same time it has conditioned the population to expect relative abundance in the midst of war. In short, consumer demand has become rather sophisticated, while the GVN's economic base and practices, despite some improvements, have not.

20. The US troop withdrawal program will tend to complicate the effort to find solutions to the GVN's economic problems. Large numbers of South Vietnamese workers are being released by US forces and their contractors. Providing additional jobs in the civilian economy would require increases in production and imports, which in turn would require increased foreign aid. Meanwhile, the reduction in US military expenditures is reducing the GVN's supply of dollars, and hence its own resources for purchasing imports and stimulating economic growth.

21. *Short-Term Economic Prospects.* Income distribution will continue to be an important issue in South Vietnam. In recent years, farmers have had a significant increase in real income, but the political will to tax the farmer directly does not seem to exist. Within the urban areas, workers in the private sector have done reasonably well despite some erosion of real income. On the other hand, the civil service and military are much worse off than several years ago despite a recent wage increase, and their unhappiness could create problems for the government in addition to making any systematic attack on corruption vastly more difficult. Despite this, the GVN probably will not attempt to redistribute income significantly through another government pay hike or by other means in this election year.

22. Grievances growing out of the maldistribution of income may cause political difficulties for Thieu in the months ahead, but are not likely to pose a critical threat to the GVN's viability during 1971. The worst of the re-

[2] The increase in prices ranged from 30 percent to 55 percent each year from 1965 through 1969 and amounted to 30 percent in 1970. Since July 1970, however, there has been almost no increase in basic prices.

[3] From an annual average of $334 million during 1963-1965, imports of goods rose to an average of $725 million during 1966-1969. On the other hand, exports declined rapidly because of reduced production of the country's two major export commodities—rice and rubber. In 1969, exports amounted to only 4 percent of imports; data for 1970 are not available.

(Continued...)

gime's other economic problems will continue to be alleviated by large-scale US assistance. Labor dislocations caused by US withdrawals will create some localized problems, but these are not likely to be critical.

C. Military Problems—Communist Strategy and United States' Withdrawals

23. *Communist Military Action in the Near Term.* The communists retain significant military capabilities in various parts of South Vietnam, particularly in the northerly provinces. But in southern South Vietnam, these capabilities are severely limited relative to the period 1967-1969 as a result of the loss of the Sihanoukville supply route, disruption and attrition of the communist support structure in South Vietnam itself, continued air interdiction, and allied cross-border operations in Cambodia and Laos. The communists recognize their weaknesses in South Vietnam and over the past year have been trying to repair the situation. Heavy emphasis has been given to beefing up the infrastructure, increasing the number of "legal" communist cadres who can operate in GVN-controlled areas, and subverting the South Vietnamese military and security forces. In the meantime, the communists have relied largely on small unit actions, terror tactics, and sabotage in an effort to conserve forces in anticipation of a prolonged struggle.

24. Most of the available evidence suggests that, for the next six months or so, the communists will continue with these same basic tactics to husband manpower and resources and to rebuild their position in the countryside. Nevertheless, occasional spurts of communist military activity will occur and there may be some military pyrotechnics prior to the South Vietnamese presidential election. But the present pattern of communist action in most of the country, the state of readiness of their forces in South Vietnam, the restrictions imposed by their logistic support capability, and the evidence drawn from captured documents, clandestine reports, and interrogation of communist prisoners and ralliers all suggest that any heightened military activity in South Vietnam over the next several months will be limited in area and duration.

25. *Impact of US Withdrawals.* South Vietnamese forces are being spread more thinly with each succeeding US withdrawal, and despite the weaknesses of communist forces, there will probably be some deterioration in local security during 1971. The combat effectiveness of ARVN may also suffer somewhat as US artillery and helicopter support is diminished. But for the next several months at least, no critical problems are likely to develop. So far, the psychological impact of the withdrawals has been limited; most South Vietnamese have by now adjusted mentally to the fact that the US will continue to scale down its military involvement in Vietnam. Even though demonstrated ARVN shortcomings may raise doubts in South Vietnam about ARVN's ability to fill the gap over the longer term as the US disengages from Indochina, such doubts are unlikely to result in any serious deterioration in the morale of ARVN or the general public during 1971.

III. MAJOR PROBLEMS OVER THE LONGER TERM

A. The Nature of the Communist Threat

26. *Prospects for 1972.* Hanoi's approach to the war in 1972 will be conditioned by certain basic elements in the situation such as continued US withdrawals, improvements in the pacification situation and in the capabilities of South Vietnam's military forces, and communist determination to gain control of South Vietnam. Certain recent developments, particularly allied operations in Laos and Cambodia, will also have some effect. On the one hand, the communists suffered

heavy casualties in these operations, lost and expended significant quantities of supplies, and had their supply lines disrupted; and this is likely to impose restrictions on the scale of military action possible during the early stages of the 1971-1972 dry season. Beyond this, allied action or the threat of action in Laos and Cambodia will impose a continuing burden on Hanoi to protect and maintain the Laos supply route.

27. On the other hand, having weathered the recent ARVN cross-border operations in southern Laos, Hanoi probably feels somewhat more confident that it can wait out the withdrawal of US forces and stay the course in Indochina. Hanoi's view is probably tempered by the realization that communist forces suffered very heavy casualties in Lam Son 719 and benefited from terrain which favored the defense, as well as from superior numbers in place on the ground. The operation did not provide any solutions to the many problems the communists face in South Vietnam. But from Hanoi's point of view, its forces contained a threat to its vital supply lines, and avoided a critical setback to the 1970-1971 supply effort. Hanoi probably calculates that ARVN, on its own, would have great difficulty in mounting further cross-border operations of this magnitude once the US is largely out of the picture.

28. Given this outlook, Hanoi might opt in 1972 for a continuation of its basically low-profile military approach in South Vietnam. In the meantime, the communists would pursue their efforts to prepare the logistical and organizational base necessary for either a long drawn-out struggle or a return to large-unit action once US forces were no longer an important factor in the war.

29. But there are other considerations which could lead Hanoi to attempt a step-up in military activity in 1972. For example, if communist fortunes took a sharp turn for the worse in the months ahead, Hanoi might hope to reverse the trend by increasing its attacks against ARVN and other government security forces during the 1971-1972 dry season campaign. Such a decision on Hanoi's part could also come later in 1972 if Hanoi at that time were convinced that the US was determined to maintain an effective residual presence in South Vietnam for an extended period.

30. Regardless of the course of the war, Hanoi's leaders might see considerable advantage in a show of military muscle prior to the US election, intended to demonstrate that Vietnamization was not working and to fan antiwar sentiment in the US. In their view, the effort could help generate increased domestic pressure on the US Administration to disengage completely from the war or, failing this, it might affect the election outcome itself. They might also calculate that the backlash in South Vietnam from negative US reactions to adverse battlefield developments would work to communist advantage by sharpening US-South Vietnamese differences.

31. On balance, we believe that Hanoi will find the arguments for some step-up in its military activity in South Vietnam persuasive. But this would be likely to differ from Hanoi's present strategy more in degree than in kind. Thus, we would not envisage an effort by Hanoi to duplicate in scale or intensity the 1968 Tet offensive. Instead, we would expect a general increase in the level of communist activity with sharp focus on a few selected areas, most likely the northern provinces and highland region of South Vietnam. The thrust of this strategy would be to attempt, with greater determination than in recent years, to score tactical victories aimed at impacting adversely on the South Vietnamese and US will to persist in the struggle.

32. Whether or not the communists initiate such increased activity, we do not believe that they will be able to reverse the military

balance in South Vietnam in 1972. Continuing communist difficulties will impose limits on how much they can accomplish, and continued allied pressures during the remainder of 1971 and pre-emptive operations in the 1971-1972 dry season could forestall communist preparations for extensive military operations. But the communists are unlikely to be frustrated at every turn; there are too many vulnerabilities in the South Vietnamese situation. For example, the adverse psychological impact in South Vietnam of increased communist military activity could be considerable, particularly if it led—or were thought by the South Vietnamese to be leading—to a weakening of US resolve. And even if—in a purely military sense—the odds seem to favor the South Vietnamese being able to contain the communist effort in 1972, the GVN will still be faced with a communist military and political organization retaining significant strength and potential.

33. *Beyond 1972.* At this point in time, there seems little doubt that the communists will continue to maintain an active challenge to the GVN well beyond 1972. Despite continued concern over the Sino-Soviet dispute, Hanoi probably assumes that it will continue to receive military and economic assistance from both Moscow and Peking as long as necessary. For its part, Hanoi has committed enormous manpower and material resources and has suffered staggering losses in attempting to gain control of South Vietnam. And while there have been shifts in strategy, Hanoi's will to persist has shown little indication of flagging. The war has been going on for over a generation—it has become a way of life for the communists and a part of their ethos. Any leader in Hanoi who advocated giving up the struggle would risk losing his position. Indeed, the present communist leadership might find it difficult to contemplate any course other than continuation of the struggle even if it meant throwing away additional resources in a basically fruitless effort. The question in their minds is not whether to continue the struggle, but how and at what level it should be pursued.

34. The "how" and "at what level" may be as difficult for Hanoi to decide as it is for us to estimate at this stage. Much would depend on how Hanoi viewed the remaining US presence and commitment to Saigon, on the strength and morale of ARVN at that time, and on what balance Hanoi struck in its willingness to continue investing resources in the struggle. There are risks and practical difficulties in any course which Hanoi might contemplate.

35. Assuming that ARVN and the territorial forces maintain or improve their capabilities over the next year or so, any communist effort in the period beyond 1972 to return to large-scale military action in South Vietnam would involve heavy manpower commitments and other strenuous demands on a North Vietnamese population already weary from the cumulative effects of the war. It would also require, as a precondition, the maintenance of secure logistic routes to the South and the rebuilding of an infrastructure in South Vietnam capable of supporting the operations of main force units in the countryside. And, of course, a large-scale military effort might fail and put at risk the ability of Hanoi to rebuild its forces once again.

36. To do too little also involves serious risk. There is no way to be sure what the impact of a long, drawn-out, low-level struggle would be on communist cadres and lower level elements in South Vietnam. Many of them might in time abandon the effort, rendering the communists unable to present a credible challenge to local security in South Vietnam. In North Vietnam, the communists might also face a decline in popular commitment to the struggle. In a sense, the war is

an "old man's" war, and whether the younger generation in the North shares the same unswerving dedication to the reunification of Vietnam as their elders cannot be determined.

37. The communists may conclude that their circumstances at home and in the South leave them little choice but to pursue a middle course, one not unlike that of the past two years. This would mean that the GVN would be faced with a continuing threat from some main force units, particularly in Military Regions (MRs) I and II, and a generalized local security threat posed by highly self-sufficient guerrillas, sappers, and terrorists throughout the country. And the political, psychological, and subversive struggle would go on at all levels of society.

38. Hanoi can also hope that developments in Laos and Cambodia will further communist objectives in South Vietnam in the years ahead. The communist position in both countries, particularly Laos, is stronger than in South Vietnam. In Laos, Hanoi probably calculates that Vang Pao's Meo guerrillas are fading as an effective fighting force; this, coupled with the possibility that the US air role in Laos may be reduced, could lead Hanoi to foresee the end of any effective indigenous resistance in Laos to communist aims. In Cambodia, on the basis of performance, the communists probably foresee little threat to their established positions from Phnom Penh's fighting forces. Thus, Hanoi probably believes that its prospects over the longer term of being able to hold the key logistical routes extending through the Laotian Panhandle and northeastern Cambodia into South Vietnam are good. And it may calculate that even a moderate level of activity in South Vietnam coupled with the permanent threat posed by communist control of the border areas would in time sap the South Vietnamese will to continue the struggle. At a minimum, Hanoi would expect this situation to impose heavy additional burdens on South Vietnamese forces, both in protecting the country's long border and in doing the work of indigenous anticommunist forces in southern Laos and Cambodia, all the while filling in for departing US forces in South Vietnam.

B. GVN Capabilities to Deal with the Communist Threat

39. *Military and Security Forces.* As the US scales down its involvement in the war, the South Vietnamese military forces will be required to assume increasing responsibilities in the struggle against the communists. Given in political requirement to provide security to the population throughout large portions of the countryside, the GVN will be forced to maintain a large military establishment to check communist activity. Progress has been made in preparing the South Vietnamese forces for the time when they are more or less on their own, but it will be years before the South Vietnamese can be self-sufficient in the military field.

40. For example, although the South Vietnamese have a significant capability for in-country air support, plans are only in the embryonic stage to provide them with a capability to mount air interdiction efforts against the communist logistical network in southern Laos. Further, ARVN has come to rely on helicopter support, and current plans call for a major reduction in the number of helicopters to remain in South Vietnam as US forces depart. Despite substantial improvements, the GVN's logistical system is not yet capable of meeting the large military establishment's needs without relying heavily on US assistance. Similarly, it will be many years before the South Vietnamese military acquires the requisite technological and managerial skills to handle the complexities of maintaining and supporting a modern fighting force.

41. The availability of technical and logistical assistance will be especially vital to the maintenance of ARVN's fighting effectiveness. ARVN has become increasingly dependent on the availability of such complex equipment as helicopters, advanced communications and fire-control equipment, and electronic monitors and sensors. The use of such equipment has given the South Vietnamese considerable advantages in combating the communists. But without substantial US assistance in maintenance, much of the modern equipment would probably deteriorate over time. ARVN might find it difficult to change its tactics and to fight without all of its technically sophisticated paraphernalia. The South Vietnamese will look to the US to continue to provide—and to assist in maintaining—the types of equipment presently available.

42. The persistence of certain basic shortcomings within the South Vietnamese military establishment is likely to impede military progress over the longer run. Despite improvements, there is little prospect that the military leadership will lose its elitist cast; high-level promotions are likely to continue to be based more on social class and personal loyalties than on military competence. Life for the common soldier will continue to be hard, and separation from families will be frequent. Military pay and allowances at all ranks, already very low, probably will not keep up with the pace of inflation. Under these conditions, military desertions are likely to continue at a fairly high rate.

43. Problems of leadership, morale, and material support are even more severe in the territorial security forces (Regional Forces and Popular Forces—RF/PF) and in the People's Self Defense Force (PSDF) than in the regular military branches. This is so even though these forces are now performing well in many parts of South Vietnam and deserve much of the credit for the improvement in local security. As the US withdraws, ARVN will have to assume the full burden of the main force war, leaving local security even more fully in the hands of the territorial forces and the PSDF. The critical importance of these forces appears to be understood at the highest levels of government, and they are receiving better training and equipment. But a considerable part of the pressure to improve the local units has come from the US. Only with a continued push from the highest national levels will the territorial security forces be assured the equipment and support needed to assume increased responsibilities. Without this support, the GVN's position in the countryside would probably suffer gradual deterioration.

44. Corruption could also continue to impair the military effectiveness of the GVN in the future. Many, possibly most, of the upper echelons of the military establishment engage in some form of corruption; in some cases, the abuses are flagrant and common knowledge. Such excesses tend to lower morale within the ranks and may contribute to the poorly paid, lower level soldier's lack of commitment and tendency to desert. The abundance of US goods has contributed to the growth of corruption and to the improper diversion of military goods and supplies. As the US scales down its effort, such diversions could leave some units short of needed supplies and vulnerable to communist attack.

45. A final critical factor in considering the GVN's military and security forces is that of will. There are no precise guidelines with which to measure the will of the South Vietnamese fighting man. To the extent that they have positive motivation, the RF, PF, and PSDF probably are fighting more from a desire to protect family and village than from any commitment to the Saigon government or aversion to communism. Within the ARVN, many senior officers and noncoms appear ideologically opposed to the communists.

(Continued...)

Moreover, while most soldiers would like to see the war come to an end, they would certainly prefer that South Vietnam remain non-communist. In general, however, the commitment of ARVN to the struggle rests more on the force of discipline and being caught up in the system than any other factor.

46. *The Attack on the Communist Apparatus.* The GVN's ability to eliminate the communist party structure is questionable. The communist apparatus has been hurt, severely in some areas, but most of the damage stems from the expanded GVN military presence in the countryside and from attrition resulting from the fighting. GVN programs against the communist apparatus have had limited success; relatively few high-level communist cadres have been eliminated as a result of direct GVN action. Moreover, much of the impetus in the GVN's effort has come from US involvement in the programs. As the US reduces its role in these programs, the GVN is unlikely to take up all the slack, and the effort against the communist apparatus would be likely to decline in effectiveness.

47. The South Vietnamese police forces are ill-equipped to take on the task of rooting out the communist apparatus; their operating procedures are inclined to be erratic, and their motivation appears low. The communists have penetrated the regime's security and police forces, and there is a widespread reluctance among the people to turn in communist cadres to the authorities. Many, perhaps most, South Vietnamese have connections, often family ties, with someone in the communist apparatus. Furthermore, the GVN's detention and judicial systems are lax; when apprehended, communists often go free because of slipshod procedures or the venality of GVN officials. As a consequence, the communists have been able to maintain a viable organization despite the GVN's counterefforts, and this is likely to continue to be the case for the foreseeable future.

C. Political Trends

48. The GVN's political cohesion will be subject to increased stress over the next few years as the US presence with its stabilizing influence declines. Frictions between the executive and the legislative branches are likely to sharpen. Though political groups will expect to participate increasingly in the politics of the nation, there is little prospect for the development of truly nationally-based political parties. It is more likely that the political groupings will continue to reflect various parochial and regional interests. The politics of South Vietnam are likely to remain basically divisive in nature much as in the past. Though these conditions may complicate the development of a cohesive political system, they need not necessarily lead to political instability.

49. In the future, there is likely to be a further shift toward a more traditional Vietnamese pattern: a centralized executive authority which nonetheless permits a considerable degree of popular participation and responsibility at the village level. The major elements of the present, foreign-inspired constitutional system, however, are likely to be retained. Continued dependence on US aid and support will provide one incentive to retain them. Additionally, the constitution tends to bestow an aura of legitimacy on whoever holds the presidency. At the same time, many groups of South Vietnamese have come to view the system as something of a barrier against extreme abuses of executive power.

50. The stronger central control envisaged for South Vietnam might well result in more efficient government; if so, it would probably be acceptable to the majority of the South Vietnamese even if democratic niceties were honored more in form than in substance. But the danger in strong central control, especially if popular political participation were severely restricted, is that it could lead to extremes in coercion, increasing grievances against the

(Continued...)

system and leading organized groups to take their complaints into the streets. The organization and skills necessary to make authoritarian controls effective have not existed in South Vietnam, and in the event of mounting popular opposition, the risk of a breakdown in public order would be high.

51. In any case, as the US phases down in South Vietnam—particularly if the communist military threat increases—the political role of the military is likely to become more open and active. Though hardly a monolith, it seems apparent that the military will remain the ultimate arbiter of power in South Vietnam; not only is it the only truly nationally organized group, but it contains most of the country's competent administrators. Moreover, as any GVN president will recognize, the government will be more secure with heavy military participation than with the generals relegated to the position of disgruntled observers or plotters. The withdrawal of US forces, however, will remove some of the inhibitions to extra-legal action by the military. If the problems confronting the GVN became particularly critical or if the generals feared that political leaders were about to make a dangerously soft settlement with the communists, they would be likely to attempt a coup. Before making such a move, however, the military leadership would probably attempt to correct such tendencies by exerting influence within the system.

52. Over the longer term, the GVN will have to face the problems of both developing and coping with nationalism. Nationalism is hardly a new emotion for the Vietnamese; in past centuries, nationalism—bordering on xenophobia—has provided strong cement for the nation in its struggle against foreign invaders. It was the ability of Ho Chi Minh to harness this force that provided the major impetus for the communist movement in the struggle for independence against the French. But the GVN has not and probably cannot, over the next few years at least, develop a sense of South Vietnamese nationalism that could be used effectively in the struggle with the North.

53. The traditional sense of Vietnamese nationalism with its xenophobic overtones, however, is alive and growing in the GVN. This is likely to pose problems for US-GVN relations. For the last decade the South Vietnamese have been forced to rely on the US for survival. Many South Vietnamese have found this dependence humiliating, and there is little doubt that a reservoir of anti-American sentiment exists in South Vietnam. Recent demonstrations, sparked by offenses—real and alleged—against South Vietnamese by US military personnel, have illustrated the volatility of the issue.

54. In the future, many issues will be given an anti-American twist by oppositionists anxious to tag the leadership as puppets of the US. Sensitive to such charges, the GVN will try to demonstrate its independence of Washington. Indeed, the government in many cases will find it convenient to shunt the blame for its own shortcomings onto the US, further feeding anti-American sentiment in the South. In short, the US is likely to be placed more frequently in the role of the villain and charged with being insensitive to the needs and interests of South Vietnam.

D. The Changing South Vietnamese Society

55. Over the longer term, the government in Saigon will be called upon to contend with other new tensions and anxieties which have developed in South Vietnamese society. Since the fall of the Diem regime, South Vietnam has been undergoing a revolutionary transformation—unanticipated, virtually unreported, and largely without guidance or objectives. Years of gradual adjustment to the stresses of war have led to vast alterations

in social organization: the displacement of large populations, the disruption and often the destruction of traditional village life, the breakdown and partial replacement of the traditional class system, and the chaotic growth of urban centers.

56. Striking changes in Vietnamese society are taking place in the countryside. In much of the country, Viet Cong and GVN-sponsored land reforms have tended to undermine the power of traditional provincial elites. Radio, television, the Honda, and other manifestations of modernization are altering the small farmer's way of life; the adoption of even a modest amount of modern farming technology is changing his role and expectations. He sees his prosperity linked to free access to GVN-controlled markets. Moreover, after years of GVN neglect, sometimes benign but often not, the Thieu government has begun to woo the villager. In addition to land reform, local leadership and village autonomy are being emphasized, and there have been promises of large investments in agricultural development.

57. The political implications of these processes cannot be defined with confidence. The rural Vietnamese are not only exceedingly weary of war and political turmoil, but also considerably more sophisticated about national developments. Thus, although the villager resents GVN corruption and abuses of power, there is reason to believe that he is also more resistant to communist blandishments. If the GVN is moderately successful in meeting rural demands for more effective administrative and economic services, and demonstrates greater overall concern with their personal well-being, it may in time alleviate many of the adversities which the farmers have suffered over the past decade and prevent the countryside from serving as the seedbed for yet another cycle of guerrilla activity.

58. While roughly 60 percent of South Vietnam's population still lives in the countryside, there has been an unprecedented influx into the country's towns and cities. Originally caused by rural insecurity, the migration was accelerated by a belief that economic opportunities were greater in the cities. Though any improvements in security and economic conditions in the countryside—and prospective GVN programs—will draw some back to their home areas, problems of rapid urban growth will not dissipate. Those who remain in the towns will still be crowded into slums, detached from their traditional communal ties, and exposed to various forms of agitation. Underemployment will be a problem, particularly as US labor needs diminish. Over time, city dwellers—especially frustrated middle class elements and veterans—could become considerably more receptive to radical appeals if the government is unable to meet their demands.

59. These changes in city and country will strain the government's relatively limited funds and expertise. The GVN's efforts to meet its "revolution of rising expectations" will also be impeded by a cumbersome administrative apparatus and widespread corruption. Even with the best of intentions, the GVN simply will not be able with its own internal resources to generate the jobs and capital needed to satisfy the level of economic demand (goods, services, and technology) already reached. While the Vietnamese are basically ambitious and hard working, industrialization can come only slowly. And it will be some time before they can export large quantities of agricultural products; in particular, the rubber industry, will take years to recover its former vigor. Moreover, prospects are not good for substantial foreign investment or large-scale economic assistance so long as the conflict with the communists remains unresolved.[4]

[4] Japan and a few European countries have shown some interest in aiding or investing in South Vietnam, but to nothing like the extent that will be required.

E. The "X" Factor: The Question of Will

60. All of the political, military, and economic factors discussed above will be important in terms of South Vietnam's future prospects. Nonetheless, an examination of these elements does not provide any certain answer to the key issue: the will of the South Vietnamese as a people and as a nation to sustain the struggle against the communists. There are times when "will" can be measured with a fair degree of confidence. By the spring of 1965, for example, it was clear that the South Vietnamese had lost the will to persist; only the large-scale intervention of US combat troops saved South Vietnam from a communist takeover. At Tet 1968, on the other hand, it became clear that ARVN—as well as some significant portion of the population—had developed a sufficient sense of commitment to offer vigorous resistance to the communist offensive. Since that time, this sense of commitment seems to have developed further.

61. The problem remains, however, of determining the extent to which the growth in commitment in South Vietnam derives from and is dependent on a continued US presence. For the past five or six years, the Americans have always been present or readily available with their manpower, materiel, and money to assist with military and economic problems. As Vietnamization proceeds, this will no longer be as true. Vietnamization is already bringing home to the South Vietnamese leaders that the time is fast approaching when they will have to cope with the communists and face the country's problems largely on their own. Developments thus far suggest that they are responding reasonably well to the challenge. But there is no way to determine how tenacious they will be a few years hence when the US is much further along the road to disengagement.

62. Thus, it is impossible at this time to offer a clear-cut estimate about South Vietnam's prospects through the mid-1970s. There are many formidable problems and no solid assurances over this period of time. In our view, the problems facing the GVN, the uncertainties in South Vietnam about the magnitude, nature, and duration of future US support, doubts concerning the South Vietnamese will to persist, the resiliency of the communist apparatus in South Vietnam, and North Vietnam's demonstrated ability and willingness to pay the price of perseverance are such that the longer term survival of the GVN is by no means yet assured.

NIE 53/14.3-73

Short-Term Prospects for Vietnam

12 October 1973

APPROVED FOR RELEASE
DATE: JAN 2005

~~Secret~~

(b)(3)

NATIONAL INTELLIGENCE ESTIMATE

Short-Term Prospects for Vietnam

~~Secret~~
NIE 53/14.3-73
12 October 1973

Copy № 303

(Continued...)

SHORT-TERM PROSPECTS FOR VIETNAM

PRÉCIS

The major judgments in this Estimate are:

A. Hanoi's actions are clearly designed to insure that it can again resort to major military action at some point to gain its objectives if other means fail. The chances of the communists gaining power through the political provisions of the Paris agreement are negligible; nor are their prospects good for achieving the GVN's collapse through a combination of political and clandestine warfare backed up by only moderate military pressure. Hanoi may not have made a final decision as to the timing of a major offensive. It must, however, believe that it will ultimately have to return to the battlefield to seek its objective of reunifying Vietnam. (Paras. 3, 54.)

B. The current military balance in South Vietnam is only slightly in favor of the GVN; with heavy infiltration and supply movements, it may have shifted to the communists' advantage by mid-1974. The political balance, however, is clearly in the GVN's favor and will remain so. (Paras. 6-19, 31-53.)

C. The forward positioning of communist forces and supplies and the improved road system give Hanoi the capability to kick off a

major military campaign with little additional preparation, perhaps less than a month. (Paras. 13-15, 55.)

D. It is a close choice whether Hanoi will opt for a major military offensive during the current dry season (October 1973-May 1974). In making its decision Hanoi must assess the following factors:

— The likelihood and extent of a US response; the positions of Moscow and Peking, particularly the consequences to the North Vietnamese position if they can not be certain of enough material support to cover losses that would accompany prolonged heavy combat; the military balance between its forces and the RVNAF; and the overall political and military situation in the South. (Para. 56.)

— The arguments for and against an offensive this dry season are presented in paragraphs 57-64.[1]

E. If there is not an offensive this dry season, Hanoi will continue to launch and no doubt accelerate carefully orchestrated significant localized, and limited-objective attacks in various regions of South Vietnam to seize territory and test the GVN's resolution. (Paras. 67-68.)

F. In the event of a major communist military effort this dry season, however, the communists would initially make substantial territorial gains in MR-1 where they would probably commit their own air assets. If the fighting were prolonged, RVNAF's continued resistance in MR-1 would be in doubt without renewed US air support. Communist gains in the rest of South Vietnam would be less dramatic, and RVNAF should be able to blunt the communist assault. (Paras. 44, 65-66.)

G. Beyond this dry season, we believe the odds favoring a major communist offensive will increase significantly in the following dry season. (Para. 76.)

— Over the long run, Hanoi may place greater weight on trends it observes in the South than on the external restraints imposed by Moscow, Peking, and Washington. (Paras. 69-75.)

[1] The Assistant Chief of Staff, Intelligence, USAF, believes that the case postulated in favor of a North Vietnamese offensive in 1974, *earlier rather than later,* merits greater weight than the case against such an offensive. His arguments in support of this position are presented in his footnote on page 16.

THE ESTIMATE

I. INTRODUCTION

1. The current situation in Vietnam is one of "less fire" rather than "cease fire", and there is no real peace. Both sides have initiated or provoked some of the fighting that has occurred since the January accords, primarily by attempting to seize or retake territory deemed strategic. In addition, the communists have replenished their southern forces, ignoring the Paris accords' strictures against personnel augmentation or equipment resupply beyond ICCS-supervised exchanges of used materiel. The communists have also engaged in a variety of activities such as road building which, while not technically a violation of the Paris agreement, enhance their military potential.

2. The ICCS has been ineffective in its peace-keeping functions. Nor is there reason to hope that the ICCS will be effective in coming months. Neither Vietnamese party will limit its actions solely because of the formal machinery of the Paris agreement. If anything, the ICCS became weaker with the withdrawal of Canada and the substitution of Iran. In essence, the governing factors for both North and South Vietnam will remain what they have always been—the perception of both Vietnamese parties of the gains and risks involved in pursuing a course of action.

II. THE VIEW FROM HANOI

3. Hanoi has made it clear that it clings to its ultimate goal of uniting Vietnam under communism and will pursue this goal by whatever means possible. But in signing the Paris agreement, North Vietnam admitted that it then faced formidable constraints—military pressure had failed to crack ARVN's resolve and the communist position was growing weaker; the US would not dissolve its commitment to Saigon (indeed, the US response in 1972 was greater than Hanoi anticipated); Hanoi's Soviet and Chinese allies were anxious for détente with Washington; and the cumulative pressures of the war were creating stresses and war-weariness in North Vietnam itself. The North Vietnamese were thus forced to make major concessions in Paris—they had to retreat from their longstanding demand for Thieu's removal, the formation of a coalition government, and an end to US military assistance.

4. Hanoi did not, however, leave Paris empty-handed. The cease-fire and bombing halt left communist forces in control of substantial, but largely unpopulated, areas in South Vietnam and allowed badly hurt units an opportunity to rest and refit. Politically, the PRG gained some aura of respectability. Military pressure on the North ceased, permitting renewed attention to reconstruction and development. And—most important—the agreement signaled the end of direct US military participation in the war.

A. Hanoi's Options

5. In weighing its strategy in the South, North Vietnam can choose from several courses of action.

— It can forego large-scale military operations and attempt to compete primarily through open political competition and clandestine warfare. Displays of military muscle would be designed primarily to protect communist personnel in the field.

— While keeping a lid on large-scale military operations, Hanoi can maintain a moderate level of main-force pressure to assess the capabilities and reactions of the other side. At the same time, it can continue to build up its forces toward the time when it might be feasible to renew all-out hostilities. Essentially, this is the course of action that Hanoi is now following.[2]

— Or, Hanoi can opt to renew offensive warfare on the scale of Tet 1968 or March 1972, either countrywide or in one or two military regions with lower levels of action elsewhere. Such actions could be preceded by a gradual escalation of military pressure—rather than an abrupt series of major assaults—on the theory that such a course would minimize the chance of US intervention.

B. Factors Influencing Hanoi's Policy Decisions

North Vietnam's Internal Strengths and Weaknesses

6. Political leadership in North Vietnam is stable, cohesive, and unchallenged. From time to time, however, there are indications of public and private debate within the ruling hierarchy over basic issues, e.g., large-scale military attacks versus guerrilla warfare tactics, reconstruction of the North versus liberation of the South, and emphasis on political tactics versus military action. Even though rivalries and policy disputes may exist within the collegial apparatus that has ruled since Ho Chi Minh's death, they are masked by a public display of unity and an apparent willingness of the Politburo members to fall in line once decisions are made.[3]

7. Since the cease-fire, Hanoi has rebuilt and strenghtened its internal military structure. The country's air defenses appear stronger than ever. Hanoi has replenished its fighter inventory by bringing most of its Mig-15s and Mig-17s home from China, is integrating Soviet SA-3 missiles into its air defense network around Hanoi, and has renovated, streamlined, and modernized its radar network. The navy also appears stronger as a result of the acquisition in late 1972 of Chi-

[2] Neither of the above options necessarily excludes an occasional flare-up of more serious fighting. An integral aspect of both would be the build-up of the political and economic viability of the communist enclave in western South Vietnam.

[3] It is not possible to speculate meaningfully on the consequences of change by death or removal of one or more of Hanoi's leaders. But in the short run, we do not think it would make much difference.

(Continued...)

nese and Soviet gunboats, including KOMARs. The ground forces have been strengthened by the addition of new armor and artillery, although it is not clear when this materiel entered the North Vietnamese inventory.

8. There is evidence as well that North Vietnamese training programs have been tailored to correct the weaknesses in leadership, discipline and tactics that hampered its army throughout last year's offensive. According to North Vietnamese military journals, conventional warfare doctrine emphasizing the combined use of armor, artillery, and infantry forces is still being stressed. (Coordination between armor and infantry was markedly lacking in the March 1972 offensive.) As in previous years, the North Vietnamese conducted their fall military conscription campaign during August 1973. There is no doubt that North Vietnam has adequate manpower resources for maintaining a large standing army, and the number of men reaching draft age each year is more than sufficient for absorbing a continuing high rate of casualties if major military action were resumed.

9. Communist propaganda continues to list reconstruction as the nation's foremost priority. The bulk of North Vietnam's efforts to date, however, has gone into activities which serve both war-related and civilian needs.

10. In making its policy decisions, the regime might give some consideration—albeit minor—to popular attitudes. There is no evidence, however, of significant popular unrest or serious opposition to the government's policies. The populace would fear that renewed US bombing would accompany a major offensive. Such potential problems, however, could almost certainly be kept in bounds by the regime, particularly if external military aid were forthcoming.

The Communists' Position in the South

11. The communists failed to capture and hold any major population centers in the 1972 offensive, but did seize territory which they are turning into relatively secure base areas in which an extensive and heavily defended interlocking road system is being constructed. (See Figure 1.) The termination of American bombing has relieved most of the pressure on communist logistics and infiltration. Communist efforts at population resettlement and economic development in PRG areas will be some time (if ever) in reaching fruition, but the communists' western enclave already provides them a forward staging area for any future offensive.

12. Since the beginning of the year, North Vietnam has also substantially increased the capabilities of its forces in South Vietnam, notably so in MR-1. Although the GVN retains a substantial manpower advantage in the other military regions, in MR-1 the communists now have a rough parity of forces with ARVN. (See Figure 2.) Moreover, the expansion of NVA firepower has been impressive throughout the country; North Vietnamese forces have a greater concentration of firepower than they had at the outset of the offensive in March 1972. There have been significant increases in AAA, armor, and artillery. North Vietnamese SAMs are deployed in northern South Vietnam. In addition, the communists have rebuilt, or can repair, a number of captured airfields.

13. Perhaps the most ominous aspect of the communist buildup is the positioning of huge stockpiles in or near South Vietnam. From a strictly materiel standpoint, stockpiles of major categories of equipment in place in the North Vietnamese Panhandle, South Vietnam, and adjacent border areas would allow communist forces to maintain heavy combat activity throughout an entire dry season and

(Continued...)

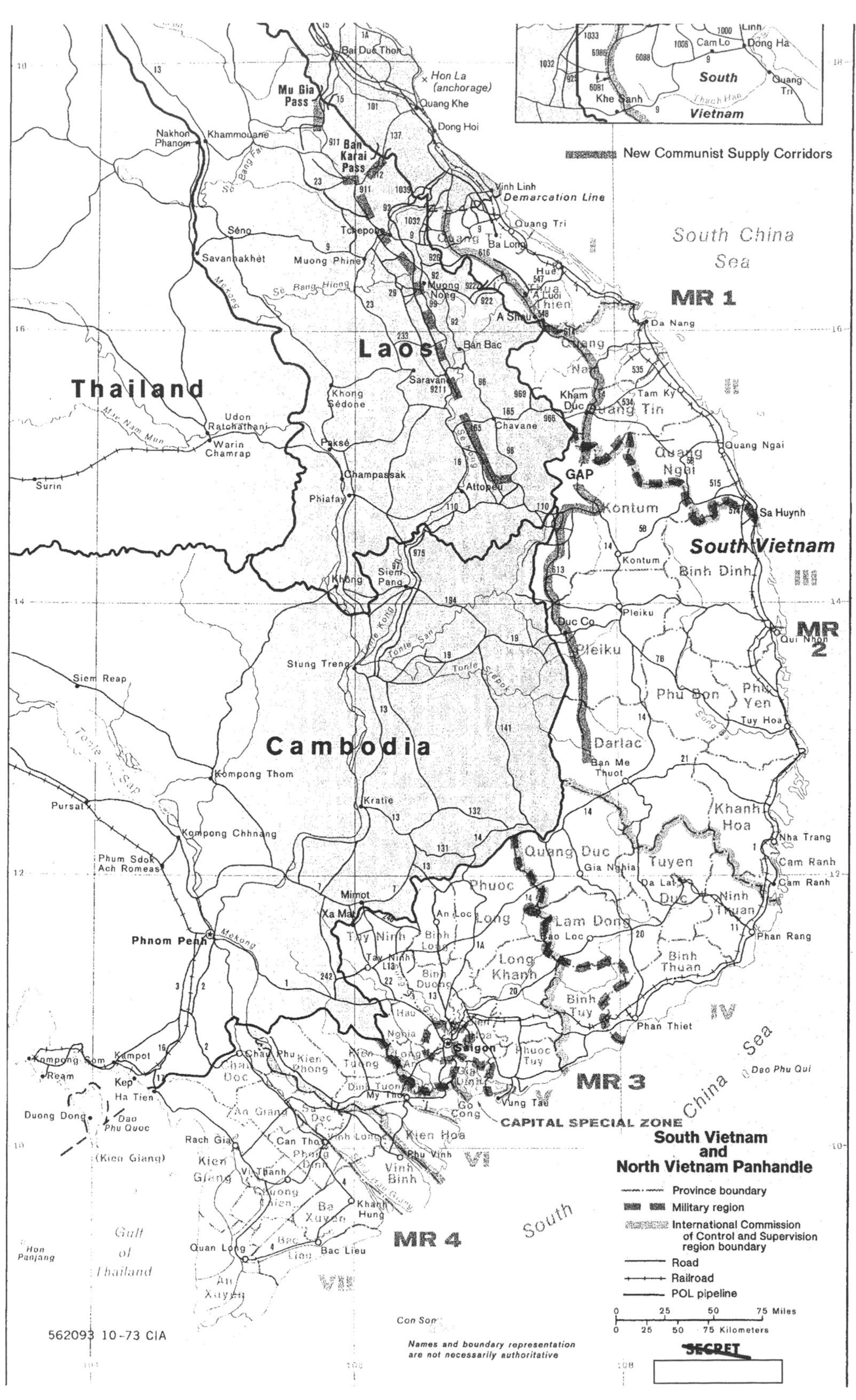
South Vietnam
and
North Vietnam Panhandle
Province boundary
Military region
International Commission of Control and Supervision region boundary
Road
Railroad
POL pipeline
0 25 50 75 Miles
0 25 50 75 Kilometers
New Communist Supply Corridors
Names and boundary representation are not necessarily authoritative
562093 10-73 CIA
SECRET
Thailand
Laos
Cambodia
South Vietnam
South China Sea
Gulf of Thailand
MR 1
MR 2
MR 3
MR 4
CAPITAL SPECIAL ZONE
GAP
Demarcation Line
Mu Gia Pass
Ban Karai Pass
Hon La (anchorage)
Quang Khe
Dong Hoi
Vinh Linh
Quang Tri
Hue
A Shau
Da Nang
Quang Ngai
Sa Huynh
Kontum
Pleiku
Qui Nhon
Tuy Hoa
Ban Me Thuot
Nha Trang
Cam Ranh
Phan Rang
Phan Thiet
Saigon
Vung Tau
Phnom Penh
Kompong Thom
Kompong Chhnang
Kratie
Stung Treng
Siem Reap
Pursat
Kampot
Kep
Ha Tien
Rach Gia
Can Tho
Bac Lieu
Quan Long
Con Son
Dao Phu Qui
Savannakhet
Tchepone
Muong Phine
Saravane
Attopeu
Chavane
Pakse
Champassak
Khong Sedone
Udon Ratchathani
Warin Chamrap
Surin
Nakhon Phanom
Khammouane
Seno
Mimot
Xa Mat
Tay Ninh
An Loc
Duc Co
Kham Duc
Khe Sanh
Dong Ha
Cam Lo

(Continued...)

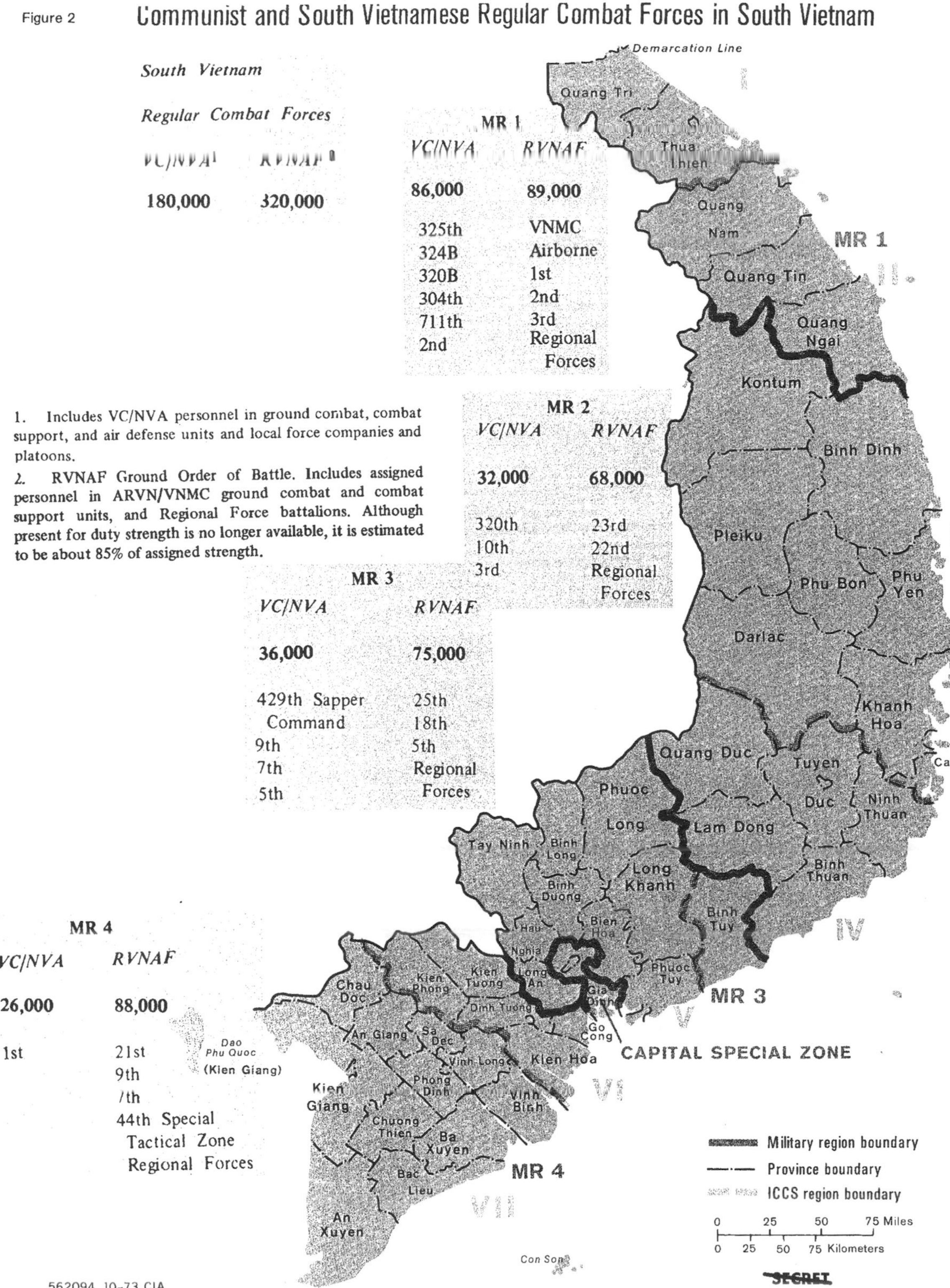

Figure 2 Communist and South Vietnamese Regular Combat Forces in South Vietnam

beyond without any overriding necessity for replenishment. The availability of POL and food is probably more limited. Despite improvements of their logistical situation, however, communist forces would still face some local distribution problems in preparing for and sustaining major military action.

14. There are now considerably more communist combat maneuver battalions and personnel in South Vietnam than at the onset of the 1972 offensive, though many of the units are not totally up to strength. Some 65,000 NVA combat and administrative services personnel have infiltrated south during the first nine months of 1973, the largest portion going to MR-1. Infiltration of combat troops picked up in September, and we expect it to continue in the coming dry season months. The level of such movement will be one clue to Hanoi's intentions. Heavy infiltration would bring NVA forces in the South up to full strength and establish a replacement pool, thus enhancing their capability to launch and sustain an offensive. A low infiltration level, on the other hand, would suggest that Hanoi did not expect heavy military activity in the winter and spring.

15. In general, the communists still have the advantage of being able to choose the time and place for military action. And with personnel and supplies in place close to the battlefield, little lead time is needed for preparing for an offensive, perhaps less than a month. A rapid buildup of personnel and supplies would be detected, but small shifts of personnel, units, or supplies might not.

16. In weighing the military factors, one clear conclusion emerges: the current military balance is only slightly in favor of the GVN.

17. On the other hand, the political balance is clearly in the GVN's favor and will remain so. The communist infrastructure is still weak as a result of the devastating losses of the 1968 offensive and subsequent government pacification campaigns, although there have been some improvements in the infrastructure in at least a few areas. Hard intelligence on the VCI is limited, but there is a generally negative cast in reports on its status, at least to the extent of strongly suggesting that the rebuilding effort will take time. The most serious problem of the VCI is its inability to maintain close contact with the population. This is most apparent in urban areas, but even in the countryside, communist access is limited.

18. The communist presence is still demonstrated by terrorism, enforced tax collection, kidnapping, and harassment. Much of the population is not firmly committed to either side and remains sensitive to any show of force or any shift in the balance of power. Local accommodations are easily arranged and are probably widespread. The North Vietnamese are making open efforts to communicate with ARVN units to consolidate ceasefire positions. Covert arrangements between the communists and local GVN defense forces in isolated villages and outposts are not easily discerned or prevented. These usually work to the communists' advantage by reducing the pressure on base areas, facilitating entry into villages and hamlets for taxing and proselyting, and reducing the flow of intelligence to the government on communist strength and activities.

19. The communist enclaves provide Hanoi a very limited potential for developing an economic base in South Vietnam. The communists are most securely ensconced in northern and western MR-1, but this is not an economically viable area. To build any type of economic infrastructure in the communist-held areas of MR-1 will require heavy imports from North Vietnam and a continued influx of civilian specialists. From a strictly eco-

nomic sense, the communist areas in MR 3 have slightly more potential. In general, however, communist holdings are in isolated areas that are sparsely populated and lacking in resources. The North Vietnamese leaders appear to realize that there is little prospect for a viable "Third Vietnam" in the South which could compete economically or politically with the GVN. Instead, the focus now seems to be on using these areas as forward staging areas for communist military forces.

External Pressures

20. *The USSR and China.* Hanoi has often ignored the advice of its major communist allies in formulating its wartime strategy and counted on forcing their support for reasons of fraternal solidarity and Sino-Soviet competition. Nonetheless, the North Vietnamese leaders are cognizant of their ultimate dependence on their allies' material assistance and have been somewhat sensitive both to their positions on the war and to their relations with each other and with the US. Chinese-Soviet rivalry offered Hanoi some insurance in the past that neither would abandon the field of fraternal support to the other. While this still holds true to some extent, their interest in détente with Washington has produced a commonality of interest between Moscow and Peking in restraining Hanoi's actions. Hanoi's latitude for playing China and the USSR off against each other has been reduced. For example, since the cease-fire, North Vietnamese leaders have made their annual pilgrimages to Moscow and Peking to review their relations and seek new aid agreements. Unlike past years, however, there was no subsequent announcement of military aid from the USSR, although military aid was mentioned after Le Duan's visit to Peking. North Vietnamese public statements (although not the most reliable weathervane) seem to indicate less than a satisfactory outcome.

21. Although Hanoi is now in a logistics position to launch and sustain prolonged heavy military operations in South Vietnam, a decision to do so in the face of opposition by Moscow and Peking and without some assurances of a continued flow of supplies would represent a major gamble unless Hanoi were confident of RVNAF's collapse.[4] To do otherwise would leave Hanoi, should its military effort fail, faced with drawn down stocks and no assurance of replacement. Over the short term, POL and foodstuffs would be the major requirements, especially in North Vietnam itself. Since these items have civilian as well as military value, China and the USSR might find it easier to rationalize supplying them to Hanoi than would be the case for purely military equipment.

22. At this point, both Moscow and Peking appear to be urging restraint on Hanoi, in part because they view détente with the US as a priority interest. They are not prepared to abandon Hanoi and will certainly continue to provide some military aid to North Vietnam, though perhaps at reduced levels.[5] (During the 1972 offensive, for example, while both allies seemed to point to the benefits of a negotiated settlement, neither attempted to

[4] Even without assurances from their allies, the North Vietnamese might consider launching an offensive limited in objectives and duration.

[5] It is virtually certain that US intelligence efforts will not be able to determine how much military equipment is actually sent to North Vietnam. There is a reasonably good chance that the dispatch of equipment to South Vietnam will be detected, unless there is a further degradation of US intelligence collection in Indochina. It will be difficult to determine—at least in the next several months—whether such equipment has only recently arrived in North Vietnam. For example, although recent intelligence noted a number of armored vehicles and artillery pieces at a military equipment transloading point northwest of Hanoi, it cannot be determined when this equipment arrived in the country. Nevertheless, since this equipment had not been noted previously, there is a strong possibility that it represents new deliveries.

force the issue by drastically reducing their logistic support.) But an offensive launched without provocation at a time when more relaxed great power relations seemed to be paying dividends would be opposed by Moscow and Peking, particularly if the offensive appeared likely to cause the US to reenter the war. Under these circumstances, Hanoi's allies would continue their aid, but would probably not increase it to cover the losses. But in view of Hanoi's sizable military stockpiles, such reluctance on the part of its allies would have more impact in political terms than on Hanoi's military capabilities in the short run.

23. *The US.* Judgments about the potential US reaction to a major military effort by the communists would be a major factor in Hanoi's policy calculations. A large-scale offensive would be a total rupture of the Paris agreement and, as such, would remove its restrictions on active American involvement. Hanoi undoubtedly views the chances of American forces reentering the war under any circumstances as greatly reduced due to domestic political pressures. In addition, if Hanoi perceived the US as being preoccupied with trying to settle a prolonged Arab-Israeli conflict, it might calculate that the US would be diverted from responding to a major communist provocation in Vietnam. But the North Vietnamese leaders would not dismiss the possibility of an American reaction, in part because they have been so wrong before in gauging the impact of American politics on the war. While the "stick" of American air power would be carefully considered before deciding whether to launch an offensive, the "carrot" of American dollars would represent no more than a minor factor in Hanoi's policy calculations.

24. *Cambodia.* Communist action in Cambodia is not likely to provide clear indications of Hanoi's intentions in South Vietnam since there are uncertainties about how much control the North Vietnamese have over the Khmer insurgents. In addition, Hanoi's encouragement of a relatively low scale of fighting in the Cambodian quadrant would not necessarily mean that Hanoi had decided to lie low in South Vietnam. Indeed, the North Vietnamese might not want to tip their hand by striking out hard in Cambodia if they were contemplating major action in South Vietnam. Conversely, prior to launching an offensive in South Vietnam, Hanoi might want to wrap up the Cambodian situation to obtain a more accurate indication at lower cost of how the US might react to stepped-up communist action.

25. A communist victory in Cambodia would not bring about an immediate or major shift in the present balance of military power in South Vietnam. Hanoi already enjoys the access it needs to the eastern Cambodian provinces along the South Vietnamese border, and the cessation of US bombing has removed most of the danger of using this region. A communist-controlled Cambodia, however, could ease communist logistical burdens by opening the port of Kompong Som to communist shipping. But Hanoi would probably hesitate to make great use of the port in the short run; it would almost certainly want to wait to see how the US and South Vietnam reacted to Cambodia's collapse, and it would not want or need to reveal its strategic plans by pouring supplies through Kompong Som.

26. In the short term, the major import of a communist victory in Cambodia on Hanoi's intentions in South Vietnam would be more psychological than military. Hanoi might hope that the fall of Cambodia would so unnerve the South Vietnamese that the stage would be set for major actions in South Vietnam. We do not believe, however, that the GVN would be so rattled by Cambodia's collapse that, by itself, this would encourage Hanoi to risk a major military push in South Vietnam.

(Continued...)

27. *Laos.* The settlement in Laos will have little effect on Hanoi's actions. It is likely that the combat structure in the Panhandle will remain essentially intact during the upcoming dry season to protect communist supply lines through Laos. Some NVA rear services units which shifted into South Vietnam earlier this year have already moved back into the eastern Panhandle, and others will probably follow.

III. THE VIEW FROM SAIGON

28. To Saigon, just as to Hanoi, the Paris agreement reflects a less than satisfactory situation. The GVN signed the agreement reluctantly and has violated it when such action seemed advantageous. The GVN believes that the January agreement left it vulnerable to communist military pressure. The GVN also has major reservations about the political aspects of the agreement and will show little interest in implementing the political arrangements called for in the accord. The GVN is determined not only to prevent the further expansion of the communists' military and political position in South Vietnam, but to reduce it as much as possible.

A. Saigon's Options

29. Despite its unhappiness with the present situation, Saigon's options for changing it are limited. Over the years, the basic strategy of the GVN has been the building of a strong nation-state able to withstand communist aggression and subversion. In this effort, the GVN has significantly improved its military and political position. It still lacks the ability to expel communist forces from South Vietnam, and it cannot effectively carry the war to the North. In sum, the GVN is still basically in the position of having to react to communist military policies and actions, while continuing its efforts to forge a strong base of support which will erode the communists' ability to pose a significant threat to South Vietnam.

30. Though not sharply defined, the GVN has several options in meeting the communist military threat:

— Quick raids could be conducted against established communist base areas—or even into Cambodia.

— The GVN could launch air strikes on NVA base areas, both within South Vietnam, and in Laos and Cambodia.

— Saigon might move on a large-scale and sustained basis to reduce communist-controlled territory.

— If the GVN concluded that the NVA were, in fact, in the preparatory stages for a new offensive, it might launch a major preemptive strike of its own.[6]

B. Factors Influencing GVN Policy and Capabilities

Political and Economic Strength of the GVN

31. President Thieu's political position has grown stronger over the past several years. Non-communist groups lack the unity or leadership to present a challenge, while the ability of the communists to mount effective political action has been very limited since the 1968 Tet offensive. The massacre in Hue turned the An Quang Buddhists, once in vigorous opposition to the government, away from thoughts of accommodation with the communists and toward working within the

[6] Concurrently with any of the above military options, Thieu would move rapidly to extend and consolidate his political controls at all levels. In addition, a nation-wide effort to gradually extend and consolidate GVN-controlled territory by military and political means would be continued.

system. There are various leftist-intellectual and student groups which are vulnerable to communist manipulation, but these groups are small and lack public support—proving little more than a nuisance to the government.

32. Thieu's power is based on the support of the government bureaucracy and the military establishment—the major instruments through which he has worked to extend his base of support throughout the country. Although basically a loner who operates through a skillful blend of patience and manipulation, Thieu is not unaware of the need to gain popular support. To this end, he has initiated a considerable number of reforms and new programs, and—probably more important—he has worked to improve his ties with village leaders and provincial councils. These efforts have borne fruit; while still not a popular figure, Thieu is accepted by most South Vietnamese as preferable to a communist alternative.

33. In the process of solidifying his position, Thieu has whittled away almost all of the political power of the individual military commanders, leaving them frequently beholden to him in the process. Thus, even though there are occasional grumblings within the military hierarchy over Thieu's political actions, there is no figure in the military who appears capable of seriously challenging him. There is little prospect of this situation changing so long as Thieu maintains the image of a firm and effective anticommunist leader who commands continuing US support, although ambitious men remain in the wings.

34. The government structure is becoming increasingly centralized and personalized, with loyalty to Thieu a prime prerequisite for any significant government assignment. The recently-formed Democracy Party—largely encadred by military officers and bureaucrats—has emerged as Thieu's instrument for extending his authority both at national and local levels. The new party has a parallel clandestine apparatus within the party organization which serves as a potential vehicle for monitoring and enforcing the loyalty of its members. While the forms of representative government may be preserved, Thieu is obviously aiming for, and already has largely achieved, a political apparatus that is wholly responsive to his direction.

35. Although the GVN will have little trouble in coping with overt communist political action, dealing with the communists' covert activities will be difficult. This task falls largely to the GVN's local paramilitary and police forces, whose effectiveness varies widely from place to place. Police effectiveness is generally good in the larger urban areas, but falls off rapidly the further one goes into the countryside. Popular Forces (PF) units and Peoples' Self Defense Forces (PSDF)—the night watchmen of the rural hamlets—often fail to resist when Viet Cong finance cadre or proselyters and their guerrilla escorts visit a village by night, particularly if there is no ARVN unit in the area.

36. Although the South Vietnamese economy has good long-term growth potential, key commodity shortages, inflation, and declining foreign exchange reserves are serious problems. The US military withdrawal has reduced both dollar inflow and employment opportunities, and the *de facto* reduction of American aid caused by the devaluation of the dollar and rising commodity prices in world markets have compounded the problem. Increased foreign and domestic investment could improve the situation, but, for the short run, it is limited because of the uncertainties of the GVN's long-term viability. The basic problems of inflation and stagnation defy quick solutions and could come to have adverse political ramifications. But for the short run, as long as US economic assistance is available, such problems are not likely to reach critical dimensions.

37. A more immediate problem, however, and one which could lead to some popular resentment against the government, is the availability of rice. The fighting in the Delta last spring contributed to a shortfall in rice production in South Vietnam. This, coupled with difficulties in obtaining immediate rice imports because of a world shortage, raises the spectre of a serious rice shortage in the late fall. This is likely to be a temporary problem, however, since additional quantities of American rice should arrive in South Vietnam by late December.

38. The communists are actively seeking to exploit the GVN's economic difficulties, while trying to reduce the economic burden on the North. Apart from enforced taxation, the communists have always maintained a shadow supply system in South Vietnam, buying foodstuffs, fuel, and pharmaceuticals on the local economy. Their recent purchases of rice and kerosene at inflated prices not only help supply their military forces and civilian residents in communist-controlled areas, but also tend to aggravate shortages and price spiraling in GVN areas. The GVN is taking stringent measures to interrupt trade with the communists, but their effectiveness has been spotty. On balance, however, it is highly unlikely over the short term that the communists will make significant gains in exploiting or even seriously aggravating Saigon's economic problems. Moreover, the severely restricted economic situation in PRG areas will reinforce the communists' need for continued taxation and commercial purchases in the GVN areas.

Can RVNAF Meet the Challenge?

39. The political strength of the GVN is clearly adequate to cope with communist subversion, but its military adequacy is a matter of concern, particularly in MR-1.

40. The South Vietnamese have large and well-equipped armed forces. Their combat effectiveness is undercut, however, by logistic and maintenance deficiencies and shortfalls in training, command and control, and manning of units. Corruption and desertion in the armed forces continue to be problems. In addition, the ground forces, including mobile reserves, are fully deployed. Faced with a communist adversary in South Vietnam which is larger and stronger than at its peak in 1972, RVNAF would probably yield substantial territory, at least initially, should the communists launch an all-out attack.

41. On the other hand, RVNAF has improved significantly in recent years, especially since the start of the 1972 campaign, as Thieu has cashiered many inept officers. Further, front-line units have gained valuable combat experience and confidence. For example, in the 1972 offensive, RVNAF (albeit with the benefit of US air support) was able to regroup and reverse many of the communists' gains. Even mediocre units hung together (excepting the disaster-struck 3rd Division) and maintained stiff resistance to the NVA. RVNAF's problems would be at least partially offset by the frequently poor tactics and performance of communist forces.

42. In terms of overall military manpower, the GVN has a substantial edge. RVNAF's 320,000 regular combat ground forces compare with a communist regular combat strength of 180,000 men. (See Figure 2, page 7.) In MR-1, however, no numerical advantage exists, as South Vietnam's 89,000 troops face a comparable communist force. Moreover, with the withdrawal of US air assets, the GVN's firepower advantage in many parts of the country is less impressive. The amount of GVN artillery tubes currently exceeds that of the communists, but the North Vietnamese have demonstrated greater proficiency in the use of such firepower. The communist tank

inventory slightly exceeds the GVN's, but this advantage is largely offset by greater RVNAF crew proficiency. It should be noted, however, that communist inventories of tanks and field and antiaircraft artillery are now at their highest level of the war owing to a significant deployment of such firepower to South Vietnam during the 1972/1973 infiltration cycle.

43. Massive air support and exclusive control of the sky have been crucial factors in ARVN's defensive and offensive capabilities. Most of this support was American; the critical question now is whether the GVN ground forces could manage without it. The South Vietnamese Air Force cannot begin to provide the abundance of air support that ground commanders were accustomed to prior to the cease-fire. Even so, VNAF ground support capabilities have improved considerably and should help to counterbalance communist firepower in most of the country.

44. In northern MR-1, however, where RVNAF is clearly most vulnerable, VNAF air operations would be severely hampered by the heavy concentration of NVA AAA/SAM forces. In addition, the North Vietnamese are in a position to mount air operations of their own in MR-1. In the event of an all-out military offensive, we believe that they would do so. The effectiveness of North Vietnamese close air support, however, would be curtailed by inexperience in ground support operations and the paucity of ground radar control facilities. In terms of air defense, North Vietnam's superior air-to-air combat experience, defense in depth, and totally integrated air defense system would probably result in an unacceptable VNAF loss rate if it attempted sustained operations over communist-controlled northern MR-1. Moreover, in the event of a major communist push in MR-1, including the forward deployment of AAA and SAMs and the possible use of Migs, VNAF would also experience serious problems in providing effective ground support.

45. Successful preemptive offensive operations of any magnitude seem well beyond GVN capabilities. The communist would undoubtedly be aware of South Vietnamese planning (as in the past) and be prepared for an attack. RVNAF could not sustain large-scale operations without a significant expansion of US military aid shipments to cover losses. Moreover, the GVN would probably be most reluctant to launch major offensive operations without the assurance of US air support.

46. Meeting lower levels of communist pressure should be well within RVNAF's capabilities. But the South Vietnamese are not likely to improve their position substantially. The communists obviously would put up a determined defense against any moves by government forces against their enclaves. As the communists continue to strengthen and consolidate their western base areas, South Vietnamese chances of successful penetration will diminish.

47. Curbing a campaign of terrorism, guerrilla warfare, and covert action would fall more to the GVN's territorial forces (the RF, PF, PSDF, and NPFF) and municipal police than to the regular forces. As in the past, certain areas can be expected to prove very resistant to communist penetration. In general, the communists are not well-prepared to undertake a significant increase in such activities.

48. Even so, the GVN's ability to stem a gradual extension of communist influence is uncertain. The communists cannot be satisfied penned up against the borders of South Vietnam. They clearly are determined to extend tendrils into GVN-controlled areas, especially in southern MR-1 and northern MR-2, which they must do if they are to support a resurgent infrastructure. And Saigon is just as deter-

mined to prevent this. Over the short run, the struggle for the "contested" areas will remain more or less stalemated.

IV. PROSPECTS THROUGH THE DRY SEASON (OCTOBER 1973-MAY 1974)

A. The GVN

49. Prospects for the GVN over the next nine months are mixed.[7] On the one hand, Thieu's political position will probably grow stronger, and the communists are unlikely to make significant political gains. On the other hand, by next summer, the GVN may no longer have a military edge over the communists if Hanoi continues its current level of buildup in the South—which we believe it will do.

50. The GVN, faced with a situation where its real options are limited, will basically devote its efforts to strengthening the country's infrastructure, maintaining and building up its military defenses, and attempting to counter Hanoi's thrusts. Continued US military and economic support will be crucial to the GVN's performance and prospects during this period.

51. The GVN will push with equal force to forestall the resurgence of the communist infrastructure, but will be faced with something of a dilemma. Aggressive local government chiefs can often interrupt communist efforts to build bridges to the local population, but government harassment often prompts communist retaliation. The ensuing rash of terrorism and military activity upsets the local population, whose lives and livelihoods are threatened by the lack of security. As a result, the local chief often loses his popular support and is hard pressed to prove that he indeed has "pacified" his territory. Caught in this situation, the local officials frequently find it preferable to seek the apparent quiet provided by accommodation. There is little reason to believe that the GVN can successfully break this longstanding pattern, although this is unlikely to be a serious problem over the short run.

52. The GVN can and will ensure that the PRG does not enhance its internal legal position through the vehicle of the Paris agreement. While a National Council of Reconciliation and Concord may eventually be formed, it will play no substantive role; the local councils will probably never be formed.

53. Militarily, RVNAF can be expected to continue its operations against communist positions, especially against enclaves not contiguous to the western corridor, and against NVA efforts to move into new areas. Main force maneuvering in areas that are not clearly controlled by either side could easily result in sporadic surges of heavy fighting. A more volatile situation could arise should the GVN, fearful that a communist military offensive was in the offing, attempt to launch a major preemptive strike against communist forces. In such a situation, there would be a high risk that the communists would retaliate in kind, and the fighting could get out of hand. It is unlikely, however, that the GVN would undertake such an action prior to consulting its American ally.

B. The Communists

54. In assessing Hanoi's military intentions, we are hobbled by a lack of firm intelligence. In fact, the communists have probably not yet

[7] Though either unpredictable or else very unlikely, there are certain factors which, if they occurred, could seriously affect judgments about the cohesion and effectiveness of the GVN. Among these are: Thieu's assassination; widespread civil disorders sparked by economic problems or a sudden revival of Buddhist opposition to the government; unexpected US Congressional action that drastically reduced or suspended entirely US assistance to South Vietnam; or clear indications that the US was no longer committed to Saigon's survival.

made a final decision whether to attempt major military action next spring. *It is clear, however, that Hanoi is acting to preserve an option to resume major military action in South Vietnam at some point.*[8] The chances for the political aspects of the Paris agreements being realized are negligible; nor can Hanoi have much hope of achieving the GVN's collapse through a combination of political and clandestine warfare backed up by only moderate military pressure. Ultimately then, Hanoi must believe that it will again have to turn to the battlefield to seek—if not the immediate military defeat of the GVN—at least a situation where new political arrangements will have to be made (e.g., coalition government) that would give the communists sufficient political leverage in the South to ensure a shift to their domination. The question, however, is when?

55. The forward positioning of communist forces and supplies and the improved road system give Hanoi the capability to kick off a major military campaign with little additional preparation. As Hanoi continues to augment its forces in South Vietnam during the coming dry season, the military balance may tilt to the communists' advantage unless there is countervailing US support for the GVN. Such a shift in the military balance could encourage Hanoi to launch major military action. In any event, with heavy infiltration, it appears likely that Hanoi would be in a position to launch—with little warning—and sustain such action by early 1974 if it so chose.

56. This means that Hanoi will probably be in a position to choose among the full range of options to attain its goals in South Vietnam. In the absence of firm information on Hanoi's short-term intentions, it is a close choice whether Hanoi will opt for a major military offensive sooner rather than later. It is such a close choice that the only prudent assessment must allow for either. This is especially so since the US role in the situation is a major one, and its position as perceived in Hanoi could well determine whether such an offensive will occur this dry season. The other major factors are the positions of Moscow and Peking, Hanoi's assessment of the military balance between its forces and RVNAF, and Hanoi's calculations about its overall military and political situation—including external considerations—should it launch or not launch a military offensive this dry season.[9]

The arguments which persuade some analysts that a major North Vietnamese offensive early next year is more likely than not are as follows:

57. The buildup of North Vietnamese manpower and war materiel in South Vietnam and adjacent border areas since January 1973 should be seen not only as an expansion of

[8] As defined in this Estimate, major military action could encompass a countrywide offensive on the scale of Tet 1968 or March 1972, or attacks on a similar level generally confined to one or two military regions, with lower levels of action elsewhere.

[9] The Assistant Chief of Staff, Intelligence, USAF, believes that the case postulated in favor of a North Vietnamese offensive in 1974, *earlier rather than later,* merits greater weight than the case against such an offensive. Inflexibly, Hanoi has always chosen to pursue the offensive—logistics permitting. Logistic preparations in the three northernmost provinces of MR-1 (Quang Tri, Thua Thien, and Quang Nam) are now virtually complete. A major offensive to seize and sever the northern provinces is almost a certainty, and will likely come earlier rather than later—especially during periods when weather would inhibit South Vietnamese air power. The South Vietnamese Air Force is a clear weather force—a fact which North Vietnam will exploit at the appropriate time. Almost certainly, an enemy thrust in MR-1 would entail diversionary offensive actions in other parts of the RVN to inhibit RVNAF reinforcement of the northern battle areas. Hanoi probably believes that a major effort to take the northern provinces entails the least risk of American reinvolvement.

communist capabilities in the South, but also as a probable sign of an intent to use these capabilities sooner rather than later. Recent indications that the beginning of the new dry season will bring additional movements of men and equipment to the South further strengthen the case that Hanoi may be preparing for a major offensive during this dry season.

58. With sufficient stocks of equipment and munitions in the South to engage in heavy combat for the duration of an entire dry season, it is unlikely that pressure from Moscow or Peking will be a decisive factor in preventing the North Vietnamese from starting an offensive. Even a complete cutoff of Soviet and Chinese exports to North Vietnam would affect Hanoi's domestic economy long before it affected the war in the South, and it is highly unlikely that Moscow or Peking would take such a step.

59. Further, Hanoi may well now regard the risk of the reinvolvement of US combat forces (air as well as ground) as fairly small. North Vietnam's view of the risk probably would not restrain its leaders from launching a major offensive if they felt other factors were favorable. Throughout the coming months, Hanoi will be constantly reevaluating its views on this matter. Political trends in the US that seemed to further restrict or to liberalize the President's power to react, would of course affect Hanoi's assessment of the risks.

60. Finally, the North Vietnamese leadership may see its chances of winning a major military victory as being greater in the spring of 1974 than later. There is an appreciable volume of evidence that the communists themselves believe they are doing badly in the political struggle in South Vietnam, and that in this struggle time is on the side of the GVN, not the communists. If this is the case, there are almost certainly elements within the Hanoi leadership which favor a resumption of military action sooner rather than later. North Vietnam's leaders might also believe that US domestic problems are likely to be greater—and the restraints on the government's actions more severe—in the next six to nine months than would be the case a year or two later. Moreover, if the Soviet Union and China are reducing arms aid to Hanoi, the North Vietnamese might consider that they would be at their maximum strength for an offensive during the coming dry season.

The arguments which persuade other analysts that the North Vietnamese will delay an offensive beyond the current dry season are as follows:

61. Hanoi will weigh a number of factors—no one of which is likely to be controlling—in deciding on the timing and scope of a military effort. A vital judgment will be what Hanoi gauges it can get away with and still avoid a crushing US response with air power. The North Vietnamese leaders almost certainly entertain major reservations on this score. Faced with uncertainties on the likelihood of a US military response to a communist offensive, the North Vietnamese would probably prefer to wait for the passage of time to provide them a better indication of the depth of the US commitment to South Vietnam.

62. In contemplating prolonged heavy combat, Hanoi would also want to be assured of enough continued material support from Moscow and Peking to cover losses. Such assurances are unlikely over the short term. Despite the heavy stockpiles in or adjacent to South Vietnam, it would be exceedingly dangerous for Hanoi to attempt a go-it-alone strategy. Given the close military balance between communist forces and RVNAF, prudence—if nothing else—would dictate to the North Vietnamese leaders that they would

have to be prepared for a possible failure of the offensive. And without assurances of sufficient supplies from Moscow and Peking to replenish battlefield losses, the communists would be left, should the offensive fail, in a weakened and vulnerable position.

63. The situation in South Vietnam will also be a compelling factor in Hanoi's policy choice. Although the communists have made significant strides in building up their military forces, their progress in the political field has been very limited. Aware of their past and present shortcomings in the political sphere, the communists are placing high priority on some strengthening of their political apparatus. To date, however, efforts at refurbishing and expanding the communist infrastructure have fallen far short of party goals, and communist leaders do not expect rapid or spectacular gains over the short term. The weakened state of the communist political apparatus would argue for the communists delaying a major military offensive until they are in a better position to take advantage of it politically.

64. Finally, there is no apparent requirement for Hanoi to act in haste in South Vietnam. Certainly the GVN will not make such rapid progress in strengthening the economic, political, and military fabric of the South over the next year or two as to become invulnerable to a later, large-scale communist offensive. The communists are in a position to maintain their position—and to strengthen it—inside the base areas in the South for the indefinite future. Thus, the communists will be in a position to carefully weigh all factors—and to entertain extended internal debate—as they shape their strategy beyond the current dry season.

If There is an Offensive

65. In the event of an all-out offensive this dry season, the communists would initially make substantial territorial gains in MR-1. Although GVN forces might be routed, it is more likely that they would fall back in reasonably good order, and they could probably hold out for some time around the major cities of Danang and Hue, though the latter would be geographically more vulnerable. Prolonged fighting would raise the crucial question of the rapidity of outside assistance for the GVN. Without renewed US air support, RVNAF's continued resistance in MR-1 would be in doubt.

66. Communist gains in the rest of South Vietnam would be less dramatic, unless their forces were significantly upgraded from present strengths. The GVN forces undoubtedly would give ground, particularly in areas where NVA units are concentrated, but should be able to blunt a communist assault.

If There Is Not an Offensive

67. If Hanoi does not mount a major offensive this dry season, there will probably be a period of internal building and testing on both sides with military action remaining generally restricted. Hanoi will continue to launch and no doubt accelerate carefully orchestrated, significant localized, and limited-objective attacks in various regions of South Vietnam during this dry season under the guise of a response to prior GVN aggression. Hanoi will limit the type and scope of such attacks to that which it believes will not provoke a US military response or a negative reaction from Peking or Moscow. Operations will be designed to seize more territory, to test GVN resolution, and for their psychological impact.

68. Hanoi will also continue to make a major effort to rebuild the communist political infrastructure, immediately in contested rural areas and more gradually in towns and cities; however, we anticipate only limited

success in this effort. The communists will, moreover, attempt to entice the population to move to PRG areas, and government officials will be approached to arrange local ad hoc trade agreements and "peace treaties." At the same time, the communists will continue trying to infiltrate the government's ranks for intelligence and subversive purposes. Some increase in terrorist and guerrilla activity is likely as the communists try to break down GVN control at the grass roots and enforce popular tolerance of their own presence.

V. OVER THE LONGER TERM

69. The foregoing summary of prospects over the short term reflects the impossibility of offering confident judgments on the timing and shape of future communist military strategy. North Vietnam's timetable—even over the short term—will be influenced by its perception of shifts in the relative balance of power, military or political, in Vietnam or in the positions of its own allies or the US. If Hanoi does not undertake a major offensive during the upcoming dry season, the question remains whether the communists are likely to opt for a return to major hostilities at some point relatively soon thereafter.

70. The strength of the American commitment to South Vietnam will continue to be a vital factor for the GVN's survival. Not only will it influence Hanoi's policy decisions, but it will also be a critical political and psychological factor in maintaining GVN confidence. Continued US military aid will be essential, even though the amounts allowed by the Paris agreement are not likely to offset the expansion of NVA strength in the South. Further large-scale US economic aid will also be required if the GVN is to have a chance to solve its economic problems. Other sources of external financing, such as offshore oil and foreign investment, offer good potential but will require several years to make a significant dent in South Vietnam's foreign aid requirements.

71. Apart from US support to South Vietnam, the overall American military posture in the Far East will also be carefully noted by Hanoi. A major US disengagement from the area, or a pulling apart of the American alliance with Thailand—now the site of American reserve forces potentially available to Vietnam—would be demoralizing to Saigon and would encourage Hanoi (and possibly its allies) to feel that the risk of confrontation with the US was negligible. Even in the absence of such signals, however, it cannot be assumed what conclusions Hanoi would draw concerning US intentions. Its record for misjudging the depth and duration of the US commitment to the GVN is well established.

72. At the same time, the willingness or reluctance of Peking and Moscow to underwrite another major military effort to topple the GVN will condition North Vietnam's strategy. At some point, the North Vietnamese are likely to press China and the USSR for substantially increased military aid. This will force these countries to weigh the impact of responding on their relationship with the US and with each other. Great power détente has contributed to a dampening of the Vietnam conflict; it has also served to undercut the North Vietnamese ability to play their allies off against each other. There are no indications now that these conditions will not continue for some time.

73. But there are conceivable developments that might make the Chinese or the Soviets (or both) more receptive to Hanoi's importunings. For example, if the Chinese and Russians came to believe that Washington was no longer so devoted to the GVN's survival as to risk progress in furthering détente, Hanoi's allies might think it safe to provide

the stepped-up aid required to sustain a major communist offensive in South Vietnam. Similarly, if Moscow and Peking become less interested in détente with the US, they might be more willing to provide increased military assistance to Hanoi. On the other hand, should the Sino-Soviet split widen, either Moscow or Peking might step up its aid to Hanoi to undercut the other's influence in Southeast Asia. None of these possibilities appears likely, but should they occur, they would isolate the American commitment to Saigon as the major external restraining force on Hanoi.

74. In weighing its longer-term strategy, Hanoi will also be sensitive to political and military trends in South Vietnam. A steady consolidation of power by Thieu, with little obvious deterioration of RVNAF capabilities, and a failure of the communists infrastructure to make inroads of any significance into the GVN's control of the population would argue—given Hanoi's determination to reunify Vietnam—for a bold military stroke even though the risks in such an offensive would be high.

75. *In Sum.* The key factor shaping Hanoi's policies will remain its perception of the likely US response, the availability of external support, the pressure imposed by Moscow and Peking, and military and political trends in South Vietnam. Over the longer run, however, Hanoi may place greater weight on the trends it observes in the South than on the external restraints imposed by Moscow, Peking, and Washington.

76. In any event, Hanoi's actions are clearly designed to insure that it can again resort to major military action to gain its objectives if other means fail. If a major communist military offensive does not occur in the upcoming dry season, we believe that the odds favoring such an action will increase significantly as the 1974-1975 dry season approaches.

NIE 53/14.3-1-74

The Likelihood of a Major North Vietnamese Offensive Against South Vietnam Before June 30, 1975

23 May 1974

APPROVED FOR RELEASE
DATE: JAN 2005

(b)(3)

~~Secret~~

NATIONAL INTELLIGENCE ESTIMATE

The Likelihood of a Major North Vietnamese Offensive Against South Vietnam Before June 30, 1975

~~Secret~~
NIE 53/14.3-1-74
23 May 1974

№ 260

THE LIKELIHOOD OF A MAJOR NORTH VIETNAMESE OFFENSIVE AGAINST SOUTH VIETNAM BEFORE JUNE 30, 1975

PRÉCIS

A major Communist offensive in South Vietnam is unlikely during 1974. The picture for the first half of 1975, however, is less clear, and there obviously is a substantial risk that Hanoi will opt for a major offensive during this period. But our best judgment now is that Hanoi will not do so.[1]

If unforeseen and dramatic new developments occurred, the Communists could easily shift course to take advantage of them.

— They have the capability to launch an offensive with little warning.

— We expect the North Vietnamese to reassess their situation this summer or fall.

[1] The Director, Defense Intelligence Agency, believes that the "best judgment" expressed in this paragraph is unduly optimistic. He believes that the chances are at least even that North Vietnam will undertake a major offensive during the first half of 1975. For his reasoning see the footnote to paragraph 15 on page 8.

The Assistant Chief of Staff, Intelligence, USAF, and the Assistant General Manager for National Security, Atomic Energy Commission, share this view.

— Changes both in South Vietnam and in the international situation, particularly in the US, will weigh heavily in their calculations.

— The North Vietnamese would also consider the views of the Soviet Union and China, but the influence of Moscow and Peking on any reassessment in Hanoi would not be decisive.

Should a major offensive occur, the Communists could retake Quang Tri City, and perhaps capture Hue in MR 1, Kontum and Pleiku cities in MR 2 and Tay Ninh City in MR 3. If the Communists persisted in their offensive, this initial situation would probably be followed by a period of inconclusive fighting and, over time, further GVN losses. ARVN might be unable to regain the initiative, and it would be questionable whether the GVN would be able to survive without combat participation by US Air Force and Navy units. At a minimum, large-scale US logistic support would be required to stop the Communist drive.

Even if there is not a major offensive during the next year, current Communist strategy does call for some increase in the tempo of the conflict.

Furthermore, it is clear that at some point Hanoi will shift back to major warfare.

SECRET

DISCUSSION

1. Hanoi continues to demonstrate its determination to impose Communist control on the South. The North Vietnamese leadership, however, presently views the task of achieving victory in the South as "complex," "difficult," and "protracted." In this sense, Hanoi is faced with a continuing dilemma. The Communist position in South Vietnam is not perceptibly improving. Even if the GVN's economy deteriorated markedly or US aid were curtailed, the Communists would still not be able to topple the GVN without major military action. Sharply increasing Communist military pressure, on the other hand, would involve a considerable gamble. Should South Vietnam successfully weather a Communist offensive, the GVN's position would be further strengthened. But should the North Vietnamese repeatedly postpone a decision in favor of major military action, they would run the risk of having the GVN's strength evolve to a point where they could not topple it.

The Military Balance [2]

2. North Vietnamese forces in South Vietnam are now stronger than they were at the time of the cease-fire:

— Hanoi is pressing ahead with its military modernization and improvement programs.

— The NVA/VC have more men, armor, artillery, and air defense weapons in South Vietnam than they did when the cease-fire went into effect.

— The Communists already have on hand sufficient materiel to support offensive operations at the 1972 level for well over a year. An improved logistics and personnel infiltration system permits year-round deliveries to South Vietnam.

[2] The military balance and the outcome of various offensive scenarios are treated in detail in an Interagency Memorandum entitled *South Vietnam: A Net Military Assessment,* SC 01984/74, dated 2 April 1974.

SECRET

— There are an additional six infantry divisions in reserve in North Vietnam which could be rapidly deployed to South Vietnam.

— Communist forces have improved with the infiltration of personnel and the institution of remedial training programs to overcome shortcomings that emerged during the fighting in 1972.

— The Communists now have wider military options during the period June to September than previously. (This is the rainy season in most of the country.) But the recent improvements in Communist capabilities do not fully alleviate the problems the NVA have traditionally encountered in operating during the wet season.

3. The South Vietnamese have also strengthened their force structure:

— South Vietnam maintains about twice as many combat troops under arms as the Communists have deployed in the South.

— The South Vietnamese received sufficient material before the cease-fire—most importantly aircraft, armor and artillery—to assure that even now they retain a country-wide edge in firepower assets.

— In the 16 months since the cease-fire, the South Vietnamese logistic command moved from almost total dependence on the US to a position where it is now able to do a creditable job.

4. In the event of a major Communist offensive, the outcome would depend on the availability of US support for South Vietnam:

— If the Communists committed a substantial portion of their six-division strategic reserve and built up replacement manpower pools in the southern part of South Vietnam:

- They could retake Quang Tri City, perhaps capture Hue, and make sizable gains in southern MR 1.

- In western MR 2, Kontum and Pleiku cities might also fall, and some gains, possibly including the fall of Tay Ninh City, would accrue to the Communists north and northwest of Saigon in MR 3.

— If the Communists persisted in their offensive, this initial situation would probably be followed by a period of inconclusive fighting and, over time, further GVN losses. ARVN might be unable to regain the initiative, and it would be questionable whether the GVN would be able to survive without combat participation by US Air Force and Navy units.

— At a minimum, large-scale US logistic support would be required to stop the Communist drive.

The Political Balance

5. Politically, the GVN is stronger than the Communists . . .

— The GVN has a generally effective governmental structure extending down to villages and hamlets. Its police and military presence in most populated areas severely limits Communist activities. President Thieu retains the backing of the army and the acceptance of most South Vietnamese; he has successfully isolated or out-maneuvered most of the non-Communist opposition.

— The Communists are not optimistic that they can extract major concessions from Thieu for the foreseeable future or that there is an early prospect for a coalition government through a "Third Force."

— Hanoi has recognized that Communist political stagnation is its most serious weakness and has instructed its southern cadre to make a maximum effort to rebuild the infrastructure and undermine the GVN. Under present circumstances, however, Communist proselyting cannot achieve quick results through recruiting new cadre or penetrating the GVN. These efforts cannot seriously erode the government's present political position, nor is there any prospect that the current Communist strategy will topple the GVN.

6. . . . but the Communists are persisting in political efforts which they still believe may yield some dividends.

— In some limited areas Communist terrorism is on the rise.

— They are infiltrating civilians from the North into Communist enclaves.

— They apparently hope their military presence in the South will add an aura of durability to the PRG.

The Economic Balance

7. Both Saigon and Hanoi face major economic problems which leave them heavily dependent on continuing assistance from their respective allies:

—North Vietnam—Although a number of critical sectors of the economy damaged by US bombing have now been restored, serious long-standing economic problem areas remain. These include inadequate food production, insufficient consumer goods, little industrial capacity, and consequently heavy dependence on foreign economic assistance.

— Although there are some signs of strains in the North Vietnamese social system, there is no indication that the leadership faces any serious challenge to its control.

— There has been no apparent curtailment in Hanoi's support for either the war or its present reconstruction efforts. Continued support for its current war effort in the South does not require significant diversion of economic resources from the North. Many of Hanoi's current economic targets, however, could not be achieved even in peaceful conditions.

— South Vietnam—The South Vietnamese economy has been in a serious slump for two years, and the outlook is for more of the same and possibly a worsening of the situation. Rapid inflation (67 percent in 1973), unemployment (between 15 and 20 percent), and a threat of declining agricultural output are major problems.

— These problems are basically the result of dislocation caused by continuing warfare in South Vietnam, increasing prices of critical imports, and declining real amounts of US assistance.

— Thus far the resilience of the South Vietnamese people as well as the protection afforded by the extended family system have prevented economic dislocation from generating political instability. But these factors of themselves do not increase the GVN's stability—they simply attenuate the negative impact of adverse economic conditions.

— Assuming continued US assistance at present levels, economic problems will not prove decisive over the next year.

— Over the longer run, however, continued economc deterioration would be likely to produce increasing corruption, possibly urban disorders, and declining GVN administrative and military effectiveness.

The Shape of Things to Come

8. Certain general considerations will affect Communist behavior:

A) Hanoi continues to see the cease-fire agreement and subsequent developments as offering some benefits which it would not jeopardize lightly:

— Militarily, the agreement, produced a US withdrawal which allowed the Communists to enhance their military capabilities in South Vietnam.

— Politically, the agreement added a degree of international respectability and legitimacy to the PRG and provided a basis for Communist insistence on being consulted about future political arrangements in Saigon.

B) The international environment continues to place certain constraints on Hanoi:

— The North Vietnamese leaders are still concerned that the US might recommit its air power if the GVN were confronted by a massive Communist military challenge.

—Hanoi cannot have full confidence in the reliability of its allies, the USSR and the PRC, as long as they remain committed to a policy of detente with the US.

C) Economic considerations also place some constraints on Hanoi:

— With continued assistance from the USSR and China, North Vietnam should be able both to step up its military action in the South and make economic progress in the North. A major increase in the level of hostilities, however, would run the risk that Moscow and Peking might reduce their assistance.

— A major offensive—while not of itself sufficient to derail Hanoi's current economic programs—would complicate the implementation of future large-scale development efforts.

D) The situation on the ground in South Vietnam cuts both ways. The Communists do not seem to be urgently preparing for a major offensive, but the very magnitude of the current Communist military presence in the South increases the danger of large-scale fighting:

— Hanoi's leaders apparently do not think that they now can take control in the South in one swift campaign. Communist ideology and experience have conditioned them to think in terms of stages.

— The Communists confront a major problem in achieving the proper mix of military and political initiatives. Given their weak political position in South Vietnam, they cannot decrease military pressure on the GVN without losing momentum. They doubt that they can significantly improve their political position without successful military action on an expanding scale against government-controlled areas of South Vietnam. On the other hand, the extension of military action would be difficult in areas where the Communist infrastructure did not provide a base for supporting such action.

— Some infiltration of men and supplies and the development of some roads and base areas over the past year has been necessary to hold territory and to support the current Communist political-military strategy.

— The Communists are, however, now equipped to move more quickly than ever before; troops can come down from the North rapidly and with very lit-

tle attrition, and the movement and prepositioning of supplies is no longer the gradual process it once was.

— On balance, the Communists do not appear to be under any immediate compulsion to go for broke; however, they would not be making such massive logistic preparations, keeping—and supporting—so many troops in the South, and moving in so many more, if they were not still seriously contemplating large-unit warfare.

Hanoi's Intentions Through June 1975

9. Available evidence now indicates that North Vietnamese leaders tentatively decided in late 1973 on a period of military, political, and economic buildup which would last well into 1975.

— The most recent COSVN instructions, which reflect decisions on the conduct of the war made at the secret 21st plenum of the Lao Dong Party in the fall of 1973, emphasize the need for a continuing military buildup in the South and a considerable period of infrastructure rebuilding. They call for a strengthening of Communist-held "liberated" areas, expanding into contested areas, and propaganda, terrorism, sabotage and subversion in government-controlled areas. A number of cadre have interpreted these instructions as applicable to the years 1974 and 1975.

— According to decisions a few months later, at the well publicized 22nd Lao Dong plenum, North Vietnamese leaders in early 1974 established guidelines for a substantial economic reconstruction program of the North in 1974 and 1975. At least one senior North Vietnamese official has publicly cautioned that Hanoi should not pay so much attention to strengthening the Communist position in the South lest the Northern reconstruction effort would be jeopardized.

— The current Communist military posture, including the measured pace of conscription and infiltration, current retraining of Communist forces, the withdrawal of some main force divisions and AAA units, does not reflect the kind of urgency that previously has preceded military escalation. There is also a marked absence in South Vietnam of tactical deployments and cadre briefings, and in North Vietnam, of mobilizations and civil defense measures. Given the advanced state of Communist military preparedness, however, it must be recognized that such indicators may provide very little warning of a new offensive.

10. In any event, the current Communist strategy calls for an increase this year in the tempo of the conflict:

— Hanoi plans to test its military prowess and probe for weaknesses in the GVN's position.

  - Main Force units are to be committed more frequently.
  - Operations to expand "liberated" areas and Communist LOCs are to increase.
  - Such action could intensify without either side actually planning for it. The Communists are bent on expanding their control and the GVN is determined to keep Communist forces bottled up in their present enclaves. Should favorable conditions develop, either side might further expand its military effort to exploit the situation.

— Hanoi may want to gauge the reactions of its major Communist allies and, more important, of the US.

11. At some point this summer or fall, we expect the North Vietnamese to reassess their strategy and initiate planning for the next stage.

— Communist officials have told their cadre in the South that they should be ready for "new developments" if the situation changes in South Vietnam or internationally. Cadre have been exhorted not to become confused if Hanoi switches to a new policy line.

12. In such a reassessment, several factors may influence Hanoi to reaffirm its policy against a major escalation.

— Hanoi may continue to see such escalation as too risky as long as it cannot count on certain victory.

— The North Vietnamese may continue to believe that any major military escalation risks a recommitment of US air support.

— Hanoi may question Soviet and Chinese willingness to support a major and prolonged military offensive.

— Hanoi may see economic deterioration in the South as in itself ultimately undermining the South Vietnamese political and social structure, and therefore believe large-scale military action to be unnecessary.

13. At the same time there are factors which may influence Hanoi toward a major escalation.

— Hanoi may decide its current strategy is costly and not working well.

— Increased RVNAF pressure, either in retaliation against Communist attacks or to forestall expected Communist initiatives, could result in erosion of important Communist base areas in the South.

— A breakdown in detente, or other international developments, could produce Soviet or Chinese encouragement for a North Vietnamese military escalation.

— Similarly, a determination that US options were seriously curtailed by domestic political developments could encourage Hanoi to escalate.

Conclusions

14. In sum, we do not believe that the Communists will undertake a major offensive this year.

15. Hanoi, however, will be reassessing its strategy as time passes, and the picture for the first half of 1975 is less clear. Changes since last fall in South Vietnam and in the international situation, particularly in the US, will weigh heavily in Hanoi's calculations, and there obviously is a substantial risk that Hanoi will opt for a major offensive. But our best judgment now is that Hanoi will not decide to do so during the first half of 1975.[3]

[3] The Director, Defense Intelligence Agency, believes that the "best judgment" expressed in this paragraph is unduly optimistic. While agreeing with the judgment in paragraph 14—i.e., that the Communists are unlikely to undertake a major offensive through the balance of 1974—he also notes that most of the supporting evidence is essentially short term in nature, and there is now no direct evidence of Hanoi's intentions for the first half of 1975. Nevertheless, North Vietnam has not only assiduously maintained its major offensive option in South Vietnam, but major sections of the Estimate make a persuasive case that Hanoi can and will readily abandon its present strategy of localized military action in the South. Expanding Communist military capabilities, coupled with Hanoi's inability to make much progress in South Vietnam under current circumstances, increase the danger of a major North Vietnamese offensive. The Director, DIA, believes that the chances are at least even that North Vietnam will undertake such action during the first half of 1975.

The Assistant Chief of Staff, Intelligence, USAF, and the Assistant General Manager for National Security, Atomic Energy Commission, share this view.

16. Nevertheless, the Communists do have the capability to launch a major offensive with little warning whenever they so choose. In the event of an unforeseen and dramatic change in the situation, the Communists could easily move militarily to take advantage of a target of opportunity. Finally, even if there is not a major offensive during the next year, it is clear that at some point Hanoi will shift back to major warfare in its effort to gain control of South Vietnam.

NIE 53/14.3-2-74

Short-Term Prospects for Vietnam

23 December 1974

Secret
NATIONAL
INTELLIGENCE
ESTIMATE
Short-Term Prospects for Vietnam
Secret
NIE 53/14.3-2-74
23 December 1974
Nº 362

(Continued...)

~~SECRET~~

SHORT-TERM PROSPECTS FOR VIETNAM

PRÉCIS

— Communist military forces in South Vietnam are more powerful than ever before.

— The South Vietnamese Armed Forces (RVNAF) are still strong and resilient and have generally acquitted themselves well since the ceasefire, but the decline to the present level of US military aid threatens to place them in a significantly weaker logistic posture than the Communists.

— Hanoi has a variety of military options, but the evidence points toward a marked increase in military action between now and mid-1975 designed to:

- defeat the GVN pacification program;
- inflict heavy casualties on the RVNAF;
- gain control of many more South Vietnamese; and
- force the GVN into new negotiations at disadvantage.

~~SECRET~~

— At a minimum the Communists will sharply increase the tempo of fighting by making greater use of their in-country forces and firepower.

— In this case, their gains would be limited, but RVNAF stockpiles of ammunition and other critical supplies would probably be depleted by April or May below the 30-day reserve required for intensive combat.

— We believe that the Communists will commit part of their strategic reserve to exploit major vulnerabilities in the South Vietnamese position or to maintain the momentum of their military effort.

— Such a commitment would carry a greater risk of major defeats for top RVNAF units and a further compounding of GVN manpower and logistic problems.

— Without an immediate increase in US military assistance, the GVN's military situation would be parlous, and Saigon might explore the possibility of new negotiations with the Communists.

— It is even possible—in response to a major opportunity—that the Communists would move to an all-out offensive by committing all or most of their strategic reserve. But our best judgment now is that they will not do so.

— Hanoi prefers to achieve its dry season goals through a military-political campaign that avoids the risks and losses of an all-out offensive.

— Hanoi probably hopes that by setting limits on its military operations there would be less likelihood of a strong reaction from Washington and that frictions with Moscow and Peking would be minimized.

— At currently appropriated levels of US military assistance, however, the level of combat that we do anticipate in the next six months will place the Communists in a position of significant advantage over RVNAF in subsequent fighting.

DISCUSSION

I. INTRODUCTION

1. Our estimates on the Vietnam problem over the past year have focused on the probability of a Communist offensive against the South that involved the commitment of NVA/VC forces now in South Vietnam and a majority of Hanoi's strategic reserve divisions in North Vietnam. The principal judgment in our last full-dress review (made in May 1974) was that such an offensive was unlikely through June 1975, although the risk would grow as June 1975 approached.[1] We also judged that such an offensive would be the only thing that could produce a decisive Communist victory.

II. THE NORTH-SOUTH BALANCE

The Communists

3. *Military.* The Vietnamese Communists now have their strongest military force in South Vietnam in the history of the war. That force is better trained and equipped than it was at the time of the 1972 offensive. In North Vietnamese military writings the emphasis on preparing for renewed large-scale conventional warfare that appeared in 1973 has been followed in 1974 by an emphasis on those aspects of combined-arms tactics that were found wanting in 1972. Also in 1974, the training cycle for new North Vietnamese conscripts was extended by several months.

4. At the same time, NVA inventories and continuing military assistance from the USSR and China have proven adequate to replace expenditures and losses in the South. In addition, the receipt since 1972 of jet fighters, SAMs, AA guns, and associated radars, and the reconstruction and modernization of airfields in the North Vietnamese panhandle have given Hanoi a more than adequate air defense capability against the South Vietnamese air threat to North Vietnam and to Communist base areas in the South.

5. In South Vietnam, there has been little change in the numerical strength or composition of NVA/VC combat forces over the past

[1] NIE 53/14.3-1-74: "The Likelihood of a Major North Vietnamese Offensive Against South Vietnam Before June 30, 1975," dated 23 May 1974 (S).

This Estimate was updated by Interagency (CIA/DIA/State) Memorandum entitled "An Assessment of the Current Military Situation in Vietnam," dated 9 August 1974 (S,). The key judgment, however, was unchanged.

year, but the rehabilitation and modernization of combat and support elements have continued apace. The NVA/VC's ability to adapt to changing situations is at an all-time high, and they can be resupplied and reinforced faster than ever. Enough replacements have been infiltrated from the North to offset the past year's combat losses. Armor levels have been kept essentially constant in the past year, and artillery levels have been increased. Sufficient supply stockpiles are available in-country to support country-wide combat operations at the 1972 offensive level for an extended period. Moreover, the Communists are sending additional large quantities of military supplies to the South. Infiltration thus far in the dry season has been heavier than last year, and we expect this pattern to continue.

6. Four new NVA corps headquarters have been identified since late 1973—one in central North Vietnam, two in South Vietnam's MR-1, and one in MR-3. Controlling several infantry division equivalents each, these headquarters are designed to give the NVA High Command greatly improved command and control. Also, during 1974 the capability of North Vietnamese MIGs to mount limited attacks against fixed installations was extended south of the principal South Vietnamese Air Force (VNAF) airbase at Danang. The presence of some 22,000 Communist air defense personnel in South Vietnam and the upgrading of equipment and weapons has resulted in an NVA SAM and AAA capability to defend base areas and key personnel infiltration and supply routes in the northern and western border regions from VNAF air strikes and reconnaissance.

7. Viet Cong guerrilla forces contribute very little to the overall Communist military strength in South Vietnam. The Viet Cong guerrillas and guerrilla support structure have been in a weakened state since the Tet 1968 offensive, and they have not regained much strength since January 1973. Today more than ever NVA main forces are the principal threat to the RVNAF.

8. *Other Considerations.* We know of no opposition on the part of the North Vietnamese people that is strong enough to affect Hanoi's ability to continue its quest to gain control over South Vietnam or that would require any significant modification of its strategy. North Vietnam basically remains a unified state run by a tightly knit party and technical elite with the dedication to pursue chosen options even in the face of great adversity.

9. There are domestic factors which could impact on Hanoi's freedom of action in the South, but we know little about their relative weight. The regime places a high priority on economic reconstruction and development, and there is a vocal element within the leadership that wishes to concentrate on these matters at the expense of the struggle in the South. The limited intelligence available on this subject, however, does not allow us to determine the depth and extent of debate over national priorities, or its probable future course and consequence.

10. Other areas of uncertainty are the weight carried by the counsels of the USSR and China in Hanoi and the degree to which either Moscow or Peking is willing to press Hanoi on the question of military action in the South. The USSR and China may see their larger interests in detente advanced by a period of relative peace in Indochina, but there is no convincing evidence that they view detente with the US as necessarily requiring them to take major steps to keep Hanoi in line. There is similarly no convincing evidence that the Soviets and Chinese have withheld or tailored their aid to North Vietnam in an effort to influence North Vietnamese strategy.

(Continued...)

In any event, whatever Moscow's and Peking's intentions, they could not restrict North Vietnam's short-term military options, although Hanoi would have to consider the longer-range implications of a Soviet and Chinese unwillingness to replace equipment and supplies lost in combat.

11. A final factor affecting Hanoi's calculations is its assessment of the US position. On the one hand, Hanoi must be encouraged that the Paris agreements not only ended direct US participation in the war, but also brought about a further reduction in the American military presence throughout Southeast Asia. In addition, the North Vietnamese leadership probably interprets recent political developments in the US as further reducing Washington's support for Saigon. On the other hand, Hanoi probably considers President Ford something of an unknown quantity on the Vietnam issue and is unsure about how he would react to a dramatic Communist military effort to upset the balance in Vietnam. There is almost certainly still some concern in Hanoi that as long as the US retains military forces in Southeast Asia, Washington would intervene to prevent a South Vietnamese military collapse.

The South Vietnamese

12. *Military.* The military performance of the RVNAF has been reasonably effective since the ceasefire agreement. At present, South Vietnamese military forces are capable of providing security sufficient to protect the bulk of the populace, despite ammunition, fuel, and equipment stringencies. Throughout this period, government forces demonstrated sophisticated command and control procedures and a high degree of tactical flexibility. This competence was evident in such diverse operations as the May 1974 MR-3 cross-border operation into Cambodia and the six-hour deployment in the late summer of 1974 of a division headquarters and a regiment from the central highlands to coastal Binh Dinh Province, where the regiment was immediately committed to open an interdicted section of Route 1.

13. Nevertheless, the quality of many RVNAF commanders is still marginal, especially at company and field-grade levels. This failing was especially evident in several units of the 1st Division in the fighting southeast of Hue in August. In addition, the RVNAF is plagued by the perennial problems of reduced manning levels in many units, a problem aggravated by high casualties, a slow replacement process, and in many cases poor quality replacements.

14. South Vietnamese military shortcomings are most apparent within the territorial forces—about half of the troops under arms. In some areas of the country the Regional Forces (RF) have performed creditably—in coastal MR-2, MR-3, and the northern delta. In southern MR-1 and in the northern highlands of MR-2, however, the territorials have performed poorly as a result of inadequate leadership, discipline, and unit manning. In the southern delta provinces of MR 4, mainly defended by territorial forces, security has deteriorated markedly since early this year, in large part because of the interplay of two major factors—increased Communist aggressiveness and a sharp rise in South Vietnamese desertions from the territorial forces and a decline in recruitment. In the delta as a whole, there was a 30 percent decline in the present-for-duty strength of RF battalion line companies during the first ten months of 1974. Another factor contributing to the spotty performance of the territorials is that they have in recent years been confronted with main force Communist units and not just VC guerrillas. The GVN is implementing plans to re-

train and upgrade the territorial forces, but it remains to be seen whether the action will be effective.

15. The most unsettling development affecting the RVNAF, however, derives from the decline in US military aid available to the GVN. In FY 1974, the RVNAF received about $1.2 billion in US military assistance, as compared with $2.3 billion in FY 1973. Funding at the $1.2 billion level was insufficient to replace all RVNAF consumption and losses of supplies and equipment.

16. Barring a supplemental appropriation, no more than $700 million in US military aid will be available to the GVN in FY 1975. In the best case, that is, combat at an overall level no greater than the average for 1974, the RVNAF could prevent Communist gains in vital population areas over the next six months or so only at the cost of drawdowns of ammunition, POL, spare parts stocks, and equipment inventories. Even at the 1974 level of combat, we would thus expect the RVNAF to be in a significantly weaker logistical position by the end of the dry season (and the Communists relatively stronger). The RVNAF's ability to cope with a subsequent sustained increase in the tempo of fighting would depend increasingly on whether the GVN received timely and large-scale US logistic support beyond presently programed levels.

17. RVNAF combat capabilities appear in retrospect to have peaked in the year or so following the ceasefire. There has been some decline in RVNAF effectiveness in recent months, but this decline has not yet reached significant proportions. The RVNAF has been forced into an increasingly defensive and reactive posture, however, and even now RVNAF shortages are limiting combat operations in some areas. It is likely that heavier combat would force the GVN to dilute further the strategy and tactics that have stood it in good stead since the ceasefire. These have included an aggressive forward posture and generous employment of air and artillery fire to break up Communist military formations and to blunt attacks.

18. As important as the current level of US assistance is the GVN's faith in a continuing US commitment to provide military assistance in the future when it is needed. A loss of confidence in the US commitment to South Vietnam would seriously affect the GVN's morale and will to continue the struggle regardless of the actual level of stocks on hand.

19. *Other Considerations.* Within the GVN there is firm commitment to maintaining South Vietnamese independence. President Thieu has used his power base—the military and the bureaucracy—to retain a strong hold on the governmental apparatus, and this apparatus has relatively little trouble in countering Communist political and clandestine subversion efforts. Moreover, the vast majority of the Vietnamese people are aware that they would fare badly under the Communist alternative.

20. But Thieu's hold on power may be somewhat less secure now than it was a year ago for three major reasons:

— The South Vietnamese reading of the US political situation, especially with regard to what is seen in Saigon as a declining US commitment to Vietnam.

— The escalation of the fighting and attendant higher casualties.

—The economic reverses since the 1972 offensive and the concomitant increases in urban unemployment and declines in living standards.

21. Political opposition groups have attempted to harness these popular frustrations in their intensified attacks against the GVN for high-level corruption, press censorship, and Thieu's and the army's monopoly of real political power. Although active political dissension is now largely limited to small groups, these issues could spur more widespread popular opposition, particularly in the upcoming election year.

22. The economic problems facing South Vietnam are not likely to lead to acute pressures on the government over the next year or so, unless the security situation markedly deteriorates. Since mid-1972, for a variety of reasons, the urban industrial and services sectors of the economy have been stalled at well below capacity, and rapid inflation has severely eroded real incomes of military personnel, civil servants, and city dwellers in general. In particular industries, such as cement and electricity, output has remained high, but the overall unemployment rate of the urban work force is at 15 to 20 percent. On the other hand, particularly in agriculture, which is the heart of the South Vietnamese economy, there have been some positive signs over the past few months. The rice crop now being harvested appears larger than last year's bumper crop because of good weather conditions and a fairly high overall use of chemical fertilizers. Stocks are large enough to assure adequate supplies without US PL-480 rice shipments for the first time in about ten years. Foreign exchange reserves are up $55 million over the start of the year to $218 million, although export growth is diminishing.[2] Reflecting the improved supply conditions, the consumer price level has held steady since August 1974, reducing the annual rate of inflation to about 40 percent. Over the longer term, the economic pressures on Thieu clearly will depend heavily on the availability of foreign aid. But they will also depend in part on how effectively the government can shift additional manpower and resources to agriculture and other industries which will, over time, make the country less dependent on foreign aid.

[2] The most important factors in the reserve increase have been a $30 million inflow from oil exploration fees and reduced import payments as a result of the urban recession.

III. WHAT NEXT?

Hanoi's Options

23. There has been little change in Hanoi's options from those of a year ago. Broadly speaking they include:

— Maintaining the 1974 strategy and level of activity in the South, in the hope that such activity would be sufficient to erode the GVN's military and political base.

— Sharply increasing military action in the South, but to a level below that of an all-out offensive.

— Launching an all-out "general" offensive in an effort to win an immediate "total" victory.

24. The GVN has demonstrated a capability to cope with the first option, and evidence of Hanoi's intentions points primarily to the second option. Reliable reports over the past 12 months or so indicated that neither North Vietnam nor its fighting forces were confident of their ability to defeat the GVN militarily. Much of the evidence, however, reflected a view in Hanoi that the stage for Thieu's ouster could be set by increasing the level of military pressure on the GVN while exploiting internal dissension.

25. More recently, a considerable volume of reliable reporting has provided details on Communist dry season intentions; these were

outlined in a COSVN resolution which laid out Communist goals for 1975. According to the resolution the Communists hope to achieve their political goals primarily by military means. In so doing, the Communists hope to use their forces to gain such objectives as:

— defeating the GVN pacification program;

— inflicting heavy casualties on RVNAF;

— gaining control of large numbers of South Vietnamese in contested or government-controlled territory; and

— forcing the GVN into new negotiations under circumstances favorable to the Communists.

As would be expected in any COSVN document, Communist plans for the northern half of South Vietnam were not detailed. Nevertheless, enough reliable reports have been received from other areas to indicate that a country-wide effort is planned. Any GVN vulnerabilities that are exposed will be exploited in follow-up action.

26. There are various levels of military pressure the Communists could apply under Option 2 within the guidelines of the COSVN resolution for 1975. At the lower end of the spectrum the Communists could rely exclusively on their in-country units. Under this scenario, GVN vulnerabilities would be most acute in the northern half of SVN and in portions of the delta. Specifically, RVNAF forces are spread thinly along Route 1—the vital supply line for Hue and other major cities near or on the coast. The road could be interdicted, and the GVN would be hard-pressed to keep it open. The central highlands would be an area in which at least initial Communist successes would be almost assured. Kontum City, for example, remains especially vulnerable to an NVA strangulation campaign. Communist gains in the southern part of the country—vital to the survival of the GVN—would probably be more limited. Some additional expansion of Communist control, however, would likely occur in the provinces north and northwest of Saigon and particularly in the southern delta where an erosion in security has already occurred.

27. Even so, under this scenario, we would expect Communist gains this dry season to be limited. The RVNAF retains sufficient strength and resiliency to contend with Communist military activity that depends only on the force structure now in-country. Both sides would be hurt, however, and the key question would then be the regenerative capability of the opposing forces. The RVNAF would be in an extremely precarious logistic position, and its ability to bounce back would depend principally on the level and timeliness of US assistance. At the level of combat called for under this scenario and at current levels of US assistance, RVNAF consumption of ammunition and other critical supplies would probably result by April or May in a depletion of stockpiles below the 30-day reserve required for intensive combat. In addition, RVNAF capabilities would doubtless be further degraded by shortages of spare parts and replacement equipment.

28. The Communists, on the other hand, would be in a far better relative logistic position. They would also still have their strategic reserve—or most of it at least—from which to draw new personnel if they so choose. Thus, by the end of this dry season a situation would be created in which the Communists would have a significant advantage over RVNAF for subsequent fighting.

29. At the upper range of military action under Option 2, Hanoi could choose during the dry season to deploy some units from its strategic reserve to the South in response to new opportunities or difficulties encountered

during the fighting. For example, up to a division might be sent to MR-1 from the reserve to exploit local successes there. A similar opportunity could emerge in the central highlands.[3] The objective of such reinforcement, however, would be limited and consistent with present Communist strategy as expressed in the COSVN resolution for 1975. Even so, there would be a risk that once embarked on this course, particularly if RVNAF appeared highly vulnerable, Hanoi might decide to commit most of its reserve forces in an effort to achieve a decisive victory over the GVN.

30. A limited commitment of the North Vietnamese strategic reserve of itself would not make the GVN's situation untenable, but it would result in greater strains on RVNAF. For example, there would be a greater danger that top RVNAF combat units might suffer major defeats, particularly since the South Vietnamese strategic reserve is already committed. Moreover, by utilizing part of their reserve force, the North Vietnamese would be in a better position to maintain a high level of combat throughout the dry season, thereby compounding RVNAF's logistic and manpower problems. In such a situation, the GVN would probably look to the US for an immediate increase in assistance. If this were not forthcoming, the GVN's military situation would be parlous, and Saigon might explore the possibility of new negotiations with the Communists.

31. Under either variant of Option 2, much will turn on RVNAF's morale and willingness to persevere. Not only will South Vietnamese forces be faced with heightened Communist aggressiveness, but they will also face the possibility that supply stringencies will constrain their ability to counter the Communist effort. Initial RVNAF successes in fending off the Communists despite these adversities would buoy morale and give the South Vietnamese increased confidence that they could stay the course. On the other hand, a series of battlefield setbacks—even if not strategically important—could set in train a feeling of defeatism which would adversely affect the RVNAF's future performance.

The Forecast

32. We expect at a minimum a sharp escalation in the fighting this dry season, with the Communists making greater use of their in-country forces and firepower than in 1974. They clearly have the flexibility to commit a portion of their strategic reserve, and we believe that they are likely to base their decisions on how the fighting evolves during the dry season. We believe that they will make such a commitment to exploit major vulnerabilities in the South Vietnamese position or to maintain the momentum of their military effort.

33. *An All-Out Offensive.* We estimate that an all-out offensive is unlikely this dry season, although there is a risk that Hanoi might move in this direction if it perceived an opportunity where it could score a decisive victory. If the Communists should choose this option there would be a major increase in Communist infiltration and most of the strategic reserve would be deployed to the South. The offensive would probably begin in the spring of the year when weather favors combined-arms operations throughout most of the country, with the major effort once again occurring in MR-1 and secondary actions elsewhere to keep the GVN from redeploying forces to meet the threat in the north. The fighting would be characterized by intense artillery duels and conventional set-piece battles extending into populated areas.

[3] These particular deployment scenarios are illustrative only and are not meant to place arbitrary restrictions on North Vietnamese military flexibility.

34. The South Vietnamese would be able to withstand the initial impact of an all-out Communist offensive only by trading space for time. They would probably lose all of MR-1 north of Danang, Pleiku and Kontum provinces in MR-2, and some territory in MR-3 and MR-4. The RVNAF would be unable to contain a sustained Communist offensive unless the US provided early and large-scale logistic assistance. Casualties and equipment losses would run high on both sides, and the RVNAF would doubtless lose more than they did during the 1972 offensive. The final outcome of a Communist general offensive, even with extensive US logistic support to the South, would hinge on such intangibles as the resourcefulness and effectiveness of ARVN unit leaders and the psychological impact of the probable early Communist successes.

35. The adverse psychological impact of Communist successes in the initial stages of the offensive might be more significant than the actual effect on the military balance. Therefore, in the worst case, a situation could develop in which the Saigon government would be unable to stabilize the situation or regain the initiative without the reintroduction of US air and naval support. If this were only a symbolic commitment, e.g., using only a small number of carrier-based aircraft, it would not have a significant impact on the Communists, but might stiffen RVNAF sufficiently to prevent a collapse in their morale and willingness to keep fighting. But a massive commitment of US airpower in the South during the early stages of the fighting would probably blunt the offensive.

IV. IN SUM

36. We believe that Hanoi prefers to achieve its goals through a political-military campaign which avoids the risks and losses of an all-out offensive. We nonetheless believe that the RVNAF will be severely tested over the next six months. Moreover, at currently appropriated levels of US military assistance, the level of combat we anticipate this dry season will place the Communists in a position of significant advantage over RVNAF in subsequent fighting.

37. Hanoi probably sees much to be gained by stepping up its efforts to inflict punishment on the RVNAF whenever and wherever it can in hope of overcoming the present military deadlock and pushing Saigon into renewed negotiations at a disadvantage. At the same time, however, Hanoi may estimate that internal problems in South Vietnam portend increasing trouble for President Thieu and therefore be reluctant to jeopardize this trend by the application of too high a level of military pressure too soon. Finally, Hanoi may calculate that by setting certain limits on its military operations in the South this dry season there would be less likelihood of a strong reaction from Washington. This course of action would also minimize friction with Moscow and Peking.

38. If the Communists were later to become dissatisfied with the results of such a course of action, they could always step up the pressure. An all-out offensive, however, would probably not occur at least until early 1976, in part because Hanoi would likely need time to gear up for such action following heightened combat in 1975 and in part because Hanoi would probably regard a US presidential year as a particularly favorable time to launch an offensive.

SNIE 53/14.3-75

Assessment of the Situation in South Vietnam

27 March 1975

APPROVED FOR RELEASE
DATE: JAN 2005

Secret

(b)(3)

SPECIAL NATIONAL INTELLIGENCE ESTIMATE

Assessment of the Situation in South Vietnam

Secret

SNIE 53/14.3-75
27 March 1975

Copy № 375

ASSESSMENT OF THE SITUATION IN SOUTH VIETNAM

The situation in South Vietnam has rapidly deteriorated since President Thieu's decision in mid-March to shift to a strategy of military retrenchment. Following is an assessment of the situation and an analysis of South Vietnam's prospects for this dry season.

I. THE MILITARY SITUATION

The Northern Coast

1. The situation is especially bleak in MR 1. The government has conceded virtually the whole region to the communists, and South Vietnamese forces are now moving to an enclave around DaNang. The remnants of two of the four South Vietnamese divisions in MR 1 are scattered, and the communists are harassing them as they pull back toward DaNang. It is questionable if the bulk of these troops will reach DaNang, and the government will be hard pressed to defend the city without them. The communists, on the other hand, have two fresh divisions west of the city, and they are preparing to attack DaNang. In addition, the North Vietnamese 320B Division—one of Hanoi's five remaining reserve divisions—is moving south.

The Central Coast

2. The government's military position in MR 2 has also deteriorated rapidly. The South Vietnamese have abandoned five highland provinces and large parts of several others, and government troops do not appear to be capable of standing up to the communists. The South Vietnamese 23rd Division and two ranger groups were badly mauled in the fighting in Darlac Province, and five of the six ranger groups withdrawing from Kontum and Pleiku are in disarray. Large quantities of munitions and fuel were abandoned at Kontum and Pleiku cities. Communist attacks on the retreating column destroyed or damaged hundreds of pieces of equipment, and South Vietnamese troops abandoned large amounts of hardware along the road—all of which was needed to defend the coastal lowlands.

3. The North Vietnamese are far stronger than the remaining government forces and are in a position to deal a decisive blow in this region. The government has just over one effective division in MR 2, compared to five North Vietnamese divisions; moreover, large numbers of replacements have arrived in the highlands from North Vietnam. Nha

Trang, the military headquarters for the region, is lightly defended and probably will fall.

The South

4. The fighting has eased somewhat north of Saigon, but the situation remains serious. The government is in the process of withdrawing from Binh Long Province and has had losses in western Binh Duong Province. The communists have thus far avoided a frontal assault on Tay Ninh City, but several communist divisions and independent regiments are pressing against government troops from three sides. Since the city will be costly to support and defend and most of the population has already fled, serious consideration is being given to abandoning this provincial capital and drawing new defensive lines in the southeastern portion of the province. In addition, recent communist gains east of Saigon have forced the GVN region commander to divert some troops from the Tay Ninh front and Saigon, and this has limited his capabilities to launch a counterattack north and west of the capital.

5. In the delta, the situation is, for the moment, relatively stable. Many of the communist main force units suffered heavy losses in the fighting around the turn of the year, but they are now rebuilding. This stable situation, however, could quickly change should Saigon move any sizable forces from the delta to bolster the defenses of MR 3.

II. THE IMPACT OF THIEU'S STRATEGY

6. Thieu decided to evacuate the highlands and concentrate his forces along the populated coast and around Saigon because he felt they were overextended, faced with a greatly superior North Vietnamese Army force, and confronted with the prospect of dwindling US aid. He clearly hoped to take the communists by surprise, extracting his forces intact and ready to fight before the communists could react. Thieu probably also calculated that by making his decision secretly and presenting it to his senior military commanders as a fait accompli he would forestall any coup plotting by them or a direct refusal to carry out his orders.

7. The result, however, was that Thieu took his own forces by surprise as much as he did the communists. His Joint General Staff and his regional commanders have all indicated that they had no prior briefing or consultation. US officials were also not notified. Without any prior planning or clear indication of the limits of the withdrawal, the redeployments have been generally disorderly. In the northern two-thirds of the country, most government forces are cut off from each other and seized with an evacuation mentality. Under these conditions some units have refused to fight.

8. The senior military leadership clearly has been caught off balance by the direction which events have taken, and their reaction has been one of dismay and depression. These attitudes also are reflected through the ranks.

9. Grumbling against Thieu's leadership has grown in the wake of military reverses, but events have moved so rapidly that there has been little coup talk. It is widely recognized that a coup at this time would be disastrous.* But the situation is such that pressures for Thieu's resignation or forcible removal could quickly emerge.

10. A source of disorder lies in the refugee problem which has caught the government ill-prepared to cope with the massive numbers of refugees generated in MRs 1 and 2. According to the latest estimates, there may now be upwards of a million displaced persons crowded into DaNang awaiting evacuation to coastal MR 2. But the government has inadequate resources to accomplish this mass evacuation in a short period, and there is a serious risk of riots and fighting in the rush to evacuate. Moreover, those who are brought out may have to be moved again—thereby creating additional pressures on the government.

11. Apart from the reverses suffered in South Vietnam, there are external factors which could further undermine the GVN. The collapse of Cambodia, for example, would bring added psychologi-

*The GVN move on March 27 to arrest "plotters" against the government was basically a warning to opposition elements; those involved did not represent any serious threat to Thieu.

cal pressure on Saigon. The continuing debate in the US on the question of US aid to South Vietnam is also an unsettling factor. Thieu probably assumes that he will have to rely on what he already has; but if the South Vietnamese in general come to believe that the US will not respond with additional assistance to meet the new situation, this will fuel defeatism.

III. PROSPECTS

12. The communists have the capability to exploit their gains, and we believe they will. In so doing, they will try to destroy the remaining government forces in MRs 1 and 2. At the moment, the situation in DaNang is chaotic. Considering the forces that North Vietnam can bring to bear against DaNang, the poor state of government defenses there, and the widespread panic in the city, its defenses could simply collapse. In any event, it will be lost within two weeks to a North Vietnamese attack, perhaps within a few days if the Marine division is removed. Thieu is already considering this move; his strategy has been to save his forces from being destroyed in overextended positions.

13. In MR 2, the thinly stretched government forces will be no match for the five North Vietnamese divisions. There are already indications that the communists are planning to attack several major population centers in the region. In the face of strong communist attacks, the South Vietnamese will be unable to maintain these enclaves.

14. In MRs 3 and 4, the government currently has a substantial edge in forces and is expected to maintain a strong defense line around the heavily populated and rice growing areas, but some retraction of defenses is probable. Tay Ninh City has been a major goal of the communists this dry season. The South Vietnamese have fought hard to hold the city thus far, and we believe they can continue to do so, although they may decide to abandon it because of the risks and costs involved in defending it.

15. In sum, the South Vietnamese withdrawals amount to a major defeat. As matters now stand, Thieu is faced with:

- — re-asserting effective control over his commanders;
- — extracting key force elements and equipment from MRs 1 and 2; and
- — organizing a strong defense of the Saigon area and MR 4.

Communist momentum, however, will be hard to stop, and the North Vietnamese may be tempted to commit the remaining portion of their strategic reserve to exploit the situation. Even if they do so, we believe that the GVN's military strength in the southern part of the country will enable it to survive the current dry season, although additional losses are certain.

16. Logistic factors, for example, would probably bar a quick assault on Saigon since the communists now lack supply stocks in forward positions in MR 3 and their prepositioning will be time consuming. In addition, even the decision to commit the strategic reserve means that forces will have to be marshalled and deployed. In so doing, the communists will run into time and distance factors, and the complexities of assembling units and moving them over long lines of communication in an environment where rapid or orderly deployment is inhibited. Finally, the South Vietnamese forces in MRs 3 and 4—including the territorial forces—remain intact and able to give a good account of themselves.

17. Even so, the GVN will probably be left with control over little more than the delta and Saigon and surrounding populated areas. It would thus face further communist pressure from a position substantially weaker than our previous estimates, with the result likely to be defeat by early 1976. The communists will keep up their military pressure to topple the GVN by outright defeat unless there have been political changes in Saigon that open the way to a new settlement on near-surrender terms.

Vietnam Document List for CD

ORE: Office of Reports and Estimates	ONE: Office of National Estimates
NIE: National Intelligence Estimate	USIB: United States Intelligence Board
SNIE: Special National Intelligence Estimate	SM: Special Memorandum
IIM: Interagency Intelligence Memorandum	SE: Special Estimate
IM: Intelligence Memorandum	M/H: Memorandum for Holders

Publication Number	Title of Publication	Date of Publication
ORE 25-48	The Breakup of the Colonial Empires and Its Implications for US Security	3 September 1948
ORE 50-50	Prospects for the Defense of Indochina Against a Chinese Communist Invasion	7 September 1950
ORE 58-50	Critical Situations in the Far East	12 October 1950
ORE 29-50	Consequences to the US of Communist Domination of Mainland Southeast Asia	13 October 1950
NIE 5	Indochina: Current Situation and Probable Developments	29 December 1950
NIE 5 (map supplement)	Indochina: Current Situation and Probable Developments	5 January 1951
Memo	The Possibility of an Early Major Viet Minh Attack in Indochina	14 March 1951
NIE 20	Resistance of Thailand, Burma and Malaya to Communist Pressures in the Event of a Commnist Victory in Indochina in 1951	20 March 1951
NIE 35	Probable Developments in Indochina During the Remainder of 1951	7 August 1951
Staff Memo 124	French Problems in Indochina	4 September 1951
Memo	Critical Developments in French Policy toward Indochina	10 January 1952
NIE 35/1	Probable Developments in Indochina Through Mid-1952	3 March 1952

NIE 35/2	Probable Developments in Indochina Through Mid-1953	29 August 1952
NIE 91	Probable Development in Indochina Through Mid-1954	4 June 1953
SE-52	Probable Consequences in Non-Communist Asia of Certain Possible Developments in Indochina Before Mid-1954	16 November 1953
SE-53	Probable Communist Reactions to Certain Possible US Courses of Action in Indochina Through 1954	18 December 1953
Memo	Current Outlook in Indochina	9 February 1954
Memo	Reactions to ROK Participation in the Indochina War	23 February 1954
NIE 10-2-54	Communist Courses of Action in Asia Through Mid-1955	15 March 1954
Memo	The Probable Outcome at Dien Bien Phu and its Implications	24 March 1954
Memo	Probable Communist Strategy and Tactics at Geneva	19 April 1954
NIE 63-54	Consequences Within Indochina of the Fall of Dien Bien Phu	30 April 1954
NIE 63-3-54	Probable Military and Political Developments in Indochina Over the Next 30 Days	21 May 1954
NIE 10-3-54	Communist Capabilitities in Indochina	1 June 1954
SNIE 63-2-54	The Effects of Certain Possible Developments on the Military Security and Political Stability of Laos and Cambodia Through 1954	9 June1954
SNIE 10-4-54	Communist Reactions to Certain US Courses of Action With Respect to Indochina	15 June 1954
NIE 63-4-54	Probable Military and Political Developments in Indochina Over the Next 30 Days (15 June-15 July)	15 June 1954
NIE 63-5-54	Post-Geneva Outlook in Indochina	3 August 1954
SNIE 63-6-54	Current Trends in South Vietnam	15 September 1954
NIE 63-7-54	Probable Developments in South Vietnam, Laos, and Cambodia Through July 1956	23 November 1954

NIE 10-7-54	Communist Courses of Action in Asia Through 1957	23 November 1954
Memo	The Crisis in Saigon	4 April 1955
NIE 10-55	Anti-Communist Resistance Potential in the Sino-Soviet Bloc	12 April 1955
Memo	(Situation in South Vietnam) untitled	23 April 1955
NIE 63.1-2-55	Possible Developments in South Vietnam	26 April 1955
SNIE 63.1-2/1-55	The Current Saigon Crisis	2 May 1955
Memo	Political Trends in Saigon	6 May 1955
NIE 63.1-55	Probable Developments in North Vietnam to July 1956	19 July 1955
NIE 63.3-55	Probable Developments in Laos to July 1956	26 July 1955
SNIE 63.1-4-55	Consequences of Possible US Courses of Action With Respect to Vietnam	13 September 1955
NIE 63.1-3-55	Probable Developments in Vietnam to July 1956	11 October 1955
NIE 63.3/1-55	Probable Developments in Laos to July 1956	20 December 1955
Memo	O/NE Comments on Present Nature of Threat to South Vietnam	6 June 1956
NIE 63-56	Probable Developments in North and South Vietnam Through Mid-1957	17 July 1956
Memo	Agrarian Reform and Internal Security in South Vietnam	30 April 1957
NIE 63.2-57	The Prospects for North Vietnam	14 May 1957
NIE 68-57	Probable Developments in Laos Over the Next Few Months	20 August 1957
NIE 68-59	The Outlook for Laos	19 May 1959
NIE 67-59	Cambodia's International Orientation	26 May 1959
NIE 63-59	Prospects for North and South Vietnam	26 May 1959
SNIE 68-2-59	The Situation in Laos	18 September 1959

SNIE 63.1-60	Short-Term Trends in South Vietnam	23 August 1960
SNIE 68-60	The Situation and Short-Term Outlook in Laos	6 December 1960
SNIE 68-2-60	Probable Communist Intentions in Laos	29 December 1960
SNIE 58-61	Probable Communist Reactions to Certain US Courses of Action with Respect to Laos	21 February 1961
NIE 50-61	Outlook in Mainland Southeast Asia	28 March 1961
SNIE 10-2-61	Likelihood of Major Communist Military Intervention in Mainland Southeast Asia	27 June 1961
SNIE 58-2-61	Probable Reactions to Certain Courses of Action Concerning Laos	5 July 1961
NIE 14.3/53-61	Prospects for North and South Vietnam	15 August 1961
SNIE 58-3-61	The Situation and Short-Run Outlook in Laos	28 September 1961
SNIE 53-2-61	Bloc Support of the Communist Effort Against the Government of Vietnam	5 October 1961
SNIE 10-3-61	Probable Communist Reactions to Certain SEATO Undertakings in South Vietnam	10 October 1961
SNIE 10-4-61	Probable Communist Reactions to Certain US Actions in South Vietnam	7 November 1961
SNIE 58-62	Relative Military Capabilities of Opposing Forces in Laos	11 January 1962
SNIE 58/1-62	Relative Military Capabilites of Opposing Forces in Laos	31 January 1962
SNIE 10-62	Communist Objectives, Capabilities, and Intentions in Southeast Asia	21 February 1962
SNIE 10-62	Annex to Communist Objectives, Capabilities, and Intentions in Southeast Asia	21 February 1962
SNIE 58-2-62	Consequences of Certain US Courses in Laos	11 April 1962
SNIE 58-3-62	Implications of the Fall of Nam Tha	9 May 1962
SNIE 58-4-62	The Current Military Situation and Outlook in Laos	14 May 1962

SNIE 58-5-62	Probable Communist Reactions to Certain Possible US Actions With Respect to Laos	31 May 1962
SNIE 58-5/1-62	Communist Reactions to Additional US Courses of Action in Laos and North Vietnam	12 June 1962
SNIE 58-6-62	Short-Run Outlook for the Laotian Coalition Government	26 September 1962
NIE 53-63	Prospects in South Vietnam	17 April 1963
SNIE 58-63	Communist Reactions to US Actions Taken With Regard to Laos	18 June 1963
SNIE 14.3-63	The Impact of the Sino-Soviet Dispute on North Vietnam and its Policies	26 June 1963
SNIE 53-2-63	The Situation in South Vietnam	10 July 1963
Memorandum about ONE Memo	South Vietnam's Leaders	4 September 1963
Memo	Probable North Vietnamese Reaction to Certain Clandestine Operations	20 December 1963
SNIE 50-64	Short-Term Prospects in Southeast Asia	12 February 1964
SNIE 14.3-64	The Outlook for North Vietnam	4 March 1964
SNIE 50-2-64	Probable Consequences of Certain US Actions with Respect to Vietnam and Laos	25 May 1964
Memo	Would the Loss of South Vietnam and Laos Precipitate a 'Domino Effect"in the Far East ?	9 June 1964
Memo	Probable Communist Reactions to Certain US or US-Sponsored Courses of Action in Vietnam and Laos	28 July 1964
SNIE 53-64	Chances for a Stable Government in South Vietnam	8 September 1964
SNIE 53-2-64	The Situation in South Vietnam	1 October 1964
SNIE 10-3-64	Probable Communist Reactions to Certain Possible US/GVN Courses of Actions	9 October 1964

SNIE 10-65	Communist Military Capabilities and Near-Term Intentions in Laos and South Vietnam	4 February 1965
SNIE 53-65	Short-Term Prospects in South Vietnam	4 February 1965
SM 7-65	The Dimensions of Kosygin's Trip	5 February 1965
SNIE 10-3-65	Communist Reactions to Possible US Actions	11 February 1965
SNIE 10-3/1-65	Communist Reactions to Possible US Courses of Action Against North Vietnam	18 February 1965
SNIE 10-4-65	Probable Communist Reactions to Deployment of an ROK Combat Division for Base Security Duty in South Vietnam	19 March 1965
USIB Memo	Recent Indications of Communist Intentions in South Vietnam	9 April 1965
Memo	Reactions to a US Course of Action in Vietnam	21 April 1965
SM 11-65	Future Soviet Moves in Vietnam	27 April 1965
SNIE 10-5-65	Communist Reactions to Certain US Actions	28 April 1965
Memo	Consequences of a Pause in Bombings of the DRV	3 May 1965
SNIE 10-6-65	Probable Communist Reactions to Certain US Actions	2 June 1965
SNIE 10-6/1-65	Probable Reactions to Certain US Courses of Action	4 June 1965
SNIE 10-7-65	Implications of a Certain US Course of Action	4 June 1965
Memo	Reactions to a Further US Buildup in South Vietnam	10 June 1965
SM 18-65	Soviet Tactics Concerning Vietnam	15 July 1965
SNIE 10-9-65	Communist and Free World Reactions to a Possible US Course of Action	23 July 1965
SNIE 58-65	Short-Term Prospects for Laos	5 August 1965
SNIE 10-10-65	Reactions to a Certain US Course of Action in Southeast Asia	10 September 1965
SNIE 10-11-65	Probable Communist Reactions to a US Course of Action	22 September 1965

Memo for DCI	Reactions to a US Course of Action in Vietnam	2 December 1965
SNIE 10-12-65	Probable Communist Reactions to a US Course of Action	10 December 1965
M/H SNIE 10-12-65	Probable Communist Reactions to a US Course of Action	16 December 1965
Memo	Three Memoranda Attached Re Vietnam	29 December 1965
Memo	Reactions to Continuation or Termination of the Pause in Air Attacks on the DRV	19 January 1966
SNIE 10-1-66	Possible Effects of a Proposed US Course of Action on DRV Capability to Support the Insurgency in South Vietnam	4 February 1966
Memo	Possible Effects of Various Programs of Air Attack Against the DRV	11 February 1966
SNIE 10-2-66	Reactions to a Possible US Course of Action	17 March 1966
Memo	Use of Nuclear Weapons in the Vietnam War	18 March 1966
SNIE 10-3-66	Probable Reactions to a Possible Course of Action in South Vietnam	19 May 1966
NIE 14.3-66	North Vietnamese Military Potential for Fighting in South Vietnam	7 July 1966
SNIE 13-66	Current Chinese Communist Intentions in the Vietnam Situation	4 August 1966
Memo	The Vietnamese Communists' Will to Persist	26 August 1966
Memo	Implications of the Current Cabinet Crisis in South Vietnam	20 October 1966
NIE 53-66	Problems of Political Development in South Vietnam Over the Next Year or So	15 December 1966
SNIE 10-67	Reactions to a Possible US Action	5 January 1967
Memo for DCI	The War in Vietnam	9 January 1967
SNIE 57-67	Significance of Cambodia to the Vietnamese Communist War Effort	26 January 1967

Memo	Communist Reactions to Certain US Courses of Action	6 February 1967
ONE Memo	Communist Policy and the Next Phase in Vietnam	12 April 1967
SNIE 11-11-67	Soviet Attitudes and Intentions Toward the Vietnam War	4 May 1967
NIE 58-67	Short-Term Political Prospects for Laos	18 May 1967
Memo 0646/67	Reaction to Various US Courses of Action	23 May 1967
Memo	Evaluation of Alternative Programs for Bombing North Vietnam	1 June 1967
SNIE 10-1-67	Reactions to a Certain US Course of Action	13 July 1967
SNIE 14.3-1-67	Problems of Viet Cong Recruitment and Morale	3 August 1967
SM 7-67	The September Presidential Election in South Vietnam	8 August 1967
Memo	Implications of an Unfavorable Outcome in Vietnam	11 September 1967
SNIE 14.3-67	Capabilities of the Vietnamese Communists for Fighting in South Vietnam	13 November 1967
SNIE 57/1-67	Significance of Cambodia to the Vietnamese Communist War Effort	14 December 1967
Memo	Communist Reactions to Certain US Military Operations in Vietnam	5 January 1968
ONE Memo	Alternative Interpretations of Hanoi's Intentions	18 January 1968
Memo for DCI	The Outlook in Vietnam	26 February 1968
Memo	Questions Concerning the Situation in Vietnam	1 March 1968
ONE Memo for DCI	Communist Reactions to Certain US Courses of Action	13 March 1968
SNIE 58-68	Communist Intentions in Laos	21 March 1968
Memo	Hanoi's Motives	3 April 1968
ONE Memo for DCI	Speculation on Hanoi's Motives	8 April 1968
IM-0587/68	Hanoi's Negotiating Position and Concept of Negotiations	6 May 1968

SNIE 53-68	The Vietnam Situation	6 June 1968
ONE Memo for DCI	The Coming Political Struggle for South Vietnam	16 September 1968
SNIE 58-1-68	Communist Capabilities and Intentions in Laos Over the Next Year	31 October 1968
NIE 50-68	Southeast Asia After Vietnam	14 November 1968
SNIE 14-69	The Pacification Effort in Vietnam	16 January 1969
Memo	Reactions to a US Course of Action	20 February 1969
SNIE 14.3-69	Capabilties of the Vietnamese Communists for Fighting in South Vietnam	17 July 1969
SNIE 14.3-70	The Outlook from Hanoi: Factors Affecting North Vietnam's Policy on the War in Vietnam	5 February 1970
SNIE 58-70	The Communist View of the Situation in Laos	5 February 1970
SNIE 13-9-70	Chinese Reactions to Possible Developments in Indochina	28 May 1970
SNIE 13-10-70	Chinese Reactions to Certain Courses of Action in Indochina	11 June 1970
SNIE 57-70	The Outlook for Cambodia	6 August 1970
SNIE 13-10-71	Communist China's Reactions to Developments in Laos	18 February 1971
NIE 53-71	South Vietnam: Problems and Prospects	29 April 1971
SNIE 57-73	The Short-Term Prospect for Cambodia	24 May 1973
NIE 53/14.3-73	Short-Term Prospects for Vietnam	12 October 1973
M/H NIE 53/14.3-73	Short-Term Prospects for Vietnam	8 November 1973
SNIE 57-1-73	The Short-Term Prospect for Cambodia Through the Current Dry Season –May 1974	5 December 1973
M/H SNIE 57-1-73	The Short-Term Prospect for Cambodia Through the Current Dry Season –May 1974	31 January 1974
IIM 74-003	South Vietnam: A Net Military Assessment	2 April 1974

SNIE 57-1-74	The Short-Term Prospect for Cambodia Through August 1974	11 April 1974
NIE 53/14.3-1-74	The Likelihood of a Major North Vietnamese Offensive Against South Vietnam Before June 30, 1975	23 May 1974
IIM 74-013	Assessment of the Curent Military Situation in Vietnam	9 August 1974
NIE 53/14.3-2-74	Short-Term Prospects for Vietnam	23 December 1974
IIM 75-016	Communist Military and Economic Aid to North Vietnam, 1970-74	3 January 1975
IIM 75-002	Imports of Military Equipment and Material by North Vietnam in 1974	10 January 1975
NIE 57-1-75	Prospects for Cambodia Through August 1975	13 February 1975
SNIE 53/14.3-75	Assessment of the Situation in South Vietnam	27 March 1975